Mickey Spillane

The Hammer Strikes Again

About the Author

Frank Morrison (Mickey) Spillane was born in Brooklyn in 1918 and later attended Kansas State College. He is one of the best-known writers of hard-boiled detective fiction, and his private eye, Mike Hammer, has been called the epitome of the breed.

Spillane has written more than twenty mystery-suspense novels, many of which have been made into movies, including *I, The Jury; My Gun Is Quick;* and *Kiss Me, Deadly.* He has also been involved with two successful television series based on his popular detective, Mike Hammer.

mickey Spillane

The Hammer Strikes Again

FIVE COMPLETE MIKE HAMMER NOVELS

One Lonely Night
The Snake
The Twisted Thing
The Body Lovers
Survival . . . Zero!

AVENEL BOOKS · NEW YORK

This omnibus was originally published in separate
volumes under the titles:
One Lonely Night, copyright © MCMLI by E. P. Dutton
& Company, Inc.
Copyright © renewed MCMLXXIX by Mickey Spillane
The Snake, copyright © MCMLXIV by Mickey Spillane
The Twisted Thing, copyright © MCMLXVI by Mickey
Spillane
The Body Lovers, copyright © MCMLXVII by Mickey
Spillane
Survival . . . Zero!, copyright © MCMLXX by Mickey
Spillane
All rights reserved.

This 1989 edition is published by Avenel Books,
distributed by Crown Publishers, Inc., 225 Park Avenue
South, New York, New York 10003, by arrangement with
E. P. Dutton, a division of NAL Penguin, Inc.

Printed in the U.S.A.

LIBRARY OF CONGRESS CATALOGING-IN-PUBLICATION
DATA
Spillane, Mickey, 1918–
    The Hammer strikes again: five complete Mike
Hammer novels-Mickey Spillane.
        p.   cm
        Contents: One lonely night—The snake—The twisted
thing—The body lovers—Survival . . . zero!
        1. Hammer, Mike (Fictitious character)—Fiction. 2.
Detective and mystery stories, American. I. Title
    PS3537.P652A6 1989
    813'.54—dc19   88-39921
                                                        CIP

ISBN 0-517-67578-1
h g f e d c b a

contents

One Lonely Night

TO MARTY

chapter one ▅▅▅▅▅▅▅▅▅▅

NOBODY EVER WALKED across the bridge, not on a night like this. The rain was misty enough to be almost fog-like, a cold gray curtain that separated me from the pale ovals of white that were faces locked behind the steamed-up windows of the cars that hissed by. Even the brilliance that was Manhattan by night was reduced to a few sleepy, yellow lights off in the distance.

Some place over there I had left my car and started walking, burying my head in the collar of my raincoat, with the night pulled in around me like a blanket. I walked and I smoked and I flipped the spent butts ahead of me and watched them arch to the pavement and fizzle out with one last wink. If there was life behind the windows of the buildings on either side of me, I didn't notice it. The street was mine, all mine. They gave it to me gladly and wondered why I wanted it so nice and all alone.

There were others like me, sharing the dark and the solitude, but they huddled in the recessions of the doorways not wanting to share the wet and the cold. I could feel their eyes follow me briefly before they turned inward to their thoughts again.

So I followed the hard concrete footpaths of the city through the towering canyons of the buildings and never noticed when the sheer cliffs of brick and masonry diminished and disappeared altogether, and the footpath led into a ramp then on to the spidery steel skeleton that was the bridge linking two states.

I climbed to the hump in the middle and stood there leaning on the handrail with a butt in my fingers, watching the red and green lights of the boats in the river below. They winked at me and called in low, throaty notes before disappearing into the night.

Like eyes and faces. And voices.

I buried my face in my hands until everything straightened itself out again, wondering what the judge would say if he could see me now. Maybe he'd laugh because I was supposed to be so damn tough, and here I was with hands that wouldn't stand still and an empty feeling inside my chest.

He was only a little judge. He was little and he was old with eyes like two berries on a bush. His hair was pure white and wavy and his skin was loose and wrinkled. But he had a voice like the avenging angel. The dignity and knowledge behind his face gave him the stature of a giant, the poise of Gabriel reading your sins aloud from the Great Book and condemning you to your fate.

He had looked at me with a loathing louder than words, lashing me with his eyes in front of a courtroom filled with people, every empty second another stroke of the steel-tipped whip. His voice, when it did come, was edged with a gentle bitterness that was given only to the righteous.

But it didn't stay righteous long. It changed into disgusted hatred because I was a licensed investigator who knocked off somebody who needed knocking off bad and he couldn't get to me. So I was a murderer by definition and all the law could do was shake its finger at definitions.

Hell, the state would have liquidated the gun anyway . . . maybe he would have pronounced sentence himself. Maybe he thought I should have stayed there and called for the cops when the bastard had a rod in his hand and it was pointing right at my gut.

Yeah, great.

If he had let it stay there it would have been all right. I'd been called a lot of things before. But no, he had to go and strip me naked in front of myself and throw the past in my face when it should have stayed dead and buried forever. He had to go back five years to a time he knew of only secondhand and tell me how it took a war to show me the power of the gun and the obscene pleasure that was brutality and force, the spicy sweetness of murder sanctified by law.

That was me. I could have made it sound better if I'd said it. There in the muck and slime of the jungle, there in the stink that hung over the beaches rising from the bodies of the dead, there in the half-light of too many dusks and dawns laced together with the crisscrossed patterns of bullets, I had gotten a taste of death and found it palatable to the extent that I could never again eat the fruits of a normal civilization.

Goddamn, he wouldn't let me alone! He went on and on cutting me down until I was nothing but scum in the gutter, his fists slamming against the bench as he prophesied a rain of purity that was going to wash me into the sewer with the other scum leaving only the good and the meek to walk in the cleanliness of law and justice.

One day I would die and the world would be benefited by my death. And to the good there was only the perplexing question: Why did I live and breathe now . . . what could possibly be the reason for existence when there was no good in me? None at all.

So he gave me back my soul of toughness, hate and bitterness and let me dress in the armor of cynicism and dismissed me before I could sneer and make the answer I had ready.

He had called the next case up even before I reached the side of the room. It had all the earmarks of a good case, but nobody seemed to be interested. All they watched was me and their eyes were bright with that peculiar kind of horrified disgust that you see in people watching some nasty, fascinating creature in a circus cage.

Only a few of them reflected a little sympathy. Pat was there. He gave me a short wave and a nod that meant everything was okay because I was his friend. But there were things the judge had said that Pat had wanted to say plenty of times too.

Then there was Pete, a reporter too old for the fast beats and just right for the job of picking up human interest items from the lower courts. He waved too, with a grimace that was a combination grin for me and a sneer for the judge. Pete was a cynic too, but he liked my kind of guy. I made bonus stories for him every once in a while.

Velda. Lovely, lovely Velda. She waited for me by the door and when I walked up to her I watched her lips purse into a ripe, momentary kiss. The rows and rows of eyes that had been following me jumped ahead to this vision in a low-cut dress who threw a challenge with every motion of her body. The eyes swept from her black pumps to legs and body and shoulders that were almost too good to be real and staggered when they met a face that was beauty capable of the extremes of every emotion. Her head moved just enough to swirl her black page-boy hair and the look she sent back to all those good people and their white-haired guardian of the law was something to be remembered. For one long second

she had the judge's eye and outraged justice flinched before outraged love.

That's right, Velda was mine. It took a long time for me to
find out just how much mine she was, much too long. But now
I knew and I'd never forget it. She was the only decent thing
about me and I was lucky.

She said, "Let's get out of here, Mike. I hate people with little
minds."

We went outside the building to the sidewalk and climbed in
my car. She knew I didn't want to talk about it and kept still.
When I let her out at her apartment it was dark and starting to
rain. Her hand went to mine and squeezed it. "A good drunk
and you can forget about it, Mike. Sometimes people are too
stupid to be grateful. Call me when you're loaded and I'll come
get you."

That was all. She knew me enough to read my mind and didn't
care what I thought. If the whole damn world climbed on my
back there would still be Velda ready to yank them off and stamp
on their faces. I didn't even tell her good-by. I just shut the door
and started driving.

No, I didn't get drunk. Twice I looked in the mirror and saw
me. I didn't look like me at all. I used to be able to look at
myself and grin without giving a damn how ugly it made me
look. Now I was looking at myself the same way those people
did back there. I was looking at a big guy with an ugly reputation,
a guy who had no earthly reason for existing in a decent, normal
society. That's what the judge had said.

I was sweating and cold at the same time. Maybe it did happen
to me over there. Maybe I did have a taste for death. Maybe I
liked it too much to taste anything else. Maybe I was twisted and
rotted inside. Maybe I would be washed down the sewer with the
rest of all the rottenness sometime. What was stopping it from
happening now? Why was I me with some kind of lucky charm
around my neck that kept me going when I was better off dead?

That's why I parked the car and started walking in the rain. I
didn't want to look in that damn mirror any more. So I walked
and smoked and climbed to the hump in the bridge where the
boats in the river made faces and spoke to me until I had to bury
my face in my hands until everything straightened itself out again.

*I was a killer. I was a murderer, legalized. I had no reason for
living. Yeah, he said that!*

The crazy music that had been in my head ever since I came
back from those dusks and dawns started again, a low steady beat

overshadowed by the screaming of brassier, shriller instruments that hadn't been invented yet. They shouted and pounded a symphony of madness and destruction while I held my hands over my ears and cursed until they stopped. Only the bells were left, a hundred bells that called for me to come closer to the music, and when I wouldn't come they stopped, one by one, all except one deep, persistent bell with a low, resonant voice. It wouldn't give up. It called me to it, and when I opened my eyes I knew the bell was from a channel marker in the river, calling whenever it swayed with the tide.

It was all right once I knew where it came from. At least it was real. That judge, that damn white-headed son-of-a-bitch got me like this. I wasn't so tough after all. It wouldn't have been so bad . . . but maybe he was right. Maybe he was dead right and I'd never be satisfied until I knew the answer myself. If there was an answer.

I don't know how long I stood there. Time was just the ticking of a watch and a blend of sound from the ramp behind me. At some point after the sixth cigarette the cold mist had turned into a fine snow that licked at my face and clung to my coat. At first it melted into damp patches on the steel and concrete, then took hold and extended itself into a coverlet of white.

Now the last shred of reality was gone completely. The girders became giant trees and the bridge an eerie forest populated by whitecapped rubber-tired monsters streaking for the end of the causeway that took them into more friendly surroundings. I leaned back into the shadow of a girder and watched them to get my mind off other things, happy to be part of the peace and quiet of the night.

It came at last, the lessening of tension. The stiffness went out of my fingers and I pulled on a smoke until it caught in my lungs the way I liked it to do. Yeah, I could grin now and watch the faces fade away until they were onto the port and starboard lights of the ships again, and the bell that called me in was only a buoy some place off in the dark.

I ought to get out of it. I ought to take Velda and my office and start up in real estate in some small community where murder and guns and dames didn't happen. Maybe I would, at that. It was wonderful to be able to think straight again. No more crazy mad hatred that tied my insides into knots. No more hunting the scum that stood behind a trigger and shot at the world. That was official police business. The duty of organized law and order. And too slow justice. No more sticks with dirty ends on them either.

That's what the snow and the quiet did for me. It had been a long time since I had felt this good. Maybe the rottenness wasn't there at all and I was a killer only by coincidence. Maybe I didn't like to kill at all.

I stuck another Lucky in my mouth and searched my pockets for matches. Something jerked my head up before I found them and I stood there listening.

The wind blew. The snow hissed to the street. A foghorn sounded. That was all.

I shrugged and tore a match out of the book when I heard it again. A little, annoying sound that didn't belong on the bridge in the peace and quiet. They were soft, irregular sounds that faded when the wind shifted, then came back stronger. Footsteps, muted by the inch or so of snow on the walk.

I would have gotten the butt lit if the feet weren't trying to run with the desperate haste that comes with fatigue. The sound came closer and closer until it was a shadow fifty feet away that turned into a girl wrapped in a coat with a big woolly collar, her hands reaching for the support of a girder and missing.

She fell face down and tried to pull herself up to run again, but she couldn't make it. Her breathing was a long, racking series of sobs that shook her body in a convulsion of despair.

I'd seen fear before, but never like this.

She was only a few steps away and I ran to her, my hands hooking under her arms to lift her to her feet.

Her eyes were like saucers, rimmed with red, overflowing with tears that blurred her pupils. She took one look at me and choked, "Lord . . . no, please!"

"Easy, honey, take it easy," I said. I propped her against the girder and her eyes searched my face through the tears unable to see me clearly. She tried to talk and I stopped her. "No words, kid. There's plenty of time for that later. Just take it easy a minute, nobody's going to hurt you."

As if that stirred something in her mind, her eyes went wide again and she turned her head to stare back down the ramp. I heard it too. Footsteps, only these weren't hurried. They came evenly and softly, as if knowing full well they'd reach their objective in a few seconds.

I felt a snarl ripple across my mouth and my eyes went half shut. Maybe you can smack a dame around all you want and make her life as miserable as hell, but nobody has the right to scare the daylights out of any woman. Not like this.

She trembled so hard I had to put my arm around her shoulder to steady her. I watched her lips trying to speak, the unholy fear spreading into her face as no sound came.

I pulled her away from the girder. "Come on, we'll get this straightened out in a hurry," She was too weak to resist. I held my arm around her and started walking toward the footsteps.

He came out of the wall of white, a short, pudgy guy in a heavy belted ulster. His homburg was set on the side of his head rakishly, and even at this distance I could see the smile on his lips. Both his hands were stuck in his pockets and he walked with a swagger. He wasn't a bit surprised when he saw the two of us. One eyebrow went up a little, but that was all. Oh yes, he had a gun in one pocket.

It was pointing at me.

Nobody had to tell me he was the one. I wouldn't even have to know he had a rod in his hand. The way the kid's body stiffened with the shock of seeing him was enough. My face couldn't have been nice to look at right then, but it didn't bother the guy.

The gun moved in the pocket so I'd know it was a gun.

His voice fitted his body, short and thick. He said, "It is not smart to be a hero. Not smart at all." His thick lips twisted into a smile of mingled satisfaction and conceit. It was so plain in his mind that I could almost hear him speak it. The girl running along, stumbling blindly into the arms of a stranger. Her pleas for help, the guy's ready agreement to protect her, only to look down the barrel of a rod.

It didn't happen like that at all, but that's what he thought. His smile widened and he said harshly, "So now they will find the two of you here tomorrow." His eyes were as cold and as deadly as those of a manta ray.

He was too cocky. All he could see was his own complete mastery of the situation. He should have looked at me a little harder and maybe he would have seen the kind of eyes I had. Maybe he would have known that I was a killer in my own way too, and he would have realized that I knew he was just the type who would go to the trouble of taking the gun out of his pocket instead of ruining a good coat.

I never really gave him a chance. All I moved was my arm and before he had his gun out I had my .45 in my fist with the safety off and the trigger back. I only gave him a second to realize what it was like to die then I blew the expression clean off his face.

He never figured the hero would have a gun, too.

Before I could get it back in the holster the girl gave a lunge and backed up against the railing. Her eyes were clear now. They darted to the mess on the ground, the gun in my hand and the tight lines that made a mask of kill-lust of my face.

She screamed. Good God, how she screamed. She screamed as if I were a monster that had come up out of the pit! She screamed and made words that sounded like, "You . . . one of them . . . no more!"

I saw what she was going to do and tried to grab her, but the brief respite she had was enough to give her the strength she needed. She twisted and slithered over the top of the rail and I felt part of her coat come away in my hand as she tumbled headlong into the white void below the bridge.

Lord, Lord, what happened? My fingers closed over the handrail and I stared down after her. Three hundred feet to the river. The little fool didn't have to do that! She was safe! Nothing could have hurt her, didn't she realize that? I was shouting it at the top of my lungs with nobody but a dead man to hear me. When I pulled away from the rail I was shaking like a leaf.

All because of that fat little bastard stretched out in the snow. I pulled back my foot and kicked what was left of him until he rolled over on his face.

I did it again, I killed somebody else! Now I could stand in the courtroom in front of the man with the white hair and the voice of the Avenging Angel and let him drag my soul out where everybody could see it and slap it with another coat of black paint.

Peace and quiet, it was great! I ought to have my head examined. Or the guy should maybe; his had a hell of a hole in it. The dirty son-of-a-bitch for trying to get away with that. The fat little slob walks right up to me with a rod in his hand figuring to get away with it. The way he strutted you'd think he didn't have a care in the world, yet just like that he was going to kill two people without batting an eye. He got part of what he wanted anyway. The girl was dead. He was the kind of a rat who would have gotten a big laugh out of the papers tomorrow. Maybe he was supposed to be the rain of purity that was going to wash me down the gutter into the sewer with the rest of the scum. Brother, would that have been a laugh.

Okay, if he wanted a laugh, he'd get it. If his ghost could laugh I'd make it real funny for him. It would be so funny that his ghost would be the laughingstock of hell and when mine got there it'd have something to laugh at too. I'm nothing but a stinking no-good killer but I get there first, Judge. I get there first and live to do it again because I have eyes that see and a hand that works without being told and I don't give a damn what you do to my soul because it's so far gone nothing can be done for it! Go to hell yourself, Judge! Get a real belly laugh!

I tore his pockets inside out and stuffed his keys and wallet in my coat. I ripped out every label on his clothes right down to the laundry marks then I kicked the snow off the pavement and rubbed his fingertips against the cold concrete until there weren't any fingertips left. When I was finished he looked like the remains of a scarecrow that had been up too many seasons. I grabbed an arm and a leg and heaved him over the rail, and when I heard a faint splash many seconds later my mouth split into a grin. I kicked the pieces of the cloth and his gun under the rail and let them get lost in the obscurity of the night and the river. I didn't even have to worry about the bullet. It was lying right there in the snow, all flattened out and glistening wetly.

I kicked that over the side too.

Now let them find him. Let them learn who it was and how it happened. Let everybody have a laugh while you're at it!

It was done and I lit a cigarette. The snow still coming down put a new layer over the tracks and the dark stain. It almost covered up the patch of cloth that had come from the girl's coat, but I picked that up and stuck it in with the rest of the stuff.

Now my footsteps were the only sound along the ramp. I walked back to the city telling myself that it was all right, it had to happen that way. I was me and I couldn't have been anything else even if there had been no war. I was all right, the world was wrong. A police car moaned through the pay station and passed me as its siren was dying down to a low whine. I didn't even give it a second thought. They weren't going anywhere, certainly not to the top of the hump because not one car had passed during those few minutes it had happened. Nobody saw me, nobody cared. If they did the hell with 'em.

I reached the streets of the city and turned back for another look at the steel forest that climbed into the sky. No, nobody ever walked across the bridge on a night like this.

Hardly nobody.

chapter two ▄▄▄▄▄▄▄▄▄▄▄▄▄▄

I DIDN'T GO HOME that night. I went to my office and sat in the big leather-covered chair behind the desk and drank without getting drunk. I held the .45 in my lap, cleaned and reloaded, watching it, feeling in it an extension of myself. How many people had it sent on the long road? My mind blocked off the thought of the past and I put the gun back in the sling under my arm and slept. I dreamt that the judge with the white hair and eyes like two berries on a bush was pointing at me, ordering me to take the long road myself, and I had the .45 in my hand and my finger worked the trigger. It clicked and wouldn't go off, and with every sharp click a host of devilish voices would take up a dirge of laughter and I threw the gun at him, but it wouldn't leave my hand. It was part of me and it stuck fast.

The key turning in the lock awakened me. Throughout that dream of violent action I hadn't moved an inch, so that when I brought my head up I was looking straight at Velda. She didn't know I was there until she tossed the day's mail on the desk. For a second she froze with startled surprise, then relaxed into a grin.

"You scared the whosis out of me, Mike." She paused and bit her lip. "Aren't you here early?"

"I didn't go home, kid."

"Oh. I thought you might call me. I stayed up pretty late."

"I didn't get drunk, either."

"No?"

"No."

Velda frowned again. She wanted to say something, but during office hours she respected my position. I was the boss and she was my secretary. Very beautiful, of course. I loved her like hell, but she didn't know how much and she was still part of the pay roll. She decided to brighten the office with a smile instead, sorted the things on my desk, and started back to the reception room.

"Velda . . ."

She stopped, her hand on the knob and looked over her shoulder. "Yes, Mike?"

"Come here." I stood up and sat on the edge of the desk tapping a Lucky against my thumbnail. "What kind of a guy am I, kitten?"

Her eyes probed into my brain and touched the discontent. For a moment her smile turned into an animal look I had seen only once before. "Mike . . . that judge was a bastard. You're an all-right guy."

"How do you know?" I stuck the butt between my lips and lit it.

She stood there spraddle-legged with her hands low on her hips like a man, her breasts rising and falling faster than they should, fighting the wispy thinness of the dress. "I could love you a little or I could love you a lot, Mike. Sometimes it's both ways but mostly it's a lot. If you weren't all right I couldn't love you at all. Is that what you wanted me to say?"

"No." I blew out a stream of smoke and looked at the ceiling. "Tell me about myself. Tell me what other people say."

"Why? You know it as well as I do. You read the papers. When you're right you're a hero. When you're wrong you're kill-happy. Why don't you ask the people who count, the ones who really know you? Ask Pat. He thinks you're a good cop. Ask all the worms in the holes, the ones who have reason to stay out of your way. They'll tell you too . . . if you can catch them."

I chucked the butt into the metal basket. "Sure, the worms'll tell me. You know why I can't catch them, Velda? Do you know why they're scared to death to tangle with me? I'll tell you why. They know damn well I'm as bad as they are . . . worse, and I operate legally."

She reached out a hand and ran it over my hair. "Mike, you're too damn big and tough to give a hang what people say. They're only little people with little minds, so forget it."

"There's an awful lot of it."

"Forget it."

"Make me," I said.

She came into my arms with a rush and I held her to me to get warm and let the moist softness of her lips make me forget. I had to push to get her away and I stood there holding her arms, breathing in a picture of what a man's woman should look like. It was a long time before I could manage a grin, but she brought it out of me. There's something a woman does without words that makes a man feel like a man and forget about the things he's been told.

"Did you bring in the paper?"

"It's on my desk."

She followed me when I went out to get it. A tabloid and a full-sized job were there. The tab was opened to a news account of the trial that was one column wide and two inches long. They had my picture, too. The other rag gave me a good spread and a good going over and they didn't have my picture. I could start picking my friends out of the pack now.

Instead of digesting the absorbing piece of news, I scanned the pages for something else. Velda scowled at my concentration and hung over my shoulder. What I was looking for wasn't there. Not a single thing about two bodies in the river.

"Something, Mike?"

I shook my head. "Nope. Just looking for customers."

She didn't believe me. "There are some excellent prospects in the letter file if you're interested. They're waiting for your answer."

"How are we fixed, Velda?" I didn't look at her.

I put the paper down and reached in my pocket for a smoke.

"We're solvent. Two accounts paid up yesterday. The money has been banked and there's no bills. Why?"

"Maybe I'll take a vacation."

"From what?"

"From paid jobs. I'm tired of being an employee."

"Think of me."

"I am," I said. "You can take a vacation too if you want to."

She grabbed my elbow and turned me around until I was fencing with her eyes again. "Whatever you're thinking isn't of fun on some beach, Mike."

"It isn't?" I tried to act surprised.

"No." She took the cigarette from my mouth, dragged on it and stuck it back. She never moved her eyes. "Mike, don't play with me, please. Either tell me or don't, but quit making up excuses. What's on your mind?"

My mouth felt tight. "You wouldn't believe it if I told you."

"Yes I would." There was nothing hidden in her answer. No laughter, no scorn. Just absolute belief in me.

"I want to find out about myself, Velda."

She must have known what was coming. I said it quietly, almost softly, and she believed me. "All right, Mike," she said. "If you need me for anything you know where to find me."

I gave her the cigarette and went back to the office. How deep can a woman go to search a man's mind? How can they know without being told when some trivial thing can suddenly become so important? What is it that gives them that look as if they know the problem and the answer too, yet hold it back because it's something you have to discover for yourself?

I sat down in the swivel chair again and pulled all the junk out of my pockets; the keys, the wallet and the change. Two of the keys were for a car. One was an ordinary house key, another for a trunk or suitcase, and another for either a tumbler padlock or another house.

If I expected to find anything in the wallet I was mistaken. There were six fives and two singles in the bill compartment, a package of three-cent stamps and a card-calendar in one pocket, and a plain green card with the edges cut off at odd angles in the other pocket. That was all.

That was enough.

The little fat boy didn't have his name in print anywhere. It wasn't a new wallet either. Fat boy didn't want identification. I didn't blame him. What killer would?

Yeah, that was enough to make me sit back and look at the scuffed folder of calfskin and make me think. It would make you think too. Take a look at your own wallet and see what's in it.

I had the stuff spread out on the desk when I remembered the other pocket of my raincoat and pulled out the huge tweed triangle that had come from the girl's coat. I laid it out on my lap with the night before shoved into some corner of my brain and looked at it as though it were just another puzzle, not a souvenir of death.

The cloth had come apart easily. I must have grabbed her at the waist because the section of the coat included the right-hand and pocket and part of the lining. I rubbed the fabric through my fingers feeling the soft texture of fine wool, taking in the details of the pattern. More out of curiosity than anything else, I stuck my hand inside the pocket and came up with a crumpled pack of cigarettes.

She didn't even have time for a last smoke, I thought. Even a condemned man gets that. She didn't. She took one look at me and saw my eyes and my face and whatever she saw there yanked a scream from her lungs and the strength to pull her over the rail.

What have I got locked up inside me that comes out at times like that? What good am I alive? Why do I have to be the one to pull the trigger and have my soul torn apart afterwards?

The cigarettes were a mashed ball of paper in my hand, a little wad of paper, cellophane and tinfoil that smelt of tobacco and death. My teeth were locked together and when I looked down at my hand my nail ripped through the paper and I saw the green underneath.

Between the cigarettes and the wrapper was another of those damnable green cards with the edges cut off at odd angles.

Two murders. Two green cards.

It was the same way backwards. Two green cards and two murders.

Which came first, the murders or the cards?

Green for death.

Murder at odd angles. Two murders. Eight odd angles. Yes, two murders. The fat boy got what he was after. Because of him the girl was murdered no matter how. So I got him. I was a murderer like they said, only to me it was different. I was just a killer. I wondered what the law would say and if they'd make that fine difference now. Yeah. I could have been smart about it; I could have done what I did, called the police and let them take over then take the dirty medicine the papers and the judge and the public would have handed me. No, I had to be smart. I had to go and mix it up so much that if those bodies were found and the finger pointed at me all I could expect was a trip on that long road to nowhere.

Was that why I did it . . . because I felt smart? No, that wasn't the reason. I didn't feel smart. I was mad. I was kill crazy mad at the bastards the boy with the scythe pointed out to me and goddamn mad at all the screwy little minds and the screwy big minds that had the power of telling me off later. They could go to hell, the judge and the jury and all the rest of them! I was getting too sick and disgusted of fighting their battles for them anyway! The boy with the scythe could go to hell with the rest and if he didn't like it he could come after me, personally. I'd love that. I wish there *was* a special agency called Death that could hear what I was thinking and make a try for me. I'd like to take that stinking black shadow and shove his own scythe down his bony throat and disjoint him with a couple of .45's! Come on, bony boy, let's see you do what you can! Get your white-haired judge and your good people tried and true and let's see just how good you are! I think I'm better, see? I think I can handle any one of you, and if you get the idea I'm kidding, then come and get me.

And if you're afraid to come after me, then I'm going after you. Maybe I'll know what I'm like then. Maybe I'll find out what's going on in my mind and why I keep on living when fat cold-blooded killers and nice warm-blooded killers are down there shaking hands with the devil!

I pulled the green card out of the cigarettes and matched it to the one from the wallet. They fitted—Twins. I put them in my shirt pocket, grabbed my coat and hat and slammed the door after me when I left the office.

At a little after ten I pulled up outside the brick building that was the house of the law. Here was where the invisible processes went on that made cops out of men and murderers out of clues. The car in front of mine was an official sedan that carried the D.A.'s sticker and I smoked a butt right down to the bottom before I decided to try to reach Pat even if the fair-haired boy of the courts was around.

I should have waited a minute longer. I had my hand on the door when he pushed through and it looked like a cold wind hit him in the face. He screwed his mouth up into a snarl, thought better of it and squeezed a smile out.

Strictly an official smile.

He said, "Morning."

I said, "Nice day."

He got in his car and slammed the door so hard it almost fell off. I waved when he drove by. He didn't wave back. The old guy on the elevator took me upstairs and when I walked into Pat's office I was grinning.

Pat started, "Did you . . ."

I answered with a nod. "I did. We met at the gate. What got into the lad, is he sore at me?"

"Sit down, Mike." Pat waved his thumb at the straight-back wooden chair reserved for official offenders about to get a reprimand. "Look, pal, the District Attorney is only an elected official, but that's a mighty big 'only.' You put him over a barrel not so long ago and he isn't going to forget it. He isn't going to forget who your friends are, either."

"Meaning you."

"Meaning me exactly. I'm a Civil Service servant, a Captain of Homicide. I have certain powers of jurisdiction, arrest and influence. He supersedes them. If the D.A. gets his hooks into you just once, you'll have a ring through your nose and I'll be handed the deal of whipping you around the arena just to give him a little satisfaction. Please quit antagonizing the guy for my sake if not for your own. Now what's on your mind?"

Pat leaned back and grinned at me. We were still buddies.

"What's new on the dockets, chum?"

"Nothing," he shrugged. "Life has been nice and dull. I come in at eight and go home at six. I like it."

"Not even a suicide?"

"Not even. Don't tell me you're soliciting work."

"Hardly. I'm on a vacation."

Pat got that look. It started behind the pupils where no look was supposed to be. A look that called me a liar and waited to hear the rest of the lie. I had to lie a little myself. "Since you have it so easy, how about taking your own vacation with me? We could have some fun."

The look retreated and disappeared altogether. "Hell, I'd love to, Mike, but we're still scratching trying to catch up on all the details around here. I don't think it's possible." He screwed up his forehead. "Don't you feel so hot?"

"Sure, I feel fine, that's why I want a vacation while I can enjoy it." I slapped my hat back on my head and stood up. "Well, since you won't come I'll hit the road alone. Too bad. Ought to be lots doing."

He rocked his chair forward and took my hand. "Have fun, Mike."

"I will." I gave it a pause, then: "Oh, by the way. I wanted to show you something before I left." I reached in my shirt pocket and took out the two green cards and tossed them on the desk. "Funny, aren't they?"

Pat dropped my hand like it had been hot. Sometimes he gets the damnedest expression on his face you ever saw. He held those cards in his fingers and walked around the desk to close and lock the door. What he said when he sat down makes dirty reading.

"Where'd you get these?" His voice had an edge to it that meant we were close to not being buddies any more.

"I found 'em."

"Nuts. Sit down, damn it." I sat down easy again and lit a smoke. It was hard to keep a grin off my mouth. "Once more, Mike, where'd they come from?"

"I told you I found them."

"Okay, I'll get very simple in my questioning. *Where* did you find them?"

I was getting tired of wearing the grin. I let it do what it wanted to do and I felt the air dry my teeth. "Look, Pat, remember me? I'm your friend. I'm a citizen and I'm a stubborn jerk who doesn't like to answer questions when he doesn't know why. Quit the cop act and ask right. So tell me I handed you a line about a vacation when all I wanted to get was some information. So tell me something you haven't told me before."

"All right, Mike, all right. All I want to know is where you got them."

"I killed a guy and took it off his body."

"Stop being sarcastic."

I must have grinned the dirtiest kind of grin there was. Pat watched me strangely, shook his head impatiently and tossed the cards back on the desk. "Are they so important I can't hear about it, Pat?"

He ran his tongue across his lips. "No, they're not so important in one way. I guess they could be lost easily enough. They're plenty of them in circulation."

"Yeah?"

He nodded briefly and fingered the edge of one. "They're Communist identification cards. One of the new fronts. The Nazi bund that used to operate in this country had cards just like 'em. They were red though. Every so often they change the cuts of the edges to try to trip up any spies. When you get in the meeting hall your card has to match up with a master card."

"Oh, just like a lodge." I picked one up and tucked it in my coat pocket.

He said, "Yeah," sourly.

"Then why all the to-do with the door? We're not in a meeting hall."

Pat smacked the desk with the flat of his hand. "I don't know, Mike. Damn it, if anybody but you came in with a couple of those cards I would have said what they were and that's all. But when it's you I go cold all over and wait for something to happen. I know it won't happen, then it does. Come on, spill it. What's behind them?" He looked tired as hell.

"Nothing, I told you that. They're curious and I found two of them. I'd never seen anything like it before and thought maybe you'd know what they were."

"And I did."

"That's right. Thanks."

I put my hat back on and stood up. He let me get as far as the door. "Mike . . ." He was looking at his hand.

"I'm on vacation now, pal."

He picked up a card and looked at the blank sides of it. "Three days ago a man was murdered. He had one of these things clutched in his hand."

I turned the knob. "I'm still on vacation."

"I just thought I'd tell you. Give you something to think about."

"Swell. I'll turn it over in my mind when I'm stretched out on a beach in Florida."

"We know who killed him."

I let the knob slip through my fingers and tried to sound casual. "Anybody I know?"

"Yes, you and eight million others. His name is Lee Deamer. He's running for State Senator next term."

My breath whistled through my teeth. Lee Deamer, the people's choice. The guy who was scheduled to sweep the state clean. The guy who was kicking the politicians all over the joint. "He's pretty big," I said.

"Very."

"Too big to touch?"

His eyes jumped to mine. "Nobody is that big, Mike. Not even Deamer."

"Then why don't you grab him?"

"Because he didn't do it."

"What a pretty circle *that* is. I had you figured for a brain, Pat. He killed a guy and he didn't do it. That's great logic, especially when it comes from you."

A slow grin started at the corner of his eyes. "When you're on vacation you can think it over, Mike. I'll wrap it up for you, just once. A dead man is found. He has one of these cards in his hand. Three people positively identified the killer. Each one saw him under favorable conditions and was able to give a complete description and identification. They came to the police with the story and we were lucky enough to hush it up.

"Lee Deamer was identified as the killer. He was described right to the scar on his nose, his picture was snapped up the second it was shown and he was identified in person. It's the most open-and-shut case you ever saw, yet we can't touch him because when he was supposed to be pulling a murder he was a mile away talking to a group of prominent citizens. I happened to be among those present."

I kicked the door closed with my foot and stood there. "Hot damn."

"Too hot to handle. Now you know why the D.A. was in such a foul mood."

"Yeah," I agreed. "But it shouldn't be too tough for you, Pat. There's only four things that could have happened."

"Tell me. See if it's what I'm thinking."

"Sure, kid. One: twins. Two: a killer disguised as Deamer. Three: a deliberate frame-up with witnesses paid to make the wrong identification. Four: it was Deamer after all."

"Which do you like, Mike?"

I laughed at his solemn tone. "Beats me, I'm on vacation." I found the knob and pulled it open. "See you when I get back."

"Sure thing, Mike." His eyes narrowed to slits. "If you run across any more cards, tell me about them, will you?"

"Yeah, anything else?"

"Just that one question. Where did you get them?"

"I killed a guy and took it off his dead body."

Pat was swearing softly to himself when I left. Just as the elevator door closed he must have begun to believe me because I heard his door open and he shouted, "Mike . . . damn it, Mike!"

I called the *Globe* office from a hash house down the street. When I asked the switchboard operator if Marty Kooperman had called in yet she plugged into a couple of circuits, asked around and told me he was just about to go to lunch. I passed the word for him to meet me in the lobby if he wanted a free chow and hung up. I wasn't in a hurry. I never knew a reporter yet who would pass up a meal he wasn't paying for.

Marty was there straddling a chair backwards, trying to keep his eyes on two blondes and a luscious redhead who was apparently waiting for someone else. When I tapped him on the shoulder he scowled and whispered, "Hell, I almost had that redhead nailed. Go away."

"Come on, I'll buy you another one," I said.

"I like this one."

The city editor came out of the elevator, said hello to the redhead and they went out together. Marty shrugged. "Okay, let's eat. A lousy political reporter doesn't stand a chance against that."

One of the blondes looked at me and smiled. I winked at her and she winked back. Marty was so disgusted he spit on the polished floor. Some day he'll learn that all you have to do is ask. They'll tell you.

He tried to steer me into a hangout around the corner, but I nixed the idea and kept going up the street to a little bar that put out a good meal without any background noise. When we had a table between us and the orders on the fire, Marty flipped me a cigarette and the angle of his eyebrows told me he was waiting.

"How much about politics do you know, Marty?"

He shook the match out. "More than I can write about."

"Know anything about Lee Deamer?"

His eyebrows came down and he leaned on his elbows. "You're an investigator, Mike. You're the lad with a gun under his coat. Who wants to know about Deamer?"

"Me."

"What for?" His hand was itching to go for the pad and pencil in his pocket.

"Because of something that's no good for a story," I said. "What do you know about him?"

"Hell, there's nothing wrong with him. The guy is going to be the next senator from this state. He packs a big punch and everybody likes him including the opposition. He's strictly a maximum of statesman and a minimum of politician. Deamer has the cleanest record of anybody, probably because he has never been mixed up in politics too much. He is independently wealthy and out of reach as far as bribery goes. He has no use for chiselers or the spoils system, so most of the sharp boys are against him."

"Are you against him, Marty?"

"Not me, feller. I'm a Deamer man through and through. He's what we need these days. Where do you stand?"

"I haven't voted since they dissolved the Whig party."

"Fine citizen you are."

"Yeah."

"Then why the sudden curiosity?"

"Suppose I sort of hinted to you . . . strictly off the record . . . that somebody was after Deamer. Would you give me a hand? It may be another of those things you'll never get to write about."

Marty balled his hands into fists and rubbed his knuckles together. His face wasn't nice to look at. "You're damn right I'll help. I'm just another little guy who's sick of being booted around the block by the bastards that get themselves elected to public office and use that office to push their own wild ideas and line their own pockets. When a good thing comes along those stinking pigs go all out to smear it. Well, not if I can help it, and not if about nine tenths of the people in this burg can help it either. What do you need, kid?"

"Not much. Just a history on Deamer. All his background from as far back as you can go. Bring it right up to date. Pictures too, if you have any."

"I have folders of the stuff."

"Good," I said. Our lunch came up then and we dug into it. Throughout the meal Marty would alternately frown at his plate then glance up at me. I ate and kept my mouth shut. He could come to his own decision. He reached it over the apple pie he had for dessert. I saw his face relax and he let out a satisfied grunt.

"Do you want the stuff now?"

"Any time will do. Stick it in an envelope and send it to my office. I'm not in a hurry."

"Okay." He eyed me carefully. "Can you let me in on the secret?"

I shook my head. "I would if I could, pal. I don't know what the score is yet myself."

"Suppose I keep my ears to the ground. Anything likely to crop up that you could use?"

"I doubt it. Let's say that Deamer is a secondary consideration to what I actually want. Knowing something about him might help both of us."

"I see." He struck a match under the table and held it to a cigarette. "Mike, if there is a news angle, will you let me in on it?"

"I'd be glad to."

"I'm not talking about publishable news."

"No?"

Marty looked through the smoke at me, his eyes bright. "In every man's past there's some dirt. It can be dirt that belongs to the past and not to the present. But it can be dirty enough to use to smear a person, smear him so good that he'll have to retreat from the public gaze. You aren't tied up in politics like I am so you haven't got any idea how really rotten it is. Everybody is out for himself and to hell with the public. Oh, sure, the public has its big heroes, but they do things just to make the people think of them as heroes. Just look what happens whenever Congress or some other organization uncovers some of the filthy tactics behind government . . . the next day or two the boys upstairs release some big news item they've been keeping in reserve and it sweeps the dirt right off the front page and out of your mind.

"Deamer's straight. Because he's straight he's a target. Everybody is after his hide except the people. Don't think it hasn't been tried. I've come across it and so have the others, but we went to the trouble of going down a little deeper than we were expected to and we came across the source of the so-called 'facts.' Because it was stuff that was supposed to come to light during any normal compilation of a man's background the only way it could reach the public without being suspected of smear tactics by the opposition was through the newspapers.

"Well, by tacit agreement we suppressed the stuff. In one way we're targets too because the big boys with the strings know how we feel. Lee Deamer's going to be in there, Mike. He's going to raise all kinds of hell with the corruption we have in our government. He'll smoke out the rats that live on the public and give this country back some of the strength that it had before we were undermined by a lot of pretty talk and pretty faces.

"That's why I want to get the story from you . . . if there is one. I want to hold a conference with the others who feel like I do and come to an honest conclusion. Hell, I don't know why I've become so damn public-spirited. Maybe it's just that I'm tired of taking all the crap that's handed out."

I put a light to my butt and said, "Has there been anything lately on the guy?"

"No. Not for a month, anyway. They're waiting until he gets done stumping the state before they pick him apart."

Pat was right then. The police had kept it quiet, not because they were part of the movement of righteousness, but because they must have suspected a smear job. Deamer couldn't have been in two places at once by any means.

"Okay, Marty. I'll get in touch with you if anything lousy comes up. Do me a favor and keep my name out of any conversation, though, will you?"

"Of course. By the way, that judge handed you a dirty one the other day."

"What the hell, he could be right, you know."

"Sure he could, it's a matter of opinion. He's just a stickler for the letter of the law, the exact science of words. He's the guy that let a jerk off on a smoking-in-the-subway charge. The sign said NO SMOKING ALLOWED, so he claimed it allowed you not to smoke, but didn't say anything about not smoking. Don't give him another thought."

I took a bill from my wallet and handed it to the waiter with a wave that meant to forget the change. Marty looked at his watch and said he had to get back, so we shook hands and left.

The afternoon papers were out and the headlines had to do with the Garden fight the night before. One of the kids was still out like a light. His manager was being indicted for letting him go into the ring with a brain injury.

There wasn't a word about any bodies being found in the river. I threw the paper in a waste barrel and got in my car.

I didn't feel so good. I wasn't sick, but I didn't feel so good. I drove to a parking lot, shoved the car into a corner and took a cab to Times Square and went to a horror movie. The lead feature had an actor with a split personality. One was a man, the other was an ape. When he was an ape he killed people and when he was a man he regretted it. I could imagine how he felt. When I stood it as long as I could I got up and went to a bar.

At five o'clock the evening editions had come out. This time the headlines were a little different. They had found one of the bodies.

Fat boy had been spotted by a ferryboat full of people and the police launch had dragged him out of the drink. He had no identification and no fingerprints. There was a sketch of what he might have looked like before the bullet got him smack in the kisser.

The police attributed it to a gang killing.

Now I was a one-man gang. Great. Just fine. Mike Hammer, Inc. A gang.

chapter three ▄▄▄▄▄▄▄▄▄▄

THE RAIN. The damned never-ending rain. It turned Manhattan into a city of deflections, a city you saw twice no matter where you looked. It was a slow, easy rain that took awhile to collect on your hat brim before it cascaded down in front of your face. The streets had an oily shine that brought the rain-walkers out, people who went native whenever the sky cried and tore off their hats to let the tears drip through their hair.

I buttoned my coat under my neck and turned the collar up around my ears. It was good walking, but not when you were soaking wet. I took it easy and let the crowd sift past me, everybody in a hurry to get nowhere and wait. I was going south on Broadway, stopping to look in the windows of the closed stores, not too conscious of where my feet were leading me. I passed Thirty-fourth still going south, walked into the Twenties with a stop for a sandwich and coffee, then kept my course until I reached the Square.

That was where my feet led me. Union Square. Green cards and pinched-faced guys arguing desperately in the middle of little groups. Green cards and people listening to the guys. What the hell could they say that was important enough to keep anybody standing in the rain? I grinned down at my feet because they had the sense that should have been in my head. They wanted to know about the kind of people who carried green cards, the kind of people who would listen to guys who carried green cards.

Or girls.

I ambled across the walk into the yellow glare of the lights. There were no soapboxes here, just those little knots of people trying to talk at once and being shouted down by the one in the middle.

A cop went by swinging his night stick. Whenever he passed a group he automatically got a grip on the thing and looked over hopefully.

I heard some of the remarks when he passed. They weren't nice.

Coming toward me a guy who looked like a girl and a girl who looked like a guy altered their course to join one group. The girl got right into things and the guy squealed with pleasure whenever she said something clever.

Maybe there were ten groups, maybe fifteen. If it hadn't been raining there might have been more. Nobody talked about the same thing. Occasionally someone would drop out of one crowd and drift over to another.

But they all had something in common. The same thing you find in a slaughterhouse. The lump of vomit in the center of each crowd was a Judas sheep trying to lead the rest to the ax. Then they'd go back and get more. The sheep were asking for it too. They were a seedy bunch in shapeless clothes, heavy with the smell of the rot they had asked for and gotten. They had a jackal look of discontent and cowardice, a hungry look that said you kill while we loot, then all will be well with the world.

Yeah.

Not all of them were like that, though. Here and there in the crowd was a pin-striped business suit and homburg. An expensive mink was flanked by a girl in a shabby gray cloth job and a guy in a hand-me-down suit with his hands stuck in the pockets.

Just for the hell of it I hung on the edge of the circle and listened. A few latecomers closed in behind me and I had to stand there and hear just why anybody that fought the war was a simple-minded fool, why anybody who tolerated the foreign policy of this country was a Fascist, why anybody who didn't devote his soul and money to the enlightenment of the masses was a traitor to the people.

The goddamn fools who listened agreed with him, too. I was ready to reach out and pluck his head off his shoulders when one of the guys behind me stood on his toes and said, "Why don't you get the hell out of this country if you don't like it?" The guy was a soldier.

I said, "Attaboy, buddy," but it got lost in the rumble from the crowd and the screech the guy let out. The soldier swore back at him and tried to push through the crowd to get at the guy, only two guys in trench coats blocked him.

Lovely, lovely, it was just what I wanted! The soldier went to shove the two guys apart and one gave him an elbow. I was just going to plant a beauty behind his ear when the cop stepped in. He was a good cop, that one. He didn't lift the night stick above his waist. He held it like a lance and when it hit it went in deep right where it took all the sound out of your body. I saw two punks fold up in the middle and one of the boys in the raincoats let out a gasp. The other one stepped back and swore.

The cop said, "Better move on, soldier."

"Ah, I'd like to take that pansy apart. Did you hear what he said?"

"I hear 'em every night, feller," the cop told him. "They got bats in their heads. Come on, it's better to let 'em talk."

"Not when they say those things!"

The cop grinned patiently. "They gotta right to say 'em. You don't *have* to listen, you know."

"I don't give a hoot. They haven't got a right to say those things. Hell, the big mouth probably was too yeller to fight a war and too lazy to take a job. I oughta slam 'im one."

"Uh-huh." The cop steered him out of the crowd. I heard him say, "That's just what they want. It makes heroes of 'em when the papers get it. We still got ways of taking care of 'em, don't worry. Every night this happens and I get in a few licks."

I started grinning and went back to listening. One boy in a trench coat was swearing under his breath. The other was holding on to him. I shifted a little to the side so I could see what I thought I had seen the first time. When the one turned around again I knew I was right the first time.

Both of them were wearing guns under their arms.

Green cards, loud-mouthed bastards, sheep, now guns.

It came together like a dealer sweeping in the cards for shuffling. The game was getting rough. But guns, why guns? This wasn't a fighting game. Who the devil was worth killing in this motley crowd? Why guns here when there was a chance of getting picked up with them?

I pulled back out of the crowd and crossed the walk into the shadows to a bench. A guy sat on the other end of it with a paper over his face, snoring. Fifteen minutes later the rain quit playing around and one by one the crowd pulled away until only a handful

was left around the nucleus. For guys who were trying to intimidate
the world they certainly were afraid of a little water. All of a
sudden the skies opened up and let loose with everything in sight.
The guy on the end of the bench jumped up, fighting the paper
that wrapped itself around his face. He made a few drunken
animal noises, swallowed hard when he saw me watching him
and scurried away into the night.

I had to sit through another five minutes of it before I got up.
The two men in the trench coats waited until the loose-jointed
guy in the black overcoat had a fifty-foot start, then they turned
around and followed him. That gave them a good reason for the
rods under their arms.

Bodyguards.

Maybe it was the rain that made my guts churn. Maybe it was
those words beating against my head, telling me that I was only
scum. Maybe it was just me, but suddenly I wanted to grab that
guy in the overcoat and slam his teeth down his throat and wait
to see what his two boys would do. I'd like to catch them reaching
for a gun! I'd like them to move their hands just one inch, then
I'd show them what practice could do when it came to snagging
a big, fat gun out of a shoulder sling! So I was a sucker for fighting
a war. I was a sap for liking my country. I was a jerk for not
thinking them a superior breed of lice!

That cop with the round Irish face should have used a knife
in their bellies instead of the butt end of a night stick.

I waited until they were blurs in the rain then tagged along in
the rear. They were a fine pair, those two, a brace of dillies. I
tailed them into the subway and out again in Brooklyn. I was
with them when they walked down Coney Island Avenue and
beside them when they turned into a store off the avenue and
they never knew I was there.

Down at the corner I crossed the street and came back up the
other side. One of the boys was still in the doorway playing
watchdog. I wanted to know how smart the people were who
wanted to run the world. I found out. I cut across the street and
walked right up to the guy without making any fuss about it. He
gave me a queer look and drew his eyebrows together in a frown,
trying to remember where he had seen me before. He was fumbling
for words when I pulled out the green card.

He didn't try to match them up. One look was enough and he
waved his head at the door. I turned the knob and went in. I'd
have to remember to tell Pat about that. They weren't being so
careful at all.

When I closed the door I changed my mind. The light went on, just like a refrigerator, and I saw the blackout shades on the windows and door, the felt padding beneath the sill so no light could escape under the door. And the switch. A home-made affair on the side of the door that cut the light when the door opened and threw it back on again when it closed.

The girl at the desk glanced up impatiently and held out her hand for the card. She matched them. She matched them damn carefully, too, and when she handed them back she had sucked hollows into her cheeks trying to think of the right thing to say.

"You're from . . .?"

"Philly," I supplied. I hoped it was a good answer. It was. She nodded and turned her head toward a door in the back of the anteroom. I had to wait for her to push a button before it opened under my hand.

There were twenty-seven people in the other room. I counted them. They were all very busy. Some of them were at desks clipping things from newspapers and magazines. One guy in a corner was taking pictures of the things they clipped and it came out on microfilm. There was a little group around a map of the city over against one wall, talking too earnestly and too low for me to catch what they were saying.

I saw the other boy in the trench coat. He still had it on and he was sticking close with the guy in the overcoat. Evidently the fellow was some kind of a wheel, checking on activities here and there, offering sharp criticism or curt words of approval.

When I had been there a full five minutes people began to notice me. At first it was just a casual glance from odd spots, then long searching looks that disappeared whenever I looked back. The man in the overcoat licked his lips nervously and smiled in my direction.

I sat down at a table and crossed my legs, a smoke dangling from my mouth. I smoked and I watched, trying to make some sense out of it. Some of them even looked like Commies, the cartoon kind. There were sharp eyes that darted from side to side, too-wise women dazzled by some meager sense of responsibility, smirking students who wore their hair long, tucked behind their heads. A few more came in while I sat and devoted themselves to some unfinished task. But sooner or later their eyes came to mine and shifted away hurriedly when I looked at them.

It became a game, that watching business. I found that if I stared at some punk who was taking his time about doing things he became overly ambitious all of a sudden. I went from one to the other and came at last to the guy in the overcoat.

He was the head man here, no doubt about it. His word was law. At twenty minutes past eleven he started his rounds of the room, pausing here and there to lay a mimeographed sheet on a desk, stopping to emphasize some obscure point.

Finally he had to pass me and for a split second he hesitated, simpered and went on. I got it and played the game to the hilt. I walked to a desk and picked up one of the sheets and read it as I sat on the edge of the desk. The scraggly blonde at the desk couldn't keep her hands from shaking.

I got the picture then. I was reading the orders for the week; I was in on the pipeline from Moscow. It was that easy. I read them all the way through, tossed the sheet down and went back to my chair.

I smiled.

Everybody smiled.

The boy in the trench coat with the gun under his arm came over and said, "You will like some coffee now?" He had an accent I couldn't place.

I smiled again and followed him to the back of the room. I didn't see the door of the place because it was hidden behind the photography equipment.

It led into a tiny conference room that held a table, six chairs and a coffee urn. When the door closed there were seven of us in the room including two dames. Trench Coat got a tray of cups from the closet and set them on the table. For me it was a fight between grinning and stamping somebody's face in. For an after-office-hours coffee deal it certainly was a high-tension deal.

To keep from grinning I shoved another Lucky in my mouth and stuck a light to it. There they were, everyone with a coffee cup, lined up at the urn. Because I took my time with the smoke I had to join the end of the line, and it was a good thing I did. It gave me time enough to get the pitch.

Everybody had been watching me covertly anyway, saying little and satisfied with me keeping my mouth shut. When they took their coffee black and wandered off to the table the two women made a face at the bitter taste. They didn't like black coffee. They weren't used to black coffee. Yet they took black coffee and kept shooting me those sidewise glances.

How simple can people get? Did they take everybody for dummies like themselves? When I drew my cup from the urn Trench Coat stood right behind me and waited. He was the only one that bothered to breathe and he breathed down my neck.

I took my sugar and milk. I took plenty of it. I turned around and lifted my cup in a mock toast and all the jerks started breathing again and the room came to life. The two women went back and got sugar and milk.

The whole play had been a signal setup a kid could have seen through.

Trench Coat smiled happily. "It is very good you are here, comrade. We cannot be too careful, of course."

"Of course." It was the first time I had said anything, but you might have thought I gave the Gettysburg Address. Overcoat came over immediately, his hand reaching out for mine.

"I am Henry Gladow, you know. Certainly you know." His chuckle was nervous and high-pitched. "We had been expecting you, but not so quickly. Of course we realize the party works quickly, but this is almost faith-inspiring! You came with incredible speed. Why, only tonight I picked up the telegram from our messenger uptown announcing your arrival. Incredible."

That was the reason for the bodyguards and the guns. My new chum was receiving party instructions from somebody else. That was why the Trench Coats closed in around the soldier, in case it had been a trap to intercept the message. Real cute, but dumb as hell.

". . . happy to have you inspect our small base of operation, comrade." I turned my attention back to him again and listened politely. "Rarely do we have such an honor. In fact, this is the first time." He turned to Trench Coat, still smiling. "This is my, er, traveling companion, Martin Romberg. Very capable man, you know. And my secretary," he indicated a girl in thick-lensed glasses who was just out of her teens, "Martha Camisole."

He went around the room introducing each one and with every nod I handed out I got back a smile that tried hard to be nice but was too scared to do a good job of it.

We finished the coffee, had another and a smoke before Gladow looked at his watch. I could see damn well he had another question coming up and I let him take his time about asking it. He said, "Er, you are quite satisfied with the operation at this point, comrade? Would you care to inspect our records and documents?"

My scowl was of surprise, but he didn't know that. His eyebrows went up and he smiled craftily. "No, comrade, not written documents. Here, in the base, we have experts who commit the documents . . ." he tapped the side of his head, "here."

"Smart," I grunted. "What happens if they talk?"

He tried to seem overcome with the preposterous. "Very funny, comrade. Quite, er . . . yes. Who is there to make them talk? That is where we have the advantage. In this country force is never used. The so-called third degree has been swept out. Even a truthful statement loses its truth if coercion is even hinted at. The fools, the despicable fools haven't the intelligence to govern a country properly! When the party is in power things will be different, eh, comrade?"

"Much, much different," I said.

Gladow nodded, pleased. "You, er, care to see anything of special importance, comrade?" His voice had a gay tone.

"No, nothing special. Just checking around." I dragged on the butt and blew a cloud of smoke in his face. He didn't seem to mind it.

"Then in your report you will state that everything *is* satisfactory here?"

"Sure, don't give it another thought."

There was more sighing. Some of the fear went out of their eyes. The Camisole kid giggled nervously. "Then may I say again that we have been deeply honored by your visit, comrade," Gladow said. "Since the sudden, untimely death of our former, er, compatriot, we have been more or less uneasy. You understand these things of course. It was gratifying to see that he was not identified with the party in any way. Even the newspapers are stupid in this country."

I had to let my eyes sink to the floor or he would have seen the hate in them. I was an inch away from killing the bastard and he didn't know it. I turned my hand over to look at the time and saw that it was close to midnight. I'd been in the pigsty long enough. I set the empty cup down on the table and walked to the door. The crumbs couldn't even make good coffee.

All but two of the lesser satellites had left, their desks clear of all papers. The guy on the photography rig was stuffing the microfilm in a small file case while a girl burned papers in a metal wastebasket. I didn't stop to see who got the film. There was enough of it that was so plain that I didn't need any pictures drawn for me.

Gladow was hoping I'd shake hands, but he got fooled. I kept them both in my pockets because I didn't like to handle snakes, not of their variety.

The outside door slammed shut and I heard some hurried conversation and the girl at the desk say, "Go right in." I was standing by the inside door when she opened it.

I had to make sure I was in the right place by taking a quick look around me. This was supposed to be a Commie setup, a joint for the masses only, not a club for babes in mink coats with hats to match. She was one of those tall, willowy blondes who reached thirty with each year an improvement.

She was almost beautiful, with a body that could take your mind off beauty and put it on other things. She smiled at Gladow as soon as she saw him and gave him her hand.

His voice took on a purr when he kissed it. "Miss Brighton, it is always a pleasure to see you." He straightened up, still smiling. "I didn't expect you to come at this hour."

"I didn't expect you to be here either, Henry. I decided to take the chance anyway. I brought the donations." Her voice was like rubbing your hand on satin. She pulled an envelope out of her pocketbook and handed it to Gladow unconcernedly. Then, for the first time, she saw me.

She squinted her eyes, trying to place me.

I grinned at her. I like to grin at a million bucks.

Ethel Brighton grinned back.

Henry Gladow coughed politely and turned to me. "Miss Brighton is one of our most earnest comrades. She is chiefly responsible for some of our most substantial contributions."

He made no attempt to introduce me. Apparently nobody seemed to care. Especially Ethel Brighton. A quick look flashed between them that brought the scowl back to her face for a brief moment. A shadow on the wall that came from one of the Trench Coats behind me was making furious gestures.

I started to get the willies. It was the damnedest thing I had ever seen. Everybody was acting like a fraternity initiation and for some reason I was the man of the moment. I took it as long as I could. I said, "I'm going uptown. If you're going back you can come along."

For a dame who had her picture in most of the Sunday supplements every few weeks, she lost her air of sophistication in a hurry. Her cheeks seemed to sink in and she looked to Gladow for approval. Evidently he gave it, for she nodded and said, "My car . . . it's right outside."

I didn't bother to leave any good nights behind me. I went through the receptionist's cubicle and yanked the door open. When Ethel Brighton was out I slammed it shut. Behind me the place was as dark as the vacant hole it was supposed to be.

Without waiting to be asked I slid behind the wheel and held out my hand for the keys. She dropped them in my palm and fidgeted against the cushions. That car . . . it was a beauty. In the daylight it would have been a maroon convertible, but under the street lights it was a mass of mirrors with the chrome reflecting every bulb in the sky.

Ethel said, "Are you from . . . New York?"

"Nope. Philly," I lied.

For some reason I was making her mighty nervous. It wasn't my driving because I was holding it to a steady thirty to keep inside the green lights. I tried another grin. This time she smiled back and worried the fingers of her gloves.

I couldn't get over it, Ethel Brighton a Commie! Her old man would tan her hide no matter how old she was if he ever heard about it. But what the hell, she wasn't the only one with plenty of rocks who got hung up on the red flag. I said, "It hasn't been too easy for you to keep all this under your hat, has it?"

Her hands stopped working the glove. "N-no. I've managed, though."

"Yeah. You've done a good job."

"Thank you."

"Oh, no thanks at all, kid. For people with intelligence it's easy. When you're, er, getting these donations, don't people sorta wonder where it's going?"

She scowled again, puzzled. "I don't think so. I thought that was explained quite fully in my report."

"It was, it was. Don't get me wrong. We have to keep track of things, you know. Situations change." It was a lot of crap to me, but it must have made sense to her way of thinking.

"Usually they're much too busy to listen to my explanations, and anyway, they can deduct the amounts from their income tax."

"They ought to be pretty easy to touch, then."

This time she smiled a little. "They are. They think it's for charity."

"Uh-huh. Suppose your father finds out what you've been doing?"

The way she recoiled you'd think I smacked her. "Oh . . . please, you wouldn't!"

"Take it easy, kid. I'm only supposing."

Even in the dull light of the dash I could see how pale she was. "Daddy would . . . never forgive me. I think . . . he'd send me some place. He'd disinherit me completely." She shuddered, her hands going back to the glove again. "He'll never know. When he does it will be too late!"

"Your emotions are showing through, kid."

"So would yours if . . . oh . . . oh, I didn't mean . . ." Her expression made a sudden switch from rage to that of fear. It wasn't a nice fear, it was more like that of the girl on the bridge.

I looked over slowly, an angle creeping into the corner of my mind. "I'm not going to bite. Maybe you can't say things back there in front of the others, but sometimes I'm not like them. I can understand problems. I have plenty of my own."

"But you . . . you're . . ."

"I'm what?"

"You know." She bit into her lip, looking at me obliquely.

I nodded as if I did.

"Will you be here long?"

"Maybe," I shrugged. "Why?"

The fear came back. "Really, I wasn't asking pointed questions. Honest I wasn't. I just meant . . . I meant with the . . . other being killed and all, well . . ."

Damn it, she let her sentence trail off as if I was supposed to know everything that went on. What the hell did they take me for anyway? It was the same thing all night!

"I'll be here," I said.

We went over the bridge and picked a path through the late traffic in Manhattan. I went north to Times Square and pulled into the curb. "This is as far as I go, sugar. Thanks for the ride. I'll probably be seeing you again."

Her eyes went wide again. Brother, she could sure do things with those eyes. She gasped, "Seeing me?"

"Sure, why not?"

"But . . . you aren't . . . I never supposed . . ."

"That I might have a personal interest in a woman?" I finished.

"Well, yes."

"I like women, sugar. I always have and always will."

For the first time she smiled a smile she meant. She said, "You aren't a bit like I thought you'd be. Really. I like you. The other . . . agent . . . he was so cold that he scared me."

"I don't scare you?"

"You could . . . but you don't."

I opened the door. "Good night, Ethel."

"Good night." She slid over under the wheel and gunned the motor. I got one last quick smile before she pulled away.

What the hell. That's all I could think of. What the hell. All right, just what the hell was going on? I walked right into a nest of Commies because I flashed a green card and they didn't say a word, not one word. They played damn fool kids' games with me that any jerk could have caught, and bowed and scraped like I was king.

Not once did anyone ask my name.

Read the papers today. See what it says about the Red Menace. See how they play up their sneaking, conniving ways. They're supposed to be clever, bright as hell. They were dumb as horse manure as far as I was concerned. They were a pack of bugs thinking they could outsmart a world. Great. That coffee-urn trick was just great.

I walked down the street to a restaurant that was still open and ordered a plate of ham and eggs.

It was almost two o'clock when I got home. The rain had stopped long ago, but it was still up there, hanging low around the buildings, reluctant to let the city alone. I walked up to my apartment and shoved the key in the lock. My mind kept going back to Gladow, trying to make sense of his words, trying to fit them into a puzzle that had no other parts.

I could remember his speaking about somebody's untimely death. Evidently I was the substitute sent on in his place. But whose death? That sketch in the paper was a lousy one. Fat boy didn't look a bit like that sketch. All right then, who? There was only one other guy with a green card who was dead, the guy Lee Deamer was supposed to have killed.

Him. He's the one, I thought. I was his replacement. But what was I supposed to be?

There was just too much to think about; I was too tired to put my mind to it. You don't kill a fat man and see a girl die because of the look on your face and get involved with a Commie organization all in two days without feeling your mind sink into a soggy ooze that drew it down deeper and deeper until it relaxed of its own accord and you were asleep.

I sat slumped in the chair, the cigarette that had dropped from my fingers had burned a path through the rug at right angles with another. The bell shrilled and shrilled until I thought it would never stop. My arm going out to the phone was an involuntary movement, my voice just happened to be there.

I said hello.

It was Pat and he had to yell at me a half-dozen times before I snapped out of it. I grunted an answer and he said, "Too late for you, Mike?"

"It's four o'clock in the morning. Are you just getting up or just going to bed?"

"Neither. I've been working."

"At this hour?"

"Since six this evening. How's the vacation?"

"I called it off."

"Really now. Just couldn't bear to leave the city, could you? By the way, did you find any more green cards with the ends snipped off?"

The palms of my hands got wet all of a sudden. "No."

"Are you interested in them at all?"

"Cut the comedy, Pat. What're you driving at? It's too damn late for riddles."

"Get over here, Mike," his voice was terse. "My apartment, and make it as fast as you can."

I came awake all at once, shaking the fatigue from my brain. "Okay, Pat," I said, "give me fifteen minutes." I hung up and slipped into my coat.

It was easier to grab a cab than wheel my car out of the garage. I shook the cabbie's shoulder and gave him Pat's address, then settled back against the cushions while we tore across town. We made it with about ten seconds to spare and I gave the cabbie a fin for his trouble.

I looked up at the sky before I went in. The clouds had broken up and let the stars come through. Maybe tomorrow will be nice, I thought. Maybe it will be a nice normal day without all the filth being raked to the top. Maybe. I pushed Pat's bell and the door buzzed almost immediately.

He was waiting outside his apartment when I got off the elevator. "You made it fast, Mike."

"You said to, didn't you?"

"Come on in."

Pat had drinks in a shaker and three glasses on the coffee table. Only one had been used so far. "Expecting company?" I asked him.

"Big company, Mike. Sit down and pour yourself a drink."

I shucked my coat and hat and stuck a Lucky in my mouth. Pat wasn't acting right. You don't go around entertaining anybody at this hour, not even your best friends. Something had etched lines into his face and put a smudge of darkness under each eye. He looked tight as a drumhead. I sat there with a drink in my hand watching Pat trying to figure out what to say.

It came halfway through my drink. "You were right the first time," he said.

I put the glass down and stared at him. "Do it over. I don't get it."

"Twins."

"What?"

"Twins," Pat repeated. "Lee Deamer had a twin brother." He stood there swirling the mixture around in his glass.

"Why tell me? I'm not in the picture."

Pat had his back to me, staring at nothing. I could barely hear his voice. "Don't ask me that, Mike. I don't know why I'm telling you when it's official business, but I am. In one way we're both alike. We're cops. Sometimes I find myself waiting to know what you'd do in a situation before I do it myself. Screwy, isn't it?"

"Pretty screwy."

"I told you once before that you have a feeling for things that I haven't got. You don't have a hundred bosses and a lot of sidelines to mess you up once you get started on a case. You're a ruthless bastard and sometimes it helps."

"So?"

"So now I find myself in one of those situations. I'm a practical cop with a lot of training and experience, but I'm in something that has a personal meaning to me too and I'm afraid of tackling it alone."

"You don't want advice from me, chum. I'm mud, and whatever I touch gets smeared with it. I don't mind dirtying myself, but I don't want any of it to rub off onto you."

"It won't, don't worry. That's why you're here now. You think I was taken in by that vacation line? Hell. You have another bug up your behind. It has to do with those green cards and don't try to talk your way out of it."

He spun around, his face taut. "Where'd you get them, Mike?"

I ignored the question. "Tell me, Pat. Tell me the story."

He threw the drink down and filled the glass again. "Lee Deamer . . . how much do you know about him?"

"Only that he's the up-and-coming champ. I don't know him personally."

"I do, Mike. I know the guy and I like him. Goddamn it, Mike, if he gets squeezed out this state, this country will lose one of its greatest assets! We can't afford to have Deamer go under!"

"I've heard that story before, Pat," I said, "a political reporter gave it to me in detail."

Pat reached for a cigarette and laid it in his lips. The tip of the flame from the lighter wavered when he held it up. "I hope it made an impression. This country is too fine to be kicked around. Deamer is the man to stop it if he can get that far.

"Politics never interested you much, Mike. You know how it

starts in the wards and works itself right up to the nation. I get a chance to see just how dirty and corrupt politics can be. You should put yourself in my shoes for a while and you'd know how I feel. I get word to lay off one thing or another . . . or else. I get word that if I do or don't do a certain thing I'll be handed a fat little present. You'd think people would respect the police, but they don't. They try to use the department to push their own lousy schemes and it happens more often than you'd imagine."

"And you, Pat, what did you do?" I leaned forward in my chair, waiting.

"I told them to go to hell. They can't touch an honest man until he makes a mistake. Then they hang him for it."

"Any mistakes yet?"

Two streams of smoke spiraled from his nostrils. "Not yet, kid. They're waiting though. I'm fed up with the tension. You can feel it in the air, like being inside a storage battery. Call me a reformer if you want to, but I'd love to see a little decency for a change. That's why I'm afraid for Deamer."

"Yeah, you were telling me about him."

"Twins. You were right, Mike. Lee Deamer was at that meeting the night he was allegedly seen killing this Charlie Moffit. He was talking to groups around the room. I was there."

I stamped the butt out in a tray and lit another. "You mean it was as simple as that . . . Lee Deamer had a twin brother?"

Pat nodded. "As simple as that."

"Then why the secrecy? Lee isn't exactly responsible for what his brother does. Even a blast in the papers couldn't smear him for that, could it?"

"No . . . not if that was all there was to it."

"Then . . ."

Pat slammed the glass down impatiently. "The brother's name was Oscar Deamer. He was an escaped inmate of a sanitarium where he was undergoing psychiatric treatment. Let that come out and Lee is finished."

I let out a slow whistle. "Who else knows about this, Pat?"

"Just you. It was too big. I couldn't keep it to myself. Lee called me tonight and said he wanted to see me. We met in a bar and he told me the story. Oscar arrived in town and told Lee that he was going to settle things for him. He demanded money to keep quiet. Lee thinks that Oscar deliberately killed this Charlie Moffit hoping to be identified as Lee, knowing that Lee wouldn't dare reveal that he had a lunatic for a brother."

"So Lee wouldn't pay off and he got the treatment."

"It looks that way."

"Hell, this Oscar could have figured Lee would have an alibi and couldn't be touched. It was just a sample, something to get him entangled. That doesn't make him much of a loony if he can think like that."

"Anybody who can kill like that is crazy, Mike."

"Yeah, I guess so."

Before he could answer me, the bell rang, two short burps and Pat got up to push the buzzer. "Lee?" I asked.

Pat nodded. "He wanted more time to think about it. I told him I'd be at home. It has him nearly crazy himself." He went to the door and stood there holding it open as he had done for me. It was so still that I heard the elevator humming in its well, the sound of the doors opening and the slow, heavy feet of a person carrying a too-heavy weight.

I stood up myself and shook hands with Lee Deamer. He wasn't big like I had expected. There was nothing outstanding about his appearance except that he looked like a schoolteacher, a very tired, middle-aged Mr. Chips.

Pat said, "This is Mike Hammer, Lee. He's a very special, capable friend of mine."

His handshake was firm, but his eyes were too tired to take me in all at once. He said to Pat very softly, "He knows?"

"He knows, Lee. He can be trusted."

I had a good look at warm gray eyes then. His hand tightened just a little around mine. "It's nice to find people that can be trusted."

I grinned my thanks and Pat pulled up a chair. Lee Deamer took the drink Pat offered him and settled back against the cushions, rubbing his hand across his face. He took a sip of the highball, then pulled a cigar from his pocket and pared the end off with a tiny knife on his watch chain.

"Oscar hasn't called back," he said dully. "I don't know what to do." He looked first at Pat, then to me. "Are you a policeman, Mr. Hammer?"

"Just call me Mike. No, I'm not a city cop. I have a Private Operator's ticket and that's all."

"Mike's been in on a lot of big stuff, Lee," Pat cut in. "He knows his way around."

"I see." He was talking to me again. "I suppose Pat told you that so far this whole affair has been kept quiet?" I nodded and he went on. "I hope it can stay that way, though if it must come out, it must. I'm leaving it all to the discretion of Pat here. I—

well, I'm really stumped. So much has happened in so short a time I hardly know where I'm at."

"Can I hear it from the beginning?" I asked.

Lee Deamer bobbed his head slowly. "Oscar and I were born in Townley, Nebraska. Although we were twins, we were worlds apart. In my younger days I thought it was because we were just separate personalities, but the truth was . . . Oscar was demented. He was a sadistic sort of person, very sly and cunning. He hated me. Yes, he hated me, his own brother. In fact, Oscar seemed to hate everyone. He was in trouble from the moment he ran off from home until he came back, then he found more trouble in our own state. He was finally committed to an institution.

"Shortly after Oscar was committed I left Nebraska and settled in New York. I did rather well in business and became active in politics. Oscar was more or less forgotten. Then I learned that he had escaped from the institution. I never heard from him again until he called me last week."

"That's all?"

"What else can there be, Mike? Oscar probably read about me in the papers and trailed me here. He knew what it would mean if I was known to have a brother who wasn't quite . . . well, normal. He made a demand for money and told me he'd have it one way or another."

Pat reached for the shaker and filled the glasses again. I held mine out and our eyes met. He answered my question before I could ask it. "Lee was afraid to mention Oscar, even when he was identified as the killer of Moffit. You can understand why, can't you?"

"Now I can," I said.

"Even the fact that Lee *was* identified, although wrongly, would have made good copy. However, the cop on the beat brought the witnesses in before they could speak to the papers and the whole thing was such an obvious mistake that nobody dared take the chance of making it public."

"Where are the witnesses now?"

"We have them under surveillance. They've been instructed to keep quiet about it. We checked into their backgrounds and found that all of them were upright citizens, plain, ordinary people who were as befuddled as we were about the whole thing. Fortunately, we were able to secure their promise of silence by proving to them where Lee was that night. They don't understand it, but they were willing to go along with us in the cause of justice."

I grunted and pulled on the cigarette. "I don't like it."

Both of them looked at me quickly. "Hell, Pat, you ought to smell the angle as well as I do."

"You tell me, Mike."

"Oscar served his warning," I said. "He'll make another stab at it. You can trap him easily enough and you know it."

"That's right. It leaves one thing wide open, too."

"Sure it does. You'll have another Lee Deamer in print and pictures, this one up for a murder rap which he will skip because he's nuts." Lee winced at the word but kept still.

"That's why I wanted you here," Pat told me.

"Fine. What good am I?"

The ice rattled against the side of his glass. Pat tried to keep his voice calm. "You aren't official, Mike. My mind works with the book. I know what I should do and I can't think of anything else."

"You mean you want me to tell you that Oscar should be run down and quietly spirited away?"

"That's right."

"And I'm the boy who could do it?"

"Right again." He took a long swallow from the glass and set it on the table.

"What happens if it doesn't work out? To you, I mean."

"I'll be looking for a job for not playing it properly."

"Gentlemen, gentlemen." Lee Deamer ran his hand through his hair nervously. "I-I can't let you do it. I can't let you jeopardize your positions. It isn't fair. The best thing is to let it come to light and let the public decide."

"Don't be jerky!" I spat out. Lee looked at me, but I wasn't seeing him. I was seeing Marty and Pat, hearing them say the same thing . . . and I was hearing that judge again.

There were two hot spaces where my eyes should have been. "I'll take care of it," I said. "I'll need all the help I can get." I looked at Pat. He nodded. "Just one thing, Pat. I'm not doing this because I'm a patriot, see? I'm doing it because I'm curious and because of it I'll be on my toes. I'm curious as hell about something else and not about right and wrong and what the public thinks."

My teeth were showing through my words and Pat had that look again. "Why, Mike?"

"Three green cards with the edges cut off, kid. I'm curious as hell about three green cards. There's more to them than you think."

I said good night and left them sitting there. I could hear the judge laughing at me. It wasn't a nice laugh. It had a nasty sound. Thirteen steps and thirteen loops that made the knot in the rope. Were there thirteen thousand volts in the chair too? Maybe I'd find out the hard way.

chapter four ████████████████████████████

I SLEPT FOR two hours before Velda called me. I told her I wouldn't be in for a good long while, and if anything important came up she could call, but unless it was a matter of life or death, either hers or mine, to leave me be.

Nothing came up and I slept once around the clock. It was five minutes to six when my eyes opened by themselves and didn't feel hot any more. While I showered and shaved I stuck a frozen steak under the broiler and ate in my shorts, still damp.

It was a good steak; I was hungry. I wanted to finish it but I never got the time. The phone rang and kept on ringing until I kicked the door shut so I wouldn't hear it. That didn't stop the phone. It went on like that for a full five minutes, demanding that I answer it. I threw down my knife with a curse and walked inside.

"What is it?" I yelled.

"It took you long enough to wake up, damn it!"

"Oh, Pat. I wasn't asleep. What's up this time?"

"It happened like we figured. Oscar made the contact. He called Lee and wants to see him tonight. Lee made an appointment to be at his apartment at eight."

"Yeah?"

"Lee called me immediately. Look, Mike, we'll have to go this alone, just the three of us. I don't want to trust anybody else."

The damp on my body seemed to turn to ice. I was cold all over, cold enough to shake just a little. "Where'll I meet you, Pat?"

"Better make it at my place. Oscar lives over on the East Side." He rattled off the address and I jotted it down. "I told Lee to go ahead and keep his appointment. We'll be right behind him. Lee is taking the subway up and we'll pick him up at the kiosk. Got that?"

"I got it. I'll be over in a little while."

We both stood waiting for the other to hang up. Finally, "Mike . . ."

"What?"

"You sure about this?"

"I'm sure." I set the receiver back in its cradle and stared at it. I was sure, all right, sure to come up with the dirty end of the stick. The dam would open and let the clean water through and they could pick me out of the sewer.

I pulled on my clothes halfheartedly. I thought of the steak in the kitchen and decided I didn't want any more of it. For a while I stood in front of the mirror looking at myself, trying to decide whether or not I should wear the artillery. Habit won and I buckled on the sling after checking the load in the clip. When I buttoned up the coat I took the box from the closet shelf that held the two spare barrels and the extra shells, scooped up a handful of loose .45s and dropped them in my pocket. If I was going to do it I might as well do it right.

Velda had just gotten in when I called her. I said, "Did you eat yet, kitten?"

"I grabbed a light bite downtown. Why, are you taking me out?"

"Yeah, but not to supper. It's business. I'll be right over. Tell you about it then."

She said all right, kissed me over the phone and hung up. I stuck my hat on, picked up another deck of Luckies and went downstairs where I whistled for a cab.

I don't know how I looked when she opened the door. She started to smile then dropped it like a hot rivet to catch her lower lip between her teeth. Velda's so tall I didn't have to bend down far to kiss her on the cheek. It was nice standing there real close to her. She was perfume and beauty and all the good things of life.

She said, "Come into the bedroom, Mike. You can tell me while I'm getting dressed."

"I can talk from out here."

Velda turned around, a grin in her eyes. "You *have* been in a woman's bedroom before, haven't you?"

"Not yours."

"I'm inviting you in to talk. Just talk."

I faked a punch at her jaw. "I'm just afraid of myself, kid. You and a bedroom could be too much. I'm saving you for something special."

"Will it cost three dollars and can you frame it?"

I laughed for an answer and went in after her. She pointed to a satin-covered boudoir chair and went behind a screen. She came out in a black wool skirt and a white blouse. God, but she was lovely.

When she sat down in front of the vanity table and started to brush her hair I caught her eyes in the mirror. They reflected the trouble that was in mine. "Now tell me, Mike."

I told her. I gave her everything Pat gave me and watched her face.

She finished with the brush and put it down. Her hand was shaking. "They want a lot of you, don't they?"

"Maybe they want too much." I pulled out a cigarette and lit one. "Velda, what does this Lee Deamer mean to you?"

This time she wouldn't meet my eyes. She spaced her words carefully. "He means a lot, Mike. Would you be mad if I said that perhaps they weren't asking too much?"

"No . . . not if you think not. Okay, kid. I'll play the hand out and see what I can do with a kill-crazy maniac. Get your coat on."

"Mike . . . you haven't told me all of it yet."

She was at it again, looking through me into my mind. "I know it."

"Are you going to?"

"Not now. Maybe later."

She stood up, a statuesque creature that had no equal, her hair a black frame for her face. "Mike, you're a bastard. You're in trouble up to your ears and you won't let anybody help you. Why do you always have to play it alone?"

"Because I'm me."

"And I'm me too, Mike. I *want* to help. Can you understand that?"

"Yes, I understand, but this isn't another case. It's more than that and I don't want to talk about it."

She came to me then, resting her hands on my shoulders. "Mike, if you *do* need me . . . ever, will you ask me to help?"

"I'll ask you."

Her mouth was full and ripe, warm with life and sparkling with a delicious wetness. I pulled her in close and tasted the fire that smoldered inside her, felt her body mold itself to mine, eager and excited.

My fingers ran into her hair and pulled her mouth away. "No more of it, Velda. Not now."

"Some day, Mike."

"Some day. Get your coat on." I shoved her away roughly, reluctant to let her go. She opened the closet and took the jacket that matched the skirt from a hanger and slipped into it. Over her shoulder she slung a shoulderstrap bag, and when it nudged the side of the dresser the gun in it made a dull clunk.

"I'm ready, Mike."

I pushed the slip of paper with Oscar's address on it into her hand. "Here's the place where he's holed up. The subway is a half-block away from the place. You go directly there and look the joint over. I don't know why, but there's something about it I don't like. We're going to tag after Lee when he goes in, but I want somebody covering the place while we're there.

"Remember, it's a rough neighborhood, so be on your toes. We don't want any extra trouble. If you spot anything that doesn't seem to be on the square, walk over to the subway kiosk and meet us. You'll have about a half-hour to look around. Be careful."

"Don't worry about me." She pulled on her gloves, a smile playing with her mouth. Hell, I wasn't going to worry about her. That rod in her bag wasn't there for ballast.

I dropped her at the subway and waited on the curb until a cab cruised by.

Pat was standing under the canopy of his apartment building when I got there. He had a cigarette cupped in the palm of his hand and dragged on it nervously. I yelled at him from the taxi and he crossed the street and got in.

It was seven-fifteen.

At ten minutes to eight we paid off the cab and walked the half-block to the kiosk. We were still fifty feet away when Lee Deamer came up. He looked neither to the right nor left, walking straight ahead as if he lived there. Pat nudged me with his elbow and I grunted an acknowledgement.

I waited to see if Velda would show, but there wasn't a sign of her.

Twice Lee stopped to look at house numbers. The third time he paused in front of an old brick building, his head going to the dim light behind the shades in the downstairs room. Briefly, he cast a quick glance behind him, then went up the three steps and disappeared into the shadowy well of the doorway.

Thirty seconds, that's all he got. Both of us were counting under our breaths, hugging the shadows of the building. The street boasted a lone light a hundred yards away, a wan, yellow eye that seemed to search for us with eerie tendrils, determined to pull us into its glare. Somewhere a voice cursed. A baby squealed and stopped abruptly. The street was too damn deserted. It should have been running with kids or something. Maybe the one light scared them off. Maybe they had a better place to hang out than a side street in nowhere.

We hit the thirty count at the same time, but too late. A door slammed above our heads and we could hear feet pounding on boards, diminishing with every step. A voice half sobbed something unintelligible and we flew up those stairs and tugged at a door that wouldn't give. Pat hit it with his shoulder, ramming it open.

Lee was standing in the doorway, hanging on to the sill, his mouth agape. He was pointing down the hall. "He ran . . . he ran. He looked out the window . . . and he ran!"

Pat muttered, "Damn . . . we can't let him get away!" I was ahead of him, my hands probing the darkness. I felt the wall give way to the inky blackness that was the night behind an open door and stumbled down the steps.

That was when I heard Velda's voice rise in a tense, "Mike . . . MIKE!"

"Over here, Pat. There's a gate in the wall. Get a light on!"

Pat swore again, yelling that he had lost it. I didn't wait. I made the gate and picked my way through the litter in the alley that ran behind the buildings. My .45 was in my hand, ready to be used. Velda yelled again and I followed her voice to the end of the alley.

When I came to the street through the two-foot space that separated the buildings I couldn't have found anybody, because the street was a funnel of people running to the subway kiosk. They ran and yelled back over their shoulders and I knew that whatever it was happened down there and I was afraid to look. If anything happened to Velda I'd tear the guts out of some son-of-a-bitch! I'd nail him to a wall and take his skin off him in inch-wide strips!

A colored fellow in a porter's outfit came up bucking the crowd yelling for someone to get a doctor. That was all I needed. I made a path through that mob pouring through the exit gates onto the station and battled my way up to the front.

Velda was all right. She was perfectly all right and I could quit shaking and let the sweat turn warm again. I shoved the gun back under my arm and walked over to her with a sad attempt of trying to look normal.

The train was almost all the way in the station. Not quite. It had to jam on the brakes too fast to make the marker farther down the platform. The driver and two trainmen were standing in front of the lead car poking at a bloody mess that was sticking out under the wheels. The driver said, "He's dead as hell. He won't need an ambulance."

Velda saw me out of the corner of her eye. I eased up to her, my breath still coming hard. "Deamer?"

She nodded.

I heard Pat busting through the crowd and saw Lee at his heels. "Beat it, kid. I'll call you later." She stepped back and the curious crowd surged around her to fill the spot. She was gone before Pat reached me.

His pants were torn and he had a dirty black smear across his cheek. He took about two minutes to get the crowd back from the edge and when a cop from the beat upstairs came through the gang was herded back to the exits like cattle, all bawling to be in on the blood.

Pat wiped his hand across his face. "What the hell happened?"

"I don't know, but I think that's our boy down there. Bring Lee over."

The trainmen were tugging the remains out. One said, "He ain't got much face left," then he puked all over the third rail.

Lee Deamer looked over the side and turned white. "My God!"

Pat steadied him with an arm around his waist. They had most of the corpse out from under the train now. "That him?" Pat asked.

Lee nodded dumbly. I could see his throat working hard.

Two more cops from the local precinct sauntered over. Pat shoved his badge out and told them to take over, then motioned me to bring Lee back to one of the benches. He folded up in one like a limp sack and buried his face in his hands. What the hell could I say? So the guy was a loony, but he was still his brother. While Pat went back to talk to the trainmen I stood there and listened to him sob.

We put Lee in a cab outside before I had a chance to say anything. The street was mobbed now, the people crowding around the ambulance waiting to see what was going in on the stretcher. They were disappointed when a wicker basket came up and was shoved into a morgue wagon instead. A kid pointed to the blood dripping from one corner and a woman fainted. Nice.

I watched the wagon pull away and reached for a butt. I needed one bad. "It was an easy way out," I said. "What did the driver say?"

Pat took a cigarette from my pack. "He didn't see him. He thinks the guy must have been hiding behind a pillar then jumped out in front of the car. He sure was messed up."

"I don't know whether to be relieved or not."

"It's a relief to me, Mike. He's dead and his name will get published but who will connect him with Lee? The trouble's over."

"He have anything on him?"

Pat stuck his hand in his pocket and pulled out some stuff. Under the light it looked as if it had been stained with ink. Sticky ink. "Here's a train ticket from Chicago. It's in a bus envelope so he must have taken a bus as far as Chi then switched to rail." It was dated the 15th, a Friday.

I turned the envelope over and saw "Deamer" printed across the back with a couple of schedule notations in pencil. There was another envelope with the stuff. It had been torn in half and used for a memo sheet, but the name Deamer, part of an address in Nebraska and a Nebraska postage mark were still visible. It was dated over a month ago. The rest of the stuff was some small change, two crumpled bills and a skeleton key for a door lock.

It was as nice an answer as we could have hoped for and I didn't like it. "What's the matter now?" Pat queried.

"I don't know. It stinks."

"You're teed off because you were done out of a kill."

"Aw, shaddup, will you!"

"Then what's so lousy about it?"

"How the hell do I know? Can't I not like something without having to explain about it?"

"Not with me you can't, pal. I stuck my neck out when I invited you in."

I sucked in on the cigarette. It was cold standing there and I turned my collar up. "Get a complete identification on that corpse, Pat. Then maybe I can tell you why I think it stinks."

"Don't worry, I intend to. I'm not taking any chances of having him laughing at us from somewhere. It would be like the crazy bastard to push someone else under that train to sidetrack us."

"Would he have time to jam that stuff in his pockets too?" I flipped my thumb at the papers Pat was holding.

"He could have. Just the same, we'll be sure. Lee has both their birth certificates and a medical certificate on Oscar that has his full description. It won't take long to find out if that's him or not."

"Let me know what you find."

"I'll call you tomorrow. I wish I knew how the devil he spotted us. I nearly killed myself in that damn alley. I thought I heard somebody yelling for you, too."

"Couldn't have been."

"Guess not. Well, I'll see you tomorrow?"

"Uh-huh." I took a last pull on the butt and tossed it at the curb. Pat went back into the station and I could hear his heels clicking on the steps.

The street was more deserted now than ever. All that was left was the one yellow light. It seemed to wink at me. I walked toward it and went up the three steps into the building. The door was still standing open, enough light from the front room seeping into the hall so I could find my way.

It wasn't much of a place, just a room. There was a chair, a closet, a single bed and a washstand. The suitcase on the bed was half filled with well-worn clothes, but I couldn't tell whether it was being packed or unpacked. I poked through the stuff and found another dollar bill stuffed in the cloth lining. Twenty pages of a mail-order catalog were under everything. Part of them showed sporting goods including all sorts of guns. The others pictured automobile accessories. Which part was used? Did he buy a gun or a tire? Why? Where?

I pulled out the shirts and shook them open, looking for any identifying marks. One had "DEA" for a laundry tag next to the label, the others had nothing so he must have done his own wash.

That was all there was to it.

Nothing.

I could breathe a little easier and tell Marty Kooperman that his boy was okay and nothing could hurt him now. Pat would be satisfied, the cops would be satisfied and everything was hunky-dory. I was the only one who still had a bug up my tail. It was a great big bug and it was kicking up a fuss. I was a hell of a way from being satisfied.

This wasn't what I was after, that's why. This didn't have to do with three green cards except that the dead man had killed a guy who carried one. What was his name . . . Moffit, Charlie Moffit. Was he dead because of a fluke or was there more to it?

I kicked at the edge of the bed in disgust and took one last look around. Pat would be here next. He'd find prints and check them against the corpse in his usual methodical way. If there was anything to be found, he'd find it and I could get it from him.

It had only been a few hours since I climbed out of the sack, but for some reason I was more tired than ever. Too much of a letdown, I guessed. You can't prime yourself for something to happen and feel right when it doesn't come off. The skin of my face felt tight and drawn, pulling away from my eyes. My back still crawled when I thought of the alley and that thing under the train.

I went into a shabby drugstore and called Velda's home. She wasn't there. I tried the office and she was. I told her to meet me in the bar downstairs and walked outside again, looking for a cab. The one that came along had a driver who had all the information about the accident in the subway secondhand and insisted on giving me a detailed account of all the gruesome details. I was glad to pay him off and get out of there.

Velda was sitting in a back booth with a Manhattan in front of her. Two guys at the bar had swung halfway around on their stools and were trying out their best leers. One said something dirty and the other laughed. Tony walked down behind the bar, but he saw me come in and stopped. The guy with the dirty mouth said something else, slid off his stool and walked over to Velda.

He set his drink down and leaned on her table, mouthing a few obscenities. Velda moved too fast for him. I saw her arm fly out, knock away the support of his hand and his face went into the table. She gave him the drink right in the eyes, glass and all.

The guy screamed, "You dirty little . . ." then she laid the heavy glass ash tray across his temple and he had it. He went down on his knees, his head almost on the floor. The other guy almost choked. He slammed his drink down and came off his stool with a rush. I let him go about two feet before I snagged the back of his coat collar with a jerk that put him right on his skinny behind.

Tony laughed and leaned on the bar.

I wasn't laughing. The one on the floor turned his head and I saw a pinched weasel face with eyes that had quick death in them. Those eyes crawled over me from top to bottom, over to Velda and back again. "A big tough guy," he said. "A big wise guy."

As if a spring exploded inside him, he came up off the floor with a knife in his hand, blade up.

A .45 can make an awful nasty sound in a quiet room when you pull the hammer back. It's just a little tiny click, but it can stop a dozen guys when they hear it. Weasel Face couldn't take his eyes off it. I let him have a good look and smashed it across his nose.

The knife hit the floor and broke when I stepped on it. Tony laughed again. I grabbed the guy by the neck and hauled him to his feet so I could drag the cold sharp metal of the rod across his face until he was a bright red mask mumbling for me to stop.

Tony helped me throw them in the street outside. He said, "They never learn, do they, Mike? Because there's two of 'em and they got a shiv they're the toughest mugs in the world. It ain't nice to get took, by a woman, neither. They never learn."

"They learn, Tony. For about ten seconds they're the smartest people in the world. But then it's always too late. After ten seconds they're dead. They only learn when they finally catch a slug where it hurts."

I walked back to the booth and sat down opposite Velda. Tony brought her another Manhattan and me a beer. "Very good," I said.

"Thanks. I knew you were watching."

She lit a cigarette and her hands were steadier than mine. "You were too rough on him."

"Nuts, he had a knife. I have an allergy against getting cut." I drained off half of the beer and laid it down on the table where I made patterns with the wet bottom. "Tell me about tonight."

Velda started to tear matches out of the book without lighting them. "I got there about seven-thirty. A light was on in the front window. Twice I saw somebody pull aside the corner of the shade and look out. A car went around the block twice, and both times it slowed down a little in front of the house. When it left I tried the door, but it was locked so I went next door and tried that one. It was locked too, but there was a cellar way under the stairs and I went down there. Just as I was going down the steps I saw a man coming up the block and I thought it might be Deamer.

"I had to take the chance that it was and that you were behind him. The cellar door was open and led through to the back yard. I was trying to crawl over a mound of boxes when I heard somebody in the back yard. I don't know how long it took me to get out there, possibly two minutes. Anyway, I heard a yell and somebody came out the door of the next house. I got through into the back alley and heard him running. He went too fast for me and I started yelling for you."

"That was Oscar Deamer, all right. He saw us coming and beat it."

"Maybe."

"What do you mean . . . 'maybe'?"

"I think there were two people in that alley ahead of me."

"Two people?" My voice had an edge to it. "Did you see them?"

"No."

"Then how do you know?"

"I don't. I just think so."

I finished the beer and waved to Tony. He brought another. Velda hadn't touched her drink yet. "Something made you think that. What was it?"

She shrugged, frowning at her glass, trying to force her mind back to that brief interval. "When I was in that cellar I thought I heard somebody in the other yard. There was a flock of cats around and I thought at the time that I was hearing them."

"Go on."

"Then when I was running after him I fell and while I lay there it didn't sound like just one person going down that alley."

"One person could sound like ten if they hit any of the junk we hit. It makes a hell of a racket."

"Maybe I'm wrong, Mike. I thought there could have been someone else and I wanted you to know about it."

"What the hell, it doesn't matter too much now anyway. The guy is dead and that should end it. Lee Deamer can go ahead and reform all he wants to now. He hasn't got a thing to worry about. As far as two people in that alley . . . well, you saw what the place was like. Nobody lives there unless he has to. They're the kind of people who scare easily, and if Lee started running somebody else could have too. Did you see him go down the subway?"

"No, he was gone when I got there, but two kids were staring down the steps and waving to another kid to come over. I took the chance that he went down and followed. The train was skidding to a stop when I reached the platform and I didn't have to be told why. When you scooted me away I looked for those kids in the crowd upstairs but they weren't around."

I hoisted my glass, turned it around in my hand and finished it. Velda downed her Manhattan and slipped her arms into her coat. "What now, Mike?"

"You go home, kid," I told her. "I'm going to take me a nice long walk."

We said good night to Tony and left. The two guys we had thrown in the street were gone. Velda grinned. "Am I safe?"

"Hell yes!"

I waved a taxi over, kissed her good night and walked off.

My heels rapped the sidewalk, a steady tap-tap that kept time with my thoughts. They reminded me of another walk I took, one that led to a bridge, and still another one that led into a deserted store that came equipped with blackout curtains, light switches on the door and coffee urns.

There lay the story behind the green cards. There was where I could find out why I had to kill a guy who had one, and see a girl die because she couldn't stand the look on my face. That was what I wanted to know . . . why it was me who was picked to pull the trigger.

I turned into a candy store and pulled the telephone directories from the rack. I found the Park Avenue Brightons and dialed the number.

Three rings later a somber voice said, "Mr. Brighton's residence."

I got right to the point. "Is Ethel there?"

"Who shall I say is calling, sir?"

"You don't. Just put her on."

"I'm sorry, sir, but . . ."

"Oh, shut up and put her on."

There was a shocked silence and a clatter as the phone was laid on a table. Off in the distance I heard the mutter of voices, then feet coming across the room. The phone clattered again, and, "Yes?"

"Hello, Ethel," I said. "I drove your car into Times Square last night. Remember?"

"Oh! Oh, but . . ." Her voice dropped almost to a whisper. "Please, I can't talk to you here. What is . . ."

"You can talk to me outside, kid. I'll be standing on your street corner in about fifteen minutes. The northeast corner. Pick me up there."

"I-I can't. Honestly . . . oh, please . . ." There was panic in her voice, a tone that held more than fear.

I said, "You'd better, baby." That was enough. I hung up and started walking toward Park Avenue. If I could read a voice right she'd be there.

She was. I saw her while I was still a half block away, crossing nervously back and forth, trying to seem busy. I came up behind her and said hello. For a moment she went rigid, held by the panic that I had sensed in her voice.

"Scared?"

"No—of course not." The hell she wasn't! Her chin was wobbling and she couldn't hold her hands still. This time I was barely smiling and dames don't usually go to pieces when I do that.

I hooked my arm through hers and steered her west where there were lights and people. Sometimes the combination is good for the soul. It makes you want to talk and laugh and be part of the grand parade.

It didn't have that effect on her.

The smile might have been pasted on her face. When she wasn't looking straight ahead her eyes darted to me and back again. We went off Broadway and into a bar that had one empty end and one full end because the television wasn't centered. The lights were down low and nobody paid any attention to us on the empty end except the bartender, and he was more interested in watching the wrestling than hustling up drinks for us.

Ethel ordered an Old Fashioned and I had a beer. She held the fingers of her one hand tightly around the glass and worked a cigarette with the other. There was nothing behind the bar to see, but she stared there anyway. I had to give up carrying the conversation. When I did and sat there as quietly as she did the knuckles of her fingers went white.

She couldn't keep this up long. I took a lungful of smoke and let it come out with my words. "Ethel . . ." She jerked, startled. "What's there about me that has you up a tree?"

She wet her lips. "Really, there's . . . there's nothing."

"You never even asked me my name."

That brought her head up. Her eyes got wide and stared at the wall. "I . . . I'm not concerned with names."

"I am."

"But you . . . I'm . . . please, what have I done? Haven't I been faithful? Must you go on. . . ." She had kept it up too long. The panic couldn't stay. It left with a rush and a pleading tone took its place. There were tears in her eyes now, tears she tried hard to hold back and being a woman, couldn't. They flooded her eyelids and ran down her cheeks.

"Ethel . . . quit being scared of me. Look in a mirror and you'll know why I called you tonight. You aren't the kind of woman a guy can see and forget. You're too damned serious."

Dames, they can louse me up every time. The tears stopped as abruptly as they came and her mouth froze in indignation. This time she was able to look at my eyes clearly. "We have to be serious. You, of all people, should know that!"

This was better. The words were her own, what was inside her and not words that I put there. "Not all the time," I grinned.

"All the time!" she said. I grinned at her and she returned it with a frown.

"You'll do, kid."

"I can't understand you." She hesitated, then a smile blossomed and grew. She was lovely when she smiled. "You were testing me," she demanded.

"Something like that."

"But . . . why?"

"I need some help. I can't take just anybody, you know." It was true. I did need help, plenty of it too.

"You mean . . . you want me to help you . . . find out who . . . who did it?"

Cripes, how I wanted her to open up. I wasn't in the mood for more of those damn silly games and yet I had to play them. "That's right."

It must have pleased her. I saw the fingers loosen up around the glass and she tasted the drink for the first time. "Could I ask a question?"

"Sure, go ahead."

"Why did you choose me?"

"I'm attracted to beauty."

"But my record . . ."

"I was attracted to that too. Being beautiful helped."

"I'm not beautiful." She was asking for more. I gave it to her.

"All I can see are your face and hands. They're beautiful, but I bet the rest of you is just as beautiful, the part I can't see."

It was too dark to tell if she had the grace to blush or not. She wet her lips again, parting them in a small smile. "Would you?"

"What?"

"Like to see the rest of me." No, she couldn't have blushed.

I laughed at her, a slow laugh that brought her head around and showed me the glitter in her eyes. "Yeah, Ethel, I want to. And I will when I want to just a little more."

Her breath came so sharply that her coat fell open and I could see the pulse in her throat. "It's warm here. Can we . . . leave?"

Neither of us bothered to finish our drinks.

She was laughing now, with her mouth and her eyes. I held her hand and felt the warm pressure of her fingers, the stilted reserve draining out of her at every step. Ethel led the way, not me. We walked toward her place almost as if we were in a hurry, out to enjoy the evening.

"Supposing your father . . . or somebody you know should come along," I suggested.

She shrugged defiantly. "Let them. You know how I feel." She held her head high, the smile crooked across her lips. "There's not one of them I care for. Any feeling I've had for my family disappeared several years ago."

"Then you haven't any feeling left for anyone?"

"I have! Oh, yes I have." Her eyes swung up to mine, half closed, revealing a sensuous glitter. "For the moment it's you."

"And other times?"

"I don't have to tell *you* that. There's no need to test me any longer."

A few doors from her building she stopped me. Her convertible was squatting there at the curb. The cars in front and behind had parking tickets on the windshield wiper. Hers bore only a club insignia.

"I'll drive this time," she said.

We got in and drove. It rained a little and it snowed a little, then, abruptly, it was clear and the stars came in full and bright, framed in the hole in the sky. The radio was a chant of pleasure, snatching the wild symphonic music from the air and offering us orchestra seats though we were far beyond the city, hugging the curves of the Hudson.

When we stopped it was to turn off the highway to a winding macadam road that led beneath the overhanging branches of evergreens. The cottage nestled on top of a bluff smiling down at the world. Ethel took my hand, led me inside to the plush little playhouse that was her own special retreat and lit the heavy wax candles that hung in brass holders from the ceiling.

I had to admire the exquisite simplicity of the place. It proclaimed wealth, but in the most humble fashion. Somebody had done a good job of decorating. Ethel pointed to the little bar that was set in the corner of the log cabin. "Drinks are there. Would you care to make us one . . . Then start the fire? The fireplace has been laid up."

I nodded, watched her leave the room, then opened the doors of the liquor cabinet. Only the best, the very best. I picked out the best of the best and poured two straight, not wanting to spoil it with any mixer, sipped mine then drank it down. I had a refill and stared at it.

A Commie. She was a jerky Red. She owned all the trimmings and she was still a Red. What the hell was she hoping for, a government order to share it all with the masses? Yeah. A joint like this would suddenly assume a new owner under a new regime. A fat little general, a ranking secret policeman, somebody. Sure, it's great to be a Commie . . . as long as you're top dog. Who the hell was supposed to be fooled by all the crap?

Yet Ethel fell for it. I shook my head at the stupid asses that are left in this world and threw a match into the fireplace. It blazed up and licked at the logs on the andirons.

Ethel came out of the other room wearing her fur coat. Her hair looked different. It seemed softer. "Cold?"

"In there it is. I'll be warm in a moment."

I handed her the glass and we touched the rims. Her eyes were bright, hot.

We had three or four more and the bottom was showing in the bottle. Maybe it was more than three or four. I wanted to ask her some questions. I wanted the right answers and I didn't want her to think about them beforehand. I wanted her just a little bit drunk.

I had to fumble with the catch to get the liquor cabinet open. There was more of the best of the best in the back and I dragged it out. Ethel found the switch on a built-in phonograph and stacked on a handful of records.

The fireplace was a leaping, dancing thing that threw shadows across the room and touched everything with a weird, demoniac light. Ethel came to me, holding her arms open to dance. I wanted to dance, but there were parts of me trying to do other things.

Ethel laughed. "You're drunk."

"I am like hell." It wasn't exactly the truth.

"Well *I'm* drunk. I'm very, very drunk and I love it!" She threw her arms up and spun around. I had to catch her. "Oo, I want to sit down. Let's sit down and enjoy the fire."

She pulled away and danced to the sofa, her hands reaching out for the black bearskin rug that was draped over the back of it. She threw it on the floor in front of the fire and turned around. "Come on over. Sit down."

"You'll roast in that coat," I said.

"I won't." She smiled slyly and flipped open the buttons that held it together. She shrugged the shoulders off first letting it fall to her waist, then swept it off and threw it aside.

Ethel didn't have anything on. Only her shoes. She kicked them off too and sunk to the softness of the bearskin, a beautiful naked creature of soft round flesh and lustrous hair that changed color with each leap of the vivid red flame behind her.

It was much too warm then for a jacket. I heard mine hit a chair and slide off. My wallet fell out of the pocket and I didn't care. The sling on my gun rack wouldn't come loose and I broke it.

She shouldn't have done it. Damn it, she shouldn't have done it! I wanted to ask her some questions.

Now I forgot what I wanted to ask her.

My fingers hurt and she didn't care. Her lips were bright red, wet. They parted slowly and her tongue flicked out over her teeth inviting me to come closer. Her mouth was a hungry thing demanding to be tasted. The warmth that seemed to come from the flames was a radiation that flowed from the sleek length of her legs and nestled in the hollow of her stomach a moment before rising over the convex beauty of her breasts. She held her arms out invitingly and took me in them.

chapter five ▬▬▬▬▬▬▬▬▬▬▬▬▬▬

I CAME AWAKE with the dawn, my throat dry and my mind groping to make sense out of what had happened. Ethel was still there, lying curled on her side up against me. Sometime during the night the fire had gone down and she had gotten up to get a blanket and throw it over us.

Somehow I got to my feet without waking her up. I pulled on my clothes, found my gun sling and my jacket on the floor. I remembered my wallet and felt around for it, getting mad when I didn't find it. I sat on the arm of the sofa and shook my head to clear out the spiders. Bending over didn't do me much good. The next time I used my foot and scooped it out from under the end table where I must have kicked it in getting dressed.

Ethel Brighton was asleep and smiling when I left. It was a good night, but not at all what I had come for. She giggled and wrapped her arms around the blankets. Maybe Ethel would quit being mad at the world now.

I climbed into my raincoat and walked out, looking up once at the sky overhead. The clouds had closed in again, but they were thinner and it was warmer than it had been.

It took twenty minutes to reach the highway and I had to wait another twenty before a truck came along and gave me a lift into town. I treated him to breakfast and we talked about the war. He agreed that it hadn't been a bad war. He had gotten nicked too, and it gave him a good excuse to cop a day off now and then.

I called Pat about ten o'clock. He gave me a fast hello, then: "Can you come up, Mike? I have something interesting."

"About last night?"

"That's right."

"I'll be up in five minutes. Stick around."

Headquarters was right up the street and I stepped it up. The D.A. was coming out of the building again. This time he didn't see me. When I rapped on Pat's door he yelled to come in and I pushed the knob.

Pat said, "Where the hell have you been?" He was grinning.

"No place." I grinned back.

"If what I suspect goes on between you and Velda, then you better get that lipstick off your face and shave."

"That bad?"

"I can smell whisky from here too."

"Velda won't like that," I said.

"No dame in love with a dope does," Pat laughed. "Park it, Mike. I have news for you." He opened his desk drawer and hauled out a large manila envelope that had CONFIDENTIAL printed across the back.

When he was draped across the arm of the chair he handed a fingerprint photostat to me. "I took these off the corpse last night."

"You don't waste time, pal."

"Couldn't afford to." He dug in the envelope and brought out a three-page document that was clipped together. It had a hospital masthead I didn't catch because Pat turned it over and showed me the fingerprints on the back. "These are Oscar Deamer's too. This is his medical case history that Lee was holding."

I didn't need to be an expert to see that they matched. "Same guy all right," I remarked.

"No doubt about it. Want to look at the report?"

"Ah, I couldn't wade through all that medical baloney. What's it say?"

"In brief, that Oscar Deamer was a dangerous neurotic, paranoiac and a few other psychiatric big words."

"Congenital?"

Pat saw what I was thinking. "No, as a matter of fact. So rest easy that no family insanity could be passed on to Lee. It seems that Oscar had an accident when he was a child. A serious skull fracture that somehow led to his condition."

"Any repercussions? Papers get any of it?" I handed the sheets back to Pat and he tucked them away.

"None at all, luckily. We were on tenterhooks for a while, but none of the newsboys connected the names. There was one fortunate aspect to the death of Oscar . . . his face wasn't recognizable. If the reporters had seen him there wouldn't have been a chance of covering up, and would some politicians like to have gotten that!"

I pulled a Lucky from my pack and tapped it on the arm of the chair. "What was the medical examiner's opinion?"

"Hell, suicide without a doubt. Oscar got scared, that's all. He tried to run knowing he was trapped. I guess he knew he'd go back to the sanitarium if he was caught . . . if he didn't stand a murder trial for Moffit's murder, and he couldn't take it."

Pat snapped his lighter open and fired my butt. "I guess that washes it up then," I said.

"For us . . . yes. For you, no."

I raised my eyebrows and looked at him quizzically.

"I saw Lee before I came to work. He called," Pat explained. "When he spoke to Oscar over the phone Oscar hinted at something. He seems to think that Oscar might have done other things than try to have him identified for a murder he didn't do. Anyway, I told him you had some unusual interest in the whole affair that you didn't want to speak about, even to me. He quizzed me about you, I told all and now he wants to see you."

"I'm to run down anything left behind?"

"I imagine so. At any rate, you'll get a fat fee out of it instead of kicking around for free."

"I don't mind. I'm on vacation anyway."

"Nuts. Stop handing me the same old thing. Think of something different. I'd give a lot to know what you have on your mind."

"You sure would, Pat." Perhaps it was the way I said it. Pat went into a piece of police steel. The cords in his neck stuck out like little fingers and his lips were just a straight, thin line.

"I've never known you to hang your hat on anything but murder, Mike."

"True, ain't it." My voice was flat as his.

"Mike, after the way I've been pitching with you, if you get in another smear you'll be taking me with you."

"I won't get smeared."

"Mike, you bastard, you have a murder tucked away somewhere."

"Sure, two of 'em. Try again."

He let his eyes relax and forced a grin. "If there were any recent

kills on the pad I'd go over them one by one and scour your
hide until you told me which one it was."

"You mean," I said sarcastically, "that the Finest haven't got
one single unsolved murder on their hands?"

Pat got red and squirmed. "Not recently."

"What about that laddie you hauled out of the drink?"

He scowled as he remembered. "Oh, that gang job. Body still
unidentified and we're tracking down his dental work. No prints
on file."

"Think you'll tag him?"

"It ought to be easy. That bridgework was unusual. One false
tooth was made of stainless steel. Never heard of that before."

The bells started in my head again. Bells, drums, the whole
damn works. The cigarette dropped out of my fingers and I bent
to pick it up, hoping the blood pounding in my veins would
pound out the crazy music.

It did. That maddening blast of silent sound went away. Slowly.

Maybe Pat never heard of stainless-steel teeth before, but I had.

I said, "Is Lee expecting me?"

"I told him you'd be over some time this morning."

"Okay." I stood up and shoved my hat on. "One other thing,
what about the guy Oscar bumped?"

"Charlie Moffit?"

"Yeah."

"Age thirty-four, light skin, dark hair. He had a scar over one
eye. During the war he was 4-F. No criminal record and not much
known about him. He lived in a room on Ninety-first Street, the
same one he's had for a year. He worked in a pie factory."

"Where?"

"A pie factory," Pat repeated, "where they make pies. Mother
Switcher's Pie Shoppe. You can find it in the directory."

"Was that card all the identification he had on him?"

"No, he had a driver's license and a few other things. During
the scuffle one pocket of his coat was torn out, but I doubt if he
would have carried anything there anyway. Now, Mike, . . . why?"

"The green cards, remember?"

"Hell, quit worrying about the reds. We have agencies who can
handle them."

I looked past Pat outside into the morning. "How many Commies are there floating around, Pat?"

"Couple hundred thousand, I think," he said.

"How many men have we got in those agencies you mentioned?"

"Oh . . . maybe a few hundred. What's that got to do with it?"

"Nothing . . . just that that's the reason I'm worried."

"Forget it. Let me know how you make out with Lee."

"Sure."

"And Mike . . . be discreet as hell about this, will you? Everybody with a press card knows your reputation and if you're spotted tagging around Lee there might be some questions asked that will be hard to answer."

"I'll wear a disguise," I said.

Lee Deamer's office was on the third floor of a modest building just off Fifth Avenue. There was nothing pretentious about the place aside from the switchboard operator. She was special. She had one of those faces that belonged in a chorus and a body she was making more effort to show than to conceal. I heard her voice and it was beautiful. But she was chewing gum like a cow and that took away any sign of pretentiousness she might have had.

There was a small anteroom that led to another office where two stenos were busy over typewriters. One wall of that room was all glass with a speaking partition built in at waist level. I had to lean down to my belt buckle to talk and gave it up as a bad job. The girl behind it laughed pleasantly and came out the door to see me.

She was a well-tailored woman in her early thirties, nice to look at and speak to. She wore an emerald ring that looked a generation older than she was. She smiled and said, "Good morning, can I do something for you?"

I remembered to be polite. "I'd like to see Mr. Deamer, please."

"Is he expecting you?"

"He sent word for me to come up."

"I see." She tapped her teeth with a pencil and frowned. "Are you in a hurry?"

"Not particularly, but I think Mr. Deamer is."

"Oh, well . . . the doctor is inside with him. He may be there a while, so . . ."

"Doctor?" I interrupted.

The girl nodded, a worried little look tugging at her eyes. "He seemed to be quite upset this morning and I called in the doctor. Mr. Deamer hasn't been too well since he had that attack awhile back."

"What kind of attack?"

"Heart. He had a telephone call one day that agitated him terribly. I was about to suggest that he go home and at that moment, he collapsed. I . . . I was awfully frightened. You see, it had never happened before, and . . ."

"What did the doctor say?"

"Apparently it wasn't a severe attack. Mr. Deamer was instructed to take it easy, but for a man of his energy it's hard to do."

"You say he had a phone call? That did it?"

"I'm sure it did. At first I thought it was the excitement of watching the Legion parade down the avenue, but Ann told me it happened right after the call came in."

Oscar's call must have hit him harder than either Pat or I thought. Lee wasn't a young man any more, a thing like that could raise a lot of hell with a guy's ticker. I was about to say something when the doctor came out of the office. He was a little guy with a white goatee out of another era.

He nodded to us both, but turned his smile on the girl. "I'm sure he'll be fine. I left a prescription. See that it's filled at once, please?"

"Thank you, I will. Is it all right for him to have visitors?"

"Certainly. Apparently he has been thinking of something that disturbed him and had a slight relapse. Nothing to worry about as long as he takes it easy. Good day."

We said so long and she turned to me with another smile, bigger this time. "I guess you can go ahead in then. But please . . . don't excite him."

I grinned and said I wouldn't. Her smile made her prettier. I pushed through the door, passed the steno and knocked on the door with Deamer's name on it.

He rose to greet me but I waved him down. His face was a little flushed and his breathing fast. "Feeling better now? I saw the doctor when he came out."

"Much better, Mike. I had to fabricate a story to tell him . . . I couldn't tell the truth."

I sat in the chair next to his and he pushed a box of cigars toward me. I said no and took out a Lucky instead. "Best to keep things to yourself. One word and the papers'll have it on page one. Pat said you wanted to see me."

Lee sat back and wiped his face with a damp handkerchief. "Yes, Mike. He told me you were interested somehow."

"I am."

"Are you one of my . . . political advocates?"

"Frankly, I don't know a hoot about politics except that it's a dirty game from any angle."

"I hope to do something about that. I hope I can, Mike, I sincerely hope I can. Now I'm afraid."

"The heart?"

He nodded. "It happened after Oscar called. I never suspected that I have a . . . condition. I'm afraid now the voters must be told. It wouldn't be fair to elect a man not physically capable of carrying out the duties of his office." He smiled wistfully, sadly. I felt sorry for the old boy.

"Anyway, I'm not concerned with the politics of the affair."

"Really? But what . . ."

"Just a loose end, Lee. They bother me."

"I see. I don't understand, but I see . . . if you can make sense of that."

I waved the smoke away from in front of him. "I know what you mean. Now about why you wanted to see me. Pat gave me part of it already, enough so I can see the rest."

"Yes. You see, Oscar intimated that no matter what happened, he was going to see to it that I was broken, completely broken. He mentioned some documents he had prepared."

I crushed the butt out and looked at him. "What kind of documents?"

Lee shook his head slowly. "The only possible thing he could compound would be our relationship as brothers. How, I don't know, because I have all the family papers. But if he could establish that I was the brother of a man committed to a mental institution, it would be a powerful weapon in the hands of the opposition."

"There's nothing else," I asked, "that could stick you?"

He spread his hands apart in appeal. "If there was it would have been brought to light long ago. No, I've never been in jail or in trouble of any sort. I'm afraid that my attention to business precluded any trouble."

"Uh-huh. How come this awful hatred?"

"I don't know, actually. As I told Pat and you previously, it may have been a matter of ideals, or because though we were twins, we weren't at all alike. Oscar was almost, well . . . sadistic in his ways. We had little to do with each other. As younger men I became established in business while Oscar got into all sorts of scrapes. I've tried to help him, but he wouldn't accept help from me at all. He hated me fiercely. I'm inclined to believe that this time Oscar had intended to bleed me for all the money he could, then make trouble for me anyway."

"You were lucky you took the attitude you did. You can't pay off, it only makes matters worse."

"I don't know, Mike; as much as he hated me I certainly didn't want that to happen to him."

"He's better off."

"Perhaps."

I reached for another cigarette. "You want me to find out what he left then, that's it."

"If there is anything to be found, yes."

When I filled my lungs with smoke I let it go slowly, watching it swirl up toward the ceiling. "Lee," I said, "you don't know me so I'll tell you something. I hate phonies. Suppose I *do* find something that ties you up into a nice little ball. Something real juicy. What do you think I should do with it?"

It wasn't the reaction I expected. He leaned forward across the desk with his fingers interlocked. His face was a study in emotions. "Mike," he said in a voice that had the crisp clarity of static electricity, "if you do, I charge you to make it public at once. Is that clear?"

I grinned and stood up. "Okay, Lee. I'm glad you said that." I reached out my hand and he took it warmly. I've seen evangelists with faces like that, unswerving, devoted to their duty. We looked at each other then he opened his desk drawer and brought out a lovely sheaf of green paper. They had big, beautiful numbers in the corners.

"Here is a thousand dollars, Mike. Shall we call it a retainer?"

I took the bills and folded them tenderly away. "Let's call it payment in full. You'll get your money's worth."

"I'm sure of it. If you need any additional information, call on me."

"Right. Want a receipt?"

"No need of it. I'm sure your word is good enough."

"Thanks. I'll send you a report if anything turns up." I flipped a card out of my pocket and laid it on his desk. "In case you want to call me. The bottom one is my home phone. It's unlisted."

We shook hands again and he walked me to the door. On the way out the cud-chewing switchboard sugar smiled between chomps then went back to her magazine. The receptionist said so long and I waved back.

Before I went to the office I grabbed a quick shave, a trim around the ears and took a shower that scraped the hide off me along with the traces of Ethel's perfume. I changed my shirt and suit but kept old Betsy in place under my arm.

Velda was working at the filing cabinet when I breezed in with a snappy hello and a grin that said I had money in my pocket. I got a quick once over for lipstick stains, whisky aromas and what not, passed and threw the stack of bills on the desk.

"Bank it, kid."

"Mike! What did *you* do?"

"Lee Deamer. We're employed." I gave it to her in short order and she listened blankly.

When I finished she said, "You'll never find a thing, Mike. I know you won't. You shouldn't have taken it."

"You're wrong, chick. It wasn't stealing. If Oscar left anything that will tie Lee up wouldn't you want me to get it?"

"Oh, Mike, you must! How long do we have to put up with the slime they call politics? Lee Deamer is the only one . . . the only one we can look to. Please, Mike, you *can't* let anything happen to him!"

I couldn't take the fear in her voice. I opened my arms out and she stepped into them. "Nobody will hurt the little guy, Velda. If there's anything I'll get it. Stop sniffling."

"I can't. It's all so nasty. You never stop to think what goes on in this country, but I do."

"Seems to me that I helped fight a war, didn't I?"

"You shouldn't have let it stop there. That's the matter with things. People forget, even the ones who *shouldn't* forget! They let others come walking in and run things any way they please, and what are they after—the welfare of the people they represent? Not a bit. All they want is to line their own pockets. Lee isn't like that, Mike. He isn't strong like the others, and he isn't smart politically. All he has to offer is his honesty and that isn't much."

"The hell it isn't. He's made a pretty big splash in this state."

"I know, and it has to stick, Mike. Do you understand?"

"I understand."

"Promise me you'll help him, Mike, promise me your word."

Her face turned up to mine, drawn yet eager to hear. "I promise," I said softly. "I'll never go back on a promise to you, nor to myself."

It made her feel better in a hurry. The tears stopped and the sniffling died away. We had a laugh over it, but behind the laughter there was a dead seriousness. The gun under my arm felt heavy.

I said, "I have a job for you. Get me a background on Charlie Moffit. He's the one Oscar Deamer bumped."

Velda stopped her filing. "Yes, I know."

"Go to his home and his job. See what kind of a guy he was. Pat didn't mention a family so he probably didn't have any. Take what cash you need to cover expenses."

She shoved the drawer in and fingered the bills on the desk. "How soon?"

"I want it by tonight if you can. If not, tomorrow will do."

I could see her curiosity coming out, but there are times when I want to keep things to myself and this was one of them. She knew it and stayed curious without asking questions.

Before she slipped the bills inside the bank book I took out two hundred in fifties. She didn't say anything then, either, but she smelt a toot coming up and I had to kiss the tip of her nose to get the scowl off her puss.

As soon as Velda left I picked up the phone and dialed Ethel Brighton's number. The flunky recognized my voice from last night and was a little more polite. He told me Ethel hadn't come in yet and hung up almost as hard as he could but not quite.

I tapped out a brief history of the case for the records, stuck it in the file and called again. Ethel had just gotten in. She grabbed the phone and made music in it, not giving a damn who heard her. "You beast. You walked right out of the cave and left me to the wolves."

"That bearskin would scare them away. You looked nice wrapped up in it."

"You liked . . . all of me, then. The parts you could see?"

"All of you, Ethel. Soft and sweet."

"We'll have to go back."

"Maybe," I said.

"Please," softly whispered.

I changed the subject. "Busy today?"

"Very busy. I have a few people to see. They promised me sizable . . . donations. Tonight I have to deliver them to Com . . . Henry Gladow."

"Yeah. Suppose I go with you?"

"If *you* think it's all right I'm sure no one will object."

"Why me?" That was one of the questions I wanted an answer to.

She didn't tell me. "Come now," she said. "Supposing I meet you in the Oboe Club at seven. Will that do?"

"Fine, Ethel. I'll save a table so we can eat."

She said so long with a pleasant laugh and waited for me to hang up. I did, then sat there with a cigarette in my fingers trying to think. The light hitting the wall broke around something on the desk making two little bright spots against the pale green.

Like two berries on a bush. The judge's eyes. They looked at me.

Something happened to the light and the eyes disappeared. I picked the phone up again and called the *Globe*. Marty was just going out on a story but had time to talk to me. I asked him, "Remember the Brighton family? Park Avenue stuff."

"Sure, Mike. That's social, but I know a little about them. Why?"

"Ethel Brighton's on the outs with her father. Did it ever make the papers?"

I heard him chuckle a second. "Getting toney, aren't you, kid? Well, part of the story was in the papers some time ago. It seems that Ethel Brighton publicly announced her engagement to a certain young man. Shortly afterwards the engagement was broken."

"Is that all?"

"Nope," he grunted, "the best is yet to come. A little prying by our diligent Miss Carpenter who writes the social chatter uncovered an interesting phase that was handled just as interestingly. The young man in question was a down-and-out artist who made speeches for the Communist Party and was quite willing to become a capitalist by marriage. He was a conscientious objector during the war though he probably could have made 4-F without trouble. The old man raised the roof but there was nothing he could do. When he threatened to cut Ethel off without a cent she said she'd marry him anyway.

"So the old man connived. He worked it so that he'd give his blessing so long as the guy enlisted in the army. They needed men bad so they took him and as soon as he was out of training camp he was shipped overseas. He was killed in action, though the truth was that he went AWOL during a battle and deserved what he got. Later Ethel found out that her father was responsible for everything but the guy's getting knocked off and he had hoped for that too. She had a couple of rows with him in public, then it died down to where they just never spoke."

"Nice girl," I mused.

"Lovely to look at anyway."

"You'll never know. Well, thanks, pal."

He stopped me before I could hang up. "Is this part of what you were driving at the other day . . . something to do with Lee Deamer?" His voice had a rasp.

"Not this," I said. "It's personal."

"Oh, well call me any time, Mike." He sounded relieved.

And so the saga of one Ethel Brighton. Nice girl turned dimwit because her old man did her out of a marriage. She was lucky and didn't know it.

I looked at my watch, remembered that I had meant to buy Velda lunch and forgot, then went downstairs and ate by myself. When I finished the dessert I sat back with a cigarette and tried to think of what it was that fought like the hammers of hell to come through my mind. Something was eating its way out and I couldn't help it. I gave up finally and paid my check. There was a movie poster behind the register advertising the latest show at the house a block over, so I ambled over and plunked in a seat before the show started. It wasn't good enough to keep me awake. I was on the second time around when I glanced at the time and hustled into the street.

The Oboe Club had been just another second-rate saloon on a side street until a wandering reporter happened in and mentioned it in his column as a good place to relax if you liked solitude and quiet. The next day it became a first-rate nightclub where you could find anything but solitude and quiet. Advertising helped plenty.

I knew the headwaiter to nod to and it was still early enough to get a table without any green passing between handshakes. The bar was lined with the usual after-office crowd having one for the road. There wasn't anyone to speak to, so I sat at the table and ordered a highball. I was on my fourth when Ethel Brighton came in, preceded by the headwaiter and a few lesser luminaries.

He bowed her into her seat, then bowed himself out. The other one helped her adjust her coat over the back of the chair. "Eat?" I asked.

"I'll have a highball first. Like yours." I signaled the waiter and called for a couple more.

"How'd the donations come?"

"Fine," she said, "even better than I expected. The best part is, there's more where that came from."

"The party will be proud of you." She looked up from her drink with a nervous little smile.

"I . . . hope so."

"They should. You've brought in a lot of mazuma."

"One must do all one can." Her voice was a flat drone, almost machine-like. She picked up her glass and took a long pull. The waiter came and took our orders, leaving another highball with us.

I caught her attention and got back on the subject. "Do you ever wonder where it all goes to?"

"You mean . . . the money?" I nodded between bites. "Why . . . no. It isn't for me to think about those things. I only do as I'm told." She licked her lips nervously and went back to her plate.

I prodded her again. "I'd be curious if I were in your shoes. Give a guess, anyway."

This time there was nothing but fear in her face. It tugged at her eyes and mouth, and made her fork rattle against the china. "Please . . ."

"You don't have to be afraid of me, Ethel. I'm not entirely like the others. You should know that."

The fear was still there, but something else overshadowed it. "I can't understand you . . . you're different. It's well. . . ."

"About the money, give a guess. Nobody should be entirely ignorant of party affairs. After all, isn't that the principle of the thing . . . everybody for everybody? Then you'd have to know everything about everybody to be able to really do the party justice."

"That's true." She squinted and a smile parted her lips. "I see what you mean. Well, I'd guess that most of the money goes to foster the schools we operate . . . and for propaganda, of course. Then there are a lot of small things that come up like office expenses here and there."

"Pretty good so far. Anything else?"

"I'm not too well informed on the business side of it so that's about as far as I can go."

"What does Gladow do for a living?"

"Isn't he a clerk in a department store?"

I nodded as if I had known all along. "Ever see his car?"

Ethel frowned again. "Yes. He has a new Packard, why?"

"Ever see his house?"

"I've been there twice," she said. "It's a big place up in Yonkers."

"And all that on a department store clerk's salary."

Her face went positively white. She had to swallow hard to get her drink down and refused to meet my eyes until I told her to look at me. She did, but hesitantly. Ethel Brighton was scared silly . . . of me. I grinned but it was lost. I talked and it went over her head. She gave all the right answers and even a laugh at one of my jokes, but Ethel was scared and she wasn't coming out of it too quickly.

She took the cigarette I offered her. The tip shook when she bent into the flame of my lighter. "What time do you have to be there?" I asked.

"Nine o'clock. There's . . . a meeting."

"We'd better go then. It'll take time getting over to Brooklyn."

"All right."

The waiter came over and took away a ten spot for his trouble while the headboy saw us to the door. Half the bar turned around to look at Ethel as she brushed by. I got a couple of glances that said I was a lucky guy to have all that mink on my arm. Real lucky.

We had to call the parking lot to get her car brought over then drove the guy back again. It was a quarter after eight before we pointed the car toward the borough across the stream. Ethel was behind the wheel, driving with a fixed intensity. She wouldn't talk unless I said something that required an answer. After a while it got tiresome so I turned on the radio and slumped back against the seat with my hat down over my eyes.

Only then did she seem to ease up. Twice I caught her head turning my way, but I couldn't see her eyes nor read the expression on her face. Fear. It was always there. Communism and Fear. Green Cards and Fear. Terror on the face of the girl on the bridge; stark, unreasoning fear when she looked at my face. Fear so bad it threw her over the rail to her death.

I'd have to remember to ask Pat about that, I thought. The body had to come up sometime.

The street was the same as before, dark, smelly, unaware of the tumor it was breeding in its belly. Trench Coat was standing outside the door seemingly enjoying the night. Past appearance didn't count. You showed your card and went in the door and showed it again. There was the same girl behind the desk and she made more of me than the card I held. Her voice was a nervous squeak and she couldn't sit still. Deliberately, I shot her the meanest grin I could dig up, letting her see my face when I pulled my lip back over my teeth. She didn't like it. Whatever it was scared her, too.

Henry Gladow was a jittery little man. He frittered around the room, stopped when he saw us and came over with a rush. "Good evening, good evening, comrades." He spoke directly to me. "I am happy to see you again, comrade. It is an honor."

It had been an honor before, too.

"There is news?" I screwed my eyebrows together and he pulled back, searching for words until he found them. "Of course. I am merely being inquisitive. Ha, ha. We are all so very concerned, you know."

"I know," I said.

Ethel handed him another of those envelopes and excused herself. I watched her walk to a table and take a seat next to two students where she began to correct some mimeographed sheets. "Wonderful worker, Miss Brighton," Gladow smiled. "You would scarcely think that she represents all that we hate."

I made an unintelligible answer.

"You are staying for the meeting?" he asked me.

"Yeah, I want to poke around a little."

This time he edged close to me, looking around to see if there was anyone close enough to hear. "Comrade, if I am not getting too inquisitive again, is there a possibility that . . . the person could be here?"

There it was again. Just what I wanted to know and I didn't dare ask the question. It was going to take some pretty careful handling. "It's possible," I said tentatively.

He was aghast. "Comrade! It is unthinkable!" He reflected a moment then: "Yet it had to come from somewhere. I simply can't understand it. Everything is so carefully screened, every member so carefully selected that it seems impossible for there to be a leak anywhere. And those filthy warmongers, doing a thing like that . . . so cold-blooded! It is simply incredible. How I wish the party was in power at this moment. Why, the one who did that would be uncovered before the sun could set!"

Gladow cursed through his teeth and pounded a puny, carefully tended fist into his palm. "Don't worry," I said slowly.

It took ten seconds for my words to sink in. Gladow's little eyes narrowed in pleasure like a hog seeing a trough full of slops. The underside of his top lip showed when he smiled. "No, comrade. I won't worry. The party is too clever to let a direct representative's death go unpunished. No, I won't worry because I realize that the punishment that comes will more than equal the crime." He beamed at me fatuously. "I am happy to realize that the higher echelon has sent a man of your capacity, comrade."

I didn't even thank him. I was thinking and this time the words made sense. They made more than sense . . . they made murder! Only death is cold-blooded, and who was dead? Three people. One hadn't been found. One was found and not identified, even by a lousy sketch. The other was dead and identified. He was cold-bloodedly murdered and he was a direct representative of the party and I was the guy looking for his killer.

Good Lord, the insane bastards thought I was an MVD man!

My hands started to shake and I kept them in my pockets. And who was the dead man but Charlie Moffit! My predecessor. A goddamned Commie gestapo man. A hatchetman, a torpedo, a lot of things you want to call him. Lee ought to be proud of his brother, damn proud. All by himself he went out and he knocked off a skunk.

But I was the prize, I was the MVD guy that came to take his place and run the killer down. Oh, brother! No wonder the jerks were afraid of me! No wonder they didn't ask my name! No wonder I was supposed to know it all.

I felt a grin trying to pull my mouth out of shape because so much of it was funny. They thought they were clever as hell and here I was right in the middle of things with an *in* that couldn't be better. Any good red would give his shirt to be where I was right this minute.

Everything started to come out right then, even the screwy test they put me through. A small-time setup like this was hardly worth the direct attention of a Moscow man unless something was wrong, so I had to prove myself.

Smart? Sure, just like road apples that happen behind horses.

Now I knew and now I could play the game. I could be one of the boys and show them some fun. There were going to be a lot of broken backs around town before I got done.

There was only one catch I could think of. Someplace was another MVD laddie, a real one. I'd have to be careful of him. At least careful that he didn't see me first, because when I met up with that stinkpot I was going to split him right down the middle with a .45!

I had been down too deep in my thoughts to catch the arrival of the party that came in behind me. I heard Gladow extending a welcome that wasn't handed out to just everybody. When I turned around to look I saw one little fat man, one big fat man and a guy who was in the newspapers every so often. His name was General Osilov and he was attached to the Russian Embassy in Washington. The big and little fat men were his aides and they did all the smiling. If anything went on in the head of the bald-headed general it didn't show in his flat, wide face.

Whatever it was Henry Gladow said swung the three heads in my direction. Two swung back again fast leaving only the general staring at me. It was a stare-down that I won. The general coughed without covering his mouth and stuck his hands in the pockets of his suitcoat. None of them seemed anxious to make my acquaintance.

From then on there was a steady flow of traffic in through the door. They came singly and in pairs, spaced about five minutes apart. Before the hour was out the place was packed. It was filled with the kind of people you'd expect to find there and it would hit you that when the cartoonists did a caricature of a pack of shabby reds lurking in the shadow of democracy they did a good job.

A few of them dragged out seats and the meeting was on. I saw Ethel Brighton slide into the last chair in the last row and waited until she was settled before I saw down beside her. She smiled, let that brief look of fear mask her face, then turned her head to the front. When I put my hand over hers I felt it tremble.

Gladow spoke. The aides spoke. Then the general spoke. He pulled his tux jacket down when he rose and glared at the audience. I had to sit there and listen to it. It was propaganda right off the latest Moscow cable and it turned me inside out. I wanted to feel the butt of an M-1 against my shoulder pointing at those bastards up there on the rostrum and feel the pleasant impact as it spit slugs into their guts.

Sure, you can sit down at night and read about the hogwash they hand out. Maybe you're fairly intelligent and can laugh at it. Believe me, it isn't funny. They use the very thing we build up, our own government and our own laws, to undermine the things we want.

It wasn't a very complicated speech the general made. It was plain, bitter poison and they cheered him noiselessly. He was making plain one thing. There were still too many people who didn't go for Communism and not enough who did and he gave a plan of organization that had worked in a dozen countries already. One armed Communist was worth twenty capitalists without guns. It was Hitler all over again. A powerful Communist government already formed would be there to take over when the big upset came, and according to him it was coming soon. Here, and he swept the room with his arm, was one phase of that government ready to go into action.

I didn't hear the rest of it. I sat there fiddling with my fingernails because I was getting ready to bust loose and spoil their plans. If I let any more words go in my ears there was going to be blood on the floor and it wasn't time for that yet. I caught snatches of things that went on, repeated intimations of how the top men were already in the core of the present government eating its vitals out so the upset would be an easy one.

For a long time I sat there working up more hatred than I had ever had at any time and I wasn't conscious of how tightly Ethel Brighton was squeezing my hand. When I looked at her tears were running down her face. That's the kind of thing the general and his party could do to decent people.

I took a long look at him, making sure that I wouldn't forget his face, because some day he'd be passing a dark alley or forget to lock his door when he went to bed. That's when he'd catch it. And I didn't want to get tagged for it either. That would be like getting the chair for squashing a spider.

The meeting ended with handshakes all around. The audience lined up along the walls taking handfuls of booklets and printed sheets to distribute later, then grouped in bunches around the room talking things over in excited murmurs. Henry Gladow and Martin Romberg were up on the rostrum having their own conference. The general said something to Henry and he must have ordered his bodyguard down into the crowd to look for his trench coat or something. Martin Romberg looked hurt. Tough.

While the seats were folded and stacked I lost track of Ethel. I saw her a few minutes later coming from the washroom and she looked a little better. She had a smile for me this time, a big one. I would have made something of it if a pimply-faced kid about twenty didn't come crawling over and tell me that the general wanted to know if I had time to speak to him.

Rather than answer I picked a hole in the crowd that had started to head for the door and walked up to the rostrum. The general stood alone, his hands behind his back. He nodded briefly and said something in a guttural tongue.

I let my eyes slide to the few who remained near by. There wasn't any respect in my tone when I said, "English. You know better than that."

The general paled a little and his mouth worked. "Yes . . . yes. I didn't expect to find anyone here. Do you have a report for me?"

I shook a cigarette out of the pack and stuck it in my mouth. "When I have you'll know about it."

His head bobbed anxiously and I knew I had the bull on him. Even a general had to be leery of the MVD. That made it nice for me. "Of course. But there should be some word to bring back to the committee."

"Then tell 'em things are looking up. It won't be long."

The general's hands came out in front where he squeezed them happily. "Then you *do* have word! The courier . . . he did have the documents? You know where they are?"

I didn't say a word. All I did was look at him and he got that same look on his face as the others had. He was thinking what I thought he was thinking, that he had taken me for granted and it was his mistake and one word to the right sources and he'd feel the ax.

He tried his first smile. "It is very all right, you know. Comrade Gladow told me."

I dragged on the cigarette and blew it in his face wishing it was some mustard gas. "You'll know soon enough," I said. I left him standing there and walked back to Ethel. She was slipping into her mink and nobody seemed to care a hoot what she wore.

"Going home?"

"Yes . . . are you?"

"I don't mind."

One of the men paused to have a word with her before she left. She excused herself to talk to him and I used the time to look around and be sure there weren't any faces there that I'd ever forget. When the time came I wanted to be able to put the finger on them and put it on good.

Maybe it was the way I stared at the babe from the desk at the door or maybe it was because I looked at her too long. Her lashes made like bird's wings for a second and everything in the room seemed to get interesting all of a sudden. Her eyes jerked around but kept coming back to mine and each time there was a little more of a blush crowding her hairline.

I kept my grin hidden because she thought I was on the make. It could have been pathetic if it wasn't so damn funny. She wasn't the kind of woman a guy would bother with if there was anything else around. Strictly the last resort type. From the way she wore her clothes you couldn't tell what was underneath and suspected probably nothing. Her face looked like nature had been tired when it made it and whatever she did to her hair certainly didn't improve things any.

Plain was the word. Stuffy was the type. And here she thought a man saw something interesting in her.

I guessed that all women were born with some conceit in them so I put on a sort of smile and walked over to her casually. A little flattery could make a woman useful sometimes.

I held out my deck of butts. "Smoke?"

It must have been her first cigarette. She choked on it, but came up smiling. "Thank you."

I said, "You've, er . . . belonged some time, Miss . . ."

"Linda Holbright." She got real fluttery then. "Oh, yes, for years, you know. And I . . . try to do anything I can for the party."

"Good, good," I said. "You seem to be . . . very capable. Pretty, too."

Her first blush had been nothing. This one went right down to her shoes. Her eyes got big and blue and round and gave me the damnedest look you ever saw. Just for the hell of it I gave one back with a punch in it. What she made of it stopped her from breathing for a second.

I heard Ethel finish her little conversation behind me and I said, "Good night, Linda. I'll see you soon." I gave her that look again. "Real soon."

Her voice sounded a little bit strained. "I . . . meant to ask you. If there is anything . . . important you should know . . . where can I reach you?"

I ripped the back off a book of matches and wrote down my address. "Here it is. Apartment 5B."

Ethel was waiting for me, so I said good night again and started for the door behind the mink coat. It made nice wiggles when she walked. I liked that.

I let her go out first then followed her. The street was empty enough so you wouldn't think anything unusual about the few couples who were making their way to the subways. Trench Coat was still at the door holding a cigarette in his mouth. His belt was too tight and the gun showed underneath. One day a cop would spot that and there'd be more trouble.

Yeah, they sure were smart.

Going back was better than going down. This time Ethel turned into a vivid conversationalist, commenting on everything she saw. I tried to get in a remark about the meeting and she brushed it off with some fast talk. I let her get it out of her system, sitting there with my mouth shut, grinning at the right places and chiming in with a grunt whenever she laughed.

About a block from my apartment I pointed to the corner and said, "I'll get off under the light, kid."

She edged into the curb and stopped. "Good night, then," she smiled. "I hope you enjoyed the meeting."

"As a matter of fact, I thought they stunk." Ethel's mouth dropped open. I kissed it and she closed it, fast. "Do you know what I'd do if I were you, Ethel?"

She shook her head, watching me strangely.

"I'd go back to being a woman and less of a dabbler in politics."

This time her eyes and mouth came open together. I kissed her again before she could get it shut. She looked at me as if I were a puzzle that couldn't be solved and let out a short, sharp laugh that had real pleasure in it.

"Aren't you a bit curious about my name, Ethel?"

Her face went soft. "Only for my own sake."

"It's Mike. Mike Hammer and it's a good name to remember."

"Mike . . ." very softly. "After last night . . . how could I forget?"

I grinned at her and opened the door. "Will I be seeing you again?"

"Do you want to?"

"Very much."

"Then you'll be seeing me again. You know where I live."

I couldn't forget her, either. On that bearskin rug with the fire behind her she was something a man never forgets. I stuck my hands in my pockets and started to whistle my way down the street.

I got as far as the door next to mine when the sedan across the street came to life. If the guy at the wheel hadn't let the clutch out so fast I wouldn't have looked up and seen the snout of the rifle that hung out the back window. What happened then came in a blur of motion and a mad blasting of sound. The long streak of flame from the rifle, the screaming of the ricocheted slug, the howl of the car engine. I dove flat out. Rolling before I hit the concrete, my hand pulling the gun out, my thumb grabbing for the hammer. The rifle barked again and gouged a hunk out of the sidewalk in front of my face, but by that time the .45 in my hand was bucking out the bullets as fast as my finger could pull the trigger, and in the light of the street lamp overhead I saw the dimples pop into the back of the car and the rear window spiderweb suddenly and smash to the ground. Somebody in the car screamed like a banshee gone mad and there were no more shots. Around me the windows were slamming up before the car had made the turn at the corner.

I kept saying it over and over to myself. "Those goddamned bastards. They got wise! Those goddamn bastards!"

A woman shrieked from a window that somebody was dead and when I looked up I saw she was pointing to me. When I climbed back on my feet she shrieked again and fell away from the window.

It hadn't been a full twenty seconds since that car had started up, and a police car was wheeling around the corner. The driver slammed on the brakes and the two of them came out with Police Specials in their hands, both of them pointed at me. I was trying to shove a fresh load into the clip when the cop snarled, "Drop that gun, damn it!"

I wasn't doing any arguing with them. I tossed the gun so it landed on my foot then shoved it away gently. The other cop picked it up. They told me to put my hands on my head and I stood there while they flashed the beam of light in my face.

"There's a ticket for that rod in my wallet along with a Private Operator's license."

The cop didn't lose any time frisking me for another rod before yanking my wallet out. He had a skeptical look on his face until he saw the ticket. "Okay, put 'em down," he said. I dropped my hands and reached for my .45. "I didn't say to pick that up yet," he added. I let it stay there. The cop who drove the buggy looked the ticket over then looked at me. He said something to his partner and motioned for me to get the gun.

"All clear?" I blew the dust off old Betsy and stowed it away. A crowd was beginning to collect and one of the cops started to herd them away.

"What happened?" He wasn't a man of many words.

"There you got me, feller. I was on my way home when the shooting started. Either it's the old yarn of mistaken identity which isn't too probable or somebody whom I thought was a friend, isn't."

"Maybe you better come with us."

"Sure, but in the meantime a black Buick sedan with no back window and a few bullets in its behind is making tracks to the nearest garage. I think I got one of the guys in the car and you can start checking the doctors."

The cop peered at me under his visor and took my word for it. The call went out on the police wires without any more talk. They were all for dragging me with them until I had a call put in to Pat and his answer relayed back to the squad car. Pat told them I was available at any time and they gave me the green light through the crowd.

I got a lot of unfriendly looks that night.

When I stood in front of my door with the key in my hand it hit me just like that. My little love scene with Ethel Brighton had had repercussions. My wallet on the floor. It wasn't in the same place in the morning. When she had gotten up for that blanket she had seen it, and my P.I. card in the holder. Tonight she passed the word.

I was lucky to get out of there with a whole skin.

Ethel, I thought, you're a cute little devil. You looked so nice in your bare skin with the fire behind you. Maybe I'll see you stripped again. Soon. When I do I'm going to take my belt off and lash your butt like it should have been lashed when you first broke into this game.

In fact, I looked forward to doing it.

chapter six ▬▬▬▬▬▬▬▬▬

I FINISHED A QUART bottle of beer before calling Velda. I got her at home and asked her what she'd found. She said, "There wasn't much *to* find, Mike. His landlady said he was on the quiet side because he was too stupid to talk. He never complained about a thing and in all the time he was living there he never once had company."

No, he wouldn't talk too much if he was an MVD agent. And he wouldn't have company for that matter, either. His kind of company was met at night and in the dark recesses of a building somewhere.

"Did you try the pie factory where he worked?"

"I did but I didn't get anywhere. The last few months he had been on deliveries and most of the guys who knew him were out selling pies. The manager told me he was a stupid egg who had to write everything down in order to remember it, but he did his job fairly well. The only driver I did see said something nasty when I mentioned Moffit and tried to date me."

The boy put on a good act. People aren't likely to get too friendly with somebody who's pretty stupid. I said, "When do the drivers leave the plant?"

"Eight A.M., Mike. Are you going back?"

"I think I'd better. Supposing you come along with me. I'll meet you on the street in front of the office about seven and that'll give us time to get over there and see some of them."

"Mike . . . what's so important about Charlie Moffit?"

"I'll tell you tomorrow."

Velda grunted her displeasure and said good night. I had hardly hung up when I heard the feet in the hall and my doorbell started to yammer. Just in case, I yanked the .45 out and dropped it in my pocket where I could keep my hand around it.

The gun wasn't necessary at all. It was the boys from the papers, four of them. Three were on the police beat and the fourth was Marty Kooperman. He wore a faint, sardonic smile that was ready to disbelieve any lie I told.

"Well, the Fourth Estate. Come on in and don't stay too long." I threw the door open.

Bill Cowan of the *News* grinned and pointed to my pocket. "Nice way to greet old friends, Mike."

"Isn't it. Come on in."

They made a straight line for the refrigerator, found it empty, but uncovered a fresh bottle of whisky that I had been saving and helped themselves. All but Marty. He closed the door himself and stood behind me.

"We hear you got shot at, Mike."

"You heard right, friend. They missed."

"I'm thinking that I could say 'too bad' and mean it."

"What's your bitch, Marty! I've been shot at before. How come you're on the police run?"

"I'm not. I came along for the ride when I heard what happened." He paused. "Mike . . . for once come clean. Has this got to do with Lee Deamer?"

The boys in the kitchen were banging their first drinks down. I had that much time at least. I said, "Marty, don't worry about your idol. Let's say that this happened as a result of my poking into something that I *thought* was connected with Deamer. He doesn't figure into it in any way."

Marty took in a breath and let it out slowly. He twisted his hat in his hands then flipped it on the coat rack. "Okay, Mike, I'll take your word for it."

"Suppose it had to do with Lee, what then, chum?"

His lips tightened over a soft voice. "We'd have to know. They're out to get Lee any way they can and there aren't many of us who can stop them."

I scowled at him. "Who's us?"

"Your Fourth Estate, Mike. Your neighbors. Maybe even you if you knew what we knew."

That was all we had time for. The boys came charging back with fresh drinks and pencils ready. I led them inside to the living room and sat down. "Shoot, laddies. What's on your mind?"

"The shooting, Mike. Good news item, ya know."

"Yeah, great news. Tomorrow the public gets my picture and another lurid account of how that Hammer character conducts a private war on a public thoroughfare and I'll get an eviction notice from my landlord and a sudden lack of clients."

Bill laughed and polished his drink off. "Just the same, it's news. We got some of it from headquarters but we want the story straight from you. Hell, man, look how lucky you are. You get to tell your side of it while the others can't say a word. Come on, give."

"Sure, I'll give." I lit up a Lucky and took a deep drag on it. "I was walking home and . . ."

"Where were you?"

"Movies. So just as I . . ."

"What movie?"

I showed him my teeth in a lopsided grin. That was an easy one. "Laurance Theatre. Bum show."

Marty showed me his teeth back. "What was playing, Mike? He was the only one not ready to take notes.

I started in on as much of the picture as I had seen and he stopped me with his hand. "That's enough. I saw it myself. Incidentally, have you still got your stub?"

Marty should have been a cop. He knows damn well that most men have an unconscious habit of dropping the things in their pockets. I pulled out an assortment and handed him one. He took it while the other boys watched, wondering what the hell it was all about. He picked up the phone, called the theatre and gave them the number on the ticket, asking if it had been sold that day. They said it had been and Marty hung up sheepishly. I let go my breath, glad that he hadn't asked what time. He wasn't such a good detective after all.

"Go on," he said.

"That's all. I was coming home when the punks in the car started to blast. I didn't get a look at any of 'em."

Bill said, "You on a case now?"

"If I was I wouldn't say so anyhow. What else?"

One of the boys from a tabloid wrinkled his nose at my story. "Come on, Mike, break down. Nobody took a shot at you without a reason."

"Look, pal, I have more enemies than I have friends. The kind of enemies I make go around loaded. Take a check on most known criminals and you'll find people who don't like me."

"In other words, we don't get a story," Bill said.

"In other words," I told him, ". . . yes. Want another drink?"

At least that was satisfactory. When they had the bottom of the bottle showing I whistled to stop their jabbering and got them together so I could get in a last word. "Don't any of you guys try tagging me around hoping for a lead about this. I'm not taking anything without paying it back. If a story crops up I'll let you in on it, meantime stick to chasing ambulances."

"Aw, Mike."

"No, 'Aw,' pally. I'm not kidding around about it, so stay out of my way."

As long as the bottle was empty and I wouldn't give with a yarn, they decided that there wasn't much sense in sticking around. They went out the door in a bunch with Marty trailing along in the rear. He said so long ruefully, his eyes warning me to be careful.

I spread the slats of the blinds apart and watched them all climb into a beat-up coupé and when I was sure they were gone for the night I took off my clothes and climbed into the shower.

I took a hot and a cold, brushed my teeth, started to put away my tools and the bell rang again. I damned a few things in general and the Fourth Estate in particular for not making sure all the boys were there when they started their inquisition. Probably a lone reporter who got the flash late and wanted to know all about it. I wrapped a towel around my lower half and made wet tracks from the bathroom to the front door.

She stood there in the dim light of the hall not knowing whether to be startled, surprised or shocked. I said, "Goddamn!"

She smiled hesitantly until I told her to come in and made a quick trip back for a bathrobe. Something had happened to Linda Holbright since the last time I had seen her and I didn't want to stand there in a towel while I found out what it was.

When I got back to the living room she was sitting in the big chair with her coat thrown over the back. This time she didn't have on a sack suit and you knew what was underneath it. It wasn't "probably nothing" either. It was a whole lot of something that showed and she wasn't making any bones about it. The angles seemed to be gone from her face and her hair was different. Before it was hair. Now it was a smooth wavy mass that trailed across her shoulders. She still wasn't pretty, but a guy didn't give a damn about that when there was a body like hers under her face.

Because of a smile she had gone to a hell of a lot of trouble. She must have taken her one asset to a perfectionist and let him build a dress around it. I think it was a dress. Paint would have done the same thing. There wasn't anything on underneath to spoil the effect and that showed. She was excited as hell and that showed too.

I was thinking that it could be very nice if she had only come a little sooner before I knew that Ethel had told what she had found in my wallet. Linda smiled at me tentatively as I sat down opposite her and lit up a smoke. I smiled back and started thinking again. This time there was a different answer. Maybe they were playing real cute and sent her in for the kicker. Maybe they had figured that their little shooting deal might get messed up and sent her around to get the score on me.

It made nice thinking because that was the way they worked and I didn't feel sorry for her any more. I got up and moved to the couch and told her to come over. I made her a drink and it must have been her first drink because she choked on it.

I kissed her and it must have been her first kiss, but she didn't choke on it. She grabbed me like the devil was inside her, bit me twice on the neck then pushed back to look at me to be sure this was happening to her.

There was no softness to her body. It was tense with the pain that was pleasure, oddly resilient under my hands. She closed her eyes, smothering the leaping fire to glowing coals. She fought to open them halfway and when she saw that I had been burnt by their flame she smiled a twisted smile as if she was laughing at herself.

If she was going to, she should have asked me then. Any woman should know when a man is nothing but a man and when he'll promise or tell anything. I knew all those things too and it didn't do me any good because I was still a man.

She asked nothing. She said, "This . . . is the first time . . . I ever . . ." and stopped there with the words choking to a hoarse whisper in her throat. She made me feel like a goddam heel. She hadn't known about Ethel's little stunt because she had been too busy getting prettied up for me.

I was going to make her put her coat on and tell her to get the hell out of there and learn more about being a woman before she tried to act like one. I would have done just that until I thought a little further and remembered that she was new to the game and didn't know when to ask the questions but figured on trying anyway. So I didn't say a damn thing.

Her hand did something at her back and the dress that looked like paint peeled off like paint with a deliberate slowness that made me go warm all over.

And she still asked nothing except to be shown how to be a woman.

She wouldn't let me go to the door with her later. She wanted to be part of the darkness and alone. Her feet were a soft whisper against the carpet and the closing of the door an almost inaudible click.

I made myself a drink, had half of it and threw the rest away. I had been right the first time and went back to feeling like a heel. Then it occurred to me that now that she had a little taste of life maybe she'd go out and seek some different company for a change.

I stopped feeling like a heel, made another drink, finished it and went to bed.

The alarm woke me up at six, giving me time to shower and shave before getting dressed. I grabbed a plate of bacon and eggs in a diner around the corner then hopped in my car and drove downtown to pick up Velda. She was standing in front of the building tucked inside a dark gray business suit, holding her coat open with her hand on her hip.

A newsboy was having trouble trying to watch her and hawk his editions too. I pulled in at the curb and tooted the horn. "Let's go, sugar."

When she climbed in next to me the newsboy sighed. "Early, isn't it?" she grinned.

"Too damned."

"You were going to tell me something today, Mike."

"I didn't say when."

"One of those deals. You're a fine one." She turned her head and looked out the window.

I tugged at her arm and made her look back at me. "I'm sorry, Velda. It doesn't make nice conversation. I'll give it to you all at once when we get back. It's important to me not to talk about it right now. Mind?"

Maybe she saw the seriousness in my eyes. She smiled and said all right, then turned on the radio so we could have some music on our way across the bridge to Brooklyn where Mother Switcher had her pie factory.

Mother Switcher turned out to be a short, squat guy with long handlebar whiskers and eyebrows that went up and down like window shades. I asked him if I could speak to a few of his drivers and he said, "If you're a union organizer it's no good. All my boys already belong to a union and get paid better'n union wages besides."

I said I was no organizer. "So what is it then?"

"I want to find out about a guy named Moffit. He worked for you."

"That dope! He owe you money?"

"Not exactly."

"Sure. Go talk to the boys, only don't stop their work."

I said thanks and took Velda with me when I went around behind the building where the trucks were lined up for their quota of pies. We waited until the first truck was filled then buttonholed the driver. He gave Velda a big smile and tipped his cap.

She took it from there. "You knew Charlie Moffit, didn't you?"

"Yeah, sure, lady. What's he done now, crawled out of his grave?"

"I imagine he's still there, but tell me, what was he like?"

The guy frowned and looked at me for the first time. "I don't get it," he grunted.

I flashed my buzzer. So did Velda. "Now I get it," he said. "Was he in trouble?"

"That's what we want to find out. What was he like?"

He leaned against his truck and chewed on a match. "Well, I'll tell ya. Charlie was a queer duck." He tapped his head and made a screwy face. "Not all there, ya know. We were forever playing all kinds of gags on him. The dope would fall for 'em too. He was always losing something. Once it was his change bag and once it was a whole load of pies. He said some kids got him in a ball game and while he played they swiped his pies. Ever hear of anything like that?"

"No, I didn't," Velda laughed.

"That wasn't all, either. He was a mean bast . . . son-of-a-gun. Once we caught him trying to set fire to a cat. One of the boys slugged him."

It didn't sound right, that picture of Charlie Moffit. I was thinking while Velda popped the questions. Some of the other men came over and added a little something that distorted the picture even more. Charlie liked women and booze. Charlie molested kids in the street. Charlie was real bright for long periods then he'd get drunk and seem to fall into a conscious coma when he'd act like a kid. He wasn't right in his dome. He had rocks in his head. He sure liked the women, though.

I took Velda out of there and started back to Manhattan, my head aching from thoughts that were too big for it. I had to squint to watch the traffic and hunch over the wheel to be sure I knew where I was going. Away in the back of my mind that devilish unseen conductor was warming up his orchestra for another of those wild symphonies. I must be mad, I thought, I must be mad. I don't think like I used to. The little things won't come through anymore and it was the little things falling into place that made big things.

My mind rambled on until Velda said, "We're here."

The attendant was waving me into the parking lot. I took my ticket and handed him the keys while she flagged a cab. All the way to the office I sat with my eyes closed and kept the curtains down on the orchestra that was trying so hard to play. Whoever was at the drums wouldn't give up. He kept up a steady beat, thumping his drum with a muted stick, trying to make me open the curtain.

Velda brought out the bottle and handed it to me. I stared at the glass, filled it and drank it down. She offered me another and I shook my head. I had to sit down. I wanted to sit down and pull something over my head to shut out the light and the sound.

"Mike." Velda ran her fingers through my hair.

"What is it, kid?" My voice didn't sound right.

"If you tell me I might be able to help you." I opened my eyes and looked at her. She had her coat off and her breasts rose high against the folds of the blouse. She pulled up the big chair and sat down, her legs flashing in the light that streamed through the window. They were beautiful legs, long, alive with smooth muscles that played through the tight fabric of her dress as she moved. It was so easy to love that woman. I ought to try it more often. It was mine whenever I wanted it.

I closed my eyes again.

There wasn't any answer or any special way to tell her. I sat there with my eyes closed and gave it to her as it happened, bit by bit. I told her how I killed on the bridge. I told her about Marty and almost all about Ethel. I told her everything that happened and waited to see what she would say.

A minute went by. I opened my eyes and saw that Velda was watching me and there was no shame, no terror in her face. She believed in me. She said, "It doesn't make sense, Mike."

"It doesn't at that," I said tiredly. "There's a flaw in it that I can see. Do you see it too?"

"Yes. Charlie Moffit."

"That's right. The man with a present and no past. Nobody knows him or knows where he comes from. He's just a present."

"Almost ideal for an MVD operative."

"That's right again. Almost. Where's the flaw?"

Velda's fingers made a little tap-tap against the arm of the chair. "The act was too nearly perfect. It was too good to be anything but true."

"Roger. Charlie Moffit was anything but MVD. I thought those Reds were figuring me to be the man who took his place. I was wrong. I was impersonating the wrong dead man. The boy on the bridge was MVD. Pat handed it to me on a platter but I let it slip by. His only identifiable mark was his bridge-work because he had a stainless-steel tooth. There's only one country where they use stainless steel for teeth . . . the U.S.S.R. Fat boy was an imported killer, a checkrein on other agents in this country. Do you know how they knew he was dead?"

"Not from the sketch in the papers. He didn't have any fingerprints, either."

"They wouldn't have found them if he did. I forgot to tell you, but I wore his fingertips to the bone on the concrete before I threw him over."

Velda bit her lip and shuddered. She said "Mike!" too softly.

"No, the reason they knew he was dead was because he dropped out of sight. I don't think they got the connection until later when some smart apple started to check the unidentified bodies in the morgue. Pat said they sent dental charts out. One of those that received them could have recognized what that stainless-steel tooth meant and there it was."

"But they knew he was dead the next night . . . or so you supposed."

"Uh-huh. Fat boy didn't check in. They must have a system for those things. There was only one answer if he didn't check in. He was dead. The dental charts only verified it."

"What must they think? Why . . ."

I kept my voice low so I wouldn't get boiling mad again. "They think it was a dirty democratic conspiracy. It was all too secret to be normal. They think it was our government playing them dirty. They're the only ones who are supposed to be able to kick you under the table."

Velda said something dirty and she wasn't smiling.

I went on: "The other night there was a new note in the party. Something happened to a courier of theirs, something about documents. They are missing. The party is very upset, the poor devils."

Velda came up out of her seat, her face tight as a drumhead. "They're at it again, Mike. Government documents and double-dealing. Damn it, Mike, why do these things have to happen?"

"They happen because we're soft. We're honorable."

"Did they say what they were?"

"No. I gathered they were pretty important."

"They must be."

"Velda, there's a lot of things that are important that we give away for free. Do you know what they were doing one night? They had a pile of technical journals and flying mags you can pick up on any newsstand. They were photographing the stuff onto microfilm for shipment back. A good intelligence man can pick out a lot of data from photos. They take a bit here and a bit there until the picture is complete and bingo, they have something we're trying to keep under the hat."

"But documents, Mike. That's government stuff! That's something the FBI should know about."

"I know, I know. Maybe they do. Maybe they know they're missing and suspect where they've gone. Maybe they don't know because the documents were photostats. They're gone and that's what counts. I'm in a muddle because they found me out and now I can't do any more snooping. They'll be looking for me with a vengeance now. They tried to kill me last night and . . ."

"Mike!"

"Oh, you didn't hear about that. You should read the papers. There's six lines about it on page four. They didn't even print my picture. Yeah, they know me now and it's every man for himself. The next time I'll start the shooting and I won't miss."

Velda had her hand over her mouth, her teeth clamped on a fingernail. "God, you get into some of the most horrible scrapes! I do wish you'd be careful." Her eyes got a little wet and she got mad at herself. "You won't tell anybody anything and you won't ask for help when you need it most. Mike . . . please . . . there are times when you have to let somebody else in on things."

I could feel my lip curling. "Sure, Velda, sure. I'll tell everybody that I go around killing people just like that. It's easy to say, but I'm the guy who's supposed to be a menace to society. Hell, I'll take it my way and the public can lump it."

She wiped away a tear that was feeling its way down her cheek. "He shouldn't have done that to you, Mike."

"Who?"

"The judge."

I swore violently and my voice was hoarse.

"Are you . . . going to keep looking?"

I nodded my head. "Indirectly, yes. I'm still on a case for Lee Deamer."

Velda's head snapped up. "Mike . . . that's it!"

"What?"

"The documents! Charlie Moffit was the courier they spoke about! He was carrying those documents the night Oscar attacked and killed him! Oscar must have taken them from him."

"Damn!" The word exploded out of me. Of course, of course! the pocket that was ripped out of his coat! I shot Velda a grin that had "thanks" written on it. "It comes clear, kid, real clear. Oscar came to town to bleed Lee and he wouldn't bleed. So he goes out and kills a guy hoping to be identified as Lee, knowing damn well Lee would have an alibi and it would just make sensational reading for the public. He figured that would bring Lee to heel when he asked for money again. The gimmick came when he killed the guy. The papers must have stuck out of his pocket and Oscar grabbed them. When he realized what they were he saw the ideal way to bring Lee around. That's what he hinted at to Lee over the phone. If Lee brought in the cops and anything happened to him, the presence of those papers was to be attributed to Lee."

Velda was white, dead-white and her breathing came too fast. "It's rotten, Mike. Good heavens, if it ever gets out . . ."

"Yeah, Lee is finished even if he *can* prove himself innocent."

"Oh, no!"

"Beautiful. No matter what happens the Commies win. If they get the documents they probably have something juicy for cruddy Uncle Joe. If they don't and somebody else finds them, their worst enemy is yanked off their necks."

"Mike . . . it can't happen!"

"Now do I go it alone, Velda? Now do I take it by myself?"

"Yes. You . . . and me. The bastards. The dirty, filthy red bastards!" They should see her now, I was thinking. Gladow, the general, the boys in the Kremlin should see her now and they'd know what they were getting into. They'd see the face of beauty that had a kill-lust in every beautiful line and they'd stick inside their cold, walled-in city and shake in their shoes!

"When do we start, Mike?"

"Tonight. Be here at nine sharp. We'll see if we can find what Oscar did with those papers." She sat back in the chair and stared at the wall.

I picked up the phone and dialed Pat's number. He came on with, "Homicide, Captain Chambers speaking."

"Mike, pal. Any new corpses today?"

"Not yet. You didn't shoot straight enough. When are you coming in to explain about last night? I went to bat for you and I want a report and not a lot of subterfuge."

"I'm practically on my way now. I'll drop by your office and pick you up for lunch."

"Okay. Make it snappy."

I said I would and cradled the receiver. Velda was waiting for orders. "Stay here," I told her. "I have to see Pat and I'll call you when I'm finished. In case I don't call or come back, be here at nine."

"That's all?"

"That's all," I repeated. I tried to look stern like a boss should, but she grinned and spoiled it. I had to kiss her good-by before she'd let me go. "There's no telling if I'll see you alive again," she laughed. Then she slapped her hand over her mouth and her eyes went wide. "What am I saying?"

"I still have a couple of lives left, kid. I'll save one for you, so don't worry." I grinned again and went out the door.

Downstairs I got tired of waiting for a cab so I walked the half mile to the lot. A car in the city could be a pain in the butt sometimes. But what the hell, it was a nice day for a change and the air felt fairly fresh if a bus or something didn't go by.

I picked up my keys when I handed over the ticket and found my heap. I was in second and heading toward the gate when I saw that the boy had cleaned off my windows, and jammed on my brakes to flip him a quarter. That two-bits saved my skin. The truck that had been idling up the street had jumped ahead to intercept me broadside, saw I was stopping and tried to get me by swerving onto the driveway and off again.

Metal being ripped out by the roots set up a shriek and the car leaped ahead before there was a nasty snap that disengaged it from the body of the truck. I let out a string of curses because the jolt had wedged me up against the wheel and I couldn't get my rod out. By the time I was back in the seat the truck was lost in the traffic.

The attendant yanked the door open, his face ashen. "Gawd, mister, you hurt?"

"No, not this time."

"Them crazy fools! Gawd, they coulda killed ya!" His teeth started to chatter violently.

"They sure coulda." I got out of the car and walked around

the front. One side of the bumper had been ripped clear off the frame and stuck out like an oversize L.

"Boy, that was close, awright. I seen 'em come up the street but I never give 'em a thought. Them crazy fools musta been fooling around the cab and hit the gas. They never stopped. You want I should call a cop?"

I kicked the bumper and it all but fell loose. "Forget it. They got away by now. Think you can get this bumper off?"

"Sure, I got some tools. Only two bolts holding it on anyway."

"Okay, take it off and pick one up for this model at a garage somewhere. I'll fix you up for your trouble."

He said, "Yessir, mister. Sure," and ran after his tools. I sat on the fender and smoked a cigarette until he finished then passed him two bucks and told him not to forget a new bumper. He said he wouldn't forget.

When I pulled away I looked up and down the one-way street just to be sure. It happened twice. I said it wouldn't but it happened again anyway. They must have had a tail on me when I came out of the office and saw a beautiful chance to nail me cold. That truck would have made hash of me if it had connected right.

They were going to all kinds of trouble, weren't they? That made me important. You have to be important if you were better off dead. The judge should like that.

Pat was sitting with his back to the door looking out the window at the city when I came in. He swung around in his chair and nodded hello. I pulled a chair up and sat down with my feet propped up on his desk. "I'm all set, Captain. Where are the bright lights?"

"Cut it out, Mike. Start talking."

"Pat, so help me, you know almost everything right now."

"Almost. Give me the rest."

"They tried again a little while ago. This time it was a truck and not bullets."

The pencil in Pat's hand tapped the desk. "Mike, I'm not a complete fool. I play along with you because we're friends, but I'm a cop, I've been a cop a long time, and I know my business. You're not telling me people are shooting you up in the streets without a reason."

"Hell, they gotta have a reason."

"Do you know what it is?" He was drawing to the end of his patience.

I took my feet off the desk and leaned toward him. "We've been through this before, Pat. I'm not a complete fool either. In your mind every crime belongs to the police, but there are times when an apparent crime is a personal affront and it isn't very satisfying not to take care of it yourself. That's how I feel about it."

"So you know then."

"I think I know. There's nothing you can do about it so quit being a cop and let's get back to being friends."

Pat tried to grin, but didn't put it over too well. "Are you straightened out with Lee?"

My feet went up on the desk again. "He gave me a tidy sum to poke around. I'm busy at it."

"Good, Mike. Be sure you make a clean sweep." He dropped his head and passed his hand over his hair. "Been reading the papers lately?"

"Not too much. I noticed one thing . . . they're pulling for Deamer in nearly every editorial column. One sheet reprints all his speeches."

"He's giving another tonight. You should go hear him."

"I'll leave that stuff up to you, chum. There's too much dribble and not enough pep talk at those meetings."

"The devil there isn't! Take the last one I was at. We had supper with the customary speeches afterward, but it was the small talk later that counted. Lee Deamer made the rounds speaking to small groups and he gave them the real stuff. It was easier for him to talk that way. Most of us had never met him until that time, but when he spoke we were sold completely. We have to have that guy in, Mike. No two ways about it. He's strong. He can't be pushed or bullied. You wouldn't know it to look at him, but he's the strength that this nation will be relying on some day."

"That was the same night Oscar pulled the stops out, wasn't it?"

"That's right. That's why we didn't want any of it to reach the public. Even a lie can be told to give the people the wrong impression."

"You've sure gotten a big interest in politics, Pat."

"Hell, why not? I'll be glad to go back to being a cop again instead of a tool in some politician's workshop. Lee gave a talk over the radio last night. You know what he did?"

I said no. I had been too busy to listen.

"He's brought some of his business sense into politics. He sat down with an adding machine and figured things up. He wanted to know why it cost the state ten million for it to have a job done when any private contractor could do it for six. He quoted

names and places and figures and told the public that if he was
elected his first order would be to sign warrants of arrest for
certain political joes who are draining the state dry."

"And?"

Pat looked at the desk and glared. "And today I heard that the
big push comes soon. Lee has to be smeared any way at all."

"It won't happen, Pat."

I shouldn't have used that tone. His head jerked up and his
eyes were tiny bright spots watching me from tight folds of skin.
His hand closed into a fist slowly and tightened until the cords
bulged out. "You know something, Mike, by God, you know
something!"

"I do?" I couldn't make it sound funny.

Pat was ready to split wide open. "Mike, you're in on it. Damn
it, you went and found something. Oh, I know you . . . no talking
until you're ready, but this isn't a murder that involved only a
handful of people . . . this is something that takes in a whole
population and you better not tip the apples over."

He stood up, his hands on the edge of the desk for support.
He spat the words out between his teeth and meant every one.
"We've been friends, Mike. You and I have been in and out of
a lot of things together and I've always valued your friendship.
And your judgment. Just remember this, if I'm guessing right and
you're in on something that might hurt Lee and won't talk about
it, and if that something *does* hurt Lee, then we can forget about
being friends. Is that clear?"

"That's clear, Pat. Would it make you feel better if I told you
that your line of reasoning is a little off? You're getting teed off
at me when you ought to be teeing off on some of the goddamn
Commies we got loose in this city."

His face had a shrewd set to it. "So they're part of it too."
Muscles stuck out in lumps along his jaws. Let him think how
he liked.

"Nothing will happen to Lee," I said. "At least nothing that
I'm concerned with." This time I got some conviction in my
voice. Pat stopped glaring and sat down.

He didn't forget the subject. "You still have those green cards
on your mind?"

"Yeah, I have. I don't like what they mean, and you shouldn't
either."

"I hate everything they stand for. I'm sorry we have to tolerate
it. We ought to do what they would have done a hundred years
ago."

"Stop talking nonsense. You're in America now."

"Sure I am, and I want to stay here. If you want a democracy you have to fight for it. Why not now before it's too late? That's the trouble, we're getting soft. They push us all around the block and we let them get away with it!"

"Calm down, will you." I hadn't realized that I was banging on his desk until he rapped my knuckles. I sat down.

"What did you do about Oscar?" I asked.

"What could we do? Nothing. It's over, finished."

"And his personal effects?"

"We went through them and there was nothing to be found. I posted a man to check his place in case any mail came in. I had the idea that Oscar might have mailed something to himself. I took the man off today when nothing showed."

I had to struggle to hold my face straight. Pat had the place watched! Neat, very neat. If we weren't the only ones who wanted to go through that apartment then we wouldn't be going in on a cold deal. Nobody else could have gotten there either!

I reached for a butt and lit it. "Let's go out to eat, Pat."

He grabbed his coat off the rack and locked the door to the office. On the way out I thought of something I should have thought of before and had him open it up again. I picked up the phone and called the office. Velda answered with a silky hello.

I said, "Mike, honey. Look, have you emptied the wastebasket by my desk yet?"

"No, there wasn't anything to empty."

"Go look if there's a cigarette pack there. Don't touch it."

She dropped the phone and I heard her heels clicking along the floor. In a moment she was back. "It's there, Mike."

"Swell. Take it out of there without touching it if you can. Put it in a box and have a boy run it down to Pat right away."

Pat watched me curiously. When I hung up he said, "What is it?"

"An almost empty pack of butts. Do me a favor and lift the prints off it. You'll find a lot of mine on them and if I'm lucky you'll find some others too."

"Whose?"

"Hell, how do I know? That's why I want you to get the prints. I need an identification. That is, if we're still friends."

"Still friends, Mike," he grinned. I socked him on the arm and started for the door again.

chapter seven ■■■■■■■

THAT NIGHT THE nation got the report on the 6:15 P.M. news broadcast. There had been a leak in the State Department and the cat was out of the bag. It seemed that we had had a secret. Somebody else was in on it now. The latest development in the process for the annihilation of man had been stolen. Supposedly secret files had been rifled and indications pointed to the duplication of the secret papers. The FBI was making every effort to track down the guilty parties.

I threw my cigarette against the wall and started swearing until I ran out of words. Then I started over again. The commentator droned on repeating what he had already said and I felt like screaming at him to tell the world who took those damn papers. Tell 'em it was the same outfit who tried to make a mockery of our courts and who squirmed into the government and tried to bring it down around our necks. Tell everybody who did it. You know you want to say it; what are you afraid of?

There wasn't any doubt of it now, those documents the general had been so anxious to get hold of were the ones we were looking for ourselves! My guts were all knotted up in a ball and my head felt like a machine shop was going on inside it. Here I had the whole lousy situation right in my hands and I had to keep it there.

Me. Mike Hammer. I was up in the big leagues now. No more plain and simple murders. I was playing ball with the big boys and they played rough. The end justified the means, that was their theory. Lie, steal, kill, do anything that was necessary to push a political philosophy that would enslave the world if we let it. Great!"

Nice picture, Judge, a beautiful picture of a world in flames. You must be one of the normal people who get the trembles when they read the papers. A philosophy like that must give you the willies. What are you thinking now . . . how that same secret that was stolen might be the cause of your death? And what would you say if you knew that I was the only one who might be able to stop it in time? Okay, Judge, sit your fanny in a chair and relax. I have a little philosophy of my own. Like you said, it's as bad as theirs. I don't give a damn for a human life any more, even my own. Want to hear that philosophy? It's simple enough. Go after the big boys. Oh, don't arrest them, don't treat them to the dignity of the democratic process of courts and law . . . do the same thing to them that they'd do to you! Treat 'em to the unglorious taste of sudden death. Get the big boys and show them the long road to nowhere and then one of those stinking little people with little minds will want to get big. Death is funny, Judge, people are afraid of it. Kill 'em left and right, show 'em that we aren't so soft after all. Kill, kill, kill, kill! They'll keep away from us then!

Hell, it was no use trying to smoke. I'd light up a butt and take a drag then throw it away because my fingers weren't steady enough to hold it. I went inside to the bedroom and took my .45 off the top of the dresser to clean it for the second time. It felt good, feeling the cold butt setting up against the palm of my hand. The deadly noses of the slugs showing in the clip looked so nice and efficient.

They liked to play dirty, I was thinking. Let's make it real dirty. I thumbed the slugs out, laying them in a neat row, then took a penknife and clipped the ends off the noses. That was real dirty. They wouldn't make too much of a hole where they went in, but the hole on the other side would be a beaut. You could stick your head in and look around without getting blood on your ears. I put the gun together, shoved the slugs back in the clip and strapped on the sling. I was ready.

It was a night to give you the meemies. Something happened to the sky and a slow, sticky fog was rolling in from the river. The cold was penetrating, indecisive as to whether to stay winter or turn into spring. I turned the collar of my coat up around my ears and started walking down the street. I didn't lose myself in any thoughts this time. My eyes looked straight ahead, but they saw behind me and to either side. They picked up figures hurrying to wherever it was they were going, and the twin yellow eyes of the cars that rolled in the street, boring holes in the fog. My ears picked up footsteps, timed their pace and direction, then discarded them for other sounds.

I was waiting for them to try again.

When I reached the corner I crossed over to my car, passed it, then walked back again. I opened the door, felt for the handle that unlocked the hood and took a quick check of the engine. I wasn't in the mood to get myself blown all over the neighborhood when I started the car. The engine was clean. So was the rest of the heap.

A car came by and I drew out behind it, getting in line to start the jaunt downtown to the office. The fog was thicker there and the traffic thinner. The subways were getting a big play. I found a place to park right outside the office and scraped my wheels against the curb then cut the engine. I sat there until a quarter to nine trying to smoke my way through a deck of Luckies. I still had a few to go when I went inside, put my name in the night register and had the elevator operator haul me up to my office floor.

At exactly nine P.M. a key turned in the lock and Velda came in. I swung my feet off the desk and walked out to the outside office and said hello. She smiled, but her heart wasn't in it. "Did you catch the news broadcast, kid?"

Her lips peeled back. "I heard it. I didn't like it."

"Neither did I, Velda. We have to get them back."

She opened her coat and perched on the edge of the desk. Her eyes were on the floor, staring at a spot on the carpet. She wasn't just a woman now. An aura of the jungle hung around her, turning her into a female animal scenting a game run and anxious to be in on the kill. "It can't stop there, Mike."

I dropped my butt and ground it into the carpet. "No, it can't." I knew what she was thinking and didn't like it.

"The papers aren't all. As far as they can go is to checkmate us. They'll try again."

"Will they?"

Her eyes moved up to meet mine, but that was all. "We can stop them, Mike."

"I can, sugar. Not you. I'm not shoving you into any front lines."

Her eyes still held mine. "There's somebody in this country who directs operations for them. It isn't anyone we know or the FBI knows or the party knows. It's somebody who can go and come like anybody else and not be interfered with. There are others who take orders and are equally dangerous because they represent the top of the chain of command and can back up their orders with force if necessary. How long will it take us to get them all, the known and the unknown?"

"It might take *me* a long time. Me, I said."

"There's a better way, Mike. We can get all those we know and any we suspect and the rest will run. They'll get the hell out of here and be afraid to come back."

It was almost funny, the way her reasoning followed mine. "Just me, Velda," I said.

Her head came up slowly and all I could think of was a big cat, a great big, luxurious cat leaning against the desk. A cat with gleaming black hair darker than the night and a hidden body of smooth skin that covered a wealth of rippling, deadly muscles that were poised for the kill. The desk light made her teeth an even row of merciless ivory, ready to rip and tear. She was still grinning, but a cat looks like it's grinning until you see its ears laid flat back against its head.

"Mike, there are men and women in this country. They made it together even when it was worse than now. Women learned how to shoot and shoot straight. They learned fast, and knew how to use a gun or a knife and use it right when the time came. I said we'd do it together. Either that or I take the whole thing to Pat."

I waited a long minute before I said, "Okay, it's us. I want it that way anyhow."

Velda slid off the desk and reached for my hand. I squeezed it hard, happy as hell I had the sense to realize that I knew what I wanted at last. She said it very simply. "I love you, Mike."

I had her in my arms, searched for her mouth and found it, a warm mouth with full, ripe lips that burned into my soul as they fused with mine. I tasted the love she offered and gave it back with all I had to give, crushing her until her breath came in short, quick jerks.

I held her face in my hands and kissed her eyes and her cheeks, listened to her moan softly and press herself closer and closer. I was lucky as hell and I knew it.

She opened her eyes when I held her off. I dropped my hand in my pocket and took out the box that I had picked up that afternoon. When I pressed the button the lid flew up and the sapphire threw back a perfect star. My fingers felt big and clumsy when I took it out and slipped it over her finger.

You don't have to speak at a time like that. Everything has been said and if anything remains it's written there in a silent promise your heart makes and that's all there is to it. Velda looked at it with a strange wonder for a long time before she kissed me again.

It was better than the last time.

It told her everything she wanted to know and no matter what happened now nothing would ever change.

"We have to go," I said.

She snapped out the lights while I waited at the door and we went down the elevator together. The watchman gave me the okay sign, so I knew nobody had been near my car while I was gone. When we were back in the fog I told her about Pat's having kept a man on Oscar's house and she picked it right up.

"Maybe . . . maybe we'll be the first."

"I'm hoping that," I said.

"What will they look like?"

"I don't know. If Moffit had them in his pocket, then they were in a package or an envelope big enough to fit in there. It may be that we're barking up the wrong tree. They might have been on microfilm."

"Let's hope we're right."

About two blocks away I ran the car in between a couple of parked trucks and waved her out. "We're taking the long way around this time."

"Through the alley?"

"Uh-huh. I don't like the idea of using the front door. When we reach the opening between the buildings duck in and keep on going."

Velda felt for my hand and held on to it. For all the world we might have been just a couple of dopes out for a walk. The fog was a white tube all around us, but it could be hiding a lot of things beside us. We crossed the street, came up around the subway kiosk and walked in the protection of the wall, the two of us searching for the narrow passageway that led behind the buildings.

As it was, we almost passed it. I stepped in holding Velda's hand and the darkness swallowed us up. For two or three minutes we stood there letting our eyes accustom themselves to this deeper gloom, then edged forward slowly, picking our way through the trash that had accumulated over the years. Animals and people had made a barely perceptible path through the center of the litter and we followed it until we stood behind the building and could feel our way along the alley by sticking close to the rotted planking that formed the wall of the yards behind the houses.

Velda was fishing in her handbag and I told her, "No lights. Just keep looking for a pile of bottles. There's a door in the wall behind it and that's the place."

I tried to judge the distance from that other night and found little to remember. Soft furry things would squeal and run across our feet whenever we disturbed the junk lying around. Tiny pairs of eyes would glare at us balefully and retreat when we came closer. A cat moved in the darkness and trapped a pair of eyes that had been paying too much attention to us and the jungle echoed with a mad death cry.

Velda tugged my hand and pointed to the ground. "Here're the bottles, Mike." She dropped my hand to walk around them. "The door is still open."

I pushed her through into the yard and we held still, taking in the black shadow of the building. The back door still swung open on one hinge. How many people lived here, I thought. How long ago was it when this dirty pile of brick and mortar was a home besides being a house? I went up the short flight of steps and took the flashlight from my pocket.

Velda flashed hers on the wall beside the door, illuminating a printed square of cardboard tacked to the framework. It read, THIS BUILDING HAS BEEN CONDEMNED FOR OCCUPANCY. A paragraph explained why and a rubber stamp signature made it official.

Ha.

The air had a musty odor of decay that collected in the long hall and clung to the walls. There was a door that led to the cellar, but the stairs were impenetrable, piled high with an unbelievable collection of scrap. Velda opened the door to the room that faced the backyard and threw her spot around the walls. I looked in over her shoulder and saw a black, charred mass and the remains of some furniture. It must have been a year or more since that room had started to burn, and nobody had been in it since. It was amazing to me that the house still stood.

Halfway down the hall there was a doorframe but no door and the room was stacked with old bedframes, a few mattresses left to the fleas and nothing worth stealing. The next room was, or had been, Oscar's. I had my hand on the knob when Velda grabbed me and we froze there.

From somewhere in the upper recesses of the house came a harsh, racking cough and the sound of someone vomiting.

I heard Velda take a deep breath of relief. "Drunk," she said.

"Yeah." I went back to the door. A plain skeleton key unlocked it and we stepped inside, locking it again behind us. Velda went to the windows, and tucked the shade in so there would be no chance of our lights being seen from the outside. Then we started to take that room apart.

Oscar's effects were collecting dust in the police storeroom, but it was unlikely that they had been in his bag or among his clothes. If they had been I would have found them the first time. We peeled the covers off the bed, found nothing and put them back. We felt in the corners and under things. I even tore the molding off the wall and shoved my hand behind it. There was nothing there, either.

Velda was working her way along the rear wall. She called softly, "Mike, come here a minute."

I followed the track of light to where she was fiddling with some aged draperies that had been tacked to the wall in a vain attempt to give a tapestry effect. She had one side pulled away and was pointing to it. "There used to be a door here. It led to that storeroom on the other side."

"Umm. This house was a one-family job at one time."

"Do you suppose. . . ."

"That it's in there?" I finished. She nodded. "We better look. This room is as bare as a baby's spanked tail."

The two of us wormed out into the hall and shut the door. Velda led the way with her light and took a cautious step over the sill into the room beyond. From upstairs the coughing came again. I banged my shin against an iron bedpost and swore softly.

It only took ten minutes to go over that room, but it was long enough to see that nothing had been put in or taken out in months. A layer of dust covered everything; the junk was attached to the walls with thousands of spider webs. The only prints in the grime on the floor were those we had made ourselves.

I hated to say it; Velda hated to hear it. "Not a damn thing. Oscar never had those papers."

"Oh, Mike!" There was a sob in her voice.

"Come on, kid, we're only wasting time now."

The flashlight hung in her hand, the penny-sized beam a small, lonely spot on the floor, listlessly trying to add a bit of brightness to a night that was darker than ever now.

"All right, Mike," she said. "There must be other places for it to be."

The guy upstairs coughed again. We would have paid no attention to him except that we heard the thump of his feet hitting the floor then the heavy thud as he fell. The guy started cursing then was still.

It wasn't a conscious thing that held us back; we just stood there and listened, not scared, not worried, just curious and cautious. If we hadn't stopped where we were at the moment we did we would have walked right into the mouth of hell.

The front door opened and for a brief interval the Trench Coats were dimly silhouetted against the gray of the fog outside. Then the door closed and they were inside, motionless against the wall.

I did two things fast. I grabbed Velda and pulled out the .45.

Why did I breathe so fast? I hadn't done a thing and yet I wanted to pant my lungs out. They were on fire, my throat was on fire, my brain was on fire. The gun that I used to be able to hold so still was shaking hard and Velda felt it too. She slid her hand over mine, the one that squeezed her arm so hard it must have hurt, and I felt some of the tension leave me.

Velda wasn't shaking at all. Trench Coats moved and I heard a whispered voice. Something Velda did made a metallic snap. My brain was telling me that now it had come, the moment I had waited for. Trench Coats. Gladow and Company: The hammer and sickle backed up with guns. The general's boys.

They came for me! Even in the fog they had managed to follow me here and now they were ready to try again. *The third time they won't miss.* That was the common superstition, wasn't it? It was to be at close quarters and a crossfire with me in the middle.

I could feel my teeth grinding together. A hot wave of hate, so violent that it shook me from top to bottom, swept through my body. Who the hell were they supposed to be? Did they expect to come in and find me with my back to the door? Was I supposed to be another sap . . . the kind of guy who'd give people like them the old fighting chance . . . a gesture of sportsmanship? I should take a chance on dying like that?

They went in the room then, softly, but not so softly that my ears couldn't follow every step they took. I could hear their breathing coming hard, the scuffle of leather against wood. I even heard the catch of the flashlight when it snapped on.

Very slowly I jacked the hammer of the .45 back. My hand told Velda to stay there. Just stay there and shut up. I bent down and unlaced my shoes, stepped out of them and into the hall. I lay on my stomach looking into the room, the .45 propped on my forearm. The light of the flash made a circuit of the wall then stopped on the draperies that covered up the opening to the other room. Trench Coat who didn't have a flash stepped forward to pull the drapes down.

And Velda was in there waiting for me.

I said, "Looking for me, Martin?" The sudden shift of the flash and the lance of flame that spit from his gun came at the same time. I heard the bullets smack the wall over my head. He fired at the door where my belly should have been, mouthing guttural, obscene curses.

Then I shot him. I aimed a little below and inside the red eye of his gun barrel and over the blast of the .45 I heard his breath leave him in a wheezing shriek that died in a bubble of blood that came to his mouth. His rod went off once, a bullet ripped into the floor, and Trench Coat dropped.

The other one didn't stay in the room. I heard cloth rip, feet stumble and a heavy body slam against the wood. The other killer had gone into the room with Velda!

I was on my feet trying to decide. I had to decide! Good God, I had to get him before he saw her. If I went in through either door he'd get me and I had to go! I could feel him waiting for me, the darkness screening him completely. He knew I'd come and he knew he'd get me.

I walked toward the door. I didn't bother trying to be quiet.

I stepped into the doorway.

The crack of the gun was a flat noise that echoed once and was gone. There was no streak of flame, only that sudden, sharp sound and a peculiar hiss that seemed out of place. I felt no shock, no pain, only a sudden tensing of the muscles and a stillness that was nearly audible.

I must have caught it, I thought. It wasn't like this before. The last time it hurt. I tried to raise my hand and it came up slowly, effortlessly. In the room a gun clattered on the bare planking and was followed immediately by a soft thunk.

She seemed far away, so far away. "Mike?"

I couldn't get the breath out of my lungs at first. "You . . . all right, Velda?"

"I killed him, Mike."

Dear God, what was there to say? I reached for her and folded her against my chest feeling her sob softly. I grabbed her flash and threw it on Trench Coat. Martin Romberg lay on his face with a hole in his back. She must have held it right against his spine when she pulled the trigger. That's why I didn't see the flash.

I straightened Velda up and pulled her toward the door. "Come on. We can't stay here." I found my shoes and yanked them on without bothering to tie them.

It was easier going out. It always is. The fog was still there, rolling in over the walls, sifting down between the buildings. Our eyes, so long in the dark, could see things that were hidden before and we raced down that back alley heading for that narrow slit a block away from the house.

The curious had already started their pilgrimage toward the sound of the shooting. A police car whined through the night, its light a blinking eye that cleared the way. We lost ourselves in the throng, came out of it and found the car. Two more police cars passed us as we started to cut back to the land of the living on the other side of town.

Velda sat stiff and straight staring out the window. When I

looked down she still held the gun in her hand. I took it away from her and laid it on the seat. "You can file another notch on it, kid. That makes two."

I gave it to her brutally hoping it might snap her out of it. She turned her head and I saw that her mouth had taken on a smile. She picked up that nasty little .32 automatic and dropped it in her handbag. The snap catch made the same metallic sound that I had heard back there in the room. "My conscience doesn't hurt me, Mike," she said softly.

I patted her hand.

"I was afraid I wouldn't be quick enough. He never saw me. He stood in the center of the room covering both entrances and I knew what he was waiting for and I knew you'd come after him. He would have killed you, Mike."

"I know, honey."

"He was standing close enough so I could reach out and put my gun right against him." Her lips tightened. "Is this how . . . you feel, Mike? Is it all right for me to feel like this? Not having a sensation of guilt?"

"I feel happy."

"So do I. Perhaps I shouldn't, Mike. Maybe I should feel ashamed and sinful, but I don't. I'm glad I shot him. I'm glad I had the chance to do it and not you. I wanted to, do you understand that?"

"I understand completely. I know how you feel because it's how I feel. There's no shame or sin in killing a killer. David did it when he knocked off Goliath. Saul did it when he slew his tens of thousands. There's no shame to killing an evil thing. As long as you have to live with the fact you might as well enjoy it."

This time Velda laughed easily. My mind turned to the judge and I could picture his face, disappointed and angry that my time still hadn't come. And we had the best alibi in the world. Self-defense. We had a gun license and they didn't. If it reached us we were still clear.

Velda said, "They were there after the same thing, weren't they?"

"What?"

She repeated it. I slammed the wheel with my hand and said something I shouldn't have. Velda looked at me, her forehead furrowed. "They were . . . weren't they?"

I shook my head in disgust at myself. "What a sap I am. Of course they were! I thought they were after me again and they were searching for those damn documents!"

"Mike! But how would they know? The papers never carried

any news of Charlie Moffit's murder. They reported it, but that was all. How could they know?"

"The same way the public knew the documents were stolen. Look, it's been a good time since he was knocked off. Just about long enough for somebody to get a loose tongue and spill something. That's how they knew . . . there was a leak. Somebody said something they shouldn't have!"

"The witnesses. They'd be the ones. Didn't Pat say they were warned to keep quiet about it?"

" 'Advised' is the word," I said. "That doesn't make them liable to any official action. Damn it, why can't people keep their big mouths shut!"

Velda fidgeted in her seat. "It was too big to keep, Mike. You don't witness a murder and just forget about it."

"Ah, maybe you're right. Maybe I give people credit for having more sense than they actually have. Hell, the leak could just as well have come out of police headquarters too. It's too late now to worry about it. The damage is done."

Velda lost herself in her thoughts for a good five minutes. I stayed hunched over the wheel trying to see through the fog. "It wasn't there, Mike. If it wasn't there then it has to be somewhere else."

"Yeah."

"You looked around the place right after Oscar died. It wasn't among his things. The police must have looked too. Then we looked again. Do you think it could possibly be that Oscar didn't have them?"

"What else is there to think? Either that or he hid them outside his room."

"Doubtful, Mike. Remember one thing, if Oscar showed himself anywhere he would have been mistaken for Lee. He couldn't have done much fooling around."

I had to grin because the girl who was wearing my ring was so smart I began to feel foolish around her. I did pretty good for myself. I picked a woman who could shoot a guy just like that and still think straight. "Go on, Velda."

"So maybe Oscar never got those documents. Charlie's ripped pocket just happened when he fell. If Charlie was the courier, and if the documents he was carrying are missing, then Charlie must have them tucked away somewhere. Remember what the men at the pie factory said . . . that he was dopey for certain periods of time? He was forgetful? Couldn't he have. . . ."

I stopped her and took it from there myself. She had tapped it right on the nose.

"When, Mike?"

I glanced at her quickly. "When what?"

"When do we go through his apartment?"

She was asking for more! Once in a night wasn't enough. "Not now," I told her. "Tomorrow's another day. Our dead friends won't be making a report tonight and the party won't be too anxious to make any more quick moves until they figure this one out first. We have time, plenty of time."

"No we don't."

I convinced her that we had by talking my head off all the way up to her apartment. When I let her out I only had one more thing to say. She waited, knowing well enough what was coming. "In case anyone asks, I was with you in your place all night, understand?"

"Can't we partially tell the truth?"

"Nope, we're engaged."

"Oh. Now I have to wait some more."

"Not long, kid, not too long. When this is all finished there'll be time for other things."

"I can wait."

"Good. Now hop upstairs and get to bed, but first, take that gun of yours and hide it somewhere. Put it where it can't be found until I tell you to take it out."

She leaned over and kissed me, a soft, light kiss that left my mouth tingling with the thought of what lay behind this girl who could be so completely lovable and so completely deadly. There were fires burning in her eyes that nothing could ever quench, but they asked me to try . . . to try hard.

I looked at her legs as she got out of the car and decided that I'd never see enough of them. They had been there all the time, mine any time I had wanted to ask and until now I never had the sense to ask. I had been stupid, all right. I was much smarter now. I waited until she was in the door before I turned the car around and crawled back to my own place.

It was late and I was tired. There had been too much in this one night again, I thought to myself. You get wound up like a watch spring, tighter and tighter until the limit is reached and you let go with a bang that leaves you empty and gasping.

When I locked the door I went directly to the closet and took down the box of parts and shells for the gun. I laid them out on the kitchen table and took the .45 apart piece by piece, cleaning and oiling every bit of it. I unwrapped the new barrel and put it in place, throwing the rest of the gun together around it. On second thought I changed the firing pin too. A microscope could pick up a lot of details from empty shell cases.

It took a half-hour to get the gun ready to go again. I shoved the old barrel and pin in a quart beer can, stuffed in some paper to keep it from rattling and dumped the works down the incinerator.

I was feeling pretty good when I crawled into the sack. Now let's see what would happen.

The alarm was about to give up when I finally woke up. There was nothing I wanted more than staying in bed, but I forced myself into a sitting position, fought a brief battle with the sheets and got my feet on the floor. A cold shower took the sleep out of my eyes and a plate of bacon and eggs put some life into my body.

I dressed and called Velda. She wasn't at home so I tried the office. She was there. I said, "How the devil do you do it?"

She laughed and came right back at me. "I'm still a working girl, Mike. Office hours are from eight to five, remember?"

"Any customers?"

"Nope."

"Any bills?"

"Nope."

"Love me?"

"Yup. Love me?"

"Yup. What a conversation. Any calls?"

"Yup. Pat called. He wants to see you. Lee Deamer called. He wants to see you, too."

I brightened up fast. "If they call back, tell them I'll check in. How about the papers?"

"Headlines, Mike. Big black headlines. It seems that a couple of rival gangs met up with each other in an old building over on the East Side. They forgot to carry their dead off when the battle was finished."

"Don't sound so smug. Did Pat mention anything about it?"

"No, but he will. He was pretty edgy with me."

"Okay, give him my love. I'll see you shortly." I hung up and laid out my working suit for the day. When I finished dressing I looked out the window and swore to myself. The fog was gone, but a drizzle had come in on its heels and the people on the street were bundled into coats trying to keep warm. The winter was dying a hard death.

On the way to the office I stopped off at a saloon and saw a friend of mine. I told him I wanted an unlicensed automatic of a certain make and .32 caliber, one that hadn't done anything except decorate somebody's dresser drawer since it was bought. My friend went to the phone and made two calls. He came back, told me to wait a few minutes, served a few customers at the bar, then went into the kitchen in the rear and I heard his voice arguing for a while. He came back with a package in his hand and said, "Twenty bucks, Mike."

I peeled off twenty, took the gun apart and removed the barrel and the pin. The rest I told my friend to dump in with his trash, thanked him and left. I stopped off at the office long enough to hand the two parts to Velda and tell her to slip them in her gun during her lunch hour. Then I went down to see Pat.

As Velda said, he wasn't happy. He said, "Hell, Mike," but his eyes raked me up and down. "Sit," he said.

I sat down and picked the paper off his desk. The headlines were big and black. There was a picture of the outside of the house with an interior shot in the middle section with white dotted lines to indicate where the bodies had been found. "Real trouble, huh, Pat?"

"Yeah, I thought maybe you could explain some of it."

"Don't be silly."

"Been shooting your gun lately?"

"Yesterday, as a matter of fact. I fired on into some waste right in my own apartment to check the ejector action. Why?"

"A paraffin test is out of order then. Mind if I see your gun?"

I said no and handed it over. Pat pressed a button on his desk and one of the technicians came in. Pat handed him the gun. "Get me a photograph of one of the slugs, Art."

"You're assuming a lot, aren't you, Pat?"

"I think so. Want to talk about it?"

"No, wait until you get your photograph."

He sat back and smiled and I read the papers. The two men were identified as Martin Romberg and Harold Valleck. They were good and dead. Both had prison records for various crimes and were suspected of being killed in a gang brawl. The police were expecting early developments in the crime. The reporters didn't have much to go on.

Art came back before I finished the funnies and handed Pat an enlarged sheet that was covered with angle shots of the slug. He laid the gun on the desk. Pat smiled again and pulled another sheet from his desk drawer. There wasn't anything funny about the way he smiled. I looked at him with a frown covering up the grin that was trying to break through, lit a butt and went back to the paper and finished the funnies.

Pat said, "You're too smart to be dumb, Mike. That or you're clean and I'm stupid as hell." His face looked empty.

I had a nice speech all ready to take him down a peg or two when I realized that he was on the spot. "You mean they were supposed to match, is that it?"

He nodded. "Something like that. A .45 killed one of them. There were only three of us who knew about Oscar's being there."

"Were they after Oscar or just there?"

"Hell, I don't know, Mike. Murder isn't uncommon in that neighborhood. Ordinarily I wouldn't give a hoot about it, but this isn't an ordinary thing. I feel about as effective as a clam right now."

"What for? Cripes, you can't help yourself if somebody gets shot. The place was empty. It was a good place for a hideout. Maybe those two eggs were holed up in there when they got caught up with."

Pat leaned back and rubbed his hands across his eyes. "Look, Mike, I'm not too dumb. Anybody can change barrels in a gun. I'll bet you the shell cases won't match your pin either."

"How'd you guess?"

"You're treating me like a kid now, feller. You're the one who's forgetting that we're friends. I know you like a book and I don't want to tear any pages out of that book because if I do I'm afraid of what the ending will be like. I know it was you, I don't know who handled the .32, I'm scared to ask questions and I hate to have you lie to me. Little lies I don't like."

I folded the paper and put it back on his desk. Pat wouldn't look at me. "Why the finger pointing at me, Pat?"

"Nuts. Just plain nuts. You should know why."

"I don't."

"One of those boys had a green Commie card on him. Now do you know why?"

"Yeah," I said. I had forgotten all about that. I lifted the cigarette and dragged the smoke down into my chest. "Now what?"

"I want to know what you're after. I want to know everything, Mike. Whenever I think about things I get cold all over and want to smash things. You've been playing cute and there's no way I can touch you. I have to absorb myself in police work and routine detail when I know I'm on the outside hoping for a look in."

"That's the trouble with the police. They have to wait until something happens. A crime has to be committed before they can make a move."

Pat watched me thoughtfully, his hands locked behind his head. "Things have happened."

"Roger, but, as you stated, they have been played very cute."

"I'm still on the outside looking in."

I snubbed the butt out and stared at the shreds of tobacco hanging out the end. "Pat . . . more things are going to happen. I know you like a book, too, but there's something else I have to know."

"Go on."

"How far can I trust you?"

"It depends on a lot of things. Never forget that I'm still a cop."

"You're still a plain citizen who likes his country and likes to see it stay the way it is, aren't you?"

"Naturally."

"All right. You're all snagged up in the ritual of written law and order. You have to follow the rules and play it square. There's a weight around your neck and you know it. If I told you what I knew you'd bust a gut trying to get something done that couldn't be done and the rats would get out of the trap.

"I'm only one guy, Pat, but I'm quite a guy and you know it. I make my own rules as I go along and I don't have to account to anybody. There's something big being kicked around and it's exactly as you said . . . it's bigger than you or me or anybody and I'm the only one who can handle it. Don't go handing me the stuff about the agencies that are equipped to handle every conceivable detail of this and that. I'm not messing with detail . . . I'm messing with people and letting them see that I'm nobody to mess with and there are a lot more like me if you want to look for them.

"What's going on isn't a case for the crime laboratory and it isn't a case for the police. The whole thing is in the hands of the people, only they don't know it yet. I'm going to show it to them because I'm the only one who has the whole works wrapped up tight trying to bring it together so we can see what it is. You can stop worrying about your law and your order and about Lee Deamer, because when I'm finished Lee can win his election and go ahead and wipe out the corruption without ever knowing that he had a greater enemy than crime plain and simple."

I picked up my gun and stuck it in the sling. Pat hadn't moved. His head bobbed slightly when I said so long, but that was all.

I was still seeing the tired smile on Pat's face, telling me that he understood and to go ahead, when I called Lee Deamer's office. His secretary told me that he was speaking at a luncheon of U.N. delegates in a midtown hotel and had already left. I got the name of the hotel, thanked her and hung up.

He must be getting anxious and I didn't blame him a bit. It was a little before noon, so I hopped in the heap and tooled it up Broadway and angled over to the hotel where it cost me a buck to park in an unloading zone with a guy to cover for me.

The clerk at the desk directed me to the hall where the luncheon was to be held and had hardly finished before I saw Lee come in the door. He swung a brief case at his side and one of the girls from his office trailed behind him carrying another. Before I could reach him a swarm of reporters came out of nowhere and took down his remarks while the photogs snapped his picture.

A covey of important-looking joes stood on the outside of the circle impatient to speak to Deamer, yet unwilling to offend the press by breaking up the party. It was Lee himself who told the boys to see him after the luncheon and walked through their midst. He had spotted me leaning against the desk and went directly into the manager's office. That little man went in after him, came out in a minute and scanned the desk. I didn't have to be told that he was looking for me.

I nodded and strode in as casually as I could. The manager smiled at me, then took up a position near the door to give us a few minutes in private. Lee Deamer was sitting in a leather-covered chair next to the desk and his face was a study in anxiety.

"Hello, Lee."

"Mike, how are you? I've been worried sick ever since I saw the papers this morning."

I offered him a butt and he shook his head. "There's nothing to worry about, Lee. Everything is fine."

"But last night. I . . . you mean you weren't connected with the doings in Oscar's place?" I grinned and lit the smoke.

"I don't know what to think. I called Captain Chambers and he led me to believe that he thought the same thing."

"He did. I talked him out of it." I raked another chair up with my foot and sat down. Murder is murder. It can be legal and it can't. No matter what it is it's still murder and the less people know about it the better. I said, "I went through Oscar's place right after the accident. Pat went through it himself. Later I took another check and I'm satisfied that if Oscar *did* leave any incriminating junk lying around, he didn't leave it in his room."

Lee sighed, relieved. "I'm glad to hear that, Mike, but I'm more than glad to hear that you didn't have anything to do with those . . . deaths. It's ugly."

"Murder is always ugly."

"Then there's nothing further to be said, I imagine. That takes a great load off my mind. Truly, Mike, I was terribly worried."

"I should think so. Well, keep your mind at rest. I'm going to backtrack on Oscar a little bit and see what comes up. It's still my opinion that he was bluffing. It's not the easiest thing in the world to frame somebody who can't be framed. If anything comes up I'll let you know, meanwhile, no news is good news, so they say."

"Fine, Mike, I'll leave everything to you. Captain Chambers will co-operate as he sees possible. I want nothing hanging over my head. If it becomes necessary I would rather the public knew about my relationship with Oscar and the facts of the case before the election."

"Forget that stuff," I told him brusquely, "there's plenty the public shouldn't know. If you went into George Washington's background you'd probably kick up a lot of dirt too. You're the one that counts, not Oscar. Remember that."

I put the chair back in place and doused the butt in a flower pot. I told Lee to give me a few minutes before he left, said so long and took off. Lee looked ten years younger than he had when he came in. I liked that guy.

There was a public phone in the lobby and I called Velda to ask her if she had switched parts in her gun. She said she had, then told me Pat had just been on the wire. I said, "But I just saw him a little while ago."

"I know, but he told me to have you contact him right away if I could reach you."

"Okay, I'll call him back. Look, I'll probably be out most of the day, so I'll pick you up sometime tonight at your place."

"Charlie Moffit?"

"Yeah, we'll take in his joint."

"I'll be ready, Mike."

I hung up, threw in another nickel and spun Pat's number when I got the dial tone. The last time I had seen him he looked tired. This time his voice was dancing.

Like on hot coals.

"Pat, feller, why the sudden rush?"

"I'll tell you later. Get your tail down here chop-chop. I have things to talk over with you. Privately."

"Am I in trouble?"

"There's a damn good chance that you'll be in jail if you don't hurry."

"Get off my back, Pat. Get a table in Louie's and I'll be down for lunch. The check is yours this time."

"I'll give you fifteen minutes."

I made it just in time. Louie was behind the bar and thumbed me toward the booths in the rear. Pat was in the last one on the aisle sucking on a cigarette as hard as he could.

Did you ever see a guy who was burned up at his wife? He was like a bomb trying hard to go off and couldn't because the powder was wet. That's what Pat reminded me of. Police efficiency was leaking out his ears and his usual suavity hung on him like a bag. If he could call those narrow slits eyes then you could say he was looking at me with intent to kill.

I walked back to the bar and had Louie make me up a drink before the session started.

He waited until I was comfortable against the back of the booth and started on my drink before he yanked an envelope out of his pocket and flipped it across the table at me. I slid the contents out and looked at him.

They were photographs of fingerprints. Most were mine.

Four weren't.

Attached to the four that weren't was a typewritten sheet, single spaced and carefully paragraphed. "They came off that cigarette pack," Pat said.

I nodded and read through the report.

Her name was Paula Riis. She was thirty-four years old, a college grad, a trained nurse and a former employee in a large Western insane asylum. Since it was a state job her prints were on file there and in Washington.

Pat let me stuff the sheets back in the envelope before he spoke. I hardly heard him say unnecessarily, "She worked in the same place that Oscar had been assigned to." A cloud of smoke circled his head again.

The music started in my head. It was different this time. It wasn't loud and it had a definite tune and rhythm. It was soft, melodious music that tried to lullaby me into drowsiness with subtle tones. It tried to keep me from thinking and I fought it back into the obscurity from which it came.

I looked at his eyes and I looked deep into twin fires that had a maddening desire to make me talk and talk fast. "What, Pat?"

"Where is she?" His voice sounded queer.

I said, "She's dead. She committed suicide by jumping off a bridge into the river. She's dead as hell."

"I don't believe you, Mike."

"That's tough. That's just too damn bad because you have to believe me. You can scour the city or the country from now to doomsday and you won't find her unless you dredge the river and by now maybe even that's too late. She's out at sea somewhere. So what?"

"I'm asking the same thing. So what, Mike? She isn't an accident, a freak coincidence that you can explain off. I want to know why and how. This thing is too big for you to have alone. You'd better start talking or I'm going to have to think one thing. You aren't the Mike Hammer I knew once. You used to have sense enough to realize that the police are set up to handle these things. You used to know that we weren't a bunch of saps. If you still want to keep still then I'm going to think those things and the friendship I had for a certain guy is ended because that guy isn't the same guy any more."

That was it. He had me and he was right. I took another sip of the drink and made circles with the wet bottom on the table.

"Her name was Paula. Like I said, she's dead. Remember when I came to you with those green cards, Pat? I took them from her. I was walking across the bridge one night when this kid was going into her dutch act. I tried to stop her. All I got was the pocket of her coat where she had the pack of butts and the cards.

"It made me mad because she jumped. I had just been dragged over the coals by that damned judge and I was feeling sour enough not to report the thing. Just the same, I wanted to know what the cards meant. When I found out she was a Commie, and that Charlie Moffit was a Commie I got interested. I couldn't help it.

"Now the picture is starting to take form. I think you've put it together already. Oscar was insane. He had to be. He and that nurse planned an escape and probably went into hiding in their little love nest a long time ago. When money became scarce they saw a way to get some through using Oscar's physical similarity to Lee.

"The first thing that happened was that Oscar killed a guy, a Commie. Now: either he took those cards off Moffit's body for some reason, or he and this Paula Riis actually were Commies themselves. Anyway when Oscar killed Moffit, Paula realized that the guy was more insane than she thought and got scared. She was afraid to do anything about it so she went over the bridge."

It was a wonderful story. It made a lot of sense. The two people that could spoil it were dead. It made a lot of sense without telling about the fat boy on the bridge and setting myself up for a murder charge.

Pat was on the last of his smokes. The dead butts littered the table and his coat was covered with ashes. The fires in his eyes had gone down . . . a little anyway. "Very neat, Mike. It fits like a glove. I'm wondering what it would fit like if there was more to it that you didn't tell me."

"Now you're getting nasty," I said.

"No, just careful. If it's the way you told it the issue's dead. If it isn't there will be a lot of hell coming your way."

"I've seen my share," I grunted.

"You'll see a lot more. I'm going to get some people on this job to poke around. They're other friends of mine and though it won't be official it will be a thorough job. These boys carry little gold badges with three words you can condense to FBI. I hope you're right, Mike. I hope you aren't giving me the business."

I grinned at him. "The only one who can get shafted is me. You . . . hell, you're worried about Lee. I told you I wouldn't line him up for a smear. He's my client and I'm mighty particular about clients. Let's order some lunch and forget about it."

Pat reached for the menu. The fires were still in his eyes.

chapter eight

I LEFT Pat at two o'clock and picked up a paper on the corner. The headlines had turned back to the cold war and the spy trials going on in New York and Washington. I read the sheet through and tossed it in a basket then got in my car.

I made a turn at the corner and cut over to an express street to head back to my place when I noticed the blue coupé behind me. The last time I had seen it it had been parked across from mine outside Pat's office. I turned off the avenue and went down a block to the next avenue and paralleled my course. The blue coupé stuck with me.

When I tried the same thing again it happened all over. This time I picked out a one-way street, crept along it behind a truck until I saw room enough at the curb to park the car. I went into the space head first and sat there at the wheel waiting. The coupé had no choice, it had to pass me.

The driver was a young kid in a pork-pie hat and he didn't give me a glance. There was a chance that I could be wrong, but just for the hell of it I jotted down his license number as he went by and swung out behind him. Only once did I see his eyes looking into his mirror, and that was when he turned on Broadway. I stuck with him a way to see what he'd do.

Five minutes later I gave it up as a bad job. He wasn't going anywhere. I made a left turn and he kept going straight ahead. I scowled at my reflection in the dirty windshield.

I was getting the jumps, I thought. I never used to get like that. Maybe Pat had put his finger on it . . . I'd changed.

When I stopped for the red light I saw the headlines on the papers laid out on a stand. More about the trials and the cold war. Politics. I felt like an ignorant bastard for not knowing what it was all about. There's no time like the present then. I swung the wheel and cut back in the other direction. I parked the car and walked up to the gray stone building where the pickets carried banners protesting the persecution of the "citizens" inside.

One of the punks carrying a placard was at the meeting in Brooklyn the other night. I crossed the line by shoving him almost on his fanny. An attendant carried my note in to Marty Kooperman and he came out to lead me back to the press seats.

Hell, you read the papers, you know what went on in there. It made me as sick to watch it as it did you to read about it. Those damned Reds pulled every trick they knew to get the case thrown out of court. They were a scurvy bunch of lice who tried to turn the court into a burlesque show.

But there was a calm patience in this judge and jury, and in the spectators too that told you what the outcome would be. Oh, the defendants didn't see it. They were too cocksure of themselves. They were The Party. They were Powerful. They represented the People.

They should have turned around and seen the faces of the people. They would have had their pants scared off. All at once I felt good. I felt swell!

Then I saw the two guys in the second row. They were dressed in ordinary business suits and they looked too damn smug. They were the boys who came in with General Osilov that night. I sat through two more hours of it before the judge broke it up for the day. The press boys made a beeline for the phones and the crowd started to scramble for the doors.

A lot of the people covered it up, but I had time to see the general's aides pass a fat brief case to another guy who saw that it reached one of the defendants.

All I could think of was the nerve they had, the gall of them to come into a court of law and directly confirm their relationship with a group accused of a crime against the people. Maybe that's why they could get ahead so fast. They were brazen. That brief case would hold one thing. Money. Cash in bills. Dough to support the trial and the accompanying propaganda.

Nuts.

I waited until they went through the doors and stayed on their heels. At least they had the sense not to come in an official car; that would have been overdoing it. They walked down a block, waved a cab to the curb and climbed in. By that time I was in a cab myself and right behind them. One nice thing about taking a taxi in New York. There're so many cabs you can't tell if you're being followed or not.

The one in front of us pulled to a stop in front of the hotel I had left not so long before. I paid off my driver and tagged after them into the lobby. The place was still jammed with reporters and the usual collection of the curious. General Osilov was standing off in a corner explaining things to four reporters through an interpreter. The two went directly up to him, interrupted and shook his hand as if they hadn't seen him in years. It was all very clubby.

The girl at the newsstand was bored. I bought a pack of Luckies and held out my hand for the change. "What's the Russky doing?"

"Him? He was a speaker at the luncheon upstairs. You should have heard him. They piped all the speeches into the lobby over the loudspeaker and he had to be translated every other sentence."

Sure, he couldn't speak English. Like hell!

I said, "Anything important come out?"

She handed me my change. "Nah, same old drivel every time. All except Lee Deamer. He jumped on that Cossack for a dozen things and called him every name that could sneak by in print. You should have heard the way the people in the lobby cheered. Gosh, the manager was fit to be tied. He tried to quiet them down, but they wouldn't shut up."

Good going, Lee. You tear the bastards apart in public and I'll do it in private. Just be careful, they're like poisonous snakes . . . quiet, stealthy and deadly. Be careful, for Pete's sake!

I opened the Luckies and shook one out. I hung it in my mouth and fumbled for a match. A hand draped with mink held a flame up to it and a voice said, "Light, mister?"

It was a silly notion, but I wondered if I could be contaminated by the fire. I said, "Hello, Ethel," and took the light.

There was something different about her face. I didn't know what it was, but it wasn't the same any more. Fine, nearly invisible lines drew it tight, giving an Oriental slant to her eyes. The mouth that had kissed so nice and spoke the word that put the finger on me seemed to be set too firm. It pulled the curve of her lips out of shape.

She had a lesson coming to her, this one. Bare skin and a leather belt. Either she was playing it bold or she didn't think I had guessed. Maybe she thought she couldn't have made it out the door without my seeing her and decided to make the first move herself. Whatever her reason, I couldn't read it in her voice or her face.

I was going to ask her what she was doing here and I saw why. The reputable Mr. Brighton of Park Avenue and Big Business was holding court next to a fluted column. A lone reporter was taking notes. A couple of big boys whose faces I recognized from newspapers were listening intently, adding a word now and then. They all smiled but two.

The sour pusses were General Osilov and his interpreter. The little guy beside the general talked fast and gesticulated freely, but the general was catching it all as it came straight from Brighton himself.

A couple hundred words later Ethel's old man said something and they all laughed, even the general. They shook hands and split up into new groups that were forming every time a discussion got started.

I took Ethel's arm and started for the door. "It's been a long time, kid. I've missed you."

She tried a smile and it didn't look good on her. "I've missed you too, Mike. I halfway expected you to call me."

"Well, you know how things are."

"Yes, I know." I threw my eyes over her face, but she was expressionless.

"Were you at the luncheon?" I asked.

"Oh . . ." she came out of it with a start. "No, I stayed in the lobby. Father was one of the speakers, you know."

"Really? No need for you to stick around, is there?"

"Oh no, none at all. I can . . . oh, Mike, just a moment. I forgot something, do you mind?"

We paused at the door and she glanced back over her shoulder. I turned her around and walked back. "Want me to go with you?"

"No, I'll be right back. Wait for me, will you?"

I watched her go and the girl at the counter smiled. I said, "There's a ten in it if you see what she does, sister." She was out of there like a shot and closed up on Ethel. I stood by the stand smoking, looking at the mirrors scattered around the walls. I could see myself in a half dozen of them. If Ethel watched to see whether or not I moved she must have been satisfied.

She was gone less than a minute. Her face looked tighter than ever.

I walked up to meet her and the girl scrambled behind her counter. I took out a dime, flipped it in my hand and went over and got a pack of gum. While the girl gave me my nickel change I dropped the ten on the counter. "She spoke to a couple of guys back in the hall. Nothing else. They were young."

I took my gum pack and offered Ethel a piece. She said she didn't want any. No wonder she looked so damned grim. She had fingered me again. Naked skin and ten extra lashes. She was going to be a sorry girl.

When we got in the cab two boys in almost identical blue suits opened the doors of a black Chevvy sedan and came out behind us. I didn't look around again until we had reached the lot where I left my car. The black Chevvy was down the street. Ethel kept up a running conversation that gave me a chance to look at her, and back over my shoulder occasionally.

If I had been paying any attention I would have gotten what she was driving at. She kept hinting for me to take her up to my place. MAN MURDERED IN OWN APARTMENT. More nice headlines. I ignored her hints and cruised around Manhattan with the black sedan always a few hundred feet behind.

Dusk came early. It drove in with the fog that seemed to like this town, a gray blind that reduced visibility to a minimum. I said to her, "Can we go back to your cabin, kid? It was pretty nice there."

I might have been mistaken, but I thought I saw the glint of tears. "It *was* nice there, wasn't it?"

"It was you, not the cabin, Ethel."

I wasn't mistaken, the tears were there. She dropped her eyes and stared at her hands. "I had forgotten . . . what it was like to live." She paused, then: "Mike . . ."

"What?"

"Nothing. We can go to the cabin if you'd like to."

.The Chevvy behind us pulled around a car and clung a little closer. I loosened the .45 with my forearm and a shrug. The dusk deepened to dark and it was easy to watch the lights in the mirror. They sat there, glowering, watching, waiting for the right moment to come.

How would it be? Ethel wanted it in my apartment. Why? So she would be out of the line of fire? Now what. They'd draw alongside and open up and they wouldn't give a hoot whether they got the both of us or not. It was a question of whether I was important enough to kill at the same time sacrificing a good party worker. Hell, there were always suckers who could rake in the dough for them. Those two headlights behind me trying to act casual said that.

We were out of the city on a wide open road that wound into the dark like a beckoning finger. The houses thinned out and there were fewer roads intersecting the main drag.

Any time now, I thought. It can happen any time. The .45 was right where I could get at it in a hurry and I was ready to haul the wheel right into them. The lights behind me flicked on bright, back to dim and on bright again, a signal they were going to pass.

I signaled an okay with my lights and gripped the wheel. The lights came closer.

I didn't watch the mirror. I had my eyes going between the road and the lightbeams on the outside lane that got brighter as they came closer when all of a sudden the beams swerved and weren't there any more. When I looked they were going in a crazy rolling pattern end over end into the field alongside the road.

I half whispered, "Cripes!" and slammed on the brakes. A handful of cars shot by the accident and began to pull in to a stop in front of me.

Ethel was rigid in her seat, her hands pushing her away from the windshield where the quick stop had thrown her. "Mike! What . . ."

I yanked the emergency up. "Stay here. A car went over behind us."

She gasped and said something I didn't catch because I was out and running back toward the car. It was upside down and both doors were open. The horn blasted, a man screamed and the lights still punched holes in the night. I was the first one there, a hundred yards ahead of anyone else.

I had time to see the tommy gun on the grass and the wallet inside the car. So that was it. That was how it was to be pulled off. One quick blast from a chatter gun that would sweep my car and it was all over. Somebody groaned in the darkness and I didn't bother to see who it was. They deserved everything they got. I grabbed that tommy gun and the wallet and ducked behind the car in the darkness and ran back down the road. The others had just reached the wreck and were hollering for somebody to get a doctor.

Ethel screamed when I threw the trunk open and I yelled for her to shut up. I tossed the tommy gun on the spare tire and shut the lid. There were more cars coasting up, threading through the jam along the road. A siren screamed its way up and two state cops started the procession moving again. I joined the line and got away from there.

"Who was it, Mike? What happened back there?"

"Just an accident," I grinned. "A couple of guys were going too fast and they rolled over."

"Were they . . . hurt?"

"I didn't stay to look. They weren't dead . . . yet." I grinned again and her face tightened. She looked at me with an intense loathing and the tears started again.

"Don't worry, baby. Don't be so damn soft-hearted. You know what the Party policies are. You have to be cold and hard. You aren't forgetting, are you?"

The "no" came through her teeth.

"Hell, the ground was soft and the car wasn't banged up much. They were probably just knocked out. You know, you have to get over being squeamish about such things."

Ethel shifted in her seat and wouldn't look at me again. We came to the drive and the trees that hung over it. We pulled up to the front of the cabin that nestled on the bluff atop the river and sat there in the dark watching the lights of the river boats.

Red and green eyes. No, they were boats. From far away came a dull booming, like a giant kettledrum. I had heard it once before, calling that way. It was only a channel marker, only a steel bell on a float that clanged when the tide and the waves swung it. I felt a shudder cross my shoulders and I said, "Shall we go in?"

She answered by opening the door. I went into the cabin behind her.

I closed the door and reached behind my back and turned the key in the lock. Ethel heard the ominous click and stopped. She looked over her shoulder at me once, smiled and went on. I watched her throw her mink on the sofa then put a match to the tapers in the holders.

She thought it was a love nest. We were locked in against the world where we could practice the human frailties without interruption. She thought I didn't know and was going to give her all for the party so as not to arouse my suspicions. She was crying softly as if the sudden passion was too much for her.

I put the key in my pocket and crossed the room to where she was and put my hands on her shoulders. She spun around, her hands locking behind my waist, her mouth reaching up for mine. I kissed her with a brutal force she'd remember and while I kissed her my fingers hooked in the fabric of her dress.

She ripped her mouth away from mine and pressed it against my cheek. She was crying hard and she said, "I love you, Mike. I never wanted to love again and I did. I love you." It was so low I hardly heard it.

My teeth were showing in a grin. I raised my hand until it was against her breast and pushed. Ethel staggered back a step and I yanked with the hand that held her dress and it came off in one piece with a quick loud tear, leaving her gasping and hurt with vivid red marks on her skin where the fabric had twisted and caught.

She gasped, pressed the back of her hand to her mouth and looked at me through eyes wide with fear. "Mike . . . you didn't have to . . ."

"Shut up." I took a step forward and she backed off, slowly, slowly, until the wall was at her back and she could retreat no more. "Am I going to rip 'em right off your hide, Ethel?"

Her head shook, unbelieving what was happening to her. It only lasted a moment, and her hands that trembled so bent up behind her back and the bra fell away and landed at her feet. Her eyes were on mine as she slid her hands inside the fragile silk of the shorts and pushed them down.

When she stepped out of them I slid my belt off and let it dangle from my hand. I watched her face. I saw the gamut of emotions flash by in swift succession, leaving a startled expression of pure animal terror.

"Maybe you should know why you're getting this, Ethel. It's something you should have gotten a long time ago. Your father should have given it to you when you started fooling around one of those Commie bastards who was after the dough you could throw his way instead of yourself. I'm going to lace the hell out of you and you can scream all you want, and nobody will be around to hear you but me and that's what I want to hear.

"You put the finger on me twice now. You fingered me when you saw the badge inside my wallet and the party put a man on my back. They put a lot of men, I guess. Two of 'em are dead already. It didn't go so good and you saw a chance to finger me again in the lobby back there. What did you expect for it, a promotion or something?"

I started to swing the belt back and forth very gently. Ethel pressed against the wall, her face a pale oval. "Mike . . . it wasn't . . ."

"Keep quiet," I said.

A naked woman and a leather belt. I looked at her, so bare and so pretty, hands pressed for support against the paneling, legs spread apart to hold a precarious balance, a flat stomach hollowed under the fear that burned her body a faint pink, lovely smooth breasts, firm with terrible excitement, rising and falling with every gasping breath. A gorgeous woman who had been touched by the hand of the devil.

I raised the belt and swung it and heard the sharp crack of the leather against her thighs and her scream and that horrible blasting roar all at once. Her body twisted and fell while I was running for the window with the .45 in my hand pumping slugs into the night and shouting at the top of my voice.

And there in the darkness I heard a body crashing through the brush, running for the road. I ran to the door that I had locked myself and cursed my own stupidity while I fumbled for the key in my pocket.

The door came open, but there was only silence outside, a dead, empty silence. I jammed a fresh clip into the gun and held it steady, deliberately standing outlined in the light of the door asking to be made a target.

I heard it again, the heavy pounding of feet going away. They were too far to catch. When they stopped a motor roared into life and he was gone. My hands had the shakes again and I had to drop the rod back in the sling. The prints of his feet were in the grass, winding around the house. I followed them to the window and bent over to pick up the hat.

A pork-pie hat. It had a U-shaped nick taken out of the crown. The boy in the blue Chevvy. Mr. MVD himself, a guy who looked like a schoolboy and could pass in a crowd for anything but what he was. I grinned because he was one thing he shouldn't have been, a lousy shot. I was duck soup there in that room with my back toward him and he missed. Maybe I was supposed to be his first corpse and he got nervous. Yeah. I turned and looked in the window.

Ethel was still on the floor and a trickle of red drained from her body.

I ran back to her, stumbling over things in the darkness. I

turned her over and saw the hole under her shoulder, a tiny blue thing that oozed blood slowly and was beginning to swell at the edges.

I said, "Ethel . . . Ethel honey!"

Her eyes came open and she looked tired, so tired. "It . . . doesn't hurt, Mike."

"I know. It won't for a while. Ethel . . . I'm sorry. God, I feel awful."

"Mike . . . don't."

She closed her eyes when I ran my hand over her cheek. "You said . . . a badge, Mike. You're not one of them, are you?"

"No. I'm a cop."

"I'm . . . glad. After . . . I met you I saw . . . the truth, Mike. I knew . . . I had been a fool."

"No more talking, Ethel. I'm going for a doctor. Don't talk."

She found my hand and hung on. "Let me, Mike . . . please. Will I die?"

"I don't know, Ethel. Let me go for a doctor."

"No . . . I want to tell you . . . I loved you. I'm glad it happened. I had to love somebody . . . else."

I forced her fingers off my hand and pushed her arm away gently. There was a phone on the bar and I lifted it to my ear. I dialed the operator and had a hard time keeping my voice level. I said I wanted a doctor and wanted one quick. She told me to wait and connected me with a crisp voice that sounded steady and alert. I told him where we were and to get here fast. He said he would hurry and broke the connection.

I knelt beside her and stroked her hair until her eyes came open, silently protesting the pain that had started. Her shoulder twitched once and the blood started again. I tried to be gentle. I got my arms under her and carried her to the couch. The wound was a deeper blue and I prayed that there was no internal hemmorrhage.

I sat beside her holding her hand. I cursed everything and everybody. I prayed a little and I swore again. I had thoughts that tried to drive me mad.

It was a long while before I realized that she was looking at me. She struggled to find words, her mind clouding from the shock of the bullet. I let her talk and heard her say, "I'm not . . . one of them any more. I told . . . everything . . . I told . . ."

Her eyes had a glazed look. "Please don't try to talk, kid, please."

She never heard me. Her lips parted, moved. "I never . . . told

them about you . . . Mike. I never saw . . . your badge. Tonight
. . . those men . . ." It was too much for her. She closed her
eyes and was still, only the cover I had thrown over her moved
enough to tell that she was still alive.

I never heard the doctor come in. He was a tall man with a
face that had looked on much of the world. He stepped past me
and leaned over her, his hand opening the bag he carried. I sat
and waited, smoking one cigarette after another. The air reeked
with a sharp chemical smell and the doctor was a tall shadow
passing back and forth across my line of vision, doing things I
wasn't aware of, desperate in his haste.

His voice came at me several times before I answered him. He
said, "She will need an ambulance."

I came out of the chair and went to the phone. The operator
said she would call and I hung up. I turned around. "How is she,
doc?"

"We won't know for a while yet. There's a slight chance that
she'll pull through." His whole body expressed what he felt. Disgust.
Anger. His voice had a demanding, exasperated tone. "What
happened?"

Perhaps it was the sharpness of his question that startled me
into a logical line of reasoning. There was a sudden clarity about
the whole thing I hadn't noticed before I heard Ethel telling me
that she had pulled out of the party and it left me with an answer
that said this time it wasn't me they were after . . . it was her
. . . and Pork Pie *had* been a good shot. He would have been a
dead shot, only Ethel had twisted when I laid the strap across her
and the bullet that was intended for her heart had missed by a
fraction and might give her life back to her.

The soft kill-music that I always hear at the wrong times took
up a beat and was joined by a multitude of ghostly instruments
that plucked at my mind to drive away any reason that I had
left.

I walked to the doctor and stared at his eyes so he could see
that I had looked on the world too, and could see the despair,
the lust, the same dirty thoughts that he had seen in so many
others and said, "Do you know who I am, doctor?"

He looked long this time, searching me. "Your face is familiar."

"It should be, doctor. You've seen it in the papers. You've read
about it many times. It's been described a hundred different ways
and there's always that reference to a certain kill-look that I have.
My name is Mike Hammer. I'm a private detective. I've killed a
lot of people."

He knew me then; his eyes asked if I were trying to buy his

silence with the price of death. "Did you do that to her too?"

"No, doctor. Somebody else did that, and for it that somebody is going to die a thousand times. It wasn't just one person who wanted that girl dead. One person ordered it, but many demanded it. I'm not going to tell you the story of what lies behind this, but I will tell you one thing. It's so damned important that it touches your life and mine and the lives of everyone in this country and unless you want to see the same thing happen again and again you'll have to hold up your report.

"You know who I am and I can show you my papers so there will never be any trouble in finding me if you think it should be done. But listen . . . if ever you believed anything, believe this . . . if I get connected with this I'll be tied up in that crazy web of police detail and a lot of other people will die. Do you understand me?"

"No." Just like that, no. I tried to keep from grabbing his neck in my hands and forcing my words down his throat. My face went wild and I couldn't control it. The doctor didn't scare, he just stood there and watched me make myself keep from killing him too.

"Perhaps I do after all." His face became sober and stern. I swallowed hard with the relief I felt. "I don't understand it at all," he said. "I'll never understand these things. I do know this though, a powerful influence motivates murder. It is never simple enough to understand. I can't understand war, either. I'll do what I can, Mr. Hammer. I do have a good understanding of people and I think that you are telling me a truth that could have some very unpleasant aspects, whatever they are."

I squeezed his hand hard and got out of there. So much to be done, I thought, so much that's still left to do. My watch said it was after ten and Velda would be waiting. Tonight we had a mission planned and after that another and another until we found the ending.

I touched the starter and the engine caught with a roar. The night had sped by and there never was enough time to do what I wanted. First Pork-Pie Hat, then those men, then Ethel. I stopped and retraced my thoughts. Ethel and those men. She was going to tell me about them; she almost did. I reached in my pocket and took out the wallet.

The card was behind some others in one of the pockets. It was an official card with all the works. The words I saw stood out as though they were written in flame. FEDERAL BUREAU OF INVESTIGATION. Good Lord, Ethel had fingered me to the FBI!

She had turned on the party and even on me! Now it *was* clear
. . . Those two Feds had tailed me hoping to be led to my
apartment and perhaps a secret cache of papers that could lead
to those missing documents! They tailed me but they in turn were
being tailed by somebody else who knew what had happened.
Pork-Pie Hat ran them off the road and came after us with the
intention of killing Ethel before she could spill anything else she
knew!

I let the music in my head play. I laughed at it and it played
harder than ever, but this time I didn't fight it. I sat back and
laughed, enjoying the symphony of madness and cheered when it
was done. So I *was* mad. I *was* a killer and I *was* looking forward
to killing again. I wanted them all, every one of them from bottom
to top and especially the one at the top even if I had to go to
the Kremlin to do it. The time for that wouldn't be now . . .
I'd only get a little way up the ladder if one of the rungs didn't
break first and throw me to my death.

But some day, maybe, some day I'd stand on the steps of the
Kremlin with a gun in my fist and I'd yell for them to come out
and if they wouldn't I'd go in and get them and when I had them
lined up against the wall I'd start shooting until all I had left was
a row of corpses that bled on the cold floors and in whose thick
red blood would be the promise of a peace that would stick for
more generations than I'd live to see.

The music gave up in a thunder of drums and I racked my
wheels against the curb outside Velda's apartment house. I looked
up at her floor when I got out and saw the lights on and I knew
she was ready and waiting.

I went on in.

She said hello and knew that something was wrong with me.
"What happened, Mike?"

I couldn't tell her the whole thing. I said simply, "They tried
again."

Her eyes narrowed down and glinted at me. They asked the
question.

I said, "They got away again, too."

"It's getting deeper, isn't it?"

"It'll go deeper before we're through. Get your coat on."

Velda went inside and reappeared with her coat on and her
handbag slung over her shoulder. It swung slowly under the weight
of the gun. "Let's go, Mike."

We went downstairs to the car and started driving. Broadway

was a madhouse of traffic that weaved and screamed, stopped for red lights and jumped away at the green. I let the flow take me past the artificial daylight of the marquees and the signs and into the dusk of uptown. When we came to the street Velda pointed and I turned up it, parking in the middle of the block under a street light.

Here was the edge of Harlem, that strange no-man's-land where the white mixed with the black and the languages overflowed into each other like that of the horde around the Tower of Babel. There were strange, foreign smells of cooking and too many people in too few rooms. There were the hostile eyes of children who became suddenly silent as you passed.

Velda stopped before an old sandstone building. "This is it."

I took her arm and went up the stairs. In the vestibule I struck a match and held it before the name plates on the mailboxes. Most were scrawled in childish writing on the backs of match books. One was an aluminum stamp and it read C. C. LOPEX, SUPT.

I pushed the button. There was no answering buzz of the door. Instead, a face showed through the dirty glass and the door was pulled open by a guy who only came up to my chest. He smoked a smelly cigar and reeked of cheap whisky. He was a hunchback. He said, "Whatta ya want?"

He saw the ten bucks I had folded in my fingers and got a greedy look on his face. "There ain't but one empty room and ya won't like that. Ya can use my place. For a tenner ya can stay all night."

Velda raised her eyebrows at that. I shook my head. "We'll take the empty."

"Sure, go ahead. Ya coulda done whatcha wanted in my place but if ya want the empty go ahead. Ya won't like it, though."

I gave him the ten and he gave me the key, telling me where the room was. He leered and looked somewhat dissatisfied because he wouldn't be able to sneak a look on something he probably never had himself. Velda started up the stairs using her flashlight to pick out the snags in the steps.

The room faced on a dark corridor that was hung heavy with the smell of age and decay. I put the key in the lock and shoved the door open. Velda found the lone bulb that dangled from the ceiling and pulled the cord to throw a dull yellow light in the room. I closed the door and locked it.

Nobody had to tell us what had happened. Somebody had been here before us. The police had impounded Charlie Moffit's personal belongings, but they hadn't ripped the room up doing it. The skinny mattress lay in the center of the floor ripped to shreds. The hollow posts of the bed had been disemboweled and lay on the springs. What had been a rug at one time lay in a heap in the corner under the pile of empty dresser drawers.

"We're too late again, Mike."

"No we're not." I was grinning and Velda grinned too. "The search didn't stop anywhere. If they found it we could have seen where they stopped looking. They tore the place apart and never came to the end. It never was here."

I kicked at the papers on the floor, old sheets from weeks back. There was a note pad with pencil sketches of girls doing things they shouldn't. We roamed around the room poking into the remains doing nothing but looking out of curiosity. Velda found a box of junk that had been spilled under the dresser, penny curios from some arcade.

There was no place else to look that hadn't already been searched. I took the dresser drawers off the rug and laid them out. They were lined with newspapers and had a few odds and ends rolling on the bottoms. There was part of a fountain pen and a broken harmonica. Velda found a few pictures of girls in next to nothing that had been cut from a magazine.

Then I found the photographs. They were between the paper lining and the side of the drawer. One was of two people, too fuzzy to identify. The other was that of a girl and had "To Charlie, with love from P." written on the bottom. I held it in my hand and looked at the face of Paula Riis. She was smiling. She was happy. She was the girl that had jumped off the bridge and was dead. I stared at her face that smiled back at me as if there never had been anything to worry about.

Velda peered over my shoulder, took the picture from me and held it under the light. "Who is she, Mike?"

"Paula Riis," I said finally. "The nurse. Charlie Moffit's girl friend. Oscar Deamer's nurse and the girl who chose to die rather than look at my face. The girl who started it all and left it hanging in mid-air while people died and killed."

I took out a cigarette and gave her one. "I had it figured wrong. I gave Pat a bum steer, then when I thought it over I got to thinking that maybe I told the truth after all. I thought that Paula and Oscar planned his escape and Oscar killed a guy . . . just any guy . . . in order to squeeze Lee. Now it seems that it wasn't just any guy that Oscar killed. It wasn't an accident. Oscar killed him for a very good reason."

"Mike . . . could it be a case of jealousy? Could Oscar have been jealous because Paula played up to Charlie?"

I dragged the smoke down, held it and let it go into the light. "I wish it happened that simply. I wish it did, sugar. I started out with a couple of green cards and took it from there. I thought I had a coincidental connection but now it looks like it wasn't so damn coincidental after all. We have too many dead people carrying those green cards."

"The answer, Mike . . . what can it be?"

I stared at the wall thoughtfully. "I'm wondering that too. I think it lies out West in an asylum for the insane. Tomorrow I want you to take the first plane out and start digging."

"For what?"

"For anything you can find. Think up the questions and look for the answers. The part we're looking for may be there and it may be here, but we haven't the time to look together. You'll have to go out alone while I plod along this end of the track."

"Mike . . . you'll be careful, won't you?"

"Very careful, Velda. I won't ask questions if I think a gun will do the job quicker. This time I'm going to live up to my reputation. I've been thinking some things I don't like and to satisfy myself I'm going to find out whether or not they're true."

"Supposing they make another try for you?"

"Oh, they will, they will. In fact, they have to. From now on I'll be sleeping with my gun in my fist and my eyes open. They'll make the play again because I know enough and think too much. I might run into a conclusion that will split things wide open. They'll be looking for me and possibly you because they know there were two guns that killed those boys in Oscar's room. They'll know I wasn't alone and they may think of you.

"I'll have to keep my apartment and the office covered while I'm away. They'll get around it somehow, but I'll try anyway."

Velda took my shoulder and made me look at her. "You aren't sending me out West just so I won't be there if there's trouble, are you?"

"No, I wouldn't do that to you. I know how much it means to be in on a thing like this."

She knew I was telling the truth for a change and dropped her hand into mine. "I'll do a good job, Mike. When I get back I won't take any chance on their finding any information I have. I'll tuck it in that trick wall lamp in the office so you can get to it without waking me from the sleep I'll probably need."

I pulled the cord and the light did a slow fade-out. Velda held her flash on the floor and stared down the corridor. A little brown face peeked out of a door and withdrew when she threw the spot on it. We held on to the banister and went down the steps that announced our descent with sharp squeals and groans.

The hunchback opened his door at the foot of the landing and took the key back. "That was quick," he said. "Pretty quick for your age. Thought ya'd take longer."

I wanted to rap him in the puss, only that would have shut him up when I had a question to ask him. "We woulda stayed only the room was a mess. Who was in there before us?"

"Some guy died who lived there."

"Yeah, but who was in there next?"

"Young kid. Said he wanted a bunk for a night. Guess he was hot or something. He gimme a ten too, plus a five for the room. Yeah, I remember him 'counta he wore a nice topcoat and one of them flat pork-pie hats. Sure woulda like to get that topcoat."

I pushed Velda outside and down to the car. The MVD had been there. No wonder the search was so complete. He looked and never looked hard enough. In his hurry to find some documents he overlooked the very thing that might have told him where they were.

I drove Velda home and went up for coffee. We talked and we smoked. I laughed at the way she looked at the ring on her finger and told her the next thing she knew there'd be a diamond to match. Her eyes sparkled brighter than the stone.

"When will it be, Mike?" Her voice was a velvet glove that caressed every inch of me.

I squirmed a little bit and managed a sick grin. "Oh, soon. Let's not go too fast, kid."

The devil came into her eyes and she pushed away from the table. I had another smoke and finished it. I started on another when she called me. When I went into the living room she was standing by the light in a gown that was nothing at all, nothing at all. I could see through it and saw things I thought existed only in a dream and the sweat popped out on my forehead and left me feeling shaky all over.

Her body was a milky flow of curves under the translucent gown and when she moved the static current of flesh against sheer cloth made it cling to her in a way that made me hold my breath to fight against the temptation I could feel tugging at my body. The inky blackness of the hair falling around her shoulders made her look taller, and the gown shrouded what was yet to come and was there for me alone.

"For our wedding night, Mike," she said. "When will it be?"

I said, "We're . . . only engaged to be engaged, you know."

I didn't dare move when she came to me. She raised herself on her toes to kiss me with a tongue of fire, then walked back to the light and turned around. I could see through that damned gown as though it weren't there at all.

She knew I'd never be able to wait long after that.

I stumbled out of the room and down to my car. I sat there awhile thinking of nothing but Velda and the brief glimpse of heaven she had showed me. I tried thinking about something else and it didn't work.

I couldn't get her out of my mind.

chapter nine

I SLEPT WITH a dream that night. It was a dream of nice things and other things that weren't so nice. There were a lot of people in the dream and not all of them were alive. There were faces from the past that mingled with those of the present, drawn silent faces turned toward me to see when I would become one of them, floating in that limbo of nonexistence.

I saw the bridge again, and two people die while the stern face of the judge looked on disapproving, uttering solemn words of condemnation. I saw flashes of fire, and men fall. I saw Ethel hovering between the void that separates life from death, teetering into the black while I screamed for her not to and tried to run to catch her, only to have my feet turn into stumps that grew from the very soil.

There were others too, bodies of dead men without faces, waiting for me to add that one missing part, to identify them with their brother dead in one sweeping blast of gunfire. I was there with them. They didn't want me because I wasn't dead, and the living didn't want me either. They couldn't figure out why I was still alive when I dwelt in the land of the dead men.

Only Velda wanted me. I could see her hovering above the others, trailing the gown of transparent fabric, her finger beckoning me to come with her where nothing would matter but the two of us.

The dead pushed me out and the living pushed me back. I tried to get up to Velda and I couldn't reach her. I screamed once for them all to shut up before there was only the land of the dead and none of the living.

Then I woke up. My head throbbed and the shout was still caught in my throat. My tongue felt thick and there was an ache across my shoulders. I staggered into the bathroom where I could duck myself under a cold shower whose stinging chill would wash away the dream.

I glanced at the clock, seeing that the morning had come and gone, leaving me only the afternoon and night. I picked up the phone, asked for long distance, then had myself connected with the hospital outside the city. I hung on for ten minutes waiting for the doctor, told him who I was when he came on and asked him how she was.

The doctor held his hand over the receiver and his voice was a slight mumble of sound. Then: "Yes, Mr. Hammer, I can talk now. The patient has passed the crisis and in my opinion she will live."

"Has she talked, doc?"

"She was conscious a few minutes but she said nothing, nothing at all. There are quite a few people waiting to hear her words." I sensed the change in his voice. "They are police, Mr. Hammer . . . and Federal men."

"I figured they'd be there. Have you said anything?"

"No. I rather believeve that you told me the truth, especially since seeing those Federal men. I told them I received an anonymous call to go to the cabin and when I did I found her."

"Good. I can say thanks but it won't mean much. Give me three days and you can say what you like if it hasn't already been explained."

"I understand."

"Is Mr. Brighton there?"

"He has been here since the girl was identified. He seems considerably upset. We had to give him a sedative."

"Just how upset is he?"

"Enough to justify medical attention . . . which he won't have."

"I see. All right, doctor, I'll call you again. Let me have those three days."

"Three days, Mr. Hammer. You may have less. Those Federal men are viewing me somewhat suspiciously." We said our goodbys and hung up. Then I went out and ate breakfast.

I got dressed and went straight to the office. Velda had left a note in her typewriter saying that she had taken the morning plane out and for me to be careful. I pulled the sheet out of the roller and tore it up. There was no mail to look at so I gave Pat a ring and caught him just as he was coming in from lunch.

He said, "Hello, Mike. What's new?"

If I told him he would have cut my throat. "Nothing much. I wanted to speak to somebody so I called. What're you doing?"

"Right now I have to go downtown. I have to see the medical examiner and he's out on a case. A suicide, I think. I'm going to meet him there and if you feel like coming along you're welcome."

"Well, I don't feel like it, but I will. Be down in a few minutes. We'll use my car."

"Okay, but shake it up."

I dumped a pack of Luckies out of the carton in my desk and shoved it in my pocket, went downstairs and took off for Pat's. He was waiting for me on the curb, talking earnestly to a couple of uniformed cops. He waved, made a final point to the cops and crossed the street.

"Somebody steal your marbles, Mike? You don't look happy."

"I'm not. I didn't get but eleven hours' sleep."

"Gosh, you poor guy. That must hurt. If you can keep awake, drive down to the foot of Third Avenue. How're you making out with Lee?"

"I'll have a definite report for him in a couple of days."

"Negative?"

I shrugged.

Pat looked at me querulously. "That's a hell of a note. What else could it be?"

"Positive."

Pat got mad. "Do you think Oscar left something behind him, Mike? By damn, if he did I want to know about it!"

"Simmer down. I'm checking every angle I know of and when my report is made you'll be able to depend on its answer. If Oscar left one thing that could frame Lee I'll be sure nobody sees it who shouldn't see it. That's the angle I'm worried about. A smear on Lee now will be fatal . . . and Pat, there's a lot of wrong guys out to smear him. If you only knew."

"I will know soon, sonny boy. I've already had a few initial reports myself and it seems that your name has cropped up pretty frequently."

"I get around," I said.

"Yeah." He relaxed into a silence he didn't break until I saw the morgue wagon and a prowl ahead of me. "Here's the place. Stop behind the car."

We hopped out and one of the cops saluted Pat and told him the medical examiner was still upstairs. Pat lugged his brief case along and met him on the stairs. I stood in the background while they rambled along about something and Pat handed him a manila folder. The M.E. tucked it under his arm and said he'd take care of it.

Pat waved his thumb toward the top of the stairs. "What is it this time?"

"Another suicide. Lieutenant Barner is on the case. Some old duck took the gas pipe. They're always doing it in this neighborhood. Go up and take a look."

"I see enough of that stuff. Let Barner handle it."

He would have followed the M.E. down the stairs if I hadn't been curious enough to step up to the landing and peer in the door. Pat came up behind me and laughed. "Curious?"

"Can't help it."

"Sure. Then let's go in and see somebody who died by their own hand instead of yours."

"That's not funny, pal. Can it." Pat laughed again and walked in.

The guy was a middle-aged average man. He had a shock of white hair and a peculiar expression and color that come from breathing too much gas. He stunk of whisky and lay in a heap on the floor with his head partially propped up against the cushioned leg of a chair.

Barner was slipping into his coat. "Damn good thing there wasn't a pilot light on that stove. Would have blown the block to bits."

Pat knelt down and took a close look at the body. "How long has he been dead?"

"Few hours, at least. There hasn't been anybody home in this building all morning. The landlady came in around noon and smelt the gas. The door was closed, but not locked, and she smashed a couple of windows out and called a doctor. There wasn't anything he could do so he called us."

"Any note?"

"Nah. The guy was tanked up. He probably got disgusted with himself and turned on the gas. He used to be an actor. Name's Jenkins, Harvey Robinson Jenkins. The landlady said he was pretty good about thirty years ago, a regular matinee idol. He dropped into character parts, got wiped out when vaudeville went out and picked up a few bucks working in small road shows now and then."

I looked around the room and took stock of his things. There was a good leather chair by the window and a new floor lamp, but the rest of the furnishings had lost their shape and luster with age. There were two rooms, a combination sitting-room-bedroom and a kitchenette. A stack of old theater posters were neatly stacked behind the bed and a new military kit decorated the top of the dresser. The kitchen was big enough to hold one person at a time. A faint odor of gas still hung up high and clung to the curtains. The refrigerator didn't work, but then it didn't have to because it was empty. A jar of jam was on the table next to an empty bottle of whisky. There were a dozen other empties under the table in a cardboard carton.

So this is death. This is the way people die if you don't help them. He was on the long road and glad of it. Too bad he had to leave his most prized possessions behind. The make-up kit was old and battered, but it was clean, unlike everything else, and the tubes and jars inside it were all neatly arranged and labeled. The mirror fastened to the back of the lid was polished clear by a careful hand. I could picture the little guy sitting there night after night playing all the great roles of history, seeing his hand transform him to the glories of his youth.

They were taking the body out in the basket when the landlady came in to see that that was all they took out. Barner said so long and left us watching the procession down the stairs. The landlady was a chubby woman whose scraggly hair fell down past her ears. Her hands were calloused and red from work and she kept rubbing them together as though they were cold.

She turned to me, clucking through her teeth. "There you see the evil of drink, young man. I lost me two husbands that way and now I lose a boarder."

"Tough. Did he owe you any money?"

"No, not one red cent. Oh, he was an honorable one was Mr. Jenkins. Lived here over three years he did but always paid his rent somehow. Too bad he got that inheritance. It was too much for him who never had any real money. He spent it all on drink and now look at him."

"Yeah."

"Well, I warned him, you can't say I didn't try. He was always making those speeches like an actor does and he told me that drink was food for the soul. Food for the soul! He never went hungry then."

Pat grunted, anxious to leave. "Let that be a lesson to you, Mike." He looked at the landlady pointedly. "How long was he on that binge?"

"Oh, for quite a while. Let me see, the letter with the money came a week after the Legion Parade. That was a Wednesday, the 13th. Yes, that's it, a week later he got the money. He paid me the three months he owed me and for two more months in advance, then he started drinking. I never did see a man drink so much. Every night he'd get carried in still mumbling one of them silly parts of his and messing up my floor."

Pat nodded thoughtfully. "See, Mike, that's what you're heading for. An untimely end."

"Nuts, I don't drink that much. Anyway, I'll shoot myself before I try to get charged up on gas. Come on, let's get out of here."

The landlady showed us to the door and watched from the stoop as we pulled away. I hunched behind the wheel when I began thinking of the old coot who took the easy way out.

I thought about it for a long time.

I let Pat out at his office, found a saloon that was half empty and perched on a stool where I could think about it some more. The rows of whisky bottles behind the bar gleamed with reflected light. They were like women. Bait. They lured you in where you forget what you were doing then sprung the trap and kicked you out.

The bartender filled my glass again, scooping up the rest of my change. I watched myself in the back mirror, wondering if I was as ugly to others as I was to myself. I grinned and the bartender scowled my way. I scowled and the bartender started grinning because my scowl isn't as pretty as most. I swirled the drink around in my glass, slopping it over the top so I could make patterns on the bar.

I made rings, ovals, faces, then overlaid the whole picture with a bridge that towered high at both ends. I stared at the hump in the middle and drained the glass in a hurry to get my mind off it.

A lot of it had fallen into place, piece by piece. Things I didn't see before were suddenly clear. It was a gigantic puzzle that only started here in Manhattan . . . the rest of it reached down to Washington, across to San Francisco, then on across the ocean. And onward still until it encompassed the world and came back to where it started.

It was a picture of hate, terror and death that had no equal in history and it was here with us now. I was the only one who could see it. There were still parts of the puzzle missing, but it had a broad, recognizable outline now. I could make up parts that would fit, but that wouldn't do. *I had to know. I had to be sure!*

This time I wasn't dealing in murder, I was dealing in war!

It was a curious puzzle that had two solutions. Every part could fit in different places, fooling you into thinking you had it. They were clever, I thought. They were clever, crafty, cunning, anything you wanted to call it.

They had a slogan that the end justified the means.

They would kill to accomplish a purpose.

They would wreck everything to gain their ends, even if they had to build again on the wreckage.

They were here and they were smart as hell. Even the Nazis were like schoolchildren as compared to them.

But that was the catch. They were smart . . . for them! I could laugh now and think rings around them all because I was smarter than the best they could offer. Torture, Death, and Lies were their brothers, but I had dealt with those triplets many times myself. They weren't strangers to me. I gave them my orders and they took them because they had to.

I was a ruthless bastard with a twisted mind who could look on death and find it pleasant. I could break an arm or smash in a face because it was easier that way than asking quesitons. I could out-fox the fox with a line of reasoning that laughed at the truth because I was the worst of the lot and never did deserve to live. That's what that damned judge thought anyway.

This time I got back in the car and drove over to the building that had the radio antenna projecting up from the roof. There were two police cars parked in front of it and I nodded to the drivers. For once I was glad to have been seen around so much with Pat. I went in and leaned on the railing that separated the room and waited until the cop in the faded alpaca coat and the eyeshade came over to me.

He nodded too.

I said, "Hello, George. I need a favor done."

"Sure, Mike. That is, if I can do it."

"You keep a record of incoming calls, don't you?"

"Yeah, why?"

"Look one up for me. A few days ago a New York prowl car crossed the George Washington bridge." I gave him the date and the approximate time. "See if it was on a call."

He went back to a stall where he rummaged around in a filing cabinet. When he returned he carried a sheet, reading from it. He looked up and raised his eyeshade farther on his forehead. "Here it is. Unidentified girl called and asked to have a police car meet her. I think I remember this one. She was in a hurry and instead of giving her address she said on the walk of the bridge. A car was dispatched to see what went on and called in that it was a wild-goose chase."

"That's all?"

"Yeah. Anything to it?"

"I don't know yet. Thanks a lot, George."

"Sure, Mike, any time. So long."

I went out and sat in the car with a cigarette drooping from my lips. Unidentified girl. That car on the bridge wasn't there by chance. I had just missed things. Too bad, too damn bad in one way that the boys in the car had gotten there late. The weather, no doubt. Then again it was lucky they didn't make it.

The engine came to life under my feet and I drove away from the curb. I took the notebook from my pocket and thumbed the pages while I was stalled in traffic, picking up Paula Riis's address from the jumble of notes. I hoped I had it right, because I had jotted it down after coming from Pat's the time he had thrown her identity at me.

It was a number in the upper Forties just off Eighth Avenue, a four-story affair with three apartments above a shoddy beauty parlor that took up the first floor. A sedan with United States Post Office Department inscribed in the door was double parked outside it. I found a place to leave my heap and got back just as two men came down the stairs and got into the car. I had seen the taller guy before; he was a postal inspector.

A dark, swarthy woman stood in the door with her hands on chunky hips muttering to herself. I took the steps two at a time and said hello to her.

She looked me up and down first. "Now what you want? You not from Post Office."

I looked past her shoulder into the vestibule and knew why those men had been here. A good-sized rectangle had been torn out of the wall. The mailbox that had been there had been ripped out by the roots and the marks of the crowbar that did it still showed in the shattered lath and plaster.

I got that cold feeling again, of being just a little bit too late. I palmed my buzzer and held it out where she could see it.

"Oh, you the police. You come about the room. Whassa matter with other police? He see everything. These crooks! When that girl comes back she be one mad cookie, you bet!"

"That's right, I came about the room. Where is it?"

"Upstairs, what's left of it. Now there's nothing but junk. Thassall, just junk. Go look."

I went and looked. I saw the same thing that had happened to Charlie Moffit's room. This was a little worse because there was more to it. I cursed softly and backed out of the room. I cursed because I was pleased that the room *was* like Charlie Moffit's room, a room ripped apart by a search that didn't have an end. They were still looking. They tore the room up then stole the mailbox because they thought that Charlie had mailed his girl friend the stuff.

Then I stopped cursing because I knew then that they did have it after all. Charlie mailed the stuff and it lay in the mailbox because she was dead. They couldn't get it out so they took the whole works. This time I cursed because I was mad, mad as hell.

I made a circuit of the room, kicking at the pieces with a frenzied futility. Clothes that had been ripped apart at the seams were everywhere. The furniture was broken, disemboweled and scattered across the floor. The bottom had been taken out of the phone and lay beneath the stand by the window. I picked it up, turned it over then chucked it away.

They had come in through the window and gouged hunks out of the sill when they pried up the sash. I threw it up and looked around, saying damn to myself because it had been so easy. There was an overturned ashcan on the ground below. They had stepped on that, then on to the roof of the extension below and right into the room.

Too bad Mr. MVD couldn't have tripped over the phone line and broken his lousy neck. I picked up the strand of wire that ran out the window to the pole and switched it out of the way. It was slack, too damn slack. I saw why in a minute. The insulator that had held it to the wall had been pulled out. I climbed out on the roof and ran my hand along the wire and the answer was in the slit that was in the insulation.

Somebody had a tap on that wire and when they pulled it off they yanked too hard and it came right off the wall. Damn! Damn it all to hell and back again! I climbed back in the room and slammed the window shut, still swearing to myself.

The woman still stood in the doorway. "You see, you see?" Her voice went higher on each word. "These damn crooks. Nobody is safe. What for are the police? What that girl going to say, eh? You know! She give me hell, you betcha. She was all paid up, too. Now whatcha think?"

"Don't get excited. Whoever searched her room took the mailbox too. They were looking for a letter."

She made a sour mouth. "Huh. They don't get it, I tell you that, for sure. She's a lose her key a month ago and I always get her mail personal. The postman he's give it to me every day and I take it inside."

My heart hammered against my ribs and I heard it send the blood driving into my head. I licked my lips to get the words out. "Maybe I better take it all along then. She can call for it when she returns."

She squinted, then bobbed her head. "That is good. I don't have to worry no more about it. From now on till I get a new mailbox I have to take everybody's mail anyhow. Come inside, I give it to you."

We went into the beauty parlor on the first floor and I waited with my hat in my hand. She came back with a handful of envelopes and one of them was a heavy job stuffed so full the flap had torn a little. I thanked her and left.

Just like that.

How simple could it get?

The murder and the wreckage that had been caused by this one fat envelope, and she drops it in my hand just like that. No trouble. No sneaking around with a gun in your hand. No tight spots that left you shaken and trembling. She hands it to me and I take it and leave.

Isn't that the way life is? You fight and struggle to get something and suddenly you're there at the end and there's nothing left to fight for any longer.

I threw the works in the glove compartment and drove back to my office. From force of habit I locked the door before I sat down to see what it was all about. There were nine letters and the big one. Of the nine three were bills, four were from female friends and had nothing to say, one was an answer to a letter she sent an employment agency and the other enclosed a Communist Party pamphlet. I threw it in the wastebasket and opened the main one.

They were photostats, ten in all, both negatives and positives, on extra thin paper. They were photos of a maze of symbols, diagrams and meaningless words, but there was something about them that practically cried out their extreme importance. They weren't for a mind like mine and I knew it.

I folded them up into a compact square and took them to the lamp on the wall. It was a tricky little job that came apart in the middle and had been given to me by a friend who dabbled in magic. At one time a bird flew out of the hidden compartment when you snapped the light on and scared the hell out of you. I stuck the photostats in there and shut it again.

There was an inch of sherry left on the bottom of the bottle in my desk and I put the mouth to my lips.

It was almost over. I had come to the pause before the end. There was little left to do but sort the parts and make sure I had them straight. I sat down again, pulling the phone over in front of me. I dialed headquarters and asked for Pat.

He had left for the weekend.

The next time I dialed Lee Deamer's office. The blonde at the switchboard was still chewing gum and threw the connection over to his secretary. She said, "I'm sorry, but Mr. Deamer has left for Washington."

"This is Mike Hammer. I was there once before. I'd like to get a call in to him."

"Oh, yes, Mr. Hammer. He's registered at the Lafayette. You can call him there. However, you had better call before six because he's speaking at a dinner meeting tonight."

"I'll call him now, and thanks."

I got long distance, gave the number and she told me the lines were all busy and I would have to wait. I hung up and went to the filing cabinet where I had the remains of another bottle of sherry stashed away. There was a box of paper cups with it and I put the makings on my desk and settled back to enjoy the wait.

After the third half-cup of sherry I snapped the radio on and caught the broadcast. The boy with the golden voice was snapping out the patter in a tone so excited that he must have been holding on to the mike to stay on his feet. It was all about the stolen documents. Suspicions were many and clues were nil. The FBI had every available man on the case and the police of every community had pledged to help in every way.

He went off and a serious-voiced commentator took his place. He told the nation of the calamity that had befallen it. The secret of our newest, most powerful weapon was now, most likely, in the hands of agents of an unfriendly power. He told of the destruction that could be wrought, hinted at the continuance of the cold war with an aftermath of a hotter one. He spoke and his voice trembled with the rage and fear he tried so hard to control.

Fifteen minutes later another commentator came on with a special bulletin that told of all ports being watched, the roundup of suspected aliens. The thing that caused the roundup was still as big a mystery as ever, but the search had turned up a lot of minor things that never would have been noticed. A government clerk was being held incommunicado. A big shot labor leader had hanged himself. A group of Communists had staged a demonstration in Brooklyn with the usual scream of persecution and had broken some windows. Twenty of them were in the clink.

I sat back and laughed and laughed. The world was in an uproar when the stuff was safe as hell not five feet away from me. The guardians of our government were jumping through hoops because the people demanded to know why the most heavily guarded secret we ever had could be swiped so easily. There were shakeups from the top to bottom and the rats were scurrying for cover, pleading for mercy. Investigations were turning up reds in the damndest spots imaginable and the senators and congressmen who recommended them for the posts were on the hot spots in their bailiwicks. Two had already sent in resignations.

Oh, it was great. Something was getting done that should have been done years ago. The heat was on and the fire was burning a lot of pants. The music I had on the radio was interrupted every five minutes now with special newscasts that said the people were getting control of the situation at last.

Of the people, for the people, by the people. We weren't so soft after all. We got pushed too far once too often and the backs were up and teeth bared.

What were the Commies doing! They must be going around in circles. The thing that would have tipped the balance back to them again had been in their hands and they'd dropped it. Was the MVD out taking care of those who had been negligent? Probably. Very probably. Pork-Pie Hat would have himself a field day. They were the only ones who knew where those documents *weren't*. Our own government knew where they started to go and still thought they were in their hands. I was the only one who knew where they *were*.

Not five feet away. Safe as pie, I thought.

The phone rang and I picked it up. The operator said, "I have your party, sir."

I said thanks, waited for the connection and heard Lee saying, "Hello, hello . . ."

"Mike Hammer, Lee."

"Yes, Mike, how are you?"

"Fine. I hear Washington is in an uproar."

"Quite. You can't imagine what it's like. They tell me the hall is filled to the rafters already, waiting to hear the speeches. I've never seen so many reporters in my life."

"Going to give 'em hell tonight?"

"I'll do my best. I have an important topic to discuss. Was there something special you wanted, Mike?"

"Yeah, sort of. I just wanted to tell you that I found it."

"It?"

"What Oscar left behind. I found it."

His voice held a bitter ring. "I knew it, I knew it! I knew he'd do something like that. Mike . . . is it bad?"

"Oh no. In fact it's pretty good. Yeah, pretty good."

He paused, and when he spoke again he sounded tired. "Remember what I told you, Mike. It's in your hands. Authenticate what you found, and if you believe that it would be better to publish the facts, then make them public."

I laughed lightly. "Not this, Lee. It isn't something you can print in a paper. It isn't anything that you nor Pat nor I expected to find. It doesn't tie you into a damn thing so you can blast 'em tonight and make it good because what I have can push you right up there where you can do a good housecleaning job."

The surprise and pleasure showed in his voice. "That *is* fine news, Mike. When can I see it?"

"When will you be back in New York?"

"Not before Monday night."

"It'll keep. I'll see you then."

I pushed the phone back across the desk and started working on the remainder of the sherry. I finished it in a half-hour and closed up the office. It was Saturday night and time to play. I had to wait until Velda came back before I made my decision. I ambled up Broadway and turned into a bar for a drink. The place was packed and noisy, except when the news bulletin came on. At seven o'clock they turned on the TV and all heads angled to watch it. They were relaying in the pics of the dinner in Washington that was to be followed by the speeches. The screen was blurred, but the sound was loud and clear.

I had a good chance to watch Mr. and Mrs. Average People take in the political situation and I felt good all over again. It was no time to come up with the documents. Not yet. Let the fire stay on full for a while. Let it scorch and purify while it could.

The bartender filled my glass and I leaned forward on my elbows to hear Lee when he spoke.

He gave them a taste of hell. He used names and quotations

and pointed to the big whiskers in the Kremlin as the brother of the devil. He threw the challenge in the faces of the people and they accepted it with cheers and applause that rocked the building.

I shouted the way I felt louder than anybody and had another drink.

At midnight I walked back to my car and drove home slowly, my mind miles away from my body. Twice I patted the .45 under my arm and out of force of habit I kept a constant check on the cars behind me.

I put the car in the garage, told the attendant to service it fully and went out the side door that led to the street. When I looked both ways and was satisfied that I wasn't going to run into another ambush I stepped out to the sidewalk and walked to my building.

Before I went upstairs I checked the little panel of lights behind the desk in the lobby. It was a burglar alarm and one of the lights was connected to the windows and doors in my apartment. They were all blank so I took the stairs up and shoved the key in the lock.

For safety's sake I went through the place and found it as empty as when I left it. Maybe Pork-Pie was afraid of a trap. Maybe he was waiting to get me on the street. He and the others had the best reason in the world to get me now. It wouldn't be too long before they figured out where the documents went to, and that was the moment I was hoping for.

I wanted them, every one of the bastards. I wanted them all to myself so I could show the sons-of-bitches what happened when they tried to play rough with somebody who likes that game himself!

The late news broadcast was on and I listened for further developments. There weren't any. I shoved the .45 under my pillow and rolled into the sack.

chapter ten

I SLEPT ALL DAY Sunday. At six-fifteen P.M. I got up to answer the persistent ringing of my doorbell and a Western Union messenger handed me a telegram. He got a buck for his persistence and I went into the living room where I opened it up.

The telegram was from Velda. It was very brief, saying the mission was accomplished and she was carrying the papers out on the first plane. I folded the yellow sheet and stuck it in the pocket of my coat that was draped on the back of the chair.

I had a combination meal, sent down for the papers and read them in bed. When I finished I slept again and didn't wake up until twelve hours later. The rain was beating against the windows with a hundred tiny fingers and the street was drenched with an overflow too great to be carried off by the sewers at the end of the block.

For a few minutes I stood at the window and looked out into the murk of the morning, not aware of the people that scurried by on the sidewalks below, or of the cars whose tires made swishing sounds on the wet pavement. Across the street, the front of the building there wavered as the water ran down the glass, assuming the shape of a face molded by ghostly hands. The face had eyes like two berries on a bush and they turned their stare on me.

This is it, Judge. Here is your rain of purity. You're a better forecaster than I thought. Now, of all times, it should rain. Cold, clear rain that was washing away the scum and the filth and pulling it into the sewer. It's here and you're waiting for me to step out into it and be washed away, aren't you? I could play it safe and stay where I am, but you know I won't. I'm me, Mike Hammer, and I'll be true to form. I'll go down with the rest of the scum.

Sure, Judge, I'll die. I've been so close to death that this time the scythe can't miss me. I've dodged too often, now I've lost the quick-step timing I had that made me duck in time. You noticed it and Pat noticed it . . . I've changed, and now I notice it myself. I don't care any more.

The hell of it is, Judge . . . your question won't get answered. You'll never know why I was endowed with the ability to think and move fast enough to keep away from the man with the reaper. I kept breaking his hour-glass and dulling his blade and he couldn't do a thing about it.

Your rain of purity has come, and out there in it is the grim specter who is determined that this time he will not miss. He'll raise his vicious scythe and swing at me with all the fury of his madness and I'll go down, but that one wild swing will take along a lot of others before it cuts me in half.

Sorry, Judge, so sorry you'll never know the answer. I was

*curious myself. I wanted to know the answer too. It's been puzzling
me a long, long time.*

I showered and dressed, packing the automatic away in the oiled
leather holster under my arm. When I finished I called long distance
and was connected with the hospital. Again I was lucky and got
the doctor while he was there. I told him my name and that was
enough.

"Miss Brighton is out of danger," he said. "For some reason
she is under police guard."

"Studious young men?"

"Yes."

"How about her father?"

"He visits her daily. His own doctor is prescribing for him."

"I see. My time is up, you know. You can talk if you like."

"For some reason I prefer not to, Mr. Hammer. I still don't
understand, but I still believe that there is more to this than I
can see. Miss Brighton asked me if you had called and I repeated
our conversation. She has taken the same attitude of silence."

"Thanks, doc. It's going to be rough when it starts, but thanks.
Tell Miss Brighton I was asking for her."

"I will. Good day."

I put the phone back and shrugged into my raincoat. Downstairs
I got my car out of the garage and backed out into the rain. The
windshield wipers were little demons working furiously, fighting
to keep me from being purified. I drove downtown hoping to see
Pat, but he had called in that his car was stuck somewhere along
the highway and he might not make it in at all.

The morning went by without my noticing its passing. When
my stomach tightened I went in and had lunch. I bought a paper
and parked the car to read it through. The headlines hadn't changed
much. There were pages devoted to the new aspect of the cold
war; pages given to the coming election, pages that told of the
shake-up in Washington, and of the greater shake-up promised by
the candidates running for election.

Lee had given 'em hell, all right. The editorial quoted excerpts
from his speech and carried a two-column cut of him shaking his
fist at the jackals who were seeking the protection of the same
government they had tried to tear down. There was another
Communist demonstration, only this one was broken up by an
outraged populace and ten of the reds had landed in the hospital.
The rest were sweeping out corridors in the city jail.

The rain let up, but it was only taking a breather before it came
down even harder. I took advantage of the momentary lull to

duck into a drugstore and put in a call to Lee's office. His secretary told me that he wasn't expected in until evening and I thanked her. I bought a fresh pack of Luckies and went back to the car and sat. I watched the rain and timed my thoughts to its intensity.

I took all the parts and let them drop, watching to see how they fit in place. They were all there, now every one. I could go out any time and show that picture around and anybody could tell that it was a big red flag with a star and a hammer and sickle. I could show it to them but I'd have to have the last piece of proof I needed and I'd have that when Velda got back. I went over it time after time until I was satisfied, then I reached for a butt.

There was only one left. I had just bought a pack and there was only one left. My watch was a round little face that laughed at me for thinking the afternoon away and I stared at it, amazed that the night had shifted in around the rain and I hadn't noticed it. I got out and went back to the same drugstore and looked up the number of the terminal.

A sugar-coated voice said that all the planes were on schedule despite the rain and the last one from the Midwest had landed at two o'clock. I smacked my hand against my head for letting time get away from me and called the office. Velda didn't answer so I hung up. I was about to call her apartment when I remembered that she'd probably be plenty tired and curled up in the sack, but she said she'd leave anything she had in the lamp if I wasn't in the office when she got in.

I started the car up and the wipers went back into action. The rain of purity was starting to give up and here I was still warm and dry. For how long?

The lights were on in the office and I practically ran in. I yelled, "Hey, Velda!" the smile I had ready died away because she wasn't there. She *had* been there, though. I smelled the faintest trace of the perfume she used. I went right to the lamp and opened the little compartment. She had laid it right on top of the other stuff for me.

I pulled it out and spread it across my desk, feeling the grin come back slowly as I read the first few lines.

It was done. Finished. I had it all ready to wrap up nice and legal now. I could call Pat and the studious-looking boys with the FBI badges and drop it in their laps. I could sit back in a ringside seat and watch the whole show and laugh at the judge because this time I was free and clear, with my hands clean of somebody's blood. The story would come out and I'd be a hero. The next time I stepped into that court of law and faced the little judge his voice would be quiet and his words more carefully chosen because I was able to prove to the world that I wasn't a bloodthirsty kill-happy bastard with a mind warped by a war of too many dawns and dusks laced by the crisscrossed patterns of bullets. I was a normal guy with normal instincts and maybe a temper that got a little out of hand at times, but was still under control when I wanted it that way.

Hell, Pat should be back now. I'll let him get the credit for it. He won't like it, but he'll have to do it. I reached for the phone.

That's when I saw the little white square of cardboard that had been sitting there in front of me all the time. I picked it up, scowling at the brief typewritten message. CALL LO 3-8099 AT EXACTLY NINE P.M. That was all. The other side was blank.

I didn't get it. Velda was the only one to have been here and she would have left more of an explanation, at least. Besides, we had memo pads for stuff like this. I frowned again and threw it back on the desk. It was ten to eight now. Hell, I wasn't going to wait another hour. I dialed the number and heard the phone ring a dozen times before I hung up.

A nasty taste was in my mouth. My shoulders kept hunching up under my coat as if I were cold. I went to the outer office to see if she had left a note in her desk typewriter and found nothing.

It wasn't right. Not at a moment like this. Nothing else could come up now. Hell, I was on my way to being a hero. The door of the washroom was standing open a little and I went to close it. The light from the lamp on the wall darted in the crack and bounced back at me with bright sparkle. I shoved the door open and every muscle in my body pulled tight as a bowstring and my breath caught in my throat.

There beside the faucet was Velda's ring . . . the sapphire ring I had given her and her wrist watch!

Velda wasn't here but her ring was and no girl is going to go off and forget her ring! No girl will wash her hands and not dry them, either . . . But Velda apparently had, for there was no crumpled paper towel in the basket under the sink!

Somehow I staggered back to my chair and sat down, the awful realization of it hitting me hard. I buried my face in my hands and said, "Oh, God . . . oh, God!" I knew what had happened now . . . *they* had her! They walked in on her and took her away.

I thought I was clever. I thought they'd try for me. But they *were* clever when the chips were down and now they had something they could trade. That's what they'd say . . . trade. Ha, that was a laugh. They'd take the documents and when I asked them to give her back I'd get a belly full of slugs. Nice trade. A stupid ass like me ought to get shot anyway.

Goddamn 'em anyway! Why couldn't they act like men and fight with me! Why did they have to pick on women! The dirty yellow bastards were afraid to tangle with me so they decided to do it the easy way. They knew the score, they knew I'd have to play ball. They seemed to know a lot of things.

All right, you conniving little punks, I'll play ball, but I'm going to make up a lot of rules you never heard of. You think I'm cornered and it'll be a soft touch. Well, you won't be playing with a guy who's a hero. You'll be up against a guy with a mind gone rotten and a lust for killing! That's the way I was and that's the way I like it!

I grabbed the phone and dialed Pat's home number. When I got him I said hello and didn't give him a chance to interrupt me. "I need a favor as fast as you can do it, kid. Find out where the phone with the number Longacre 3-8099 is located and call me right back. Shake it because I need it right away."

Pat let out a startled answer that I cut off by slamming the phone back. Five minutes later the phone rang and I picked it up.

"What goes on with you, Mike? That number is a pay station in the Times Square subway station."

"Fine," I answered, "that's all I need to know. See you later."

"Mike . . . hey . . ." I cut him off again and picked up my coat.

They thought they were smart but they forgot I had a fast brain and a lot of connections. Maybe they thought I wouldn't take the chance.

I was downstairs and in the car like a shot. Going up Broadway I pulled out all the stops and forgot there was such a thing as a red light. When I turned off Broadway onto Times Square I saw a patrolman standing in front of the subway entrance idly swinging his stick in his hands.

Tonight was my night and I was going to play it all the way to the hilt. I yanked out the wallet I had taken from that overturned car the other night, plucked the FBI card from the pocket and fitted it into mine. The cop was coming out into the rain to tell me I couldn't park there when I stepped out and shoved the wallet under his nose.

I didn't let him have more than a peek at it, but it was enough.

I said, "Stay here and watch that car. I don't want it gone when I come back."

He drew himself all the way up with a look that only public servants old in the service can get and passed me a snappy salute. With the headlines blaring from all the papers he didn't have to ask questions to know what was up. "I'll take care of it," he shot back.

I ran down the stairs and slipped a dime in the turnstile. I had fifteen minutes to find the right booth, fifteen short minutes. I made a tour of the place poking my head into the empties hoping the one I was looking for wouldn't be occupied.

It wasn't. I found it over near the steps that led to the BMT line, the last one on the end of five booths. I stepped into one and shut the door. The light above my head was too damn bright, but one crack with the nose of the .45 took care of that. I lifted the receiver off the hook without dropping a nickel in and started conversation with an imaginary person on an imaginary phone.

At five minutes to nine he walked up to the end booth, obviously ignoring the others, and closed the door. I let the minutes tick off until the hands of my watch were at right angles to each other, then shoved a nickel in the slot and dialed LO 3-8099.

It rang just once. "Yes?"

I forced a bluff into my voice, keeping it low. "This is Mike Hammer. Who the hell are you and what's this business with the card?"

"Ah, yes, Mr. Hammer. You got our card. That is very fortunate indeed. Need I tell you who is speaking?"

"You damn well better, friend."

"No, certainly not a friend. Just the opposite, I would think. I'm calling about a matter of documents you have, Mr. Hammer. They're very important documents, you know. We have taken a hostage to insure their safe delivery to us."

"What . . ."

"Please, Mr. Hammer. I'm speaking about your very lovely secretary. A very obstinate woman. I think we can force her to talk if you refuse, you know."

"You bastard!"

"Well?"

My voice changed pitch and stuttered into the mouthpiece. "What can I say? I know when I'm licked. You . . . can have them."

"I was sure you'd see the light, Mr. Hammer. You will take those documents to the Pennsylvania Station on Thirty-fourth

Street and deposit them in one of the pay lockers at the end of the waiting room. You will then take the key and walk about on the streets outside until someone says, 'Wonderful night, friend,' and give that person the key. Keep your hands in plain sight and be absolutely alone. I don't think I have to warn you that you will be under constant observation by certain people who will be armed."

"And the girl . . . Velda?" I asked.

"Provided you do as you are told, and we receive the documents, the girl shall be released, of course."

"Okay. What time do I do all this?"

"Midnight, Mr. Hammer. A fitting hour, don't you think?"

He hung up without waiting for an answer. I grinned and watched him squirm out of the booth, a guy who fitted his voice to perfection. Short, soft and fat, wearing clothes that tried without success to make him look tall, hard and slim.

I grinned again and gave him a good lead, then climbed out of the booth and stayed on his tail. He hesitated at the passages, settled on the route that led up the northwest corner of the block and started up the stairs. My grin like to have split my face open. The famous Hammer luck was riding high, wide and handsome. I could call his shots before he made them and I knew it.

When he reached the street I brushed by him and gave him the elbow for luck. He was so intent upon waving to a cab that he never gave me a tumble. I waited for him to get in then started my car. The cop waved me off with his night stick and I was on my way.

Three hours before the deadline.

How much time was that? Not much, yet plenty when it counted. The cab in front of me weaved around the traffic and I stayed right with it. I could see the back of his head in the rear window and I didn't give a hoot whether or not he turned around.

He didn't. He was so sure that I was on the end of the stick that it never occurred to him that he was being tailed. He was going to get that stick up the tail himself when the time came.

So the judge was right all the while. I could feel the madness in my brain eating its way through my veins, chewing the edges of my nerves raw, leaving me something that resembled a man and that was all. *The judge had been right!* There *had* been too many of those dusks and dawns; there *had* been pleasure in all that killing, an obscene pleasure that froze your face in a grin even when you were charged with fear. Like when I cut down that Jap with his own machete and laughed like hell while I made

slices of his scrawny body, then went on to do the same thing
again because it got to be fun. The little bastards wanted my hide
and I gave them a hard time when they tried to take it. Sure,
my mind was going rotten even then. I remember the ways the
guys used to look at me. You'd think I had fangs. *And it hung
on and rotted even further!* How long had it been since I had
taken my face out of the ground? How long had it been since
they handed me the paper that said it was over and we could go
back to being normal people again? And since . . . how many
had died while I backed up the gun? Now who was I trying to
fool—me? I enjoyed that killing, every bit of it. I killed because
I had to and I killed things that needed killing. But that wasn't
the point. *I enjoyed killing those things and I knew the judge was
right!* I was rotten right through and I knew that at that moment
my face was twisted out of shape into a grin that was half sneer
and my heart beat fast because it was nice sitting back there with
a rod under my arm and somebody was going to hurt pretty quick
now, then die. And it might even be me and I didn't give a good
damn one way or another.

I tried to figure out where the hell we were. We had passed
over a viaduct and a few other things that were vague outlines,
but I couldn't tell where we were. If I didn't see the name on
the movie house I would have been screwed up, but I caught it
in time along with the smell of the river and knew we were some
place in Astoria heading down toward the water where the people
gave way to the rats and the trash that littered the shore.

There wasn't much more to the block. I cut my lights and
drifted in to the curb, snatching the keys out of the ignition as I
opened the door. Ahead of me the tail light of the cab was a red
dot getting smaller and for one second I thought I had been too
soon.

The red dot stopped moving away from me.

Of all the fates who were out for my skin, only one backed me
up. It was a lovely fate that turned over a heap and spilled the
pair of studious-looking boys out, the ones who had the FBI cards
and that gorgeous black tommy gun that was still in the trunk
of my car. I held the lid open and yanked it out, shucking the
case on the pavement. It nestled in my hands like a woman,
loaded and cocked, with two spare clips that made a pleasant
weight in my pocket.

I got in close to the buildings and took off at a half-trot. A
drunk watched me go by, then scurried back into his doorway.

The dot up front disappeared, turned into two headlights on dim and came back and past me.

I ran faster. I ran like a guy with three feet and reached the corner in time to see the guy angling up the rutted street that paralleled the river.

How nice it is when it gets dark. It's all around you, a black coat that hides the good and the bad, and lets you stay shouting distance behind somebody else and never gives you away. My little man stepped right along as if he knew where he was going.

There weren't any houses now. There was a smell of decay, noises that didn't belong to a city. Far away the lights of cars snaked along a bridge happily unaware of this other part of New York.

Then the rain began again. The glorious rain of purity was nothing but light tears . . . the sky protesting because I was walking and thinking when I should be dead. Long dead. I spit on the ground to show what I thought of it.

My little man was gone. The constant, even grinding of his shoes in the gravel had stopped and now there was a silence that shut out all other noises, even the rain.

I was alone in the darkness and my time had come. It had to come, there was only an hour left and never time to undo it if it had all been a mistake! For about ten seconds I stood still, watching those cars in the distance. They wormed ahead, they disappeared as if going into a tunnel, emerging again many seconds later. I knew where my little man was now.

Not far off was a building. That was what stopped those lights. There was a building and I saw it when I took a dozen more steps. It was the remains of a building, anyway. Three floors staggered up from the ground in uneven rows of bricks. Only the windows on the top floors showed a few panes whole and unbroken, most likely because they were beyond stone's throw. The rest were plastered with boards that seemed to be there to keep things in rather than out.

I was back in the jungle again. I had that feeling. There was a guy at my shoulder in deeper black than the night and he carried a scythe and a map to point out the long road. I didn't walk, I stalked and the guy stalked with me, waiting patiently for that one fatal misstep.

He was death and I knew him well. I had seen him plenty of times before and I laughed in his face because I was me, see? I was Mike Hammer and I could laugh because what did I give a damn about death? He could laugh back at me with his grisly, bony laugh, and even if we didn't make any sound at all my laugh was louder than his. Stick with me, man in black. Stick close because some customers are going to be made that should have been made a long time ago. You thought I was bad when there was a jungle around me for cover and I learned how to kill and kill and kill and walk away and remind myself that killing was nice. Yeah, you thought I was a wise guy. Stick around, old man, maybe you'll see me for the first time doing something I really enjoy. Maybe some day I'll pick on you and we'll have it out, a hot .45 against that blade of yours.

All the instincts came back. The chatter gun was slung just right for easy carrying and quick action. Without me telling it to, my hand had scooped up gobs of mud and daubed my face and hands, even blanking out the luminous dial of my watch.

The pleasure of the hunt, the wonderful knowledge that you're hot and right! The timing was there, that sense of alertness that gets bred into you when there's blood in the air. I liked it!

I stood in the shadow of the building, melting into the wall with the rain, watching the two men. One was there at the doorway, an invisible figure I sensed rather than saw. The other was coming toward me just as I planned it. It had taken a long while just to get this far. I knew without looking that the hands of my watch would be overlapping. Somewhere back in Manhattan a guy would be looking for me to call me friend. Somewhere inside Velda would be sitting, a hostage who would never talk.

The guy came nearer and I knew he had a gun in his hand. I let him come.

Now I could see him plainly. He stopped three feet away and looked back uncertainly. I had the tommy gun in one hand and the nose of the .45 in the other. I let him look back again and this time I let him see me.

No, it wasn't me he saw, it was the other guy, the one with the cowl and the scythe. I swung that gun butt so hard it made a wet smack and almost twisted out of my hand. The guy didn't have any forehead left. There was nothing but a black hole from his eyes to his hair and I was grinning. I eased him down without a sound and picked up the tommy gun. Then I started around the building.

It goes that way. One guy makes one lousy error and everybody falls into the trap. The guy at the door thought it was the other one when I walked out of the murk. He grunted the last sound he ever made because I wrapped my arm under his neck and started bending him over backwards. I had my knee in his spine, pulling him into a living bow that clawed at my hands to release the scream that sudden fear had driven into his throat.

The goddamn grin wouldn't come off my face even when I heard his spine snap and felt that sickening lurch that comes when the bow is bent too far. Two of them. A pair of bastards who had wanted to play in the Big Game. Slimy, squirmy worms who had visions of being on top where they could rule with the whip.

I went into the building with death at my shoulder and he was made because I was giving the orders. He was waiting for the mistake he knew I'd have to make sooner or later.

My breath wasn't coming easy now. It was hot and coarse in my throat, rasping into my lungs. I stood inside the door, listening, waiting, letting my eyes use precious seconds to orient themselves to this new gloom. My watch made a mad ticking to remind me that now it had to be quick. Time, it had gone. There was nothing left!

I saw the empty packing boxes that had been smashed and left to rot. I saw the welter of machinery, glazed with rust, lying in heaps under the high, vaulted roof. Long ago it had been a factory of some sort. I wondered incongruously what had been made here. Then the smell of turpentine gave it to me. Paint. There was three hundred feet of length to it, almost that in width. I could make out the partitions of wood and brick separating it into compartments.

But I didn't have time to look through it all, not all three floors of it!

The sons-of-bitches had picked the best spot on earth, not a sound would penetrate these walls! In that maze of partitions and cubicles even the brightest beam of light that could escape would be dulled and unseen. I wanted to pull the trigger of the gun and blast the whole dump to bits and wade into the wreckage with my bare hands. I wanted to scream just like the guys outside wanted to scream and I couldn't.

Another minute to make myself cool off. Another minute to let instinct and training take over.

Another minute for my eyes to see and they picked out the path that led through the rubbish, a path I should have seen sooner because it had been deliberately made and often used. Old paint cans had been pushed aside and spilled their thick, gooey mess on the floor. The larger drums had been slop pails for left-over stuff and marked the turns in the trail.

My eyes saw it, my feet followed it. They took me around the bend and through a hall then up the stairs.

And the path that was cleared through the dirt on the floor led to the middle, then the top story. It led to rooms that reeked of turpentine so strong it almost took my breath away. It led to a corridor and another man who stepped out of the shadows to die. It led to a door that swung open easily and into a room that faced on other rooms where I was able to stand in my invisible cloak of blackness with barely the strength to hold the gun.

I stood there and looked at what I was, hearing myself say, "Good God, no, please . . . no!" I had to stand there for a moment of time that turned into eternity while I was helpless to intervene and see things my mind wanted to shut out . . . hear things my ears didn't want to hear.

For an eternal moment I had to look at them all, everyone. General Osilov in a business suit leaning on his cane almost casually, an unholy leer lighting his face. My boy of the subway slobbering all over his chin, puking a little without noticing it, his hands pressed against his belly while his face was a study in obscene fascination.

And the guy in the pork-pie hat!

Velda.

She was stark naked.

She hung from the rafters overhead by a rope that chewed into her wrists, while her body twisted slowly in the single light of the electric lantern! The guy in the pork-pie hat waited until she turned to face him then brought the knotted rope around with all the strength of his arm and I heard it bite into her flesh with a sickening sound that brought her head up long enough for me to see that even the pain was dulling under the evil of this thing.

He said, "Where is it? You'll die if you don't tell me!"

She never opened her mouth. Her eyes came open, but she never opened her mouth!

Then there was only beauty to the nakedness of her body. A beauty of the flesh that was more than the sensuous curve of her hips, more than the sharp curve of breasts drawn high under the weight of her body, more than those long, full legs, more than the ebony of her hair. There was the beauty of the flesh that was the beauty of the soul and the guy in the pork-pie hat grimaced with hate and raised the rope to smash it down while the rest slobbered with the lust and pleasure of this example of what was yet to come, even drooled with the passion that was death made slow in the fulfillment of the philosophy that lived under a red flag!

And in that moment of eternity I heard the problem asked and knew the answer! I knew why I was allowed to live while others died! I knew why my rottenness was tolerated and kept alive and why the guy with the reaper couldn't catch me and I smashed through the door of the room with the tommy gun in my hands spitting out the answer at the same time my voice screamed it to the heavens!

I lived only to kill the scum and the lice that wanted to kill themselves. I lived to kill so that others could live. I lived to kill because my soul was a hardened thing that reveled in the thought of taking the blood of the bastards who made murder their business. I lived because I could laugh it off and others couldn't. I was the evil that opposed other evil, leaving the good and the meek in the middle to live and inherit the earth!

They heard my scream and the awful roar of the gun and the slugs tearing into bone and guts and it was the last they heard. They went down as they tried to run and felt their insides tear out and spray against the walls.

I saw the general's head splinter into shiny wet fragments and splatter over the floor. The guy from the subway tried to stop the bullets with his hands and dissolved into a nightmare of blue holes.

There was only the guy in the pork-pie hat who made a crazy try for a gun in his pocket. I aimed the tommy gun for the first time and took his arm off at the shoulder. It dropped on the floor next to him and I let him have a good look at it. He couldn't believe it happened. I proved it by shooting him in the belly. They were all so damned clever!

They were all so damned dead!

I laughed and laughed while I put the second clip in the gun. I knew the music in my head was going wild this time, but I was laughing too hard to enjoy it. I went around the room and kicked them over on their backs and if they had faces left I made sure they didn't. I saved the last burst for the bastard who was MVD in a pork-pie hat and who looked like a kid. A college boy. He was still alive when he stared into the flame that spit out of the muzzle only an inch away from his nose.

I cut her down carefully, dressed her, cradled her in my arms like a baby and knew that I was crying. Me. I could still do that. I felt her fingers come up and touch one of the wet spots on my cheek, heard her say the three words that blessed everything I did, then I went back to the path that led out into the night that was still cold and rainy, but still free to be enjoyed. There was a soft spot on the ground where I laid her with my coat under her head while I went back to do what I had to do. I went back to the room where death had visited and walked under the rafters until I reached the pork-pie hat that lay next to the remains of the thing that wore it. I lifted his wallet out of his back pocket and flipped his coat open so I could rip the inside lining pocket out along with some shreds of the coat fabric. That was all. Except for one thing. When I went down the stairs once more I found a drum of paint whose spilled contents made a sticky flow into some empty cans. When I built up a mound of old papers around the stuff I touched a match to it, stood there until I was satisfied with its flame, then went back to Velda. Her eyes were closed and her breathing heavy. She came up in my arms and I fixed my coat around her.

I carried her that way to my car and drove her home, and stayed while a doctor hovered above her. I prayed. It was answered when the doctor came out of the room and smiled. I said another prayer of thankfulness and did the things that had to be done to make her comfortable. When the nurse came to sit by her side I picked up my hat and went downstairs.

The rain came down steadily. It was clear and pure. It swept by the curb carrying the filth into the sewer.

We know now, don't we, Judge? We know the answer.

There were only a few hours left of the night. I drove to the office and opened the lamp. I took out the two envelopes in there and spread them out on my desk. The beginning and the end. The complexities and the simplicities. It was all so clever and so rotten.

And to think that they might have gotten away with it!

It was over and done with now. Miles away an abandoned paint factory would be a purgatory of flame and explosions that would leave only the faintest trace of what had been there. It was a hell that wiped away all sins leaving only the good and the pure. The faintest trace that it left would be looked into and expounded upon. There would be nothing left but wonder and the two big words, WHY and HOW. There were no cars at the scene. They wouldn't have been foolish enough to get there that way. The flames would char and blacken. They would leave remains that would take months to straighten out, and in that straightening they would come across melted leaden slugs and a twisted gun that was the property of the investigating bureau in Washington. There would be cover-up and more wonder and more speculation, then, eventually, someone would stumble on part of the truth. Yet even then, it was a truth only half-known and too big to be told.

Only I knew the whole thing and it was too big for me. I was going to tell it to the only person who would understand what it meant.

I picked up the phone.

chapter eleven ▰▰▰▰▰▰▰▰▰▰▰▰▰▰▰

THE SIXTH TIME it rang I heard it come off the cradle. A sharp click was the light coming on then Lee Deamer's voice gave me a sleepy hello.

I said, "This is Mike Hammer, Lee." My voice had a tired drag too. "Hate to call you at this hour, but I have to speak to you."

"Well, that's all right, Mike. I was expecting you to call. My secretary told me you had called earlier."

"Can you get dressed?"

"Yes. Are you coming over here?"

"I'd rather not, Lee. I don't want to be cooped up right now. I need the smell of air. A hell of a lot has happened. It isn't anything I can broadcast and I can't keep it to myself. You're the only one I can talk to. I want to show you where it started and how it happened. I want you to see the works. I have something very special to show you."

"What Oscar left behind?"

"No, what somebody else did. Lee, you know those government documents that were copied?"

"Mike! It can't be!"

"It is."

"This is . . . why, it's. . . ."

"I know what you mean. I'll pick you up in a few minutes. Hurry up."

"I'll be ready by the time you get here. Really, Mike, I don't know what to say."

"Neither do I, that's why I want you to tell me what to do. I'll be right over."

I put the phone back slowly, then gathered the envelopes into a neat pack and stuck them in my pocket. I went downstairs and stood on the sidewalk with my face turned toward the sky.

It was still raining.

It was a night just like that first one.

The rain had a hint of snow in it.

Before I reached Lee's house I made a stop. The place was a rooming house that had a NO VACANCY sign in front and a row of rooms with private entrances. I went in and knocked on the second door. I knocked again and a bed squeaked. I knocked the third time and a muffled voice swore and fcct shuffled across the floor.

The door went open an inch and I saw one eye and part of a crooked nose. "Hello, Archie," I said.

Archie threw the door open and I stepped in. Archie owed me a lot of favors and now I was collecting one. I told him to get dressed and it took him about two minutes to climb into his clothes.

He waited until we were in the car before he opened his yap. "Trouble?" That was all he said.

"Nope. All you're going to do is drive a car. No trouble."

We went over to Lee's place and I rang the bell. They have one of those speaking-tube gadgets there and Lee said he'd be right down. I saw him hurry through the lobby and open the door.

He grinned when we shook hands. I was too tired to grin back. "Is it pretty bad, Mike? You look like you're out on your feet."

"I am. I'm bushed but I can't go to bed with this on my mind. My car is out front."

The two of us went down the walk and I opened the door for him. We got in the back together and I told Archie to head for the bridge. Lee sat back and let his eyes ask me if we could talk with Archie in the car. I shook my head no so we just sat there watching the rain streak across the windows.

At the entrance to the bridge I passed Archie a half a buck and he handed it to the cop on duty at the toll booth. We started up the incline when I tapped him on the shoulder.

"Stop here, Archie. We're going to walk the rest of the way. Go on over to Jersey and stop up some beer. Come back in a half-hour. We'll be at the top of the hump on the other side waiting for you." I dropped a fin on the seat beside him to pay for the beer and climbed out with Lee behind me.

It was colder now and the rain was giving birth to a snowflake here and there. The steel girders of the bridge towered into the sky and were lost, giant man-made trees that glistened at the top as the ice started to form.

Our feet made slow clicking sounds against the concrete of the walk and the boats on the river below called back to them. I could see the red and green eyes staring at me. They weren't faces this time.

"This is where it started, Lee," I said.

He glanced at me and his face was puzzled.

"No, I don't expect you to understand, because you don't know about it." We had our hands stuffed in our pockets against the cold, and our collars turned up to keep out the wet. The hump was ahead of us, rising high into the night.

"Right up there is where it happened. I thought I'd be alone that night, but there were two other people. One was a girl. The other was a little fat guy with a stainless-steel tooth. They both died."

I took the fat envelope out of my pocket and shook out the pages inside. "It's amazing, isn't it? Here the best minds in the country are looking for this and I fell right into it. It's the detailed plans of the greatest weapon ever made and I have it right here in my hand."

Lee's mouth fell open. He recovered and reached for it. "How, Mike? How could this come to you?"

There wasn't any doubting its authenticity. He shook his head, completely bewildered, and gave it back to me. "That's the story, Lee. That's what I wanted to tell you, but first I want to make sure this country has a secret that's safe."

I took my lighter out and spun the little wheel. There was a spark, then a blue flame that wavered in the wind. I touched it to the papers and watched them smolder and suddenly flame up. The yellow light reflected from our faces, dying down to a soft red glow. When there was nothing left but a corner that still held the remnants of the symbols and numbers, I flicked the papers over the edge and watched them go to the wind. That one corner I put in my pocket.

"If it had happened to anyone else, I wonder what the answer would have been?"

I shook my head and reached for a Lucky. "Nobody will ever know that, Lee." We reached the top of the hump and I stopped.

The winter was with us again. The girders were tall white fingers that grew from the floor of the bridge, scratching the sky open. Through the rift the snow drifted down and made wet patches on the ground.

I leaned on the handrail, looking out over the river. "It was the same kind of night: it was cold and wet and all alone. A girl came running up that ramp with a guy behind her who had a gun in his pocket. I shot the guy and the girl jumped over the railing. That's how simple it was. The only things they left behind were two green cards that identified them as members of the Communist Party.

"So I was interested. I was interested in anything that toted around a green card. That's how I got interested in Oscar. The guy he killed had a green card too. Hell, you know the rest of the story. There's a few things only I know and that's the main thing. I know how many people died tonight. I know what the papers will look like tomorrow and the month after. You know what, Lee, I killed more people tonight than I have fingers on my hands. I shot them in cold blood and enjoyed every minute of it. I pumped slugs in the nastiest bunch of bastards you ever saw and here I am calmer than I've ever been and happy too. They were Commies, Lee. They were red sons-of-bitches who should have died long ago, and part of the gang who are going to be dying in the very near future unless they get smart and take the gas pipe. Pretty soon what's left of Russia and the slime that breeds there won't be worth mentioning and I'm glad because I had a part in the killing.

"God, but it was fun! It was the way I liked it. No arguing, no talking to the stupid peasants. I just walked into that room with a tommy gun and shot their guts out. They never thought that there were people like me in this country. They figured us all to be soft as horse manure and just as stupid."

It was too much for Lee. He held onto the rail and looked sick.

I said, "What's the matter, Oscar?"

His eyes were glazed and he coughed. "You mean . . . Lee."

"No I don't. I mean Oscar. Lee's dead."

It was all there, the night, the cold and the fear. The unholy fear. He was looking at my face and he had the same look of unholy fear as the girl had that other night so long ago.

I said it slow. I let him hear every word. "The girl that died here that night was Paula Riis. She was a nurse in an asylum for the insane. I had it wrong . . . she didn't help Oscar to escape . . . she just quit and Oscar escaped later by himself. Paula came to New York and got tied up with a lot of crappy propaganda the Commies handed out and went overboard for it. She thought it was great. She worked like hell and wound up in a good spot.

"Then it happened. Somehow she saw the records or was introduced to the big boy in this country. She knew it was you.

What happened, did she approach you thinking you were Oscar's brother? *Whatever happened she recognized you as Oscar and all her illusions were shattered. She knew you were Oscar Deamer and demented as hell!*

"That's why you were a Commie, Oscar, because you were batty. It was the only philosophy that would appeal to your crazy mind. It justified everything you did and you saw a chance of getting back at the world. You escaped from that sanitarium, took Lee's private papers and made yourself a name in the world while Lee was off in the woods where he never saw a paper of any kind and never knew what you did. You must have had an expert dummy the fingerprints on that medical record . . . but then, you had access to that kind of expert, didn't you?

"It was rough when Paula recognized you. She lost her ideals and managed to contact Lee. She told him to come East and expose you, but she did something else first. She had a boy friend in the party. His name was Charlie Moffit and she told him the story hoping to drag him out of the Commie net.

"Charlie was the stupid one. He saw a play of his own and made it. He saw how he could line you up for some ready cash and gave you the story over the phone. It was right after the Legion Parade, the 13th, that you had a heart attack according to your secretary . . . not because your brother contacted you because his ticket was dated the 15th, a Friday, and he didn't arrive until the day after. *You had a heart attack when Charlie Moffit called you!*

"You contacted the torpedo that went under the MVD title and you worried about it, but there was no out until Lee arrived himself and gave you a buzz. That was the best touch of all! Then you saw how you could kill Charlie yourself, have the blame shifted to your brother with a reasonable story that would make it look good. You knew you had a way to kill two birds with one stone . . . and get rid of a brother who could have stood in your way. There was only one thing you didn't foresee. Charlie Moffit was a courier in the chain that passed along those documents. During one of his more lucid moments he recognized that they were important and held onto them for life insurance. He mailed them to his girl friend, Paula, to take care of."

He was white. He hung on to the rail and shook. He was scared stiff.

"So you waited until Charlie called again and arranged to meet him. You had it all figured out beforehand and it looked good as gold. You got hold of an old actor and had him impersonate you while you went out and killed Charlie Moffit. The actor was good, too. He knew how to make speeches. You paid him off, but you didn't know then that he liked to drink. He never did before because he had no money. Later you found that he had a loose tongue when he drank and he had to go too. But that was an easy kill and it's getting ahead of the story.

"You killed Charlie, switched with the actor at the dinner meeting, and made yourself a wonderful alibi. It happened after the supper when you were going around speaking to the groups, a time when nobody would be conscious of the switch, espcially since none of them knew you too well anyway.

"I don't know what the play was at your brother's place when Pat and I went after him, but I'll try to set it up. See if I'm right. Mr. MVD went there first and got him running. He got him in the subway and shoved him under the train so his identity would be washed out."

As casually as I could I took Velda's envelope from my pocket and fingered out the sheet inside. He didn't bother to look at it.

I said, "My secretary dug up this story. She went back to your home state and went through the records. She found out that you and your brother were twins, all right, but you weren't identical twins. *You were fraternal twins and he didn't look like you at all!*

"But to get back to the beginning. You knew when Lee called you that there was more to it than you thought. You knew Charlie wasn't smart enough to dig up the stuff by himself, so you and fat boy did some fast snooping and found out about Paula. During that time she saw you or the other guy and got scared. She wanted to talk and called the police, asking them to meet her on the bridge where they could be alone.

"Your MVD pal was a little shrewder. He tapped her phone line and moved in to intercept her, but she moved a little faster and got out of the house before he came around. She had just enough lead to make it to the top of the bridge right where we're standing when he arrived. It was pretty—you should have been here. You should have seen what I did to him. The sour note was Paula. She thought I was one of them looking for a cut of the loot or something, because she couldn't picture any decent person hauling out a rod just like that and blowing a guy's face off. She went over the bridge.

"It would have been so nice for you if I hadn't had a conscience and wanted to find out what the green card meant. You knew my reputation but never thought I could go that far. You hired me so you could keep tabs on me and now look what happened.

"Maybe nothing would have happened if those documents hadn't turned up missing. Those people would have died just to keep your identity a secret. But one of those dead men was a critical link connected with the missing documents, so you cooked up the story of your brother's having left something incriminating behind him, thinking that maybe I'd come across the documents and hand them over to you. Well, Oscar, I did. You had your boys try to run them down first, but they didn't quite make it.

"I got to be a very dangerous guy in your little game. I was all over the picture with my nose picking up a lot of smells. You passed the orders to get me out of the way at any price and damn near succeeded. Too bad your new MVD boy didn't get me instead of Ethel Brighton up in the cabin there. She was dangerous too. She finally got wise to how foolish she had been and talked to the right people. She was even going to turn me in, but your MVD boy stopped that.

"You know, I thought Ethel put the finger on me when she saw my identification in my wallet. But it wasn't Ethel, it was you. You fingered me because I was getting in there. You thought that I had gone too far already and didn't want to take any more chances. So out come the strong-arm boys and the MVD lad.

"He sure was a busy little beaver. He wanted to kill me in the worst way. When you guys discovered that I had those documents you must have gone nuts. Maybe it even occurred to you that in the process of getting them I would have uncovered all the angles to the thing. I did that, little man, I did just that.

"You got real gay at the end, though. You pulled a real smartie when you put the snatch on Velda. For that there was only one answer . . . I wanted to see you die. I saw them die. You should have seen what I saw and you would have died yourself even before a bullet reached you.

"But none of that is bad when you compare it to the big thing. That's you, Mr. Deamer. You, the little man whom the public loves and trusts . . . you who are to lead the people into the ways of justice . . . you who shouted against the diabolic policies of the Communists . . . you are the biggest Communist of them all!

"You know the theory . . . the ends justify the means. So you fought the Commie bastards and on the strength of that you hoped to be elected, and from there the Politburo took over. With you in where it counted you could appoint party members to key positions, right in there where they could wreck this country without a bit of trouble. Brother, that was a scheme. I bet the boys in the Kremlin are proud of you."

I saw the gun snake out of his pocket and I reached over and plucked it out of his fingers. Just like that. He stared after it as it arched out and down into the river.

"Tomorrow," I said, "the boys in the Kremlin are going to be wondering what the hell happened. They'll wonder where their boys are and they'll put up a yell, but there will be fear behind that yell because when they learn what happened they'll have to revise their whole opinion of what kind of people are over here. They'll think it was a tough government that uncovered the thing secretly. They'll think it was one of Uncle's boys who chopped down that whole filthy mob, and they won't complain too much because they can't afford to admit those same boys who were here on diplomatic passes were actually spying. The Kremlin mob will really stand on their heads when they get my final touch. It's a beauty, Mr. Deamer. Do you know what I'm going to do?"

He was staring at my face. His eyes couldn't leave my eyes and his flesh was already dying with the fear inside him. He tried to talk and made only harsh breathing sounds. He raised his hands as if I were something evil and he had to keep me away. I was evil. I was evil for the good. I was evil and he knew it. I was worse than they were, so much worse that they couldn't stand the comparison. I had one, good, efficient, enjoyable way of getting rid of cancerous Commies. I killed them.

I said, "The touch is this, Oscar. You, the greatest Commie louse of them all, will be responsible for the destruction of your own party. You're going to die and the blame will go to the Kremlin. I'm going to stick a wallet and some shreds of cloth in your fist when you're dead. In your other hand will be the remains of those documents, enough to show what they were. Enough to make the coppers think that somehow you alone, in a burst of patriotic effort, managed to get hold of those important papers and destroyed them. It'll make them think that just as you were destroying them the killer came up and you fought it out. You came out second best, but in the struggle you managed to rip out the pocket that held his wallet and the cops will track it down thinking it came from your murderer, and what they find will be this . . . they'll find that it came from a guy who was an MVD man. He'll be dead, but that won't matter. If they manage to tie it in with the bodies in the paint shop they'll think that the killer went back to report without the papers he was sent after and the party, in their usual manner of not tolerating inefficiency, started to liquidate him and they smeared each other in the process. No, the Kremlin won't think that. They'll think it was all a very clever plan, an ingenious jumble that will never be straightened out, which it is. You're going to be a big hero. You saved the day and died in the saving. When the news is made public and the people know their favorite hero has been knocked off by the reds they'll go on a hunt that won't stop until the issue is decided, and brother, when the people in this country finally do get around to moving, they move fast!"

The irony of it brought a scream to his lips. He made a sudden mad lurch and tried to run, but the snow that came down so white and pure tripped him and I only had to reach out to get his throat in my hand.

I turned him around to face me, to let him look at what I was and see how I enjoyed his dying. The man who had thrown a lot of people on the long road to nowhere was a gibbering idiot slobbering at the mouth. I had his neck in my one hand and I leaned on the railing while I did it. I squeezed and squeezed and squeezed until my fingers were buried in the flesh of his throat and his hands clawed at my arm frantically, trying to tear me away.

I laughed a little bit. It was the only sound in the night. I laughed while his tongue swelled up and bulged out with his eyes and his face turned black. I held him until he was down on his knees and dead as he was ever going to be, then I took my hand away and watched while he fell forward into the snow. I had to pry his fingers apart to get the wallet in them. I made sure he had a good hold on the thing then I laughed again.

Maybe Archie would guess, I thought. He could guess all he wanted to, but he couldn't talk. I was holding a murder over his head, too. A justified killing that only he and I knew about. I saw the headlights of my car coming from the other end of the bridge and I walked across the steel walk to be there when Archie drove up.

The snow was coming down harder now. Soon that dark mass over there would be just a mound. And when the sun shone again the thaw would provide the deluge that would sweep everything into the sewer where it belonged.

It was lonely standing there. But I wouldn't be here long now. The car had almost reached the top of the ramp. I saw Archie bent over the wheel and took a last look around.

No, nobody ever walked across the bridge, especially not on a night like this.

Well, hardly nobody.

The Snake

chapter one ▬▬▬▬▬▬▬▬▬▬

YOU WALK DOWN the street at night. It's raining out. The only sound is that of your own feet. There are city sounds too, but these you don't hear because at the end of the street is the woman you've been waiting for for seven long years and each muffled tread of your footsteps takes you closer and closer and the sound of them marks off seconds and days and months of waiting.

Then, suddenly, you're there, outside a dark-faced building, a brownstone anachronism that stares back dully with the defiant expression of the moronic and you have an impending sense of being challenged.

What would it be like, I thought. *Was she still beautiful? Had seven years of hell changed her as it had me? And what did you say to a woman you loved and thought was killed because you pulled a stupid play? How do you go from seven years ago to now?*

Only a little while ago a lot of other feet were pointing this way, searching for this one house on this one street, but now mine were the only ones left to find it because the rest belonged to dead men or those about to die.

The woman inside was important now. Perhaps the most important in the world. What she knew would help destroy an enemy when she told it. My hands in my pockets balled into hard knots to keep from shaking and for a moment the throbbing ache of the welts and cuts that laced my skin stopped.

And I took the first step.

There were five more, then the V code on the doorbell marked *Case,* the automatic clicking of the lock and I was in the vestibule of the building under a dim yellow light from a single overhead bulb and down the shadowed hallway to the rear was the big door. Behind it lay seven years ago.

I tapped out a **Y** on the panel and waited, then tapped a slow **R** and the bolt slid back and the knob turned and there she stood with the gun still ready if something had gone wrong.

Even in that pale light I could see that she was more beautiful than ever, the black shadow of her hair framing a face I had seen every night in the misery of sleep for so long. Those deep brown eyes still had that hungry look when they watched mine and the lush fullness of her mouth glistened with a damp warmth of invitation.

Then, as though there had never been those seven years, I said, "Hello, Velda."

For a long second she just stood there, somehow telling me that it was only the *now* that counted and with that same rich voice that could make music with a simple word, she answered, "Mike . . ."

She came into my arms with a rush and buried her face in my neck, barely able to whisper my name over and over because my arms were so tight around her. Even though I knew I was hurting her I couldn't stop and she didn't ask me to. It was like we were trying to get inside each other and in the frenzy of it found a way when our mouths met in a predatory coupling we had never known before. I tasted the fire and beauty of her, my fingers probing the flesh of her back and arms and shoulders, leaving marks wherever they touched. That familiar resiliency was still in her body, tightening gradually into a passionate tautness that rippled and quivered, crying out soundlessly for more, more, more.

I took the gun from her hand, dropped it in a chair, then pushed the door closed with my foot and felt for the light switch. A lamp on the table seemed to come alive with the unreal slowness of a movie prop, gradually highlighting the classic beauty of her face and the provocative thrust of her breasts.

There was a subtle leanness about her now, like you saw in those fresh from a battle area, every gesture a precision movement, every sense totally alert. And now she was just beginning to realize that it was over and she could be free again.

"Hello, kitten," I said, and watched her smile.

There wasn't much we could say. That would take time, but now we had all the time in the world. She looked at me, talking through those crazy eyes, then her expression went soft and a frown made small creases across her forehead. Her fingers went out and touched my face and the white edge of her teeth went into her lip.

"Mike . . .?"

"It's okay, baby."

"You're not . . . hurt?"

I shook my head. "Not any more."

"There's something about you now . . . I can't quite tell what . . ."

"Seven years, Velda," I interrupted. "It was downhill all the way until I found out you were still alive. It leaves marks, but none that can't be wiped out."

Her eyes blurred under tears that came too quickly to control. "Mike, darling, . . . I couldn't reach you. It was all too impossible and big . . ."

"I know it, kid. You don't have to explain."

Her hair swirled in a dark arc when she shook her head. "But I do."

"Later."

"Now." Her fingers touched my mouth to silence me and I let them. "It took seven years to learn a man's secret and escape Communist Europe with information that will keep us equal or better than they are. I know I could have gotten away earlier . . . but I had to make a choice."

"You made the right one."

"There was no way to tell you."

"I know it."

"Truly . . ."

"I understand, kitten."

She wouldn't listen. Her voice was softly insistent, almost pleading. "I could have, Mike. I know I could have some way, but I couldn't afford the chance. There were millions of lives at stake." She paused a second, then pulled my cheek against hers. "I know how you must have felt, thinking you had me killed. I thought of it so often I nearly went out of my mind, but I still couldn't have changed things."

"Forget it," I told her.

"What did happen to you, Mike?"

She pushed away, holding me at arm's length to study me.

"I got to be a drunk," I said.

"You?"

"Me, kitten."

Her expression was one of curious bewilderment. "But when I told them . . . they had to find you . . . only you could do it . . ."

"One mentioned your name and I changed, honey. When you came alive again, so did I."

"Oh, Mike . . ."

As big as she was, I picked her up easily, kissed her again, and took her across the room to the gaudy mohair couch that nestled in the bay of an airshaft window. She quivered against me, smiled when I laid her down, then pulled my mouth to hers with a desperation that told me of the loneliness of seven years and the gnawing wanting inside her now.

Finally she said, "I'm a virgin, Mike."

"I know."

"I've always waited for you. It's been a pretty long wait."

I grinned down at her. "I was crazy to make you wait."

"And now?"

Then I wasn't grinning any more. She was all mine whenever I wanted her, a big, beautiful animal of a woman who loved me and was ready to be taken *now, now.* Even touching was a painful emotion and the fire that had been dormant was one I didn't want to put out.

I said, "Can you wait a little bit more?"

"Mike?" There was a quick hurt in her eyes, then the question.

"Let's do it right, kitten. Always I do the wrong things. Let's make this one right." Before she could answer I said, "Don't argue. Don't even talk about it. We do it, that's all, then we can explode into a million pieces. We do the bit at City Hall with the license and do it right."

Velda smiled back impishly, the happiness of knowing what I wanted plain in her face. "That really doesn't matter," she told me. "First I want you. Now. More than ever."

"Crazy broad," I said, then fought her mouth with mine, knowing we were both going to win. My hand drifted across the satiny expanse of her naked shoulder, feeling the minute trembling throughout her body. She twisted so she pressed against me, moaning softly, demanding things we never had from each other.

"Pretty," he said from the door. *"Real pretty."*

I still had the .45 in my belt but I never could have made it. Velda's convulsive grip around my neck slowed the action enough so that I saw the Police Positive in his hand and didn't get killed after all. The hammer was back for faster shooting and the look on his face was one I had seen before on other cheap killers, and knew that he'd drop me the second he thought I might be trouble.

"Go on, don't stop," he said. "I like good shows."

I made my grin as simpering as I could, rolling away from Velda until I sat perched on the edge of the couch. I was going wild inside and fought to keep my hands dangling at my sides while I tried to look like an idiot caught in the act until I could think my way past this thing.

"I didn't know there'd be two, but it figures a babe like you'd have something going for her." He nudged the gun toward me. "But why grab off a mutt like this, baby?"

When she spoke from behind me her voice was completely changed. "When I could have had you?"

"That's the way, baby. I've been watching you through that window four days and right now I'm ready. How about that?"

I would have gone for the rod right then, but I felt the pressure of her knee against my back.

"How about that?" Velda repeated.

The guy let out a jerky laugh and looked at me through slitted eyes. "So maybe we'll make music after all, kid. Just as soon as I dump the mutt here."

Then I couldn't keep quiet any longer. "You're going to have to do it the hard way."

The gun shifted just enough so it pointed straight at my head. "That's the way I always do things, mutt."

He was ready. The gun was tight in his hand and the look was there and he was ready. Velda said, "Once that gun goes off you won't have me."

It wasn't enough. The guy laughed again and nodded. "That's okay too, baby. This is what I came for anyway."

"Why?" she asked him.

"Games, baby?" The gun swung gently toward her, then back to me, ready to take either or both of us when he wanted to. I tried to let fear bust through the hate inside me and hoped it showed like that when I slumped a little on the couch. My hand was an inch nearer the .45 now, but still too far away.

"I want the kid, baby, ya know?" he said. "So no games. Trot her out, I take off, and you stay alive."

"Maybe," I said.

His eyes roved over me. "Yeah, maybe," he grinned. "You know something, mutt? You ain't scared enough. You're thinking."

"Why not?"

"Sure, why not? But whatever you think it just ain't there for you, mutt. This ain't your day."

There were only seconds now. He was past being ready and his eyes said it was as good as done and I was dead and he started that final squeeze as Velda and I moved together.

We never would have made it if the door hadn't slammed open into him and knocked his arm up. The shot went into the ceiling and with a startled yell he spun around toward the two guys in the doorway, dropping as he fired, but the smaller guy got him first with two quick shots in the chest and he started to tumble backwards with the blood bubbling in his throat.

I was tangled in the raincoat trying to get at my gun when the bigger one saw me, streaked off a shot that went by my head, and in the light of the blast I knew they weren't cops because I recognized a face of a hood I knew a long time. It was the last shot he ever made. I caught him head on with a .45 that pitched him back through the door. The other one tried to nail me while I was rolling away from Velda and forgot about the guy dying on the floor. The mug let one go from the Police Positive that ripped into the hood's belly and with a choking yell he tumbled out the door, tripped, and hobbled off out of sight, calling to someone that he'd been hit.

I kicked the gun out of the hand of the guy on the floor, stepped over him, and went out in the hall gun first. It was too late. The car was pulling away from the curb and all that was left was the peculiar silence of the street.

He was on his way out when I got back to him, the sag of death on his face. There were things I wanted to ask him, but I never got the chance. Through bloody froth he said, "You'll . . . get yours, mutt."

I didn't want him to die happy. I said, "No chance, punk. This is my day after all."

His mouth opened in a grimace of hate and frustration that was the last living thing he ever did.

From where to where, I thought. *Why are there always dead men around me? I came back, all right. Just like in the old days. Love and death going hand in hand.*

There was something familiar about his face. I turned his head with my toe, looked at him closely and caught it. Velda said, "Do you know him?"

"Yeah. His name is Basil Levitt. He used to be a private dick until he tried a shakedown on somebody who wouldn't take it, then he did time for second-degree murder."

"What about the other one?"

"They call him Kid Hand. He was a free-lance gun that did muscle for small bookies on bettors who didn't want to pay off. He's had a fall before too."

I looked at Velda and saw the way she was breathing and the set expression on her face. There was a strange sort of wildness there you find on animals suddenly having to fight for their lives. I said, "They aren't from the other side, kitten. These are new ones. These want something different." I waited a moment, then: "Who's the kid, honey?"

"Mike . . ."

I pointed to the one on the floor. "He came for a kid. He came here ready to shoot you up. Now who's the kid?"

Again, she gave me an anguished glance. "A girl . . . she's only a young girl."

I snapped my fingers impatiently. "Come on, give me, damn it. You know where you stand! How many people have died because of what you know and right now you haven't got rid of it. You want to get killed after everything that happened, for some stupid reason?"

"All right, Mike." Anguish gave way to concern then and she glanced upward. "Right now she's in an empty room on the top floor. Directly over this one."

"Okay, who is she?"

"I . . . don't know. She came here the day after . . . I was brought here. I heard her crying outside and took her in."

"That wasn't very smart."

"Mike . . . there were times when I wish someone had done that to me."

"Sorry."

"She was young, desperate, in trouble. I took care of her. It was like taking in a scared rabbit. Whatever her trouble was, it was big enough. I thought I'd give her time to quiet down, then perhaps be able to help her."

"What happened?"

"She's scared, Mike. Terrified. She's all mixed up and I'm the only one she can hang on to."

"Good, I'll take your word for it. Now get me up to her before this place is crawling with cops. We have about five minutes before somebody is going to be curious enough to make a phone call."

From the third floor you could hear the rhythmic tap of her feet dancing a staccato number that made you think of an Eleanor

Powell routine when prettylegs were queen of the boards. There was no music, yet you knew *she* heard some and was in a never-never land of her own.

Velda knocked, but the dancing didn't stop. She turned the knob and pushed the door open and with a soft cry the girl in the middle of the room twisted around, her hand going to her mouth when she saw me, huge eyes darting from Velda's to mine. She threw one glance toward the window when Velda said, "It's all right, Sue. This is our friend."

It was going to take more than that to convince her and there wasn't enough time. "My name is Mike Hammer, Sue. I'm going to help you. Can you understand that?"

Whatever it was, it worked. The fear left her face and she tried on a tentative smile and nodded. "Will you . . . really?"

"Really," I nodded back. To Velda I said, "Can we get her out of here?"

"Yes. I know of a place I can take her."

"Where?"

"Do you remember Connie Lewis' restaurant on Forty-first?"

"Just off Ninth?"

"That's it. I'll be there. She has the upper three floors to herself."

"That was seven years ago."

"She'll be there," Velda told me.

"Okay," I said, "you get there with the kid. I'll do the talking on the bit downstairs, then in about an hour you show up at Pat's office. I'm being a damn fool for letting you out on the street again but I can't see any other way of doing it."

Her hand squeezed mine and she smiled. "It'll be all right, Mike."

Then the kid walked up and I looked into the face of the prettiest little Lolita-type I ever saw. She was a tiny blonde with enormous brown eyes and a lovely mouth in a pert pointed face that made you want to pick her up like a doll. Her hair was silk-soft and hung loosely to her shoulders, and when she moved all you could see was girl-woman, and if you weren't careful you'd feel the wrong kind of feel.

But I was an old soldier who had been there and back, so I said, "How old are you, chicken?"

She smiled and said, "Twenty-one."

I grinned at Velda. "She's not lying. You thought she was kidding when she told you that, didn't you?"

Velda nodded.

"We'll get straight on this later. Right now take off." I looked at Sue, reaching out to feel her hair. "I don't know what your trouble is, girl, but first things first. I'm going to lay something on the line with you though."

"Oh?"

"Downstairs there are two dead men because of you. So play it the way you're told and we'll make it. Try using your own little head and there may be more dead people. Me, I've had it. I'll help you all the way as long as you do it like I say, but go on your own and you're like out, kid, understand? There aren't any more people who can make this boy tumble again, big or little. I'm telling you this because you're not as little as you look. You can fool a lot of slobs, but not this slob, so we're starting off square, okay?"

"Okay, Mr. Hammer." There was no hesitation at all.

"Call me Mike."

"Sure, Mike."

"Get her out of here, Velda."

The sirens converged from both directions. They locked the street in on either end and two more took the street to the front of the house. The floods hit the doorway and the uniformed cops came in with .38's in their hands.

I had the door open, the lights lit, and both hands in view when the first pair stepped through the doorway. Before they asked I took the position, let them see my .45 on the table beside the other guns, and watched patiently while they flipped open my wallet with the very special ticket in the identification window.

The reaction was slow at first. They weren't about to take any chances with two dead men on the floor, but they couldn't go too far the other way either. Finally the older one handed my wallet back. "I knew you back in the old days, Mike."

"Times haven't changed much."

"I wonder." He nodded toward the two bodies. "I don't suppose you want to explain about all this now?"

"That's right."

"You got a big ticket there. When?"

"Call Captain Chambers. This is his baby."

"I guess it is."

"There's a new Inspector in the division. He might not like the action."

"No sweat, friend. Don't worry."

"I'm not worrying. I just remember you and Captain Chambers were friends."

"No more."

"I heard that too." He holstered his gun. Behind him another pair came in cautiously, ready. "This is a big one?" he asked.

"Yeah. Can I make a call?"

"Mind if I make it for you?"

"Nope." I gave him a number that he already knew and watched his face go flat when I handed him the name. He went outside to the car, put the call through, and when he came back there was a subtle touch of deference in his attitude. Whatever he had said to the others took the bull off me, and by the time the M.E. got there it was like someone had diplomatic immunity.

Pat came in five minutes later. He waited until the pictures were taken and the bodies removed, then waved everybody else out except the little man in gray whom nobody was big enough to wave out. Then he studiously examined my big fat .45 and said, "The same one, isn't it?"

"It's the only one I ever needed."

"How many men have you killed with it?"

"Nine," I said. Then added, "With that gun."

"Good score."

"I'm still alive."

"Sometimes I wonder."

I grinned at him. "You hate me, buddy, but you're glad, aren't you?"

"That you're still alive?"

"Uh-huh."

He turned slowly, his eyes searching for some obscure answer. "I don't know," he said. "Sometimes I can't tell who is the worse off. Right now I'm not sure. It's hard to kill friendships. I tried hard enough with you and I almost made it work. Even with a woman between us I can't be sure any more. You crazy bastard, I watch what you do, see you get shot and beat to hell and wonder why it has to happen like that, and I'm afraid to tell myself the answer. I know it but I can't say it."

"So say it."

"Later."

"Okay."

"Now what happened?" He looked at Art Rickerby sitting in the chair.

I said, "Velda was here. I came for her. These two guys bust in, this one here first. The other came in time to break up the play."

"Nicely parlayed."

"Well put, buddy."

"For an ex-drunk you're doing all right." He glanced at Rickerby again.

"Some people have foresight," I reminded him.

"Do I leave now?" Pat said. "Do I go along with the Federal bit and take off?"

For the first time Art Rickerby spoke. He was quiet as always and I knew that there were no ends left untied in the past I had just left. He said, "Captain . . . there are times when . . . there are times. It was you who forced Mr. Hammer into circumstances he could hardly cope with. It was a dead man and me who made him stick to it. If he's anathema out of the past, then it's our fault. We brought a man back who should have died a long time ago. The present can't stand a man like that any more. Now they want indecision and compromise and reluctance and fear . . . and we've dropped a hot iron in society's lap. We've brought a man back who almost shouldn't be here and now you and me and society are stuck with him."

"Thanks a bunch," I said.

"Sure," Pat said to Art, "he's always been in the special-privilege class, but now it's over my head. You got the pull, Rickerby. I don't get all the picture, but I've been around long enough to figure a few things out. Just clue me on this one."

"Pat . . ." I started.

"Not you, Mike. *Him.*" He smiled with that gentle deceptiveness. "And make it good. We have two dead men here and I'm not writing that off for anybody. No more I'm not."

Art nodded and glanced at his watch. "The girl Velda," he said, "she was the crux. She has information this country depends upon. A team of assassins was assigned to kill her and nobody could get to that team we called "The Dragon" but him, because nobody could be as terrible as they were. It turned out that he was even worse. If that is a good word. For that information this country would pay any price and part of the cost was to rehabilitate this man in a sense and give him back his privilege and his gun.

"The Dragon team is gone now. There is only the girl Velda. There is still that price to pay and he can call the tune. You have no choice but to back him up. Is that clear?"

"No, but it's coming through," Pat said. "I know most of the story but I find it hard to believe."

I said, "Pat . . ."

"What?"

"Let's leave it, kid. We were both right. So she's still mine. If you want her then take her away, but you have to fight me for her and you haven't got a chance in the world of winning."

"Not as long as you're alive," he told me.

"Sure, Pat."

"And the law of averages is on my side."

"Why, sure."

I didn't think he could do it, but he did. He grinned and stuck out his hand and instinctively I took it. "Okay, boy. It's like before now. We start fresh. Do I get the story or does he?"

"First him, buddy," I said, nodding toward Art, "then you. It's bigger than local and I'm not just a private cop any more."

"They told me about your ticket. Smart."

"You know me. Never travel small."

"That's right. Somebody's got to be the hero."

"Nuts. If I'm on a dead play, then I want odds that will pay off."

"They did."

"Damn right they did. I stuck it up and broke it off. Everybody wanted me dead and instead it turned all the way around. So I got the payoff. A big ticket and the rod back and nobody puts the bull on me until I flub it royally . . . and this, friend, I'm not about to do again."

"No?"

"Watch."

"My pleasure, big buddy." He grinned. Again. "Mind if I leave and talk it out with Mister Government here?"

"No. But be at your office soon. She'll be there and so will I."

"Soon?"

"An hour."

"I'll be waiting, hero."

When he left, Art Rickerby said, "She has to talk right away. Where is she?"

"I told you . . . in an hour . . . at Pat's office."

"There were dead men here."

"So . . ."

"Don't piddle with me, Mike."

"Don't piddle with me, Art."

"Who are they?"

"I damn well don't know, but this you'll do and damn well do it right."

"Don't tell me what to do."

"No? I shove it up your tail if I want to, Art, and don't you forget it. You do this one my way. This is something else from your personal angle and leave it alone. Let those dead men be.

As far as anybody is concerned they're part of The Dragon group
and the last part at that. There ain't no more, the end, finis. They
came for Velda and I was here to lay on the gravy like I did the
rest and you go along with it. What's here is not part of your
business at all, but for the moment you can cover me. Do it."
"Mike . . ."
"Just do it and shut up."
"Mike . . ."
I said softly, "I gave you The Dragon, didn't I?"
"Yes."
"I was dead. You exhumed me. You made me do things that
were goddamned near impossible, and when I didn't die doing
them you were surprised. So be surprised now. Do like I tell you."
"Or . . .?"
"Or Velda won't come in."
"You're sure?"
"Positive, friend."
"It will be done."
"Thanks."
"No trouble."

And Velda told them the next day. She spelled it out in detail
and a government organization collapsed. In Moscow thirty men
died, and in the East Zone of Berlin five more disappeared, and
in South America there was a series of accidents and several
untimely deaths, and across the face of the globe the living went
to the dead in unaccountable numbers and codes and files were
rearranged and meetings hastily brought about and summit con-
ferences planned and in the U.N. buildings whole new philosophies
were adopted and decisions brought about in a changed light, and
as suddenly as she had been a threat to a different world, she had
become a person again. She had nothing more to give and in the
world of politics there was no retribution as long as you knew
nothing new and really didn't care at all.
But there *was* something new. There were two dead men to tell
about it and somewhere in the city was another with a bullet in
his gut looking for somebody to take it out and if the little blonde
didn't tell, one of these would.
You just didn't lay dead men at your feet without someone
coming looking for you.
And I had them at my feet.

chapter two ▰▰▰▰▰

I KNEW I had a tail on me when I left the D.A.'s office. It had been nicely set up even though Rickerby had put the fix in for me. No local police force likes to be queered out of a deal in their own back yard, and if they could move in, orders or not, they were going to give it the big try. If Pat had set the tail it would have been hard to spot, but the new D.A. was too ambitious to figure out there were civilian-type pros in the police business too.

For an hour I let him wait outside bars, fool around a department store while I picked up a few goodies, then went in one door of the Blue Ribbon Restaurant on Forty-fourth, around through the bar, and out that door while he was looking for me at the tables. I was back on Seventh Avenue before he knew I was gone, flagged down a cab, and had him cut over to Forty-ninth and Ninth.

Connie Lewis' place was called "La Sabre" and turned out to be a downstairs supper place for the neighborhood trade. It specialized in steaks and chops and seemed to be built around a huge charcoal grill that smoked and sizzled into a copper canopy. Connie was a round little woman with a perpetual smile and wrinkles at the corners of her eyes and mouth that said it was for real. It had been years since I had seen her and she hadn't changed a bit.

But me she didn't recognize at first. When it did come she beamed all over, tried to get me to drink, then eat, and when I wouldn't do either, showed me the way to the staircase going upstairs, and told me Velda was on the second floor rear with her company.

I used the same VY knock and she opened the door. There was no gun in her hand this time, but I knew it wasn't far out of reach. She pulled me in, closed the door, and locked it. I grinned at her, grabbed her by the shoulders, and touched her mouth with mine. Lightly. I couldn't afford any more. Her eyes laughed back at me and told me I could pick my own time and place. Any time, any place.

I said, "Hello, beautiful. Where's the kid?"

"Here I am, Mike."

She eased into the room impishly, hands clasped behind her back. She stood at the corner of the bedroom door watching, seemingly unafraid, but inside those huge brown eyes was a worm of fear that had been there too long to be plucked out easily.

I took Velda's arm, steered her to the table, and motioned the kid to come over too. Automatically, the kid slid closer to Velda, knowing she was protected there, never taking her eyes from my face.

"Let's have it," I said.

Velda nodded. "You can tell him."

"I . . . don't know."

For what it was worth I took out my new wallet and flipped it open. The blue and gold card with the embossed seal in the plastic window did the trick again. She studied it, frowned, then made up her mind.

"All right," she finally told me. "My name is Sue Devon." When she said it there was a challenge in her voice I couldn't ignore.

"Am I supposed to know you?"

She flicked her eyes to her hands, to Velda, then to me. "I have another name."

"Oh?"

"Torrence. I never use it. He had me legally adopted a long time ago but I never use his name. I hate it."

I shook my head. "Sorry, kid. I don't make you at all."

Velda reached out and touched my hand. "Sim Torrence. He was the District Attorney once; now he's running in the primaries for governor of the state."

"Win with Sim?"

"That's right."

"I remember seeing posters around, but I never tied him up with the D.A.'s office." I let a grin ease out. "It's been a rough seven years. I didn't keep up with politics. Now let's hear the rest of this."

Sue nodded, her hair tumbling around her face. She bit at her lip with even white teeth, her hands clasped so tight the knuckles showed white. "I ran away from him."

"Why?"

The fear was a live thing in her eyes. "I think . . . he killed my mother. Now he wants to kill me."

When I glanced at Velda I knew she was thinking the same thing I was. I said, "People running for governor don't usually kill people."

"He killed my mother," she repeated.

"You said you *thought* he did." She didn't answer, so I asked, "When was this supposed to have happened?"

"A long time ago."

"How long?"

"I . . . was a baby. Eighteen years ago."

"How do you know he did this?"

She wouldn't look at me. "I just know it, that's all."

"Honey," I said, "you can't accuse a man of murder with a reason like that."

She made a little shrug and worked her fingers together.

I said, "You have something else on your mind. What is it?"

Velda slipped her arm around her shoulders and squeezed. Sue looked at her gratefully and turned back to me again. "I remember Mama talking. Before she died. Whatever she said . . . is in my mind . . . but I can't pick out the words. I was terribly frightened. She was dying and she talked to me and told me something and I don't remember what it was!" She sucked her breath in and held it while the tears welled up in her eyes.

When she relaxed I said, "And what makes you think he wants to kill you?"

"I know . . . the way he looks at me. He . . . touches me."

"Better, baby. You'll have to do better than that."

"Very well. There was a car. It almost hit me."

"Did you recognize it?"

"No."

"Go on."

"There was a man one night. He followed me home from the theater. He tried to cut me off but I knew the roads and lost him not far from the house."

"Did you recognize him or his car?"

"No."

"Did you report the incidents?"

"No," she said softly.

"Okay, Sue, my turn. Do you know you're an exceptionally pretty girl?" She looked up at me. "Sure you do. Men are going to follow you, so get used to dodging. Nearly everybody has a close call with a car, so don't put too much store in that. And so far as your stepfather is concerned, he'd look at you like any man would his daughter and touch you the same way. You haven't said anything concrete yet."

"Then what about that man you killed and the other one?"

"*Touché,*" I said. But I couldn't let it lay there. She was waiting and she was scared. I looked at Velda. "Did you tell her where you've been for seven years and what happened?"

"She knows."

"And about me?"

"Everything."

"Then maybe this is an answer . . . those men were part of an enemy organization who had to destroy Velda before she talked. They moved in to get her, not you. And now it's over. Nobody's going to kill her because now she's said her piece and it's too late. What do you think about that?"

"I'm not going back," she said simply.

"Supposing I go to see your stepfather. Suppose I can really find out the truth, even to what your mother told you. Would that help any?"

"Maybe." Her voice was a whisper.

"Okay, kid, I'll play Big Daddy."

Velda looked up with eyes so full of thanks I had to laugh at her. She scooted the kid off to the other end of the room, took my arm, and walked me to the door. "You'll do all you can?"

"You know, you'd think I'd know better by now."

"Mike . . . don't change."

"No chance, baby."

She opened the door. "Do you . . . believe that about . . . those men coming for me?"

After a few seconds I said, "No. Basil Levitt said he wanted both you and the kid, so it wasn't anything to do with the last operation. She's in it someplace." I knew I was frowning.

"What are you thinking of?"

"Something he said, damn it." I wiped my face with my hand and grimaced. "I've been away too long. I'm not clicking."

"It will come."

"Sure, honey," I said. I touched her face lightly. "Later?"

"I'll be waiting."

"Put the kid to bed."

She made a face at me, grinned, and nodded.

It was like there had never been those seven years at all.

There wasn't much trouble getting background material on Simpson Torrence. He had been making headlines since the '30s, was featured in several of the latest magazines, and was the subject of three editorials in opposition newspapers. I took two hours to go over the bits and pieces and what I came up with made him a likely candidate for governor. In fact, several of his high-ranking constituents were looking past the mansion at Albany to the White House in Washington.

But good points I wasn't looking for. If there was anything to the kid's story at all, then something would have to point to another side of the guy's character. People just don't come all good.

I called Hy Gardner and asked him to meet me at the Blue Ribbon with anything he might have on Torrence. All he said was, "Now what?" But it meant he'd be there.

He showed up with Pete Ladero, who did legwork for a political columnist, and over lunch I picked out all the information on Torrence I could get. Substantially, it was the same as the better magazines had reported. Sim Torrence was a product of New York schools, had graduated *magna cum laude* and gone into public service immediately afterward. He had a small inheritance that made him independent enough to be able to afford the work and a determination that took him from an assistant D.A. through the main office into the State Legislature and Senate, and now he was standing at the threshold of the governorship. I said, "What's wrong with the guy?"

"Nothing," Pete told me. "Find out something and I'll peddle it to the opposition for a million bucks."

"Didn't they try?"

"You kidding?"

Hy shoved his glasses up on his forehead. "So what's the business then, Mike? What are you laying into Torrence for?"

"Curiosity right now. His name came up in a little deal a while back."

"This for publication?"

"No. It's strictly for curiosity value."

"I wish to hell you'd say what you're going to say."

"Okay," I agreed. "What about his marriage?"

Pete and Hy looked at each other, shrugged, and Pete said, "His wife died years ago. He never remarried."

"Who was she?"

Pete thought for a moment, then: "Her name was Devon, Sally Devon. If I remember right she was a fairly pretty showgirl when it was fashionable to marry showgirls. But hell, she died not long after the war. There was never any scandal connected with his marriage."

"What about the kid?" I asked.

Pete shook his head. "Nothing. I've met her several times. Torrence adopted her when her mother died, sent her to pretty good schools, and she's lived with him since."

"She ran away."

"You don't run away when you're over twenty-one," he reminded me. "Sim probably has given her a checking account that will keep her provided for wherever she goes." He paused a moment. "I don't get the angle there."

"Because I haven't got one," I said. "In my business names and people get dropped into funny places and no matter who they are they get checked out. Hell, it never hurts to prove a clean man clean."

Pete agreed with a nod, finished his coffee, and told us so long. Hy said, "Satisfied?"

"I'm getting there."

"Do I get a hint at least?"

"Sure. The two dead men the night I found Velda."

Hy frowned and pulled his glasses off, his cigar working across his mouth. "The ones who followed you and tried to nail Velda at the last minute?"

"That's the story the papers got, friend."

He waited, staring at me.

I said, "They had nothing to do with the espionage bit. They were part of another story."

"Brother!" Hy poked the cigar out in the ash tray and reached for his pencil and scratch sheets.

"No story yet, Hy. Hold it back. I'll tell you when."

Reluctantly, he put them back. "Okay, I'll wait."

"Velda had Torrence's kid with her. She took her in like a stray cat. Strictly coincidence, but there we are. The kid said she was hiding out from her old man, but whether she's lying or not, we know one thing: two dead men and a possible third say trouble's there."

"How the hell can you suppress stuff like that!" Hy exploded.

"Angles, buddy."

"Boy, you sure come on like Gangbusters. I hope you're protecting yourself."

"Don't worry about me."

"Don't worry, I won't."

Hy had to get back to his desk at the *Tribune* building so I dropped him off and went ahead to Pat's office. The uniformed sergeant at the desk waved to me, said Pat was upstairs in new quarters and to go ahead up.

He was eating at his desk as usual, too crammed with work to take time out at a lunch counter. But not too busy to talk to me. I was part of his work. He grinned and said, "How is Velda?"

"Fine, but not for you."

"Who knows?" He reached for the coffee container. "What's up?"

"What did you get on Levitt and the other guy?"

"Nothing new on Levitt. He'd been sporting some fresh money lately without saying where it came from. It was assumed that he picked up his old blackmail operations."

"And the other one?"

"Kid Hand. You knew him, didn't you?"

"I've seen him around. Small-time muscle."

"Then you haven't seen him lately. He's gone up in the world. Word has it that he's been handling all the bookie operations on the upper west side."

"Tillson's old run?"

"Hell, Tillson was knocked off a year ago."

"So who's Hand working for?"

"I wish I knew. Mr. Big has been given the innocuous-sounding name of Mr. Dickerson, but nobody seems to know any more about him."

"Somebody's going to be taking over Hand's end. There'll be a shake-up somewhere."

"Mike . . . you just don't know the rackets any more. It's all I.B.M.-style now. Business, purely business, and they're not being caught without a chain of command. No, there won't be a shake-up. It'll all happen nice and normally. Somebody else will be appointed to Kid Hand's job and that will be that."

"You guessed the bug, though, didn't you?"

Pat nodded. "Certainly. What's a wheel like Hand taking on a muscle job for anyway? You know the answer?"

"Sure. I'd say he was doing somebody a favor. Like somebody big."

"Yeah," Pat said sourly. "Now the question is, who was killing who? You nailed Hand, Levitt fired two shots, and we recovered one out of the ceiling."

"Another one got Hand's friend in the gut. You might check the hospitals."

"*Now* you tell me."

"Nuts, Pat. You figured it right after it happened."

He swung around idly in his chair, sipping at the coffee container. When he was ready he said, "What were they really after, Mike?"

I took my time too. "I don't know. Not yet I don't. But I'll find out."

"Great. And with all that top cover you got I have to sweat you out."

"Something like that."

"Let me clue you, Mike. We have a new Inspector. He's a tough nut and a smart one. Between him and the D.A., you're liable to find your tail in a jam. Right now they're trying hard to bust you loose for them to work over, so you'd better have pretty powerful friends in that office you seem to be working for."

I put my hat on and stood up. "Anything I come up with, you'll get."

"Gee, thanks," he said sarcastically, then grinned.

Sim Torrence lived inside a walled estate in Westchester that reflected the quiet dignity of real wealth and importance. A pair of ornate iron gates were opened wide, welcoming visitors, and I turned my rented Ford up the drive.

The house, a brick colonial type, was surrounded by blue spruces that reached to the eaves. Two black Caddies were parked in front of one wing and I pulled up behind them, got out, touched the doorbell, and waited.

I had expected a maid or a butler, but not a stunning brunette with electric blue eyes that seemed to spark at you. She had an early season tan that made her eyes and the red of her mouth jump right at you and when she smiled and said quizzically, "Yes?" it was like touching a hot line.

I grinned crookedly. "My name is Hammer. I'm looking for Mr. Torrence."

"Is he expecting you?"

"No, but I think he'll see me. It's about his daughter."

The eyes sparked again with some peculiar fear. "Is she . . . all right?"

"Fine."

Then relief took over and she held out her hand to me. "Please come in, Mr. Hammer. I'm Geraldine King, Mr. Torrence's secretary. He's going to be awfully glad to see you. Since Sue ran off again he's been so upset he can't do a thing."

"Again?"

She glanced up at me and nodded. "She's gone off several times before. If she only knew what she does to Mr. Torrence when she gets in one of her peeves she'd be more considerate. In here, Mr. Hammer." She pointed into a large study that smelled of cigars and old leather. "Make yourself at home, please."

There wasn't much time for that. Before I had a chance to make a circuit of the room I heard the sound of hurried feet and Big Sim Torrence, the Man-Most-Likely-To-Succeed, came in looking not at all like a politician, but with the genuine worry of any distraught father.

He held out his hand, grabbed mine, and said, "Thanks for coming, Mr. Hammer." He paused, offered me a chair, and sat down. "Now, where is Sue? Is she all right?"

"Sure. Right now she's with a friend of mine."

"Where, Mr. Hammer?"

"In the city."

He perched on the edge of the chair and frowned. "She . . . *does* intend to come back here?"

"Maybe."

His face hardened then. It was a face that had an expression I had seen a thousand times in courtrooms. It became a prosecuting attorney's face who suddenly found himself with a hostile witness and was determined to drag out the right answers the hard way.

Torrence said, "Perhaps I don't understand your concern in this matter."

"Perhaps not. First, let me tell you that it's by accident that I'm here at all. Sue was sort of taken in hand by my secretary and I made a promise to look into things before letting her return."

"Oh?" He looked down into his hands. "You are . . . qualified for this matter then?"

The wallet worked its magic again and the hostility faded from his face. His expression was serious, yet touched with impatience. "Then please get to the point, Mr. Hammer. I've worried enough about Sue so . . ."

"It's simple enough. The kid says she's scared stiff of you."

A look of pain flitted across his eyes. He held up his hand to stop me, nodded, and looked toward the window. "I know, I know. She says I killed her mother."

He caught me a little off base. When he looked around once more I said, "That's right."

"May I explain something?"

"I wish somebody would."

Torrence settled back in his chair, rubbing his face with one hand. His voice was flat, as though he had gone through the routine countless times before. "I married Sally Devon six months after her husband died. Sue was less than a year old at the time. I had known Sally for years then and it was like . . . well, we were old friends. What I didn't know was that Sally had become an alcoholic. In the first years of our marriage she grew worse in spite of everything we tried to do. Sally took to staying at my place in the Catskills with an old lady for a housekeeper, refusing to come into the city, refusing any help . . . just drinking herself to death. She kept Sue with her although it was old Mrs. Lee who really took care of the child. One night she drank herself into a stupor, went outside into the bitter cold for something, and passed out. She was unconscious when Mrs. Lee found her and dead before either a doctor or I could get to her. For some reason the child thinks I had something to do with it."

"She says her mother told her something before she died."

"I know that too. She can't recall anything, but continues to make the charge against me." He paused and rubbed his temples. "Sue has been a problem. I've tried the best schools and let her follow her own desires, but nothing seems to help matters any. She wants to be a showgirl like her mother was." He looked up at me slowly. "I wish I knew the answer."

This time I was pretty direct. "She says you're trying to kill her."

His reaction was one of amazement. *"What?"* Very slowly he came to the edge of his seat. *"What's that?"*

"A car tried to run her down, she was deliberately followed, and somebody took a shot at her."

"Are you sure?"

"I am about the last time. I was there when it happened." I didn't bother giving him any of the details.

"But . . . why haven't I heard . . .?"

"Because it involved another matter too. In time you'll hear about it. Not now. Just let's say it happened."

For the first time his courtroom composure left him. He waved his hands like a lost person and shook his head.

I said, "Mr. Torrence, do you have any enemies?"

"Enemies?"

"That's right."

"I . . . don't think so." He reflected a moment and went on. "Political enemies, perhaps. There are two parties and . . ."

"Would they want to kill you?" I interrupted.

"No . . . certainly not. Disagree, but that's all."

"What about women?" I asked bluntly.

He paid no attention to my tone. "Mr. Hammer . . . I haven't kept company with a woman since Sally died. This is a pretty well-known fact."

I looked toward the door meaningfully. "You keep pretty company."

"Geraldine King was assigned to me by our state chairman. She has been with me through three political campaigns. Between times she works with others in the party running for office."

"No offense," I said. "But how about other possibles? Could

you have made any special enemies during your political career?"

"Again, none that I know of who would want to kill me."

"You were a D.A. once."

"That was twenty-some years ago."

"So go back that far."

Torrence shrugged impatiently. "There were a dozen threats, some made right in the courtroom. Two attempts that were unsuccessful."

"What happened?"

"Nothing," he said. "Police routine stopped the action. Both persons were apprehended and sent back to prison. Since then both have died, one of T.B., the other of an ulcer."

"You kept track of them?"

"No, the police did. They thought it best to inform me. I wasn't particularly worried."

"Particularly?"

"Not for myself. For Sue and anyone else, yes. Personally, my recourse is to the law and the police. But remember this, Mr. Hammer, it isn't unusual for a District Attorney to be a target. There was a man named Dewey the mobs could have used dead, but to kill him would have meant that such pressure would be brought on organized crime that when Dutch Schultz wanted to kill him the mob killed Dutch instead. This is a precarious business and I realize it. At the same time, I won't alter my own philosophies by conforming to standards of the scared."

"How often have you been scared?"

"Often. And you?"

"Too often, buddy." I grinned at him and he smiled back slowly, his eyes showing me he knew what I meant.

"Now, about Sue."

"I'll speak to her."

"You'll bring her home?"

"That's up to Sue. I'll see what she says. Supposing she won't come?"

Torrence was silent a moment, thinking. "That's up to her then. She's a . . . child who isn't a child. Do you know what I mean?"

"Uh-huh."

He nodded. "She's well provided for financially and, frankly, I don't see what else I can do for her. I'm at a point where I need advice."

"From whom?"

His eyes twinkled at me. "Perhaps from you, Mr. Hammer."

"Could be."

"May I ask your status first?"

"I hold a very peculiar legal authorization. At the moment it allows me to do damn near anything I want to. Within reason, of course."

"For how long?"

"You're quick, friend." He nodded and I said, "Until somebody cuts me out of it or I make a mistake."

"Oh?"

"And the day of mistakes is over."

"Then advise me. I need advice from someone who doesn't make mistakes any more." There was no sarcasm in his tone at all.

"I'll keep her with me until she wants out."

A full ten seconds passed before he thought it over, then he nodded, went to the other side of his desk and pulled out a checkbook. When he finished writing he handed me a pretty green paper made out for five thousand dollars and watched while I folded it lengthwise.

"That's pretty big," I said.

"Big men don't come little. Nor do big things. I want Sue safe. I want Sue back. It's up to you now, Mr. Hammer. Where do you start?"

"By getting you to remember the names of the other guys who threatened to kill you."

"I doubt if those matters are of any importance."

"Suppose you let me do the deciding. A lot of trouble can come out of the past. A lot of dirt too. If you don't want me probing you can take your loot back. Then just for fun I might do it anyway."

"There's something personal about this with you, isn't there, Mr. Hammer? It isn't that you need the money or the practice. You needn't tell me, but there is something else."

We studied each other for the few ticks of time that it took for two pros in the same bit of business to realize that there wasn't much that could be hidden.

"You know me, Torrence."

"I know you, Mike. Doesn't everybody?"

I grinned and stuck the check in my pocket. "Not really," I said.

chapter three ━━━━━━━━━━━━━

YOU CAN ALWAYS make a start with a dead man. It's an ultimate end and a perfect beginning. Death is too definite to be ambiguous and when you deal with it your toes are in the chocks and not looking for a place to grab hold.

But death can be trouble too. It had been a long time and in seven years people could forget or stop worrying or rather play the odds and get themselves a name in the dark shadows of the never land of the night people.

Kid Hand was dead. Somebody would be mad. Somebody would be worried. By now everybody would know what happened in that tenement room and would be waiting. There would be those who remembered seven years ago and would wonder what came next. Some would know. Some would have to find out.

Me, maybe.

Off Broadway on Forty-ninth there's a hotel sandwiched in between slices of other buildings and on the street it has a screwy bar with a funny name filled with screwier people and even funnier names. They were new people, mostly, but some were still there after seven years and when I spotted Jersey Toby I nodded and watched him almost drop his beer and went to the bar and ordered a Four Roses and ginger.

The bartender was a silent old dog who mixed the drink, took my buck, and said, "Hello, Mike."

I said, "Hello, Charlie."

"You ain't been around."

"Didn't have to be."

"Glad you dumped the slop chutes."

"You hear too much."

"Bartenders like to talk too."

"To who?"

"Whom," he said.

"So whom?"

"Like other bartenders."

"Anybody else?"

"Nobody else," he said gently.

"Business is business," I grinned.

"So be it, Mike."

"Sure, Charlie," I told him.

He walked away and set up a couple for the hookers working the tourist traffic at the other end, then sort of stayed in the middle with a small worried expression on his face. Outside it was hot and sticky and here it was cool and quiet with the dramatic music of Franck's Symphony in D Minor coming through the stereo speakers too softly to be as aggressive as it should. It could have been a logical place for anybody to drop in for a break from the wild city outside.

One of the hookers spotted my two twenties on the bar and broke away from her tourist friend long enough to hit the cigarette machine behind me. Without looking around she said, "Lonely?"

I didn't look around either. "Sometimes."

"Now?"

"Not now," I said.

She turned around, grinned, and popped a butt in her pretty mouth. "Crazy native," she said.

"A real aborigine."

She laughed down in her throat. "So back to the flatland foreigners."

Jersey Toby waited until she left, then did the cigarette-machine bit himself before taking his place beside me. He made it look nice and natural, even to getting into a set routine of being a sudden bar friend and buying a drink.

When the act was over he said, "Look, Mike . . ."

"Quit sweating, buddy."

"You come for me or just anybody?"

"Just anybody."

"I don't like it when you don't come on hard."

"A new technique, Toby."

"Knock it off, Mike. Hell, I know you from the old days. You think I don't know what happened already?"

"Like what?"

"Like what's with Levitt and Kid Hand. You got rocks in your head? You think you can come shooting into the city any more? Man, things ain't like before. You been away and you should've stayed away. Now before you get me involved, let me tell you one big thing. Don't make me out a patsy. I ain't telling you nothing. Not one goddamn thing. Lay off me. I been doing a lot of small-time crap that don't get me no heat from either direction and that's the way I like it."

"Great."

"And no soft stuff too. Save that bull for the enlisted men."

"What are you pitching now?"

"I'm a pimp."

"You came down in the world."

"Yeah? Well maybe I did, but I got bucks going for me now and a couple of broads who like the bit. I do it square and not like some of the creeps and on top there's enough juice to pay off who needs paying off, like. Y'know?"

"I won't eat your bread, kiddo."

"Goddamn right."

He sat there glowering into his drink, satisfied that he had made his point, then I reached over and took his hand and held it against my side where the .45 was strung and said, "Remember?"

When he took his hand back he was shaking. "You're still nuts," he said. "You ain't nothing no more. One push with that rod and you've had it. I'm still paying juice."

This time I pulled the other cork. I took out the wallet and opened it like I was going to put my money back only I let him see the card in the window. He took a good look, his eyes going wide, then reached for his drink. "An ace, Toby," I said. "Now do we go to your place or my place?"

"I got a room upstairs," he told me.

"Where?"

"313."

"Ten minutes. You take off first."

It was a back-alley room that had the antiseptic appearance of all revamped hotel rooms, but still smelled of stale beer, old clothes, and tired air. Jersey Toby opened a beer for himself when I waved one off, then sat down with a resigned shrug and said, "Spill it, Mike."

"Kid Hand."

"He's dead."

"I know. I shot him. The top of his head came off and left a mess on the wall. He wasn't the first and he probably won't be the last."

Toby put the beer down slowly. *"You're nuts."*

"That's the best you can say?"

"No," he repeated. *"You're nuts.* I think you got a death wish."

"Toby . . ."

"I mean it, Mike. Like word goes around fast. You don't make a hit in this town without everybody knowing. You was crazy enough in those old days, but now you're real nuts. You think I don't know already? Hell, like everybody knows. I don't even want to be in the same room with you."

"You don't have a choice, Toby."

"Sure, so I'll pay later. So will you. Damn, Mike . . ."

"Kid Hand," I repeated.

"He took Tillson's job. Everybody knew about that."

"More."

"Like what, you nut! How the hell should I know about Kid? We ain't in the same game. I'm pimping. You know what he was? Like a big shot! Mr. Dickerson's right-hand boy. You think I'm going to . . .?"

"Who?"

"Knock it off . . . you know."

"Who, Toby?"

"Mr. Dickerson."

"Who's he, buddy?"

"Mike . . ."

"Don't screw around with me."

"Okay. So who knows from Dickerson? He's the new one in. He's the big one. He comes in with power and all the hard boys are flocking back. Hell, man, I can't tell you more. All I know is Mr. Dickerson and he's the gas."

"Political?"

"Not him, you nut. This one's power. Like firepower, man. You know what's happening in this town? They're coming in from the burgs, man. Big shooters and they're gathering around waiting for orders. I feel the stream going by but I ain't fishing. Too long the mobs have been dead . . . now it's like Indians again. A chief is back and the crazy Soos is rejoicing. That's all I can say."

"Kid Hand?"

"Crazy, man. A shooter and he knew where his bread was. He was on the way up until he decided to get back in the ranks again. He should've stayed where he was."

"Why?"

"Why what?"

"He pulled on me. I don't take that crap."

"He knew it was you, maybe? He knew it was anybody?"

"Somebody said he might have been doing a personal favor."

Toby got up and faced the blank window. "Sure, why not? Favors are important. It makes you look big. It proves like you're not a punk. It proves . . ."

"It proves how fast you can get killed, too."

Slowly, he turned around. "Am I in the middle, Mike?"

"I don't see how."

"Ask it straight."

"Who is Dickerson?"

"Nobody knows. Just that he's big."

"Money?"

"I guess."

"Who takes Kid Hand's place?"

"Whoever can grab it. I'd say Del Penner. He's pretty tough. He had a fall ten years ago, but came back to grab off the jukes in Chi, then moved into the bolita and hi-li in Miami. He was pushing Kid pretty hard."

"Then maybe Kid's move in on me was part of a power grab."

"Favors don't hurt nobody."

"It killed Kid."

"So he didn't know it was you."

I looked at him a long time, then his face got tight and he turned away. When he gulped down his beer he looked at me, shrugged, and said, "Word goes it was a personal favor. You were a surprise. You just don't know what kind of a surprise. It wasn't with you. It was something else. That's all. I don't know . . . I don't want to know. Let me make my bucks my own way, only stay loose, man."

"Why?"

"You're hot now, man. Everybody knows. Everybody's looking."

"I've had heat before."

"Not like this." He looked into his beer, shrugged, and decided. "You ever hear of Marv Kania?"

"No."

"He's a contract man from St. Loo. Punk about twenty-eight, got a fall for murder second when he was a teen-ager, joined with Pax in K.C., then did the route with Arnold Philips on the coast and back to St. Loo. They figured he was the contract kill on Shulburger, Angelo, and Vince Pago and the big Carlysle hit in L.A. He's got plenty of cover and is as nuts as you are."

"What does that make me, Toby?"

"A target, man. He's in town with a slug in his gut and everybody knows how it happened. If he dies you're lucky. If he don't you're dead."

I got up and put on my hat. "My luck's been pretty good lately," I said.

He nodded gravely. "I hope it holds."

When I went to open the door he added, "Maybe I don't, too."

"Why?"

"I don't want to be around when it stops. You'll make an awful splash."

"It figures."

"Sure it does," he said.

Then I went back to her, the beautiful one whose hair hung dark and long, whose body was a quiet concert in curves and colors of white and shadow that rose softly under a single sheet into a woman's fulfillment of mounded breasts and soft clefts.

She didn't hear me come in until I said, "Velda . . ."

Then her eyes opened, slowly at first, then with the startled suddenness of a deer awakened and her hand moved and I knew what she had in it. When she knew it was me her fingers relaxed, came out from under the cover, and reached for mine.

"You can lose that way, kid," I said.

"Not when you're here."

"It wasn't always me."

"This is *now*, Mike," she said. It was almost me thinking again when I walked up the steps a couple of days ago.

I took her hand, then in one full sweep flipped the sheet off her body and looked at her.

What is it when you see woman naked? *Woman*. Long. Lovely. Tousled. Skin that looks slippery in the small light. Pink things that are the summit. A wide shadowy mass that is the crest. Desire that rests in the soft fold of flesh that can speak and taste and tell that it wants you with the sudden contractions and quickening intake of breath. A mouth that opens wetly and moves with soundless words of love.

I sat on the edge of the bed and let my fingers explore her. The invitation had always been there, but for the first time it was accepted. Now I could touch and feel and enjoy and know that this was mine. She gasped once, and said, "Your eyes are crazy, Mike."

"You can't see them."

"But I know. They're wild Irish brown green and they're crazy."

"I know."

"Then do what I want."

"Not me, kid. You're only a broad and I do what I want."

"Then do it."

"Are you ready?" I asked.

"I've always been ready."

"No you haven't."

"I am now."

Her face was turned toward mine, the high planes in her cheeks throwing dark shades toward her lips, her eyes bright with a strange wetness, and when I bent forward and kissed her it was like tasting the animal wildness of a tiger filled with an insensate hunger that wanted to swallow its victim whole and I knew what woman was like. Pure woman.

Across the room, muffled because of the alcove, came a peculiar distant tone that made the scales, rising and falling with an eerie quality that had a banshee touch, and Velda said, "She's awake."

I pulled the sheet up and tucked it around her shoulders. "She isn't."

"We can go somewhere."

"No. The biggest word."

"Mike . . ."

"First we get rid of the trouble. It won't be right until then."

I could feel her eyes. "With you there will always be trouble."

"Not this trouble."

"Haven't we had enough?"

I shook my head. "Some people it's always with. You know me now. It comes fast, it lasts awhile, then it ends fast."

"You never change, do you?"

"Kitten, I don't expect to. Things happen, but they never change."

"Will it be us?"

"It has to be. In the meantime there are things to do. You ready?"

She grinned at me, the implication clear. "I've always been ready. You just never asked before."

"I never ask. I take."

"Take."

"When I'm ready. Not now. Get up."

Velda was a woman. She slid out of bed and dressed, deliberately, so I could watch everything she did, then reached into the top drawer of the dresser and pulled out a clip holster and slid it inside her skirt, the slide going over the wide belt she wore. The flat-sided Browning didn't even make a bulge.

I said, "If anybody ever shot me with that I'd tear their arms off."

"Not if you got shot in the head," she told me.

I called Rickerby from downstairs and he had a man stand by while we were gone. Sue was asleep, I thought, but I couldn't be sure. At least she wasn't going anyplace until we got back. We walked to the parking lot where I picked up the rented Ford and cut over to the West Side Highway.

She waited until I was on the ramp to ask, "Where are we going?"

"There's a place called 'The Angus Bull.' " It's a new one for the racket boys."

"Who told you?"

"Pat."

"And whom do I con?"

"A man named Del Penner. If he isn't there you'll pick up a lead if you work it right. He was pushing Kid Hand and will probably take his place in the group. What you want to know is this . . . who is Mr. Dickerson?"

She threw me a funny glance and I filled her in on the small details. I watched her out of the corner of my eyes while she picked it all apart and put it back together again. There was something new about her now that wasn't there seven years ago. Then she had been a secretary, a girl with her own P.I. ticket and the right to carry a gun. Then she had been a girl with a peculiar past I hadn't known about. Now she was a woman, still with a peculiar past and a gun, but with a strange new subtlety added that was nurtured during those years behind the Iron Curtain in the biggest chase scene civilization had ever known.

"Where do we clear?"

"Through Pat."

"Or your friend Rickerby?"

"Keep him as an alternate. It isn't his field yet, so we'll stay local."

"Where will you be?"

"Running down the immediate past of a guy called Basil Levitt. Pat came up with nothing. They're still on the job, but he had no office and no records. Whatever he carried he carried in his hat, but he sure was working for somebody. He was after you and the kid and was four days watching your joint. I don't know what we have going, but these are the only leads we have."

"There's Sue."

"She has nothing to say yet."

"Did you believe what she said about her father trying to kill her?"

"No."

"Why not?"

"Because it isn't logical. The kid's a neurotic type and until something proves out I'm not going along with childish notions."

"Two dead men aren't notions."

"There's more to it than that, baby. Let me do it my way, okay?"

"Sure. It's always your way, isn't it?"

"Sure."

"Is that why I love you?"

"Sure."

"And you love me because I think that way?"

"Why sure."

"I'm home, Mike."

I touched her knee and felt her leg harden. "You never were away, kid."

She was on her own when I dropped her downtown. She grinned at me, waved, and I let her go. There was something relaxing about the whole thing now. No more tight feeling in the gut. No more of that big empty hole that was her. She was there and bigger than ever, still with the gun on her belt and ready to follow.

Going through Levitt's place was only a matter of curiosity. It was a room, nothing more. The landlady said he had been there six months and never caused trouble, paid his rent, and she didn't want to talk to any more cops. The neighbors didn't know anything about him at all and didn't want to find out. The local tavern owner had never served him and couldn't care less. But up in his room the ash trays had been full of butts and there were two empty cartons in the garbage and anyone who smokes that much had to pick up cigarettes somewhere.

Basil Levitt did it two blocks away. He got his papers there too. The old lady who ran the place remembered him well and didn't mind talking about it.

"I know the one," she told me. "I wondered when the cops would get down here. I even woulda seen them only I wanted to see how fast they'd get here. Sure took you long enough. Where you from, son?"

"Uptown."

"You know what happened?"

"Not yet."

"So what do you want with me?"

"Just talk, Mom."

"So ask."

"Suppose you tell." I grinned at her. "Maybe you want the third degree, sweetie, just like in TV . . . okay?"

She waved her hand at me. "That stuff is dead. Who hits old ladies any more except delinquents?"

"Me. I hit old ladies."

"You look like the type. So ask me."

"Okay . . . any friends?"

She shook her head. "No, but he makes phone calls. One of the hot boys . . . never shuts the door." She nodded toward the pay booth in back.

"You listened?"

"Why not? I'm too old to screw so I get a kick out of love talk."

"How about that?"

"Yeah, how?" She smiled crookedly and opened herself a Coke. "He never talked love talk, never. Just money and always mad."

"More, Mom."

"He'd talk pretty big loot. Five G's was the last . . . like he was a betting man. Was he, son?"

"He bet his skin and lost. Now more."

She made a gesture with her shoulders. "Last time he was real mad. Said something was taking too long and wanted more loot. I don't think he got it."

"Any names?"

"Nope. He didn't call somebody's house, either."

I waited and she grinned broadly.

"He only called at a certain time. He had to speak up like wherever the other party was, it was damn noisy. That's how come I heard him."

"You'd make a good cop, Mom."

"I been around long enough, son. You want to know something else?"

"That's what I'm here for."

"He carried a package once. It was all done up in brown paper and it wasn't light. It was a gun. Rifle all taken down, I'd say. You like that bit?"

"You're doing great. How'd you know?"

"Easy. It *clunked* when he set it down. Besides, I could smell the gun oil. My old man was a nut on those things before he kicked off. I smelled that stuff around the house for years."

Then I knew what bugged me right after Basil Levitt died. I said my thanks and turned to go. She said, "Hey . . ."

"What?"

"Would you really hit an old lady?"

I grinned at her. "Only when they need it," I said.

I stood in the room that had been Velda's and scanned the other side of the street. It didn't take long to sort out the only windows that were set right for an ambush. Ten bucks to a fat old man got me the key with no questions asked and when I opened the door to the first one that was it.

The gun was an expensive sporting rifle with a load in the chamber, blocked in on a tripod screwed to a tabletop and the telescopic sights were centered on the same window I had looked out of a few minutes before. There were two empty cigarette cartons beside the gun, a tomato-juice can full of butts and spent matches, and the remains of a dozen sandwiches scattered around.

Basil's vigil had been a four-day one. For that long a time he had waited. At any time he could have had Velda. He knew she was there. He told me so. He had watched her that long but couldn't move in.

The reason for his wait was plain now. It wasn't her he was after at all. It was the kid. He wanted her. He was on a contract to knock her off and had to wait for her to show.

Only she didn't. Velda had kept her upstairs out of sight. It was only when I came on the scene that he had to break his pattern. He didn't know why I was there but couldn't take any chances. I might be after the same target he was after but for a different reason: to get her out.

So now it was back to the little Lolita-type again.

chapter four ▅▅▅▅▅▅▅▅▅▅

IT HAD BEEN a long time since I had seen Joey Adams and his wife Cindy. Now, besides doing his major night-club routines with time off for tent-circus Broadway musicals and world-wide junkets, he was president of AGVA. But he hadn't changed a bit. Neither had Cindy. She was still her same stunning self in the trademark colors of scarlet and midnight whamming out a column for *TV Guide*.

I told the girl not to announce me and when I went in Joey was perched on the edge of his desk trying to talk Cindy out of something new in minks. He wasn't getting anywhere. I said, "Hello, buddy."

He looked over his shoulder, grinned, and hopped off the desk with his hand out. "I'll be damned," he said, "you finally picked up the rain check. Where you been?"

"On the wrong street." I looked past him. "Hello, beautiful."

Cindy threw me a flashing smile. "I told Joey you'd show up. We've been following the obituaries. You leave a trail, Mike."

"I was following one."

"That's what Hy said. You big fink, why didn't you come visit when you needed help?"

"Hell, kid, I didn't need any help to stay drunk."

"That's not what I meant."

Joey waved at her impatiently. "Come on, come on, what's new? Look, suppose we . . ."

"I need help now, pal."

It caught him off balance a second. "Listen, I'm no AA, but . . ."

"Not that kind of help," I grinned.

"Oh?"

"You've been bugging me to play cop for how long, Joey?"

His eyes lit up like a marquee but Cindy got there first.

"Listen, old friend, you keep my boy away from the shooters. Like he's mine and I want to keep him in one piece. He's just a comedian and those gun routines are hard on the complexion."

"Cut it out, Cindy. If Mike wants . . ."

"Don't sweat it, friend. Just a simple favor."

He looked disappointed.

"But it's something you can get to where I can't," I added.

Joey laughed and faked a swing at my gut. "So name it, kid."

"How far back do your files go?"

"Well," he shrugged, "what do you want to know?"

I sat on the edge of the desk and lined things up in my mind. "There was a showgirl named Sally Devon who was in business over twenty years ago. Name mean anything?"

Joey squinted and shook his head. "Should it?"

"Not necessarily. I doubt if she was a headliner."

"Mike . . ." Cindy uncoiled from her chair and stood beside Joey. "Wasn't she Sim Torrence's wife at one time?"

I nodded.

"How'd you know?" Joey asked.

"I'm just clever."

"What do you know about her, honey?"

"Nothing at all, but I happened to be talking politics to one of Joey's friends and he dropped her name in the hat. He had worked with her at one time."

"Now she's in politics," Joey grunted. "So who were you talking to?"

"Bert Reese."

"What do you think, Joey? Do a rundown for me? Maybe Bert can steer you to somebody else that would know about her."

"Sure, but if it's politics you want, Cindy can . . ."

"It's not politics. Just get a line on her show-biz activities. She would've been in from twenty to thirty years back. Somebody at Equity might know her or the old chorus-line bunch. She was married to Sim Torrence while he was still a small-timer so the connection might bring somebody's memory back. Seem possible?"

"Sure, Mike, sure. The kids always keep in touch. They never forget. Hell, you know show business. I'll dig around."

"How long will it take?"

"I ought to have something by tomorrow. Where'll I get in touch?"

"My old office. I'm back in business, or reach me through the Blue Ribbon Restaurant."

He gave me that big grin again and winked. Now he was doing an act he liked. There are always frustrated cops and firemen. I shook hands with Joey, waved at Cindy, and left them to battle about the mink bit again.

Rickerby's man gave me a funny look and a curt nod when I showed, asked if there were anything else, and when I said no, made his phone call to clear and took off. Then I went upstairs.

I could hear her all the way, like a wild bird singing a crazy melody. She had an incredible range to her voice and just let it go, trilling some strange tune that had a familiar note, but was being interpreted out of its symphonic character.

The singing didn't come from the floor where I had left her, either. It was higher up and I made the last flight in a rush and stood at the end of the corridor with the .45 in my hand wondering what the hell was going on. She had everything wrapped up in that voice, fear, hate, anxiety, but no hope at all.

When I pushed the door open slowly her voice came flooding out from the peculiar echo chamber of the empty room. She stood facing the corner, both hands against the wall, her head down, her shoulders weaving gently with the rhythm of her voice, her silken blonde hair a gold reflection from the small bulb overhead.

I said, "Sue . . ." and she turned slowly, never stopping, but, seeing me there, went into a quiet ballet step until she stopped and let her voice die out on a high lilting note. There was something gone in her eyes and it took a half minute for her to realize just who I was.

"What are you doing up here?"

"It's empty," she said finally.

"Why do you want it like that?"

She let her hands drift behind her back. "Furniture looks at you. It means people and I don't want any people."

"Why, Sue?"

"They hurt you."

"Did somebody hurt you?"

"You know."

"I know that nobody has hurt you so far."

"So far. They killed my mother."

"You don't know that."

"Yes I do. A snake killed her."

"A what?"

"A snake."

"Your mother died of natural causes. She was . . . a sick woman."

This time Sue shook her head patiently. "I've been remembering. She was afraid of a snake. She told me so. She said it was the snake."

"You were too young to remember."

"No I wasn't."

I held out my hand to her and she took it. "Let's go downstairs, sugar. I want to talk to you."

"All right. Can I come back up here when I want to?"

"Sure. No trouble. Just don't go outside."

Those big brown eyes came up to mine with a sudden hunted look. "You know somebody wants to hurt me too, don't you?"

"Okay, kid, I won't try to con you. Maybe it will make you a little cautious. I think somebody is after you. Why, I don't know, but stick it out the way I tell you to, all right?"

"All right, Mike."

I waited until she had finished her coffee before I dropped the bomb on her. I said, "Sue . . ."

Then her eyes looked up and with a sudden intuition she knew what I was going to say.

"Would you mind going home?"

"I won't go," she said simply.

"You want to find out what really happened to your mother, don't you?"

She nodded.

"You can help if you do what I ask."

"How will that help?"

"You got big ears, kid. I'm an old soldier who knows his way around this business and you just don't fool me, baby. You can do anything you want to. Go back there and stay with it. Somebody wants you nailed, sugar, and if I can get you in a safe place I can scrounge without having you to worry about."

Sue smiled without meaning and looked down at her hands. "*He* wants me dead."

"Okay, we'll play it your way. *If* he does there's nothing he can do about it now. There's too many eyes watching you."

"Are yours, Mike?"

I grinned. "Hell, I can't take 'em off you."

"Don't fool with me, Mike."

"All right, Sue. Now listen. Your old man paid me five grand to handle this mess. It isn't like he's caught in a trap and is trying to con me because he knows all about me. I'm no mouse. I've knocked over too many punks and broke too many big ones to play little-boy games with."

"Are you *really* convinced, Mike?"

"Honey, until it's all locked up, tight, I'm never convinced, but at this stage we have to work the angles. Now, will you go back?"

She waited a moment, then looked up again. "If you want me to."

"I want you to."

"Will I see you again?"

Those big brown eyes were a little too much. "Sure, but what's a guy like me going to do with a girl like you?"

A smile touched her mouth. "Plenty, I think," she said.

Sim Torrence was out, but Geraldine King made the arrangements for a limousine to pick up Sue. I waited for it to arrive, watched her leave, then went back to my office. I got out at the eighth floor, edged around the guy leaning up against the wall beside the buttons with his back to me, and if it didn't suddenly occur to me that his position was a little too awkward to be normal and that he might be sick I never would have turned around and I would have died face down on the marble floor.

I had that one split-second glance at a pain- and hate-contorted

face before I threw myself back toward the wall scratching for the
.45 when his gun blasted twice and both shots rocketed off the
floor beside my face.

Then I had the .45 out and ready but it was too late. He had
stepped back into the elevator I had just left and the doors were
closing. There wasn't any sense chasing him. The exit stairs were
down the far end of the corridor and the elevator was a quick
one. I got up, dusted myself off, and looked up at the guy who
stuck his head out of a neighboring door. He said, "What was
that?"

"Be damned if I know. Sounded like it was in the elevator."

"Something's always happening to that thing," he said passively,
then closed his door.

Both slugs were imbedded in the plaster at the end of the hall,
flattened at the nose and scratched, but with enough rifling marks
showing for the lab to make something out of it. I dropped them
in my pocket and went to my office. I dialed Pat, told him what
had happened, and heard him let out a short laugh. "You're still
lucky, Mike. For how long?"

"Who knows?"

"You recognize him?"

"He's the guy Basil Levitt shot, buddy. I'd say his name was
Marv Kania."

"Mike . . ."

"I know his history. You got something out on him?"

"For a month. He's wanted all over. You sure about this?"

"I'm sure."

"He must want you pretty badly."

"Pat, he's got a bullet in him. He's not going to last like he is
and if he's staying alive it's to get me first. If we can nail him
we can find out what this is all about. If he knows he's wanted
he can't go to a doctor and if he knows he's dying he'll do anything
to come at me again. Now damn it, a shot-up guy can't go
prancing around the streets, you know that."

"He's doing it."

"So he'll fall. Somebody'll try to help him and he'll nail them
too. He just can't follow me around, I move too fast."

"He'll wait you out, Mike."

"How?"

"You're not thinking straight. If he knows what this operation
is about he'll know where you'll be looking sooner or later. All
he has to do is wait there."

"What about in the meantime?"

"I'll get on it right away. If he left a trail we'll find it. There aren't too many places he can hole up."

"Okay."

"And, buddy . . ."

"What, Pat?"

"Hands off if you nail him, understand? I got enough people on my back right now. This new D.A. is trying to. break your license."

"Can he?"

"It can be done."

"Well hell, tell him I'm cooperating all the way. If you look in the downstairs apartment in the building across the street from where Velda was staying you'll find a sniper's rifle that belonged to Basil Levitt. Maybe you can backtrack that."

"Now you tell me," he said softly.

"I just located it."

"What does it mean?"

I didn't tell him what I thought at all. "Got me. You figure it out."

"Maybe I will. Now you get those slugs down to me as fast as you can."

"By messenger service right now."

When I hung up I called Arrow, had a boy pick up the envelope with the two chunks of lead, got them off, then stretched out on the couch.

I slept for three hours, a hard, tight sleep that was almost dreamless, and when the phone went off it didn't awaken me until the fourth or fifth time. When I said hello, Velda's voice said, "Mike . . ."

"Here, kitten. What's up?"

"Can you meet me for some small talk, honey?"

My fingers tightened involuntarily around the receiver. *Small talk* was a simple code. *Trouble,* it meant, *be careful.*

In case somebody was on an extension I kept my voice light. "Sure, kid. Where are you?"

"A little place on Eighth Avenue near the Garden . . . Lew Green's Bar."

"I know where it is. Be right down."

"And, Mike . . . come alone."

"Okay."

On the way out I stopped by Nat Drutman's office and talked him out of a .32 automatic he kept in his desk, shoved it under my belt behind my back, and grabbed a cab for Lew Green's Bar. There was a dampness in the air and a slick was showing on the streets, reflecting the lights of the city back from all angles. It was one of those nights that had a bad smell to it.

Inside the bar a pair of chunkers were swapping stories in a half-drunken tone while a TV blared from the wall. A small archway led into the back room that was nestled in semi-darkness and when I went in a thin, reedy voice said from one side, "Walk easy, mister."

He had his hands in his side pockets and would have been easy to take, loaded or not, but I went along with him. He steered me past the booths to the side entrance where another one waited who grinned in an insolent way and said, "He carries a heavy piece. You look for it?"

"You do it," the thin guy said.

He knew right where to look. He dragged the .45 out, said, "Nice," grinned again, and stuck it in his pocket. "Now outside. We got transportation waiting. You're real V.I.P."

The place they took me to was in Long Island City, a section ready to be torn down to make way for a new factory building. The car stopped outside an abandoned store and when the smart one nodded I followed him around the back with the thin one six feet behind me and went on inside.

They sat at a table, three of them, with Velda in a chair at the end. A single Coleman lamp threw everything into sharp lights and shadows, making their faces look unreal.

I looked past them to Velda. "You okay, honey?"

She nodded, but there was a tight cast to her mouth.

The heavy-set guy in the homburg said, "So you're Mike Hammer."

I took a wild guess. "Del Penner."

His face hardened. "He clean?"

Both the guys at the door behind him nodded and the one took my .45 out and showed it. Del said, "You came too easy, Hammer."

"Who expected trouble?"

"In your business you should always expect it."

"I'll remember it. What's the action, Penner?"

"You sent her asking about me. Why?"

"Because I'm getting my toes stepped on. A guy named Kid Hand got shot and I hear you're taking his place. I don't like to get pushed. Now what?"

"You'll get more than pushed, Hammer. Word's around that you got yourself some top cover and knocking you off can make too much noise. Not that it can't be handled, but who needs noise? Okay, you're after something, so spill it."

"Sure. You are stepping up then?"

Penner shrugged elaborately. "Somebody takes over. What else?"

"Who's Dickerson?"

Everybody looked at everybody else before Del Penner decided to answer me. He finally made up his mind. "You know that much, then you can have this. *Nobody* knows who Mr. Dickerson is."

"Somebody knows."

"Maybe, but not you and not us. What else?"

"You pull this stunt on your own?"

"That you can bet your life on. When this broad started nosing around I wanted to know why. So I asked her and she told me. She said they were your orders. Now get this . . . I know about the whole schmear with you knocking off Kid Hand and getting Levitt bumped and leaving Marv Kania running around with a slug in his gut. I ain't got orders on you yet but like I said, when anybody noses around me I want to know why."

"Supposing I put it this way then, Penner . . . I'm the same way. Anybody tries to shoot me up is in for a hard time. You looked like a good place to start with and don't figure I'm the only one who'll think of it. You don't commit murder in this town and just walk away from it. If you're stepping into Kid Hand's job then you should know that too."

Penner smiled tightly. "The picture's clear, Hammer. I'm just stopping it before it gets started."

"Then this bit is supposed to be a warning?"

"Something like that."

"Or maybe you're doing a favor ahead of time."

"What's that mean?"

"Like Kid Hand was maybe doing a personal favor and stepped down off his pedestal to look like a big man."

The silence was tight. Del Penner just stared at me, not bothered at all by what I said. His hand reached up and touched his homburg and he sat back in his chair. "Warning then, Hammer. Don't make any more noise around me. I imagine you'd be about a fifteen-hundred-buck job. One thousand five hundred bucks can buy both of you dead and no mud on my hands. Clear?"

I put both hands on the table and leaned right into his face. "How much would you cost, Del?" I asked him. He glared at me, his eyes hard and bright. I said, "Come on, Velda. They're giving us a ride home."

We sat in the front next to the driver, the skinny guy in the back. All the way into Manhattan he kept playing with my gun. When we got to my office the one behind the wheel said, "Out, mac."

"Let's have the rod."

"Nah, it's too good a piece for a punk like you. I want a souvenir."

So I put the .32 up against his neck while Velda swung around in her seat and pointed the automatic at the skinny guy and his whine was a tinny nasal sound he had trouble making. He handed over the .45 real easy, licking his lips and trying to say something. The one beside me said, "Look, mac . . ."

"I never come easy, buddy. You tell them all."

His eyes showed white all the way around and he knew. He knew all right. The car pulled away with a squeal of tires and I looked at Velda and laughed. "You play it that way by accident, honey?"

"I've had to read a lot of minds the past seven years. I knew how it would work. I just wanted you ready."

"I don't know whether to kiss you or smack your ass."

She grinned impishly. "You can *always* kiss me."

"Don't ask for it."

"Why not? It's the only way I'm going to get it, I think."

Teddy's place is a lush restaurant about as far downtown as it's possible to get without falling in the river. It seemed an unlikely spot for good food and celebrities, but there you got both. Hy Gardner was having a late supper with Joey and Cindy Adams, and when he spotted us, waved us over to the table.

Before we could talk he ordered up scampi and a steak for both of us, then: "You come down for supper or information?"

"Both."

"You got Joey really researching. He comes to me, I go to somebody else, and little by little I'm beginning to get some mighty curious ideas. When are you going to recite for publication?"

"When I have it where it should be."

"So what's the pitch on Sally Devon?"

"All yours, Joey," I said.

He could hardly wait to get it out. "Boy, what a deal you handed me. You threw an old broad my way. There was more dust on her records than a Joe Miller joke. Then you know who comes up with the answers?"

"Sure, Cindy."

"How'd you know?"

"Who else?"

"Drop dead. Anyway, we contacted some of the kids who worked with her only like now they're ready for the old ladies' home. Sure, she was in show business, but with her it didn't last long and was more of a front. Her old friends wouldn't say too much, being old friends and all, but you knew what they were thinking. Sally Devon was a high-priced whore. She ran with some of the big ones for a while, then got busted and wound up with some of the racket boys."

Velda looked at me, puzzled. "If she was involved with the rackets, how'd she end up with Sim Torrence who was supposed to be so clean? That doesn't make sense."

"Sure it does," Hy told her. "He got her off a hook when he was still an assistant D.A. Look, she was still a beautiful doll then and you know the power of a doll. So they became friends. Later he married her. I can name a couple of other top politicos who are married to women who used to be in the business. It isn't as uncommon as you think."

He put his fork down and sipped at his drink. "What do you make of it now?" When I didn't answer he said, "Blackmail?"

"I don't know," I admitted.

"Well, what else do you want?"

For a moment I sat there thinking. "Torrence is a pretty big wheel now, isn't he?"

"As big as they get without being in office."

"Okay, he said repeated threats were made on him by guys he helped put away."

"Ah, they all get that."

"They all don't have a mess like this either."

"So what?"

"This, Hy . . . I'd like a rundown on his big cases, on everyone who ever laid a threat on him. You ought to have that much in your morgue."

Hy shrugged and grinned at me. "I suppose you want it tonight."

"Why not?"

"So we'll finish the party in my office. Come on."

Hy's file on Sim Torrence was a thick one composed of hundreds of clippings. We all took a handful and found desk space to look them over. A little after one we had everything classified and cross-indexed. Joey had four cases of threats on Sim's life, Cindy had six, Velda and I both had three, and Hy one. He put all the clips in a Thermofax machine, pulled copies, handed them over, and put the files back.

"Now can we go home?" he said.

Joey wanted to go on with it until Cindy gave him a poke in the ribs.

"So let's all go home," I told him.

We said so long downstairs and Velda and I headed back toward the Stem. In the lower Forties I checked both of us into a hotel, kissed her at the door, and went down to my room. She didn't like it, but I still had work to do.

After a shower I sat on the bed and started through the clips. One by one I threw them all down until I had four left. All the rest who had threatened Sim Torrence were either dead or back in prison. Four were free, three on parole, and one having served a life sentence of thirty years.

Life.

Thirty years.

He was forty-two when he went in, seventy-two when he came out. His name was Sonny Motley and there was a picture of him in a shoe repair shop he ran on Amsterdam Avenue. I put the clips in the discard pile and looked at the others.

Sherman Buff, a two-time loser that Sim had put the screws to in court so that he caught a big fall. He threatened everybody including the judge, but Torrence in particular.

Arnold Goodwin who liked to be called Stud. Sex artist. Rapist. He put the full blame for his fall on Torrence, who not only prosecuted his case but processed it from the first complaint until his capture. No known address, but his parole officer could supply that.

Nicholas Beckhaus, burglar with a record who wound up cutting a cop during his capture. He and two others broke out of a police van during a routine transfer and it was Sim Torrence's office who ran him down until he was trapped in a rooming house. He shot a cop in that capture too. He promised to kill Torrence on sight when he got out. Address unknown, but he would have a parole officer too.

I folded the clips, put three in my pants pocket, and leaned back on the bed. Then there was a knock on the door.

I had the .45 in my hand, threw the bolt back, and moved to the side. Velda walked in grinning, closed the door, and stood there with her back against it. "Going to shoot me, Mike?"

"You crazy!"

"Uh-huh."

"What do you want?"

"You don't know?"

I reached out and pulled her in close, kissed her hair, then felt the fire of her mouth again. She leaned against me, her breasts firm and insistent against my naked chest, her body forming itself to mine.

"I'm going to treat you rough, my love . . . until you break down."

"You're going back to bed."

"To bed, yes, but not back." She smiled, pulled away, and walked to my sack. Little by little, slowly, every motion a time-honored motion, she took off her clothes. Then she stood there naked and smiling a moment before sliding into the bed where she lay there waiting.

"Let's see who's the roughest," I said, and lay down beside her. I punched out the light, got between the top sheet and the cover, turned on my side and closed my eyes.

"You big bastard," she said softly. "If I didn't love you I'd kill you."

chapter five ▋▋▋▋▋▋▋▋▋▋▋▋▋▋

I WAS UP AND dressed before eight. The big, beautiful, tousled black-haired thing who had lain so comfortably against me all night stirred and looked at me through sleepy-lidded eyes, then stretched languidly and smiled.

"Frustrated?" I asked her.

"Determined." She stuck her tongue out at me. "You'll pay for last night."

"Get out of the sack. We have plenty to do."

"Watch."

I turned toward the mirror and put on my tie. "No, damn it."

But I couldn't help seeing her, either. It wasn't something you could take your eyes off very easily. She was too big, too lovely, her body a pattern of symmetry that was frightening. She posed deliberately, knowing I would watch her, then walked into the shower without bothering to close the door. And this time I saw something new. There was a fine, livid scar that ran diagonally across one hip and several parallel lines that traced themselves across the small of her back. I had seen those kind of marks before. Knives made them. Whips made them. My hands knotted up for a second and I yanked at my tie.

When she came out she had a towel wrapped sarong-fashion around her, smelling of soap and hot water, and this time I didn't watch her. Instead I pulled the clips out, made a pretense of reading them until she was dressed, gave them to her to keep in her handbag, and led her out the door.

At the elevator I punched the down button and put my hand through her arm. "Don't do that to me again, kitten."

Her teeth flashed through the smile. "Oh no, Mike. You've kept me waiting too long. I'll do anything to get you. You see . . . I'm not done with you yet. You can marry me right now or put up with some persecution."

"We haven't got time right now."

"Then get ready to suffer, gentleman." She gave my arm a squeeze and got on the elevator.

After breakfast I bypassed Pat's office to get a line on the parole officers handling Buff, Goodwin, and Beckhaus. Both Buff and Beckhaus were reporting to the same officer and he was glad to give me a rundown on their histories.

Sherman Buff was married, lived in Brooklyn, and operated a successful electronics shop that subcontracted jobs from larger companies. His address was good, his income sizable, and he had a woman he was crazy about and no desire to go back to the old life. The parole officer considered him a totally rehabilitated man.

Nicholas Beckhaus reported regularly, but he had to come in on the arm of his brother, a dentist, who supported him. At some time in prison he had been assaulted and his back permanently damaged so that he was a partial cripple. But more than that, there was brain damage too, so that his mental status was reduced to that of a ten-year-old.

The officer who handled Arnold Goodwin was more than anxious to talk about his charge. Goodwin had been trouble all the way and had stopped reporting in three months ago. Any information we could dig up on his whereabouts he'd appreciate. He was afraid of only one thing . . . that before Goodwin was found he'd kill somebody.

Arnold Goodwin looked like a good bet.

Velda said, "Did you want to see the other probable?"

"Sonny Motley?"

"It will only take a few minutes."

"He's in his seventies. Why?"

She moved her shoulders in thought. "He was a good story. The three-million-dollar killer."

"He wasn't in for murder. He was a three-time loser when they caught him in that robbery and he drew an automatic life sentence."

"That could make a man pretty mad," she reminded me.

"Sure, but guys in their seventies aren't going to hustle on a kill after thirty years in the pen. Be reasonable."

"Okay, but it wouldn't take long."

"Oh, hell," I said.

Sonny Motley's shoe repair shop had been open at seven as usual, the newsboy said, and pointed the place out to us. He was sitting in the window, a tired-looking old man bent over a metal foot a woman's shoe was fitted to, tapping on a heel. He nodded, peering up over his glasses at us like a shaven and partially bald Santa Claus.

Velda and I got up in the chairs and he put down his work to shuffle over to us, automatically beginning the routine of a shine. It wasn't a new place and the rack to one side of the machines was filled with completed and new jobs.

When he finished I gave him a buck and said, "Been here long?"

He rang the money up and smiled when I refused the change. "Year and a half." Then he pulled his glasses down a little more and looked at me closely. "Reporter?"

"Nope."

"Well, you look like a cop, but cops aren't interested in me any more. Not city cops. So that makes you independent, doesn't it?"

When I didn't answer him he chuckled. "I've had lots of experience with cops, son. Don't let it discourage you. What do you want to know?"

"You own this place?"

"Yup. Thirty years of saving a few cents a day the state paid me and making belts and wallets for the civilian trade outside bought me this. Really didn't cost much and it was the only trade I learned in the pen. But that's not what you want to know."

I laughed and nodded. "Okay, Sonny, it's about a promise you made a long time ago to kill Sim Torrence."

"Yeah, I get asked that lots of times. Mostly by reporters though." He pulled his stool over and squatted on it. "Guess I was pretty mad back then." He smiled patiently and pushed his glasses up.

"Let's say that if he up and died I wouldn't shed any tears, but I'll tell you Mr. . . ."

"Hammer. Mike Hammer."

"Yes, Mr. Hammer . . . well, I'm just not about to go back inside walls again. Not that this is any different. Same work, same hours. But I'm on the outside. You understand?"

"Sure."

"Something else too. I'm old. I think different. I don't have those old feelings." He looked at Velda, then me. "Like with the women. Was a time when even thinking of one drove me nuts, knowing I couldn't have one. Oh, how I wanted to kill old Torrence then. But like I told you, once you get old the fire goes out and you don't care any more. Same way I feel about Torrence. I just don't care. Haven't even thought about him until somebody like you or a reporter shows up. Then I think of him and it gets funny. Sound silly to you?"

"Not so silly, Sonny."

He giggled and coughed, then looked up. "Silly like my name. Sonny. I was a heller with the women in them days. Looked young as hell and they loved to mother me. Made a lot of scores like that." For a moment his eyes grew dreamy, then he came back to the present. "Sonny. Ah, yeah, they were the days, but the fire is out now."

"Well . . ." I took Velda's arm and he caught the motion.

Eagerly, a man looking for company, he said, "If you want I could show you the papers on what happened. I had somebody save 'em. You wait here a minute." He got up, shuffled off through a curtained door, and we could hear him rummaging through his things. When he came back he laid out a pitiful few front pages of the old *World* and there he was spread all over the columns.

According to the testimony, in 1932 the Sonny Motley mob, with Black Conley second in command, were approached secretly by an unknown expert on heisting through an unrevealed medium. The offer was a beautifully engineered armored-car stickup. Sonny accepted and was given the intimate details of the robbery including facets known only to insiders which would make the thing come off.

Unfortunately, a young Assistant District Attorney named Sim Torrence got wind of the deal, checked it out, and with a squad of cops, broke up the robbery . . . but only after it had been accomplished. The transfer of three million dollars in cash had been made to a commandeered cab and in what looked like a spectacular double cross, or possibly an attempt to save his own skin, Black Conley had jumped in the cab when the shooting started and taken off, still firing back into the action with the rifle he had liked so well. One shot caught Sonny Motley and it was this that stopped his escape more than anything else. In an outburst of violence in the courtroom Sonny shouted that he had shot back at the bastard who double-crossed him and if he didn't hit him, then he'd get him and Torrence someday for sure. They never found the cab, the driver, the money, or Black Conley.

Sonny let me finish, and when I handed the papers back said, "It would've gone if Blackie didn't pull out."

"Still sore?"

"Hell no."

"What do you think happened?"

"Tell you what, Mr. Hammer. I got me a guess. That was a double cross somehow, only a triple cross got thrown in. I think old Blackie wound up cab and all at the bottom of the river someplace."

"The money never showed."

"Nope. That went with Blackie too. Everybody lost. I just hope I did shoot the bastard before he died. I don't see how I coulda missed."

"You're still mad, Sonny."

"Naw, not really. Just annoyed about them thirty years he made me take. That Torrence really laid it on, but hell, he had it made. I was a three-timer by then anyway and would have taken life on any conviction. It sure made Torrence though." He pulled his glasses off, looked at the papers once with disgust, rolled them into a ball, and threw them away from him into a refuse carton. "Frig it. What's the sense thinking of them things?"

He looked older and more tired in that moment than when we came in. I said, "Sure, Sonny, sorry we bothered you."

"No trouble at all, Mr. Hammer. Come in for a shine any time."

On the street Velda said, "Pathetic, wasn't he?"

"Aren't they all?"

We waited there a few minutes trying to flag a cab, then walked two blocks before one cut over to our side and squealed to a stop. A blue panel truck almost caught him broadside, but the driver was used to those simple occupational hazards and didn't blink an eye.

I let Velda off at the office with instructions to get what she could from Pat concerning Basil Levitt and Kid Hand and to try to re-establish some old pipelines. If there were new faces showing in town like Jersey Toby said, there was a reason for it. There was a reason for two dead men and a murder attempt on me. There was a reason for an assassination layout with Sue Devon the target and somebody somewhere was going to know the answers.

When Velda got out I gave the cabbie Sim Torrence's Westchester address and sat back to try and think it out. Traffic was light on the ride north and didn't tighten up until we got to the upper end of Manhattan.

Then it was too thick. Just as the cab slowed for a light somebody outside let out a scream and I had time to turn my head, see the nose of a truck almost in the window, and threw myself across the seat as the cab took a tremendous jar that crushed in the side and sent glass and metal fragments ripping above my head. There was one awful moment as the cab tipped, rolled onto its side, and lay there in that almost total silence that follows the second after an accident.

Up front the cabbie moaned softly and I could smell the sharp odor of gasoline. Somebody already had the front door open and arms were reaching in for the driver. I helped lift him, crawled out the opening, and stood there in the crowd brushing myself off. A couple dozen people grouped around the driver, who seemed more shaken than hurt, and for a change a few were telling him they'd be willing to be witnesses. The driver of the truck had cut across and deliberately slammed into the cab like it was intentional or the driver was drunk.

But there wasn't any driver in the truck at all. Somebody said he had jumped out and gone down into a subway kiosk across the street and acted like he was hurt. He was holding his belly and stumbled as he ran. Then I noticed the truck. It was a blue panel job and almost identical to the one which almost nailed the cab when Velda and I first got in it.

Nobody noticed me leave at all. I took the number of the cab and would check back later, but right now there wasn't time enough to get caught up in a traffic accident. A block down I got another cab and gave him the same address. At the Torrence estate I told the driver to wait, went up, and pushed the bell chime.

Seeing Geraldine King again was as startling as it was the first time. She was in a sweater and skirt combination that set off the titian highlights in her hair, giving a velvet touch to the bright blue of her eyes. There was nothing businesslike about the way she was dressed. It was there only to enhance a lovely body and delight the viewer. I had seen too many strap marks not to know she was skin naked beneath the sweater.

She caught my eyes, let me look a moment longer, and smiled gently. "Stickler for convention?"

"Not me, honey."

"Women should be like pictures . . . nice to look at."

"Not if you haven't got the price to afford to take them home."

"Sometimes you don't have to buy. There are always free gifts."

"Thanks," I grunted. Then I laughed at her. "You sure must be one hell of a political advantage to have around."

"It helps." She held the door open. "Come on in. Mr. Torrence is in the study."

When I went in Sim pushed some papers aside, stood up, and shook hands. "Glad to see you again, Mike. What can I do for you?"

"Some gal you got there."

"What?" He frowned behind his glasses. "Oh . . . oh, yes, indeed. Now . . ."

"I've been checking out your enemies, Mr. Torrence. Those who wanted to kill you."

"Oh?"

"You said you knew of a dozen persons who threatened to kill you. Would Arnold Goodwin be one?"

"The sex offender?"

"Among other things."

"Yes . . . he made threats. Since he was so young I paid no attention to them. Why?"

"Because he's out and is in violation of his parole. He hasn't reported in for some time."

"He was quite an emotionally disturbed young man. Do you think . . .?"

I shrugged. "Those guys can do anything. They'd hurt anybody to get to the primary object of their hate. I haven't followed through on him, but I will."

"Well, the police should be informed immediately . . ."

"They will be. His parole officer has him listed already. The thing is, he can cut a wide path before they nail him. Meantime, any protection for Sue or yourself should be direct and personal. I'd suggest an armed guard."

"Mr. Hammer . . . we're coming into an election year. If this kind of thing gets out do you know what it means?"

"So take your chances then."

"I'll have to. Nevertheless, it may be sensible to keep somebody here in the house with me. I think Geraldine can arrange for someone."

"You want me to?"

"No, we'll take care of it."

"Okay then. Incidentally, I saw Sonny Motley."

"Sonny Motley?" He tugged at his glasses and pulled them off. "He was given a life sentence."

"Life ends at thirty years in the pen. He's out. You remember him then?"

"I certainly do! It was that case that made me a public figure. You don't think . . ."

"He's an old guy who runs a shoe shop uptown now. No, he's safe enough. You don't play tough when you're over seventy. Those brick walls took too much out of him. It was a pretty interesting case. Neither Blackie Conley or the loot ever showed up, did it?"

"Mike, we covered every avenue possible looking for that money. We alerted every state, every foreign government . . . but whatever happened to Conley or the money has never come to light."

"What do you think happened?" I asked him. Torrence made a vague gesture with his hands. "If he could have gotten out of the country, effected a successful new identity, and didn't try to make too much of a splash so as to attract attention he could have made it. Others have done it on a smaller scale. So might he. That job was well engineered. Whether or not Conley actually planned a double cross or took off when he saw how the fighting was going, we'll never know, but he got away."

"There was the cab."

"He could have killed the driver and dumped the cab somewhere. He was a ruthless man."

"Sonny seemed to think somebody else got to him."

Torrence shook his head, thinking. "I doubt it. There was still the cab and driver, still the money whose serial numbers were recorded. No, I think Conley made a successful escape. If he did, he's probably dead by now. He was eight years older than Sonny, if I remember right. That would put him in his eighties at the end of this time." He looked at me steadily. "Funny you should bring that up."

"Something's come out of the past, buddy. There's trouble. I'm in the middle of it."

"Yes," he nodded, "you are. Now, how can I be of further help?"

"Look back. No matter how slight it might seem, see who wants you badly enough to try to hurt Sue or yourself."

"I will, Mr. Hammer."

"One more thing."

"What's that?"

"Your former wife."

"Yes?"

"How much did you know about her?" I asked him.

Torrence flinched visibly, dropped his eyes to his hands, then brought them back to my face again. "I assume you went to the trouble of looking into her background."

"I heard a few things."

"Then let me say this . . . I was well aware of Sally's history before marrying her. In way of explanation I'll tell you that I loved her. In way of an excuse you might understand, say there's no accounting for taste. We met when she was in trouble. A business relationship developed into friendship that became love. Unfortunately, she maintained her alcoholism and died because of it. Why do you ask?"

"I was thinking of blackmail possibilities."

"Discard them. Everything is a matter of public record. I wouldn't tolerate blackmail."

"Maybe it hasn't been tried yet."

"What does that mean?"

"I don't know," I said. "There are just some interesting possibilities that have developed. You try to stay ahead of them." I got up and put on my hat. "Okay, if I need anything else I'll stop by."

"I'm always available, Mr. Hammer." With a gesture of dismissal he went back to his papers, so I eased out the door and looked for Geraldine King.

She was in a smaller room toward the front, one that had been converted into a small, but efficiently equipped office. Behind a typewriter, with black-rimmed glasses perched on her nose, she looked like a calendar artist's idea of what a secretary should be. Through the knee well in the desk I could see her skirt hiked halfway up her thighs for comfort and the first thing she did when she saw me in the doorway was reach for the hem and tug it down.

I let out a half-silent wolf whistle and grinned. "Man," I said.

She pulled her glasses off and dropped them in front of her. "Distracting, aren't I?"

"Tell me, honey, how the hell does Torrence work with you around?"

Geraldine chuckled and shrugged. "With ease, that's how. I am a fixture, a political associate and nothing more. I can prance around this house in the buff and he'd never notice."

"Want to bet?"

"No, I mean it. Mr. Torrence is dedicated. His political life is all he knows and all he wants. He's been in public service so long that he thinks of nothing else. Any time he is seen with a woman having supper or at some social function is for a political advantage."

"The female votes?"

"Certainly. Women don't mind widowers who seem to still have a family instinct but they do seem to resent confirmed bachelors."

"That's what the men get for giving them the vote. Look, kid, Sim tells me you've been through a few of his political campaigns."

"That's right."

"He ever have any trouble before?"

"Like what?"

"Something from his past coming out to shake him. Any blackmail attempts or threats against his personal life. He says no, but sometimes these things go through the party rather than the individual."

She sat back, frowning, then shook her head. "I think I'd know of anything like that. The organization is well knit and knows the implications of these things and I would have been told, but as far as I know nothing can interfere with his career. He's exceptionally clean. That's why we were so concerned about Sue's running off. Even a thing like that can affect voting. A man who can't run his own house can hardly be expected to run a state."

"You know he's in a position to be hurt now."

"I realize that." She got up, pushed her chair back, and walked toward me with a swaying stride, not conscious at all of the subtle undulations beneath the tight-fitting sweater and skirt. "Do you think Sue will be all right?"

"She's a big girl. She may not look it, but don't be fooled."

"This business . . . about Mr. Torrence killing her mother."

"That's an idea she'll have to get out of her mind."

Geraldine said, "She dreams it. Dreams can be pretty real sometimes. Her very early childhood couldn't have been very nice. I don't think she ever knew who her father was. If she makes open accusations it can damage Mr. Torrence."

"I'll speak to her. She around?"

"There's a summer house on the south side where she practices. She practically lives there."

She was standing in front of me now, concern deep inside those wild blue eyes. I said, "I'll see what I can do."

Geraldine smiled, reached up slowly, and put her arms around my neck. With the same deliberate slowness she pulled herself on her toes, wet her lips with her tongue, and brought my mouth down to hers. It was a soft teasing, tasting kiss, as if she were sampling the juice from a plum before buying the lot. Her mouth was a warm cavern filled with life and promise, then just as slowly she drew away, smiling.

"Thank you," she said.

I grinned at her. "Thank *you*."

"I could hate you easier than I could like you."

"Which is worse?"

"That you'll have to find out for yourself."

"Maybe I will, baby."

At first I didn't think she was there, then I heard the sounds of a cabinet opening and I knocked on the door. Her smile was like the sun breaking open a cloud and she reached for my hand. "Hello, Mike. Gee I'm glad to see you." She looked past me. "Isn't Velda with you?"

"Not this time. Can I come in?"

She made a face at me and stepped aside, then closed the door.

It was a funny little place, apparently done over to her specifications. One wall was all mirror with a dancer's practice bar against it. Opposite was a record player with a shelf of LP's, a shoe rack with all the implements of the trade, a standup microphone attached to a record player, a spinet piano covered with lead sheets of popular music and Broadway hits, with a few stuffed animals keeping them in place.

The rest of the room was a girl-style den with a studio couch, dresser, cabinets, and a small conference table. Cardboard boxes, books, and a few old-fashioned paper files covered the table and it was these she was going through when I found her.

"What're you up to, Sue?"

"Going through my mother's things."

"She's a long time dead. Face it."

"I know. Would you like to see what she looked like?"

"Sure."

There were a few clippings from the trade papers of the time and some framed night-club shots taken by the usual club photographers and they all showed a well-built blonde with a slightly vacuous expression. Whether it was intended or built in I couldn't tell, but she almost typified the beautiful but dumb showgirl. There were four photos, all taken in night spots long since gone. In two of them she was with a party of six. In the other two there were four people, and in those she was with the same man, a lanky dark-haired guy with deep-set eyes who almost seemed like a hell-fire preacher touring the sin spots for material for a sermon.

"She was pretty," I said.

"She was beautiful," Sue said softly. "I can still remember her face."

"These were taken before you were born." I pointed to the dates on the back of the photos.

"I know. But I can remember her. I remember her talking to me. I remember her talking about *him*."

"Come on, kid."

Her hair swirled as she made a small negative gesture. "I mean it. She hated him."

"Sue . . . they were married."

"I don't care."

I looked at her sharply. "Want me to be blunt?"

She shrugged and bit into her lip.

"Your mother was an alcoholic. Sim tried everything to dry her out. Alcoholics hate that. If she hated him it was because he wanted to help. Get it out of your mind that he killed her."

"She told me the snake killed her."

"Drunks see snakes and elephants and everything else. Don't go getting wrapped up in an obsession."

"She told me to look for a letter. Someday I'll find it."

"You were three years old. How could you remember those things?"

"I just do."

"Okay, you look for it then. Meanwhile, I want you to do something for me."

"What?"

"Don't cause trouble. You stay out of his hair until we clear this thing up. Promise me?"

"Maybe." She was smiling at me.

"What do you want?"

"Kiss me."

I grunted. "I just got done kissing Geraldine King."

"You're nasty, but I don't care." She sidled around the desk and stood there with her hands behind her back. "I'll take seconds," she said.

So I kissed her.

"Not like that."

"How?" The damn game was getting out of hand. The big broads I could handle, but how do you get the kids off your back?

Then she showed me how in a moment of sudden violence that was all soft and tender yet filled with some latent fury I couldn't understand. The contact was brief, but it shook me and left her trembling, her eyes darkly languid and her face flushed.

"I hope you like seconds best."

"By far, kid, only don't do it again." I faked a laugh and held her away. "Stay cool, okay?"

"Okay, Mike."

Then I got out of there and back into the taxi where I gave the driver Pat's address.

chapter six ▰▰▰▰▰▰▰▰▰▰▰

THE NEW INSPECTOR was a transfer from another division, a hard apple I had seen around years ago. His name was Spencer Grebb and one of his passionate hatreds was personnel from other fields poking around in his domain, with first cut going to private investigators and police reporters. From the look he gave me, I seemed to have a special place in his book and was target one on his big S list.

Charles Force was a D.A. out for Charlie Force. He was young, talented, on the way up, and nothing was going to deter his ambition. He was a nice-looking guy, but you couldn't tell what was going on behind his face. He had made it the hard way, in the courtrooms, and was a pro at the game right down the line.

Now they both sat at one side of the room with Pat in the middle, looking at me like I was game they were going to let out of the box long enough to get a running start so that hunting me down would be a pleasure.

After the introductions I said, "You check those slugs out, Pat?"

"Both from the same gun that killed Basil Levitt. You mentioned Marv Kania. Could you identify the guy, the guy who pulled the trigger?"

"If he's Kania I could."

"Try this." Pat flipped a four-by-five photo across the desk and I picked it up.

I looked at it and tossed it back. "That's the one."

"Positive?"

"Positive. He's made two passes at me, once in the office building and today with a truck. It rammed a taxi I was in."

Inspector Grebb had a hard, low voice. "This you reported right away."

"Now I'm doing it. At the moment it could have been a simple traffic accident. I ducked out because I had something to do. Now I'm tying it all in."

His smile was a twisted thing. "You know, it wouldn't be too hard to find a charge to press there, would it, Mr. Force?"

Charlie Force smiled too, but pleasantly. A courtroom smile. "I don't think so, Inspector."

As insolently as I could make it, I perched on the edge of Pat's desk and faced them. "Let's get something straight. I know what you guys would like to see, but I'm not going to fall easily. The agency I represent is Federal. It's obscure, but pulls a lot of weight, and if you want to see just how much weight is there, push me a little. I'm operating in an official capacity whether you like it or not, which gives me certain latitudes. I've been around long enough to know the score on both ends so play it straight, friends. I'm cooperating with all departments as Captain Chambers will tell you. Just don't push. You'd be surprised what kind of a stink I can raise if I want to."

I looked at Charlie Force deliberately. "Especially in the publicity circuit, buddy."

His eyebrows pulled together. "Are you threatening me, Mr. Hammer?"

I nodded and grinned at him. "That I am, buster. That's one edge I have on you. A bad schmear and you can go down a notch and never hit the big-time. So play ball."

They didn't like it, but they had to take it. In a way, I couldn't blame them a bit. An ex private jingle coming in with a big ticket isn't easy to take. Especially not one with a reputation like mine.

The D.A. seemed to relax. He was still smiling, but it wasn't for real. "We've been advised to cooperate."

Thanks, Rickerby, I thought. *You're still paying for The Dragon.*

Pat said, "We ran a pretty thorough check on Basil Levitt."

"Anything?"

"We located a girl he used to shack up with. She told us he was on a job but wouldn't say what it was. He said he was getting paid well for it but there would be more later and he was already making big plans. Outside of a few others who knew he had fresh money on him, nothing."

"What about the rifle?"

"Stolen from a sporting goods store upstate about a month ago. We had the numbers on file. He must have worn gloves in the room where he had the gun set up, but got careless when he loaded the clip. There was a single print that tied him in with it."

Before I could answer, Charlie Force said, "Now what we are interested in knowing is who he was shooting at."

I looked at my watch and then at his face. "Art Rickerby clued you in. You know what Velda was involved with."

"Yes," he agreed pleasantly. "We know. But I'm beginning to wonder about it all."

"Well, stop wondering."

"You were there too. Right in the middle."

"Fresh on the scene. Levitt had been there some time. Days."

"Waiting for you?"

Let them think it, I figured. I wasn't cutting him in on anything. "I'm trying to find that out too," I told him. "When I do you'll get the word."

Grebb and Force got up together and headed for the door. Their inspection trip was over. They were satisfied now that I'd make a good target. Grebb looked at me through those cold eyes, still smiling twistedly. "Be sure to do that," he said.

When they were gone Pat shook his head. "You don't make friends easily."

"Who needs them?"

"Someday you will."

"I'll wait until then. Look, buddy, you know what the action is in town?"

Pat just nodded.

"Dickerson?"

He spread his hands. "We're working on it."

"How can a wheel come in already operating and not be known?"

"It isn't hard. You want to know what we have?"

"Damn right."

"Hoods are showing up from all over the country. They're all clean, at least clean enough so we can't tumble them. We can roust them when we want to, but they have nothing we can pin on them."

"How many?"

"Not an army, but let a dozen wrong types hit town at once and it sets a pattern. Something's about to happen."

"They're not holding a convention."

"No, they're getting paid somehow. Either there's loot being laid out or they're operating under orders. There are Syndicate men in and sitting by nice and quietly waiting for the word. All we can do is wait too. In the meantime there's a shake-up in the rackets. Somebody's got the power to pull strings long enough to get action out of the Midwest and the coast. There's a power play going on and a big one. I wish I could figure it out."

He sat there drumming his fingertips on the desk top. "What do *you* think, Mike?"

I gave it to him straight, right down the line, laying the facts face up from the time I walked into the apartment until I reached his office. I watched his mind close around the details and put them into mental cubbyholes to hold there until he had time to assimilate them. But I gave him no opinions, nothing more than facts.

Finally he said, "There are some strange implications."

"Too many."

"I suppose you want something from me now."

"Yeah. Get a killer off my back."

His eyes touched mine and narrowed. "We'll do all we can. He can't get around too long with a bullet in him."

"Up to now he's been doing great."

I got up off the desk and put on my hat. "This Arnold Goodwin . . ."

"I'll get a team out on it. This is one of the implications I don't like. These are the real potential killers. Whether Torrence likes it or not, I'll see that somebody is staked out around his house. We'll keep it quiet, so what he doesn't know won't hurt him."

"Good deal. I'll see you later."

"By the way, Joey Adams called here for you. He wants to see you about something." He grinned at me. "Said he got stopped on a traffic violation and flashed his honorary badge with all the little diamonds and just found out from the arresting officer what it was good for."

"Old joke."

"Funny though."

I called Joey from downstairs and had him meet me in the Blue Ribbon. It was between the meal hours and nobody was there, so George and I sipped coffee until he got there.

After he ordered milk and cake I said, "What's the bit?"

"Look you had me chasing down Sally Devon's old friends. Well, I'm up in the office when Pauline Coulter comes in to tell me what she forgot. About a week ago she ran into Annette Lee who was with Sally when she died."

"Man, she was old then."

"She's older now, but still kicking. Annette Lee used to be a wardrobe mistress in a show Sally worked in and afterward worked for Sally as sort of personal maid. Now how about that? You think I'll make a cop yet?"

"Not if you keep flashing that police badge." I grinned.

"Come on!"

"Okay, it was a joke." I laughed. "No kidding though . . . this Lee gal might clean up a few things. It's nice to have friends in important places."

"Anytime, Mike." He pulled out a card and scribbled down an address. "Here's where she is. It's a rooming house across town. She never goes anywhere so you can always find her home."

I stuck the card in my pocket. "How about now? You free?"

"Like a bird, man."

Annette Lee had a front room downstairs in one of the countless brownstones along the street. Her pension money kept her adequately, her cat kept her company, and whatever went on outside her window was enough to keep her busy. She was a small woman, shrunken with age, but in the straight-back rocker, with tiny feet pushing against the floor with tireless rhythm to keep her in motion, she had a funny pixyish quality that was reflected in her faded gray eyes.

There was no telling her accurate age, but it had crept up on her so that her talk wandered into peculiar directions and it was difficult to keep her on one track. But she remembered Sally Devon well. They had been good friends and it was Sally who had taken her in when she was sick and needed an operation, and Sally who cared for her and paid her expenses, so that when Sally needed her, she was glad to go.

She eyed us sharply when I questioned her about Sally's background, but until she was aware that I knew about her past, was reluctant to talk about it. It was Sally's earnings in the seamier side of life that paid her expenses and she was grateful. Little by little she gave it to us. Sally had left show business to take up with men, had gotten involved with the wrong ones and found herself in trouble.

Yes, she knew Sim Torrence, and although she didn't like him, thought he had done well by Sally. He had taken her in when she needed help, and if it hadn't been for Sally's drinking the marriage might have been successful. What she thought was that Sally's guilt complex for bringing a tarnished background into Sim Torrence's life drove her to alcoholism.

She remembered the night Sally died, too. Outside in the cold. Drunk. It was a shame. She couldn't revive her. I asked her directly if she thought Sim Torrence had anything to do with Sally's death.

Annette Lee gave me a shriveling glance. "Don't be silly," she said.

"Just clearing up a point," I told her.

"Then what's this all about, young man?"

"Sue thinks so."

"Sally's little baby?"

"That's right."

"Rubbish. She was only a mite."

"Maybe," I said, "But she's pretty insistent about it. One minute she has the idea Torrence was responsible, the next she says it was a snake."

Annette's face pulled into a tight expression and for a moment her eyes were less faded-looking. "Snake? Sally used to talk about that. When she was drunk. She kept mentioning the snake. Funny you should bring it up. Never thought it would make an impression on a child. Yes, she used to talk about the snake all right. But no snake killed her. She died right there in the front yard, right in my arms. Like to froze, the poor thing did, all drunk up and sick. Maybe it was for the best though."

She sat back in the rocker and closed her eyes. Too much talking was wearing her down. I motioned to Joey and we got up. "Well," I said, "thanks for the talk. Maybe I'll come back again sometime."

"Please do."

We walked to the door as the rhythm of her rocking slowed down. Just as I was about to leave it picked up again and she said, "Young man . . ."

"Ma'am?"

"They ever catch him?"

"Who's that?"

"The one who ran off with all that money. A whole lot of money. Sally's old boy friend."

I called Joey back in and shut the door. "A lot of money?"

"Indeed. Three million dollars. Conley, I think his name was. Blackie Conley. He was a mean one. He was the meanest of them all. They ever catch him?"

"No, they never did."

With her eyes still closed she shook her head. "Never thought they would. He was a thinker. Even heard where he was going after they stole it."

"Where, Miss Lee?" I asked softly.

She didn't answer. She was asleep.

"*Damn,*" I said.

The picture was suddenly getting a sharp outline.

I dropped Joey at his AGVA office and went back to my own where Velda was waiting. She had compiled a report on Del Penner for me and from what it looked like he was in solidly now, a natural inheritor of Kid Hand's old territory. It was a step up and he was ready for it, taking advantage of an occupational hazard. Nothing was solidified yet, but he was there and holding on.

When I finished it I got Pat on the phone, asked him if he could pull a package on Blackie Conley from the file, then told Velda to run over and pick it up. When she left I was back in my chair and swung around so I could stare out the window at the concrete escarpment that was New York.

It was getting dark out and a mist was closing in. Another hour and it would be raining again. The multicolor neons of the city were bursting against the gray overcast like summer heat lightning and someplace across town a siren wailed. Another followed it.

Trouble out there. Trouble all over, but trouble out there all the time. Someplace was a guy with a slug in him and a gun in his hand. Someplace was Marv Kania, hurting like hell, waiting for me to show up so he could put one in my gut too. It was Levitt who had done it, but me in his mind. I was the living one, so I did it. Screw him. Let him hurt.

Three million dollars. That could bring trouble to a city. That could bring a man back to power and buy muscle. That was big starter money and a prize for anybody.

Sim Torrence thought Blackie Conley could have made it. Okay, suppose he did. Suppose he sat on that three million all these years, afraid to spend it, not wanting to convert it because of the loss he'd take in the transaction. He just sat on it. It was power to him. Brother, he sure waited for the heat to cool, but it happens like that sometimes. Harmony Brothers sat on a million and a half for forty-one years and only told where it was on his deathbed.

Frankie Boyle kept seventy thousand in his mattress for sixteen years, sleeping happily on it every night without ever touching it, then went out of his mind when the rooming house was burned down along with his unspent fortune.

So Blackie Conley got away and sat on three million for thirty years. In the last of his life he gets a power complex and wants to buy his way back in. He'd know how to do it all right. If he could stay under cover thirty years he could still do it.

Blackie Conley! Mr. Dickerson.

A big, fat possible.

Question: *Why try to knock off Sue Devon?*

Answer: A cute possible here too. If Blackie was in love with Sally, and IF Sally had a child by another man, there might be enough hatred to want the child destroyed.

There was only one thing wrong with the premise. Too many people wanted Sue dead. Basil Levitt was trying for it when Kid Hand and Marv Kania came in.

But there was an answer to that one too, a money answer. Sue was a target with a price on her head and if it were big enough the shooters would fight each other for a crack at her. Kid Hand could use the dough and make himself a big one in somebody's eyes at the same time. That could explain why Levitt came in so fast after I got there. He thought I was after head money too.

Blackie Conley, Mr. Dickerson, three million bucks. And the vultures.

Velda came in then and laid the package on my desk. Inside the folder was a picture of Conley. I had seen one like it not too long before in Sue's room. Blackie Conley was the guy in the night clubs with Sally Devon.

His arrest history went back to when he was a child and if he were alive today he'd be eighty-two years old. There were a lot older people still around and some of them right up there with the best. Age doesn't hit everybody the same way.

Pat had included some notes for me suggesting I go into a transcript of the trial if I wanted more information on Conley since it was the last that he was ever mentioned. He was tied in with the gang and his history brought out, but since the trial was a prolonged affair it would take a lot of reading to pick out the pieces.

I looked up at Velda and she stuck her tongue out at me. "I know, you want me to do it."

"You mind?"

"No, but what am I looking for?"

"Background on Conley."

"Why don't you ask Sonny Motley?"

"I intend to, kitten. We have to hit it from all sides."

I filled in the picture for her, watching her face put it together like I did. She nodded finally and said, "You could have it, Mike. It . . . seems right."

"But not quite?"

She ran the tip of her tongue between her teeth. "I just have a feeling."

"I know. Missing pieces. Suppose you meet Annette Lee and see if you can get any more out of her. It won't come easy, but try. She might give you someplace to start with Conley too."

"Okay, lover."

"And be careful, honey. That nut Kania is still loose. So is Arnold Goodwin. Those guys could be keys to this thing."

"Pat said he'd call you if anything came in on them."

"Good."

"And he said to tell you Charlie Force is protesting your association with the agency you work for."

"He knows what he can do."

"That Inspector Grebb is trouble. He's covering you like a blanket. Do you know you have a tail waiting downstairs?"

"I expected it. I know a way out too."

"You're asking for it, wise guy. I just don't want to see you get killed, that's all. I want to kill you myself. It'll take days and days."

"Knock it off." I swung off my chair and stood up. She grinned, kissed me lightly, and picked up her handbag.

"I arranged for an apartment for you. It's furnished and the key's in the desk. It's got a big double bed."

"It's polite to wait till you're asked."

Velda cocked her head and smiled. "There's a couch in the living room if you still want to be the gentleman."

"Can't you wait until we get married?"

"No." She pulled on her raincoat and belted it. "If I don't push you you'll never come."

"I suppose you have a key."

"Naturally."

"Change the damn lock."

She made a face and walked to the door. "So I'll do like you and shoot it off. *Adios,* doll."

* * *

Sonny Motley had closed his shop an hour ago, but the newsboy was still in his kiosk and told me the old guy had a beer or so every night in a joint two blocks down.

It was a sleazy little bar that had sort of just withered within the neighborhood, making enough to keep going, but nothing more. A half-dozen tables lined one wall and the air smelled of beer and greasy hamburgers. Two old broads were yakking it up at the bar, a couple of kids were at the other end watching the fights on TV while they pulled at their drinks, and Sonny Motley sat alone at the last table with a beer in front of him and a late-edition tabloid open in front of him. Beside his feet was a lunchbox and change of a dollar on the table.

I sat down opposite him and said, "Hello, Sonny."

He looked up, closed the paper, and gave me a half-toothless smile. "By damn, didn't expect you. Good you should come. I don't see many people socially."

"This isn't exactly social."

"'Course not. When does a private cop and a con get social? But for me any talk is social. Sometimes I wish I didn't finish my time. At least then I'd get to see a parole officer for a chat once in a while. But who the hell has time for an old guy like me?"

"Ever see any of your old mob, Sonny?"

"Come on . . . what's your name? Hammer . . ." He ticked off his fingers, "Gleason, Tippy Wells, Harry the Fox, Guido Sunchi . . . all dead. Vinny Pauncho is in the nuthouse up by Beacon and that crazy Willie Fingers is doing his big stretch yet in Atlanta. I wrote to Willie once and never even heard back. Who's left?"

"Blackie Conley."

"Yeah, he's left dead."

"Sim Torrence thinks he might have made it."

"Baloney."

I told the bartender to bring me a beer and turned back to Sonny. "Suppose he did."

"So let him."

"Suppose he came back with the three million bucks you guys heisted?"

Sonny laughed abruptly and smacked his hands on the table. "That would be the funniest yet. What the hell could he do with it? All that stud wanted was broads and at his age it would be like shoving a wet noodle up a tiger's . . . no, Hammer, it wouldn't do him no good at all." He sat back and chuckled at the thought and waved for another beer.

"Let's consider it," I insisted.

"Sure, go ahead."

"So he's old. He wants one more crack at the big-time."

"Who the hell would listen to him?"

"You could pull a power play from behind the scenes. Three million bucks can do a lot of talking and if somebody is fronting for you who knows what you look like?"

Sonny stopped smiling then, his face wrapped in thought. Then he dragged on the beer and put half of it down at once. "No," he said, "Blackie ain't coming back, Hammer. He never ain't."

"Why not?"

His grin was tight-lipped, satisfied with what he was thinking. "Because I nailed old Blackie, I did. Man, with a rod I was good. I mean good, Hammer. You know he got me with that damn rifle. It put me down and stopped me, but I had one chance at him when he took off in that taxi and let one go while he still had the rifle poked out the window. I didn't miss with that shot. I think I got old Blackie and he crawled off and died or wound himself and the taxi both up in the drink."

"Maybe."

"Okay, so I'm wrong. Hope I am." He chuckled again and finished the beer. "Like to see old Blackie again. I'd like to find out if I really did get him or not."

"Ever hear of Mr. Dickerson?" I asked him.

"Nope. Should I?"

"Not especially."

"Who is he?"

"I don't know either."

"Like hell you don't."

"Why do you say that?" I asked him.

"Because I've lived with cons too damn long, Hammer. You get so you can tell things without them having to be said. Take now, f'instance. You ain't asked all you came here to ask yet, have you?"

It was my turn to buy and I yelled for another brew. "Okay, old-timer, I'll put it straight. You remember Sally Devon?"

Sonny frowned slightly and wiped his mouth with the back of his hand. "Sure. Used to be my broad."

"I thought she was Conley's."

"That bastard would go after anything in skirts no matter who she belonged to."

"Even yours?"

"Sure. I warned him off a few times. Had to knock him on

his kiester once. But hell, what difference does it make? In those days he was a sharp article. Older than we were and pretty smooth. Sally was always sweet on him. If I didn't bounce her around she woulda left me for him any day."

He stopped suddenly, his eyes going cold. "You're thinking maybe because of her Blackie dumped the heist and tried to take me?"

"Could be."

Then the coldness left his eyes and the age came back. He let out a muted cackle and shook his head at the joke. "Damn," he said, "that guy was always thinking."

"Where were you going with the money if that job paid off, Sonny?"

"What's the matter, don't you read?"

"You tell me."

He bobbed his head, relishing the moment. "I even see it done on some TV shows now, but it woulda worked. We had a truck with a tailgate ramped down. We was to drive the cab right in there and take off. So the cops found the truck and another one we was going to change to. It's all down. Instead that Bastard Blackie crossed us."

"What were you going to do to the driver?"

"Toss him out, bump him. Who knows? We woulda figured somethin'."

"You had a hideout?"

"Yeah, a house in the Catskills we had rented ahead of time. The cops plastered that looking for Blackie. He made all the arrangements on that end and never got to use 'em. Coulda been the crime of the century."

"Maybe it was," I said.

Sonny was reaching for his glass and stopped short. "What're you thinking, boy?"

"Maybe while Blackie was making plans for you he was making other plans for himself. Suppose he arranged for an alternate hideout and made it after all. Suppose he bumped the driver, ditched the car, and holed up all these years and finally decided to come back again. Now he's here with three million bucks taking his last fling, buying himself an organization."

He listened, sat silent a moment, then shook his head and picked up his beer. "Not old Blackie. He couldn't live without the broads and now he's too old."

"Ever hear of a voyeur?"

"What's that?"

"They can't do it so they just watch. I know a few old jokers who get their kicks that way. They got millions too."

"I think you're nuts," he said, "but any time you want to talk about it come back and talk. You're the first company I had around in a long time."

"Sure." I wrote down my new address on a matchbook cover and passed it to him. "Reach me here or at the office if you get any ideas. You can earn some cash."

I put a buck on the table and left. Behind me Sonny was still chuckling. I'd like to be there if he ever got to meet Blackie face to face.

chapter seven

I CALLED Hy from a drugstore on the avenue and got Pete Ladero's address from him. I reached him at home and asked him if he could get the newspaper clips on the Motley-Conley job thirty years ago and bring them up to the office. He griped about leaving his favorite TV program, but his nose for news was too big and he said it would take an hour, but he'd be there.

At the Automat on Sixth between Forty-fourth and Forty-fifth I picked up a tray, loaded it with goodies, and went upstairs to think for a while. It wasn't accidental. I knew Jersey Toby would be there the same as he had been there at the same time every night the past ten years. I let him finish his meal, picked up my coffee, and joined him at his table. When he saw me he almost choked, gave a quick look around, and tightened up.

"Damn, can't you get off my neck? Whatta you want?"

"Talk, Toby, just talk."

"Well, I said all I'm gonna say. Scratch off, Mike. I don't want no part of you, buddy. You know I got asked questions already?"

"Who asked?"

"Some broad in the other joint. She knew you all right. I tried to lie out of it and said you was looking for a dame for that night but she wouldn't buy it. Said she knew you too well. You're hooked for somebody else. You're putting my tail in a sling."

"So I'll make it short."

"Like hell. You won't make nothing."

"Okay, Toby, then tomorrow a pickup goes out on you. You get rousted every time you step on the street. Lineup twice a week, complaints . . ."

Jersey Toby looked at me, his face white and drawn. "Come on, you wouldn't do that."

"Try me."

He finished his coffee, looked around nervously again until he was assured we were alone, and nodded. "You would at that. Okay, spill it."

"Let's go back to Dickerson again, Toby."

"We went through that once."

"You get the word."

"Sure . . . secondhand through the broads."

"Good enough. What's the word on the money angle? If out-of-town hoods are moving in, something's drawing them. Who's spreading the green around?"

Toby's tongue flicked at dry lips and he pulled on the butt. "Look . . . if I prime you, this is the last?"

I shrugged.

"Let's hear it, Mike."

"You bought it. I'll back off."

"Okay then, Marge . . . she's the redhead. She was with . . . a guy one night. No names, Mike. I ain't giving you names. I specialize in that end of the trade. Marge, she's a favorite with the hard boys. Does a lot of fancy tricks for them, see? Well, this guy . . . like he's representing somebody big. He's like muscle on lend. He comes in to do a favor. He's Chicago and ready. He ain't saying what's to do, but he stands ready. Now his boss man lends him out because a favor was asked, only his boss man don't *do* no favors. It's got to be bought or got to be forced. Somebody's got something on his boss man and is making a trade.

"Don't ask what it is. Who am I to know? I just put two and two together until it works out. Somebody is building an organization and although money is there it's the pressure that's bringing the boys in."

I tipped back in the chair watching him. "It plays if somebody is building an organization. Whatever the pressure is, it brings muscle in that can't be bought, then the muscle can be used to square the money."

"You play it," Toby said. "I don't even want to think on it no more."

"How many are in?"

"Enough. With a mob like's here I could damn near run the town single-handed."

"These boys all come from big sources?"

Toby's head bobbed once. "The biggest. The Syndicate's lending men. They come out of the individual operations, but the boss men are the Syndicate men. You're trouble, boy."

"Thanks, kiddo. You've been a help."

"For that I ain't happy. I hope they get you before they tie me into anything."

"Forget it," I said and got up from the table.

I left him there and walked out into the rain back toward my office. If Jersey Toby was right Mr. Dickerson was pulling off a cute trick. It figured right, too, because he'd be smart enough and would have had the time to work it out. Little by little he could have built the things he needed to pressure the big ones into line. He had the background, experience, and the desire. One thing led to another. Once the mob was in, an organization could be built that could utilize three million bucks properly.

If Mr. Dickerson was Blackie Conley it fitted just right.

Up in the office I had to wait only fifteen minutes before Pete Ladero came in with a folio under his arm. He laid the stuff on the table and opened it up. "Do I get an explanation first?"

"Research on Blackie Conley," I said.

"Aw, for crying out loud, he's been dead for years."

"Has he?"

"Well . . ." He paused and searched my face. "You on to something?"

"You familiar with this case?"

"I ran over it. The magazine writers rehashed it enough so I know the general background. Give."

"If Conley's alive he's got three million bucks in his kick. He might be old and fiesty enough to start trouble with it."

"Boy, bring-'em-back-alive Hammer." He reached for the paper. "You looking for anything special?"

"Conley's connection with the heist. Take half and we'll go through them."

So we sat down and read. Velda called and I told her to hop over, then went back to the papers again.

The prosecution had a cut-and-dried case. Sonny Motley pleaded guilty since he was nailed in the act and faced an automatic sentence anyway. He ranted and raved all the way through the trial, cursing everybody from the judge down, but Torrence and Conley in particular. Torrence because he wouldn't let him alone, but kept hammering for details, and Conley for the big double-cross and a bullet in his shoulder.

The main item of interest was the missing three million dollars, but despite the speculation and the nationwide police search, not one thing was turning up. Sonny Motley didn't mind spilling his guts if it meant nailing Blackie Conley and the unseen face who engineered the deal. Right then he figured they pulled the double-cross together, but Sim Torrence couldn't get any evidence whatsoever on the one behind the action.

There was another witness. Her name was Sally Devon and she was called because she was assumed to be a confederate of Sonny's. Her testimony was such that she turned out to be the beautiful but dumb type after all, knowing nothing of the mob's operation. Sonny and the others all admitted she was only a shack job as far as they were concerned and that seemed to end her part in the affair. Only one reporter mentioned a statement that had any significance. Just before she was discharged from the stand she said that *"she'd like to get the snake that was responsible."*

And that was what had bothered me. Sue had said the same thing, only there had been a minor discrepancy in her statements. First she said it was *a* snake that had killed her mother. Later she said *the* snake! Sue Devon remembered something, all right. Sally had raved in her drunkenness too . . . not about snakes . . . but about *the* snake. Old Mrs. Lee just hadn't understood right.

Now The Snake was emerging. It was the one who engineered the whole damn business. The one nobody knew about or saw. The one who could have engineered it into a massive double-cross to start with.

Blackie Conley. He really played it cute. He stood by as a lieutenant to Sonny Motley, but it was his plan to start with. He worked it into a cross and took off with the profits. He was bigger than anybody gave him credit for being. He was big enough to hold on until he felt like it and make the most incredible comeback in the history of crime.

If it worked.

And it was working.

I had been looking over the paper too long. Pete said, "You found it, didn't you?"

"I think I have."

"Do I get it?"

"Why not?" I put the paper down and looked at him. "Can you hold it?"

"Better tell me about it first."

When I did he whistled softly and started writing. I said, "If it goes out now this guy might withdraw and we'll never get him. You can call the shots, buddy, but I'd advise you to wait. It could be bigger."

He put the pencil away, grinning. "This is bonus stuff, Mike. I'll sit on it. Make it mine though, will you?"

"Done."

"Want Hy in?"

"Damn right. The office can use the publicity. Give him the same poop."

"Sure, Mike." He folded the news clips together and headed for the door. "Call me when you need anything."

I waved when he left, then picked up the phone and dialed Pat. He was home for a change, and sore about being dragged out of bed. I said, "How'd you make out, Pat?"

"Got something new for you."

"Oh?"

"Write off Arnold Goodwin. He's dead."

"What happened?"

"He was killed a couple of months ago in an automobile accident near Saratoga. His body's been lying in a morgue up there unclaimed. The report just came in with his prints."

"Positive?"

"Look it was a stiff with good prints. He was on file. He checked out. The dead man was Goodwin. The accident involved a local car and was just that . . . an accident."

"Then it narrows things down. You still working on Basil Levitt?"

"All the way. We've gone over his record in detail and are trying to backtrack him up to the minute he died. It won't be easy. That guy knew how to cover a trail. Two of my men are working from a point they picked up three months ago and might be able to run it through. Incidentally, I have an interesting item in his history."

"What's that?"

"After he lost his P.I. license he had an arrest record of nineteen. Only two convictions, but some of the charges were pretty serious. He was lucky enough each time to have a good lawyer. The eleventh time he was picked up for assault and it was Sim Torrence who defended him and got him off."

"I don't like it, Pat."

"Don't worry about it. Sim was in civil practice at the time and it was one of hundreds he handled. Levitt never used the same lawyer twice, but the ones he used were good ones. Torrence had a damn good record and the chances are the tie-in was accidental. We got on this thing this morning and I called Torrence personally. He sent Geraldine King up here with the complete file on the case. It meant an hour in court to him, that's all, and the fee was five hundred bucks."

"Who made the complaint?"

"Some monkey who owned a gin mill but who had a record himself. It boils down to a street fight, but Torrence was able to prove that Levitt was merely defending himself. Here's another cute kick. Our present D.A., Charlie Force, defended Levitt on charge seventeen. Same complaint and he got him off too."

"Just funny that those two ever met."

"Mike, in the crime business they get to meet criminals. He does, I do, and you do. Now there's one other thing. The team I have out are circulating pictures of Levitt. Tonight I get a call from somebody who evidently saw the photo and wanted to know what it was all about. He wouldn't give his name and there wasn't time to get a tracer on the call. I didn't tell him anything but said that if he had any pertinent information on Levitt to bring it to us. I was stalling, trying for a tracer. I think he got wise. He said sure, then hung up. As far as we got was that the call came from Flatbush."

"Hell, Pat, that's where Levitt comes from."

"So do a couple million other people. We'll wait it out. All I knew was that it was an open phone, not a booth unless the door was left open, and probably in a bar. I could hear general background talk and a juke going."

"We'll wait that one out then. He has something on his mind."

"They usually call again," Pat said. "You have anything special?"

"Some ideas."

"When do I hear them?"

"Maybe tomorrow."

"I'll stand by."

When I hung up I stared at the phone, then leaned my face into my hands trying to make the ends meet in my mind. Screwy, that's all I could think of. Screwy, but it was making sense.

The phone rang once, jarring me out of my thought. I picked it up, said hello, and the voice that answered was tense. "Geraldine King, Mike. Can you come out here right away?"

"What's up, Geraldine?"

She was too agitated to try to talk. She simply said, "Please,

Mike, come right away. *Now*. It's very important." Then she gave me no choice. She hung up.

"I wrote a note to Velda telling where I was going and that I'd head right back for the apartment when I was done, then left it in the middle of her desk.

Downstairs I cut around back of the cop assigned to watch me, took the side way out without being seen, and picked up a cruising cab at the street corner. The rain was heavier now, a steady, straight-down New York rain that always seemed to come in with the trouble. Heading north on the West Side Highway I leaned back into the cushions and tried to grab a nap. Sleep was out of the question, even for a little while, so I just sat there and remembered back to those last seven years when forgetting was such a simple thing to do.

All you needed was a bottle.

The cop on the beat outside Torrence's house checked my identity before letting me go through. Two reporters were already there talking to a plainclothesman and a fire captain, but not seeming to be getting much out of either one of them.

Geraldine King met me at the door, her face tight and worried.

I said, "What happened?"

"Sue's place . . . it burned."

"What about the kid?"

"She's all right. I have her upstairs in bed. Come on inside."

"No, let's see that building first."

She pulled a sweater on and closed the door behind us. Floodlights on the grounds illuminated the area, the rain slanting through it obliquely.

There wasn't much left, just charred ruins and the concrete foundation. Fire hoses and the rain had squelched every trace of smoldering except for one tendril of smoke that drifted out of one corner, and I could see the remains of the record player and the lone finger that was her microphone stand. Scattered across the floor were tiny bits of light bouncing back from the shattered mirror that had lined the one wall. But there was nothing else. Whatever had been there was gone now.

I said, "We can go back now."

When we were inside Geraldine made us both a drink and stood in the den looking out the window. I let her wait until she was ready to talk, finishing half my drink on the way. Finally she said, "This morning Sue came inside. I . . . don't know what started it, but she came out openly and accused Mr. Torrence of having killed her mother. She kept saying her mother told her."

"How could she say her mother told her she was murdered when she was alive to tell her?" I interrupted.

"I know, I know, but she insisted her mother wrote something and she was going to find it. You know she kept all her mother's old personal things out there."

"Yes, I saw some of them."

"Mr. Torrence is in the middle of an important campaign. He was quite angry and wanted this thing settled once and for all, so while Sue was in here he went out and went through her things, trying to prove that there was nothing.

"Sue must have seen him from upstairs. She came down crying, ran outside, and told him to leave. Neither one of us could quiet her down. She locked herself inside and wouldn't come out and as long as she was there we didn't worry about it. This . . . wasn't exactly the first time this has happened. We were both used to her outbursts.

"Late this afternoon Mr. Torrence got a call and had to leave for his office on some campaign matter. It was about two hours later that I happened to look out and saw the smoke. The building was burning from the inside and Sue was still there. The record player was going and when I looked in the window she was doing some crazy kind of dance with one of those big stuffed toys that used to belong to her mother.

"She wouldn't come out, wouldn't answer me . . . nothing. I . . . guess I started screaming. There was a policeman outside the fence, fortunately. He just happened to be there."

I shook my head. "No, he wasn't. This department was co-operating with the requests of the city police. He was there purposely. Go on."

"He came in and broke down the door. By that time Sue was almost unconscious, lying there on the floor with the flames shooting up the walls. We dragged her out, got her in the house, and I put her to bed. One of the neighbors saw the flames and called the fire department. They came, but there was nothing to do. The damage was not really important . . . except now we'll never know what Sue had of her mother's that she was always searching for."

"Where was Torrence at this time?"

Slowly, she turned around, fingering the drink in her hand. "I know what you're thinking, but perhaps twenty minutes before that I spoke to him on the phone. He was in the city."

"How can you be sure?"

"Because I spoke to two others in his office on some party matters."

"Where is he now?"

"On the way to Albany with some of his constituents. If you want I'll see that he's notified and we'll get him right back."

"I don't think it's necessary. Can I see Sue?"

"She'll be asleep. She was totally worn out. She started the fire, you know."

"I don't."

"But I do."

"How?"

"She told me. She'll tell you too when she's awake."

"Then we'll awaken her."

"All right."

Sue's bedroom was a composite of little girl and grownup. There were framed still pictures of Sally Devon on her dresser and vanity along with some of herself in leotards and ballet costumes. There was another record player here and an almost identical stack of classical L.P.'s. Scattered here and there were toys from another year, mostly fuzzy animals and dolls in dancing clothes.

She lay in bed like a child, her yellow hair spilling around her face, one arm snuggling an oversized animal whose fur had been partially burned off, the face charred so that it was almost unrecognizable for whatever it was. She smiled dreamily, held the toy close to her, and buried her face against it. Some of the straw was sticking out on one side and she pushed it out of the way.

I touched her arm. "Sue . . ."

She didn't awaken immediately. I spoke her name twice again before she opened her eyes.

She said, "Hello, Mike."

"Sue . . . did you set the fire?"

"Yes, I was . . . burning Mother's old papers. I didn't want him to see anything of hers."

"What happened?"

She smiled again. "I . . . don't know. Everything . . . seemed to start burning. I sort of felt happy then. I didn't care. I sang and danced while it was burning and felt good. That's all I remember."

"Okay, go back to sleep."

"Mike . . ."

"What?"

"I'm sorry."

"That's all right."

"He'll . . . put me away or something now, won't he?"

"I don't think so. It *was* an accident."

"Not really it wasn't. I meant it."

I sat on the edge of the bed and took her hand. She was still in a state of semi-shock and sometimes that's the time when they can say the right thing. I said, "Sue . . . you remember telling me your mother was killed by the snake?"

Her eyes drifted away momentarily, then came back to mine. "The snake did it. She said so. The snake would kill her because he had to."

"Who is the snake, honey?"

"She said the snake would kill her," she repeated. "I remember." Her eyes started to widen and under my hand her arm grew taut. "She said . . ."

But I wouldn't let her talk any more. She was too near the breaking point, so I leaned over and kissed her and the fear left her face as suddenly as it appeared and she smiled.

"Go back to sleep, honey. I'll see you in the morning."

"Don't leave, Mike."

"I'll be around."

"Please, Mike."

I winked and stood up. "Sleep, baby, for me."

"All right, Mike."

I left a night light on and the door partly open and went back downstairs with Geraldine. I sat back on the couch and took the drink she made me, sipping it slowly.

Outside the rain slapped at the windows, massaging them with streaky, wet fingers. She turned on the record player, drew the heavy draperies across the windows, and turned out all the lights except one. Then she sat down beside me.

Only then did she say, "What shall we do, Mike?"

"Nothing yet."

"There were reporters out there."

"What did you tell them?"

"That it was accidental. It really wasn't too important . . . just a small outbuilding. If it weren't Mr. Torrence's place it would never draw a mention, but . . . well, you understand."

"They won't make much out of it."

"But if Sue keeps making these accusations . . . it's an election year, Mike. The campaign for governor of a state is of maximum importance. You know how both parties look at it. This is a key state. From here a governor can go into the White House or at least have a major effect on national policy. If anything . . .

anything at all comes up that can be detrimental to a selected candidate it can be disastrous. This . . . this business with Sue is getting out of hand."

"Your bunch knows about it then?"

She nodded, then took a swallow of her drink. "Yes . . . in a way it's why I'm here. I've been with Sim Torrence on his other campaigns as much as a guardian for Sue as an assistant to Mr. Torrence. She doesn't realize all this and I've made it a point to keep it almost businesslike, but I do manage to find things for Sue to do and distract this antagonistic attitude she has. All her life she's been trying to emulate her mother . . . trying to be a showgirl. She's been coached in singing, dancing, and arts . . . given the very best Mr. Torrence can give her. She's taken advantage of those opportunities, not just to help her into show business but it gets her away from him. Sad, but true."

"You speculating now?"

She looked at me over her glass. "No, she's told me that. You can ask her."

"I believe it."

"What can we do? It's critical now."

"I'll think of something."

"Will you, Mike? We need help badly."

"You sure love this political crap, don't you?"

"My life, Mike. I gave my life to it."

"Hell, you're too young to die. Maybe you should have been born a man."

"There's a place for women in politics."

"Bull."

"You just like them to be women, don't you?"

"That's what they are."

"All right. For you I'll be a woman."

She put her drink down on the coffee table, took mine from my hand and put it next to hers, both unfinished. There was a sudden hunger in her eyes and a warmth to her face that made her mouth seem to blossom into a new fullness. Her fingers went to her throat and one by one she unbuttoned her blouse until it lay open, then with the slightest shrug of her shoulders it slid away so that her fingers could work more magic with the soft fabric of the bra. She whisked it away and it floated to the floor where it lay unnoticed.

I looked at her, not touching her, taking in the lovely slope of her breasts that were swelled with emotion and tipped with the firm pinkness of passion. I could smell the fragrant heat of her only inches away, and as I watched, her stomach undulated and moved spasmodically against the waistband of her skirt.

"How am I . . . as a woman, Mike?"

"Lovely," I told her. I reached for her, turned her around, then lay her as she was, half naked, across my lap, my fingers caught in her hair, touching her gently at first, then with firm insistence that made her shudder.

She raised herself against me, twisting her head, searching for my mouth until she found it, then with a small whimper she was part of me, her lips a ripe, succulent fruit, her tongue an alive, vital organ that was a soul seeking another soul. I let her fall away from me reluctantly, her mouth still working as though it were kissing mine yet, her eyes closed, her breath coming heavily.

Someplace in the house a clock chimed and a dull rumble of thunder outside echoed it. I let my hand run down the naked expanse of her stomach until the tips of my fingers traced a path across her waist under the skirt. She moaned softly and sucked in her breath so there would be a looseness at her belt. I felt her briefly, kneaded the pliant flesh, then took my hand away.

Her eyes opened, she smiled once and closed them again. Then she was asleep. It had been a hard day for her too. I held her until I was sure she wouldn't awaken, then raised her, propped a cushion beneath her shoulders, and let her down onto it. I covered her with her blouse and a plaid car blanket that was folded over the back of a chair.

In the morning she'd feel better. She'd hate me maybe, but then again, maybe not. I went upstairs and checked Sue. She had turned on her side and the oversized stuffed toy was almost crushed beneath her.

I called a cab in from town, let myself out, and waited by the gate. The cop on the beat asked me if everything was all right and I told him the women were both asleep and to stay on his toes. He still couldn't read me but with the card I carried he wasn't taking any chances. He saluted cordially and walked off into the darkness.

Inspector Grebb should have seen that, I thought. He'd flip. He'd sooner I got a boot in the tail.

When the cab came he didn't want to take me clean into the city so I changed cabs at the George Washington Bridge and gave that driver the address of my new apartment. I started to grin, thinking of what Velda would do if she knew where I was an hour ago. Hell, she never would believe me if I told her the truth anyway, so why say a word? But you can't go through two of those deals in one night and stand up to it. If Velda were there I hoped she was sacked out tight. Right then I needed sleep more than anything I could think of.

I paid the cab off and went inside. The place was freshly renovated and smelled of paint. I took the automatic elevator to the third floor, found my new apartment at the very end of the hall, and stuck the key in the lock. There was a soft glow from a table lamp at the end of the couch in the living room and a radio was playing softly. From where I stood I could see her stretched out comfortable and laughed to myself. Velda had determination, but sleep had won out. She got the couch and I got the bed this time. Tomorrow she'd sizzle, but she'd still be waiting.

I went in on the balls of my feet, walking quietly so as not to waken her, but I couldn't help looking at her as I passed. And when I saw her I turned ice cold inside because she wasn't just asleep at all. Somebody had brought something down across her temple turning it into a livid welt that oozed dark blood under her ear into her hairline.

I grabbed her, said *"Velda!"* once, then she let out a little meowing sound and her eyes flicked open. She tried to talk but couldn't and it was her eyes that got the message across. I looked up to the side where he stood with one hand holding his belly and the other a gun and he had it pointed right at my head.

Marv Kania had finally found me.

His eyes had death in them, his and mine. His belly was bloated and I could smell the stench of a festering wound, the sickening odor of old blood impregnated into cloth. There was a wildness in his face and his mouth was a tight slash that showed all his teeth. Marv Kania was young, but right there he was as old as death itself.

"I was waiting for you, mister."

Slowly, I got up. I was going to have to pull against a drawn gun and there wasn't a chance I could make it. He was dying, but the gun in his hand was there with the deft skill of the professional and it never wavered an inch. He let the muzzle drift down from my head until it pointed at my stomach.

"Right where I got it, man, and there's no coming back after that. Everything inside goes. You'll live a little while and you'll hurt like I hurt. You try to move away from it and I put one more in your head."

I was thinking fast, wondering how fast I could move away from the shot. He knew what I was going to do and grinned through the pain he felt. Just to let me know it was no good he made two quick wrist motions to show he still had it and I had it, then he thumbed the hammer back.

"The girl. What about her?"

"What do you care? You'll be dead."

"What about her?"

His face was a mask of pain and hate. "I'll tell you what I'm going to do. With her she gets one shot. Same as you. Then I go outside and die. Out in the rain, just so long as I don't die in no crummy room. In the park, that's where I die. I always wanted to die there." His eyes half shut momentarily as a spasm of pain took him, then he snapped them open and grinned, his teeth bare against his gums.

Velda turned on the couch, whispering my name softly. She must have come in when he was there. He held a gun on her, belted her out, and kept on waiting. Now he was going to kill her along with me.

"You ready, you bastard?"

I didn't move. I just stood there hoping Velda could do something while my own body half shielded her from him, hoping she could move fast enough to get the hell out. He saw that too and started to laugh. It was so funny to him with all the hate bottled up inside he laughed even harder as he aimed the rod with every ounce of professional technique he ever had.

And it was the laugh that did it. The laugh that broke the last thing inside. The laugh that burst the lifeline. He felt it go and his eyes went so wide the whites of them showed the horror he felt because he was still a loser and before he could put that final fraction of pressure on the trigger the gun dropped from his hand and he pitched face down on the floor with a sickening squashing sound as some ghastly, putrescent fluid burst from his belly.

I picked Velda up, carried her into the bedroom, and washed the blood from her temple. Then I loosened her clothes and pulled the blanket over her before flopping down on the bed beside her.

Outside I had another dead man at my feet, but he was going to have to wait until morning.

chapter eight ▰▰▰▰▰▰▰

PAT WAS THERE at nine in the morning. So was Inspector Grebb and Charles Force. Pat's face told me he had no choice so I threw him a brief nod so he knew I got the picture.

The police photographers got all the shots they wanted, the body was carried out, Velda had a doctor in with her, and Grebb pointed at a chair for me and sat down himself.

"You've been a thorn in our side, Hammer," he said pleasantly.

"Tough."

"But I think we have you nailed now."

"For failing to report a body?"

"It's enough. You don't step that far outside and still get a gun-carrying privilege. It will break you with that fancy agency because they like closed mouths about their operations. They lift your ticket and you're back in the ranks again."

Charlie Force was standing there with that same old courtroom smile, like his bait had caught the fish. I said, "I warned you, Charlie."

"Mr. Force, if you don't mind?"

This time I let him see the kind of grin I had, the one with teeth in it. I said, "Okay, buddy, I'll come to your party, only I'm bringing my friends. I'm bringing in pressures you never heard of. Get something in your goddamn heads . . . you're two public servants and all you're looking for is another step up. If you got the idea you'll get it over me you're wrong. Don't think that agency is going to back down a bit. I gave them too much and they're still paying off for it. I'll keep giving them more and more until they can't afford to lose me. The agency is bigger than both you guys and now you're going to find it out the hard way.

"As for you, Force, before you were playing in courtrooms I was pushing a legal gun around this town and there are guys I know and friends I made who'd like nothing better than to wipe your nose in a mess. Believe me, buddy, if you ever did one lousy thing in your life . . . and you can bet your ass you did because everybody does, I'll nail it down and you'll go with it. It won't even be a hard job. But I'll do even better than that to you, kid. I'll pull the stool right out from under you. This little bugger I'm on now is a hot little bugger and it's mine. You get no slice of it at all. I'll make the action and get the yaks."

I spun around and looked at Pat. "Tell them, friend."

"You did a pretty good job. I'm still a Captain."

"Well, maybe we'll get you raised one after this, okay, Inspector?"

He didn't say anything. He sat there glowering at me, not knowing what to think. But he was an old hand and knew when the wind was blowing bad. It showed in his eyes, only he didn't want me to see it. Finally he looked at his watch, then up to me. "We'll wait some more," he said. "It's bound to happen sometime."

"Don't hold your breath waiting," I said.

"You take care of things here, Captain," he said to Pat. "I'll want to see the report later."

"I'll have it on your desk, Inspector."

They left then, two quiet men with one idea in their minds nobody was ever going to shake loose. When they were out I said to Pat, "Why the heat?"

"Because the city is on edge, Mike. They haven't got the answers and neither have I. Somehow you always get thrown in the middle of things so that you're the one to pull the switch."

"You got everything I know."

Pat nodded sagely. "Great. Facts are one thing, but there's still that crazy mind of yours. You make the same facts come out different answers somehow." He held up his hand to shut me up. "Oh, I agree, you're cooperative and all that jazz. You lay it on the line like you're requested to do and still make it look like your own idea. But all the time you're following a strange line of reasoning nobody who looks at the facts would take. I always said you should have been a straight cop in the first place."

"I tried it a long time ago and it didn't work."

"You would have made a perfect crook. Sometimes I wonder just what the hell you really are inside. You live in a half world of your own, never in, never out, always on the edge."

"Nuts to you, Pat. It works."

"The hard way."

Pat walked to the window, stared down into the courtyard a moment, then came back. "Kania say anything to you before he died?"

"Only how he was going to enjoy killing me."

"You didn't ask him any questions?"

"With a gun on me and him ready to shoot? There wasn't anything to ask."

"There wasn't any chance you could have taken him?"

"Not a one."

"So I'll buy it. Now, how'd he find you?"

"I'm not that hard to find. He did it twice before. He probably picked up Velda at my office and followed her here."

"She talk yet?"

"No," I told him, "but maybe she will now. Let's ask her."

The doctor had finished with Velda, assuring us both that it was only a minor concussion that should leave no after-effects, gave me a prescription for a sedative, and left us alone with her.

She smiled up at me crookedly, her face hurting with the effort. "Think you can talk, kitten?"

"I'm all right."

"How'd that punk get in here?"

She shook her head and winced. "I don't know. I left the door unlocked thinking you'd be in shortly, then I went to the bathroom. When I went back into the living room he stepped out of the bedroom. He held the gun on me . . . then made me lie on the couch. I knew he was afraid I'd scream or something so he just swung the gun at me. I remember . . . coming awake once, then he hit me again. That's all I remember until you spoke to me."

I glanced at Pat. "That's how he did it then. He waited at the office."

"Did you know Grebb kept a man staked out there?"

"Didn't everybody? I told you to stay off my neck."

"It wasn't my idea."

"Kania must have spotted him the same as I did. He simply waited outside or across the street until Velda came out. When she came alone he figured she could lead him to me and stayed with her. She made the job easy by leaving the door open."

"I'm sorry, Mike."

"No sweat, baby," I said. "It won't happen again."

"Mike . . ."

"What?"

"Miss Lee. She'd like to see you again."

She was bypassing Pat, but he caught it and grinned. "I haven't heard about her."

"An old lady. Sally Devon's old wardrobe mistress. She was with her when she died. She'll talk to anybody for company's sake but she might come up with something."

"Still going back thirty years?"

"Does money get old?" I asked him.

There was a jack next to the bed so I got the phone from the living room and plugged it in and laid it on the nightstand where Velda could reach it. "You stay put all day, honey. I'll check in with you every now and then and if you want anything, just call down for it. I'll leave your key with the super and he can check on anybody who comes in."

"Mike . . . I'll be fine. You don't have to . . ."

I cut her off. "Look, if I want you for anything, I'll call. There's a lot you can do without getting out of bed. Relax until I need you. Shall I get somebody to stay with you?"

"No."

"I'll be moving fast. I don't know where I'll be. But I'll check in every couple of hours. Maybe Pat here can give you a buzz too."

"Be glad to," he said. There was restraint in his voice and I knew how he was hurting. It isn't easy for a guy who loves a woman to see her going down the road with somebody else. War, love . . . somebody's got to be the loser.

So I covered her up and went outside with Pat. About twenty minutes later two men from his division came in, got a rundown on Kania, and started backtracking him. A contract killer wasn't notorious for leaving a trail, but Marv Kania had a record, he was known. He might have been tight-lipped about his operation, but somewhere somebody was going to know something.

One thing. That's all we needed. You could start with dead men, all right, but it won't do you any good if they only lead to other dead men. Mr. Dickerson had played some smart cards. He had picked his people well. The ones here were clean. The ones who weren't were dead. The hoods in town could be taken in and questioned, but if they knew nothing because the orders hadn't been issued yet, they couldn't say anything. It was still a free country and you couldn't make them leave the state as long as they stayed clean. The men behind them were power who could still turn on the heat through odd but important channels so you couldn't roust them too far.

I told Pat I'd see him sometime after lunch, walked him downstairs, left a key with the super, and gave him a fin for his trouble. Pat went on downtown and I hopped a cab across town to Annette Lee's place, got the landlady to let me in, and stepped into her living room.

The old gal was still in her rocker, still going through that same perpetual rhythm, stopping only when her chair had inched against another piece of furniture. Her curtains were drawn back, letting in the early light, and she smiled a big hello when she saw me.

"How nice of you to come back, young man," she said. She held out her hand without getting up and I took it. "Sit down, please."

I tossed my hat on a table and pulled up another straight-back chair and perched on the end of it.

"Your young lady was here yesterday. We had a lovely visit. It isn't often I get company, you know."

I said, "She mentioned you wanted to see me."

"Yes." Annette Lee nodded, then leaned her head back against the chair with her eyes half shut. "We were talking. I . . ." She waved her hand vaguely in front of her face. "Sometimes I forget things. I'm going on ninety now. I think I've lived too long already."

"You never live too long."

"Perhaps so. I can still enjoy things. I can dream. Do you dream, Mr. . . .?"

"Hammer."

"Mr. Hammer. Do you dream?"

"Sometimes."

"You're not old enough to dream back like I do. It's something like being reborn. I like to dream. They were good days then. I dream about them because they're all I have to dream about. Yes, they were fine days."

"What was it you wanted to tell me, Miss Lee?" I asked her gently.

"Oh?" She thought a moment, then: "There was something. Your young lady and I talked about Sally and Sue. Yes, that was it. Dear Sally, she was so lovely. It was a pity she died."

"Miss Lee . . ."

"Yes?"

"The night she died . . . do you remember it well?"

"Oh yes. Oh yes indeed." Her rocking slowed momentarily so she could shift positions, then started again.

"Was she drunk, really drunk?"

"Dear me, yes. Sally drank all the time. From very early in the morning. There was nothing I could do so I tried to keep her company and talk to her. She didn't want to talk too much, you know. When she did it was drunk talk I couldn't always understand. Do you know what I mean?"

"I've heard it."

"There was that thing with the snakes you mentioned. It was rather an obsession with her."

"She was frightened of the snake?"

Annette Lee lifted her head and peered at me. "No, that was the strange thing. She wasn't afraid. It was . . . well, she hated it."

"Was the snake a person?"

"Excuse me?"

"Could she have been referring to a person as The Snake? Not snakes or a snake. *The Snake.*"

The rocking stopped completely. She looked at me curiously in the semi-darkened room, her fingertip touching her lips. "So that was what she meant."

"Go on."

"No wonder I didn't understand. My goodness, I never understood in all this time. Yes, she said *the* snake. It was always *the* snake. She hated *the* snake, that was why she wanted to live so far away from the city. She never wanted to go back."

"Annette . . . who was Sue's father?"

The old girl made a face at me and raised the thin line of her eyebrows. "Does it matter?"

"It might."

"But I'm afraid I couldn't tell you."

"Why not?"

"Simply because I don't know. Sue has Sally's maiden name, you know. She never got her father's name because she doesn't know who he is. I'm afraid Sally was . . . a bit promiscuous. She had many men and among them would be Sue's father. I doubt if Sally ever really knew either. A pity. Sue was such a lovely baby."

"Could it have been Blackie Conley?"

For the first time Annette Lee giggled. "Dear no. Not him. Never Blackie."

"Why?"

"Simply because he wasn't capable. I think that was one of the reasons Blackie was so . . . so frustrated. He *did* like the ladies, you know. He slept with one after the other. He even married two of them but it never worked out. He always wanted an heir but he wasn't capable. Why . . . the boys used to kid him about it."

Her feet pushed harder until she had to edge the chair away from the wall so that she faced me more directly. "Do you ever remember Bud Packer?"

"Just the name."

"Bud was . . . joshing him one day about his . . . impotence and Blackie shot him. You know where. I think Blackie did time for that but I don't rightly remember. No, Blackie was not Sue's father by any means. Besides, you're forgetting one big thing."

I let her say it.

"Blackie's been gone . . . for years. Long before Sue was born. Blackie is dead somewhere."

She put her head back and closed her eyes. I said, "Tired?"

"No, just thinking. Daydreaming."

"How about this angle . . . could Sim Torrence have been the father?"

Her giggle broke into a soft cackle only the old can make. "Sim Torrence? I'm afraid not. Sue was born before they were married."

"He could still be the father."

"You don't understand, Mr. . . . ."

"Hammer."

"Mr. Hammer. You see, I was with Sally always before. I knew the many faces she was with. I know who she slept with and none of them were Sim Torrence. It wasn't until after the baby was born that they were married when he took her in and provided for them." The flat laugh came out again. "Those two could never have a baby of their own though."

"Why not?"

"Because she and Sim never slept together. After the baby was born Sally never let a man near her. She underwent a change. All she thought of was the baby, making plans for her, hoping for her to grow up and be somebody. You know, I hate to give away women-secrets, but Sally deliberately cultivated Sim Torrence. They knew each other for some time earlier. Some court case. She managed to meet him somehow and I remember them going out for a couple of weeks before she brought him to our apartment and told me they were going to get married."

"Did Torrence take it well?"

"How does any man take it who is going to lose his bachelor-hood?" She smiled knowingly. "He was rather shaken. Almost embarrassed. But he did provide well for Sally and Sue. They had a simple ceremony and moved into his town house."

"Were you with them?"

"Oh yes. Sally wouldn't leave me. Why, I was the only one who could take care of her and the baby. She wasn't very domestic, you know. She wasn't supposed to be. Yes, those were different women then. Showgirls. They had to be pampered."

"Why wouldn't she let Torrence near her in bed?"

"Does it sound strange that a woman who was a . . . a whore would be afraid of sex?"

I shook my head. "Most of them are frigid anyway," I said bluntly.

"So true, so true. Well, that was Sally. Frigid. Having the baby scared her. Even having a man scared her."

"Was she scared of Torrence?"

"Of every man, Mr. . . .," and this time she remembered my name and smiled, ". . . Hammer. Yes, Sim Torrence scared her but I think he understood. He let her stay at that place in the country. He came up on occasions and it was very strained but he was very understanding about it too. Of course, like all men, he could bury himself in his work. That was his real wife, his work."

"Miss Lee . . . the last time I was here we talked about Blackie Conley, remember?"

"I remember."

"You said you knew about the plans he made for that robbery he and Sonny Motley were involved in. What were they?"

She stopped rocking, her face curious again. "Are you looking for the money?"

"I'm a cop, Miss Lee. I'm looking for a killer, for the money . . . for anything that will help keep trouble from Sue."

"Sue? But that was before she was born."

"It can come back to hurt her. Now what did you hear?"

She nodded, pressing her lips together, her hands grasping the arms of the rockers. "Do you really think . . .?"

"It might help."

"I see." She paused, thought a moment, then said, "You know that Sonny really didn't plan the robbery. It was his gang, but he didn't plan it. They were . . . acting for someone."

"I know about that."

"Blackie had instructions to find a place where they were going to hide out. He was told where to go and how to do it. I remember because I listened to the call." She chuckled at the thought. "I never did like Blackie. He was at Sally's place when he took the call. In fact, that was where they did all their planning, at Sally's apartment. Sonny was going with her then when she wasn't sneaking off with Blackie."

"I see."

"Really," she told me, "I wasn't supposed to know about these things. I was always in the other room out of sight, but I was worried about Sally and tried to find out what was going on. I listened in and they didn't know it."

"None of this came out at the trial," I reminded her.

"Nor was it about to, young man. I didn't want to involve Sally any more than she was. She *did* appear in court, you know."

"Briefly. She wasn't implicated. She was treated as an innocent victim."

Those watery old eyes found mine and laughed in their depths.

"No, Sally wasn't so innocent. She knew everything that went on. Sally's pose was very deliberate. Very deliberate. She was a better actress than anyone imagined."

Annette Lee leaned forward like some old conspirator. "Now that it can't hurt her, let me tell you something. It was through dear Sally that this robbery came about. All arrangements, all contacts were made through her. Sonny was quite a man in those days and ran a sizable operation. But it was through Sally Devon that another party interested Sonny in that robbery. No, Sally was hardly the innocent victim."

I didn't let her see me take it in. I passed it off quickly to get her back on the track again, but now the angles were starting to show. I said, "When Blackie Conley got this call . . . what happened?"

Jerked suddenly from one train of thought, she sat back frowning. "Oh . . . Blackie . . . well, I heard this voice . . ."

"A man?"

"Yes. He told Blackie to see a man in a certain real estate agency, one that could be trusted. He gave him the phone number."

I added, "And Blackie arranged to rent a house in the Catskills?"

"That's right. He made the call right then and said he'd be in the next day." She opened her eyes again, now her fingers tapping a silent tune on the chair. "But then he made another call to Howie Green."

"Who?"

"Howie Green. He was a bootlegger, dearie, but he owned properties here in the city. He invested his money wisely, Howie did, and always had something to show for it. Howie was as crooked as they come, but smarter than most of them. One of Howie's enterprises was a real estate agency that used to be someplace on Broadway. Oh yes, Howie was a big man, but he owed Blackie Conley a favor. Blackie killed a man for Howie and held it over his head. He told Howie he wanted a place to hole up in somewhere away from the city and to pick it out."

"Where was it, Annette?"

"I don't know, young man. Howie merely said he'd do it for him. That was all. I suppose Blackie took care of it later. However, it's all over now. Howie Green's dead too. He died in an accident not long afterward."

"Before the robbery?"

"I really don't remember that."

I reached for my hat and stood up. "You've been a great help, Annette."

"Have I really?"

I nodded.

"Will Sue be . . . all right?"

"I'm sure she will."

"Someday," she asked me, "will you bring her to me? I would like to see her again."

"We'll make a point of it."

"Good-by then. It was nice of you to come over."

"My pleasure, Miss Lee."

At two o'clock I contacted Pat and made a date to meet him at his office. He didn't like the idea because he knew Grebb would want to sit in on the conversation but thought he could arrange it so we could be alone.

I took a cab downtown, found Pat alone at his desk buried in the usual paperwork, waited for him to finish, then said, "What officers were in on the Motley holdup? Any still around?"

"This your day for surprises?"

"Hit me."

"Inspector Grebb was one. He was a beat cop who was alerted for the action."

"Oh hell."

"Why?"

"Think he'd remember the details?"

"I don't remember Grebb ever forgetting anything."

"Then let's call him in."

"You sure about this?" Pat asked me.

"It's the easy way. So we give him a bite after all."

Pat nodded, lifted the phone, and made a call. When he hung up he said, "The Inspector will be happy to see you."

"I bet."

It didn't take him long to get up there. He didn't have Charlie Force with him either. He came in with the patient attitude of the professional cop, always ready to wait, always ready to act when the time came. He might have been a tough, sour old apple, but he made it the hard way and you couldn't take it away from him.

Inwardly I laughed at myself because if I wasn't careful I could almost like him.

"Whose party is it this time?" he asked.

Pat said, "He's throwing it."

"I never thought you'd ask, Hammer." He dragged a chair out with his foot, sat in it heavily and sighed, but it was all an act.

He was no more tired or bored than I was. "Shoot," he said.

"Pat tells me you were in on the Motley thing thirty years ago."

"My second day on the beat, Hammer. That show you how close to retirement I am. My present job is a gratuity. One last fling for the old dog in a department he always wanted to run."

"Better luck in your next one."

"We aren't talking about that. What's with the Motley job?"

"How did the cops get wise?"

"Why don't you read the transcript of the trial? It was mentioned."

"This is easier. Besides, I wanted to be sure."

Grebb pulled a cigar from his pocket, snapped off the end, and fired it up. "Like a lot of big ones that went bust," he said, "somebody pulled the cork. The department got a call. It went through the D.A.'s office."

"Torrence?"

"No, one of the others got it and passed it to him. Torrence handled it personally though."

"Where were you?"

"Staked out where the truck was hidden in case they got through somehow. They never made it. We got the truck and the driver. Second day on the beat too, I'll never forget it. Fresh out of school, still hardly shaving, and I get a hot one right off. Made me decide to stay in the department."

"How long did you have to get ready?"

"About an hour, if I remember right. It was plenty of time. We could have done it in fifteen minutes."

"They ever find out who made the call?"

"Nope."

"They look very hard?"

Grebb just shrugged noncommittally. Then he said, "Let's face it, we'd sooner have stoolies on the outside where they can call these things in than a live guy testifying in court who winds up a dead squealer a day later. We didn't break our backs running down anybody. Whoever it was played it the way we liked it. The job was a bust and we nailed the crew."

"It wasn't a bust, Inspector."

He stared at me until his face hurt.

"Nobody ever located the money."

"That's happened before. One of those things."

"Blackie Conley simply disappeared."

The cigar bobbed in his mouth. "And if he lived very long afterward he's a better man than I am. By now he'd be dead anyway." He took the cigar away from his mouth and flipped the ash off with his pinky. "But let's get back to the money . . . that's the interesting part."

"I have an idea it might show up."

"Maybe we better listen to your idea."

"Uh-uh. Facts I'll give you, ideas stay in my pocket until I can prove them out."

"Facts then."

"None you don't already have if you want to check the transcript like you suggested. I just make something different out of them, that's all."

Grebb put the cigar back between his teeth and pushed himself out of his chair. When he was on his feet he glanced at Pat meaningfully, said, "don't let me wait too long, Captain," then went out.

"I wish you'd quit pushing him," Pat told me. "Now what's with this bit?"

I sat in the chair Grebb had vacated and propped my feet on Pat's desk. "I think Blackie Conley's alive."

"How'd he do it?"

"He was the planner behind the operation. He set it up, then phoned in a double-cross. Trouble was, he should have cut it shorter. He almost lost it himself. He laid out one escape plan, but took an alternate. He got away in that cab with the three million bucks and sat on it someplace."

Pat tapped a pencil on the desk as I gave him the information Annette Lee gave me. Every once in a while he'd make a note on a pad, study it, then make another.

"We'll have to locate whatever records are left of Howie Green's business. If he was dealing in real estate it will be a matter of public record."

"You don't think Blackie would use his own name, do you?"

"We can narrow it down. Look, check your file on Green."

Pat put in another call and for the twenty minutes it took to get the papers up we went over the angles of the case. I still wouldn't lay it out the way I saw it, but he had enough to reach the same conclusion if he thought the same way.

The uniformed officer handed Pat a yellowed folder and Pat opened it on his desk. Howie Green, deceased. Known bootlegger, six arrests, two minor convictions. Suspected of duplicity in a murder of one Francis Gorman, another bootlegger who moved into his territory. Charge dropped. Known to have large holdings that were legally acquired as far as the law could prove. His annual income made him a rich man for the times. He was killed by a hit-and-run driver not far from his own house and the date given was three days before the robbery of the three million bucks.

"Pretty angle, Pat."

"Spell it out."

"If Conley did get hideout property from Green, paid for it, made the transaction, and accepted the papers in a phony name and took possession, then killed him before Green knew what he wanted it for, who could say where he was? Chances were that nobody but Conley and Green ever saw each other and Green wasn't around to talk any more."

Pat closed the folder and shoved it in his desk. "We could check all the transactions Green made in the few weeks prior to his death."

"Time, buddy. We haven't got the time."

"But I have one thing you don't have."

I knew what he was going to say.

"Men. We can put enough troops on it to shorten the time."

"It'll still be a long job."

"You know a better way?"

The phone rang before I could answer and although I could hear the hurried chatter at the other end I couldn't make it out. When he cradled the phone Pat said, "One of my squad in Brooklyn on that Levitt rundown."

"Oh?"

"He was eating with one of the men from the precinct over there when a call came in about a body. He went along with his friend and apparently the dead guy is one of the ones he showed Basil Levitt's picture to."

"A starter," I said.

"Could be. Want to take a run over?"

"Why not?"

Pat got his car from the lot and we hopped in, cutting over the bridge into the Brooklyn section. The address was in the heart of Flatbush, one block off the Avenue, a neighborhood bar and grill that was squeezed in between a grocery and a dry cleaning place.

A squad car was at the curb and a uniformed patrolman stood by the door. Two more, obviously detectives from the local precinct, were in the doorway talking. Pat knew the Lieutenant in charge, shook hands with him, introduced him to me as Joe Cavello, then went inside.

Squatting nervously on a stool, the bartender watched us, trying to be casual about the whole thing. Lieutenant Cavello nodded toward him and said, "He found the body."

"When?"

"About an hour ago. He had to go down to hook into some fresh beer kegs and found the guy on the floor. He'd been shot once in the head with a small-caliber gun . . . I'd say about a .32."

"The M.E. set the time of death?" I asked him.

"About twelve to fifteen hours. He'll be more specific after an autopsy."

"Who was he?" Pat said.

"The owner of the place."

"You know him?"

"Somewhat," Cavello said. "We've had him down to the precinct a few times. Twice on wife beating and another when he was picked up in a raid on a card game. This is kind of a chintzy joint. Local bums hang out here because the drinks are cheap. But that's all they sell anyway, cheap booze. We've had a few complaints about some fights in here but nothing ever happened. You know, the usual garbage that goes with these slop chutes."

Pat said, "I had Nelson and Kiley over here doing a rundown on Basil Levitt. You hear about it?"

"Yeah, Lew Nelson checked in with me right after it happened. He saw the body. It was the guy he spoke to all right. I asked around but nobody here seemed to know Levitt."

"How about the bartender?" I said.

Cavello shook his head. "Nothing there. He does the day work and nothing more. When the boss came on, he went off. He doesn't know the night crowd at all."

"He live around here?"

"Red Hook. Not his neighborhood here and he couldn't care less."

While Pat went over the details of what the police picked up I wandered back to the end of the bar. There was a back room used as a storeroom and a place for the food locker with a doorway to one side that opened into the cellar. The lights were on downstairs and I went down to the spot behind the stairs where the chalk marks outlined the position of the body. They were half on the floor and half on the wall, so the guy was found in a sitting position.

Back upstairs Cavello had taken Pat to the end of the bar and I got back in on the conversation. Cavello said, "Near as we could figure it out, this guy Thomas Kline closed the bar earlier than usual, making the few customers he had leave. It was something he had never done before apparently. He'd stick it out if there was a dime in the joint left to be spent. This time he bitched about a headache, closed up, and shut off the lights. That was it. We spoke to the ones who were here then, but they all went off to another place and closed it down much later, then went home. Clean alibis. All working men for a change. No records.

"We think he met somebody here for some purpose. Come here." He led the way to a table in one corner and pointed to the floor. A small stain showed against the oiled wood. "Blood. It matched the victim's. Here's where he was shot. The killer took the body downstairs, dumped it behind the staircase where it couldn't be seen very easily, then left. The door locks by simply closing it so it was simple enough to do. One block down he's in traffic, and any place along the Avenue he could have picked up a cab if he didn't have his own car. We're checking all the cabbies' sheets now."

But I had stopped listening to him about then. I was looking at the back corner of the wall. I tapped Pat on the arm and pointed. "You remember the call you got from someone inquiring about Levitt?"

"Yeah," he said.

There was an open pay phone on the wall about four feet away from a jukebox.

Pat walked over to it, looked at the records on the juke, but who could tell rock-and-roll from the titles? He said to Cavello, "Many places got these open phones?"

"Sure," Cavello told him, "most of the spots that haven't got room for a booth. Mean anything?"

"I don't know. It could."

"Anything I could help with?"

Pat explained the situation and Cavello said he'd try to find anyone who saw Kline making a phone call about that time. He didn't expect much luck though. People in that neighborhood didn't talk too freely to the police. It was more likely that they wouldn't remember anything rather than get themselves involved.

Another plainclothes officer came in then, said hello to Pat, and he introduced me to Lew Nelson. He didn't have anything to add to the story and so far that day hadn't found anybody who knew much about Levitt at all.

I tapped his shoulder and said, "How did Kline react when you showed him Levitt's photo?"

"Well, he jumped a little. He said he couldn't be sure and I figured he was lying. I got the same reaction from others beside him. That Levitt was a mean son and I don't think anybody wanted to mess around with him. He wanted to know what he was wanted for and I wouldn't say anything except that he was dead and he seemed pretty satisfied at that.

"Tell you one thing. That guy was thinking of something. He studied that photo until he was sure he knew him and then told me he never saw him before. Maybe he thought he had an angle somewhere."

There wasn't much left there for us. Pat left a few instructions, sent Nelson back on the streets again, and started outside. He stopped for a final word to Cavello so I went on alone and stood on the sidewalk beside the cop on guard there. It wasn't until he went to answer the radio in the squad car that I saw the thing his position had obscured.

In the window of the bar was a campaign poster and on it a full-face picture of a smiling Torrence who was running in the primaries for governor and under it was the slogan, WIN WITH SIM.

chapter nine

I MADE THE call from the drugstore on the corner. I dialed the Torrence estate and waited while the phone rang a half-dozen times, each time feeling the cold go through me deeper and deeper.

Damn, it couldn't be too late!

Then a sleepy voice said, "Yes?" and there was no worry in it at all.

"Geraldine?"

"Mike, you thing you.".

"Look . . ."

"Why did you leave me? How could you leave me?"

"I'll tell you later. Has Torrence come home yet?"

My voice startled her into wakefulness. "But . . . no, he's due here in an hour though. He called this morning from Albany to tell me when he'd be home."

"Good, now listen. Is Sue all right?"

"Yes . . . she's still in bed. I gave her another sedative."

"Well, get her out of it. Both of you hop in a car and get out of there. Now . . . not later, now."

"But, Mike . . ."

"Damn it, shut up and do what I say. There's going to be trouble I can't explain."

"Where can we go? Mike, I don't . . ."

I gave her my new address and added, "Go right there and stay there. The super has the key and will let you in. Don't open that door for anybody until you're sure it's me, understand? I can't tell you any more except that your neck and Sue's neck are out a mile. We have another dead man on our hands and we don't need any more. You got that?"

She knew I wasn't kidding. There was too much stark urgency in my voice. She said she'd leave in a few minutes and when she did I could sense the fear that touched her.

I tapped the receiver cradle down, broke the connection, dropped in a dime, and dialed my own number. Velda came on after the first ring with a guarded hello.

I said, "It's breaking, baby. How do you feel?"

"Not too bad. I can get around."

"Swell. You go downstairs and tell the super that a Geraldine King and Sue Devon are to be admitted to my apartment. Nobody else. Let him keep the key. Then you get down to Sim Torrence's headquarters and check up on his movements all day yesterday. I want every minute of the day spelled out and make it as specific as you can. He got a phone call yesterday. See if it originated from there. I don't care if he took ten minutes out to go to the can . . . you find out about it. I'm chiefly interested in any time he took off last night."

"Got it, Mike. Where can I reach you?"

"At the apartment. When I get through I'll go right there. Shake it up."

"Chop chop. Love me?"

"What a time to ask."

"Well?"

"Certainly, you nut."

She laughed that deep, throaty laugh and hung up on me and I had a quick picture of her sliding out of bed, those beautiful long legs rippling into a body . . . oh hell.

I put the phone back and went back to Pat.

"Where'd you go?" he said.

"We got a killer, buddy."

He froze for a second. "You didn't find anything?"

"No? Then make sense out of this." I pointed to the picture of Sim Torrence in the window.

"Go ahead."

"Sim's on the way up. He's getting where he always wanted to be. He's got just one bug in his life and that's the kid, Sue Devon. All her life she's been on his back about something in their past and there was always that chance she might find it.

"One time he defended a hard case and when he needed one he called on the guy. Basil Levitt. He wanted Sue knocked off. Some instinct told Sue what he intended to do and she ran for it and wound up at Velda's. She didn't know it, but it was already too late. Levitt was on her tail all the while, followed her, set up in a place opposite the house, and waited for her to show.

"The trouble was, Velda was in hiding too. She respected the kid's fears and kept her under cover until she was out of trouble herself, then she would have left the place with her. Hell, Pat, Levitt didn't come in there for Velda . . . he was after the kid. When he saw me he must have figured Torrence sent somebody else because he was taking too long and he wasn't about to lose his contract money. That's why Levitt bust in like that.

"Anyway, when Torrence made the deal he must have met Levitt in this joint here thinking he'd never be recognized. But he forgot that his picture is plastered all over on posters throughout the city. Maybe Kline never gave it a thought if he recognized him then. Maybe Kline only got the full picture when he saw Levitt's photo. But he put the thing together. First he called your department for information and grew suspicious when nobody gave him anything concrete.

"Right here he saw Torrence over a barrel, so yesterday he called him and told him to meet him. Sim must have jumped out of his skin. He dummied an excuse and probably even led into a trip to Albany for further cover . . . this we'll know about when I see Velda. But he got here all right. He saw Kline and that was the last Kline saw of anything."

"You think too much, Mike."

"The last guy that said that is dead." I grinned.

"We'd better get up there then."

New York, when the traffic is thick, is a maddening place. From high above the streets the cars look like a winding line of ants, but when you are in the convoy it becomes a raucous noise, a composite of horns and engines and voices cursing at other voices. It's a heavy smell of exhaust fumes and unburned hydrocarbons and in the desire to compress time and space the distance between cars is infinitesimal.

The running lights designed to keep traffic moving at a steady pace seem to break down then. They all become red. Always, there is a bus or truck ahead, or an out-of-town driver searching for street signs. There are pedestrians who take their time, sometimes deliberately blocking the lights in the never-ceasing battle against the enemy, those who are mounted.

In the city the average speed of a fire truck breaks down to eighteen miles an hour with all its warning devices going, so imagine what happens to time and distance when the end-of-day rush is on. Add to that the rain that fogged the windshields and made every sudden stop hazardous.

Ordinarily from Brooklyn the Torrence place would have been an hour away. But not this night. No, this was a special night of delay and frustration, and if Pat hadn't been able to swing around two barriers with his badge held out the window it would have been an hour longer still.

It was a quarter to eight when we turned in the street Sim Torrence lived on. Behind the wall and the shrubbery I could see lights on in the house and outside that there was no activity at all. From the end of the street, walking toward us, was the patrolman assigned to the beat on special duty, and when we stopped, his pace quickened so that he was there when we got out.

Pat held his badge out again, but the cop recognized me. Pat said, "Everything all right here?"

"Yes, sir. Miss King and the girl left some time ago and Torrence arrived, but there has been no trouble. Anything I can help with?"

"No, just routine. We have to see Torrence."

"Sure. He left the gate open."

We left the car on the street and walked in, staying on the grass. I had the .45 in my hand and Pat had his Police Positive out and ready. Sim Torrence's Cadillac was parked in front of the door and when I felt it the hood was still warm.

Both of us knew what to do. We checked the windows and the back, met again around the front, then I went up to the door while Pat stood in the shadows.

I touched the buzzer and heard the chime from inside.

Nobody answered so I did it again.

I didn't bother for a third try. I reached out, leaned against the door latch, and it swung in quietly. I went in first, Pat right behind me covering the blind spots. First I motioned him to be quiet, then to follow me since I knew the layout.

There was a deathly stillness about the house that didn't belong there. With all the lights that were going there should have been some sort of sound. But there was nothing.

We checked through the downstairs room, opening closets and probing behind the furniture. Pat looked across the room at me, shook his head, and I pointed toward the stairs.

The master bedroom was the first door on the right. The door was partly open and there was a light on there too. We took that one first.

And that was where we found Sim Torrence. He wasn't winning any more.

He lay face down on the floor with a bullet through his head and a puddle of blood running away from him like juice from a stepped-on tomato. We didn't stop there. We went into every room in the house looking for a killer before we finally came back to Sim.

Pat wrapped the phone in a handkerchief, called the local department, and reported in. When he hung up he said, "You know we're in a sling, don't you?"

"Why?"

"We should have called in from Brooklyn and let them cover it from this end."

"My foot, buddy. Getting in a jam won't help anything. As far as anyone is concerned we came up here on a social call. I was here last night helping out during an emergency and I came back to check, that's all."

"And what about the women?"

"We'll get to them before anybody else will."

"You'd better be right."

"Quit worrying."

While we waited we checked the area around the body for anything that might tie in with the murder. There were no spent cartridges so we both assumed the killer used a revolver. I prowled around the house looking for a sign of entry, since Geraldine would have locked the door going out and Sim behind him, coming in. The killer must have already been here and made his own entry the easy way through the front door.

The sirens were screaming up the street outside when I found out where he got in. The window in Sue's room had been neatly jemmied from the trellis outside and was a perfect, quiet entry into the house. Anybody could have come over the walls without being seen by the lone cop on the beat. From there up that solid trellis was as easy as taking the steps.

Sue's bed was still rumpled. Geraldine must have literally dragged her out of it because the burned stuffed toy was still there crammed under the covers, almost like a body itself.

Then I could see that something new had been added. There was a bullet hole and powder burns on the sheet and when I flipped it back I saw the hole drilled into the huge toy.

Somebody had mistaken that charred ruin for Sue under the covers and tried to put a bullet through her!

Back to Lolita again. Damn, where would it end?

What kind of a person were we dealing with?

I went to put the covers back in their original position before calling Pat in when I saw the stuffed bear up close for the first time. It had been her mother's and the fire had burned it stiff. The straw sticking out was hard and crisp with age, the ends black from the heat. During the night Sue must have lain on it and her weight split open a seam.

An edge of a letter stuck out of it.

I tugged it loose, didn't bother to look at it then because they were coming in downstairs now, racing up the stairs. I stuck the letter in my pocket and called for Pat.

He got the import of it right away but didn't say anything. From all appearances this was a break-in and anybody could have done it. The implications were too big to let the thing out now and he wasn't going to do much explaining until we had time to go over it.

The reporters had already gathered and were yelling for admittance. Tomorrow this kill would make every headline in the country and the one in Brooklyn would be lucky if it got a squib in any sheet at all. There was going to be some high-level talk before this one broke straight and Pat knew it too.

It was an hour before we got out of there and back in the car. Some of the bigwigs of the political party had arrived and were being pressed by the reporters, but they had nothing to say. They got in on VIP status and were immediately sent into the den to be quizzed by the officers in charge and as long as there was plenty to do we could ride for a while.

Pat didn't speak until we were halfway back to the city, then all he said was, "One of your theories went out the window today."

"Which one?"

"If Sim planned to kill Sue, how would he excuse it?"

"I fell into that one with no trouble, Pat," I said. "You know how many times he has been threatened?"

"I know."

"So somebody was trying to get even. Revenge motive. They hit the kid."

"But Sue is still alive."

"Somebody thought he got her tonight. I'll tell you this . . . I bet the first shot fired was into that bed. The killer turned on the light to make sure and saw what happened. He didn't dare let it stand like that so he waited around. Then in came Sim. Now it could be passed off as a burglary attempt while the real motive gets lost in the rush."

I tapped his arm. "There's one other thing too. The night of the first try there were two groups. Levitt and Kid Hand. They weren't working together and they were both after the same thing . . . the kid."

"All right, sharpie, what's the answer?"

"I think it's going to be three million bucks," I said.

"You have more than that to sell."

"There's Blackie Conley."

"And you think he's got the money?"

"Want to bet?"

"Name it."

"A night on the town. A foursome. We'll find you a broad. Loser picks up all the tabs."

Pat nodded. "You got it, but forget finding me a broad. I'll get my own."

"You'll probably bring a policewoman."

"With you around it wouldn't be a bad idea," he said.

He let me out in front of my apartment and I promised to call him as soon as I heard from Velda. He was going to run the Torrence thing through higher channels and let them handle this hotcake.

I went upstairs, called through the door, and let Geraldine open it. Velda still hadn't gotten back. Sue was inside on the couch, awake, but still drowsy from the sedatives she had taken. I made Geraldine sit down next to her, then broke the news.

At first Sue didn't react. Finally she said, "He's really dead?"

"Really, sugar."

Somehow a few years seemed to drape themselves around her. She looked at the floor, made a wry face, and shrugged. "I'm sorry, Mike. I don't feel anything. Just free. I feel free."

Geraldine looked like she was about to break, but she came through it. There was a stricken expression in her eyes and her mouth hung slackly. She kept repeating, "Oh, no!" over and over again and that was all. When she finally accepted it she asked, "Who, Mike, who did it?"

"We don't know."

"This is terrible. The whole political . . ."

"It's more terrible than that, kid. Politicians can always be replaced. I suggest you contact your office when you feel up to it. There's going to be hell to pay and if your outfit gets into power this time it'll be by a miracle . . . and those days, believe me, are over."

She started asking me something else, but the phone rang and I jumped to answer it. Velda said, "Mike . . . I just heard. Is it true?"

"He's had it. What did you come up with?"

"About the time you mentioned . . . nobody could account for Torrence's whereabouts for almost two hours. Nobody really looked for him and they all supposed he was with somebody else, but nobody could clear him for that time."

"That does it then. Come on back."

"Twenty minutes."

"Shake it."

In a little while I was going to be tied in with this mess and would be getting plenty of visitors and I didn't want either Geraldine or Sue around. Their time would come, but not right now. I called a hotel, made reservations for them both, dialed for a cab, and told them to get ready. Neither wanted to leave until I told them there was no choice. I wanted them completely out of sight and told Geraldine to stay put again, having her meals sent up until I called for her.

Events had moved too quickly and she couldn't think for herself any longer. She agreed dumbly, the girls got into their coats, and I walked them out to the cab.

Upstairs I sat at the desk and took the letter out of my pocket. Like the straw, it was crisp with age, but still sealed, and after all these years smelled faintly of some feminine perfume. I slid my finger under the flap and opened it.

The handwriting was the scrawl of a drunk trying hard for sobriety. The lines were uneven and ran to the edge of the page, but it was legible enough.

It read:

Darling Sue:
    My husband Sim is the one we called The Snake. Hate
him, darling, because he wants us dead. Be careful of him.
Someday he will try to kill us both. Sim Torrence could
prove I helped deliver narcotics at one time. He could
have sent me to prison. We made a deal that I was to
be the go-between for him and Sonny Motley and he was
going to arrange the robbery. He could do it because he
knew every detail of the money exchange. What he really
wanted was for Sonny and the rest to be caught so he
could boost his career. That happened, didn't it, darling?
He never should have left me out in the cold. After I had
you I wanted security for you and knew how to get it. I
didn't love Sim Torrence. He hated me like he hates
anybody in his way. I made him do it for you, dearest.
I will hide this letter where he won't find it but you will
someday. He searches everything I have to be sure this
can't happen. Be careful my darling. He is The Snake and
he will try to kill you if he can. Be careful of accidents.
He will have to make it look like one.

                                        All My Love,
                                        Mother

    The Snake . . . the one thing they all feared . . . and now he
was dead. Dedicated old Win with Sim, an engineer of robberies,
hirer of murderers, a killer himself . . . what a candidate for
governor. The people would never know how lucky they were.
    The Snake. A good name for him. I was right . . . it worked
the way I figured it. The votes weren't all counted yet, but the
deck was stacked against Sim Torrence. In death he was going to
take a fall bigger than the one he would have taken in life.
    Torrence never got the three million. He never gave a damn
about it in the first place. All breaking up that robbery did was
earn him prestige and some political titles. It was his first step
into the big-time and he made it himself. He put everybody's life
on the block including his own and swung it. I wondered what
plans he had made for Sally if she hadn't nipped into him first.
In fact, marrying her was even a good deal for him. It gave him
a chance to keep her under wraps and lay the groundwork for a
murder.
    Hell, if I could check back that far with accuracy I knew what
I would find. Sim paid the house upstate a visit, found Annette
Lee asleep and Sally in a dead drunk. He simply dragged her out
into the winter night and the weather did the rest. He couldn't
have done anything with the kid right then without starting an

investigation. Sally would have been a tragic accident; the kid too meant trouble.

So he waited. Like a good father, which added to his political image, he adopted her into his house. When it was not expedient for him to have her around any longer he arranged for her execution through Levitt. He sure was a lousy planner there. Levitt talked too much. Enough to die before he could do the job.

In one way Sue forced her own near-death with her crazy behavior. Whatever she couldn't get out of her mind were the things her mother told her repeatedly in her drunken moods. It had an effect all right. She made it clear to Sim that he was going to have to kill her if he didn't want her shooting her mouth off.

Sim would have known who The Snake was. Sally had referred to him by that often enough. No wonder he ducked it at the trial. No wonder it seared him silly when Sue kept insisting her mother left something for her to read. No wonder he searched her things. That last time in Sue's little house was one of desperation. He knew that sooner or later something would come to light and if it happened he was politically dead, which to him was death *in toto.*

But somebody made a mistake. There was a bigger snake loose than Torrence ever was. There was a snake with three million bucks buried in its hole and that could be the worst kind of snake of all. Hell, Sim wasn't a snake at all. He was a goddamn worm.

I folded the letter and put it back in my pocket when the bell rang. When I opened the door Velda folded into my arms like a big cat, kicked it shut with her heel, and buried her face against my neck.

"You big slob," she said.

While she made coffee I told her about it, taking her right through from the beginning. She read the letter twice, getting the full implication of it all.

"Does Pat know all this?"

"Not yet. He'd better take first things first."

"What are you going to do?"

"Call Art Rickerby."

I picked the unlisted number out of memory and got Art on the phone. It took a full thirty minutes to rehash the entire situation, but he listened patiently, letting me get it across. It was the political side of it he was more concerned with at the moment, realizing what propaganda ammunition the other side could use against us.

One thing about truth . . . let it shine and you were all right.

It was the lies that could hurt you. But there were ways of letting the truth come out so as to nullify the awkward side of it and this was what the striped-pants boys were for.

Art said he'd get into it right away, but only because of my standing as a representative of the agency he was part of.

I said, "Where do I go from here, Art?"

"Now who's going to tell you, big man?"

"It isn't over yet."

"It's never over, Mike. When this is over there will be something else."

"There will be some big heat coming my way. I'd hate to lose my pretty little ticket. It's all I have."

He was silent for a moment, then he said, "I'll let you in on a confidence. There are people here who like you. We can't all operate the same way. Put a football player on the diamond and he'd never get around the bases. A baseball player in the middle of a pileup would never get up. You've never been a total unknown and now that you're back, stay back. When we need you, we'll yell. Meanwhile nobody's going to pick up your ticket as long as you stay clean enough. I didn't say legal . . . I said clean. One day we'll talk some more about this, but not now. You do what you have to do. Just remember that everybody's watching so make it good."

"Great, all I have to do is stay alive."

"Well, if you do get knocked off, let me repeat a favorite old saying of yours, 'Kismet, buddy.'"

He hung up and left me staring at the phone. I grinned, then put it down and started to laugh. Velda said, "What's so funny?"

"I don't know," I told her. "It's just funny. Grebb and Charlie Force are going to come at me like tigers when this is over to get my official status changed and if I can make it work they don't have a chance."

That big, beautiful thing walked over next to me and slid her arms around my waist and said, "They never did have a chance. You're the tiger, man."

I turned around slowly and ran my hands under her sweater, up the warm flesh of her back. She pulled herself closer to me so that every curve of hers matched my own and her breasts became rigid against my chest.

There was a tenderness to her mouth that was only at the beginning, then her lips parted with a gentle searching motion and her tongue flicked at mine with the wordless gestures of love. Somehow the couch was behind us and we sank down on it together. There was no restraint at all, simply the knowledge that it was going to happen here and now at our own time and choosing.

No fumbling motions. Each move was deliberate, inviting, provoking the thing we both wanted so badly. Very slowly there was a release from the clothes that covered us, each in his own way doing what he wanted to do. I kissed her neck, uncovered her shoulders, and ran my mouth along them. When my hands cradled her breasts and caressed them they quivered at my touch, nuzzling my palms for more like a hungry animal.

Her stomach swelled gently against my fingers as I explored her, making her breath come in short, hard gasps. But even then there was no passiveness in her. She was as alive as I was, as demanding and as anxious. Her eyes told me of all the love she had for so long and the dreams she had had of its fulfillment.

The fiery contact of living flesh against living flesh was almost too much to stand and we had gone too far to refuse the demand any longer. She was mine and I was hers and we had to belong to each other.

But it didn't happen that way.

The doorbell rang like some damn screaming banshee and the suddenness of it wiped the *big now* right out of existence. I swore under my breath, then grinned at Velda, who swore back the same words and grinned too.

"When will it be, Mike?"

"Someday, kitten."

Before I could leave she grabbed my hand. "Make it happen."

"I will. Go get your clothes on."

The bell rang again, longer this time, and I heard Pat's voice calling out in the hall.

I yelled, "All right, damn it, hold on a minute."

He didn't take his finger off the bell until I had opened the door.

"I was on the phone," I explained. "Come on in."

There were four others with him, all men I had seen around the precinct. Two I knew from the old days and nodded to them. The others went through a handshake.

"Velda here?"

"Inside, why?"

"She was down asking questions around the party headquarters. They want an explanation. Charlie Force is pushing everybody around on this."

"So sit down and I'll explain."

Velda came out as they were pulling up chairs, met the officers and perched on the arm of the couch next to me. I laid it out for Pat to save him the time of digging himself, supplied him with Velda's notes and the names of the persons she spoke to, and wrapped it up with Art's little speech to me.

When Pat put his book away he said, "That's one reason why I'm here. We're going to see what we can get on Howie Green. These officers have been working on it already and have come up with something that might get us started."

"Like what?"

"The real estate agency Howie Green operated went into the hands of his partner after his death. The guy's name was Quincy Malek. About a year later he contracted T.B. and died in six months. Now from a nephew we gather that Malek was damn near broke when he kicked off. He had sold out everything and his family picked over what was left. The original records left over from his partnership with Green went into storage somewhere, either private or commercial.

"Right now I have one bunch checking all the warehouses to see what they can dig up. The nephew does remember Malek asking that the records be kept so it's likely that they were. It wouldn't take up much room and a few hundred bucks would cover a storage bill on a small package for a long, long time.

"Now that's a supposition, the commercial angle. Malek and Green had a few other properties still in existence and we'll go through them too. Until everything is checked out you can't tell what we'll find. Meanwhile, we're taking another angle. We're checking all property transactions carried out by Green within a certain time of his death. If you're right something will show up. We'll check every damn one of them if we have to."

"You know how long it will take, Pat?"

"That's what I want to know. You got a better idea in that screwy mind of yours?"

"I don't know," I told him. "I'll have to think about it."

"Oh no, not you, boy. If you got anything you have it now. You just aren't the prolonged-thinking type. You got something going this minute and I want to know what it is."

"Stow it."

"Like that?"

"Like that. If it proves out I'll get it to you right away. The only reason I'm slamming it to you like this is because you're in deep enough as it is. Let me try my way. If there's trouble I'll take it alone."

"Mike . . . I don't like it. We have a killer running loose."

"Then let me be the target."

His eyes drifted to Velda beside me.

I said, "She'll stay safe. I went through that once before."

"Watch her," Pat said softly, and I knew he was never going to change about the way he felt for her.

"How many men you going to put going through the files?"

"As many as I can spare."

"Suppose you get to it first?" I queried.

He smiled crookedly. "Well, with your official status I imagine I can pass on a tip to you. Just make sure it works both ways."

"Deal. How will we make contact?"

"Keep in touch with my office. If anything looks promising I'll leave word."

He got up to go and I reached for my coat. I picked the letter out and handed it to him. "It was in Sue's teddy bear. It puts a lock on Sim all the way. I don't advise showing it to the kid though."

Pat read it through once, shook his head, and put it in his inside coat pocket. "You're a card, man, a real card. What kind of luck have you got?"

"The best kind."

"Don't pull that kind of stunt on Grebb, buddy."

"You know me."

"Sure I know you."

I let them out and went back and stretched out on the couch. Velda made me some coffee and had one with me. I drank mine staring at the ceiling while I tried to visualize the picture from front to back. It was all there except the face. Blackie Conley's face. I knew I was going to see it soon. It was a feeling I had.

"Mike . . . where are we going?"

"You're thinking ahead of me, kiddo."

"Sometimes I have to."

"You're not going anyway."

"Don't cut me out, Mike." Her hand touched the side of my jaw, then traced a tingling line down my chin.

"Okay, doll."

"Want to tell me what you have in your mind?"

"A thought. The only thing that's wrong with the picture."

"Oh? What?"

"Why Blackie Conley would want to kill Sim."

"Mike . . ." She was looking past me, deep in thought. "Since it was Torrence who engineered that robbery and not Conley as you first thought, perhaps Conley suspected what was going to come off. Supposing he outguessed Torrence. In that case, he would have had the whole bundle to himself. He would have made his own getaway plans and broken out at the right time. Don't forget, Conley was older than Sonny and he was no patsy. There was no love between the pair either. In fact, Conley might even have guessed who the brain was behind the whole thing and had reasons for revenge."

"You might have something there, kitten."

"The first try was for Sue," she went on. "That really was an indirect blow at Sim. The next try was for them both."

"There's a possible flaw in your picture too, but I can supply an answer."

She waited. I said, "It's hard to picture a guy in his eighties going up that trellis. He'd have to hire it done . . . but that's why the hoods are in town."

"I don't know, Mike. Remember Bernard MacFadden making his first parachute jump into the river when he was about the same age?"

"Uh-huh. It could be done."

"Then the answer is still to find Blackie Conley."

"That's right."

"How?"

"If we can restore another old man's memory we might get the answer."

"Sonny Motley?"

"Yup."

"Tonight?"

"Right now, sugar."

chapter ten ▬▬▬▬▬▬▬▬

FINDING SONNY MOTLEY'S apartment wasn't easy. Nobody in the gin mills knew where he lived; the cop on the beat around his store knew him but not his address. I checked the few newsstands that were open and they gave me a negative. It was at the last one that a hackie standing by heard me mention the name and said, "You mean that old con?"

"Yeah, the one who has the shoe shop."

"What's the matter?"

"Nothing. We need some information about a missing person and he might be able to help us."

"Ha, I'd like to see those old cons talk. They won't give nobody the right time."

"You know where he lives?"

"Sure. Took him home plenty of times. Hop in."

We climbed in the cab, went angling up to a shoddy section that bordered on the edge of Harlem, and the cabbie pointed out the place. "He's downstairs there on this side. Probably in bed by now."

"I'll get him up." I gave him a buck tip for his trouble and led the way down the sandstone steps to the iron gate at the bottom. I pushed the bell four or five times before a light came on inside.

A voice said, "Yeah, whatta ya want?"

"Sonny?"

"Who're you?"

"Mike Hammer."

"Oh, fer . . ." He came to the door, opened it, and reached for the grilled gate that held us out. He had a faded old robe wrapped around his body and a scowl on his face as black as night. Then he saw Velda and the sky lightened. "Hey . . . how about that."

"This is Velda, my secretary. Sonny Motley."

"Hello, Sonny."

"Well, don't just stand there. Come on in. Hot damn, I ain't had a broad in my joint since before I went to stir. Hot damn, this is great!" He slammed the gate, locked the door, and led the way down the hall. He pushed his door open and said, "Don't mind the place, huh? So it's a crummy place and who comes here? I'm a crummy old man anyway. Sure feel good to have a broad in the joint. Want a drink?"

"I'll pass," I said.

"Not me." He grinned. "A sexy broad comes in like her and I'm gonna have me a drink."

"I thought you were all over the sex angle, Sonny."

"Maybe inside I am, but my eyes don't know it. No, sir. You sit down and let me get dressed. Be right back."

Sit down? We had a choice of box seats. Egg boxes or apple boxes. There was one old sofa that didn't look safe and a chair to match that had no cushion in it. The best bet was the arms of the chair so Velda took one side and I took the other.

A choice between living here or a nice comfortable prison would be easy to make. But like the man said, at least he was free. Sonny was back in a minute, hitching suspenders over bony shoulders, a bottle of cheap booze in his hand.

"You sure you don't want nothing?"

"No, thanks."

"No need to break out glasses then." He took a long pull from the bottle, ambled over to the couch, and sat down facing us. "Hot damn," he said, "those are the prettiest legs I ever saw."

Velda shifted uncomfortably, but I said, "That's what I keep telling her."

"You keep telling her, boy. They love to hear that kind of talk. Right, lady?"

She laughed at the impish look on his face. "I guess we can stand it."

"Damn right you can. Used to be a real killer with the ladies myself. All gone now though." He pulled at the bottle again. "'Cept for looking. Guess a man never tires of looking." He set the bottle down on the floor between his feet and leaned back, his eyes glowing. "Now, what can I do for you?"

"I'm still asking questions, Sonny."

He waved his hands expansively. "Go ahead. If I can answer 'em it's all free."

"I can't get rid of the idea your old partner's still alive."

His shoulders jerked with a silent laugh. "Can't, eh? Well, you better, because that no-good is gone. Dead. I don't know where or how, but he's dead."

"Let's make like he isn't."

"I got lots of time."

"And I got news for you."

"How's that?"

"Sim Torrence is dead."

Briefly, his eyes widened. "True?"

"True."

Then he started to cackle again. "Good. Had it coming, the bugger. He put the screws on enough guys. I hope it wasn't easy."

"He was shot."

"Good. Bring the guy in and I'll fix his shoes free every time. I mean that. Free shine too."

"I thought you didn't care any more."

"Hell, I said I didn't hate him, not that I didn't care. So he's dead. I'm glad. Tomorrow I'll forget he was even alive. So what else is new?"

"Sim Torrence was the big brain who engineered your last job."

He was reaching for the bottle and stopped bent over. He looked up, not believing me. "Who says?"

"You'll read about it in the papers."

He straightened, the bottle entirely forgotten. "You mean . . ."

"Not only that, he engineered it right into a deliberate frame-up. That case made him the D.A. After that coup he was a landslide candidate."

"This is square, what you're telling me?"

"On the level, Sonny."

"The dirty son of a bitch. Sorry, lady."

"Here's an added note I want you to think about. If Blackie Conley got wise in time he could have worked the double-cross to his own advantage, taking the loot and dumping you guys."

Sonny sounded almost out of breath. "I'll be damned," he said. Some of the old fire was in his voice. "A real switcheroo. How do you like that? Sure, now I get what the score is. Blackie laid out the getaway route. Hell, he never followed through with the plan. He had something else schemed up and got away." Abruptly he dropped his head and laughed at the floor. "Boy, he was smarter than I figured. How do you like that?" he repeated.

"Sonny . . ."

He looked up, a silly grin on his face. Egg. He couldn't get over it. I said, "Blackie rented the property you were supposed to hole up in from Howie Green."

"That's right."

"He must have bought another place at the same time for his own purpose using another name."

"Just like that bastard Green to fall in with him. He'd do anything for a buck. I'm glad Blackie knocked him off!"

"He did?"

"Sure he did. Before the heist. You think we wanted somebody knowing where we was headed?"

I looked at him, puzzled.

He caught the look and said, "Yeah, I know. There ain't no statute of limitations on murder. So they could still take me for being in it. Hell, you think I really care? Look around here. What do I have? Nothing. That's what. I already served life. What could they do that's worse? Maybe at the best I can live ten years, but what can I do with ten years? Live in a crummy rat hole? Beat on shoes all day? No friends? Man, it was better doin' time. You just don't know."

I waved him down. "Look, I don't care about Green. He asked for it, so he got it. I want Blackie Conley."

"How you gonna find him?"

"Did you know Green?"

"You kiddin'? Him and me grew up together on the same block. I took more raps for that punk when I was a kid . . . aw, forget it."

"Okay, now Green was a stickler for detail. He kept records somewhere. He passed on his business to his partner, Quincy Malek."

"I knew him too."

"Now Quincy kept the records. Wherever they are, they'll have a notation of the transactions carried out by the business. It will show the property locations and we can run them down one by one until we get the place Blackie bought from him."

"You think Blackie'll still be there?"

"He hasn't showed up any place else, has he?"

"That just ain't like Blackie." He rubbed his hands together and stared at them. "Maybe I didn't know Blackie so good after all. Now what?"

"Did you know Quincy Malek?"

"Sure. From kids yet. Him too. He was another punk."

"Where would he put something for safekeeping?"

"Quincy? Man, who knows?" He chuckled and leaned back against the cushions. "He had places all over. You know he operated a couple of houses without paying off? The boys closed him on that one."

"The records, Sonny. Right now we're checking up on all of Quincy's former properties and every commercial warehouse in the city, but if you remember anything about what he had you can cut the time right down."

"Mister, you're dragging me back thirty years."

"What did you have to think about all the time you were in prison, Sonny? Whatever it was belonged back there too because in prison there was nothing to think about."

"Broads," he grinned. "Until I was sixty all I thought about was broads. Not the used ones I had before, but ones that didn't even exist. Maybe after sixty I went back, but it took some time."

"Now you got something to think about."

Sonny sat there a long moment, then his mouth twisted into a sour grimace. "Tell me, mister. What would it get me? You it would get something. Me? Nothing. Trouble, that's all it would bring. Right now I ain't got nothin' but I ain't got trouble either.

Nope. Don't think I can help you. I've had my belly full of trouble and now it's over. I don't want no more."

"There won't be trouble, Sonny."

"No? You think with all the papers down my throat I'd get any peace? You think I'd keep the lease on the shoe shop? It's bad enough I'm a con and a few people know it, but let everybody know it and I get booted right out of the neighborhood. No business, nothin'. Sorry, mister."

"There might be a reward in it."

"No dice. I'd have everybody in the racket chiseling it outa me. I'd wind up a drunk or dead. Somebody'd try to take me for the poke and I'd be out. Not me, Mister Hammer. I'm too old to even worry about it."

Damn, he was tying me up tight and he was right. There had to be a way. I said, "If I wanted to I could put the heat on you for the Howie Green kill. The way things stand I wouldn't be a bit surprised if we got some quick and total cooperation from the police."

Sonny stared a second, then grunted. "What a guest *you* are. You sure want me to fall bad."

"Not that bad. If you want to push it I'd probably lay back. I'm just trying you, Sonny."

Once again his eyes caught Velda's legs. She had swung them out deliberately and the dress had pulled up over her knee. It was enough to make Sonny giggle again. "Oh, hell, why not? So maybe I can feed you something. What's it they call it? Public duty or some kind of crap like that."

"Quincy Malek, Sonny."

He sat back and squinted his eyes shut. "Now let's see. What would that punk do? He up and died but he never expected to, I bet. He was the kind who'd keep everything for himself if he could. Even if he left something to his family I bet they'd have to dig for it.

"Quincy owned property around town. Tenements, stuff like that. He'd buy cheap and hold. Got plenty in rentals and he seemed to know what was coming down and what was going up. Always had a hot iron in the fire."

"Would he keep any records there?"

"Nope, don't think so. Something might happen to 'em. My guess is he'd leave 'em with somebody."

"Who?"

"Something about old Quincy nobody knew. He kept a pair of sisters in an apartment building he owned. Tricky pair that. Real queer for anything different. I got the word once that he had a double deal with them. They owned the apartment with some papers signed so that he could take it back any time he wanted. He couldn't get screwed that way. Me, I'd look for those sisters. That building would be the only income they had and they couldn't dump it so they were stuck with it, but since it was a good deal all around, why not, eh?"

"Who were they, Sonny?"

"Now you got me, mister. I think if you poke around you'll find out who. I remember the deal, but not the dames. That any help?"

"It's a lead."

"Maybe I'll think of it later. You want me to call if I do?"

I picked a scrap of paper off the table, wrote down the office and home numbers, and gave them to him. "Keep calling these numbers until you get me or Velda here."

"Sure." He tucked the paper in his pants pocket. Then he got an idea. "Hey," he said, "if you find that crumb Blackie, you let me know. Hell, I'd even like a feel of that money. Just a feel. I think I'm entitled. It cost me thirty years."

"Okay, a feel," I said kiddingly.

Then Velda swung her legs out again and he grinned. "You know what I'd really like to feel, don't you?"

With a laugh Velda said, "You're a dirty old man."

"You bet, lady. But I'd sure like to see you with your clothes off just once."

"If you did you'd drop dead," I told him.

"What a way to go," he said.

Pat wasn't bothering to get any sleep either. I reached him at the office and gave him the dope Sonny passed on to me. He thought it had merit enough to start working on and was going to put two men on it right away. Nothing else had paid off yet, although they had come up with a few former properties Malek had owned. They had made a search of the premises, but nothing showed. A team of experts were on a twenty-four-hour detail in the records section digging up old titles, checking possibles, and having no luck at all so far.

Offhand I asked for Quincy's old address and Pat gave me the location of his home and the building the real estate agency was housed in. He had checked them both personally and they were clean.

I hung up the phone and asked Velda if she wanted something

to eat. The Automat was right down the street so she settled for a cup of coffee and a sandwich. We waited for the light, cut over, and ducked inside.

Right at the front table Jersey Toby was having coffee and when he saw me he simply got up and left with his coffee practically untouched.

We fed nickels into the slots, got what we wanted, and picked a table.

Outside the damn rain had started again.

Velda said, "What's on your mind?"

"How can you tell?"

"Your poker face slipped. You're trying to think of something."

I slammed the coffee cup down. "One lousy thing. I can feel it. One simple goddamn thing I can't put my finger on and it's right there in front of me. I keep forgetting things."

"It'll come back."

"Now is when I need it."

"Will talking about it help?"

"No."

"You're close, aren't you?"

"We're sitting right on top of it, baby. We're riding three million bucks into the ground and have a killer right in front of us someplace. The damn guy is laughing all the way too."

"Suppose the money isn't there?"

"Honey . . . you don't just *lose* that kind of capital. You don't misplace it. You put it someplace for a purpose. Somebody is ready to move in this town and that money is going to buy that person a big piece of action. If that one is as smart as all this, the action is going to be rough and expensive."

"Why don't you call Pat again? They might have something."

"I don't want to bug him to death."

"He won't mind."

We pushed away from the table and found a phone booth. Pat was still at his desk and it was three A.M. He hadn't found anything yet. He did have one piece of news for me and I asked what it was.

"We picked up one of the out-of-town boys who came in from Detroit. He was getting ready to mainline one when he got grabbed and lost his fix. He sweated plenty before he talked; now he's flipping because he's in trouble. The people who sent him here won't have anything to do with a junkie and if they know he's on H he's dead. Now he's yelling for protection."

"Something hot?"

"We know the prime factor behind the move into town. Somebody has spent a lot of time collecting choice items about key men in the Syndicate operation. He's holding it over their heads and won't let go. The payoff is for them to send in the best enforcers who are to be the nucleus of something new and for this they're paying and keeping still about it. None of them wants to be caught in a bind by the Syndicate itself so they go with the demand."

"Funny he'd know that angle."

"Not so funny. Their security isn't that good. Word travels fast in those circles. I bet we'll get the same story if we can put enough pressure on any of the others."

"You said they were clean."

"Maybe we can dirty them up a little. In the interest of justice, that is."

"Sometimes it's the only way. But tell me this, Pat . . . who could pull a play like that? You'd need to know the in of the whole operation. That takes some big smarts. You'd have to pinpoint your sucker and concentrate on him. This isn't a keyhole game."

"It's been done."

"Blackie Conley could have done it," I suggested. "He could have used a bit of the loot for expenses and he would have had the time and the know-how."

"That's what I think too."

"Anything on Malek's women?"

"Hold it a minute." I heard him put the phone down, speak to somebody, then he picked it up again. "Got a note here from a retired officer who was contacted. He remembers the girls Malek used to run with but can't recall the building. His second wife put in a complaint to have it raided for being a disorderly house at one time and he was on the call. Turned out to be a nuisance complaint and nothing more. He can't place the building any more though."

"Hell," I said.

"We'll keep trying. Where will you be?"

"Home. I've had it."

"See you tomorrow," Pat said.

I hung up and looked at Velda. "Malek," I said. "Nobody can find where he spent his time."

"Why don't you try the yellow pages?" Velda kidded.

I paused and nodded. "You just might be right at that, kid."

"It was a joke, Mike."

I shook my head. "Pat just told me he had a second wife. That meant he had a first. Let's look it up."

There were sixteen Maleks in the directory and I got sixteen dimes to make the calls. Thirteen of them told me everything from drop dead to come on up for a party, but it was the squeaky old voice of the fourteenth that said yes, she was Mrs. Malek who used to be married to Quincy Malek. No, she never used the Quincy or the initial because she never cared for the name. She didn't think it was the proper time to call, but yes, if it was as important as I said it was, I could come right over.

"We hit something, baby," I said.

"Pat?"

"Not yet. Let's check this one out ourselves first."

The cab let us out on the corner of Eighth and Forty-ninth. Somewhere along the line over one of the store fronts was the home of Mrs. Quincy Malek the first. Velda spotted the number over the darkened hallway and we went in, found the right button, and pushed it. Seconds later a buzzer clicked and I opened the door.

It was only one flight up. The stairs creaked and the place reeked of fish, but the end could be up there.

She was waiting at the top of the landing, a garishly rouged old lady in a feathered wrapper that smelled of the twenties and looked it. Her hair was twisted into cloth curlers with a scarf hurriedly thrown over it and she had that querulous look of all little old ladies suddenly yanked out of bed at a strange hour.

She forced a smile, asked us in after we introduced ourselves, and had us sit at the kitchen table while she made tea. Neither Velda nor I wanted it, but if she were going to put up with us we'd have to go along with her.

Only when the tea was served properly did she ask us what we wanted.

I said, "Mrs. Malek . . . it's about your husband."

"Oh, he died a long time ago."

"I know. We're looking for something he left behind."

"He left very little, very little. What he left me ran out years ago. I'm on my pension now."

"We're looking for some records he might have kept."

"My goodness, isn't that funny?"

"What is?"

"That you should want them too."

"Who else wanted them, Mrs. Malek?"

She poured another cup of tea for me and put the pot down daintily. "Dear me, I don't know. I had a call . . . oh, some months ago. They wanted to know if Quincy left any of his business records with me. Seems that they needed something to clear up a title."

"Did he, Mrs. Malek?"

"Certainly, sir. I was the only one he could ever trust. He left a large box with me years ago and I kept it for him as I said I would in case it was ever needed."

"This party who called . . ."

"I told him what I'm telling you."

"Him?"

"Well . . . I really couldn't say. It was neither a man's nor a woman's voice. They offered me one hundred dollars if they could inspect the box and another hundred if I were instrumental in proving their claim."

"You take it?"

Her pale blue eyes studied me intently. "Mr. Hammer, I am no longer a woman able to fend for herself. At my age two hundred dollars could be quite an asset. And since those records had been sitting there for years untouched, I saw no reason why I shouldn't let them have them."

It was like having a tub of ice water dumped over you. Velda sat there, the knuckles of her hand white around the teacup.

"Who did you give it to, Mrs. Malek?"

"A delivery boy. He left me an envelope with one hundred dollars in it."

"You know the boy?"

"Oh dear no. He was just . . . a boy. Spanish, I think. His English was very bad."

"Damn," I said.

"Another cup of tea, Mr. Hammer?"

"No, thanks." Another cup of tea would just make me sick. I looked at Velda and shook my head.

"The box was returned, of course," she said suddenly.

"What!"

"With another hundred dollars. Another boy brought it to me."

"Look, Mrs. Malek . . . if we can take a look at that box and find what we're looking for, I'll make a cash grant of five hundred bucks. How does that sound to you?"

"Lovely. More tea?"

I took another cup of tea. This one didn't make me sick. But she almost did. She sat there until I finished the cup, then excused herself and disappeared a few minutes. When she came back she was carrying a large cardboard carton with the top folded down and wrapped in coarse twine.

"Here you are, Mr. Hammer."

Velda and I opened the carton carefully, flipped open the top, and looked down at the stacked sheafs of notations that filled the entire thing. Each one was an independent sales record that listed prices, names, and descriptions and there were hundreds of them. I checked the dates and they were spread through the months I wanted.

"Are you satisfied, sir?"

I reached for my wallet and took out five bills. There were three singles left. I laid them on the table but she didn't touch them.

She said, "One of those pieces of paper is missing, I must tell you."

All of a sudden I had that sick feeling again. I looked at the five hundred bucks lying on the table and so did Mrs. Malek.

"How do you know?" I asked her.

"Because I counted them. Gracious, when Quincy trusted me with them I wanted to be sure they were always there. Twice a year I used to go through them to make sure the tally was identical with the original one. Then when I got them back I counted them again and one was missing." She looked at me and nodded firmly. "I'm positive. I counted twice."

"That was the one we wanted, Mrs. Malek."

"I may still be of help." She was smiling at some private secret. "Some years back I was sick. Quite sick. I was here in bed for some months and for lack of something to do I decided to make my own record of Quincy's papers. I listed each and every piece much as he did."

She reached into the folds of her wrapper and brought out a thick, cheap note pad and laid it down on the table. "You'll have to go through them all one by one and find the piece that's missing, but it's here, Mr. Hammer."

I picked up the pad, hefted it, and stuck it in my pocket. "One question, Mrs. Malek. Why are you going so far with us?"

"Because I don't like to be stolen from. That other party deliberately stole something of value from me. That person was dishonest. Therefore I assume you are honest. Am I wrong?"

"You aren't wrong, Mrs. Malek. You may get more out of this than you think."

"This is sufficient for my needs, sir."

I picked up the box and put on my hat. "You'll get them all back this time. The police may want to hold them for a while, but eventually they'll be returned."

"I'm sure they will. And I thank you, sir."

I grinned at her. "I could kiss you."

"That would be a pleasure." She glanced at Velda. "Do you mind?"

"Be my guest," Velda said.

So I kissed her.

Damn if the blush didn't make the rouge spots fade right out.

The last three bucks bought a cab ride back to the apartment and two hamburgers apiece. We dumped the contents of the box on the floor, spread them out into piles, opened the notebook, and started to go through them.

At dawn I called Pat without telling him what I had. So far he had nothing. Then we went back to the scoreboard. It could have taken a few days but we got lucky. At three in the afternoon Velda instituted a quick system of cross-checking and we found the missing item.

It was a deed made out to one Carl Sullivan for a piece of property in Ulster County, New York, and the location was accurately described. Beneath it, apparently copied from the original notation, were the initials, B.C. *Blackie Conley!*

chapter eleven ▰▰▰▰▰▰▰▰▰▰

I HAD TO BORROW fifty bucks from George over at the Blue Ribbon to get on my way, but he came up with the dough and no questions. Down the street I rented a Ford and Velda got in it for the drive upstate. Instead of taking the Thruway I got on old Route 17 and stopped at Central Valley to see a real estate dealer I knew. It wasn't easy to keep the glad-handing of old-times talk to a minimum, but we managed. I gave him my property location and he pulled down a wall map and started locating it on the grid.

He found it quickly enough. Then he looked at me strangely and said, "You own this?"

"No, but I'm interested in it."

"Well, if you're thinking of buying it, forget it. This is in the area they located those gas wells on and several big companies have been going nuts trying to find the owner. It's practically jungle up there and they want to take exploration teams in and can't do it without permission. The taxes have been paid in advance so there's no squawk from the state and nobody can move an inch until the owner shows up."

"Tough."

His face got a little bit hungry. "Mike . . . do you know the owner?"

"I know him."

"Think we can swing a deal?"

"I doubt it."

His face fell at the thought of the money he was losing. "Well, if he wants to sell, put in a word for me, okay?"

"I'll mention it to him."

That seemed to satisfy him. We shook hands back at the car and took off. An hour and ten minutes later we were at the turnoff that led to the property. The first road was a shale and dirt one that we took for a mile, looking for a stream. We found that too, and the barely visible indentation that showed where another road had been a long time back.

I drove down the road and backed the Ford into the bushes, hiding it from casual observation, then came back to Velda and looked at the jungle we were going into.

The trees were thick and high, pines intermingled with oaks and maples, almost hopelessly tangled at their bases with heavy brush and thorny creepers. Towering overhead was the uneven roll of the mountain range.

It was getting late and we wouldn't have too much sun left.

"It's someplace in there," I said. "I don't know how he did it, but it was done. He's in there."

Animals had made their way in ahead of us. The trail was barely visible and some of the brush was fuzzed with the hair of deer, the earth, where it was soft in spots, showing the print of their hoofs. We made it crawling sometimes, fighting the undergrowth constantly. But little by little we got inside.

The ground slope ranged upward, leveled off, then slanted down again. We saw the remains of a shack and headed toward it, but that was all it was, a vermin-infested building that had long ago fallen into ruin. At one side there was a carton of rusted tins that had spilled over and rotted out, and another wooden crate of cooking utensils, still nested inside each other. The remains of a mattress had been scattered over the floor making permanent nests for thousands of mice.

It didn't make sense.

We started down the slope and burst through the brush into a clearing that was shaped like a bowl. Nature had somehow started something growing there, a peculiar soft grass that refused to allow anything else to intrude on its domain.

Velda said, "Mike . . ."

I stopped and looked back.

"I'm tired, Mike. Can't we rest a minute?"

"Sure, honey. This is a good place."

She sank to the ground with a long sigh and stretched out languidly looking at the sky. The clouds were tinged with a deep red and the shadows were beginning to creep down the mountainside. "This is lovely, Mike."

"Not much like the city, is it?"

She laughed, said, "No," and lifted her legs to strip off the ruins of her nylons. She stopped with one leg pointed toward the mountain. "You do it."

What a broad.

I held her foot against my stomach, unhooked the snaps that held the stockings, and peeled one down, then the other. She said, "Ummm," and patted the ground beside her. I crossed my legs and sat down, but she grabbed for me, tipped me over toward her, and held my face in her hands. "It's going to be dark soon, Mike. We can't go back through that again. Not until morning." Her smile was impish.

"Any time, any place. You're crazy."

"I want you, Mike. Now."

"It's going to get cold."

"Then we'll suffer."

I kissed her then, her mouth slippery against mine.

"It's awfully warm now," she murmured. She raised her legs and the dress slid down her thighs.

"Stop that."

Her hand took mine and held it against the roundness of one thigh, keeping it there until she could take hers away and knew mine would stay. Ever so slowly my hand began a movement of its own, sensing the way to love, unable to stop the motion.

With an age-old feminine motion she made it easier for me,

her entire being trying to bring me into its vortex and I tried to fill the void. There was something I was fighting against, but it wasn't a fight I knew I could win. There was a bulk between us and Velda's hand reached inside my coat and pulled out the .45 and laid it on the ground in back of her.

The sun was low now, the rays angling into the trees. One of them picked up a strange color in the brush at the foot of the hill, an odd color that never should have been there. I stared at it, trying to make out what it was.

Then I knew.

The fingers of my hand squeezed involuntarily and Velda let out a little cry, the pain of it shocking her. I said, "Stay here," and snapped to my feet.

"Mike . . ."

I didn't take the time to answer her. I ran down the hill toward the color and with each step it took shape and form until it was what I knew it had to be.

A thirty-year-old taxi cab. A yellow and black taxi that had been stolen off the streets back in the thirties.

The tires were rotted shreds now, but the rest of it was intact. Only a few spots of rust showed through the heavy layers of paint that the cab had been coated with to protect it against the destruction of the wind-driven grit in the city.

I looked it over carefully and almost wanted to say that they sure didn't make them like this any more. The windows were still rolled shut hard against their rubber cushions so that the stuff fused them right into the body of the car with age. The car had been new when it was stolen, and they made that model to last for years. It was an airtight vault now, a bright yellow, wheeled mausoleum for two people.

At least they had been two people.

Now they were two mummies. The one in the front was slumped across the wheel, hat perched jauntily on a skeletal head covered with drawn, leathery flesh. There wasn't much to the back of the head. That had been blown away.

The guy who did it was the other mummy in the back seat. He leaned against the other side of the car, his mouth gaping open so that every tooth showed, his clothes hanging from his withered limbs. Where his eyes were I could see two little dried bits of things that still had the appearance of watching me.

He still held the rifle across his lap aimed at the door in front of me, fingers clutched around its stock and his right forefinger still on the trigger. There was a black stain of blood on the shirt that could still give it a startlingly white background.

Between his feet were three canvas sacks.

A million dollars in each.

I had finally found Blackie Conley.

She came up on bare feet and I didn't hear her until her breath hissed with the horror of what she saw. She pressed the back of her hand against her mouth to stop the scream that started to come, her eyes wide open for long moments.

"Mike . . . who . . . ?"

"Our killer, Velda. The Target. The one we were after. That's Blackie Conley in the back seat there. He almost made it. How close can a guy come?"

"Pretty close, Mr. Hammer. Some of us come all the way."

I didn't hear him either! He had come up the side of the hill on sneakered feet and stood there with a gun on us and I felt like the biggest fool in the world! My .45 was back there in the love nest and now we were about to be as dead as the others. It was like being right back at the beginning again.

I said, "Hello, Sonny."

The Snake. The real snake, as deadly as they come. The only one that had real fangs and knew how to use them. His face had lost the tired look and his eyes were bright with the desirous things he saw in his future. There was nothing stooped about him now, nothing of the old man there. Old, yes, but he wasn't the type who grew old easily. It had all been a pose, a cute game, and he was the winner.

"You scared me, Mr. Hammer. When you got as far as Malek you really scared me. I was taking my time about coming here because I wasn't ready yet and then I knew it was time to move. You damn near ruined everything." What I used to call a cackle was a pose too. He did have a laugh. He thought it was funny.

Velda reached for my arm and I knew she was scared. It was too much too fast all over again and she could only take so much.

"Smart," he said to me. "You're a clever bastard. If all I had was the cops to worry about it would have been no trouble, but I had to draw you." His mouth pulled into a semblance of a grin. "Those nice talks we had. You kept me right up to date. Tell me, did you think I had a nice face?"

"I thought you had more sense, Sonny."

He dropped the grin then. "Get off it, guy. More sense? For what? You think I was going to spend all my life in the cooler without getting some satisfaction? Mister, that's where you made your mistake. You should have gone a little further into my case history. I always was a mean one because it paid off. If I had to play pretty-face to make it pay off I could do that too."

"You won't make it, Sonny."

"No? Well, just lose that idea. For thirty years I worked this one out. I had all the time in the world to do it too. With the contacts I had in the can I got enough on the big boys to make them jump my way when I was ready. I put together a mob and now I'll have to move to get it rolling. You think I won't live big for what little time I have left? Well, you're making a mistake when you think that. A lot of planning went into this dodge, kid."

"You still hate, don't you?"

Sonny Motley nodded slowly, a smile of pure pleasure forming. "You're goddamn right. I hated that bastard Torrence and tried to get at him through this kid. Mistake there . . . I thought he loved the kid. I would've been doin' him a favor to rub her out, right?"

"He was trying for her too."

"I got the picture fast enough. When I knocked him off in his house I thought I'd get the kid just for the fun of it. She fooled me. Where was she, mister?"

I shrugged.

"Hell, it don't matter none now." He lifted the gun so I could see down the barrel. "I thought sure you'd get on to me sooner. I pulled a boner, you know that, don't you?"

I knew it now, all right. When Marv Kania tried to nail me with the cab, it was because Sonny had called him from the back room when he faked getting me old clippings of his crime and told him where I was going. When Marv almost got me in my apartment it was because Sonny told him my new address and that I'd be there. I made it easy because I told Sonny both times.

I said, "Marv Kania was holed up in your place, wasn't he?"

"That's right, dying every minute, and all he wanted was to get that last crack at you. It was the one thing that kept him alive."

"It was the thing that killed him too, Sonny."

"Nobody'll miss him but me. The kid had guts. He knew nobody could help him, but he stuck the job out."

"You got the guts too, Sonny?"

"I got the guts, Hammer." He laughed again. "You gave old Blackie credit for having my guts though. That was pretty funny. You were so sure it was him. Never me. Blackie the slob. You know, I figured out that cross when I was in stir. It came through to me and when I put the pieces together bit by bit I knew what I was going to do. I even figured out how Blackie got wise at the last minute and what he'd do to plan a getaway. He wasn't such a hard guy to second-guess. After all, I had thirty years to do it in. Now it's the big loot I waited all that time to spend."

"You won't do it, Sonny."

"How do you figure to stop me? You got no gun and you're under one. I can pump a fast one into you both and nobody will hear a sound. Blackie picked this place pretty well. You're gonna die, you know. I can't let you two run around."

Velda's fingers bit into my arm harder. "See the money in the car, Hammer? It still there? It wasn't in the shack so it's gotta be there or around here somewhere."

"Look for yourself."

"Step back."

We moved slowly, two steps, then stood there while Sonny grinned and looked into the window of the cab.

It was hard to tell what was happening to his face. For one second I thought I'd have a chance to jump him but he caught himself in time and swung the gun back on us. His eyes were dancing with the joy of the moment and the laugh in his throat was real.

Sonny Motley was doing what he had wanted to do for so long, meeting Blackie Conley face to face.

"Look at him. It's him back there! Look at that dirty double-crosser sitting there just like I shot him. Goddamn, I didn't miss with that shot. I killed the son of a bitch thirty years ago! See that, Hammer . . . see the guy I killed thirty years ago. Damn, if that isn't a pretty sight."

He paused, sucking in his breath, his chest heaving, "Just like he was, still got that rifle he loved. See where I got him, Hammer . . . right in the chest. Right through the open window before he could get his second shot off.

"Hello, Blackie, you dirty bastard!" he shrieked. "How'd you like that shot? How'd it feel to die, Blackie? This is worth waiting all the thirty years for!"

Sonny turned and grimaced at me, his eyes burning. "Always figured to make it, Blackie did. Had the driver pull him into his hidey hole and shot him in the head. But he never lived through my shot. No chance of that. Man, this is my *big* day . . . the biggest damn day in my life! Now I got everything!"

He drew himself erect at the thought, a funny expression changing his face. He said, "Only one thing I ain't got any more," and this time he was looking at Velda.

"Take those clothes off, lady."

Her fingers that were so tight on my arm seemed to relax and I knew she was thinking the same thing as I was. It could be a diversion. If she could step aside and do it so we were split up I might get the chance to jump him.

I didn't watch her. I couldn't. I had to watch him. But I could tell from his eyes just what she was doing. I knew when she took the skirt off, then the bra. I watched his eyes follow her hands as she slid the skirt down over her ankles and I knew by the quick intake of his breath and the sudden brightness of his eyes when she had stepped out of the last thing she wore.

She made the slightest motion to one side then, but he was with it. He said, "Just stay there, lady. Stay here close where I can get to you both."

Not much time was left now. The fire in his eyes was still burning, but it wouldn't last.

"Real nice, lady," he said. "I like brunettes. Always have. Now you can die like that, right together."

No time at all now.

"Too bad you didn't get the money, Sonny."

He shook his head at me, surprised that I'd make such a bad attempt. "It's right on the floor there."

"You'd better be sure, Sonny. We got here ahead of you."

If he had trouble opening the door I might be able to make the move. All he had to do was falter once and if I could get past the first shot I could take him even if he caught me with it. Velda would hit the ground the second he pulled the trigger and together we'd have him.

"No good, Hammer. It's right there and Old Blackie is still guarding it with his rifle. You saw it."

"You didn't."

"Okay, so you get one last look." He reached for the door handle and gave it a tentative tug. It didn't budge. He laughed again, knowing what I was waiting for but not playing it my way at all. The gun never wavered and I knew I'd never get the chance. From where he stood he could kill us both with ease and we all knew it.

The next time he gave the door a sharp jerk and it swung open, the hinges groaning as the rust ground into them. He was watching us with the damndest grin I ever saw and never bothered to see what was happening in the cab. The pull on the door was enough to rock the car and ever so steadily the corpse of Blackie Conley seemed to come to life, sitting up in the seat momentarily. I could see the eyes and the mouth open in a soundless scream with the teeth bared in a grimace of wild hatred.

Sonny knew something was happening and barely turned his head to look . . . just enough to see the man he had killed collapse into dust fragments, and as it did the bony finger touched the trigger that had been filed to react to the smallest of pressures and the rifle squirted a blossom of roaring flame that took Sonny Motley square in the chest and dropped him lifeless four feet away.

While the echo still rumbled across the mountainside, the leather-covered skull of Blackie Conley bounced out of the cab and rolled to a stop face to face with Sonny and lay there grinning at him idiotically.

You can only sustain emotion so long. You can only stay scared so long. It stops and suddenly it's like nothing happened at all. You don't shake, you don't break up. You're just glad it's over. You're a little surprised that your hands aren't trembling and wonder why it is you feel almost perfectly normal.

Velda said quietly, "It's finished now, isn't it?"

Her clothes were in a heap beside her and in the dying rays of the sun she looked like a statuesque wood nymph, a lovely naked wood nymph with beautiful black hair as dark as a raven against a sheen of molded flesh that rose and dipped in curves that were unbelievable.

Up there on the hill the grass was soft where we had lain in the nest. It smelled flowery and green and the night was going to be a warm night. I looked at her, then toward the spot on the hill. Tomorrow it would be something else, but this was now.

I said, "You ready?"

She smiled at me, savoring what was to come. "I'm ready."

I took her hand, stepped over the bodies, new and old, on the ground, and we started up the slope.

"Then let's go," I said.

The Twisted Thing

TO SID GRAEDON
WHO SAW THE CHARRED EDGES

chapter one ▬▬▬▬▬▬▬▬▬▬▬▬▬

THE LITTLE GUY'S face was a bloody mess. Between the puffballs of blue-black flesh that used to be eyelids, the dull gleam of shock-deadened pupils watched Dilwick uncomprehendingly. His lips were swollen things of lacerated skin, with slow trickles of blood making crooked paths from the corners of his mouth through the stubble of a beard to his chin, dripping onto a stained shirt.

Dilwick stood just outside the glare of the lamp, dangling like the Sword of Damocles over the guy's head. He was sweating too. His shirt clung to the meaty expanse of his back, the collar wilted into wrinkles around his huge neck. He pushed his beefy hand further into the leather glove and swung. The solid smack of his open hand on the little guy's jaw was nasty. His chair went over backward and his head cracked against the concrete floor of the room like a ripe melon. Dilwick put his hands on his hips and glared down at the caricature that once was human.

"Take him out and clean 'im up. Then get 'im back here." Two other cops came out of the darkness and righted the chair. One yanked the guy to his feet and dragged him to the door.

Lord, how I hated their guts. Grown men, they were supposed to be. Four of them in there taking turns pounding a confession from a guy who had nothing to say. And I had to watch it.

It was supposed to be a warning to me. Be careful, it said, when you try to withhold information from Dilwick you're looking for a broken skull. Take a look at this guy for example, then spill what you know and stick around so I, the Great Dilwick, can get at you when I want you.

I worked up a husky mouthful of saliva and spat it as close to his feet as I could. The fat cop spun on his heel and let his lips fold back over his teeth in a sneer. "You gettin' snotty, Hammer?"

I stayed slouched in my seat. "Any way you call it, Dilwick," I said insolently. "Just sitting here thinking."

Big stuff gave me a dirty grimace. "Thinking . . . you?"

"Yeah. Thinking what you'd look like the next day if you tried that stuff on me."

The two cops dragging the little guy out stopped dead still. The other one washing the bloodstains from the seat quit swishing the brush over the wicker and held his breath. Nobody ever spoke that way to Dilwick. Nobody from the biggest politician in the state to the hardest apple that ever stepped out of a pen. Nobody ever did because Dilwick would cut them up into fine pieces with his bare hands and enjoy it. That was Dilwick, the dirtiest, roughest cop who ever walked a beat or swung a nightstick over a skull. Crude, he was. Crude, hard and dirty and afraid of nothing. He'd sooner draw blood from a face than eat and everybody knew it. That's why nobody ever spoke to him that way. That is, nobody except me.

Because I'm the same way myself.

Dilwick let out his breath with a rush. The next second he was reaching down for me, but I never gave him the chance to hook his hairy paws in my shirt. I stood up in front of him and sneered in his face. Dilwick was too damn big to be used in meeting guys eye to eye. He liked to look down at them. Not this time.

"What do you think you'll do?" he snarled.

"Try me and see," I said.

I saw his shoulder go back and didn't wait. My knee came up and landed in his groin with a sickening smash. When he doubled over my fist caught him in the mouth and I felt his teeth pop. His face was starting to turn blue by the time he hit the floor. One cop dropped the little guy and went for his gun.

"Cut it, stupid," I said, "before I blow your goddamn head off. I still got my rod." He let his hand fall back to his side. I turned and walked out of the room. None of them tried to stop me.

Upstairs I passed the desk sergeant still bent over his paper. He looked up in time to see me and let his hand snake under the desk. Right then I had my own hand six inches from my armpit practically inviting him to call me. Maybe he had a family at home. He brought his hand up on top of the desk where I could see it. I've seen eyes like his peering out of a rathole when there was a cat in the room. He still had enough I AM THE LAW in him to bluster it out.

"Did Dilwick release you?" he demanded.

I snatched the paper from his hand and threw it to the floor, trying to hold my temper. "Dilwick didn't release me," I told him. "He's downstairs vomiting his guts out the same way you'll be doing if you pull a deal like that again. Dilwick doesn't want *me*. He just wanted me to sit in on a cellar séance in legal torture to show me how tough he is. I wasn't impressed. But get this, I came to Sidon to legally represent a client who used his one phone call on arrest to contact me, not to be intimidated by a fat louse that was kicked off the New York force and bought his way into the cops in this hick town just to use his position for a rake-off."

The sergeant started to interrupt, licking his loose lips nervously, but I cut him short. "Furthermore, I'm going to give you just one hour to get Billy Parks out of here and back to his house. If you don't," and I said it slowly, "I'm going to call the State's Attorney and drop this affair in his lap. After that I'll come back here and mash your damn face to a pulp. Understand now? No habeas corpus, no nothing. Just get him out of here."

For a cop he stunk. His lower lip was trembling with fear. I pushed my hat on the back of my head and stamped out of the station house. My heap was parked across the street and I got in and turned it over. Damn, I was mad.

Billy Parks, just a nice little ex-con trying to go straight, but do you think the law would help him out? Hell no. Let one thing off-color pop up and they drag him in to get his brains kicked out because he had a record. Sure, he put in three semesters in the college on the Hudson, and he wasn't too anxious to do anything that would put him in his senior year where it took a lifetime to matriculate. Ever since he wrangled that chauffeur's job from Rudolph York I hadn't heard from him . . . until now, after York's little genius of a son had been snatched.

Rain started to spatter against the windshield when I turned into the drive. The headlights picked out the roadway and I followed it up to the house. Every light in the place was on as if the occupants were afraid a dark corner might conceal some unseen terror.

It was a big place, a product of wealth and good engineering, but in spite of its stately appearance and wrought-iron gates, somebody had managed to sneak in, grab the kid and beat it.

Hell, the kid was perfect snatch bait. He was more than a son to his father, he was the result of a fourteen-year experiment. Then, that's what he got for bringing the kid up to be a genius. I bet he'd shell out plenty of his millions to see him safe and sound.

The front door was answered by one of those tailored flunkies who must always count up to fifty before they open up. He gave me a curt nod and allowed me to come in out of the rain anyway.

"I'm Mike Hammer," I said, handing him a card. "I'd like to see your boss. And right away," I added.

The flunky barely glanced at the pasteboard. "I'm awfully sorry, sir, but Mr. York is temporarily indisposed."

When I shoved a cigarette in my mouth and lit it I said, "You tell him it's about his kid. He'll un-indispose himself in a hurry."

I guess I might as well have told him I wanted a ransom payment right then the way he looked at me. I've been taken for a lot of things in my life, but this was the first for a snatch artist. He started to stutter, swallowed, then waved his hand in the general direction of the living room. I followed him in.

Have you ever seen a pack of alley cats all set for a midnight brawl when something interrupts them? They spin on a dime with the hair still up their backs and watch the intruder through hostile eye slits as though they were ready to tear him so they could continue their own fight. An intense, watchful stare of mutual hate and fear.

That's what I ran into, only instead of cats it was people. Their expressions were the same. A few had been sitting, others stopped their quiet pacing and stood poised, ready. A tableau of hate. I looked at them only long enough to make a mental count of a round dozen and tab them as a group of ghouls whose morals had been eaten into by dry rot a long time.

Rudolph York was slumped in a chair gazing blankly into an empty fireplace. The photos in the rags always showed him to be a big man, but he was small and tired-looking this night. He kept muttering to himself, but I couldn't hear him. The butler handed him my card. He took it, not bothering to look at it.

"A Mr. Hammer, sir."

No answer.

"It . . . It's about Master Ruston, sir."

Rudolph York came to life. His head jerked around and he looked at me with eyes that spat fire. Very slowly he came to his feet, his hands trembling. "Have you got him?"

Two boys who might have been good-looking if it weren't for the nightclub pallor and the squeegy skin came out of a settee together. One had his fists balled up, the other plunked his highball glass on a coffee table. They came at me together. Saps. All I had to do was look over my shoulder and let them see what was on my face and they called it quits outside of swinging distance.

I turned my attention back to Rudolph York. "No."

"Then what do you want?"

"Look at my card."

He read, "Michael Hammer, Private Investigator," very slowly, then crushed the card in his hand. The contortions in his face were weird. He breathed silent, unspeakable words through tight lips, afraid to let himself be heard. One look at the butler and the flunky withdrew quietly, then he turned back to me. "How did you find out about this?" he charged.

I didn't like this guy. As brilliant a scientist as he might be, as wealthy and important, I still didn't like him. I blew a cloud of smoke in his direction. "Not hard," I answered, "not hard at all. I got a telephone call."

He kept beating his fist into an open palm. "I don't want the police involved, do you hear! This is a private matter."

"Cool off, doc. I'm not the police. However, if you try to keep me out of this I'll buzz one of the papers, then your privacy will really be shot to hell."

"Whom do you represent?" he asked coldly.

"Your chauffeur, Billy Parks."

"So?"

"So I'd like to know why you put the finger on him when you found out your kid was missing. I'd like to know why you let them mangle him without a formal charge even being lodged, and why you're keeping all this under your hat. And by damn you better start speaking and pretty loud at that."

"Please, Mr. Hammer."

A hand hit my shoulder and spun me, another came up from the side and cracked across my face. The punk said, "How dare you talk to Uncle like that!"

I let him get it out then backhanded him across the mouth with all I had. This time the other one grabbed my coat. He got a short jab in the ribs that bent him over, then the palm of my hand across his puss that straightened him up again. I shoved him away and got the punk's tie in my hand. When I was breathing in his face I twisted on the tie until the blue started running up his neck, then I smacked him on each side of that whisky-sodden face until my hand hurt. When I dropped him he lay on the floor crying, trying to cover his face with his hands.

I spoke to the general assembly rather than to him. "In case anyone else has ideas like that, he'd better have more in his hands than a whisky glass."

York hadn't missed a trick. He looked old again. The fire left his eyes and he groped for the arm of the chair. York was having a pretty rough time of it, but after having seen Billy I didn't feel sorry for him.

I threw my butt in the fireplace and parked in the chair opposite him. He didn't need any prompting. "Ruston was not in his bed in the morning. It had been slept in, but he was not there. We searched the house and the grounds for him, but found no trace of his presence. I must have become excited. The first thing that entered my head was that I had an ex-convict in my employ. I called the local police and reported what had taken place. They led Parks away. I've since regretted the incident."

"I imagine," I remarked dryly. "How much is it costing you to keep this quiet?"

He shuddered. "Nothing. I did offer them a reward if they could locate Ruston."

"Oh, swell. Great. That's all they needed. Cripes, you got a brain like a fly!" His eyes widened at that. "These local jokers aren't cops. Sure, they'd be quiet, who wouldn't? Do you think they'd split the kind of reward money you'd be offering if they could help it?"

I felt like rapping him in the teeth. "Throwing Billy to the wolves was stupid. Suppose he was an ex-con. With three convictions to his credit he wasn't likely to stick his neck out for that offense. He'd be the first suspect as it was. Damn, I'd angle for Dilwick before I would Billy. He's more the type."

York was sweating freely. He buried his face in his hands and swayed from side to side, moaning to himself. He stopped finally, then looked up at me. "What will I do, Mr. Hammer? What *can* be done?"

I shook my head.

"But something must be done! I must find Ruston. After all these years . . . I can't call the police. He's such a sensitive boy . . . I—I'm afraid."

"I merely represent Billy Parks, Mr. York. He called me because he was in a jam and I'm his friend. What I want from you is to give him back his job. Either that or I call the papers."

"All right. It really doesn't matter." His head dropped again. I put on my hat and stood up, then, "But you? Mr. Hammer, you aren't the police as you say. Perhaps you could help me, too."

I threw him a straw. "Perhaps."

He grabbed at it. "Would you? I need somebody . . . who will keep this matter silent."

"It'll cost you."

"Very well, how much?"

"How much did you offer Dilwick?"

"Ten thousand dollars."

I let out a whistle, then told him, "Okay, ten G's plus expenses."

Relief flooded his face like sunlight. The price was plenty steep but he didn't bat an eye. He had been holding this inside himself too long and was glad to hand it to someone else.

But he still had something to say. "You drive a hard bargain, Mr. Hammer, and in my position I am forced, more or less, to accept. However, for my own satisfaction I would like to know one thing, how good a detective are you?"

He said it in a brittle tone and I answered him the same way. An answer that made him pull back away from me as though I had a contagious disease. I said, "York, I've killed a lot of men. I shot the guts out of two of them in Times Square. Once I let six hundred people in a nightclub see what some crook had for dinner when he tried to gun me. He got it with a steak knife. I remember because I don't want to remember. They were too nasty. I hate the bastards that make society a thing to be laughed at and preyed upon. I hate them so much I can kill without the slightest compunction. The papers call me dirty names and the kind of rats I monkey with are scared stiff of me, but I don't give a damn. When I kill I make it legal. The courts accuse me of being too quick on the trigger but they can't revoke my license because I do it right. I think fast, I shoot fast, I've been shot at plenty. And I'm still alive. That's how good a detective I am."

For a full ten seconds he stood speechless, staring at me with an undisguised horror. There wasn't a sound from the room. It isn't often that I make a speech like that, but when I do it must be convincing. If thoughts could be heard that house would be a babble of fearful confusion. The two punks I biffed looked like they had just missed being bitten by a snake. York was the first one to compose himself. "I suppose you'd like to see the boy's room?"

"Uh-uh."

"Why not? I thought . . ."

"The kid's gone, that's enough. Seeing the room won't do any good. I don't have the equipment to fool around with clues, York.

Fingerprints and stuff are for technical men. I deal with motives and people."

"But the motive . . ."

I shrugged. "Money, probably. That's what it usually is. Let's start at the beginning first." I indicated the chair and York settled back. I drew up closer to him. "When did you discover him to be missing?"

"Yesterday morning. At eight o'clock, his regular rising hour, Miss Malcom, his governess, went into his room. He was not in bed. She looked for him throughout the house, then told me he could not be found. With the aid of the gardener and Parks we searched the grounds. He was not there."

"I see. What about the gatekeeper?"

"Henry saw nothing, heard nothing."

"Then you called the police, I suppose?" He nodded. "Why did you think he was kidnapped?"

York gave an involuntary start. "But what other reason could account for his disappearance?"

I leaned forward in my seat. "According to all I've ever read about your son, Mr. York, he is the most brilliant thing this side of heaven. Wouldn't a young genius be inclined to be highly strung?"

He gripped the arms of the chair until the veins stood out on the back of his hands. The fire was in his eyes again. "If you are referring to his mental health, you are mistaken. Ruston was in excellent spirits as he has been all his life. Besides being his father and a scientist, I am also a doctor."

It was easy to see that he didn't want any doubts cast upon the mind of one he had conditioned so carefully so long. I let it go for the time being.

"Okay, describe him to me. Everything. I have to start somewhere."

"Yes. He is fourteen. In appearance he is quite like other boys. By appearance I mean expressions, manners and attitudes. He is five feet one-inch tall, light brown hair, ruddy complexion. He weighs one hundred twelve pounds stripped. Eyes, brown, slight scar high on the left side of his forehead as the result of a fall when he was younger."

"Got a picture of him?" The scientist nodded, reached inside his jacket pocket and came out with a snapshot. I took it. The boy was evidently standing in the yard, hands behind his back in a typically shy-youth manner. He was a good-looking kid at that. A slight smile played around his mouth and he seemed to be pretty self-conscious. He had on shorts and a dark sweater. Romping in the background was a spotted spaniel.

"Mind if I keep it?" I asked.

York waved his hand. "Not at all. If you want them, there are others."

When I pocketed the snap I lit another cigarette. "Who else is in the house? Give me all the servants, where they sleep, anyone who has been here recently. Friends, enemies, people you work with."

"Of course." He cleared his throat and listed the household. "Besides myself, there is Miss Malcom, Parks, Henry, two cooks, two maids and Harvey. Miss Grange works for me as a laboratory assistant, but lives at home in town. As for friends, I have few left that I ever see since I stopped teaching at the university. No enemies I can think of. I believe the only ones who have been inside the gate the past few weeks were tradesmen from town. That is," he indicated the gang in the room with a thumb, "outside these, my closest relatives. They are here and gone constantly."

"You are quite wealthy?" The question was unnecessary, but I made my point.

York cast a quick look about him, then a grimace that was half disgust passed over him. "Yes, but my health is still good."

I let the ghouls hear it. "Too bad for them."

"The servants all sleep in the north wing. Miss Malcom has a room adjoining Ruston's and connected to it. I occupy a combination study and bedroom at the front of the house.

"I work with no one and for no one. The nature of my work you must be familiar with; it is that of giving my son a mind capable of greater thought and intelligence than is normally found. He may be a genius to you and others, but to me he is merely one who makes full use of his mind. Naturally, my methods are closely guarded secrets. Miss Grange shares them with me, but I trust her completely. She is as devoted to my son as I am. Since the death of my wife when the child was born, she has aided me in every way. I think that is all?"

"Yeah, I guess that'll do."

"May I ask how you will proceed?"

"Sure. Until we get a sign from whoever kidnapped your son I'm going to sit tight. The ones that grabbed the kid must think they know what they're doing, otherwise they wouldn't pick someone like your boy who is always in the public eye. If you wanted to you could have every cop in the state beating the bushes. I take it there was no note . . ."

"None at all."

". . . so they're playing it close to see what you'll do. Call the cops and they're liable to take a powder. Hold off a bit and they will contact you. Then I'll go to work . . . that is if it's really a snatch."

He bit into his lip and gave me another of those fierce looks. "You say that as though you don't think he was kidnapped."

"I say that because I don't *know* he was kidnapped. It could be anything. I'll tell you better when I see a ransom note."

York didn't get a chance to answer, for at that moment the butler reappeared, and between him and the luscious redhead they supported a bloody, limp figure. "It's Parks, sir. Miss Malcom and I found him outside the door!"

We ran to him together. York gasped when he saw Parks' face then sent the butler scurrying off for some hot water and bandages. Most of the gore had been wiped off, but the swellings were as large as ever. The desk sergeant had done as I told him, the hour wasn't up yet, but somebody was still going to pay for this. I carried Billy to a chair and sat him down gently.

I stepped back and let York go to work when the butler returned with a first-aid kit. It was the first good chance I had to give Miss Malcom the once-over all the way from a beautiful set of legs through a lot of natural curves to an extraordinarily pretty face. Miss Malcom they called her.

I call her Roxy Coulter. She used to be a strip artist in the flesh circuit of New York and Miami.

chapter two

BUT ROXY HAD missed her profession. Hollywood should have had her. Maybe she didn't remember Atlantic City or that New Year's Eve party in Charlie Drew's apartment. If she did she held a dandy deadpan and all I got in return for my stare was one of those go ahead peeks, but don't touch looks.

A peek was all I got, because Billy came around with a groan and made an effort to sit up. York put his hand against his chest and forced him down again. "You'll have to be quiet," he cautioned him in a professional tone.

"My face," his eyes rolled in his head, "jeez, what happened to my face?"

I knelt beside him and turned over the cold compress on his forehead. His eyes gleamed when he recognized me. "Hello, Mike. What happened?"

"Hi, Billy. They beat up on you. Feel any better?"

"I feel awful. Oh, that bastard. If only I was bigger, Mike . . . damn, why couldn't I be big like you? That dirty . . ."

"Forget about him, kid." I patted his shoulder. "I handed him a little of the same dish. His map'll never be the same."

"Cripes! I bet you did! I thought something funny happened down there. Thanks, Mike, thanks a lot."

"Sure."

Then his face froze in a frightened grimace. "Suppose . . . suppose they come back again? Mike . . . I—I can't stand that stuff. I'll talk, I'll say anything. I can't take it, Mike!"

"Ease off. I'm not going anywhere. I'll be around."

Billy tried to smile and he gripped my arm. "You will?"

"Yup, I'm working for your boss now."

"Mr. Hammer." York was making motions from the side of the room. I walked over to him. "It would be better if he didn't get too excited. I gave him a sedative and he should sleep. Do you think you can manage to carry him to his room? Miss Malcom will show you the way."

"Certainly," I nodded. "And if you don't mind, I'd like to do a little prowling afterward. Maybe question the servants."

"Of course. The house is at your disposal."

Billy's eyes had closed and his head had fallen on his chin when I picked him up. He'd had a rough time of it all right. Without a word Miss Malcom indicated that I was to follow her and led me through an arch at the end of the room. After passing through a library, a study and a trophy room that looked like something out of a museum, we wound up in a kitchen. Billy's room was off an alcove behind the pantry. As gently as I could I laid him under the covers. He was sound asleep.

Then I stood up. "Okay, Roxy, now we can say hello."

"Hello, Mike."

"Now why the disguise and the new handle? Hiding out?"

"Not at all. The handle as you call it is my real name. Roxy was something I used on the stage."

"Really? Don't tell me you gave up the stage to be a diaper changer. What are you doing here?"

"I don't like your tone, Mike. You change it or go to hell."

This was something. The Roxy I knew never had enough self-respect to throw her pride in my face. Might as well play it her way.

"Okay, baby, don't get teed off on me. I have a right to be just a little bit curious, haven't I? It isn't very often that you catch somebody jumping as far out of character as you have. Does the old man know about the old life?"

"Don't be silly. He'd can me if he did."

"I guessed as much. How did you tie up in this place?"

"Easy. When I finally got wise to the fact that I was getting my brains knocked out in the big city I went to an agency and signed up as a registered nurse. I was one before I got talked into tossing my torso around for two hundred a week. Three days later Mr. York accepted me to take care of his child. That was two years ago. Anything else you want to know?"

I grinned at her. "Nope. It was just funny meeting you, that's all."

"Then may I leave?"

I let my grin fade and eased her out through the door. "Look, Roxy, is there somewhere we can go talk?"

"I don't play those games anymore, Mike."

"Get off my back, will you? I mean talk."

She arched her eyebrows and watched me steadily a second, then seeing that I meant it, said, "My room. We can be alone there. But only talk, remember?"

"Roger, bunny, let's go."

This time we went into the outer foyer and up a stairway that seemed to have been carved out of a solid piece of mahogany. We turned left on the landing and Roxy opened the door for me.

"In here," she said.

While I picked out a comfortable chair she turned on a table lamp then offered me a smoke from a gold box. I took one and lit it. "Nice place you got here."

"Thank you. It's quite comfortable. Mr. York sees that I have every convenience. Now shall we talk?"

She was making sure I got the point in a hurry. "The kid. What is he like?"

Roxy smiled a little bit, and the last traces of hardness left her face. She looked almost maternal. "He's wonderful. A charming boy."

"You seem to like him."

"I do. You'd like him too." She paused, then, "Mike . . . do you really think he was kidnapped?"

"I don't know, that's why I want to talk about him. Downstairs I suggested that he might have become temporarily unbalanced and the old man nearly chewed my head off. Hell, it isn't unreasonable to figure that. He's supposed to be a genius and that automatically puts him out of the normal class. What do you think?"

She tossed her hair back and rubbed her forehead with one hand. "I can't understand it. His room is next door, and I heard nothing although I'm usually a light sleeper. Ruston was perfectly all right up to then. He wouldn't simply walk out."

"No? And why not?"

"Because he is an intelligent boy. He likes everyone, is satisfied with his environment and has been very happy all the time I've known him."

"Uh-huh. What about his training? How did he get to be a genius?"

"That you'll have to find out from Mr. York. Both he and Miss Grange take care of that department."

I squashed the butt into the ashtray. "Nuts, it doesn't seem likely that a genius can be made. They have to be born. You've been around him a lot. Tell me, just how much of a genius is he? I know only what the papers print."

"Then you know all I know. It isn't what he knows that makes him a genius, it's what he is capable of learning. In one week he mastered every phase of the violin. The next week it was the piano. Oh, I realize that it seems impossible, but it's quite true. Even the music critics accept him as a master of several instruments. It doesn't stop there, either. Once he showed an interest in astronomy. A few days later he exhausted every book on the subject. His father and I took him to the observatory where he proceeded to amaze the experts with his uncanny knowledge. He's a mathematical wizard besides. It doesn't take him a second to give you the cube root of a six-figure number to three decimal points. What more can I say? There is no field that he doesn't excel in. He grasps fundamentals at the snap of the fingers and learns in five minutes what would take you or me years of study. That, Mike, is the genius in a nutshell, but that's omitting the true boy part of him. In all respects he is exactly like other boys."

"The old man said that too."

"He's quite right. Ruston loves games, toys and books. He has a pony, a bicycle, skates and a sled. We go for long walks around the estate every once in a while and do nothing but talk. If he wanted to he could expound on nuclear physics in ten-syllable words, but that isn't his nature. He'd sooner talk football."

I picked another cigarette out of the box and flicked a match with my thumbnail. "That about covers it, I guess. Maybe he didn't go off his nut at that. Let's take a look at his room."

Roxy nodded and stood up. She walked to the end of the room and opened a door. "This is it." When she clicked on the light switch I walked in. I don't know what I expected, but this wasn't it. There were pennants on the walls and pictures tucked into the corners of the dresser mirror. Clothes were scattered in typical boyish confusion over the backs of chairs and the desk.

In one corner was the bed. The covers had been thrown to the foot and the pillow still bore the head print of its occupant. If the kid had really been snatched I felt for him. It was no night to be out in your pajamas, especially when you left the top of them hanging on the bedpost.

I tried the window. It gave easily enough, though it was evident from the dust on the outside of the sill that it hadn't been opened recently.

"Keep the kid's door locked at night?" I asked Roxy.

She shook her head. "No. There's no reason to."

"Notice any tracks around here, outside the door or window?"

Another negative. "If there were any," she added, "they would have been wiped out in the excitement."

I dragged slowly on the cigarette, letting all the facts sink in. It seemed simple enough, but was it? "Who are all the twerps downstairs, bunny?"

"Relatives, mostly."

"Know 'em?"

Roxy nodded. "Mr. York's sister and her husband, their son and daughter, and a cousin are his only blood relations. The rest are his wife's folks. They've been hanging around here as long as I've been here, just waiting for something to happen to York."

"Does he know it?"

"I imagine so, but he doesn't seem bothered by them. They try to outdo each other to get in the old boy's favor. I suppose there's a will involved. There usually is."

"Yeah, but they're going to have a long wait. York told me his health was perfect."

Roxy looked at me curiously, then dropped her eyes. She fidgeted with her fingernails a moment and I let her stew a bit before I spoke.

"Say it, kid."

"Say what?"

"What you have on your mind and almost said."

She bit her lip, hesitating then, "This is between you and me, Mike. If Mr. York knew I told you this I'd be out of a job. You won't mention it, will you?"

"I promise."

"About the second week I was here I happened to overhear Mr. York and his doctor after an examination. Apparently Mr. York knew what had happened, but called in another doctor to verify it. For some time he had been working with special apparatus in his laboratory and in some way became overexposed to radiation. It was enough to cause some internal complications and shorten his life-span. Of course, he isn't in any immediate danger of dying, but you never can tell. He wasn't burned seriously, yet considering his age, and the fact that his injury has had a chance to work on him for two years, there's a possibility that any emotional or physical excitement could be fatal."

"Now isn't that nice," I said. "Do you get what that means, Roxy?" She shook her head. "It might mean that somebody else knows that too and tried to stir the old boy up by kidnapping the one closest to him in the hope that he kicks off during the fun. Great . . . that's a nice subtle sort of murder."

"But that's throwing it right on the doorstep of the beneficiary of his estate."

"Is it? I bet even a minor beneficiary would get enough of the long green to make murder worthwhile. York has plenty."

"There are other angles too, Mike."

"Been giving it some thought, haven't you?" I grinned at her. "For instance, one of the family might locate the kid and thus become number-one boy to the old man. Or perhaps the kid was the chief beneficiary and one of them wanted to eliminate him to push himself further up the list. Yeah, kid, there's a lot of angles, and I don't like any of 'em."

"It still might be a plain kidnapping."

"Roger. That it might. It's just that there're a lot more possibilities to it that could make it interesting. We'll know soon enough." I opened the door and hesitated, looking over my shoulder. " 'Night, Roxy."

"Good night."

York was back by the fireplace again, still brooding. I would have felt better if he had been pacing the floor. I walked over and threw myself in a big chair. "Where'll I spend the night?" I asked him.

He turned very slowly. "The guest room. I'll ring for Harvey."

"Never mind. I'll get him myself when I'm ready."

We sat in silence a few minutes then York began a nervous tapping of his fingers. Finally, "When do you think we'll have word?"

"Two, three days maybe. Never can tell."

"But he's been gone a day already."

"Tomorrow, then. I don't know."

"Perhaps I should call the police again."

"Go ahead, but you'll probably be burying the boy after they find him. Those punks aren't cops, they're political appointees. You ought to know these small towns. They couldn't find their way out of a paper bag."

For the first time he showed a little parental anxiety. His fist came down on the arm of the chair. "Damn it, man, I can't simply sit here! What do you think it's like for me? Waiting. Waiting. He may be dead now for all we know."

"Perhaps, but I don't think so. Kidnapping's one thing, murder's another. How about introducing me to those people?"

He nodded. "Very well." Every eye in the room was on me as we made the rounds. I didn't suppose there would be anyone too anxious to meet me after the demonstration a little while ago.

The two gladiators were first. They were sitting on the love seat trying not to look shaky. Both of them still had red welts across their cheeks. The introduction was simple enough. York merely pointed in obvious disdain. "My nephews, Arthur and William Graham."

We moved on. "My niece, Alice Nichols." A pair of deep brown eyes kissed mine so hard I nearly lost my balance. She swept them up and down the full length of me. It couldn't have been any better if she did it with a wet paintbrush. She was tall and she had seen thirty, but she saw it with a face and body that were as fresh as a new daisy. Her clothes made no attempt at concealment; they barely covered. On some people skin is skin, but on her it was an invitation to dine. She told me things with a smile that most girls since Eve have been trying to put into words without being obvious or seeming too eager and I gave her my answer the same way. I can run the ball a little myself.

York's sister and her husband were next. She was a middle-aged woman with "Matron" written all over her. The type that wants to entertain visiting dignitaries and look down at "peepul" through a lorgnette. Her husband was the type you'd find paired off with such a specimen. He was short and bulgy in the middle. His single-breasted gray suit didn't quite manage to cross the equator without putting a strain on the button. He might have had hair, but you'd never know it now. One point of his collar had jumped the tab and stuck out like an accusing finger.

York said, "My sister, Martha Ghent, her husband, Richard." Richard went to stick out his hand but the old biddie shot him a hasty frown and he drew back, then she tried to freeze me out. Failing in this she turned to York. "Really, Rudolph, I hardly think we should meet this . . . this person."

York turned an appealing look my way, in apology. "I'm sorry, Martha, but Mr. Hammer considers it necessary."

"Nevertheless, I don't see why the police can't handle this."

I sneered at her in my finest manner. "I can't see why you don't keep your mouth shut, Mrs. Ghent."

The way her husband tried to keep the smile back, I thought he'd split a gut. Martha stammered, turned blue and stalked off. York looked at me critically, though approvingly.

A young kid in his early twenties came walking up as though the carpet was made of eggs. He had Ghent in his features, but strictly on his mother's side. A pipe stuck out of his pocket and he sported a set of thick-lensed glasses. The girl at his side didn't resemble anyone, but seeing the way she put her arm around Richard I took it that she was the daughter.

She was. Her name was Rhoda, she was friendly and smiled. The boy was Richard, Junior. He raised his eyebrows until they drew his eyes over the rims of his glasses and peered at me disapprovingly. He perched his hands on his hips and "Humphed" at me. One push and he would be over the line that divides a man and a pansy.

The introductions over, I cornered York out of earshot of the others. "Under the circumstances, it might be best if you kept this gang here until things settle down a bit. Think you can put them up?"

"I imagine so. I've been doing it at one time or another for the last ten years. I'll see Harvey and have the rooms made up."

"When you get them placed, have Harvey bring me a diagram showing where their rooms are. And tell him to keep it under his hat. I want to be able to reach anyone anytime. Now, is there anyone closely connected with the household we've missed?"

He thought a moment. "Oh, Miss Grange. She went home this afternoon."

"Where was she during the kidnapping?"

"Why . . . at home, I suppose. She leaves here between five and six every evening. She is a very reserved woman. Apparently has very little social activity. Generally she furthers her studies in the library rather than go out anywhere."

"Okay, I'll get to her. How about the others? Have they alibis?"

"Alibis?"

"Just checking, York. Do you know where they were the night before last?"

"Well . . . I can't speak for all of them, but Arthur and William were here. Alice Nichols came in about nine o'clock then left about an hour later."

This part I jotted down on a pad. "How did you collect the family . . . or did they all just drift in?"

"No, I called them. They helped me search, although it did no good. Mr. Hammer, what are we going to do? Please . . ."

Very slowly, York was starting to go to pieces. He'd stood up under this too calmly too long. His face was pale and withered-looking, drawn into a mask of tragedy.

"First of all, you're going to bed. It won't do any good for you to be knocking yourself out. That's what I'm here for." I reached over his shoulder and pulled a velvet cord. The flunky came in immediately and hurried over to us. "Take him upstairs," I said.

York gave the butler instructions about putting the family up and Harvey seemed a little surprised and pleased that he'd be allowed in on the conspiracy of the room diagram.

I walked to the middle of the floor and let the funeral buzz down before speaking. I wasn't nice about it. "You're all staying here tonight. If it interferes with other plans you've made it's too bad. Anyone that tries to duck out will answer to me. Harvey will give you your rooms and be sure you stay in them. That's all."

Lady sex appeal waited until I finished then edged up to me with a grin. "See if you can grab the end bedroom in the north wing," she said, "and I'll get the one connected to it."

I said in mock surprise, "Alice, you can get hurt doing things like that."

She laughed. "Oh, I bruise easily, but I heal fast as hell."

Swell girl. I hadn't been seduced in a long time.

I wormed out through a cross fire of nasty looks to the foyer and winked at Richard Ghent on the way. He winked back; his wife wasn't looking.

I slung on my coat and hat and went out to the car. When I rolled it through the gate I turned toward town and stepped on the gas. When I picked up to seventy I held it there until I hit the main drag. Just before the city line I pulled up to a gas station and swung in front of a pump. An attendant in his early twenties came out of the miniature Swiss Alpine cottage that served as a service station and automatically began unscrewing the gas cap. "Put in five," I told him.

He snaked out the hose and shoved the nose in the tank, watching the gauge. "Open all night?" I quizzed.

"Yeah."

"On duty yourself?"

"Yup. 'Cept on Sundays."

"Don't suppose you get much to do at night around here."

"Not very much."

This guy was as talkative as a pea pod. "Say, was much traffic along here night before last?"

He shut off the pump, put the cap back on and looked at me coldly. "Mister, I don't know from nothing," he said.

It didn't take me long to catch on to that remark. I handed him a ten-spot and followed him inside while he changed it. I let go a flyer. "So the cops kind of hinted that somebody would be nosing around, huh?"

No answer. He rang the cash register and began counting out bills. "Er . . . did you happen to notice Dilwick's puss? Or was it one of the others?"

He glanced at me sharply, curiously. "It was Dilwick. I saw his face."

Instead of replying I held out my right hand. He peered at it and saw where the skin had been peeled back off half the knuckles. This time I got a great big grin.

"Did you do that?"

"Uh-huh."

"Okay, pal, for that we're buddies. What do you want to know?"

"About traffic along here night before last."

"Sure, I remember it. Between nine o'clock and dawn the next morning about a dozen cars went past. See, I know most of 'em. A couple was from out of town. All but two belonged to the up-country farmers making milk runs to the separator at the other end of town."

"What about the other two?"

"One was a Caddy. I seen it around a few times. Remember it because it had one side dented in. The other was that Grange dame's two-door sedan. Guess she was out wolfing." He laughed at that.

"Grange?"

"Yeah, the old bag that works out at York's place. She's a stiff one."

"Thanks for the info, kid." I slipped him a buck and he grinned. "By the way, did you pass that on to the cops too?"

"Not me. I wouldn't give them the right time."

"Why?"

"Lousy bunch of bastards." He explained it in a nutshell without going into detail.

I hopped in and started up, but before I drove off I stuck my head out the window. "Where's this Grange babe live?"

"At the Glenwood Apartments. You can't miss it. It's the only apartment house in this burg."

Well, it wouldn't hurt to drop up and see her anyway. Maybe she had been on her way home from work. I gunned the engine and got back on the main drag, driving slowly past the shaded fronts of the stores. Just outside the business section a large green canopy extended from the curb to the marquee of a modern three-story building. Across the side in small, neat letters was GLEN-WOOD APARTMENTS. I crawled in behind a black Ford sedan and hopped out.

Grange, Myra, was the second name down. I pushed the bell and waited for the buzzer to unlatch the door. When it didn't come I pushed it again. This time there was a series of clicks and I shoved the door open. One flight of stairs put me in front of her apartment. Before I could ring, the metal peephole was pulled back and a pair of dark eyes threw insults at me.

"Miss Grange?"

"Yes."

"I'd like to speak to you if you can spare a few moments."

"Very well, go ahead." Her voice sounded as if it came out of a tree trunk. This made the third person I didn't like in Sidon.

"I work for York," I explained patiently, "I'd like to speak to you about the boy."

"There's nothing I care to discuss."

Why is it that some dames can work me up into a lather so fast with so little is beyond me, but this one did. I quit playing around. I pulled out the .45 and let her get a good look at it. "You open that door or I'll shoot the lock off," I said.

THE TWISTED THING 337

She opened it. The insults in her eyes turned to terror until I put the rod back under cover. Then I looked at her. If she was an old bag I was Queen of the May. Almost as tall as I was, nice brown hair cut short enough to be nearly mannish and a figure that seemed to be well molded, except that I couldn't tell too well because she was wearing slacks and a house jacket. Maybe she was thirty, maybe forty. Her face had a built-in lack of expression like an old painting. Wearing no makeup didn't help it any, but it didn't hurt, either.

I tossed my hat on a side table and went inside without being invited. Myra Grange followed me closely, letting her wooden-soled sandals drag along the carpet. It was a nice dump, but small. There was something to it that didn't sit right, as though the choice of furniture didn't fit her personality. Hell, maybe she just sublet.

The living room was ultramodern. The chairs and the couch were surrealist dreams of squares and angles. Even the coffee table was balanced precariously on little pyramids that served as legs. Two framed wood nymphs seemed cold in their nudity against the background of the chilled blue walls. I wouldn't live in a room like this for anything.

Myra held her position in the middle of the floor, legs spread, hands shoved in her side pockets. I picked a leather-covered ottoman and sat down.

She watched every move I made with eyes that scarcely concealed her rage. "Now that you've forced your way in here," she said between tight lips, "perhaps you'll explain why, or do I call the police?"

"I don't think the police would bother me much, kiddo." I pulled my badge from my pocket and let her see it. "I'm a private dick myself."

"Go on." She was a cool tomato.

"My name is Hammer. Mike Hammer. York wants me to find the kid. What do you think happened?"

"I believe he was kidnapped, Mr. Hammer. Surely that is evident."

"Nothing's evident. You were seen on the road fairly late the night the boy disappeared. Why?"

Instead of answering me she said, "I didn't think the time of his disappearance was established."

"As far as I'm concerned it is. It happened that night. Where were you?"

She began to raise herself up and down on her toes like a British major. "I was right here. If anyone said he saw me that night he was mistaken."

"I don't think he was." I watched her intently. "He's got sharp eyes."

"He was mistaken," she repeated.

"All right, we'll let it drop there. What time did you leave York's house?"

"Six o'clock, as usual. I came straight home." She began to kick at the rug impatiently, then pulled a cigarette from a pocket and stuck it in her mouth. Damn it, every time she moved she did something that was familiar to me but I couldn't place it. When she lit the cigarette she sat down on the couch and watched me some more.

"Let's quit the cat and mouse, Miss Grange. York said you were like a mother to the kid and I should suppose you'd like to see him safe. I'm only trying to do what I can to locate him."

"Then don't classify me as a suspect, Mr. Hammer."

"It's strictly temporary. You're a suspect until you alibi yourself satisfactorily then I won't have to waste my time and yours fooling around."

"Am I alibied?"

"Sure," I lied. "Now can you answer some questions civilly?"

"Ask them."

"Number one. Suspicious characters loitering about the house anytime preceding the disappearance."

She thought a moment, furrowing her eyebrows. "None that I can recall. Then again, I am inside all day working in the lab. I wouldn't see anyone."

"York's enemies. Do you know them?"

"Rudolph . . . Mr. York has no enemies I know of. Certain persons working in the same field have expressed what you might call professional jealousy, but that is all."

"To what extent?"

She leaned back against the cushions and blew a smoke ring at the ceiling. "Oh, the usual bantering at the clubs. Making light of his work. You know."

I didn't know anything of the kind, but I nodded. "Anything serious?"

"Nothing that would incite a kidnapping. There were heated discussions, yes, but few and far between. Mr. York was loathe to discuss his work. Besides, a scientist is not a person who would resort to violence."

"That's on the outside. Let's hear a little bit about his family.

You've been connected with York long enough to pick up a little something on his relatives."

"I'd rather not discuss them, Mr. Hammer. They are none of my affair."

"Don't be cute. We're talking about a kidnapping."

"I still don't see where they could possibly enter into it."

"Damn it," I exploded, "you're not supposed to. I want information and everybody wants to play repartee. Before long I'm going to start choking it out of people like you."

"Please, Mr. Hammer, that isn't necessary."

"So I've been told. Then give."

"I've met the family very often. I know nothing about them although they all try to press me for details of our work. I've told them nothing. Needless to say, I like none of them. Perhaps that is a biased opinion but it is my only one."

"Do they feel the same toward you?"

"I imagine they are very jealous of anyone so closely connected with Mr. York as I am," she answered with a caustic grimace. "You might surmise that of any rich man's relatives. However, for your information and unknown to them, I enjoy a personal income outside the salary Mr. York pays me and I am quite unconcerned with the disposition of his fortune in the event that anything should happen to him. The only possession he has that I am interested in is the boy. I have been with him all his life, and as you say, he is like a son to me. Is there anything else?"

"Just what is York's work . . . and yours?"

"If he hasn't told you, I'm not at liberty to. Naturally, you realize that it centered around the child."

"Naturally." I stood up and looked at my watch. It was nine-fifteen. "I think that covers it, Miss Grange. Sorry to set you on your ear to get in, but maybe I can make it up sometime. What do you do nights around here?"

Her eyebrows went up and she smiled for the first time. It was more of a stifled laugh than a smile and I had the silly feeling that the joke was on me. "Nothing you'd care to do with me," she said.

I got sore again and didn't know why. I fought a battle with the look, stuck my hat on and got out of there. Behind me I heard a muffled chuckle.

The first thing I did was make a quick trip back to the filling station. I waited until a car pulled out then drove up to the door. The kid recognized me and waved. "Any luck?" he grinned.

"Yeah, I saw her. Thought she was an old bag?"

"Well, she's a stuffy thing. Hardly ever speaks."

"Listen," I said, "are you sure you saw her the other night?"

"Natch, why?"

"She said no. Think hard now. Did you see her or the car?"

"Well, it was her car. I know that. She's the only one that ever drives it."

"How would you know it?"

"The aerial. It's got a bend in it so it can only be telescoped down halfway. Been like that ever since she got the heap."

"Then you can't be certain she was in it. You wouldn't swear to it?"

"Well . . . no. Guess not when you put it that way. But it was her car," he insisted.

"Thanks a lot." I shoved another buck at him. "Forget I was around, will you?"

"Never saw you in my life," he grinned. Nice kid.

This time I took off rather aimlessly. It was only to pacify York that I left the house in the first place. The rain had let up and I shut off the windshield wipers while I turned onto the highway and cruised north toward the estate. If the snatch ran true to form there would be a letter or a call sometime soon. All I could do would be to advise York to follow through to get the kid back again then go after the ones that had him.

If it weren't for York's damn craving for secrecy I could buzz the state police and have a seven-state alarm sent out, but that meant the house would crawl with cops. Let a spotter get a load of that and they'd dump the kid and that'd be the end of it until some campers came across his remains sometime. As long as the local police had a sizable reward to shoot for they wouldn't let it slip. Not after York told them not to.

I wasn't underestimating Dilwick any. I'd bet my bottom dollar he'd had York's lines tapped already, ready to go to town the moment a call came through. Unless I got that call at the same time I was liable to get scratched. Not me, brother. Ten G's was a lot of mazuma in any language.

The lights were still on en masse when I breezed by the estate. It was still too early to go back, and as long as I could keep the old boy happy by doing a little snooping I figured I was earning my keep, at least. About ten miles down the highway the town of Bayview squatted along the water's edge waiting for summer to liven things up.

A kidnap car could have gone in either direction, although this route was unlikely. Outside Bayview the highway petered off into a tar road that completely disappeared under drifting winter sands. Anything was worth trying, though. I dodged an old flivver that was standing in the middle of the road and swerved into the gravel parking place of a two-bit honky-tonk. The place was badly run down at the heels and sadly in need of a paint job. A good deodorant would have helped, too. I no sooner got my foot on the rail when a frowsy blonde sidled up to me and I got a quick once-over. "You're new around here ain't you?"

"Just passing through."

"Through to where? That road outside winds up in the drink."

"Maybe that's where I'm going."

"Aw now, Buster, that ain't no way to feel. We all got our troubles but you don't wanna do nothing like that. Lemme buy you a drink, it'll make you feel better."

She whistled through her teeth and when that got no response, cupped her hands and yelled to the bartender who was busy shooting crap on the bar. "Hey, Andy, get your tail over here and serve your customers."

Andy took his time. "What'll you have, pal?"

"Beer."

"Me too."

"You too nothing. Beat it, Janie, you had too much already."

"Say, see here, I can pay my own way."

"Not in my joint."

I grinned at the two of them and chimed in. "Give her a beer why don't you?"

"Listen pal, you don't know her. She's half tanked already. One more and she'll be making like a Copa cutie. Not that I don't like the Copa, but the dames there are one thing and she's another, just like night and day. Instead of watching, my customers all get the dry heaves and trot down to Charlie's on the waterfront."

"Well, I like that!" Janie hit an indignant pose and waved her finger in Andy's face. "You give me my beer right now or I'll make better'n the Copa. I'll make like . . . like . . ."

"Okay, okay, Janie, one more and that's all."

The bartender drew two beers, took my dough instead of Janie's and rang it up. I put mine away in one gulp. Janie never reached completely around her glass. Before Andy could pick out the change Janie had spilled hers halfway down the bar.

Andy said something under his breath, took the glass away then fished around under the counter for a rag. He started to mop up the mess.

I watched. In my head the little bells were going off, slowly at first like chimes on a cold night. They got louder and louder, playing another scrambled, soundless symphony. A muscle in my neck twitched. I could almost feel that ten grand in my pocket already. Very deliberately I reached out across the bar and gathered a handful of Andy's stained apron in my fist. With my other hand I yanked out the .45 and held it an inch away from his eye. He was staring death in the face and knew it.

I had trouble keeping my voice down. "Where did you get that bar rag, Andy?"

His eyes shifted to the blue-striped pajama bottoms that he held in his hand, beer soaked now, but recognizable. The other half to them were in Ruston York's bedroom hanging on the foot of the bed.

Janie's mouth was open to scream. I pointed the gun at her and said, "Shut up." The scream died before it was born. She held the edge of the bar with both hands, shaking like a leaf. Ours was a play offstage; no one saw it, no one cared. "Where, Andy?"

". . . Don't know, mister. Honest . . ."

I thumbed the hammer back. He saw me do it. "Only one more chance, Andy. Think hard."

His breath came in little jerks, fright thickened his tongue. "Some . . . guy. He brought it in. Wanted to know . . . if they were mine. It . . . was supposed to be a joke. Honest, I just use it for a bar rag, that's all."

"When?"

". . .'s afternoon."

"Who, Andy?"

"Bill. Bill Cuddy. He's a clam digger. Lives in a shack on the bay."

I put the safety back on, but I still held his apron. "Andy," I told him, "if you're leveling with me it's okay, but if you're not, I'm going to shoot your head off. You know that, don't you?"

His eyes rolled in his head then came back to meet mine. "Yeah, mister. I know. I'm not kidding. Honest, I got two kids . . ."

"And Janie here. I think maybe you better keep her with you for a while. I wouldn't want anyone to hear about this, understand?"

Andy understood, all right. He didn't miss a word. I let him go and he had to hang on to his bar to keep from crumbling. I slid the rod back under my coat, wrung out the pajamas and folded them into a square.

When I straightened my hat and tie I said, "Where is Cuddy's place?"

Andy's voice was so weak I could hardly hear it. "Straight . . . down the road to the water. Turn left. It's the deck . . . deckhouse of an old boat pulled up on the . . . beach."

I left them standing there like Hansel and Gretel in the woods, scared right down to their toes. Poor Andy. He didn't have anymore to do with it than I did, but in this game it's best not to take any chances.

As Janie had said, the road led right to the drink. I parked the car beside a boarded-up house and waded through the wet sand on foot. Ten feet from the water I turned left and faced a line of broken-down shacks that were rudely constructed from the junk that comes in on the tide. Some of them had tin roofs, with the advertisements for soft drinks and hot dogs still showing through.

Every once in a while the moon would shine through a rift in the clouds, and I took advantage of it to get a better look at the homemade village.

Cuddy's place was easier to find than I expected. It was the only dump that ever had seen paint, and on the south side hung a ship's name plate with Carmine spelled out in large block letters. It was a deckhouse, all right, probably washed off during a storm. I edged up to a window and looked in. All I could see were a few vague outlines. I tried the door. It opened outward noiselessly. From one corner of the room came the raspy snore of a back-sleeper with a load under his belt.

A match lit the place up. Cuddy never moved, even when I put the match to the ship's lantern swinging from the center of the ceiling. It was a one-room affair with a few chairs, a table and a double-decker bed along the side. He had rigged up a kerosene stove with the pipe shooting through the roof and used two wooden crates for a larder. Beside the stove was a barrel of clams.

Lots of stuff, but no kid.

Bill Cuddy was a hard man to awaken. He twitched a few times, pawed the covers and grunted. When I shook him some more his eyelids flickered, went up. No pupils. They came down ten seconds later. A pair of bleary, bloodshot eyes moved separately until they came to an accidental focus on me.

Bill sat up. "Who're you?"

I gave him a few seconds to study me, then palmed my badge in front of his face. "Cop. Get up."

His legs swung to the floor, he grabbed my arm. "What's the

matter, officer? I ain't been poachin'. All I got is clams, go look." He pointed to the barrel. "See?"

"I'm no game warden," I told him.

"Then whatcha want of me?"

"I want you for kidnapping. Murder maybe."

"Oh . . . No!" His voice was a hoarse croak. "But . . . I ain't killed nobody atall. I wouldn't do that."

He didn't have to tell me that. There are types that kill and he wasn't one of them. I didn't let him know I thought so.

"You brought a set of pajamas into Andy's place this afternoon. Where did you get them?"

He wrinkled his nose, trying to understand what I was talking about. "Pajamas?"

"You heard me."

He remembered then. His face relaxed into a relieved grin. "Oh, that. Sure, I found 'em lying on Shore Road. Thought I'd kid Andy with 'em."

"You almost kidded him to death. Put on your pants. I want you to show me the spot."

He stuck his feet into a pair of dungarees and pulled the suspenders over his bony shoulders, then dragged a pair of boots out from under the bed. A faded denim shirt and a battered hat and he was dressed. He kept shooting me sidewise glances, trying to figure it out but wasn't getting anyplace.

"You won't throw me in the jug, will you?"

"Not if you tell the truth."

"But I did."

"We'll see. Come on." I let him lead the way. The sand had drifted too deep along the road to take the car so we plodded along slowly, keeping away from the other shacks. Shore Road was a road in name only. It was a strip of wet Sahara that separated the tree line from the water. A hundred yards up and the shacks had more room between them. Bill Cuddy pointed ahead.

"Up there is the cove where I bring the boat in. I was coming down there and where the old cistern is I see the pants lying right in the middle of the road."

I nodded. A few minutes later we had reached the cistern, a huge, barrel-shaped thing lying on its side. It was big enough to make a two-car garage. Evidently it, like everything else around here, had been picked up during a storm and deposited along the shore. Bill indicated a spot on the ground with a gnarled forefinger.

"Right here's the spot, officer, they was lying right here."

"Fine. See anyone?"

"Naw. Who would be out here? They was washed up, I guess."

I looked at him, then the water. Although the tide was high the water was a good forty yards from the spot. He saw what I meant and he shifted uneasily.

"Maybe they blew up."

"Bill?"

"Huh?"

"Did you ever see wet clothes blow along the ground? Dry clothes, maybe, but wet?"

He paused. "Nope."

"Then they didn't blow up or wash up. Somebody dropped them there."

He got jittery then, his face was worried. "But I didn't do it. No kidding, I just found them there. They was new-looking so I brung 'em to Andy's. You won't jug me, will you? I . . ."

"Forget it, Bill. I believe you. If you want to keep your nose clean turn around and trot home. Remember this, though. Keep your mouth shut, you hear?"

"Gee, yeah. Thanks . . . thanks, officer. I won't say nothing to nobody." Bill broke into a fast shuffle and disappeared into the night.

Alone like that you can see that what you mistook for silence was really a jungle of undertones, subdued, foreign, but distinct. The wind whispering over the sand, the waves keeping time with a steady lap, lap. Tree sounds, for which there is no word to describe bark rubbing against bark, and the things that lived in the trees. The watch on my wrist made an audible tick.

Somewhere oars dipped into the water and scraped in the oarlocks. There was no telling how far away it was. Sounds over water carry far on the wind.

I tried to see into the night, wondering how the pajamas got there. A road that came from the cove and went nowhere. The trees and the bay. A couple of shacks and a cistern.

The open end faced away from me, making it necessary to push through yards of saw grass to reach it. Two rats ran out making ugly squeaking noises. When I lit a match I seemed to be in a hall of green slime. Droplets of water ran down the curved sides of the cistern and collected in a stinking pool of scum in the middle. Some papers had blown in, but that was all. The only things that left their footprints in the muck had tails. When I couldn't hold my breath any longer I backed out and followed the path I had made to the road.

Right back where I started. Twenty-five yards away was the

remains of a shack. The roof had fallen in, the sides bulged out like it had been squeezed by a giant hand. Further down was another. I took the first one. The closer I came to it the worse it looked. Holes in the side passed for windows, the door hung open on one hinge and was wedged that way by a pile of sand that had blown around the corner. No tracks, no nothing. It was as empty as the cistern.

Or so I thought.

Just then someone whimpered inside. The .45 leaped into my hand. I took a few wooden matches, lit them all together and threw them inside and went in after them.

I didn't need my gun. Ruston York was all alone, trussed up like a Christmas turkey over in the corner, his naked body covered with bruises.

In a moment I was on my knees beside him, working the knots loose. I took it easy on the adhesive tape that covered his mouth so I wouldn't tear the skin off. His body shook with sobs. Tears of fright and relief filled his large, expressive eyes, and when he had his arms free he threw them around my neck. "Go ahead and cry, kid," I said.

He did, then. Hard, body-racking gasps that must have hurt. I wiggled out of my jacket and put it around him, talking quickly and low to comfort him. The poor kid was a mess.

It came with jarring suddenness, that sound. I shoved the kid on his back and pivoted on my heels. I was shooting before I completed the turn. Someone let out a short scream. A heavy body crashed into my chest and slammed my back against the wall. I kicked out with both feet and we spilled to the floor. Before I could get my gun up a heavy boot ripped it out of my hand.

They were all over me. I gave it everything I had, feet, fingernails and teeth, there wasn't enough room to swing. Somehow I managed to hook my first two fingers in a mouth and yank, and I felt a cheek rip clear to the ear.

There was no more for me. Something smashed down on my skull and I stopped fighting. It was a peaceful feeling, as if I were completely adrift from my body. Feet thudded into my ribs and pounded my back raw, but there was no pain, merely vague impressions. Then even the impressions began to fade.

chapter three ▰▰▰▰▰▰▰▰▰▰

I CAME BACK together like a squadron of flak-eaten bombers reforming. I heard the din of their motors, a deafening, pulsating roar that grew louder and louder. Pieces of their skin, fragments of their armor drifted to earth and imbedded themselves in my flesh until I thought I was on fire.

Bombs thudded into the earth and threw great flashes of flame into my face and rocked my body back and forth, back and forth. I opened my eyes with an effort.

It was the kid shaking me. "Mister. Can you get up? They all ran away looking for me. If you don't get up they'll be back and find us. Hurry, please hurry."

I tried to stand up, but I didn't do too good a job. Ruston York got his arms around me and boosted. Between the two of us I got my feet in position where I could shove with my legs and raise myself. He still had on my coat, but that was all.

I patted his shoulder. "Thanks, kid. Thanks a lot."

It was enough talk for a while. He steered me outside and up into the bushes along the trees where we melted into the darkness. The sand muffled our footsteps well. For once I was grateful for the steady drip of rain from the trees; it covered any other noises we made.

"I found your gun on the floor. Here, do you want it?" He held the .45 out gingerly by the handle. I took it in a shaking hand and stowed it in the holster. "I think you shot somebody. There's an awful lot of blood by the door."

"Maybe it's mine," I grunted.

"No, I don't think so. It's on the wall, too, and there's a big hole in the wall where it looks like a bullet went through."

I prayed that he was right. Right now I half-hoped they'd show again so I could have a chance to really place a few where they'd hurt.

I don't know how long it took to reach the car, but it seemed like hours. Every once in a while I thought I could discern shouts and guarded words of caution. By the time Ruston helped slide me under the wheel I felt as though I had been on the Death March.

We sat there in silence a few moments while I fumbled for a cigarette. The first drag was worth a million dollars. "There's a robe in the back," I told the kid. He knelt on the seat, got it and draped it over his legs.

"What happened?"

"Gosh, mister, I hardly know. When you pushed me away I ran out the door. The man I think you shot nearly grabbed me, but he didn't. I hid behind the door for a while. They must have thought I ran off because when they followed me out one man told the others to scatter and search the beach, then he went away too. That's when I came in and got you."

I turned the key and reached for the starter. It hurt. "Before that. What happened then?"

"You mean the other night?"

"Yeah."

"Well, I woke up when the door opened. I thought maybe it was Miss Malcom. She always looks in before she goes to bed, but it wasn't her. It was a man. I wanted to ask him who he was when he hit me. Right here." Ruston rubbed the top of his head and winced.

"Which door did he come in?"

"The one off the hall, I think. I was pretty sleepy."

Cute. Someone sneaks past the guard at the gate, through a houseful of people and puts the slug on the kid and walks off with him.

"Go on." While he spoke I let in the clutch and swung around, then headed the car toward the estate.

"I woke up in a boat. They had me in a little room and the door was locked. I could hear the men talking in the stern and one called the man who was steering, Mallory. That's the only time I heard a name at all."

The name didn't strike any responsive chord as far as I was concerned, so I let him continue.

"Then I picked the lock and . . ."

"Wait a second, son." I looked at him hard. "Say that again."

"I picked the lock. Why?"

"Just like that you picked the lock. No trouble to it or anything?"

"Uh-uh." He flashed a boyish grin at me, shyly. "I learned all about locks when I was little. This one was just a plain lock."

He *must* be a genius. It takes me an hour with respectable burglar tools to open a closet door.

". . . and as soon as I got out I opened a little hatch and crawled up on the deck. I saw the lights from shore and jumped overboard. Boy, was that water cold. They never even heard me at all. I nearly made it at that. After I jumped the boat kept right on going and disappeared, but I guess they found the door open down below. I should have locked it again but I was sort of scared and forgot. Just when I got up on the shore some man came running at me and they had me again. He said he'd figured I'd head for the lights, then he slapped me. He was waiting for the others to come and he made me go into the stack with him. Seems like they tied up in the cove and had to wait awhile before they could take me back to the boat.

"He had a bottle and started drinking from it, and pretty soon he was almost asleep. I waited until he was sort of dopey then threw my pajama pants out the window with a rock in them hoping someone would find them. He never noticed what I did. But he did know he was getting drunk, and he didn't have any more in the bottle. He hit me a few times and I tried to get away. Then he really gave it to me. When he got done he took some rope and tied me up and went down the beach after the others. That was when you came in."

"And I went out," I added.

"Gee, mister, I hope you didn't get hurt too badly." His face was anxious, truly anxious. It's been a long time since someone worried about me getting hurt. I ran my fingers through his hair and shook his head gently.

"It isn't too bad, kid," I said. He grinned again, pulled the robe tighter and moved closer to me. Every few seconds he'd throw me a searching glance, half curious, half serious.

"What's your name?"

"Mike Hammer."

"Why do you carry a gun?"

"I'm a detective, Ruston. A private detective."

A sigh of relief escaped him. He'd probably figured me for one of the mob who didn't like the game, I guess."

"How did you happen to find me?"

"I was looking for you."

"I'm . . . I'm glad it was you, Mr. Hammer, and not somebody else. I don't think anyone would have been brave enough to do what you did."

I laughed at that. He was a good kid. If any bravery was involved he had it all. Coming back in after me took plenty of nerve. I told him so, but he chuckled and blushed. Damn, you couldn't help but like him. In spite of a face full of bruises and all the hell he had been through he could still smile. He sat there beside me completely at ease, watching me out of the corner of his eye as though I was a tin god or something.

For a change some of the lights were off in the house. Henry, the gatekeeper, poked a flashlight in the car and his mouth fell open. All he got out was, "M . . . Master Ruston!"

"Yeah, it's him. Open the gates." He pulled a bar at the side and the iron grillwork rolled back. I pushed the buggy through, but by the time I reached the house Henry's call had the whole family waiting on the porch.

York didn't even wait until I stopped. He yanked the door open and reached for his son. Ruston's arms went around his neck and he kept repeating, "Dad . . . Dad."

I wormed out of the car and limped around to the other side. The family was shooting questions at the kid a mile a minute and completely ignored me, not that it mattered. I shoved them aside and took York by the arm. "Get the kid in the house and away from this mob. He's had enough excitement for a while."

The scientist nodded. Ruston said, "I can walk, Dad." He held the robe around himself and we went in together.

Before the others could follow, York turned. "If you don't mind, please go to your rooms. You will hear what happened in the morning."

There was no disputing who was master in that house. They looked at one another then slouched off in a huff. I drew a few nasty looks myself.

I slammed the door on the whole pack of them and started for the living room, but Harvey interrupted me en route. Having once disrupted his composure, events weren't likely to do it a second time. When he handed me the tray with the diagram of the bedroom layout neatly worked up he was the perfect flunky.

"The guest plan, sir," he said. "I trust it is satisfactory?"

I took it without looking at it and thanked him, then stuck it in my pocket.

York was in an anteroom with his son. The kid was stretched out on a table while his father went over each bruise carefully, searching for abrasions. Those he daubed with antiseptic and applied small bandages. This done he began a thorough examination in the most professional manner.

When he finished I asked, "How is he?"

"All right, apparently," he answered, "but it will be difficult to tell for a few days. I'm going to put him to bed now. His physical condition has always been wonderful, thank goodness."

He wrapped Ruston in a robe and rang for Harvey. I picked up the wreckage that was my coat and slipped into it. The butler came in and at York's direction, picked the kid up and they left the room. On the way out Ruston smiled a good-night at me over the butler's shoulder.

York was back in five minutes. Without a word he pointed at the table and I climbed on. By the time he finished with me I felt like I had been in a battle all over again. The open cuts on my face and back stung from iodine, and with a few layers of six-inch tape around my ribs I could hardly breathe. He told me to get up in a voice shaky from suppressed emotion, swallowed a tablet from a bottle in his kit and sat down in a cold sweat.

When I finished getting dressed I said, "Don't you think you ought to climb into the sack yourself? It's nearly daybreak."

He shook his head. "No. I want to hear about it. Everything. Please, if you don't mind . . . the living room."

We went in and sat down together. While I ran over the story he poured me a stiff shot of brandy and I put it away neat.

"I don't understand it. Mr. Hammer . . . it is beyond me."

"I know. It doesn't seem civilized, does it?"

"Hardly." He got up and walked over to a Sheraton secretary, opened it and took out a book. He wrote briefly and returned waving ten thousand dollars in my face. "Your fee, Mr. Hammer. I scarcely need say how grateful I am."

I tried not to look too eager when I took that check, but ten G's is ten G's. As unconcernedly as I could, I shoved it in my wallet. "Of course, I suppose you want me to put a report in to the state police," I remarked. "They ought to be able to tie into that crew, especially with the boat. A thing like that can't be hidden very easily."

"Yes, yes, they will have to be apprehended. I can't imagine why they chose to abduct Ruston. It's incredible."

"You are rich, Mr. York. That is the primary reason."

"Yes. Wealth does bring disadvantages sometimes, though I have tried to guard against it."

I stood up. "I'll call them then. We have one lead that might mean something. One of the kidnappers was called Mallory. Your boy brought that up."

"What did you say?"

I repeated it.

His voice was barely audible. "Mallory . . . No!"

As if in a trance he hurried to the side of the fireplace. A pressure on some concealed spring-activated hidden mechanism and the side swung outward. He thrust his hand into the opening. Even at this distance I could see him pale. He withdrew his hand empty. A muscular spasm racked his body. He pressed his hands against his chest and sagged forward. I ran over and eased him into a chair.

"Vest . . . pocket."

I poked my fingers under his coat and brought out a small envelope of capsules. York picked one out with trembling fingers and put it on his tongue. He swallowed it, stared blankly at the wall. Very slowly a line of muscles along his jaw hardened into knots, his lips curled back in an animal-like snarl. "The bitch," he said, "the dirty man-hating bitch has sold me out."

"Who, Mr. York? Who was it?"

He suddenly became aware of me standing there. The snarl faded. A hunted-quarry look replaced it. "I said nothing, you understand? Nothing."

I dropped my hand from his shoulder. I was starting to get a dirty taste in my mouth again. "Go to hell," I said. "I'm going to report it."

"You wouldn't dare!"

"Wouldn't I? York, old boy, that son of yours pulled me out of a nasty mess. I like him. You hear that? I like him more than I do a lot of people. If you want to expose him to more danger that's your affair, but I'm not going to have it."

"No . . . that's not it. This can't be made public."

"Listen, York, why don't you stow that publicity stuff and think of your kid for a change? Keep this under your hat and you'll invite another snatch and maybe you won't be so lucky. Especially," I added, "since somebody in your household has sold you out."

York shuddered from head to foot.

"Who was it, York? Who's got the bull on you?"

"I . . . have nothing to say."

"No? Who else knows you're counting your hours because of those radiation burns? What's going to happen to the kid when you kick off?"

That did it. He turned a sick color. "How did you find out about that?"

"It doesn't matter. If I know it others probably do. You still didn't tell me who's putting the squeeze on you."

"Sit down, Mr. Hammer. Please."

I pulled up a chair and parked.

"Could I," he began, "retain you as sort of a guardian instead of reporting this incident? It would be much simpler for me. You see, there are certain scientific aspects of my son's training that you, as a layman, would not understand, but if brought to light under the merciless scrutiny of the newspapers and a police investigation might completely ruin the chances of a successful result.

"I'm not asking you to understand, I'm merely asking that you cooperate. You will be well paid, I assure you. I realize that my son is in danger, but it will be better if we can repel any danger rather than prevent it at its source. Will you do this for me?"

Very deliberately I leaned back in my chair and thought it over. Something stunk. It smelled like Rudolph York. But I still owed the kid a debt.

"I'll take it, York, but if there's going to be trouble I'd like to know where it will come from. Who's the man-hating turnip that has you in a brace?"

His lips tightened. "I'm afraid I cannot reveal that, either. You need not do any investigating. Simply protect my interests, and my son."

"Okay," I said as I rose. "Have it your own way. I'll play dummy. But right now I'm going to beat the sheet. It's been a tough day. You'd better hit it yourself."

"I'll call Harvey."

"Never mind, I'll find it." I walked out. In the foyer I pulled the diagram out of my pocket and checked it. The directions were clear enough. I went upstairs, turned left at the landing and followed the hand-carved balustrade to the other side. My room was next to last and my name was on white cardboard, neatly typed, and framed in a small brass holder on the door. I turned the knob, reached for the light and flicked it on.

"You took long enough getting here."

I grinned. I wondered what Alice Nichols had used as a bribe to get Harvey to put me in next to her. "Hello, kitten."

Alice smiled through a cloud of smoke. "You were better-looking the last time I saw you."

"So? Do I need a shave?"

"You need a new face. But I'll take you like you are." She shrugged her shoulders and the spider web of a negligee fell down to her waist. What she had on under it wasn't worth mentioning. It looked like spun moonbeams with a weave as big as chicken wire. "Let's go to bed."

"Scram, kitten. Get back in your own hive."

"That's a corny line, Mike, don't play hard to get."

I started to climb out of my clothes. "It's not a line, kitten, I'm beat."

"Not that much."

I draped my shirt and pants over the back of the chair and flopped in the sack. Alice stood up slowly. No, that's not the word. It was more like a low-pressure spring unwinding. The negligee was all the way off now. She was a concert of savage beauty.

"Still tired?"

"Turn off the light when you go out, honey." Before I rolled over she gave me a malicious grin. It told me that there were other nights. The lights went out. Before I corked off one thought hit me. It couldn't have been Alice Nichols he had meant when he called some babe a man-hating bitch.

Going to sleep with a thought like that is a funny thing. It sticks with you. I could see Alice over and over again, getting up out of that chair and walking across the room, only this time she didn't even wear moonbeams. Her body was lithe, seductive. She did a little dance. Then someone else came into my dream, too. Another dame. This one was familiar, but I couldn't place her. She did a dance too, but a different kind. There was none of that animal grace, no fluid motion. She took off her clothes and moved about stiffly, ill at ease. The two of them started dancing together, stark narked, and this new one was leading. They came closer, the mist about their faces parted and I got a fleeting glimpse of the one I couldn't see before.

I sat bolt upright in bed. No wonder Miss Grange did things that bothered me. It wasn't the woman I recognized in her apartment, it was her motions. Even to striking a match toward her the way a man would. Sure, she'd be a man-hater, why not? She was a Lesbian.

"Damn!"

I hopped out of bed and climbed into my pants. I picked out York's room from the diagram and tiptoed to the other side of the house. His door was partly opened. I tapped gently. No answer.

I went in and felt for the switch. Light flooded the room, but it didn't do me any good. York's bed had never been slept in. One drawer of his desk was half-open and the contents pushed aside. I looked at the oil blot on the bottom of the drawer. I didn't need a second look at the hastily opened box of .32 cartridges to tell me what had been in there. York was out to do murder.

Time, time, there wasn't enough of it. I finished dressing on the way out. If anyone heard the door slam after me or the motor start up they didn't care much. No lights came on at all. I slowed up by the gates, but they were gaping open. From inside the house I could hear a steady snore. Henry was a fine gatekeeper.

I didn't know how much of a lead he had. Sometime hours ago my watch had stopped and I didn't reset it. It could have been too long ago. The night was fast fading away. I don't think I had been in bed a full hour.

On that race to town I didn't pass a car. The lights of the kid's filling station showed briefly and swept by. The unlit head lamps of parked cars glared in the reflection of my own brights and went back to sleep.

I pulled in behind a line of cars outside the Glenwood Apartments, switched off the engine and climbed out. There wasn't a sign of life anywhere. When this town went to bed it did a good job.

It was one time I couldn't ring doorbells to get in. If Ruston had been with me it wouldn't have taken so long; the set of skeleton keys I had didn't come up with the right answer until I tried two dozen of them.

The .45 was in my fist. I flicked the safety off as I ran up the stairs. Miss Grange's door was closed, but it wasn't locked; it gave when I turned the knob.

No light flared out the door when I kicked it open. No sound broke the funeral quiet of the hall. I stepped in and eased the door shut behind me.

Very slowly I bent down and unlaced my shoes, then put them beside the wall. There was no sense sending in an invitation. With my hand I felt along the wall until I came to the end of the hall. A switch was to the right. Cautiously, I reached around and threw it up, ready for anything.

I needn't have been so quiet. Nobody would have yelled. I found York, all right. He sat there grinning at me like a blooming idiot with the top of his head holding up a meat cleaver.

chapter four ▰▰▰▰▰▰▰▰▰▰

NOW IT WAS murder. First it was kidnapping, then murder. There seems to be no end to crime. It starts off as a little thing, then gets bigger and bigger like an over-inflated tire until it busts all to hell and gone.

I looked at him, the blood running red on his face, seeping out under the clots, dripping from the back of his head to the floor.

It was only a guess, but I figured I had been about ten minutes too late.

The room was a mess, a topsy-turvy cell of ripped-up furniture and emptied drawers. The carpet was littered with trash and stuffing from the pillows. York still clutched a handful of papers, sitting there on the floor where he had fallen, staring blankly at the wall. If he had found what he was searching for it wasn't here now. The papers in his hand were only old receipted electric bills made out to Myra Grange.

First I went back and got my shoes, then I picked up the phone. "Give me the state police," I told the operator.

A Sergeant Price answered. I gave it to him briefly. "This is Mike Hammer, Sergeant," I said. "There's been a murder at the Glenwood Apartments and as far as I can tell it's only a few minutes old. You'd better check the highways. Look for a Ford two-door sedan with a bent radio antenna. Belongs to a woman named Myra Grange. Guy that's been bumped is Rudolph York. She works for him. Around thirty, I'd say, five, six or seven, short hair, well built. Not a bad-looking tomato. No, I don't know what she was wearing. Yeah . . . yeah, I'll stay here. You want me to inform the city cops?"

The sergeant said some nasty things about the city boys and told me to go ahead.

I did. The news must have jarred the guy on the desk awake because he started yelling his fool head off all over the place. When he asked for more information I told him to come look for himself, grinned into the mouthpiece and hung up.

I had to figure this thing out. Maybe I could have let it go right then, but I didn't think that way. My client was dead, true, but he had overpaid me in the first place. I could still render him a little service gratis.

I checked the other rooms, but they were as scrambled as the first one. Nothing was in place anywhere. I had to step over piles of clothes in the bedroom that had been carefully, though hurriedly, turned inside out.

The kitchen was the only room not torn apart. The reason for that was easy to see. Dishes and pans crashing against the floor would bring someone running. Here York had felt around, moved articles, but not swept them clear of the shelves. A dumbwaiter door was built into the wall. It was closed and locked. I left it that way. The killer couldn't have left by that exit and still locked it behind him, not with a hook-and-eye clasp. I opened the drawers and peered inside. The fourth one turned up something I hadn't expected to see. A meat cleaver.

That's one piece of cutlery that is rarely duplicated in a small apartment. In fact, it's more or less outdated. Now there were two of them.

The question was: Who did York surprise in this room? No, it wasn't logical. Rather, who surprised York? It had to be that way. If York had burst in here on Grange there would have been a scene, but at least she would have been here too. It was hard picturing her stepping out to let York smash up the joint.

When York came in the place was empty. He came to kill, but finding his intended victim gone, forgot his primary purpose and began his search. Kill. Kill. That was it. I looked at the body again. What I looked for wasn't there anymore.

Somebody had swiped the dead man's gun.

Why? Damn these murderers anyway, why must they mess things up so? Why the hell can't they just kill and be done with it? York sat there grinning for all he was worth, defying me to find the answer. I said, "Cut it out, pal. I'm on your side."

Two cleavers and a grinning dead man. Two cleavers, one in the kitchen and one in his head. What kind of a killer would use a cleaver? It's too big to put in a pocket, too heavy to swing properly unless you had a fairly decent wrist. It would have to be a man, no dame likes to kill when there's a chance of getting spattered with blood.

But Myra Grange . . . the almost woman. She was more half man. Perhaps her sensibilities wouldn't object to crunching a skull or getting smeared with gore. But where the hell did the cleaver come from?

York grinned. I grinned back. It was falling into place now. Not the motive, but the action of the crime, and something akin to motive. The killer knew York was on his way here and knew Grange was out. The killer carried the cleaver for several reasons. It might have just been handy. Having aimed and swung it was certain to do the job. It was a weapon to which no definite personality could be attached.

Above all things, it was far from being an accidental murder. I hate premeditation. I hate those little thoughts of evil that are suppressed in the mind and are being constantly superimposed upon by other thoughts of even greater evil until they squeeze out over the top and drive a person to the depths of infamy.

And this murder was premeditated. Perhaps that cleaver was supposed to have come from the kitchen, but no one could have gone past York to the kitchen without his seeing him, and York had a gun. The killer had chosen his weapon, followed York here and caught him in the act of rifling the place. He didn't even have to be silent about it. In the confusion of tearing the place apart York would never have noticed little sounds . . . until it was too late.

The old man half-stooping over the desk, the upraised meat-ax, one stroke and it was over. Not even a hard stroke. With all that potential energy in a three-pound piece of razor-sharp steel, not much force was needed to deliver a killing blow. Instantaneous death, the body twisting as it fell to face the door and grin at the killer.

I got no further. There was a stamping in the hall, the door was pushed open and Dilwick came in like a summer storm. He didn't waste any time. He walked up to me and stood three inches away, breathing hard. He wasn't pretty to look at.

"I ought to kill you, Hammer," he grated.

We stood there in that tableau a moment. "Why don't you?"

"Maybe I will. The slightest excuse, any excuse. Nobody's going to pull that on me and get away with it. Not you or anybody."

I sneered at him. "Whenever you're ready, Dilwick, here or in the mayor's office, I don't care."

Dilwick would have liked to have said more, but a young giant in the gray and brown leather of the state police strode over to me with his hand out. "You Mike Hammer?" I nodded.

"Sergeant Price," he smiled. "I'm one of your fans. I had occasion to work with Captain Chambers in New York one time and he spent most of the time talking you up."

The lad gave me a bone-crushing handshake that was good to feel.

I indicated the body. "Here's your case, Sergeant."

Dilwick wasn't to be ignored like that. "Since when do the state police have jurisdiction over us?"

Price was nice about it. "Ever since you proved yourselves to be inadequately supplied with material . . . and men." Dilwick flushed with rage. Price continued, addressing his remarks to me. "Nearly a year ago the people of Sidon petitioned the state to assist in all police matters when the town in general and the county in particular was being used as a rendezvous and sporting place by a lot of out-of-state gamblers and crooks."

The state cop stripped off his leather gloves and took out a pad. He noted a general description of the place, time, then asked me for a statement. Dilwick focused his glare on me, letting every word sink in.

"Mr. York seemed extremely disturbed after his son had been returned to him. He . . ."

"One moment, Mr. Hammer. Where was his son?"

"He had been kidnapped."

"So?" Price's reply was querulous. "It was never reported to us."

"It was reported to the city police." I jerked my thumb at Dilwick. "He can tell you that."

Price didn't doubt me, he was looking for Dilwick's reaction. "Is this true?"

"Yes."

"Why didn't we hear about it?"

Dilwick almost blew his top. "Because we didn't feel like telling you, that's why." He took a step nearer Price, his fists clenched, but the state trooper never budged. "York wanted it kept quiet and that's the way we handled it, so what?"

It came back to me again. "Who found the boy?"

"I did." Dilwick was closer to apoplexy than ever. I guess he wanted that ten grand as badly as I did. "Earlier this evening I found the boy in an abandoned shack near the waterfront. I brought him home. Mr. York decided to keep me handy in case another attempt was made to abduct the kid."

Dilwick butted in. "How did you know York was here?"

"I didn't." I hated to answer him, but he was still the police. "I just thought he might be. The boy had been kicked around and I figured that he wanted Miss Grange in the house."

The fat cop sneered. "Isn't York big enough to go out alone anymore?"

"Not in his condition. He had an attack of some sort earlier in the evening."

Price said, "How did you find out he was gone, Mr. Hammer?"

"Before I went to sleep I decided to look in to see how he was. He hadn't gone to bed. I knew he'd mentioned Miss Grange and, as I said, figured he had come here."

Price nodded. "The door . . .?"

"It was open. I came in and found . . . this." I swept my hand around. "I called you, then the city police. That's all."

Dilwick made a face and bared what was left of his front teeth. "It stinks."

So it did, but I was the only one who was sure of it.

"Couldn't it have been like this, Mr. Hammer." Dilwick emphasized the *mister* sarcastically. "You find the kid, York doesn't like to pay out ten thousand for hardly any work, he blows after you threaten him, only you followed him and make good the threat."

"Sure, it could," I said, "except that it wasn't." I poked a butt in my mouth and held a match to it. "When I kill people I don't have to use a meat hatchet. If they got a gun, I use a gun. If they don't I use my mitts." I shifted my eyes to the body. "I could kill him with my fingers. On bigger guys . . . I'd use both hands. But no cleaver."

"How did York get here, Mr. Hammer?"

"Drove, I imagine. You better detail a couple of boys to lock up his car. A blue '64 Caddy sedan."

Price called a man in plain clothes over with his forefinger and repeated the instructions. The guy nodded and left.

The coroner decided that it was time to get there with the photo guys and the wicker basket. For ten minutes they went around dusting the place and snapping flashes of the remains from all positions until they ran out of bulbs. I showed Price where I'd touched the wall and the switch so there wouldn't be a confusion of the prints. For the record he asked me if I'd give him a set of impressions. It was all right with me. He took out a cardboard over which had been spread a light paraffin of some sort and I laid both hands on it and pressed. Price wrote my name on the bottom, took the number off my license and stowed it back in his pocket.

Dilwick was busy going through the papers York had scattered about, but finding nothing of importance returned his attention to the body. The coroner had spread the contents of the pockets out of an end table and Price rifled through them. I watched over his shoulder. Just the usual junk: a key ring, some small change, a wallet with two twenties and four threes and membership cards in several organizations. Under the wallet was the envelope with the capsules.

"Anything missing?" Price asked.

I shook my head. "Not that I know of, but then, I never went through his pockets."

The body was stuffed into a wicker basket, the cleaver wrapped in a towel and the coroner left with his boys. More troopers came in with a few city guys tagging along and I had to repeat my story all over again. Standing outside the crowd was a lone newspaperman, writing like fury in a note pad. If this was New York they'd have to bar the doors to hold back the press. Just wait until the story reached the wires. This town wouldn't be able to hold them all.

Price called me over to him. "You'll be where I'll be able to reach you?"

"Yeah, at York's estate."

"Good enough. I'll be out sometme this morning."

"I'll be with him," Dilwick cut in. "You keep your nose out of things, too, understand?"

"Blow it," I said. "I know my legal rights."

I shoved my hat on and stamped my butt out in an ashtray. There was nothing for me here. I walked to the door, but before I could leave Price hurried after me. "Mr. Hammer."

"Yeah, Sergeant?"

"Will I be able to expect some cooperation from you?"

I broke out a smile. "You mean, if I uncover anything will I let you in on it, don't you?"

"That covers it pretty well." He was quite serious.

"Okay," I agreed, "but on one condition."

"Name it."

"If I come across something that demands immediate action, I'm going to go ahead on it. You can have it too as soon as I can get it to you, but I won't sacrifice a chance to follow a lead to put it in your hands."

He thought a moment, then, "That sounds fair enough. You realize, of course, that this isn't a permit to do as you choose. The reason I'm willing to let you help out is because of your reputation. You've been in this racket longer than I have, you've had the benefit of wide experience and are familiar with New York police methods. I know your history, otherwise you'd be shut out of this case entirely. Shorthanded as we are, I'm personally glad to have you help out."

"Thanks, Sergeant. If I can help, I will. But you'd better not let Dilwick get wise. He'd do anything to stymie you if he heard about this."

"That pig," Price grunted. "Tell me, what are you going to do?"

"The same thing you are. See what became of the Grange dame. She seems to be the key figure right now. You putting out a dragnet?"

"When you called, a roadblock was thrown across the highways. A seven-state alarm is on the Teletype this minute. She won't get far. Do you know anything of her personally?"

"Only that she's supposed to be the quiet type. York told me that she frequents the library a lot, but I doubt if you'll find her

there. I'll see what I can pick up at the house. If I latch on to
anything about her I'll buzz you."

I said so long and went downstairs. Right now the most important thing in my life was getting some sleep. I felt like I hadn't
seen a pillow in months. A pair of young troopers leaned against
the fender of a blue Caddy sedan parked down further from my
heap. They were comparing notes and talking back and forth. I'd
better remind Billy to come get it.

The sun was thumbing its nose at the night when I reached
the estate. Early-morning trucks that the gas station attendant had
spoken of were on the road to town, whizzing by at a good clip.
I honked my horn at the gate until Henry came out, still chewing
on his breakfast.

He waved. "So it was you. I wondered who opened the gates.
Why didn't you get me up?"

I drove alongside him and waited until he swallowed. "Henry,
did you hear me go out last night?"

"Me? Naw, I slept like a log. Ever since the kid was gone I
couldn't sleep thinking that it was all my fault because I sleep so
sound, but last night I felt pretty good."

"You must have. Two cars went out, the first one was your
boss."

"York? Where'd he go?"

"To town."

He shifted uneasily from one foot to the other. "Do . . . do
you think he'll be sore because I didn't hear him?"

I shook my head. "I don't think so. In fact, I don't think he
wanted to be heard."

"When's he coming back?"

"He won't. He's dead." I left him standing there with his mouth
open. The next time he'd be more careful of those gates.

I raced the engine outside the house and cut it. If that didn't
wake everyone in the house the way I slammed the door did.
Upstairs I heard a few indignant voices sounding off behind closed
doors. I ran up the stairs and met Roxy at the top, holding a
quilted robe together at her middle.

She shushed me with her hand. "Be quiet, please. The boy is
still asleep." It was going to be hard on him when he woke up.

"Just get up, Roxy?"

"A moment ago when you made all the noise out front. What
are you doing up?"

"Never mind. Everybody still around?"

"How should I know? Why, what's the matter?"

"York's been murdered."

Her hand flew to her mouth. For a long second her breath caught in her throat. "W . . . who did it?" she stammered.

"That's what I'd like to know, Roxy."

She bit her lip. "It . . . it was like we were talking about, wasn't it?"

"Seems to be. The finger's on Myra Grange now. It happened in her apartment and she took a powder."

"Well, what will we do?"

"You get the gang up. Don't tell them anything, just that I want to see them downstairs in the living room. Go ahead."

Roxy was glad to be doing something. She half ran to the far end of the hall and threw herself into the first room. I walked around to Ruston's door and tried it. Locked. Roxy's door was open and I went in that way, closing it behind me, then stepped softly to the door of the adjoining room and went in.

Ruston was fast asleep, a slight smile on his face as he played in his dreams. The covers were pulled up under his chin making him look younger than his fourteen years. I blew a wisp of hair away that had drifted across his brow and shook him lightly. "Ruston."

I rocked him again. "Ruston."

His eyes came open slowly. When he saw me he smiled. "Hello, Mr. Hammer."

"Call me Mike, kid, we're pals, aren't we?"

"You bet . . . Mike." He freed one arm and stretched. "Is it time to get up?"

"No, Ruston, not yet. There's something I have to tell you." I wondered how to put it. It wasn't easy to tell a kid that the father he loved had just been butchered by a blood-crazy killer.

"What is it? You look awfully worried, Mike, is something wrong?"

"Something is very wrong, kid, are you pretty tough?"

Another shy smile. "I'm not tough, not really. I wish I were, like people in stories."

I decided to give it to him the hard way and get it over with. "Your dad's dead, son."

He didn't grasp the meaning of it at first. He looked at me, puzzled, as though he had misinterpreted what I had said.

"Dead?"

I nodded. Realization came like a flood. The tears started in the corners. One rolled down his cheek. "No . . . he can't be dead. He can't be!" I put my arms around him for a second time. He hung on to me and sobbed.

"Oh . . . Dad. What happened to him, Mike? What happened?"

Softly, I stroked his head, trying to remember what my own father did with me when I hurt myself. I couldn't give him the details. "He's . . . just dead, Ruston."

"Something happened, I know." He tried to fight the tears, but it was no use. He drew away and rubbed his eyes. "What happened, Mike, please tell me?"

I handed him my handkerchief. He'd find out later, and it was better he heard it from me than one of the ghouls. "Someone killed him. Here, blow your nose." He blew, never taking his eyes from mine. I've seen puppies look at me that way when they've been kicked and didn't understand why.

"Killed? No . . . nobody would kill Dad . . . not my dad." I didn't say a word after that. I let it sink in and watched his face contort with the pain of the thought until I began to hurt in the chest myself.

For maybe ten minutes we sat like that, quietly, before the kid dried his eyes. He seemed older now. A thing like that will age anyone. His hand went to my arm. I patted his shoulder.

"Mike?"

"Yes, Ruston?"

"Do you think you can find the one who did it?"

"I'm going to try, kid."

His lips tightened fiercely. "I want you to. I wish I were big enough to. I'd shoot him, that's what I'd do!" He broke into tears again after that outburst. "Oh . . . Mike."

"You lay there, kid. Get a little rest, then when you feel better get dressed and come downstairs and we'll have a little talk. Think of something, only don't think of . . . that. It takes time to get over these things, but you will. Right now it hurts worse than anything in the world, but time will fix it up. You're tough, Ruston. After last night I'd say that you were the toughest kid that ever lived. Be tough now and don't cry anymore. Okay?"

"I'll try, Mike, honest, I'll try."

He rolled over in the bed and buried his face in the pillow. I unlocked his door to the hall and went out. I had to stick around now whether I wanted to or not. I promised the kid. And it was a promise I meant to keep.

Once before I made a promise, and I kept it. It killed my soul, but I kept it. I thought of all the blood that had run in the war, all that I had seen and had dripped on me, but none was redder or more repulsive than that blood I had seen when I kept my last promise.

chapter five ▬▬▬▬▬▬▬▬▬▬▬

THEIR FACES WERE those that stare at you from the walls of a museum; severe, hostile, expectant. They stood in various attitudes waiting to see what apology I had to offer for dragging them from their beds at this early hour.

Arthur Graham awkwardly sipped a glass of orange juice between swollen lips. His brother puffed nervously at a cigarette. The Ghents sat as one family in the far corner, Martha trying to be aloof as was Junior. Rhoda and her father felt conspicuous in their hurried dressing and fidgeted on the edge of their chairs.

Alice Nichols was . . . Alice. When I came into the living room she threw an eyeful of passion at me and said under her breath, "Lo, lover." It was too early for that stuff. I let the bags under my eyes tell her so. Roxy, sporting a worried frown, stopped me to say that there would be coffee ready in a few minutes. Good. They were going to need it.

I threw the ball from the scrimmage line before the opposition could break through with any bright remarks. "Rudolph York is dead. Somebody parted his hair with a cleaver up in Miss Grange's apartment."

I waited.

Martha gasped. Her husband's eyes nearly popped out. Junior and Rhoda looked at each other. Arthur choked on his orange juice and William dropped his cigarette. Behind me Alice said, "Tsk, tsk."

The silence was like an explosion, but before the echo died away Martha Ghent recovered enough to say coldly, "And where was Miss Grange?"

I shrugged. "Your guess is as good as mine." I laid it on the table then. "It's quite possible that she had nothing to do with it. Could be that someone here did the slaughtering. Before long the police are going to pay us a little visit. It's kind of late to start fixing up an alibi, but if you haven't any, you'd better think of one, fast."

While they swallowed that I turned on my heel and went out to the kitchen. Roxy had the coffee on a tray and I lifted a cup and carried it into Billy's room. He woke up as soon as I turned the knob.

"Hi, Mike." He looked at the clock. "What're you doing up?"

"I haven't been to bed yet. York's dead."

"What!"

"Last night. Got it with a cleaver."

"Good night! What happens now?"

"The usual routine for a while, I guess. Listen, were you in the sack all this time?"

"Hell, yes. Wait a minute, Mike, you . . ."

"Can you prove it? I mean did anyone see you there?"

"No. I've been alone. You don't think . . ."

"Quit worrying, Billy. Dilwick will be on this case and he's liable to have it in for you. That skunk will get back at you if he can't at me. He's got what little law there is in this town on his side now. What I want to do is establish some way you can prove you were here. Think of any?"

He put his finger to his mouth. "Yeah, I might at that. Twice last night I thought I heard a car go out."

"That'd be York then me."

"Right after the first car, someone came downstairs. I heard 'em inside, then there was some funny sound like somebody coughing real softly, then it died out. I couldn't figure out what it was."

"That might do it if we can find out who came down. Just forget all about it until you're asked, understand?"

"Sure, Mike. Geez, why did this have to happen? I'll be out on my ear now." His head dropped into his hands. "What'll I do?"

"We'll think of something. If you feel okay you'd better get dressed. York's car is still downtown, and when the cops get done with it you'll have to drive it back."

I handed him the coffee and he drank it gratefully. When he finished I took it away and went into the kitchen. Harvey was there drying his eyes on a handkerchief. He saw me and sniffed, "It's terrible, sir. Miss Malcom just told me. Who could have done such a thing?"

"I don't know, Harvey. Whoever it was will pay for it. Look,

I'm going to climb into bed. When the police come, get me up, will you?"

"Of course, sir. Will you eat first?"

"No thanks, later."

I skirted the living room and pushed myself up the stairs. The old legs were tired out. The bedclothes were where I had thrown them, in a heap at the foot of the bed. I didn't even bother to take off my shoes. When I put my head down I didn't care if the house burned to the ground as long as nobody awakened me.

The police came and went. Their voices came to me through the veil of sleep, only partially coherent. Voices of insistence, voices of protest and indignation. A woman's voice raised in anger and a meeker man's voice supporting it. Nobody seemed to care whether I was there or not, so I let the veil swirl into a gray shroud that shut off all sounds and thoughts.

It was the music that woke me. A terrible storm of music that reverberated through the house like a hurricane, shrieking in a wonderful agony. There had never been music like that before. I listened to the composition, wondering. For a space of seconds it was a song of rage, then it dwindled to a dirge of sorrow. No bar or theme was repeated.

I slipped out of the bed and opened the door, letting the full force of it hit me. It was impossible to conceive that a piano could tell such a story as this one was telling.

He sat there at the keyboard, a pitiful little figure clad in a Prussian blue bathrobe. His head was thrown back, the eyes shut tightly as if in pain, his fingers beating notes of anguish from the keys.

He was torturing himself with it. I sat beside him. "Ruston, don't."

Abruptly, he ceased in the middle of the concert and let his head fall to his chest. The critics were right when they acclaimed him a genius. If only they could have heard his latest recital.

"You have to take it easy, kid. Remember what I told you."

"I know, Mike, I'll try to be better. I just keep thinking of Dad all the time."

"He meant a lot to you, didn't he?"

"Everything. He taught me so many things, music, art . . . things that it takes people so long to get to know. He was wonderful, the best dad ever."

Without speaking I walked him over to the big chair beside the fireplace and sat down on the arm of the chair beside him. "Ruston," I started, "your father isn't here anymore, but he wouldn't want you to grieve about it. I think he'd rather you went on with all those things he was teaching you, and be what he wanted you to be."

"I will be, Mike," he said. His voice lacked color, but it rang earnestly. "Dad wanted me to excel in everything. He often told me that a man never lived long enough to accomplish nearly anything he was capable of because it took too long to learn the fundamentals. That's why he wanted me to know all these things while I was young. Then when I was a doctor or a scientist maybe I would be ahead of myself, sort of."

He was better as long as he could talk. Let him get it out of his system, I thought. It's the only way. "You've done fine, kid. I bet he was proud of you."

"Oh, he was. I only wish he could have been able to make his report."

"What report?"

"To the College of Scientists. They meet every five years to turn in reports, then one is selected as being the best one and the winner is elected President of the College for a term. He wanted that awfully badly. His report was going to be on me."

"I see," I said. "Maybe Miss Grange will do it for him."

I shouldn't have said that. He looked up at me woefully. "I don't think she will, not after the police find her."

It hit me right between the eyes. "Who's been telling you things, kid?"

"The policemen were here this morning. The big one made us all tell where we were last night and everything. Then he told us about Miss Grange."

"What about her?"

"They found her car down by the creek. They think she drowned herself."

I could have tossed a brick through a window right then. "Harvey!" I yelled. "Hey, Harvey."

The butler came in on the double. "I thought I asked you to wake me up when the police got here. What the hell happened?"

"Yes, sir. I meant to, but Officer Dilwick suggested that I let you sleep. I'm sorry, sir, it was more an order than a request."

So that was how things stood. I'd get even with that fat slob. "Where is everybody?"

"After the police took their statements he directed the family to return to their own homes. Miss Malcom and Parks are bringing Mr. York's car home. Sergeant Price wished me to tell you that he will be at the headquarters on the highway this evening and he would like to see you."

"I'm glad someone would like to see me," I remarked. I turned to Ruston. "I'm going to leave, son. How about you going to your room until Roxy . . . I mean Miss Malcom gets here? Okay?"

"All right, Mike. Why did you call her Roxy?"

"I have pet names for everybody."

"Do you have one for me?" he asked, little lights dancing in his eyes.

"You bet."

"What?"

"Sir Lancelot. He was the bravest of the brave."

As I walked out of the room I heard him repeat it softly, "Sir Lancelot, the bravest of the brave."

I reached the low fieldstone building set back from the road at a little after eight. The sky was threatening again, the air chilly and humid. Little beads of sweat were running down the windshield on the side. A sign across the drive read, STATE POLICE HEAD-QUARTERS, and I parked beside it.

Sergeant Price was waiting for me. He nodded when I came in and lay down the sheaf of papers he was examining. I threw my hat on an empty desk and helped myself to a chair. "Harvey gave me your message," I said. "What's the story?"

He leaned back in the swivel seat and tapped the desk with a pen. "We found Grange's car."

"So I heard. Find her yet?"

"No. The door was open and her body may have washed out. If it did we won't find it so easily. The tide was running out and would have taken the body with it. The river runs directly into the bay, you know."

"That's all supposition. She may not have been in the car."

He put the pencil between his teeth. "Every indication points to the fact that she was. There are clear tire marks showing where the car was deliberately wrenched off the road before the guardrails to the bridge. The car was going fast, besides. It landed thirty feet out in the water."

"That's not what you wanted to see me about?" I put in.

"You're on the ball, Mr. Hammer."

"Mike. I hate titles."

"Okay, Mike. What I want is this kidnapping deal."

"Figuring a connection?"

"There may be one if Grange was murdered."

I grinned. "You're on the ball yourself." Once again I went over the whole story, starting will Billy's call when he was arrested. He listened intently without saying a word until I was finished.

"What do you think?" he asked.

"Somebody's going to a lot of trouble."

"Do you smell a correlation between the two?"

I squinted at him. "I don't know . . . yet. That kidnapping came at the wrong time. A kidnapper wants money. This one never got away with his victim. Generally speaking, it isn't likely that a second try would be made on the same person, but York wanted the whole affair hushed up ostensibly for fear of the publicity it would bring. That would leave the kid open again. It is possible that the kidnapper, enraged at having his deal busted open, would hang around waiting to get even with York and saw his chance when he took off at that hour of the morning to see Grange."

Price shook out a cig from his pack and offered me one. "If that was the case, money would not have been the primary motive. A kidnapper who has muffed his snatch wants to get far away fast."

I lit up and blew a cloud of smoke at the ceiling. "Sounds screwed up, doesn't it?" He agreed. "Did you find out that York didn't have long to live anyway?"

He seemed startled at the change of subject. "No. Why?"

"Let's do it this way," I said. "York was on the list. He had only a few years at best to live. At the bottom of every crime there's a motive no matter how remote, and nine times out of ten that motive is cold, hard cash. He's got a bunch of relations that have been hanging around waiting for him to kick the bucket for a long time. One of them might have known that his condition was so bad that any excitement might knock him off. That one arranges a kidnapping, then when it fails takes direct action by knocking off York, making it look like Grange did it, then kills Grange to further the case by making it appear that she was a suicide in a fit of remorse."

Price smiled gently. "Are you testing me? I could shoot holes in that with a popgun. Arranging for a kidnapping means that you invite blackmail and lose everything you tried to get. York comes into it somewhere along the line because he was searching for something in that apartment. Try me again."

I laughed. "No good. You got all the answers."

He shoved the papers across the desk to me. "There are the statements of everybody in the house. They seem to support each other pretty well. Nobody left the house according to them so nobody had a chance to knock off York. That puts it outside the house again."

I looked them over. Not much there. Each sheet was an individual statement and it barely covered a quarter of the page. Besides a brief personal history was the report that once in bed, each person had remained there until I called them into the living room that morning.

I handed them back. "Somebody's lying. Is this all you got?"

"We didn't press for information although Dilwick wanted to. Who lied?"

"Somebody. Billy Parks told me he heard someone come downstairs during the night."

"Could it have been you?"

"No, it was before I followed York."

"He made no mention of it to me."

"Probably because he's afraid somebody will refute it if he does just to blacken him. I half promised him I'd check on it first."

"I see. Did York take you into his confidence at any time?"

"Nope. I didn't know him that long. After the snatch he hired me to stick around until he was certain his son was safe."

Price threw the pencil on the desk. "We're climbing a tree," he said tersely. "York was killed for a reason. Myra Grange was killed for the same reason. I think that for the time being we'll concentrate our efforts on locating Grange's body. When we're sure of her death we can have something definite to work on. Meanwhile I'm taking it for granted that she is dead."

I stood up to leave. "I'm not taking anything for granted, Sergeant. If she's dead she's out of it; if not the finger is still on her. I'm going to play around a little bit and see what happens. What's Dilwick doing?"

"Like you. He won't believe she's dead until he sees her either."

"Don't underestimate that hulk," I told him. "He's had a lot of police work and he's shrewd. Too shrewd, in fact, that's why he was booted off the New York force. He'll be looking out for himself when the time comes. If anything develops I'll let you know."

"Do that. See you later."

That ended the visit. I went out to the car and sat behind the wheel a while, thinking. Kidnapping, murder, a disappearance. A house full of black sheep. One nice kid, an ex-stripper for a nurse and a chauffeur with a record. The butler, maybe the butler did it. Someday a butler would do it for a change. A distraught father who stuck his hand in a hole in the fireplace and found something gone. He sets out to kill and gets killed instead. The one he wanted to kill is gone, perhaps dead too. Mallory. That was the name that started the ball of murder rolling. But Mallory figured in the kidnapping.

Okay, first things first. The kidnapping was first and I'd take it that way. It was a hell of a mess. The only thing that could make it any worse was to have Grange show up with an airtight alibi. I hated to hold out on Price about Mallory, but if he had it Dilwick would have to get it too, and that would put the kibosh on me. Like hell. I promised the kid.

I shoved the car in gear and spun out on the highway. Initial clue, the cops call it, the hand that puts the hound on the trail, that's what I had to have. York thought it was in Grange's apartment. Find what he was searching for and you had the answer. Swell, let's find it.

This time I parked around the block. The rain had started again, a light mist that you breathed into your lungs and dampened matches in your pocket. From the back of the car I pulled a slicker and climbed into it, turning the collar up high. I walked back to Main Street, crossed over to the side of the street opposite the apartment and joined the few late workers in their dash toward home.

I saw what I was looking for, a black, unmarked sedan occupied by a pair of cigar-smoking gentlemen who were trying their best to remain unnoticed. They did a lousy job. I circled the block until I was behind the apartment. A row of modest one-family houses faced me, their windows lighted with gaiety and cheer. Each house was flanked by a driveway.

Without waiting I picked the right one and turned down the cinder drive, staying to the side in the shadow of a hedgerow where the grass partially muffled my feet. Somehow I slipped between the garage and the hedges to the back fence without making too much of a racket. For ten minutes I stood that way, motionless. It wasn't a new experience for me. I remembered other pits of blackness where little brown men waited and threw jeers into our faces to draw us out. That was a real test of patience. This guy was easier. When another ten minutes passed the match lit his face briefly, then subsided into the ill-concealed glow of a cigarette tip.

Dilwick wasn't taking any chances on Myra Grange slipping back to her apartment. Or anyone else for that matter.

Once I had him spotted I kept my eyes a few feet to the side of him so I wouldn't lose him. Look directly at an object in the dark and you draw a blank spot. I went over the fence easily enough, then flanked the lookout by staying in the shadows again. By the time I reached the apartment building I had him silhouetted against the lights of another house. The janitor had very conveniently left a row of ash barrels stacked by the cellar entrance. I got up that close, at least. Six feet away on the other side of the gaping cavern of the entrance the law stood on flat feet, breathing heavily, cursing the rain under his breath.

My fingers snaked over the lip of a barrel, came away with a piece of ash the size of a marble. I balanced it on my thumb, then flipped it. I heard nothing, but he heard it and turned his head, that was all. I tried again with the same results. The next time I used a bigger piece. I got better results, too. He dropped the butt, ground it under his heel and walked away from the spot.

As soon as he moved I ducked around the barrels and down the stairs, then waited again, flattened against the wall. Finding nothing, the cop resumed his post. I went on tiptoes down the corridor, my hand out in front like a sleepwalker.

This part was going to take clever thinking. If they had both exits covered it was a sure bet that the apartment door was covered, too. I came to a bend in the tunnel and found myself in the furnace room. Overhead a dim bulb struggled against dust and cobwebs to send out a feeble glow. On the other side of the room a flight of metal steps led to the floor above. Sweet, but not practical. If I could make the roof I might be able to come down the fire escape, but that meant a racket or being seen by the occupants.

Right then I was grateful to the inventor of the dumbwaiter. The empty box yawned at me with a sleepy invitation. The smell was bad, but it was worth it. I climbed aboard and gave the rope a tentative pull to see if the pulleys squealed. They were well oiled. *Danke Schön*, janitor. You get an *A*.

When I passed the first floor I was beginning to doubt whether I could make it all the way. Crouching there like that I had no leverage to bear on the ropes. I was all wrist motion. I took a hitch in the rope around the catch on the sliding door and rested a second, then began hauling away again. Somewhere above me voices passed back and forth. Someone yelled, "Put it on the dumbwaiter."

I held my breath. Let them catch me here and I was sunk. Dilwick would like nothing better than to get me on attempted burglary and work me over with a few of his boys.

A moment went by, two, then, "Later, honey, it's only half-full."

Thanks, pal. Remind me to scratch your back. I got another grip on the rope and pulled away. By the time I reached Myra's door I was exhausted. Fortunately, one of the cops had forgotten to lock it after taking a peek down the well, not that it mattered. I didn't care whether anyone was inside or not. I shoved the two-bit door open and tumbled to the floor. I was lucky. The house was quiet as a tomb. If I ever see that trick pulled in a movie and the hero steps out looking fresh as a daisy I'll throw rocks at the screen. I lay there until I got my wind back.

The flash I used had the lens taped, so the only light it shed was a round disk the size of a quarter. I poked around the kitchen a bit taking it all in. Nobody had cleaned up since the murder as far as I could see. I went into the living room, avoiding the litter on the floor. The place was even worse than it was before. The police had finished what York had started, pulling drawers open further, tearing the pictures from the walls and scuffling up the rug.

But they hadn't found it. If they had I wouldn't've had to use the dumbwaiter to get in. Dilwick was better than shrewd. He was waiting for Grange to come back and find it for him.

Which meant that he was pretty certain Grange was alive. Dilwick knew something that Price and I didn't know, in that case.

In the first half hour I went through every piece of junk that had been dragged out without coming across anything worthwhile. I kicked at the pile and tried the drawers in the desk again. My luck stunk; Grange didn't go in for false bottoms or double walls. I thought of every place a dame hides things, but the cops had thought of them too. Every corner had been poked into, every closet emptied out. Women think of cute places like the hollows of bedposts and the inside of lamps, but the bedposts turned out to be solid and the lamps of modern transparent glass.

Hell, she had to have important things around. College degrees, insurance policies and that sort of stuff. I finally realized what was wrong. My psychology. Or hers. She only resembled a woman. She looked like one and dressed like one, physically, she was one, but Myra Grange had one of those twisted complexes. If she thought it was like a man. That was better. Being partially a woman she would want to secrete things; being part man she would hide them in a place not easily accessible, where it would take force, and not deduction to locate the cache.

I started grinning then. I pulled the cabinets away from the walls and tried the sills of the doors. When I found a hollow behind the radiator I felt better. It was dust-filled and hadn't been used for some time, mainly because a hand reaching in there could be burned if the heat was on, but I knew I was on the right track.

It took time, but I found it when I was on my hands and knees, shooting light along the baseboards under the bed. It wasn't even a good job of concealment. I saw where a claw hammer had probably knocked a hole in the plaster behind it.

A package of envelopes held together by a large rubber band was the treasure. It was four-inches thick, at least, with corners of stock certificates showing in the middle. A nice little pile.

I didn't waste time going through them then. I stuck the package inside my coat and buttoned the slicker over it. I had one end of the baseboard in place when I thought what a fine joke it would be to pull on slobbermouth to leave a calling card. With a wrench I pulled it loose, laid it on the floor where it couldn't be missed and got out to the kitchen. Let my fat friend figure that one out. He'd have the jokers at the doors shaking in their shoes by the time he was done with them.

The trip down was better. All I had to do was hang on and let the rope slide through my hands. Between the first floor and the basement I tightened up on the hemp and cut down the descent. It was a good landing, just a slight jar and I walked away from there. Getting out was easier than coming in. I poked my head out the cellar window on the side where the walk led around to the back and the concrete stared me in the face, gave a short whistle and called, "Hey, Mac."

It was enough. Heavy feet came pounding around the side and I made a dash up the corridor, out the door and dived into the bushes before the puzzled cop got back to his post scratching his head in bewilderment. The fence, the driveway, and I was in my car pulling up the street behind a trailer truck.

The package was burning a hole in my pocket. I turned down a side street where the neon of an open diner provided a stopping-off place, parked and went in and occupied a corner booth. When a skinny waiter in an oversized apron took my order I extracted the bundle. I rifled through the deck, ignoring the bonds and policies. I found what I was after.

It was York's will, made out two years ago, leaving every cent of his dough to Grange. If that female was still alive this put her on the spot for sure. Here was motive, pure, raw motive. A several-million-dollar motive, but it might as well be a can tied to her tail. She was a lucky one indeed if she lived to enjoy it.

Sloppy Joe came back with my hamburgers and coffee. I shelved the package while he dished out the slop, then forced it down my gullet, with the coffee as a lubricant. I was nearly through when I noticed my hands. They were dusty as hell. I noticed something else, too. The rubber band that had been around the package lay beside my coffee cup, stiff and rotted, and in two pieces.

Then I didn't get it after all, at least not what York was searching for. This package hadn't been opened for a hell of a long time, and it was a good bet that whatever had been in the fireplace had been there until the other night. The will had been placed in the package years ago.

Damn. Say it again, Mike, you outsmarted yourself that time. Damn.

chapter six ▰▰▰▰▰▰▰▰▰▰▰▰▰▰▰▰

I SET MY WATCH by the clock on the corner while I waited for the light to change. Nine-fifteen, and all was far from well. Just what the hell was it that threw York into a spasm? I knew damn well now that whatever it was, either Grange had it with her or she never had it at all. I was right back where I started from. Which left two things to be done. Find Mallory, or see who came downstairs the night of the murder and why that movement was denied in the statements. All right, let it be Mallory. Maybe Roxy could supply some answers. I pulled the will from the package and slipped it inside my jacket, then tossed the rest of the things in the back of the glove compartment.

Henry had the gates open as soon as I turned off the road. When he shut them behind me I called him over. "Anyone been here while I was gone?"

"Yes, sir. The undertaker came, but that was all."

I thanked him and drove up the drive. Harvey nodded solemnly when he opened the door and took my hat. "Have there been any developments, sir?"

"Not a thing. Where's Miss Malcom?"

"Upstairs, I believe. She took Master Ruston to his room a little while ago. Shall I call her for you?"

"Never mind, I'll go up myself."

I rapped lightly and opened the door at the same time. Roxy took a quick breath, grabbed the negligee off the bed and held it in front of her. That split second of visioning nudity that was classic beauty made the blood pound in my ears. I shut my eyes against it. "Easy, Roxy," I said, "I can't see so don't scream and don't throw things. I didn't mean it."

She laughed lightly. "Oh, for heaven's sake, open them up. You've seen me like this before." I looked just as she tied the wrapper around her. That kind of stuff could drive a guy bats.

"Don't tempt me. I thought you'd changed?"

"Mike . . . don't say it that way. Maybe I have gone modest, but I like it better. In your rough way you respected it too, but I can't very well heave things at you for seeing again what you saw so many times before."

"The kid asleep?"

"I think so." The door was open a few inches, the other room dark. I closed it softly, then went back and sat on the edge of the bed. Roxy dragged the chair from in front of her vanity and set it down before me.

"Do I get sworn in first?" she asked with a fake pout.

"This is serious."

"Shoot."

"I'm going to mention a name to you. Don't answer me right away. Let it sink in, think about it, think of any time since you've been here that you might have heard it, no matter when. Roll it around on your tongue a few times until it becomes familiar, then if you recognize it tell me where or when you heard it and who said it . . . if you can."

"I see. Who is it?"

I handed her a cigarette and plucked one myself. "Mallory," I said as I lit it for her. I hooked my hands around my knee and waited. Roxy blew smoke at the floor. She looked up at me a couple of times, her eyes vacant with thought, mouthing the name to herself. I watched her chew on her lip and suck in a lungful of smoke.

Finally she rubbed her hand across her forehead and grimaced. "I can't remember ever having heard it," she told me. "Is it very important?"

"I think it might be. I don't know."

"I'm sorry, Mike." She leaned forward and patted my knee.

"Hell, don't take it to heart. He's just a name to me. Do you think any of the characters might know anything?"

"That I couldn't say. York was a quiet one, you know."

"I didn't know. Did he seem to favor any of them?"

She stood up and stretched on her toes. Under the sheer fabric little muscles played in her body. "As far as I could see, he had an evident distaste for the lot of them. When I first came here he apparently liked his niece, Rhoda. He remembered her with gifts upon the slightest provocation. Expensive ones, too. I know, I bought them for him."

I snubbed my butt. "Uh-huh. Did he turn to someone else?"

"Why, yes." She looked at me in faint surprise. "The other niece, Alice Nichols."

"I would have looked at her first to begin with."

"Yes, you would," she grinned. "Shall I go on?"

"Please."

"For quite a while she got all the attention which threw the Ghents into an uproar. I imagine they saw Rhoda being his heir and didn't like the switch. Mr. York's partiality to Alice continued for several months then fell off somewhat. He paid little attention to her after that, but never forgot her on birthdays or holidays. His gifts were as great as ever. And that," she concluded, "is the only unusual situation that ever existed as far as I know."

"Alice and York, huh? How far did the relationship go?"

"Not that far. His feelings were paternal, I think."

"Are you sure?"

"Pretty sure. Mr. York was long past his prime. If sex meant anything to him it was no more than a biological difference between the species."

"It might mean something to Alice."

"Of that I'm sure. She likes anything with muscles, but with Mr. York she didn't need it. She did all right without it. I noticed that she cast a hook in your direction."

"She didn't use the right bait," I stated briefly. "She showed up in my room with nothing on but a prayer and wanted to play. I like to be teased a little. Besides, I was tired. Did York know she acted that way?"

Roxy plugged in a tiny radio set and fiddled with the dial. "If he did he didn't care."

"Kitten, did York ever mention a will?"

An old Benny Goodman tune came on. She brought it in clearer and turned around with a dance step. "Yes, he had one. He kept the family on the verge of a nervous breakdown every time he alluded to it, but he never came right out and said where his money would go."

She began to spin with the music. "Hold still a second will you. Didn't he hand out any hints at all?"

The hem of her negligee brushed past my face, higher than any hem had a right to be. "None at all, except that it would go where it was most deserving."

Her legs flashed in the light. My heart began beating faster again. They were lovely legs, long, firm. "Did Grange ever hear that statement?"

She stopped, poised dramatically and threw her belt at me. "Yes." She began to dance again. The music was a rhumba now and her body swayed to it, jerking rhythmically. "Once during a heated discussion Mr. York told them all that Miss Grange was the only one he could trust and she would be the one to handle his estate."

There was no answer to that. How the devil could she handle it if she got it all? I never got a chance to think about it. The robe came off and she used it like a fan, almost disclosing everything, showing nothing. Her skin was fair, cream-colored, her body graceful. She circled in front of me, letting her hair fall to her shoulders. At the height of that furious dance I stood up.

Roxy flew into my arms. "Kiss me . . . you thing."

I didn't need any urging.

Her mouth melted into mine like butter. I felt her nails digging into my arms. Roughly, I pushed her away, held her there at arm's length. "What was that for?"

She gave me a delightfully evil grin. "That is because I could love you if I wanted to, Mike. I did once, you know."

"I know. What made you stop?"

"You're Broadway, Mike. You're the bright lights and big money . . . sometimes. You're bullets when there should be kisses. That's why I stopped. I wanted someone with a normal life expectancy."

"Then why this?"

"I missed you. Funny as it sounds, someplace inside me I have a spot that's always reserved for you. I didn't want you to ever know it, but there it is."

I kissed her again, longer and closer this time. Her body was talking to me, screaming to me. There would have been more if Ruston hadn't called out.

Roxy slipped into the robe again, the cold static making it snap. "Let me go," I said. She nodded.

I opened the door and hit the light switch. "Hello, Sir Lancelot."

The kid had been crying in his sleep, but he smiled at me.

"Hello, Mike. When did you come?"

"A little while ago. Want something?"

"Can I have some water, please? My throat's awfully dry."

A pitcher half-full of ice was on the desk. I poured it into a glass, and handed it to him and he drank deeply. "Have enough?"

He gave the glass back to me. "Yes, thank you."

I gave his chin a little twist. "Then back to bed with you. Get a good sleep."

Ruston squirmed back under the covers. "I will. Good night, Mike."

"'Night, pal." I closed the door behind me. Roxy had changed into a deep maroon quilted job and sat in the chair smoking a cigarette. The moment had passed. I could see that she was sorry, too. She handed me my deck of butts and I pocketed them, then waved a good-night. Neither of us felt like saying anything.

Evidently Harvey had retired for the night. The staircase was lit only by tiny night-lights shaped to resemble candle flames, while the foyer below was a dim challenge to the eyesight. I picked my way through the rooms and found Billy's without upsetting anything. He was in bed, but awake. "It's Mike, Billy," I said.

He snapped on the bed lamp. "Come on in."

I shut the door and slumped in a chair next to him. "More questions. I know it's late, but I hope you don't mind."

"Not at all, Mike. What's new?"

"Oh, you know how these things are. Haven't found Miss Grange yet and things are settling around her. Dilwick's got his men covering her place like a blanket."

"Yeah? What for? Ain't she supposed to be drowned?"

"Somebody wants it to look that way, I think. Listen, Billy, you told me before that you heard someone come downstairs between York and me the night of the murder. It wasn't important before except to establish an alibi for you if it was needed, but now what you heard may have a bearing on the case. Go over it again, will you? Do it in as much detail as you can."

"Let's see. I didn't really hear York leave, I just remember a car crunching the gravel. It woke me up. I had a headache and a bad taste in my mouth from something York gave me. Pills, I think."

"It was supposed to keep you asleep. He gave you a sedative."

"Whatever it was I puked up in bed, that's why it didn't do me any good. Anyway, I lay here half-awake when I heard somebody come down the last two stairs. They squeak, they do. This room is set funny, see. Any noise outside the room travels right in here. They got a name for it."

"Acoustics."

"Yeah, that's it. That's why nobody ever used this room but me. They couldn't stand the noise all the time. Not only loud noises, any kind of noises. This was like whoever it was didn't want to make a sound, but it didn't do any good because I heard it. Only I thought it was one of the family trying to be quiet so they wouldn't wake anyone up and I didn't pay any attention to it. About two or three minutes after that comes this noise like someone coughing with their head under a coat and it died out real slow and that's all. I was just getting back to sleep when there was another car tearing out the drive. That was you, I guess."

"That all?"

"Yeah, that's all, Mike. I went back to sleep after that."

This was the ace. It had its face down so I couldn't tell whether it was red or black, but it was the ace. The bells were going off in my head again, those little tinkles that promised to become the pealing of chimes. The cart was before the horse, but if I could find the right buckle to unloosen I could put them right back.

"Billy, say nothing to nobody about this, understand? If the local police question you, say nothing. If Sergeant Price wants to know things, have him see me. If you value your head, keep your mouth shut and your door locked."

His eyes popped wide open. "Geez, Mike, is it that important?"

I nodded. "I have a funny feeling, Billy, that the noises you heard were made by the murderer."

"Good Golly!" It left him breathless. Then, "You . . . you think the killer . . ." he swallowed, ". . . might make a try for me?"

"No, Billy, not the killer. You aren't that important to him. Someone else might, though. I think we have a lot more on our hands than just plain murder."

"What?" It was a hoarse whisper.

"Kidnapping, for one thing. That comes in somewhere. You sit tight until you hear from me." Before I left I turned with my hand on the knob and looked into his scared face again. "Who's Mallory, Billy?"

"Mallory who?"

"Just Mallory."

"Gosh, I don't know."

"Okay, kid, thanks."

Mallory. He might as well be Smith or Jones. So far he was

just a word. I navigated the gloom again half consciously, thinking of him. Mallory of the kidnapping; Mallory whose very name turned York white and added a link to the chain of crime. Somewhere Mallory was sitting on his fanny getting a large charge out of the whole filthy mess. York knew who he was, but York was dead. Could that be the reason for his murder? Likely. York, by indirect implication and his peculiar action intimated that Myra Grange knew of him too, but she was dead or missing. Was that Mallory's doing? Likely. Hell, I couldn't put my finger on anything more definite than a vague possibility. Something had to blow up, somebody would have to try to take the corners out of one of the angles. I gathered all the facts together, but they didn't make sense. A name spoken, the speaker unseen; someone who came downstairs at night, unseen too, and denying it; a search for a stolen something-or-other, whose theft was laid at the feet of the vanished woman. I muttered a string of curses under my breath and kicked aimlessly at empty air. Where was there to start? Dilwick would have his feelers out for Grange and so would Price. With that many men they could get around much too fast for me. Besides, I had the feeling that she was only part of it all, not the key figure that would unlock the mystery, but more like one whose testimony would cut down a lot of time and work. I still couldn't see her putting the cleaver into York then doing the Dutch afterward. If she was associated with him professionally she would have to be brilliant, and great minds either turn at murder or attempt to conceive of a flawless plot. York's death was brutal. It was something you might find committed in a dark alley in a slum section for a few paltry dollars, or in a hotel room when a husband returns to find his woman in the arms of her lover. A passion kill, a revenge kill, a crude murder for small money, yes, but did any of these motives fit here? For whom did York hold passion . . . or vice versa? Roxy hit it when she said he was too old. Small money? None was gone from his wallet apparently. That kind of kill would take place outside on a lonely road or on a deserted street anyway. Revenge . . . revenge. Grange said he had no enemies. That was now. Could anything have happened in the past? You could almost rule that out too, on the basis of precedent. Revenge murders usually happen soon after the event that caused the desire for revenge. If the would-be murderer has time to think he realizes the penalty for murder and it doesn't happen. Unless, of course, the victim, realizing what might happen, keeps on the move. That accentuates the importance of the event to the killer and spurs him on. Negative. York was a public figure for years. He had lived in the same house almost twenty years. Big money, a motive for anything. Was that it? Grange came into that. Why did she have the will? Those things are kept in a safe deposit box or lawyer's files. The chief beneficiary rarely ever got to see the document much less have it hidden among her personal effects for so long a time. Damn, Grange had told me she had a large income aside from what York gave her. She didn't care what he did with his money. What a very pretty attitude to take, especially when you know where it's going. She could afford to be snotty with me. I remembered her face when she said it, aloof, the hell-with-it attitude. Why the act if it wasn't important then? What was she trying to put across?

Myra Grange. I didn't want it to, but it came back to her every time. Missing the night of the kidnapping; seen on the road, but she said no. Why? I started to grin a little. An unmarried person goes out at night for what reason? Natch . . . a date. Grange had a date, and her kind of dates had to be kept behind closed doors, that's why she was rarely seen about. York wouldn't want it to get around either for fear of criticism, that's why he was nice about it. Grange would deny it for a lot of reasons. It would hurt her professionally, or worse, she might lose a perfectly good girl friend. It was all supposition, but I bet I was close.

The night air hit me in the face. I hadn't realized I was standing outside the door until a chilly mist ran up the steps and hugged me. I stuck my hands in my pockets and walked down the drive. Behind me the house watched with staring eyes. I wished it could talk. The gravel path encircled the gloomy old place with gray arms and I followed it aimlessly, trying to straighten out my thoughts. When I came to the fork I stood motionless a moment then followed the turn off to the right.

Fifty yards later the colorless bulk of the laboratory grew out of the darkness like a crypt. It was a drab cinder-block building, the only incongruous thing on the estate. No windows broke the contours of the walls on either of the two sides visible, no place where prying eyes might observe what occurred within. At the far end a thirty-foot chimney poked a skinny finger skyward, stretching to clear the treetops. Upon closer inspection a ventilation system showed just under the eaves, screened air intakes and outlets above eye level.

I went around the building once, a hundred-by-fifty-foot structure, but the only opening was the single steel door in the front, a door built to withstand weather or siege. But it was not built to withstand curiosity. The first master key I used turned the lock.

It was a laugh. The double tongue had prongs as thick as my thumb, but the tumbler arrangement was as uncomplicated as a glass of milk.

Fortunately, the light pulls had tiny phosphorescent tips that cast a greenish glow. I reached up and yanked one. Overhead a hundred-watt bulb flared into daylight brilliance. I checked the door and shut it, then looked about me. Architecturally, the building was a study in simplicity. One long corridor ran the length of it. Off each side were rooms, perhaps sixteen in all. No dirt marred the shining marble floor, no streaks on the enameled white walls. Each door was shut, the brass of the knobs gleaming, the woodwork smiling in varnished austerity. For all its rough exterior, the inside was spotless.

The first room on the one side was an office, fitted with a desk, several filing cabinets, a big chair and a water cooler. The room opposite was its mate. So far so good. I could tell by the pipe rack which had been York's.

Next came some sort of supply room. In racks along the walls were hundreds of labeled bottles, chemicals unknown to me. I opened the bins below. Electrical fittings, tubes, meaningless coils of copper tubing lay neatly placed on shelves alongside instruments and parts of unusual design. This time the room opposite was no mate. Crouched in one corner was a generator, snuggling up to a transformer. Wrist-thick power lines came in through the door, passed through the two units and into the walls. I had seen affairs like this on portable electric chairs in some of our more rural states. I couldn't figure this one out. If the education of Ruston was York's sole work, why all the gadgets? Or was that merely a shield for something bigger?

The following room turned everything into a cockeyed mess. Here was a lounge that was sheer luxury. Overstuffed chairs, a seven-foot couch, a chair shaped like a French curve that went down your back, up under your knees and ended in a cushioned foot rest. Handy to everything were magazine racks of popular titles and some of more obscure titles. Books in foreign languages rested between costly jade bookends. A combination radio-phonograph sat in the corner, flanked by cabinets of symphonic and pop records. Opposite it at the other end of the room was a grand piano with operatic scores concealed in the seat. Cleverly contrived furniture turned into art boards and reading tables. A miniature refrigerator housed a bottle of ice water and several frosted glasses. Along the wall several Petri dishes held agar—agar with yellow bacteria cultures mottling the tops. Next to them was a double-lensed microscope of the best manufacture.

What a playpen. Here anyone could relax in comfort with his favorite hobby. Was this where Ruston spent his idle hours? There was nothing here for a boy, but his mind would appreciate it.

It was getting late. I shut the door and moved on, taking quick peeks into each room. A full-scale lab, test tubes, retorts, a room of books, nothing but books, then more electrical equipment. I crossed the corridor and stuck my head in. I had to take a second look to be sure I was right. If that wasn't the hot seat standing in the middle of the floor it was a good imitation.

I didn't get a chance to go over it. Very faintly I heard metal scratching against metal. I pulled the door shut and ran down the corridor, pulling at the light cords as I went. I wasn't the only one that was curious this night.

Just as I closed the door of Grange's office behind me the outside door swung inward. Someone was standing there in the dark waiting. I heard his breath coming hard with an attempt to control it. The door shut, and a sliver of light ran along the floor, shining through the crack onto my shoes. The intruder wasn't bothering with the overheads, he was using a flash.

A hand touched the knob. In two shakes I was palming my rod, holding it above my head ready to bring it down the second he stepped in the door. It never opened. He moved to the other side and went into York's office instead.

As slowly as I could I eased the knob around, then brought it toward my stomach. An inch, two, then there was room enough to squeeze out. I kept the dark paneling of the door at my back, stood there in the darkness, letting my breath in and out silently while I watched Junior Ghent rifle York's room.

He had the flashlight propped on the top of the desk, working in its beam. He didn't seem to be in a hurry. He pulled out every drawer of the files, scattering their contents on the floor in individual piles. When he finished with one row he moved to another until the empty cabinet gaped like a toothless old man.

For a second I thought he was leaving and faded to one side, but all he did was turn the flash to focus on the other side of the room. Again, he repeated the procedure. I watched.

At the end of twenty minutes his patience began to give out. He yanked things viciously from place and kicked at the chair, then obviously holding himself in check tried to be calm about it. In another fifteen minutes he had circled the room, making it look like a bomb had gone off in there. He hadn't found what he was after.

That came by accident.

The chair got in his way again. He pushed it so hard it skidded along the marble, hit an empty drawer and toppled over. I even noticed it before he did.

The chair had a false bottom.

Very clever. Search a room for hours and you'll push furniture all over the place, but how often will you turn up a chair and inspect it. Junior let out a surprised gasp and went down on his knees, his fingers running over the paneling. When his fingernails didn't work he took a screwdriver from his pocket and forced it into the wood. There was a sharp snap and the bottom was off.

A thick envelope was fastened to a wire clasp. He smacked his lips and wrenched it free. With his forefinger he lifted the flap and drew out a sheaf of papers. These he scanned quickly, let out a sarcastic snort, and discarded them on the floor. He dug into the envelope and brought out something else. He studied it closely, rubbing his hand over his stomach. Twice he adjusted his glasses and held them closer to the light. I saw his face flush. As though he knew he was being watched he threw a furtive glance toward the door, then shoved the stuff back in the envelope and put it in his side pocket.

I ducked back in the corridor while he went out the door, waited until it closed then snapped the light on and stepped over the junk. One quick look at the papers he had found in the envelope told me what it was. This will was made out only a few months ago, and it left three-quarters of his estate to Ruston and one-quarter to Alice. York had cut the rest out with a single buck.

Junior Ghent had something more important, though. I folded the will into my pocket and ran to the door. I didn't want my little pal to get away.

He didn't. Fifty yards up the drive he was getting the life beat out of him.

I heard his muffled screams, and other voices, too. I got the .45 in my hand and thumbed the safety off and made a dash for them.

Maybe I should have stayed on the grass, but I didn't have that much time. Two figures detached themselves from the one on the ground and broke for the trees. I let one go over their heads that echoed over the grounds like the rolling of thunder, but neither stopped. They went across a clearing and I put on speed to get free of the brush line so I could take aim. Junior stopped that.

I tripped over his sprawled figure and went flat on my kisser. The pair scrambled over the wall before I was up. From the ground I tried a snap shot that went wild. On the other side of the wall a car roared into life and shot down the road.

A woman's quick, sharp scream split the air like a knife and caught me flat-footed. Everything happened at once. Briars ripped at my clothes when I went through the brush and whipped at my face. Lights went on in the house and Harvey's voice rang out for help. By the time I reached the porch Billy was standing beside the door in his pajamas.

"Upstairs, Mike, it's Miss Malcom. Somebody shot her!"

Harvey was waving frantically, pointing to her room. I raced inside. Roxy was lying on the floor with blood making a bright red picture on the shoulder of her nightgown. Harvey stood over me, shaking with fear as I ripped the cloth away. I breathed with relief. The bullet had only passed through the flesh under her arm.

I carried her to bed and called to the butler over my shoulder. "Get some hot water and bandages. Get a doctor up here."

Harvey said, "Yes, sir," and scurried away.

Billy came in. "Can I do anything, Mike? I . . . I don't want to be alone."

"Okay, stay with her. I want to see the kid."

I opened the door to Ruston's room and turned on the light. He was sitting up, holding himself erect with his hands, his eyes were fixed on the wall in a blank stare, his mouth open. He never saw me. I shook him, he was stiff as a board, every muscle in his body as rigid as a piece of steel. He jerked convulsively once or twice, never taking his eyes from the wall. It took a lot of force to pull his arms up and straighten him out.

"Harvey, did you call that doctor?"

Billy sang out, "He's doing it now, Mike."

"Damn it, tell him to hurry. The kid's having a fit or something."

He hollered down the stairs to Harvey; I could hear the excited stuttering over the telephone, but it would be awhile before a medic would reach the house. Ruston began to tremble, his eyes rolled back in his head. Leaning over I slapped him sharply across the cheek.

"Ruston, snap out of it." I slapped him again. "Ruston."

This time his eyelids flickered, he came back to normal with a sob. His mouth twitched and he covered his face with his hands. Suddenly he sat up in bed and shouted, "Mike!"

"I'm right here, kid," I said, "take it easy." His face found mine and he reached for my hand. He was trembling from head to foot, his body bathed in cold sweat.

"Miss Malcom . . . ?"

"Is all right," I answered. "She just got a good scare, that's all." I didn't want to frighten him any more than he was. "Did someone come in here?"

He squeezed my hand. "No . . . there was a noise, and Miss Malcom screamed. Mike, I'm not very brave at all. I'm scared."

The kid had a right to be. "It was nothing. Cover up and be still. I'll be in the next room. Want me to leave the door open?"

"Please, Mike."

I left the light on and put a rubber wedge under the door to keep it open. Billy was standing by the bed holding a handkerchief to Roxy's shoulder. I took it away and looked at it. Not much of a wound, the bullet was of small caliber and had gone in and come out clean. Billy poked me and pointed to the window. The pane had spider-webbed into a thousand cracks with a neat hole at the bottom a few inches above the sill. Tiny glass fragments winked up from the floor. The shot had come in from below, traveling upward. Behind me in the wall was the bullet hole, a small puncture head high. I dug out the slug from the plaster and rolled it over in my hand. A neat piece of lead whose shape had hardly been deformed by the wall, caliber .32. York's gun had found its way home.

I tucked it in my watch pocket. "Stay here, Billy, I'll be right back."

"Where are you going?" He didn't like me to leave.

"I got a friend downstairs."

Junior was struggling to his feet when I reached him. I helped him with a fist in his collar. This little twerp had a lot of explaining to do. He was a sorry-looking sight. Pieces of gravel were imbedded in the flesh of his face and blood matted the hair of his scalp. One lens of his specs was smashed. I watched him while he detached his lower lip from his teeth, swearing incoherently. The belting he took had left him half-dazed, and he didn't try to resist at all when I walked him toward the house.

When I sat him in a chair he shook his head, touching the cut on his temple. He kept repeating a four-letter word over and over until realization of what had happened hit him. His head came up and I thought he was going to spit at me.

"You got it!" he said accusingly on the verge of tears now.

"Got what?" I leaned forward to get every word. His eyes narrowed.

Junior said sullenly, "Nothing."

Very deliberately I took his tie in my hand and pulled it. He tried to draw back, but I held him close. "Little chum," I said, "you are in a bad spot, very bad. You've been caught breaking and entering. You stole something from York's private hideaway and Miss Malcom has been shot. If you know what's good for you, you'll talk."

"Shot . . . killed?"

There was no sense letting him know the truth. "She's not dead yet. If she dies you're liable to face a murder charge."

"No. No. I didn't do it. I admit I was in the laboratory, but I didn't shoot her. I . . . I didn't get a chance to. Those men jumped on me. I fought for my life."

"Did you? Were you really unconscious? Maybe. I went after them until I heard Miss Malcom scream. Did she scream because you shot her, then faked being knocked out all the while?"

He turned white. A little vein in his forehead throbbed, his hands tightened until his nails drew blood from the palms. "You can't pin it on me," he said. "I didn't do it, I swear."

"No? What did you take from the room back there?"

A pause, then, "Nothing."

I reached for his pockets, daring him to move. Each one I turned inside out, dumping their contents around the bottom of the chair. A wallet, theater stubs, two old letters, some keys and fifty-five cents in change. That was all.

"So somebody else wanted what you found, didn't they?" He didn't answer. "They got it, too."

"I didn't have anything," he repeated.

He was lying through his teeth. "Then why did they wait for you and beat your brains out? Answer that one." He was quiet. I took the will out and waved it at him. "It went with this. It was more important than this, though. But what would be more important to you than a will? You're stupid, Junior. You aren't in this at all, are you? If you had sense enough to burn it you might have come into big dough when the estate was split up, especially with the kid under age. But no, you didn't care whether the will was found and probated or not, because the other thing was more important. It meant more money. How, Junior, how?"

For my little speech I had a sneer thrown at me. "All right," I told him, "I'll tell you what I'm going to do. Right now you look like hell, but you're beautiful compared to what you'll look like in ten minutes. I'm going to slap the crap out of you until you talk. Yell all you want to, it won't do any good."

I pulled back my hand. Junior didn't wait, he started speaking. "Don't. It was nothing. I . . . I stole some money from my uncle once. He caught me and made me sign a statement. I didn't want it to be found or I'd never get a cent. That was it."

"Yes? What made it so important that someone else would want it?"

"I don't know. There was something else attached to the statement that I didn't look at. Maybe they wanted that."

It could have been a lie, but I wasn't sure. What he said made sense. "Did you shoot Miss Malcom?"

"That's silly." I tightened up on the tie again. "Please, you're choking me. I didn't shoot anyone. I never saw her. You can tell, the police have a test haven't they?"

"Yes, a paraffin test. Would you submit to it?"

Relief flooded his face and he nodded. I let him go. If he had pulled the trigger he wouldn't be so damn anxious. Besides, I knew for sure that he hadn't been wearing gloves.

A car pulled up outside and Harvey admitted a short, stout man carrying the bag of his profession. They disappeared upstairs. I turned to Junior. "Get out of here, but stay where you can be reached. If you take a powder I'll squeeze your skinny neck until you turn blue. Remember one thing, if Miss Malcom dies you're it, see, so you better start praying."

He shot out of the chair and half ran for the door. I heard his feet pounding down the drive. I went upstairs.

"How is she?" The doctor applied the last of the tape over the compress and turned.

"Nothing serious. Fainted from shock." He put his instruments back in his bag and took out a notebook. Roxy stirred and woke up.

"Of course you know I'll have to report this. The police must have a record of all gunshot wounds. Her name, please."

Roxy watched me from the bed. I passed it to her. She murmured, "Helen Malcom."

"Address?"

"Here." She gave her age and the doctor noted a general description then asked me if I had found the bullet.

"Yeah, it was in the wall. A .32 lead-nose job. I'll give it to the police." He snapped the book shut and stuck it in his bag.

"I'd like you to see the boy, too, Doctor," I mentioned. "He was in a bad way."

Briefly, I went over what had happened the past few days. The doctor picked his bag up and followed me inside. "I know the boy," he said. "Too much excitement is bad for any youngster, particularly one as finely trained as he is."

"You've seen him before? I thought his father was his doctor."

"Not the boy. However I had occasion to speak to his father several times in town and he spoke rather proudly of his son."

"I should imagine. Here he is."

The doctor took his pulse and I winked over his shoulder. Ruston grinned back. While the doctor examined him I sat at the desk and looked at nine-by-twelve photos of popular cowboy actors Ruston had in a folder. He was a genius, but the boy kept coming out around the seams. A few of the books in the lower shelves were current Western novels and some books on American geography in the 1800s. Beside the desk was a used ten-gallon hat and lariat with the crown of the skimmer autographed by Hollywood's foremost heroic cattle hand. I don't know why York didn't let his kid alone to enjoy himself the way boys should. Ruston would rather be a cowboy than a child prodigy any day, I'd bet. He saw me going over his stuff and smiled.

"Were you ever out West, Mike?" he asked.

"I took some training in the desert when I was with Uncle Whiskers."

"Did you ever see a real cowboy?"

"Nope, but I bunked with one for six months. He used to wear high-heeled boots until the sergeant cracked down on him. Some card. Wanted to wear his hat in the shower. First thing he'd do when he'd get up in the morning was to put on his hat. He couldn't get used to one without a six-inch brim and was forever wanting to tip his hat to the Lieutenant instead of saluting."

Ruston chuckled. "Did he carry a six-shooter?"

"Naw, but he was a dead shot. He could pick the eyes out of a beetle at thirty yards."

The doctor broke up our chitchat by handing the kid some pills. He filled a box with them, printed the time to take them on the side and dashed off a prescription. He handed it to me. "Have this filled. One teaspoonful every two hours for twenty-four hours. There's nothing wrong with him except a slight nervous condition. I'll come back tomorrow to see Miss Malcom again. If her wound starts bleeding call me at once. I gave them both a sedative so they should sleep well until morning."

"Okay, Doctor, thanks." I gave him over to Harvey who ushered him to the door.

Roxy forced a smile. "Did you get them, Mike?"

"Forget about it," I said. "How did you get in the way?"

"I heard a gun go off and turned on the light. I guess I shouldn't have done that. I ran to the window but with the light on I couldn't see a thing. The next thing I knew something hit me in the shoulder. I didn't realize it was a bullet until I saw the hole in the window. That's when I screamed," she added sheepishly.

"I don't blame you, I'd scream too. Did you see the flash of the gun?"

Her head shook on the pillow. "I heard it I think, but it sounded sort of far off. I never dreamed . . ."

"You weren't hurt badly, that's one thing."

"Ruston, how . . ."

"Okay. You scared the hell out of him when you yelled. He's had too much already. That set him off. He was stiff as a fence post when I went in to him."

The sedative was beginning to take effect. Roxy's eyes closed sleepily. I whispered to Billy, "Get me a broom handle or something long and straight, will you?"

He went out and down the corridor. While I waited I looked at the hole the bullet had made, and in my mind pictured where Roxy had stood when she was shot. Billy came in with a long brass tube.

"Couldn't find a broom, but would this curtain rod do?"

"Fine," I said softly. Roxy was asleep now. "Stand over here by the window."

"What you going to do?"

"Figure out where that shot came from."

I had him hold the rod under his armpit and I sighted along the length of it, lining the tube up with the hole in the wall and the one in the window. This done I told him to keep it that way then threw the window up. More pieces of glass tinkled to the floor. I moved around behind him and peered down the rod.

I was looking at the base of the wall about where the two assailants had climbed the top. That put Junior out of it by a hundred feet. The picture was changing again, nothing balanced. It was like trying to make a mural with a kaleidoscope. Hell's bells. Neither of those two had shot at me, yet that was where the bullet came from. A silencer maybe? A wild shot at someone or a shot carefully aimed. With a .32 it would take an expert to hit the window from that range much less Roxy behind it. Or was the shot actually aimed at her?

"Thanks, Billy, that's all."

He lowered the rod and I shut the window. I called him to one side, away from the bed. "What is it, Mike?"

"Look, I want to think. How about you staying up here in the kid's room tonight. We'll fix some chair cushions up on the floor."

"Okay, if you say so."

"I think it will be best. Somebody will have to keep an eye on them in case they wake up, and Ruston has to take his medicine," I looked at the box, "every three hours. I'll give Harvey the prescription to be filled. Do you mind?"

"No, I think I'll like it here better'n the room downstairs."

"Keep the doors locked."

"And how. I'll push a chair up against them too."

I laughed. "I don't think there will be any more trouble for a while."

His face grew serious. "You can laugh, you got a rod under your arm."

"I'll leave it here for you if you want."

"Not me, Mike. One more strike and I'm out. If I get caught within ten feet of a heater they'll toss me in the clink. I'd sooner take my chances."

He began pulling the cushions from the chairs and I went out. Behind me the lock clicked and a chair went under the knob. Billy wasn't kidding. Nobody was going to get in there tonight.

chapter seven ▰▰▰▰▰▰▰▰

DOWNSTAIRS I DIALED the operator and asked for the highway patrol. She connected me with headquarters and a sharp voice crackled at me. "Sergeant Price, please."

"He's not here right now, is there a message?"

"Yeah, this is Mike Hammer. Tell him that Miss Malcom, the York kid's nurse, was shot through the shoulder by a thirty-two-caliber bullet. Her condition isn't serious and she'll be able to answer questions in the morning. The shot was fired from somewhere on the grounds but the one who fired it escaped."

"I got it. Anything else?"

"Yes, but I'll give it to him in person. Have they found any trace of Grange yet?"

"They picked up her hat along the shore of the inlet. Sergeant Price told me to tell you if you called."

"Thanks. They still looking for her?"

"A boat's grappling the mouth of the channel right now."

"Okay, if I get time I'll call back later." The cop thanked me and hung up. Harvey waited to see whether I was going out or not, and when I headed for the door got my hat.

"Will you be back tonight, sir?"

"I don't know. Lock the door anyway."

"Yes, sir."

I tooled my car up the drive and honked for Henry to come out and open the gates. Although there was a light on in his cottage, Henry didn't appear. I climbed out again and walked in the place. The gatekeeper was sound asleep in his chair, a paper folded across his lap.

After I shook him and swore a little his eyes opened, but not the way a waking person's do. They were heavy and dull, he was barely able to raise his head. The shock of seeing me there did more to put some life in him than the shaking. He blinked a few times and ran his hand over his forehead.

"I'm . . . sorry, sir. Can't understand myself . . . lately. These awful headaches, and going to sleep like that."

"What's the matter with you, Henry?"

"It's . . . nothing, sir. Perhaps it's the aspirin." He pointed to a bottle of common aspirin tablets on the table. I picked it up and looked at the label. A well-known brand. I looked again, then shook some out on my palm. There were no manufacturer's initials on the tablets at all. There were supposed to be, I used enough of them myself.

"Where did you get these, Henry?"

"Mr. York gave them to me last week. I had several fierce headaches. The aspirin relieved me."

"Did you take these the night of the kidnapping?"

His eyes drifted to mine, held. "Why, yes. Yes, I did."

"Better lay off them. They aren't good for you. Did you hear anything tonight?"

"No, I don't believe I did. Why?"

"Oh, no reason. Mind if I take some of these with me?" He

shook his head and I pocketed a few tablets. "Stay here," I said, "I'll open the gates."

Henry nodded and was asleep before I left the room. That was why the kidnapper got in so easily. That was why York left and the killer left and I left without being heard at the gate.

It was a good bet that someone substituted sleeping tablets for the aspirins. Oh, brother, the killer was getting cuter all the time.

But the pieces were coming together one by one. They didn't fit the slots, but they were there, ready to be assembled as soon as someone said the wrong word, or made a wrong move. The puzzle was closer to the house now, but it was outside, too. Who wanted Henry to be asleep while Ruston was snatched? Who wanted it so bad that his habits were studied and sleeping pills slipped into his aspirin bottle? If someone was that thorough they could have given him something to cause the headaches to start with. And who was in league with that person on the outside?

A wrong move or a wrong word. Someone would slip sometime. Maybe they just needed a little push. I had Junior where the hair was short now, that meant I had the old lady, too. Jump the fence to the other side now. Alice. She said *tsk, tsk* when I told them York was dead. Sweet thing.

I had to make another phone call to trooper headquarters to collect the list of addresses from the statements. Price still hadn't come in, but evidently he had passed the word to give me any help I needed, for there was no hesitation about handing me the information.

Alice lived west of town in a suburb called Wooster. It was little less than a crossroad off the main highway, but from the size of the mansions that dotted the estates it was a refuge of the wealthy. The town itself boasted a block of storefronts whose windows showed nothing but the best. Above each store was an apartment. The bricks were white, the metal work bright and new. There was an aura of dignity and pomp in the way they nestled there. Alice lived above the fur shop, two stores from the end.

I parked between a new Ford and a Caddy convertible. There were no lights on in Alice's apartment, but I didn't doubt that she'd want to see me. I slid out and went into the tiny foyer and looked at the bell. It was hers. For a good five seconds I held my finger on it, then opened the door and went up the steps. Before I reached the top, Alice, in the last stages of closing her robe, opened the door, sending a shaft of light in my face.

"Well, I'll be damned," she exclaimed. "You certainly pick an awful time to visit your friends."

"Aren't you glad to see me?" I grinned.

"Silly, come on in. Of course I'm glad to see you."

"I hate to get you up like this."

"You didn't. I was lying in bed reading, that's all." She paused just inside the door. "This isn't a professional visit, is it?"

"Hardly. I finally got sick and tired of the whole damn setup and decided to give my mind a rest."

She shut the door. "Kiss me."

I pecked her on the nose. "Can't I even take my hat off?"

"Oooo," she gasped, "the way you said that!"

I dropped my slicker and hat on a rack by the door and trailed her to the living room. "Have a drink?" she asked me.

I made with three fingers together. "So much, and ginger."

When she went for the ice I took the place in with a sweep of my head. Swell, strictly swell. It was better than the best Park Avenue apartment I'd ever been in, even if it was above a store. The furniture cost money and the oils on the wall even more. There were books and books, first editions and costly manuscripts. York had done very well by his niece.

Alice came back with two highballs in her hand. "Take one," she offered. I picked the big one. We toasted silently, she with the devil in her eyes, and drank.

"Good?"

I bobbed my head. "Old stuff, isn't it?"

"Over twenty years. Uncle Rudy gave it to me." She put her drink down and turned off the overhead lights, switching on a shaded table lamp instead. From a cabinet she selected an assortment of records and put them in the player. "Atmosphere," she explained impishly.

I didn't see why we needed it. When she had the lamp at her back the robe became transparent enough to create its own atmosphere. She was all woman, this one, bigger than I thought. Her carriage was seduction itself and she knew it. The needle came down and soft Oriental music filled the room. I closed my eyes and visualized women in scarlet veils dancing for the sultan. The sultan was me. Alice said something I didn't catch and left.

When she came back she was wearing the cobwebs. Nothing else.

"You aren't too tired tonight?"

"Not tonight," I said.

She sat down beside me. "I think you were faking the last time, and after all my trouble."

Her skin was soft and velvety-looking under the cobwebs, a

vein in her throat pulsed steadily. I let my eyes follow the contours of her shoulders and down her body. Impertinent breasts that mocked my former hesitance, a flat stomach waiting for the touch to set off the fuse, thighs that wanted no part of shielding cloth.

I had difficulty getting it out. "I *had* to be tired."

She crossed her legs, the cobwebs parted. "Or crazy," she added.

I finished the drink off in a hurry and held out the glass for another. I needed something to steady my nerves.

Ice clinked, glass rang against glass. She measured the whisky and poured it in. This time she pulled the coffee table over so she wouldn't have to get up again. The record changed and the gentle strains of a violin ran through the *Hungarian Rhapsody*. Alice moved closer to me. I could feel the warmth of her body through my clothes. The drinks went down. When the record changed again she had her head on my shoulder.

"Have you been working hard, Mike?"

"No, just legwork."

Her hair brushed my face; soft, lovely hair that smelled of jasmine. "Do you think they'll find her?"

I stroked her neck, letting my fingers bite in just a little. "I think so. Sidon is too small a town to try to hide in. Did you know her well?"

"Ummm. What? Oh, no. She was very distant to all of us."

More jasmine. She buried her face in my shoulder. "You're a thing yourself," I grinned. "Shouldn't you be wearing black?"

"No. It doesn't become me."

I blew in her ear. "No respect for the dead."

"Uncle never liked all those post-funeral displays anyway."

"Well, you should do something since you were his favorite niece. He left you a nice lump of cash."

She ran her fingers through my hair, bending my head close to hers. "Did he?" Lightly, her tongue ran over her lips, a pink, darting temptation.

"Uh-huh." We rubbed noses, getting closer all the time. "I saw his will. He must have liked you."

"Just you like me, Mike, that's all I want." Her mouth opened slightly. I couldn't take anymore. I grabbed her in my arms and crushed her lips against mine. She was a living heartbeat, an endless fire that burned hot and deep. Her arms went about me, holding tightly. Once, out of sheer passion, she bit me like a cat would bite.

She tore her mouth away and pressed it against my neck, then rubbed her shoulders from side to side against my chest until the cobwebs slipped down her arms and pinioned them there. I touched her flesh, bruised her until she moaned in painful ecstasy, demanding more. Her fingers fumbled with the buttons of my coat. Somehow I got it off and draped it over a chair, then she started on my tie. "So many clothes, Mike, you have so many clothes." She kissed me again.

"Carry me inside." I scooped her off the couch, cradling her in my arms, the cobwebs trailing beneath her. She pointed with her finger, her eyes almost closed. "In there."

No lights. The comforter was cool and fluffy. She told me to stay there and kissed my eyes shut. I felt her leave the bed and go into the living room. The record changed and a louder piece sent notes of triumph cascading into the room. Agonizing minutes passed waiting until she returned, bearing two half-full glasses on a tray like a gorgeous slave girl. Gone now were even the cobwebs.

"To us, Mike, and this night." We drank. She came to me with arms outstretched. The music came and went, piece after piece, but we heard nothing nor cared. Then there was no sound at all except the breathing.

It was well into morning before we stirred. Alice said no, but I had to leave. She coaxed, but now the sight of her meant less and I could refuse. I found my shoes, laced them, and tucked the covers under her chin.

"Kiss me." She held her mouth up.

"No."

"Just one?"

"All right, just one." She wasn't making it any too easy. I pushed her back against the pillows and said good night.

"You're so ugly, Mike. So ugly you're beautiful."

"Thanks, so are you." I waved and left her. In the living room I picked my coat up from the floor and dusted it off. My aim was getting worse, I thought I had it on the chair.

On the way out I dropped the night latch and shut the door softly. Alice, lovely, lovely Alice. She had a body out of this world. I ran down the stairs pulling on my slicker. Outside the sheen of the rain glimmered from the streets. I gave the brim of my hat a final tug and stepped out.

There were no flashes of light, no final moments of distortion. Simply that one sickening, hollow-sounding smash on the back of the head and the sidewalk came up and hit me in the face.

* * *

I was sick. It ran down my chin and wet my shirt. The smell of it made me sicker. My head was a huge balloon that kept getting bigger and bigger until it was taut and ready to burst into a thousand fragments. Something cold and metallic jarred my face repeatedly. I was cramped, horribly cramped. Even when I tried to move I stayed cramped. Ropes bit into my wrists leaving hempen splinters imbedded under the skin, burning like darts. Whenever the car hit a bump the jack on the floor would slam into my nose.

No one else was with me back there. The empty shoulder holster bit into my side. Nice going, I thought, you walked into that with your mouth open and your eyes shut. I tried to see over the back of the seat, but I couldn't raise myself that far. We turned off the smooth concrete of the highway and the roadway became sloshy and irregular. The jack bounced around more often. First I tried to hold it down with my forehead, but it didn't work, then I drew back from it. That was worse. The muscles in my back ached with the torture of the rack.

I got mad as hell. Sucker. That's what I was. Sucker. Someone was taking me for a damn newcomer at this racket. Working me over with a billy then tossing me in the back of a car. Just like the prohibition days, going for a ride. What the hell did I look like? I had been tied up before and I had been in the back of a car before, but I didn't stay there long. After the first time I learned my lesson. Boy Scout stuff, be prepared. Some son of a bitch was going to get his brains kicked out.

The car skidded to a stop. The driver got out and opened the door. His hands went under my armpits and I was thrown into the mud. Feet straddled me, feet that merged into a dark overcoat and a masked face, and a hand holding my own gun so that I was looking down the muzzle.

"Where is it?" the guy said. His voice carried an obvious attempt at disguise.

"What are you talking about?"

"Damn you anyway, what did you do with it? Don't try to stall me, what did you do with it? You hid it somewhere, you bastard, it wasn't in your pocket. Start talking or I'll shoot your head off!"

The guy was working himself up into a kill-crazy mood. "How do I know where it is if you won't tell me what you want," I snarled.

"All right, you bastard, get smart. You stuck your neck out once too often. I'll show you." He stuck the gun in his pocket and bent over, his hands fastening in my coat collar and under my arm. I didn't help him any. I gave him damn near two hundred pounds of dead weight to drag into the trees.

Twice the guy snagged himself in the brush and half-fell. He took it out on me with a slap in the head and a nasty boot in the ribs. Every once in a while he'd curse and get a better grip on my coat, muttering under his breath what was going to happen to me. Fifty yards into the woods was enough. He dropped me in a heap and dragged the rod out again, fighting for his breath. The guy knew guns. The safety was off and the rod was ready to spit.

"Say it. Say it now, damn you, or you'll never say it. What did you do with them . . . or should I work you over first?"

"Go to hell, you pig."

His hand went up quickly. The gun described a chopping arc toward my jaw. That was what I was waiting for. I grabbed the gun with both hands and yanked, twisting at the same time. He screamed when his shoulder jumped out of the socket, screamed again when I clubbed the edge of my palm against his neck.

Feet jabbed out and ripped into my side, he scrambled to get up. In the middle of it I lost the gun. I held on with one arm and sank my fist into him, but the power of the blow was lost in that awkward position.

But it was enough. He wrenched away, regained his feet and went scrambling through the underbrush. By the time I found the gun he was gone. Time again. If I had had only a minute more I could have chased him, but I hadn't had time to cut my feet loose. Yeah, I'd been on the floor of a car before with my hands tied behind my back. After that first time I have always carried a safety-razor blade slipped through the open seam into the double layer of cloth under my belt. It works nice, very handy. Someday I'd get tied up with my hands in front and I'd be stuck.

The knots were soft. A few minutes with them and I was on my feet. I tried to follow his tracks a few yards, but gave it up as a bad job. He had fallen into a couple of soft spots and left hunks of his clothes hanging on some tree limbs. He didn't know where he was going and didn't care. All he knew was that if he stopped and I caught him he'd die in that swamp as sure as he was born. It was almost funny. I turned around and waded back through the tangled underbrush, dodging snaky low-hanging branches that tried to whip my eyes out.

At least I had the car. My erstwhile friend was going to have to hoof it back to camp. I walked around the job, a late Chevvy sedan. The glove compartment was empty, the interior in need of a cleaning. Wrapped around the steering post was the ownership card with the owner's name: Mrs. Margaret Murphy, age fifty-two, address in Wooster, occupation, cook. A hell of a note, lifting some poor servant's buggy. I started it up. It would be back in town before it was missed.

When I turned around I plowed through the ruts of a country road for five minutes before reaching the main highway. My lights hit a sign pointing north to Wooster. I must have been out some time, it was over fifteen miles to the city. Once on the concrete I stepped on the gas. More pieces of the puzzle. I had something. I felt in my pocket; the later will was still there. Then what the hell was it? What was so almighty important that I'd been taken for a ride and threatened to make me talk?

Ordinarily I'm not stupid, on the contrary, my mind can pick up threads and weave them into whole cloth, but now I felt like putting on the dunce cap and sitting in the corner.

Nuts.

Twenty minutes to nine I was on the outskirts of Wooster. I turned down the first side street I came to, parked and got out of the car after wiping off any prints I might have made. I didn't know just how the local police operated, but I wasn't in the mood to do any explaining. I picked up the main road again and strode uphill toward Alice's. If she was up there was no indication of it. I recovered my hat from the foyer, cast one look up to the shuttered window and got in my own car. Things were breaking all around my head and I couldn't make any sense out of anything. It was like taking an exam with the answer sheet in front of you and failing because you forgot your glasses.

Going back to Sidon I had time to think. No traffic, just the steady hum of the engine and the sharp whirr of the tires. I was supposed to have something. I didn't have it. Yet certain parties were so sure I did have it they put the buzz on me. *It, it,* for Pete's sake, why don't they name the name? I had two wills and some ideas. They didn't want the wills and they didn't know about the ideas. Something else I might have picked up . . . or didn't pick up.

Of course. Of all the potted, tin-headed fools, I took the cake. Junior Ghent got more than the one will. That was all he had left after the two boys got done with him. They took something else, but whatever it was Junior didn't want me messing in his plans by telling me about it. They took it all right, but somewhere between me and the wall they dropped that important something, and figuring me to be smarter than I should have been, thought I must have found it.

I grinned at myself in the rearview mirror. I'm thick sometimes, but hit me often enough and I get the idea. I didn't even have to worry about Junior beating me to it. He *knew* they had it . . . he wouldn't plan on them dropping it. My curiosity was getting tired of thinking in terms of *its*. This had better be good or I was going to be pretty teed off.

Nice, sweet little case. Two hostile camps. Both fighting each other, both fighting me. In between a lot of people getting shot at and Ruston kidnapped to boot. Instead of a logical starting place it traveled in circles. I kicked the gas pedal a little harder.

Harvey was waiting with the door open when I turned up the drive. I waved him inside and followed the gravel drive to the spot where Junior had taken his shellacking. After a few false starts, I picked out the trail the two had taken across the yard and began tracking. Here and there a footprint was still visible in the soft sod; a twig broken off, flower stalks bent, a stone kicked aside. I let my eyes read over every inch of the path and six feet to the sides, too. If I knew what I was looking for it wouldn't have been so bad. As it was, it took me a good twenty minutes to reach the wall.

That was where it was. Lying face up in full view of anybody who cared to look. A glaring white patch against the shrubbery, a slightly crinkled, but still sealed envelope.

The IT.

Under my fingers I felt a handful of what felt like postcards. With a shrug I shoved the envelope unopened into my pocket. Item one. I poked around in the grass and held the shrubs aside with my feet. Nothing. I got down on the ground and looked across the grass at a low angle, hoping to catch the sunlight glinting off metal. The rough calculations I took from Roxy's room showed this to be the point of origin of the bullet, but nowhere could I see an empty shell. Hell, it could have been a revolver, then there would be no ejected shell. Or it could have been another gun instead of York's. Nuts there. A .32 is a defensive weapon. Anybody who wants to kill uses a .38 or better, especially at that range. I checked the distance to Roxy's window again. Just to hit the house would mean an elevation of thirty degrees. The lad who made the window was good. Better than that, he was perfect. Only he must have fired from a hole in the ground, because there was no place he could have hidden in this area. That is, if it wasn't one of the two who went over the wall.

I gave up and went back to the car and drove around to the front of the house.

Dutiful Harvey stared at the dirt on my clothes and said, "There's been an accident, sir?"

"You might call it that," I agreed pleasantly. "How is Miss Malcom?"

"Fine, sir. The doctor was here this morning and said she was not in any danger at all."

"The boy?"

"Still quite agitated after his experience. The doctor gave him another sedative. Parks has remained with them all this while. He hasn't set foot out of the room since you left."

"Good. Has anyone been here at all?"

"No, sir. Sergeant Price called several times and wants you to call him back."

"Okay, Harvey, thanks. Think you can find me something to eat? I'm starved."

"Certainly, sir."

I trotted upstairs and knocked on the door. Billy's voice cautiously inquired who it was, and when I answered pulled a chair away from the door and unlocked it.

"Hi, Billy."

"Hello, Mike . . . what the hell happened?"

"Somebody took me for a ride."

"Cripes, don't be so calm about it."

"Why not? The other guy has to walk back."

"Who?"

"I don't know yet."

Roxy was grinning at me from the bed. "Come over and kiss me, Mike." I gave her a playful tap on the jaw.

"You heal fast."

"I'll do better if you kiss me." I did. Her mouth was a field of burning poppies.

"Okay?"

"I want more."

"When you get better." I squeezed her hand. Before I went into Ruston's room I dusted myself off in front of the mirror. He had heard me come in and was all smiles.

"Hello, Mike. Can you stay here awhile this time?"

"Oh, maybe. Feeling good?"

"I feel all right, but I've been in bed too long. My back is tired."

"I think you'll be able to get up today. I'll have Billy take you for a stroll around the house. I'd do it myself only I have some work to clean up."

"Mike . . . how is everything coming? I mean . . ."

"Don't think about it, Ruston."

"That's all I can do when I lie here awake. I keep thinking of that night, and Dad and Miss Grange. If only there was something I could do I'd feel better."

"The best you can do is stay right here until everything's settled."

"I read in books . . . they were books of no account . . . but sometimes in cases like this the police used the victim as bait. That is, they exposed a person to the advantage of the criminal to see if the criminal would make another attempt. Do you think . . ."

"I think you have a lot of spunk to suggest a thing like that, but the answer is no. You aren't being the target for another snatch, not if I can help it. There're too many other ways. Now how about you hopping into your clothes and getting that airing." I peeled the covers back and helped him out of bed. For a few seconds he was a bit unsteady, but he settled down with a grin and went to the closet. I called Billy in and told him what to do. Billy wasn't too crazy about the idea, but it being daylight, and since I said that I'd stick around, he agreed.

I left the two of them there, winked at Roxy and went downstairs in time to lift a pair of sandwiches and a cup of coffee from Harvey's tray. Grunting my thanks through a mouthful of food I went into the living room and parked in the big chair. For the first time since I had been there a fire blazed away in the fireplace. Good old Harvey. I wolfed down the first sandwich and drowned it in coffee. Only then did I take the envelope out of my pocket. The flap was pasted on crooked, so it had to be the morning dew that had held it shut. I remembered that look on Junior's face when he had seen what was in it. I wondered if *it* was so good mine would look the same way.

I ran my finger under the flap and drew out six pictures.

Now I saw why Junior got so excited. Of the two women in the photos, the only clothes in evidence were shoes. And Myra Grange only had one on at that. Mostly, she wore a leer. A big juicy leer. Alice Nichols looked expectant. The pictures were pornography of the worst sort. Six of them, every one different, both parties fully recognizable, yet the views were of a candid sort, not deliberately posed. No, that wasn't quite it, they were posed, yet unposed . . . at least Myra Grange wasn't posing.

I had to study the shots a good ten minutes before I got the connection. What I had taken to be a border around the pictures done in the printing was really part of the shot. These pics were taken with a hidden camera, one concealed behind a dresser, with the supposed border being some books that did the concealing. A hidden camera and a time arrangement to trip it every so often.

No, Myra Grange wasn't posing, but Alice Nichols was. She had deliberately maneuvered for position each time so Grange was sure to be in perfect focus.

How nice, Alice. How very nicely you and York framed Grange. A frame to neutralize another frame. So?

I fired up a butt and shoved the pics back in my pocket. The outer rim of the puzzle was falling into the grooves in my mind now. Grange had an old will. Why? Would York have settled his entire estate on her voluntarily? Or could he have been forced into it? If Grange had something on her boss . . . something big . . . it had to be big . . . then she could call the squeeze play, and be reasonably sure of making a touchdown, especially when York didn't have long to go anyway. But sometime later York had found out about Grange and her habits and saw a way out. Damn, it was making sense now. He played up to Rhoda Ghent, plied her with gifts, then asked her to proposition Grange. She refused and he dropped her like a hot potato then started on Alice. York should have talked to her first. Alice had no inhibitions anyway, and a cut of York's will meant plenty of action to her. She makes eyes at Grange, Grange makes eyes at Alice and the show is on with the lights properly fed and the camera in position. Alice hands York the negatives, York has a showdown with Grange, threatening to make the pictures public and Grange folds up, yet holds onto the old will in the hope something would happen to make York change his mind. Something like a meat cleaver perhaps? It tied in with what Roxy told me. It could even explain the big play after the pictures. Junior had found out about them somehow, possibly from his sister. If he could get the shots in a law court he could prove how Alice came by her share and get her kicked right out of the show. At least then the family might have some chance to split the quarter of the estate. One hostile camp taken care of. Alice had to be the other. She had to have the pictures before Junior could get them . . . or anybody else for that matter. What could be better than promising a future split of her quarter if they agreed to get the pictures for her? That fit, too. Except that they came too late and saw Junior, knew that he had beaten them to it, so they waylay him, take the stuff and blow. Only I happened in at the wrong time and in the excitement the package gets lost.

I dragged heavily on the cigarette and ran over it again, checking every detail. It stayed the same way. I liked it. Billy and Ruston yelled to me on their way out, but I only waved to them. I was trying to reason out what it was that Grange had on York in the beginning to start a snowball as big as this one rolling downhill.

Flames were licking the top of their sooty cavern. Dante's own inferno, hot, roasting, destroying. It would have been so nice if I could only have known what York had hidden in the pillar of the fireplace. York's secret hiding place, that and the chair bottom. Why two places unless he didn't want to have all his eggs in one basket. Or was it another case of first things first? He could have put something in the fireplace years ago and not cared to change it.

With a show of impatience I flipped the remains of the butt into the flames, then stretched my legs out toward the fireplace. Secrets, secrets, so damn many secrets. I moved my head to one side so I could see the brick posts on the end of the smoke-blackened pit. It was well concealed, that cache. Curiosity again. I got up and looked it over more closely. Not a brick out of line, not a seam visible. Unless you saw it open you would never guess it to be there.

I went over every inch of it, rapping the bricks with my bare knuckles, but unlike wood, they gave off no sound. There had to be a trip for it somewhere. I looked again where the stone joined the wall. One place shoulder-high was smudged. I pressed.

The tiny door clicked and swung open.

Nice. It was faced with whole brick that joined with a fit in a recess of the concrete that the eye couldn't discern. To get my hand in I had to hold the door open against the force of a spring. I fished around, but felt nothing except cold masonry until I went to take my hand out. A piece of paper caught in the hinge mechanism brushed my fingers. I worked it out slowly, because at the first attempt to dislodge it, part of the paper crumbled to dust. When I let the door go it snapped shut, and I was holding a piece of an ancient newspaper.

It was brown with age, ready to fall apart at the slightest pressure. The print was faded, but legible. It bore the dateline of a New York edition, one that was on the stands October 9, fourteen years ago. What happened fourteen years ago? The rest of the paper had been stolen, this was a piece torn off when it was lifted from the well in the fireplace. A dateline, nothing but a fourteen-year-old dateline.

I'm getting old, I thought. These things ought to make an impression sooner. Fourteen years ago Ruston had been born.

chapter eight ▰▰▰▰▰▰▰▰▰▰▰▰

SOMEHOW, THE LIBRARY had an unused look. An ageless caretaker shuffled up the aisle carrying a broom and a dustpan, looking for something to sweep. The librarian, untrue to type, was busy painting her mouth an unholy red, and never looked up until I rapped on the desk. That got me a quick smile, a fast once-over, then an even bigger smile.

"Good morning. Can I help you?"

"Maybe. Do you keep back copies of New York papers?"

She stood up and smoothed out her dress around her hips where it didn't need smoothing at all. "This way, please."

I followed her at a six-foot interval, enough so I could watch her legs that so obviously wanted watching. They were pretty nice legs. I couldn't blame her a bit for wanting to show them off. We angled around behind ceiling-high bookcases until we came to a stairwell. Legs threw a light switch and took me downstairs. A musty odor of old leather and paper hit me on the last step. Little trickles of moisture beaded the metal bins and left dark stains on the concrete walls. A hell of a place for books.

"Here they are." She pointed to a tier of shelves, stacked with newspapers, separated by layers of cardboard. Together we located the old *Globe* editions then began peeling off the layers. In ten minutes we both looked like we had been playing in coal. Legs threw me a pout. "I certainly hope that whatever you're after is worth all this trouble."

"It is, honey," I told her, "it is. Keep your eyes open for October 9."

Another five minutes, then, "This it?"

I would have kissed her if she didn't have such a dirty face. "That's the one. Thanks."

She handed it over. I glanced at the dateline, then at the one in my hand. They matched. We laid the paper out on a reading desk and pulled on the overhead light. I thumbed through the leaves, turning them over as I scanned each column. Legs couldn't stand it any longer. "Please . . . what are you looking for?"

I said a nasty word and tapped the bottom of the page. "This."

"But . . ."

"I know. It's gone. Somebody ripped it out."

She said the same nasty word, then asked, "What was it?"

"Beats me, honey. Got any duplicates around?"

"No, we only keep one copy. There's rarely any call for them except from an occasional high-school history student who is writing a thesis on something or other."

"Uh-huh." Tearing that spot out wasn't going to do any good. There were other libraries. Somebody was trying to stall me for time. Okay, okay, I have all the time in the world. More time than you have, brother.

I helped her stack the papers back on their shelves before going upstairs. We both ducked into washrooms to get years of dust off our skin, only she beat me out. I half expected it anyway.

When we were walking toward the door I dropped a flyer. "Say, do you know Myra Grange?" Her breath caught and held. "Why . . . no. That is, isn't she the one . . . I mean with Mr. York?"

I nodded. She had made a good job of covering up, but I didn't miss that violent blush of emotion that surged into her cheeks at the mention of Grange's name. So this was why the vanishing lady spent so many hours in the library. "The same," I said. "Did she ever go down there?"

"No." A pause. "No, I don't think so. Oh, yes. She did once. She took the boy . . . Mr. York's son down there, but that was when I first came here. I went with them. They looked over some old manuscripts, but that was all."

"When was she here last?"

"Who are you?" She looked scared.

My badge was in my hand. She didn't have to read it. All she needed was the sight of the shield to start shaking. "She was here . . . about a week ago."

Very carefully, I looked at her. "No good. That was too long ago. Let's put it this way. When did you *see* her last?" Legs got the point. She knew I knew about Myra and guessed as much about her. Another blush, only this one faded with the fear behind it.

"A . . . a week ago, I told you." I thanked her and went out. Legs was lying through her teeth and I couldn't blame her.

The water was starting to bubble now. It wouldn't be long before it started to boil. Two things to do before I went to New York, one just for the pleasure of it. I made my first stop at a drugstore. A short, squat pharmacist came out from behind the glass partition and murmured his greetings. I threw the pills I had taken from Henry's bottle on the counter in front of me.

"These were being taken for aspirin," I said. "Can you tell me what they are?"

He looked at me and shrugged, picking up one in his fingers. He touched a cautious tongue to the white surface, then smelled it. "Not aspirin," he told me. "Have you any idea what they might be?"

"I'd say sleeping pills. One of the barbiturates." The druggist nodded and went back behind his glass. I waited perhaps five minutes before he came back again.

"You were right," he said. I threw two five-dollar bills on the counter and scooped up the rest of the pills. Very snazzy, killer, you got a lot of tricks up your sleeve. A very thorough guy. It was going to be funny when I had that killer at the end of my rod. I wondered if he was thorough enough to try to get rid of me.

Back and forth, back and forth. Like a swing. From kidnapping to murder to petty conniving and back to the kidnapping again. Run, run, run. Shuttle train stuff. Too many details. They were like a shroud that the killer was trying to draw around the original motive. That, there had to be. Only it was getting lost in the mess. It could have been an accident, this eruption of pointless crimes, or they might have happened anyway, or they could have been foreseen by the killer and used to his own advantage. No, nobody could be that smart. There's something about crime that's like a disease. It spreads worse than the flu once it gets started. It already had a good start when Ruston was kidnapped. It seemed like that was months ago, but it wasn't . . . just a few short days.

I reviewed every detail on my way to Wooster, but the answer always came up the same. Either I was dumb or the killer was pretty cagey. I had to find Mallory, I had to find Grange, I had to find the killer if he wasn't one of those two. So far all I found was a play behind the curtain.

Halfway there I gave up thinking and concentrated on the road. With every mile I'd gotten madder until I was chain-smoking right through my deck of butts. Wooster was alive this time. People walked along the streets in noisy contentment, limousines blared indignantly at lesser cars in front of them, and a steady stream

of traffic went in and out of the shop doors. There was plenty of
room in front of Alice's house. I parked the car and went into
the foyer, remembering vividly the crack on my skull.

This time the buzz was a short one. I took the stairs fast, but
she was faster. She stood in the door with a smile, ready to be
kissed. I said, "Hello, Alice," but I didn't kiss her. Her smile broke
nervously.

"What's the matter, Mike?"

"Nothing, kid, nothing at all. Why?"

"You look displeased about something." That was putting it
mildly.

I went inside without lifting my hat. Alice went to reach for
the decanter, but I stopped her by throwing the envelope on the
coffee table. "You were looking for these, I think."

"I?" She pulled one of the pictures out of the wrapper, then
shoved it back hastily, her face going white. I grinned.

Then I got nasty. "In payment for last night."

"You can go now."

"Uh-uh. Not yet." Her eyes followed mine to the ashtray. There
were four butts there, two of them had lipstick on them and the
other two weren't my brand.

Alice tried to scream a warning, but it never got past her lips.
The back of my hand caught her across the mouth and she rolled
into the sofa, gasping with the sting of the blow. I turned on my
heels and went to the bedroom and kicked the door open. William
Graham was sitting on the edge of the bed as nice as you please
smoking a cigarette. His face was scratched in a dozen places and
hunks torn out of his clothes from the briars in the woods.

Every bit of color drained out of his skin. I grabbed him before
he could stand up and smashed him right in the nose. Blood
spurted all over my coat. His arms flailed out, trying to push me
away, but I clipped him again on the nose, and again, until there
was nothing but a soggy, pulpy mass of flesh to hit. Then I went
to work on the rest of his puss. Slapping, punching, then a nasty
cut with the side of my hand. He was limp in my grasp, his head
thrown back and his eyes wide open. I let him go and he sagged
into a shapeless heap on the floor. It was going to take a thousand
dollars worth of surgery to make his face the same.

Alice had seen and heard. When I went into the living room
she was crouched in terror behind a chair. That didn't stop me.
I yanked her out; her dress split down the middle. "Lie to me,
Alice," I warned, "and you'll look just like him. Maybe worse.
You put him up to bumping me, didn't you?"

All she could do was nod soundlessly.

"You told him he wasn't in the will, but if he and his brother found the pictures and gave them to you you'd cut them in for your share?"

She nodded again. I pushed her back. "York made the will," I said. "It was his dough and I don't care what he did with it. Take your share and go to hell with it. You probably will anyway. Tell Arthur I'll be looking for him. When I find him he's going to look like his brother."

I left her looking eighty years old. William was moaning through his own blood when I went out the door. Good party. I liked it. There would be no more rides from that enemy camp. The redskins have left, vamoosed, departed.

There was only one angle to the Graham boys that I couldn't cover. Which one of them took the shot at Roxy and why? I'll be damned if I heard a shot. They didn't stop long enough to say boo far less than snap off a quickie. And they certainly would have shot at me, not toward the window. I wasn't sure of anything, but if there was money on the table I'd say that neither one had used a gun at all that night. It was details like that that creased me up. I had to make a choice one way or the other and follow it to a conclusion. All right, it was made. The Graham boys were out. Someone else fired it.

New York was a dismal sight after the country. I hadn't thought the grass and the trees with their ugly bilious color of green could have made such an impression on me. Somehow the crowded streets and the endless babble of voices gave me a dirty taste in my mouth. I rolled into a parking lot, pocketed my ticket, then turned into a chain drugstore on the stem. My first call was back to Sidon. Harvey answered and I told him to keep the kid in the room with Roxy and Billy until I got back and take any calls that came for me. My next dime got Pat Chambers, Captain of Homicide.

"Greetings, chum," I said, "this is Uncle Mike."

"It's about time you buzzed me. I was beginning to think you cooled off another citizen and were on the fly. Where are you?"

"Right off Times Square."

"Coming down?"

"No, Pat. I have some business to attend to. Look, how about meeting me on the steps of the library. West Forty-third Street entrance. It's important."

"Okay. Say in about half an hour. Will that do?"

I told him fine and hung up. Pat was tops in my book. A careful, crafty cop, and all cop. He looked more like a gentleman-about-town, but there it ended. Pat had a mind like an adding machine and a talent for police work backed up by the finest department in the world. Ordinarily a city cop has no truck with a private eye, but Pat and I had been buddies a long time with one exception. It was a case of mutual respect, I guess.

At a stand-up-and-eat joint I grabbed a couple dogs and a lemonade then beat it to the library in time to see Pat step out of a prowl car. We shook hands and tossed some remarks back and forth before Pat asked, "What's the story?"

"Let's go inside where we can talk."

We went through the two sets of doors and into the reading room. Holding my voice down I said, "Ever hear of Rudolph York, Pat?"

"So?" He had.

I gave him the story in brief, adding at the end, "Now I want to see what was attached to the rest of this dateline. It'll be here somewhere, and it's liable to turn up something you can help me with."

"For instance?"

"I don't know yet, but police records go back pretty far, don't they? What I want to know may have happened fourteen years ago. My memory isn't that good."

"Okay, let's see what we can dig up."

Instead of going through the regular library routine, Pat flashed his shield and we got an escort to where the papers were filed. The old gentleman in the faded blue serge went unerringly to the right bin, pulled out a drawer and selected the edition I wanted all on the first try. He pointed to a table and pulled out chairs for us. My hands were trembling with the excitement of it when I opened the paper.

It was there. Two columns right down the side of the page. Two columns about six-inches long with a photo of York when he was a lot younger. Fourteen years younger. A twenty-four-point heading smacked me between the eyes with its implications.

FATHER ACCUSES SCIENTIST OF BABY SWITCH

Herron Mallory, whose wife gave birth to a seven-pound boy that died two days later, has accused Rudolph York, renowned scientist, of switching babies. Mallory alleged that it was York's son, not his, who died. His claim is based on the fact that he saw his own child soon after

> birth, and recognized it again when it was shown to York, his own having been pronounced dead earlier. Authorities denied that such a mistake could have happened. Head Nurse, Rita Cambell, verified their denials by assuring both York and Mallory that she had been in complete charge during the two days, and recognized both babies by sight, confirming identification by their bracelets. Mrs. York died during childbirth.

I let out a long, low whistle. The ball had moved up to midfield. Pat suggested a follow-up and we brought out the following day's sheet. On page four was a small, one-column spread. It was stated very simply. Herron Mallory, a small-time petty thief and former bootlegger, had been persuaded to drop the charges against Rudolph York. Apparently it was suspected that he couldn't make any headway against a solid citizen like York in the face of his previous convictions. That was where it ended. At least for the time being.

York had a damn good reason then to turn green when Mallory's name was mentioned. Pat tapped the clipping. "What do you think?"

"It might be the real McCoy . . . then again it might be an accident. I can't see why York would pull a stunt like that."

"There're possibilities here. York was no young man when his son was born. He might have wanted an heir awfully bad."

"I thought of that, Pat, but there's one strike against it. If York was going to pull a switch, with his knowledge of genetics he certainly would have taken one with a more favorable family history, don't you think?"

"Yes, if he made the switch himself. But if it were left up to someone else . . . the nurse, for instance, the choice might have been pretty casual."

"But the nurse stated . . ."

"York was very wealthy, Mike."

"I get it. But there's another side too. Mallory, being a cheap chiseler, might have realized the possibilities in setting up a squawk after his own child died, and picked on York. Mallory would figure York would come across with some hard cash just to keep down that kind of publicity. How does that read?"

"Clever, Mike, very clever. But which one do you *believe?*"

The picture of York's face when he heard the name Mallory flashed across my mind. The terror, the stark terror; the hate. York the strong. He wouldn't budge an inch if Mallory had simply been trying some judicious blackmail. Instead, he would have been the one to bring the matter to the police. I said: "It was a switch, Pat."

"That puts it on Mallory."

I nodded. "He must have waited a long time for his chance. Waited until the kid was worth his weight in gold to York and the public, then put the snatch on him. Only he underestimated the kid and bungled the job. When York went to Grange's place, Mallory followed him, thinking that York might have figured where the kidnapping came from and split his skull."

"Did you try to trace the cleaver, Mike?"

"No, it was the kind you could buy in any hardware store, and it was well handled, besides. A tool like that would be nearly impossible to trace. There was no sense in my fooling around with it. Price will track it down if it's possible. Frankly, I don't think it'll work. What's got me now is why someone ripped out this clipping in the Sidon library. Even as a stall it wouldn't mean much."

"It's bound to have a bearing."

"It'll come, it'll come. How about trying to run down Mallory for me? Think you can find anything on him?"

"We should, Mike. Let's go down to headquarters. If he was pinched at all we'll have a record of it."

"Roger." We were lucky enough to nab a cab waiting for the red light on the corner of Fifth and Forty-second. Pat gave him the downtown address and we leaned back into the cushions. Fifteen minutes later we got out in front of an old-fashioned red brick building and took the elevator to the third floor. I waited in an office until Pat returned bearing a folder under his arm. He cleared off the desk with a sweep of his hand and shook the contents out on the blotter.

The sheaf was fastened with a clip. The typewritten notation read, Herron Mallory. As dossiers go, it wasn't thick. The first page gave Mallory's history and record of his first booking. Age, 20 in 1927; born in New York City of Irish-Russian parents. Charged with operating a vehicle without a license. That was the starter. He came up on bootlegging, petty larceny; he was suspected of participating in a hijack-killing and a holdup. Plenty of charges, but a fine list of cases suspended and a terse "not convicted" written across the bottom of the page. Mr. Mallory either had a good lawyer or friends where it counted. The last page bore his picture, a profile and front view shot of a dark fellow slightly on the thin side with eyes and mouth carrying an inbred sneer.

I held it under the light to get a better look at it, studying it from every angle, but nothing clicked.

Pat said, "Well?"

"No good, chum. Either I never saw him before or the years have changed him a lot. I don't know the guy from Adam."

He held out a typewritten report. One that had never gotten past a police desk. I read it over. In short, it was the charges that Mallory had wanted filed against York for kidnapping his kid. No matter who Mallory was or had been, there was a note of sincerity in that statement. There was also a handwritten note on hospital stationery from Head Nurse Rita Cambell briefly decrying the charge as absolutely false. There was no doubt about it. Rita Cambell's note was aggressive and assuring enough to convince anyone that Mallory was all wet. Fine state of affairs. I had never participated in the mechanics of becoming a father, but I did know that the male parent was Johnny-the-Gom as far as the hospital was concerned. He saw his baby maybe once for two minutes through a tiny glass plate set in the door. Sure, it would be possible to recognize your child even in that time, but all babies do look alike in most ways. To the nurse actually in charge of the child's entire life, however, each one has the separate identity of a person. It was unlikely that she would make a mistake . . . unless paid for it. Damn, it *could* happen unless you knew nurses. Doubt again. Nurses had a code of ethics as rigid as a doctor's. Any woman who gave her life to the profession wasn't the type that would succumb to a show of long green.

Hell, I was getting all balled up. First I was sure it was a switch, now I wasn't so sure. Pat had seen the indecision in my face. He can figure things, too. "There it is, Mike. I can't do anything more because it's outside my jurisdiction, but if I can help you in any way, say the word."

"Thanks, kid. It really doesn't make much difference whether it was a switch or not. Someplace Mallory figures in it. Before I can go any further I'll have to find either Mallory or Grange, but don't ask me how. If Price turns up Grange I'll get a chance to talk to her, but if Dilwick is the one I'll be out in the cold."

Pat looked sour. "Dilwick ought to be in jail."

"Dilwick ought to be dead. He's a bastard."

"He's still the law, though, and you know what that means."

"Yeah."

Pat started stuffing the papers back in the folder, but I stopped him. "Let me take another look at them, will you?"

"Sure."

I rifled through them quickly, then shook my head.

"Something familiar?"

"No . . . I don't think so. There's something in there that's ringing a bell, but I can't put my finger on it. Oh, nuts, put 'em away."

We went downstairs together and shook hands in the doorway. Pat hailed a cab and I took the next one up to Fifty-fourth and Eighth, then out over to the parking lot. The day was far from being wasted; I was getting closer to the theme of the thing. On top of everything else there was a possible baby switch. It was looking up now. Here was an underlying motive that was as deep and unending as the ocean. The groping, the fumbling after ends that led nowhere was finished. This was meat that could be eaten. But first it had to be chewed; chewed and ground up fine before it could be swallowed.

My mind was hammering itself silly. The dossier. What was in the dossier? I saw something there, but what? I went over it carefully enough; I checked everything against everything else, but what did I forget?

The hell with it. I shoved the key in the ignition and stepped on the starter.

chapter nine ◼◼◼◼◼◼◼◼◼◼

GOING BACK TO Sidon I held it down to a slow fifty, stopping only once for a quick bite and a tank of gas. Someday I was going to get me a decent meal. Someday. Three miles from the city I turned off the back road to a clover leaf, then swung onto the main artery. When I reached the state police headquarters I cut across the concrete and onto the gravel.

For once Price was in when I wanted him.

So was Dilwick.

I said hello to Price and barely nodded to Dilwick.

"You lousy slob!" he muttered softly.

"Shut up, pig."

"Maybe you both better shut up," Price put in quietly. I threw my hat on the desk and pushed a butt between my lips. Price waited until I lit it, then jerked his thumb toward the fat cop.

"He wants words with you, Mike."

"Let's hear 'em," I offered.

"Not here, wise guy. I think you'd do better at the station. I don't want to be interrupted."

That was a nasty dig at Price, and the sergeant took it right up. "Forget that stuff," he barked, "while he's here he's under my jurisdiction. Don't forget it."

For a minute I thought Dilwick was going to swing and I was hoping he would. I'd love to be in a two-way scramble over that guy. The odds were too great. He looked daggers at Price. "I won't forget it," he repeated.

Price led off. "Dilwick says you broke into the Grange apartment and confiscated something of importance. What about it, Mike?"

I let Dilwick have a lopsided grin. "Did I?"

"You know damn well you did! You'd better . . ."

"How do you know it was important?"

"It's gone, that's reason enough."

"Hell."

"Wait a minute, Mike," Price cut in. "What did you take?"

I saw him trying to keep his face straight. Price liked this game of baiting Dilwick.

"I could say nothing, pal, and he couldn't prove a thing. I bet you never found any prints of mine, did you, Dilwick?" The cop's face was getting redder. ". . . and the way you had that building bottled up nobody *should* have been able to get in, should they?" Dilwick would split his seams if I kept it up any longer. "Sure, I was there, so what? I found what a dozen of you missed."

I reached in my pocket and yanked out the two wills. Dilwick reached a shaking hand for them but I passed them to Price. "This old one was in Grange's apartment. It isn't good because this is the later one. Maybe it had better be filed someplace."

Dilwick was watching me closely. "Where did the second one come from?"

"Wouldn't you like to know?"

I was too slow. The back of Dilwick's hand nearly rocked my head off my shoulders. The arm of a chair hit my side and before I could spill over into it Dilwick had my shirt front. Price caught his hand before he could swing again.

I kicked the chair away and pulled free as Price stepped between us. "Let me go, Price!" I yelled.

"Damn it, I said to turn it off!"

Dilwick backed off reluctantly. "I'll play that back to you,

Dilwick," I said. Nobody was pulling that trick on me and getting by with it. It's a wonder he had the nerve to start something after that last pasting I gave him. Maybe he was hoping I'd try to use my rod . . . that would be swell. He could knock me off as nice as anything and call it police business.

"Maybe you'll answer the next time you're spoken to, Hammer. You've pulled a lot of shady deals around here lately and I'm sick of it. As for you, Price, you're treating him like he's carrying a badge. You've got me hogtied, but that won't last long if I want to work on it."

The sergeant's voice was almost a whisper. "One day you're going to go too far. I think you know what I mean."

Evidently Dilwick did. His lips tightened into a thin line and his eyes blazed, but he shut up just the same. "Now if you have anything to say, say it properly."

With an obvious attempt at controlling his rage, Dilwick nodded. He turned to me again. "Where did you get the other will?"

"Wouldn't you like to know?" I repeated.

"You letting him get away with this, Price?"

The trooper was on the spot. "Tell him, Mike."

"I'll tell you, Price. He can listen in. I found it among York's personal effects."

For a full ten minutes I stood by while the two of them went over the contents of the wills. Price was satisfied with a cursory examination, but not so Dilwick. He read every line, then reread them. I could see the muscles of his mouth twitch as he worked the thing out in his mind. No, I was not underestimating Dilwick one bit. There wasn't much that went on that he didn't know about. Twice, he let his eyes slide off the paper and meet mine. It was coming. Any minute now.

Then it was here. "I could read murder into this," he grated.

Price turned sharply. "Yes?"

"Hammer, I think I'm going to put you on the spot."

"Swell. You'd like that. Okay, go ahead."

"Pull up your ears and get a load of this, Price. This punk and the Nichols dame could make a nice team. Damn nice. You didn't think I'd find out about those pictures, did you, Hammer? Well, I did. You know what it looks like to me? It looks like the Nichols babe blackmailed Grange into making York change his will. Let York see those shots and Grange's reputation would be shot to hell, she'd be fired and lose out on the will to boot. At least if she came through on the deal, all she'd lose was the will."

I nodded. "Pretty, but where do I come in?"

"Right now. Grange got hold of those pictures somehow. Only Nichols pulls a fast one and tells York that Grange was the one who was blackmailing her. York takes off for Grange's apartment in a rage because he had a yen for his pretty little niece, only Grange bumps him. Then Nichols corners you and you bump Grange and get the stuff off her, and the will. Now you turn it up, Nichols comes into a wad of cash and you split it."

It wasn't as bad as I thought. Dilwick had squeezed a lot of straight facts out of somebody, only he was putting it together wrong. Yeah, he had gotten around, all right. He had reached a lot of people to get that much and he'd like to make it stick.

Price said, "What about it, Mike?"

I grinned. "He's got a real sweet case there." I looked at the cop. "How're you going to prove it?"

"Never mind," he snarled, "I will, I will. Maybe I ought to book you right now on what I have. It'll hold up and Price knows it, too."

"Uh-uh. It'll hold up . . . for about five minutes. Did you find Grange yet?"

He said nothing.

"Nuts," I laughed, "no corpus delicti, no Mike Hammer."

"Wrong, Hammer. After a reasonable length of time and sufficient evidence to substantiate death, a corpse can be assumed."

"He's right, Mike."

"Then he's got to shoot holes in my alibi, Price. I have a pretty tight one."

"Where did you go after you left Alice's apartment the other night?" Brother, I should have guessed it. Dilwick had put the bee on the Graham kid and the bastard copped a sneak. It was ten to one he told Dilwick he hadn't seen me.

That's what I get for making enemies. If the Graham kid thought he could put me on the spot he'd do it. So would Alice for that matter.

But there were still angles. "Go ahead and work on my alibi, Dilwick. You know what it is. Only I'll give you odds that I can make your witness see the light sooner than you can."

"Not if you're in the can."

"First get me there. I don't think you can. Even if you did a good lawyer could rip those phonies apart on the stand and you know it. You're stalling, Dilwick. What're you scared of? Me? Afraid I'll put a crimp in your doings?"

"You're asking for it, punk."

Price came back into the argument. "Skip it, Dilwick. If you have the goods on him then present it through the regular channels, only don't slip up. Let you and your gang go too far and there'll be trouble. I'm satisfied to let Mr. Hammer operate unhampered because I'm familiar with him . . . and you, too."

"Thanks, pal."

Dilwick jammed his hat on and stamped out of the room. If I wanted to get anywhere I was going to have to act fast, because my fat friend wasn't going to let any grass grow under his feet finding enough dope to toss me in the clink. When the door slammed I let Price have my biggest smile. He smiled right back.

"Where've you been?"

"New York. I tried to get you before I left but you weren't around."

"I know. We've had a dozen reports of Grange being seen and I've been running them down."

"Any luck?"

"Nothing. A lot of mistaken identities and a few cranks who wanted to see the police in action. What did you get?"

"Plenty. We're back to the kidnapping again. This whole pot of stew started there and is going to end there. Ruston wasn't York's kid at all. His died in childbirth and another was switched to take its place. The father of the baby was a small-time hoodlum and tried to make a complaint but was dissuaded along the line. All very nicely covered up, but I think it's a case of murder that's been brewing for fourteen years."

During the next half hour I gave him everything I knew, starting with my trip to the local library. Price was a lot like Pat. He sat there saying nothing, taking it all in and letting it digest in his mind. Occasionally he would nod, but never interrupted until I had finished.

He said: "That throws the ball to this Mallory character."

"Roger, and the guy is completely unknown. The last time he showed up was a few days after the switch took place."

"A man can change a lot in fourteen years."

"That's what I'm thinking," I agreed. "The first thing we have to do is concentrate on locating Grange. Alive or dead she can bring us further up to date. She didn't disappear for nothing."

"All right, Mike, I'll do my share. I still have men dragging the channel and on the dragnet. What are you going to do?"

"There are a few members of the loyal York clan that I'd like to see. In the meantime do you think you can keep Dilwick off my neck?"

"I'll try, but I can't promise much. Unfortunately, the law is made up of words which have to be abided more by the letter than the spirit therein, so to speak. If I can sidetrack him I will, but you had better keep him under observation if you can. I don't have to tell you what he's up to. He's a stinker."

"Twice over. Okay, I'll keep in touch with you. Thanks for the boost. The way things are I'm going to have to be sharp on my end to beat Dilwick out of putting me up at the expense of the city."

Dusk had settled around the countryside like a gray blanket when I left headquarters. I stepped into the car and rolled out the drive to the highway. I turned toward the full glow that marked the lights of Sidon and pulled into the town at suppertime. I would have gone straight to the estate if I hadn't passed the library which was still lit up.

It was just an idea, but I've had them before and they'd paid off. I slammed the brakes on, backed up and parked in front of the building. Inside the door I noticed the girl at the desk, but she wasn't the same one I had spoken to before. This one had legs like a bridge lamp. Thinking that perhaps Legs was in one of the reading rooms, I toured the place, but aside from an elderly gentleman, two schoolteacher types and some kids, the place was empty.

Just to be sure I checked the cellar, too, but the light was off and I didn't think she'd be down there in the dark even if Grange was with her. Not with that musty-tomb odor anyway.

The girl at the desk said, "Can I help you find something, sir?"

"Maybe you can."

"What book was it?"

I tried to look puzzled. "That is what I forgot. The girl that was here this morning had it all picked out for me. Now I can't find her."

"Oh, you mean Miss Cook?"

"Yeah," I faked, "that's the one. Is she around now?"

This time the girl was the one to be puzzled. "No, she isn't. She went home for lunch this afternoon and never returned. I came on duty early to replace her. We've tried to locate her all over town, but she seems to have dropped from sight. It's so very strange."

It was getting hot now, hotter than ever. The little bells were going off inside my skull. Little bells that tinkled and rang and chimed and beat themselves into shattered pieces of nothing. It was getting hotter, this broth, and I was holding onto the handle.

"This Miss Cook. Where does she live?"

"Why, two blocks down on Snyder Avenue. Shall I call her apartment again? Perhaps she's home now."

I didn't think she'd have any luck, but I said, "Please do."

She lifted the receiver and dialed a number. I heard the buzz of the bell on the other end, then the voice of the landlady answering. No, Miss Cook hadn't come in yet. Yes, she would tell her to call as soon as she did. Yes. Yes. Good night.

"She isn't there."

"So I gathered. Oh, well, she's probably had one of her boy friends drop in on her. I'll come back tomorrow."

"Very well, I'm sorry I couldn't help you."

Sorry, everybody was being sorry. Pretty soon somebody was going to be so sorry they died of it. Snyder Avenue was a quiet residential section of old brownstone houses that had undergone many a face-lifting and emerged looking the same as ever. On one corner a tiny grocery store was squeezed in between buildings. The stout man in the dirty white apron was taking in some boxes of vegetables as he prepared to close up shop. I drew abreast of him and whistled.

When he stopped I asked, "Know a Miss Cook? She's the librarian. I forgot which house it was."

"Yeah, sure." He pointed down the block. "See that car sitting under the streetlight? Well the house just past it and on the other side is the one. Old Mrs. Baxter is the landlady and she don't like noise, so you better not honk for her."

I yelled my thanks and went up the street and parked behind the car he had indicated. Except for the light in the first floor front, the place was in darkness. I ran up the steps and looked over the doorbell. Mrs. Baxter's name was there, along with four others, but only one bell.

I pushed it.

She must have been waiting for me to make up my mind, because she came out like a jack-in-the-box.

"Well?"

"Mrs. Baxter?"

"That's me."

"I'm looking for Miss Cook. They . . ."

"Who ain't been looking for her. All day long the phone's been driving me crazy, first one fellow then another. When she gets back here I'm going to give her a good piece of my mind."

"May I come in, Mrs. Baxter?"

"What for? She isn't home. If she didn't leave all her things here I'd say she skipped out. Heaven only knows why."

I couldn't stand there and argue with her. My wallet slipped into my palm and I let her see the glint of the metal. Badges are wonderful things even when they don't mean a thing. Her eyes went from my hand to my face before she moistened her lips nervously and stood aside in the doorway.

"Has . . . has there been trouble?"

"We don't know." I shut the door and followed her into the living room. "What time did she leave here today?"

"Right after lunch. About a quarter to one."

"Does she always eat at home?"

"Only her lunch. She brings in things and . . . you know. At night she goes out with her boy friends for supper."

"Did you see her go?"

"Yes. Well, no. I didn't see her, but I heard her upstairs and heard her come down. The way she always takes the stairs two at a time in those high heels I couldn't very well not hear her."

"I see. Do you mind if I take a look at her room? There's a chance that she might be involved in a case we're working on and we don't want anything to happen to her."

"Do you think . . ."

"Your guess is as good as mine, Mrs. Baxter. Where's her room?"

"Next floor in the rear. She never locks her door so you can go right in."

I nodded and went up the stairs with the old lady's eyes boring holes in my back. She was right about the door. It swung in when I turned the knob. I shut the door behind me and switched on the light, standing there in the middle of the room for a minute taking it all in. Just a room, a nice, neat girl's room. Everything was in its place, nothing was disarranged. The closet was well stocked with clothes including a fairly decent mink coat inside a plastic bag. The drawers in the dresser were the same way. Tidy. Nothing gone.

Son of a bitch, *she* was snatched too! I slammed the drawer shut so hard a row of bottles went over. Why didn't I pick her up sooner. She was Myra Grange's alibi! Of course! And somebody was fighting pretty hard to keep Myra Grange's face in the mud. She didn't skip out on her own . . . not and leave all her clothes here. She went out that front door on her way back to work and she was picked up somewhere between here and the library. Fine, swell. I'd made a monkey of myself by letting things slide just a little longer. I wasn't the only one who knew that she and Grange were on more than just speaking terms. That somebody was either following me around or getting there on his own hook.

A small desk and chair occupied one corner of the room beside the bed. A small letter-writing affair with a flap front was on the desk. I pulled the cover down and glanced at the papers neatly placed in the pigeonholes. Bills, receipted bills. A few notes and some letters. In the middle of the blotter a writing tablet looked at me with a blank stare.

The first three letters were from a sailor out of town. Very factual letters quite unlike a sailor. Evidently a relative. Or a sap. The next letter was the payoff. I breezed through it and felt the sweat pop out on my face. Paragraph after paragraph of lurid, torrid love . . . words of endearment . . . more love, exotic, fantastic.

Grange had signed only her initials at the bottom.

When I slid the letter back I whistled through my teeth. Grange had certainly gone whole hog with her little partner. I would have closed the desk up after rifling through the rest of the stuff if I hadn't felt that squeegy feeling crawling around my neck. It wasn't new. I had had it in Pat's office.

Something I was supposed to remember. Something I was supposed to see. Damn. I went back through the stuff, but as far as I could see there wasn't anything there that I had seen before I came into the room. Or was there?

Roger . . . there was! It was in my hand. I was staring at Grange's bold signature. It was the handwriting that I had recognized. The first time I had seen it was on some of her papers I had taken from that little cache in her apartment. The next time I had seen it was on the bottom of a statement certifying that Ruston was York's son and not Mallory's, only that time the signature read *Rita Cambell.*

It hit me like a pile driver, hard, crushing. It had been dangling in front of my face all this time and I hadn't seen it. But I wasn't alone with the knowledge, hell no. Somebody else had it too, that's why Grange was dead or missing and Cook on the lam.

Motive, at last the motive. I stood alone in the middle of the room and spun the thing around in my mind. This was raw, bitter motive. It was motive that incited kidnapping and caused murder and this was proof of it. The switch, the payoff. York taking Grange under his wing to keep the thing quiet. Crime that touched off crime that touched off more crime like a string of firecrackers. When you put money into it the thing got bigger and more scrambled than ever.

I had gotten to the center of it. The nucleus. Right on the target were Ruston and Grange. Somebody was aiming at both of them.

Winged the kid and got Grange. Mallory, but who the hell was he? Just a figure known to have existed, and without doubt still existing.

I needed bait to catch this fish, yet I couldn't use the kid; he had seen too much already. That is, unless he was willing. I felt like a heel to put it up to him. But it was that or try to track Grange down. Senseless? I didn't know. Maybe a dozen cops *had* dragged the river, and maybe the dragnet *was* all over the state, but maybe they were going at it the wrong way. Sure, maybe it would be best to try for Grange. She was bound to have the story if anyone had, and I wouldn't be taking a chance with the kid's neck either.

Mrs. Baxter was waiting for me at the foot of the stairs, wringing her hands like a nervous hen. "Find anything?" she asked.

I nodded. "Evidence that she expected to come back here. She didn't just run off."

"Oh, dear."

"If anyone calls, try to get their names, and keep a record of all calls. Either Sergeant Price of the state police will check on it or me personally. Under no conditions give out the information to anyone else, understand?"

She muttered her assent and nodded. I didn't want Dilwick to pull another fasty on me. As soon as I left, all the lights on the lower floor blazed on. Mrs. Baxter was the scary type, I guess.

I swung my heap around in a U-turn, then got on the main street and stopped outside a drugstore. My dime got me police headquarters and headquarters reached Price on the radio. We had a brief chitchat through the medium of the desk cop and I told him to meet me at the post in fifteen minutes.

Price beat me there by ten feet and came over to see what was up.

"You have the pictures of Grange's car after it went in the drink?"

"Yeah, inside, want to see them?"

"Yes."

On the way in I told him what had happened. The first thing he did was go to the radio and put out a call on the Cook girl. I supplied the information the best I could, but my description centered mainly about her legs. They were things you couldn't miss. For a few minutes Price disappeared into the back room and I heard him fiddling around with a filing cabinet.

He came out with a dozen good shots of the wrecked sedan. "If you don't mind, tell me what you're going to do with these?"

"Beats me," I answered. "It's just a jumping-off place. Since she's still among the missing she can still be found. This is where she was last seen apparently."

"There've been a lot of men looking for her."

I grinned at him. "Now there's going to be another." Each one of the shots I went over in detail, trying to pick out the spot where it went in, and visualizing just how it turned in the air to land like it did. Price watched me closely, trying to see what I was getting at.

"Price . . ."

"Yes."

"When you pulled the car out, was the door on the right open?"

"It was, but the seat had come loose and was jammed in the doorway. She would have had some time trying to climb out that way."

"The other door was open too?"

His head bobbed. "The lock had snapped when the door was wrenched open, probably by the force of hitting the water, although being on the left, it could have happened when her car was forced off the road."

"Think she might have gotten out that way?"

"Gotten out . . . or floated out?"

"Either one."

"More like it was the other way."

"Was the car scratched up much?"

The sergeant looked thoughtful. "Not as much as it should have been. The side was punched in from the water, and the front fender partially crumpled where it hit the bottom, but the only new marks were short ones along the bottom of the door and on the very edge of the fender, and at that we can't be sure that they didn't come from the riverbed."

"I get it," I said. "You think that she was scared off the road. I've seen enough women drivers to believe that, even if she was only half a dame. Why not? Another car threatening to slam into her would be reason enough to make her jump the curb. Well, it's enough for me. If she was dead there wouldn't be much sense keeping her body hidden, and if it weren't hidden it would have shown up by now, so I'm assuming that Grange is still alive somewhere and if she's alive she can be found."

I tossed the sheaf of pictures back to Price. "Thanks, chum. No reflection on any of you, but I think you've been looking for Grange the wrong way. You've been looking for a body."

He smiled a bit and we said good night. What had to be done

had to wait until morning . . . the first thing in the morning. I tooled my car back to town and called the estate. Harvey was glad to hear from me, yes, everything was all right. Billy had been in the yard with Ruston all day and Miss Malcom had stayed in her room. The doctor had been there again and there was nothing to worry about. Ruston had been asking for me. I told Harvey to tell the kid I'd drop up as soon as I could and not to worry. My last instructions still went. Be sure the place was locked up tight, and that Billy stayed near the kid and Roxy. One thing I did make sure of. Harvey was to tell the gatekeeper what was in the bottle that he thought contained aspirin.

When I hung up I picked up another pack of butts, a clean set of underwear, shirt and socks in a dry goods store, then threw the stuff in the back of the car and drove out around town until I came to the bay. Under the light of the half-moon it was black and shimmering, an oily, snaky tongue that searched the edges of the shore with frightened, whimpering sounds. The shadows were black as pitch, not a soul was on the streets. Three-quarters of a mile down the road one lone window winked with a yellow, baleful eye.

I took advantage of the swath Grange had cut in the restraining wire and pulled up almost to the brink of the drop-off, changed my mind, pulled out and backed in, just in case I had to get out of there in a hurry. When I figured I was well set I opened my fresh deck of butts, chain-smoked four of them in utter silence, then closed up the windows to within an inch of the top, pulled my hat down over my eyes and went to sleep.

The sun was fighting back the night when I woke up. Outside the steamed-up windows a gray fog was drifting up from the waters, coiling and uncoiling until the tendrils blended into a low-hanging blanket of haze that hung four feet over the ground.

It looked cold. It was cold. I was going to be kicking myself a long time if nothing came of this. I stripped off my clothes throwing them into the car until I was standing shivering in my underwear. Well, it was one way to get a bath, anyway. I could think of better ways.

A quick plunge. It had to be quick or I would change my mind. I swam out to the spot I had fixed in my mind; the spot where Grange's car had landed. Then I stopped swimming. I let myself go as limp as possible, treading water just enough to keep my head above the surface. You got it. I was supposed to be playing dead, or almost dead. Half knocked out maybe. The tide was the same, I had checked on that. If this had been just another river it wouldn't have mattered, but this part was more an inlet than anything else. It emptied and filled with the tides, having its own peculiarities and eddies. It swirled and washed around objects long sunk in the cove of the bottom. I could feel it tug at my feet, trying to drag me down with little monkey hands, gentle, tugging hands that would mean nothing to a swimmer, but could have a noticeable effect on someone half dazed.

Just a few minutes had passed and I was already out of sight of the car around the bend. Here the shores drew away as the riverbed widened until it reached the mouth of the inlet opening into the bay. I thought that I was going to keep right on drifting by, and had about made up my mind to quit all this damn foolishness when I felt the first effect of the eddy.

It was pulling me toward the north shore. A little thrill of excitement shot through me, and although I was numb I felt an emotional warmth dart into my bones. The shore was closer now. I began to spin in a slow, tight circle as something underneath me kicked up a fuss with the water. In another moment I saw what was causing the drag. A tiny U-bend in the shoreline jutted out far enough to cause a suction in the main flow and create enough disturbance to pull in anything not too far out.

Closer . . . closer . . . I reached out and got hold of some finger-thick reeds and held on, then steadied myself with one hand in the mud and clambered up on the shore. There were no tracks save mine, but then again there wouldn't be. Behind me the muck was already filling in the holes my feet had made. I parted the reeds, picking my way through the remains of shellfish and stubble. They were tough reeds, all right. When I let them go they snapped back in place like a whip. If anyone had come out of the river it would have been here. It *had* to be here!

The reeds changed into scrub trees and thorny brush that clawed at my skin, raking me with their needlepoints. I used a stick as a club and beat at them, trying to hold my temper down. When they continued to eat their way into my flesh I cursed them up and down.

But the next second I took it all back. They were nice briars. Beautiful briars. The loveliest briars I had ever seen, because one of them was sporting part of a woman's dress.

I could have kissed that torn piece of fabric. It was stained, but fresh. And nobody was going to go through those reeds and briars except the little sweetheart I was after. This time I was gentler with the bushes and crawled through them as best I could without getting myself torn apart. Then the brush gave way to grass. That green stuff felt better than a Persian rug under my sore feet. I sat down on the edge of the clearing and picked the thorns out of my skin.

Then I stood up and shoved the tail end of my T-shirt down into my shorts. Straight ahead of me was a shack. If ever there was an ideal hiding place, this was it, and as long as I was going to visit its occupant I might as well look my charming best.

I knocked, then kicked the door open. A rat scurried along the edge of the wall and shot past my feet into the light. The place was as empty as a tomb. But it *had* been occupied. Someone had turned the one room into a shambles. A box seat was freshly splintered into sharp fragments on the floor, and the makeshift stove in the middle of the room lay on its side. Over in the corner a bottle lay smashed in a million pieces, throwing jagged glints of light to the walls. She had been here. There was no doubt of it. Two more pieces of the same fabric I held in my hand were caught on the frayed end of the wooden table. She had put up a hell of a fight, all right, but it didn't do her any good.

When the voice behind me said, "Hey, you!" I pivoted on my heel and my hand clawed for the gun I didn't have. A little old guy in baggy pants was peering at me through the one lens of his glasses, wiping his nose on a dirty hunk of rag at the same time.

"That's not healthy, Pop."

"You one of them there college kids?" he asked.

I eased him out the door and came out beside him. "No, why?"

"Always you college kids what go around in yer shorts. Seed some uptown once." He raised his glasses and took a good look at my face. "Say . . . you ain't no college kid."

"Didn't say I was."

"Well, what you guys joining? I seed ya swimming in the crick, just like the other one."

I went after that *other one* like a bird after a bug. "What other one?" My hands were shaking like mad. It was all I could do to keep my hands off his shirt and shake the facts out of him.

"The one what come up t'other day. Maybe it was yesterday. I disremember days. What ya joining?"

"Er . . . a club. We have to swim the river then reach the house without being seen. Guess they won't let me join now that somebody saw me. Did you see the other guy too?"

"Sure. I seed him, but I don't say nothing. I seed lotta funny things go on and I don't ask no questions. It's just that this was kinda funny, that's all."

"What did he look like?"

"Well, I couldn't see him too good. He was big and fat. I heered him puffing plenty after he come out of the weeds. Yeah, he was a big feller. I didn't know who he was so I went back through the woods to my boat."

"Just the other guy, that's all you saw?"

"Yep."

"Nobody else?"

"Nope."

"Anybody live in that shack?"

"Not now. Comes next month and Pee Wee'll move in. He's a tramp. Don't do nothing but fish and live like a pig. He's been living there three summers now."

"This other one you saw, did he have a mean-looking face, sort of scowling?"

"Ummmm. Now that you mention it, he looked kinda mad. Guess that was one reason why I left."

Dilwick. It was Dilwick. The fat slob had gotten the jump on me again. I knew he was smart . . . he had to be to get along the way he did, but I didn't think he was that smart. Dilwick had put the puzzle together and come out on top. Dilwick had found Grange in the shack and carted her off. Then why the hell didn't he produce her? Maybe the rest of the case stunk, but this part raised a putrid odor to high heaven. Everybody under the sun wanted in on the act, now it was Dilwick. Crime upon crime upon crime upon crime. Wasn't it ever going to end? Okay, fat boy, start playing games with me. You think you pulled a quickie, don't you? You think nobody knows about this . . . T.S., junior, I know about it now, and brother, I think I'm beginning to see where I'm going.

"How can I get back to the bridge without swimming, Pop?"

He pointed a gnarled finger toward the tree line. "A path runs through there. Keeps right along the bank, but stick to it and nobody'll see ya in ya jeans. Hope they let ya join that club."

"I think I can fix it." I batted away the bugs that were beginning to swarm around me and took off for the path. Damn Dilwick anyway.

chapter ten ▰▰▰▰▰▰

GOING BACK WAS rough. My feet were bleeding at the end of the
first hundred yards and the blue-tailed flies were making my back
a bas-relief of red lumps. Some good samaritan had left a dirty
burlap bag that reeked of fish and glinted with dried scales in the
path and I ripped it in half and wrapped the pieces over my
instep and around my ankles. It wasn't so bad after that.

By the time I reached the bridge the sun was hanging well up
in the sky and a few office workers were rolling along the road
on their way to town. I waited until the road was clear, then made
a dash across the bridge to the car and climbed into some dry
clothes. My feet were so sore I could hardly get into my shoes,
but leaving the laces open helped a little. I threw the wet shorts
in the back with the rest of the junk and reached for a butt. There
are times when a guy wants a cigarette in the worst way, and this
was one of them.

I finished two, threw the car in gear and plowed out to the
concrete. Now the fun began. Me and Dilwick were going to be
as inseparable as clamshells. Grange was the key to unlock this
mess. Only Dilwick had Grange. Just to be certain I pulled into
a dog wagon and went to the pay phone. Sergeant Price was in
again. It was getting to be a habit.

I said hello, then: "Get a report on Grange yet, Sergeant?"

He replied in the negative.

"How about the city cops?"

"Nothing there either. I thought you were looking for her?"

"Yeah . . . I am. Look, do me a favor. Buzz the city bulls and
see if they've turned up anything in the last few hours. I'll hold
on."

"But they would have called me if . . ."

"Go on, try it anyway."

Price picked up another phone and dialed. I heard him ask the
cop on the desk the question, then he slammed the receiver down.
"Not a thing, Mike."

"Okay, that's all I want to know." I grinned to myself. It was
more than a feud between the city and the state police; it
was monkey business. But it was all right with me. In fact, I was
happier about it than I should have been. I was looking forward
to kicking Dilwick's teeth right down his big fat yap.

But before I did anything I was going to get some breakfast. I
went through my first order, had seconds, then went for another

431

round. By that time the counterman was looking at the stubble of the beard on my face and wondering whether or not I was a half-starved tramp filling my belly then going to ask to work out the check.

When I threw him a ten his eyes rolled a little. If he didn't check the serial number of that bill to see if it was stolen I didn't know people. I collected my change and glanced at the time. Ten-fifteen. Dilwick would be getting to his office about now. Swell.

This time I found a spot on the corner and pulled in behind a pickup truck. I shut off the motor then buried my nose in a magazine with one eye on the station house across the street. Dilwick came waddling up five minutes later. He disappeared inside and didn't show his face for two hours. When he did come out he was with one of the boys that had worked over Billy that night.

The pair stepped into an official car and drove down the street, turning onto Main. I was two cars behind. A half mile down they stopped, got out and went into a saloon. I took up a position where I could cover the entrance.

That was the way the day went; from one joint to another. By five o'clock I was dying for a short beer and a sandwich, and the two decided to call it quits. Dilwick dumped his partner off in front of a modern, two-story brick building, then cut across town, beating out a red light on the way. By the time I had caught up with him he was locking the car up in front of a trim duplex. He never saw me, not because I slouched down in my seat as I shot by, but because he was waving to a blonde in the window.

I only got a glimpse of her well-rounded shoulders and ample bust, but the look on her face told me that I had might as well go home because this was going to be an all-night affair.

No sense taking any chances. I bought a container of coffee and some sandwiches in a delicatessen then circled the block until I eased into the curb across the street and fifty yards behind the police buggy. The sandwiches went in a hurry. On top of the dash I laid out my cigs and a pack of matches, then worked the seat around until I was comfortable. At nine o'clock the lights went out in the duplex. Twenty cigarettes later they were still out. I curled up on the seat and conked off.

I was getting to hate the morning. My back ached from the swim yesterday and the cramped position behind the wheel. I opened the door and stretched my legs, getting a peek at myself in the rear-vision mirror. I didn't look pretty. Dilwick's car was still in front of the duplex.

"Have a rough night?"

I raised my eyebrows at the milkman. He was grinning like a fool.

"See a lot of you guys around this morning. Want a bottle of milk? It's good and cold."

"Hell yeah, hand one over." I fished in my pocket and threw him a half.

"Someday," he said, "I'm going to sell sandwiches on this route. I'll make a million."

He walked off whistling as I yanked the stopper out and raised the bottle to my lips. It was the best drink I ever had. Just as I reached the bottom the door opened in the duplex. A face came out, peered around, then Dilwick walked out hurriedly. I threw the empty bottle to the grass beside the curb then waited until the black sedan had turned the corner before I left my position. When I reached the intersection Dilwick was two blocks ahead. Tailing him was too easy. There were no cars out that early to screen me. When he stopped at a diner I kept right on going to the station house and got my old spot back, hoping that I hadn't made a mistake in figuring that Dilwick would come back to his castle after he had breakfast.

This time I was lucky. He drove up a half hour later.

Forcing myself to be patient was brutal. For four solid hours Dilwick went through the saloon routine solo, then he picked up his previous companion. At two in the afternoon he acquired another rummy and the circus continued. I was never far behind. Twice, I hopped out and followed them on foot, then scrambled for my heap when they came out of a joint. Six o'clock they stopped in a chop suey joint for supper and I found a chance to get a shave and watch them at the same time from a spot on the other side of the avenue. If this kept up I'd blow my top. What the hell was Dilwick doing with Grange anyway? What goes on in a town where all the cops do is tour the bars and spend their nights shacking up with blondes? If Grange was such a hot potato why wasn't Dilwick working on her? Or did he have her stashed away somewhere . . . or what could be worse, maybe I was all wet in thinking Dilwick had her in the first place.

Nuts.

I had a coffee and was two cigarettes to the good when the trio came out of the restaurant, only this time they split up in front of the door, shaking hands all around. Dilwick got in the car, changed his mind and walked down to a liquor store. When he came out with a wrapped bottle under his arm the other two were gone. Good, this was better. He slid under the wheel and pulled out. I let a convertible get between us and went after him. No blonde tonight. Dilwick went through town taking his time until he reached the highway, stopped at one of those last chance places for a beer while I watched from the spacious driveway, unwrapped his bottle before he started again and had a swig.

By the time he was on the highway it was getting dark. What a day. Five miles out of Sidon he turned right on a black macadam road that wound around the fringes of some good-sized estates and snapped on his lights. I left mine off. Wherever he was going, he wasn't in a hurry. Apparently the road went nowhere, twisting around hills and cutting a swath through the oaks lining the roads. After a while the estates petered out and the countryside, what was visible of it, became a little wild.

Ahead of me his taillight was a red eye, one that paced itself at an even thirty-five. On either side of me were walls of Stygian blackness, and I was having all I could do to stay on the road. I had to drive with one eye on the taillight and the other on the macadam, but Dilwick was making it easy for me by taking it slow.

Too easy. I was so busy driving I didn't see the other car slide up behind me until it was too late. They had their lights out too.

I hit the brakes as they cut across my nose, my hand fumbling for my rod. Even before I stopped the guy had leaped out of the car and was reaching through my window for me. I batted the hand away from my neck then got slammed across my eyes with a gun barrel. The door flew open. I kicked out with my feet and somebody grunted. Somehow I got the gun in my hand, but another gun lashed out of the darkness and smashed across my wrist.

Damn, I was stupid! I got mousetrapped! Somehow I kicked free of the car and swung. A formless shape in front of me cursed and grunted. Then a light hit me full in the face. I kicked it out of a hand, but the damage had been done. I couldn't see at all. A fist caught me high on the head as a pair of arms slipped around my waist and threw me into a fender. With all my strength I jerked my head back and caught the guy's nose. The bone splintered and hot blood gushed down my collar.

It was kick and gouge and try to get your teeth in something. The only sounds were of fists on flesh and feet on the road. Heavy breathing. I broke free for a moment, ducked, and came in punching. I doubled one up when I planted my knuckles in his belly up to the wrist. A billy swooshed in the air, missed and swooshed again. I thought my shoulder was broken. I got so damn mad I let somebody have it in the shins and he screamed in pain when I nearly busted the bone with my toe. The billy caught me in the bad shoulder again and I hit the ground, stumbling over the guy who was holding his leg. He let go long enough to try for my throat, but I brought my knee up and dug it in his groin.

All three of us were on the ground, rolling in the dirt. I felt cold steel under my hand and wrapped my fingers around a gun butt as a foot nearly ripped me in half. The guy with the billy sent one tearing into my side that took the breath out of my lungs. He tried again as I rolled and grazed me, then landed full on my gut with both his knees. Outlined against the sky I could see him straddling me, the billy raised in the air, ready to crush in my skull. Little balls of fire were popping in my brain and my breath was still a tight knot in my belly when that shot-weighted billy started to come down.

I raised the gun and shot him square in the face, blowing his brains all over the road.

But the billy was too much to stop. It was pulled off course yet it managed to knock me half-senseless when it grazed my temple. Before I went completely out I heard feet pounding on the road and an engine start up. The other guy wasn't taking any chances. He was clearing out.

I lay there under a corpse for three-quarters of an hour before I had enough strength to crawl away. On my hands and knees I reached my car and pulled myself erect. My breath came in hot, jerky gasps. I had to bend to one side to breathe at all. My face felt like a truck went over it and I was sticky with blood and guts, but I couldn't tell how much of it was my own. From the dash I pulled a flashlight and played its beam over the body in the road. Unless he had some identifying scars, nobody would ever be able to tell who he was. Ten feet away from his feet his brainpan lay like a gooey ashtray on the road.

His pockets held over a hundred bucks in cash, a wallet with a Sidon police shield pinned to it and a greasy deck of cards. The billy was still in his hand. I found my own gun, cleaned off the one I had used and tossed it into the bushes. It didn't matter whether they found it or not. I was going to be number-one client in a murder case.

Lousy? It was stinking. I was supposed to have been rubbed

out. All very legal, of course. I was suspiciously tailing a cop down a dark road with my lights out, and when ordered to halt put up a fight and during it got myself killed. Except it didn't happen that way. I nailed one and the other got away to tell about it. Maybe Dilwick would like it better this way.

So they caught me. They knew I was trailing them all day and laid a lot of elaborate plans to catch me in the trap. I had to get out of there before that other one got back with reinforcements. I let the body stay as it was, then crawled under the wheel and drove onto the grass, swinging around the corpse, then back on the highway. This time I used my lights and the gas pedal, hightailing it away as fast as I could hold the turns. Whenever I reached an intersection I cut off on it, hoping it wasn't a dead end. It took me a good two hours to circle the town and come out in the general vicinity of York's place, but I couldn't afford using the highway.

The car was in my way now; it could be spotted too easily. If they saw me it would be shoot to kill and I didn't have the kind of artillery necessary to fight a gang war. Dilwick would have every cop in town on the lookout, reporting the incident to Price only after they cornered me somewhere and punched me full of holes, or the death of the cop was printed in the papers.

There was only one reason for all the hoodah . . . Grange was still the key, and Dilwick knew I knew he had her.

Trusting luck that I wasn't too far from home, I ran the car off the road between the trees, pulling as far into the bushes as I could get. Using some cut branches for camouflage I covered up the hood and any part that could be seen by casual observation from the road. When I was satisfied I stepped out and began walking in a northerly direction.

A road finally crossed the one I was on with phone wires paralleling it. A lead from a pole a hundred yards down left the main line and went into the trees. When I reached it I saw the sleepy little bungalow hidden in the shadows. If my feet on the pavement didn't wake the occupants, my sharp rapping did.

Inside someone said, "George . . . the door."

Bedsprings creaked and the guy mumbled something then crossed the room to the door. A light went on overhead and when the guy in the faded bathrobe took a look at me he almost choked.

"I had an accident. Do you have a phone?"

"Accident? Yeah . . . yeah. Come in."

He gulped and glancing at me nervously, called, "Mary. It's a man who's had an accident. Anything I can do for you, mister? Anybody else hurt?"

The guy back there would never feel anything again. "No, nobody else is hurt."

"Here's the phone." His wife came out while I dialed Price's number. She tried to fuss around with a wet rag, wiping the blood off my face, but I waved her off. Price wasn't there; but I got his home number. He wasn't there either, he had left for headquarters. The woman was too excited. I insisted that I didn't need a doctor, but let her go over my battered face with the rag, then dialed headquarters again.

Price was there. He nearly exploded when he heard my voice. "What the hell happened? Where are you?"

"Out of town. What are you doing up at this hour?"

"Are you kidding? A police reporter slipped me the news that a cop was killed south of town. I got the rest from Dilwick. You're in a jam now."

"You're not telling me anything new," I said. "Has he got the police combing the town for me?"

"Everyone on the force is out. I had to put you on the Teletype myself. All the roads are blocked and they have a cordon around York's house. Are you giving yourself up?"

"Don't be silly. I'd be sticking my head in a noose. As far as Dilwick is concerned I have to be knocked off. It's a screw pitch, pal, and I'm in it deep, but don't believe all you hear."

"You killed him, didn't you?"

"You're damn right. If I hadn't it would have been me lying back there with my head in sections all over the ground. They squeezed me good. I was tailing Dilwick, but they got wise and tailed me. Like a damn fool I let Dilwick lead me out in the sticks and they jumped me. What was I supposed to do, take it lying down? They didn't have orders to pick me up, they were supposed to knock me off."

"Where are you? I'll come out and get you."

"No dice, buddy, I have work to do."

"You'd better give yourself up, Mike. You'll be safer in the custody of the law."

"Like hell. Dilwick will have me held under his jurisdiction and that's what he wants. He'll be able to finish the job then."

"Just the same, Mike . . ."

"Say, whose side are you on?"

He didn't say a word for a full minute. "I'm a policeman, Mike. I'll have to take you in."

He was making it hard for me. "Listen, don't be a sap, Price, something's come up that I have to follow."

"What?"

I glanced at the two faces that were taking in every word. "I can't tell you now."

"The police can handle it."

"In a pig's eye. Now listen. If you want to see this case solved you'll have to stay off my back as much as you can. I know something that only the killer knows and I have to use it while it's hot. If you take me in it'll be too late for both of us. You know what Dilwick and his outfit are like. So I shot one of them. That's hardly killing a cop, is it? Then don't get so upset about me blasting a cheap crook. Do you want to see this case wrapped up or not?"

"Of course."

"Then keep your boys out of this. I'm not worried about the rest."

There was another silent period while he thought it over, then he spoke. "Mike, I shouldn't do this; it's against all rules and regulations. But I know how things stand and I still want to be a good cop. Sometimes to do that you have to fall in line. I'll stay off you. I don't know how long it will be before the pressure gets put on me, but until then I'll do what I can."

"Thanks, pal. I won't run out on you."

"I know that."

"Expect to hear from me every once in a while. Just keep the calls under your hat. If I need you I'll yell for help."

"I'll be around, Mike. You'd better steer clear of York's place. That place is alive with city cops."

"Roger . . . and thanks again."

When I cradled the phone I could see a thousand questions getting ready to come my way. The guy and his wife were all eyes and ears and couldn't make sense out of my conversation. It had to be a good lie to be believed.

I shoved my badge under their noses. "You've overheard an official phone conversation," I said brusquely. "Under no circumstances repeat any part of it. A band of thieves has been operating in this neighborhood under the guise of being policemen and we almost got them. Unfortunately one got away. There's been difficulty getting cooperation from the local police, and we have been operating under cover. In case they show up here you saw nothing, heard nothing. Understand?"

Wide-eyed, their heads bobbed in unison and I let myself out through the door. If they believed that one they were crazy.

As soon as I was in the shadows I turned up the road toward York's estate. Cops or no cops I had to get in there someway. From the top of a knoll I looked down the surrounding countryside. In the distance the lights of Sidon threw a glow into the sky, and here and there other lights twinkled as invisible trees flickered between us in the night breeze. But the one I was interested in was the house a bare mile off that was ablaze with lights in every window and ringed with the twin beams of headlights from the cars patroling the grounds. Occasionally one would throw a spotlight into the bushes, a bright finger of light trying to pin down a furtive figure. Me.

The hell with them. This was one time I couldn't afford a run-in with the bulls. I cut across the fields until the dark shape of a barn loomed ahead. Behind it was a haystack. It was either one or the other. I chose the stack and crawled in. It would take longer for the cows to eat me out than it would for some up-with-the-sun farmer to spot me shacking up with bossy. Three feet into the hay I shoved an armload of the stuff into the tunnel I had made, kicked my feet around until I had a fair-sized cave and went to sleep.

The sun rose, hit its midpoint then went down before I moved. My belly was rumbling with hunger and my tongue was parched from breathing chaff. If a million ants were inside my shirt I couldn't have felt more uncomfortable. Keeping the stack between me and the house, I crawled through the grass to the watering trough and brushed away the dirt that had settled on top of the water. If I thought that last bottle of milk was the best drink I ever had, I was wrong. When I could hold no more I splashed my face and neck, letting it soak my shirt, grinning with pleasure.

I heard the back door of the house slam and took a flying dive to the other side of the trough. Footsteps came closer, heavy, boot-shod feet. When I was getting set to make a jump I noticed that the steps were going right on by. My breath came a little easier. Sticking my head out from behind the trough I saw the broad back of my host disappearing into the barn. He was carrying a pail in either hand. That could mean he was coming over to the trough. I had it right then. Trying to step softly, I ducked into a crouch and made a dash for the darkness of the tree line.

Once there I stripped to the skin and dusted myself off with my shirt. Much better. A bath and something to eat and I would feel almost human. Sometime during the night my watch had stopped and I could only guess at the time. I put it at an arbitrary nine-thirty and wound it up. Still too early. I had one cigarette left, the mashed, battered remains of a smoke. Shielding the match I fired it up and dragged it down to my fingernails. For two hours I sat on a stump watching a scud of clouds blot out the stars and feeling little crawling things climb up my pants leg.

The bugs were too much. I'd as soon run the risk of bumping into a cordon of Dilwick's thugs. When my watch said ten after eleven I skirted the edge of the farm and got back on the road. If anyone came along I'd see them a mile away. I found my knoll again. The lights were still on in York's house, but not in force like they had been. Only one pair of headlights peered balefully around the grounds.

An hour later I stood opposite the east wall leaning over the edge of a five-foot drainage ditch with my watch in my hands. At regular six-minute intervals the outlines of a man in a slouch hat and raincoat would drift past. When he reached the end of the wall he turned and came back. There were two of them on this side. Always, when they met at the middle of the wall, there would be some smart retort that I couldn't catch. But their pacing was regular. Dilwick should have been in the Army. A regular beat like that was a cinch to sneak through. Once a car drove by checking up on the men and tossing a spot into the bushes, but from that angle the ditch itself was completely concealed by the foot-high weeds that grew along its lip.

It had to be quick. And noiseless.

It took the guy three minutes to reach the end of the wall, three minutes to get back to me again. Maybe three-quarters of a minute. if he ran. When he passed the next time I checked my watch, keeping my eyes on the second hand. One, two, two and a half. I gripped the edge of the ditch. Ten seconds, five . . . I crouched . . . now! Vaulting the ditch I ducked across the road to the wall. Ten feet away, the tree I had chosen waved to me with leafy fingers. I jumped, grabbed the lowest limb and swung up, then picked my way up until I was even with the wall. My clothes caught on spikelike branches, ripped loose, then caught again.

Feet were swishing the grass. Feet that had a copper over them. This was the second phase. If he looked up and saw me outlined against the sky I was sunk. I palmed the .45 and threw the safety off, waiting. They came closer. I heard him singing a tuneless song under his breath, swearing at briars that bit at his ankles.

He was under the tree now, in the shadows. The singing stopped. The feet stopped. My hand tightened around the butt of the gun, aiming it where his head would be. If he saw me he was held in his tracks. I would have let one go at him if I didn't see the flare of the match in time. When his butt was lit he breathed the smoke in deeply then continued on his rounds. I shoved the gun back and put the watch on him again until it read another three minutes.

Button your coat . . . be sure nothing was going to jingle in your pockets . . . keep your watch face blacked out . . . hold tight . . . get ready . . . and jump. For one brief moment I was airborne before my fingers felt the cold stone wall. The corner caught me in the chest and I almost fell. Somehow I kicked my feet to the top and felt broken glass cemented in the surface shatter under my heels. Whether or not anybody was under me, I had to jump, I was too much of a target there on the wall. Keeping low I stepped over the glass and dropped off.

I landed in soft turf with hardly a sound, doubled up and rolled into a thorny rosebush. The house was right in front of me now; I could pick out Roxy's window. The pane was still shattered from the bullet that had pierced it and nicked her.

Ruston's window was lit, too, but the shade was drawn. Behind the house the police car stopped, some loud talking ensued, then it went forward again. No chance to check schedules now. I had to hope that I wasn't seen. Just as soon as the car passed I ran for the wall of the building, keeping in whatever cover the bushes and hedgerows afforded. It wasn't much, but I made the house without an alarm going off. The wrist-thick vine that ran up the side wasn't as good as a ladder, but it served the purpose. I went up it like a monkey until I was just below Roxy's window.

I reached up for the sill, grabbed it and as I did the damn brick pulled loose and tumbled down past me landing with a raucous clatter in the bushes below and then bounced sickeningly into other bricks with a noise as loud as thunder in my ears. I froze against the wall, heard somebody call out, then saw a bright shaft of light leap out from a spot in someone's hand below and watched it probe the area where the brick had landed.

Whoever he was didn't look up, not expecting anyone above him. His stupidity was making me feel a little better and I figured I had it made. I wasn't that lucky. There was too much weight on the vine and I felt it beginning to pull loose from wherever it was anchored in the wall above my head.

I didn't bother trying to be careful. Down below a couple of voices were going back and forth and their own sounds covered mine. I scrambled up, reached and got hold of an awning hook imbedded in the concrete of the exterior frame of the window and hung on with one hand, my knee reaching for the sill before I could pull the hook out of the wall.

Down below everybody was suddenly satisfied and the lights went out. In the darkness I heard feet taking up the vigil again. I waited a full minute, tried the window, realized that it was locked then tapped on the pane. I did it again, not a frantic tapping, but a gentle signaling that got a response I could hear right through the glass. I hoped she wouldn't scream, but would think it out long enough to look first.

She did.

There was enough reflected light from a bed lamp to highlight my face and I heard her gasp, reach for the latch and ease the window up. I rolled over the sill, dropped to the floor and let her shut the window behind me and pull down the blind. Only then did she snap on the light.

"Mike!"

"Quiet, kid, they're all over the place downstairs."

"Yes, I know." Her eyes filled up suddenly and she half-ran to me, her arms folding me to her.

Behind us there was a startled little gasp. I swung, pushed Roxy away from me, then grinned. Ruston was standing there in his pajamas, his face a dead white. "Mike!" he started to say, then swayed against the doorjamb. I walked over, grabbed him and rubbed his head until he started to smile at me.

"You take it easy, little buddy . . . you've had it rough. How about letting me be the only casualty around here. By the way, where is Billy?"

Roxy answered. "Dilwick took him downstairs and is making him stay there."

"Did he get rough with him?"

"No . . . Billy said he'd better lay off or he'd get a lawyer that would take care of that fat goon and Dilwick didn't touch him. For once Billy stood up for himself."

Ruston was shaking under my hand. His eyes would dart from the door to the window and he'd listen attentively to the heavy footsteps wandering down in the rooms below. "Mike, why did you come? I don't want them to see you. I don't care what you did, but you can't let them get you."

"I came to see you, kid."

"Me?"

"Uh-huh."

"Why?"

"I have something big to ask you."

The two of them stared at me, wondering what could be so great as to bring me through that army of cops. Roxy, quizzically; Ruston with his eyes filled with awe. "What is it, Mike?"

"You're pretty smart, kid, try to understand this. Something has come up, something that I didn't expect. How would you like to point out the killer for me? Be a target. Lead the killer to you so I can get him?"

"Mike, you can't!"

I looked at Roxy. "Why not?"

"It isn't fair. You can't ask him to do that!"

I slumped in a chair and rubbed my head. "Maybe you're right. It is a lot to expect."

Ruston was tugging at my sleeve. "I'll do it, Mike. I'm not afraid."

I didn't know what to say. If I missed I'd never be able to look at myself in the face again, yet here was the kid, ready and trusting me not to miss. Roxy sank to the edge of the bed, her face pale, waiting for my answer. But I couldn't let a killer run around loose.

"Okay, Lancelot, it's a deal." Roxy was hating me with her eyes. "Before we go over it, do you think you can get me something to eat?"

"Sure, Mike. I'll get it. The policemen won't bother me." Ruston smiled and left. I heard him going down the stairs, then tell the cop he was hungry and so was his governess. The cop growled and let him go.

Roxy said, "You're a louse, Mike, but I guess it has to be that way. We almost lost Ruston once, and it's liable to happen again if somebody doesn't think of something. Well, you did. I just hope it works, that's all."

"So do I, kid."

Ruston came running up the stairs and slipped into the room, bearing a pair of enormous sandwiches. I all but snatched them out of his hand and tore into them wolfishly. Once, the cop came upstairs and prowled past the door and I almost choked. After he went by, the two of them laughed silently at me standing there with my rod in my hand and the remains of a sandwich sticking out of my mouth.

Roxy went over and pressed her ear to the door, then slowly turned the key in the lock. "I suppose you'll leave the same way you came in, Mike, so maybe that'll give you more time if you have to go quickly."

"Gee, I hope nothing happens to you, Mike. I'm not afraid for myself, I'm just afraid what those policemen will do. They say you shot a cop and now you have to die."

"Lancelot, you worry too much."

"But even if you find out who's been causing all the trouble the police will still be looking for you, won't they?"

"Perhaps not," I laughed. "They're going to be pretty fed up with me when I bust this case."

The kid shuddered, his eyes closed tightly for a second. "I keep thinking of that night in the shack. The night you shot one of those men that kidnapped me. It was an awful fight."

I felt as though a mule had kicked me in the stomach. "What did you say?"

"That night . . . you remember. When you shot that man and . . ."

I cut him off. "You can get off that target, Ruston," I said softly. "I won't need you for a decoy after all."

Roxy twisted toward me, watching the expression in my eyes. "Why, Mike?"

"I just remembered that I shot a guy, that's why. I had forgotten all about it." I jammed on my hat and picked up a pack of Roxy's butts from the dresser. "You two stay here and keep the door locked. I can get the killer, now, by damn, and I won't have to make him come to me either. Roxy, turn that light off. Give me five minutes after I leave before you turn it on again. Forget you ever saw me up here or Dilwick will have your scalp."

The urgency in my voice moved her to action. Without a word in reply she reached out for the light and snapped it off. Ruston gasped and moved toward the door, with the slightest tremor of excitement creeping into his breathing. I saw him silhouetted there for an instant, a floor lamp right in front of him. Before I could caution him the shade struck him in the face. His hand went out . . . hit the lamp and it toppled to the floor with the popping of the bulb and the crash of a fallen tree. Or so it seemed.

Downstairs a gruff voice barked out. Before it could call again I threw the window up and went out, groping for the vine. Someplace in the house a whistle shrilled and angry fists beat at the door. Half-sliding, half-climbing, I went down the side of the building. Another whistle and somebody got nervous and let a shot blast into the confusion. From every side came the shouts and the whistles. Just before I reached the ground a car raced up and two figures leaped out. But I was lucky. The racket was all centered on the inside of the house and the coppers were taking it for granted that I was trapped there.

As fast as I could go, I beat it across the drive to the lawn, then into the trees. Now I knew where I was. One tree ahead formed the perfect ladder over the wall. I had my gun out now in case that patrol was waiting. There would be no command to halt, just a volley of shots until one of us dropped. All right, I was ready. Behind me a window smashed and Roxy screamed. Then there was a loud "There he goes!" and a pair of pistols spit fire. With the trees in the way and the distance opening between us, I wasn't concerned about getting hit.

The tree was a godsend. I went up its inclined trunk thanking whatever lightning bolt had split it in such a handy fashion, made the top of the wall and jumped for the grass. The sentries weren't there anymore. Probably trying to be in on the kill.

A siren screamed inside the wall and the chase was on, but it would be a futile chase now. Once in the tree line on the other side of the road I took it easy. They'd be looking for a car and the search would be along the road. So long, suckers!

chapter eleven ▰▰▰▰▰▰▰▰▰▰▰▰▰▰

I SLEPT IN MY car all night. It wasn't until noon that I was ready to roll. Now the streets would be packed with traffic and my buggy would be just another vehicle. There were hundreds like it on the road. Superficially it was a five-year-old heap that had seen plenty of service, but the souped-up motor under the hood came out of a limousine that had packed a lot of speed and power. Once on the road nothing the city cops had was going to catch me.

Good old Ruston. If my memory had been working right I wouldn't have forgotten my little pal I plugged. Guys who are shot need doctors, and need them quick, and in Sidon there wouldn't be that many medics that I couldn't run them all down. A crooked doc, that's what I wanted. If a gunshot had been treated Price would have known about it and told me, but none had been entered in the books. Either a crooked doc or a threatened doc. He was the one to find.

I stripped the branches from the fenders and cleared a path to the road, and then eased out onto the macadam. At the first crossroad a sign pointed to the highway and I took the turn. Two miles down I turned into a stream of traffic, picked out a guy going along at a medium clip and nosed in behind him.

We both turned off into the city, only I parked on a side street and went into a candy store that had a public phone. Fiddling through the Yellow Pages, I ripped out the sheet of doctors listed there, and went through the motions of making a phone call. Nobody bothered to so much as glance at me.

Back in the car I laid out my course and drove to the first on my list. It wasn't an impressive list. Seven names. Dr. Griffin was stepping out of his car when I pulled in.

"Doctor . . ."

"Yes?"

His eyes went up and down the ruin of my suit. "Don't mind me," I said. "I've been out all night chasing down the dick that shot that cop. I'm a reporter."

"Oh, yes, I heard about that. What can I do for you?"

"The police fired several shots at him. There's a chance that he might have been hit. Have you treated any gunshot wounds lately?"

He drew himself up in indignant pride. "Certainly not! I would have reported it immediately had I done so."

"Thank you, Doctor."

The next one wasn't home, but his housekeeper was. Yes, she knew all about the doctor's affairs. No, there had been no gunshot wounds since Mr. Dillon shot himself in the foot like a silly fool when loading his shotgun. Yes, she was very glad to be of service.

Dr. Pierce ushered me into his very modern office personally. I pulled the same reporter routine on him. "A gunshot wound, you say?"

"Yes. It wasn't likely that he'd treat it himself."

He folded his hands across his paunch and leaned back in his chair. "There was one the day before yesterday, but I reported that. Certainly you know about it. A .22-caliber bullet. The man was hit while driving out in the country. Said he didn't know where it came from."

I covered up quickly. "Oh, that one. No, this would have been a larger shell. The cops don't pack .22's these days."

"I expect not," he laughed.

"Well, thanks anyway, Doctor."

"Don't mention it."

Four names left. It was past three o'clock. The next two weren't

THE TWISTED THING   447

home, but the wife of one assured me that her husband would not have treated any wounds of the sort because he had been on a case in the hospital during the entire week.

The other one was in Florida on a vacation.

Dr. Clark had offices a block away from police headquarters, a very unhealthy place right now. Cars drove up and away in a constant procession, but I had to chance it. I parked pointing away from the area, making sure I had plenty of room to pull out, my wheels turned away from the curb. A woman came out of the office holding a baby. Then a man walking on a cane. I didn't want to enter an office full of people if I could help it, but if he didn't get rid of his patients in a hurry I was going to have to bust in anyway. A boy went in crying, holding his arm. Damn it, I was losing time!

As I went to reach for the ignition switch another guy came out, a four-inch wide bandage going from the corner of his mouth to his ear. The bells again. They went off all at once inside my skull until I wanted to scream. The bandage. The hell with the gunshot wound, he was probably dead. The bandage. My fingers hooking in a mouth and ripping the skin wide open. Of course, he'd need a doctor too! You wouldn't find two freak accidents like that happening at once. He was a ratty-looking guy dressed in a sharp gray suit with eyes that were everywhere at once. He went down the steps easily and walked to a car a couple ahead of me. I felt my heart beginning to pound, beating like a heavy hammer, an incredible excitement that made my blood race in my veins like a river about to flood.

He pulled out and I was right behind him, our bumpers almost touching. There was no subtlety about this tail job, maybe that's why I got away with it so long. He didn't notice me until we were on the back road six miles out of town ripping off seventy miles an hour. Just the two of us. We had left all other traffic miles behind. I saw his eyes go to the rear-vision mirror and his car spurted ahead. I grinned evilly to myself and stepped down harder on the accelerator until I was pushing him again.

His eyes hardly left the mirror. There was fright in them now. A hand went out and he signaled me to pass. I ignored it. Eighty-five now. A four-store town went by with the wind. I barely heard the whistle of the town cop blast as I passed him. Eighty-seven. The other car was having trouble holding the turns. It leaned until the tires screamed as the driver jerked it around. I grinned again. The frame of my car was rigged for just such emergencies. Ninety. Trees shot by like a huge picket fence. Another town. A rapid parade of identical billboards advertising a casino in Brocton. Ninety-five. A straightaway came up lined with more billboards. A nice flat stretch was ahead, he would have opened up on it if he could have, but his load was doing all it could. At the end of the straightaway was the outline of a town.

My little friend, you have had it, I said to myself. I went down on the gas, the car leaped ahead, we rubbed fenders. For a split second I was looking into those eyes and remembering that night, before I cut across his hood. He took to the shoulder, fought the wheel furiously but couldn't control it. The back end skidded around and the car went over on its side like a pinwheel. I stood on the brake, but his car was still rolling as I stopped.

I backed up and got out without shutting the engine off. The punk was lucky, damn lucky. His car had rolled but never up-ended, and those steel turret top jobs could take it on a roll in soft earth. He was crawling out of the door reaching under his coat for a rod when I jumped him. When I slapped him across that bandage he screamed and dropped the gun. I straddled him and picked it up, a snub-nosed .38, and thrust it in my waistband.

"Hello, pal," I said.

Little bubbles of pink foam oozed from the corners of his mouth. "Don't . . . don't do nothing . . ."

"Shut up."

"Please . . ."

"Shut up." I looked at him, looked at him good. If my face said anything he could read it. "Remember me? Remember that night in the shack? Remember the kid?"

Recognition dawned on him. A terrible, fearful recognition and he shuddered the entire length of his body. "What're ya gonna do?"

I brought my hand down across his face as hard as I could. He moaned and whimpered, "Don't!" Blood started to seep through the bandage, bright red now.

"Where's the guy I shot?"

He breathed, "Dead," through a mouthful of gore. It ran out of his mouth and dribbled down his chin.

"Who's Mallory?"

He closed his eyes and shook his head. All right, don't talk. Make me make you. This would be fun. I worked my nails under the adhesive of the bandage and ripped it off with one tug. Clotted blood pulled at his skin and he screamed again. A huge half-open tear went from the corner of his mouth up his jawline, giving him a perpetual grin like a clown.

"Open your eyes." He forced his lids up, his chest heaved for air. Twitches of pain gripped his face. "Now listen to me, chum. I asked you who Mallory was. I'm going to put my fingers in your mouth and rip out those stitches one by one until you tell me. Then I'm going to open you up on the other side. If you'd sooner look like a clam, don't talk."

"No! I . . . I don't know no Mallory."

I slapped him across the cheek, then did as I promised. More blood welled out of the cut. He screamed once more, a short scream of intolerable agony. "Who's Mallory?"

"Honest . . . don't know . . ."

Another stitch went. He passed out cold.

I could wait. He came to groaning senselessly. I shook his head until his eyes opened. "Who do you work for, pal?"

His lips moved, but no sound came forth. I nudged him again. "The boss . . . Nelson . . . at the casino."

Nelson. I hadn't heard it before. "Who's Mallory?"

"No more. I don't know . . ." His voice faded out to nothing and his eyes shut. Except for the steady flow of blood seeping down his chin he looked as dead as they come.

It was getting dark again. I hadn't noticed the cars driving up until the lights of one shone on me. People were piling out of the first car and running across the field, shouting at each other and pointing to the overturned car.

The first one was all out of breath when he reached me. "What happened, mister? Is he dead? God, look at his face!"

"He'll be all right," I told him. "He just passed out." By that time the others were crowded around. One guy broke through the ring and flipped his coat open to show a badge.

"Better get him to a hospital. Ain't none here. Nearest one's in Sidon." He yanked a pad out of his pocket and wet the tip of a pencil with his tongue. "What's your name, mister?"

I almost blurted it out without thinking. If he heard it I'd be under his gun in a second, and there wasn't much I could do with this mob around. I stood up and motioned him away from the crowd. On the other side of the upturned car I looked him square in the eye.

"This wasn't an accident," I said, "I ran him off the road."

"You what?"

"Keep quiet and listen. This guy is a kidnapper. He may be a killer. I want you to get to the nearest phone and call Sergeant Price of the state police, understand? His headquarters is on the highway outside of Sidon. If you can't get him, keep trying until you do."

His hands gripped my lapels. "Say, buster, what are you trying to pull? Who the hell are you, anyway?"

"My name is Mike . . . Mike Hammer. I'm wanted by every crooked cop in this part of the state and if you don't get your paws off me I'll break your arm!"

His jaw sagged, but he let go my coat, then his brows wrinkled. "I'll be damned," he said. "I always did want to meet you. Read all the New York papers y' know. By damn. Say, you *did* kill that Sidon cop, didn't you?"

"Yes, I did."

"By damn, that's good. He put a bullet into one of our local lads one night when he was driving back from the casino. Shot him while he was dead drunk because he didn't like his looks. He got away with it too, by damn. What was that you wanted me to tell the police?"

I breathed a lot easier. I never thought I'd find a friend this far out. "You call Price and tell him to get out to the casino as fast as his car will bring him. And tell him to take along some boys."

"Gonna be trouble?"

"There's liable to be."

"Maybe I should go." He pulled at his chin, thinking hard. "I don't know. The casino is all we got around here. It ain't doing us no good, but the guy that runs it runs the town."

"Stay out of it if you can help it. Get an ambulance if you want to for that guy back there, but forget the hospital. Stick him in the cooler. Then get on the phone and call Price."

"Okay, Mike. I'll do that for you. Didn't think you shot that cop in cold blood like the notices said. You didn't, did you?"

"He was sitting on top of me about to bash my brains out with a billy when I shot the top of his head off."

"A good thing, by damn."

I didn't hang around. Twenty pairs of eyes followed me across the field to my car, but if there was any explaining to be done the cop was making a good job of it. Before I climbed under the wheel he had hands helping to right the car and six people carrying the figure of The Face to the road.

Nelson, the Boss. Another character. Where did he come in? He wasn't on the level if rat-puss was working for him. Nelson, but no Mallory. I stepped on the starter and ran the engine up. Nelson, but no Mallory. Something cold rolled down my temple and I wiped it away. Sweat. Hell, it couldn't be true, not what I was thinking, but it made sense! Oh, hell, it was impossible, people just aren't made that way! The pieces didn't have to be fitted into place any longer . . . they were being drawn into a pattern of murder as if by a magnet under the board, a pattern of death as complicated as a Persian tapestry, ugly enough to hang in Hitler's own parlor. Nelson, but no Mallory. The rest would be only incidental, a necessary incidental. I sweated so freely that my shirt was matted to my body.

I didn't have to look for the killer any longer. I knew who the killer was now.

The early crowd had arrived at the casino in force. Dozens of cars with plates from three states were already falling into neat rows at the direction of the attendant and their occupants in evening dress and rich business clothes were making their way across the lawn to the doors. It was an imposing place built like an old colonial mansion with twenty-foot pillars circling the entire house. From inside came the strains of a decent orchestra and a lot of loud talk from the bar on the west side. Floodlights played about the grounds, lighting up the trees in the back and glancing off the waters of the bay with sparkling fingers. The outlines of a boathouse made a dark blot in the trees, and out in the channel the lights from some moored yachts danced with the roll of the ships.

For five minutes I sat in the car with a butt hanging between my lips, taking in every part of the joint. When I had the layout pretty well in my mind I stepped out and flipped the attendant a buck. The guy's watery eyes went up and down my clothes, wondering what the hell I was doing there.

"Where'll I find Nelson, friend?"

He didn't like my tone, but he didn't argue about it. "What do you want him for?"

"We got a load of special stuff coming in on a truck and I want to find out what he wants done with it."

"Booze?"

"Yeah."

"Hell, ain't he taking the stuff off Carmen?"

"This is something special, but I'm not jawing about it out here. Where is he?"

"If he ain't on the floor he'll be upstairs in his office."

I nodded and angled over to the door. Two boys in shabby tuxedos stood on either side throwing greetings to the customers. They didn't throw any to me. I saw them exchange glances when they both caught the outlines of the rod under my coat. One started drifting toward me and I muttered, "I got a truckload of stuff for the boss. When it comes up get it around the back. We had a police escort all the way out of Jersey until we lost them."

The pair gave me blank stares wondering what I was talking about, but when I brushed by them they fingered me an okay thinking I was on the in. Bar noises came from my left, noises you couldn't mistake. They were the same from the crummiest joint in the Bronx to the swankiest supper club uptown. I went in, grabbed a spot at the end and ordered a brew. The punk gave me a five-ounce glass and soaked me six bits for it. When he passed me my change I asked for the boss.

"Just went upstairs a minute ago." I downed the drink and threaded my way out again. In what had been the main living room at one time were the bobbing heads of the dancers, keeping time to the orchestra on the raised dais at one end. Dozens of white-coated waiters scurried about like ants getting ready for winter, carrying trays loaded to the rims with every size glass there was. A serving bar took up one whole end of the corridor with three bartenders passing out drinks. This place was a gold mine.

I went up the plush-carpeted stairs with traffic. It was mostly male. Big fat guys chewing on three-buck cigars carrying dough in their jeans. An occasional dame with a fortune in jewelry dangling from her extremities. At the top of the landing the whir of the wheels and the click of the dice came clearly over the subdued babble of tense voices seated around the tables. Such a beautiful setup. It would be a shame to spoil it. So this was what Price had referred to. Protected gambling. Even with a hundred-way split to stay covered the boss was getting a million-dollar income.

The crowd went into the game rooms, but I continued down the dimly lit hallway past the rest rooms until I reached another staircase. This one was smaller, less bright, but just as plush and just as well used. Upstairs someone had a spasm of coughing and water splashed in a cooler.

I looked around me, pressing flat against the wall, then ducked around the corner and stood on the first step. The gun was in my hand, fitting into its accustomed spot. One by one I went up the stairs, softly, very softly. At the top, light from a doorway set into the wall threw a yellow light on the paneling opposite it. Three steps from the landing I felt the board drop a fraction of an inch under my foot. That was what I was waiting for.

I hit the door, threw it open and jammed the rod in the face of the monkey in the tux who was about to throw the bolt. "You should have done that sooner." I sneered at him.

He tried to bluff it out. "What the hell do you think you're doing?"

"Shut up and lay down on the floor. Over here away from the door."

I guess he knew what would happen if he didn't. His face went white right down into his collar and he fell to his knees then stretched out on the floor like he was told. Before he buried his map in the nap of the carpet he threw me one of those "you'll-be-sorry" looks.

Like hell I'd be sorry. I wasn't born yesterday. I turned the gun around in my hand and got behind the door. I didn't have long to wait. The knob turned, a gun poked in with a guy behind it looking for a target, a leer of pure sadistic pleasure on his face. When I brought the butt of the .45 across his head the leer turned to amazement as he spilled forward like a sack of wet cement. The skin on his bald dome was split a good three inches from the thong hook on the handle and pulled apart like a gaping mouth. He would be a long time in sleepy town.

"You ought to get that trip fixed in the stairs," I said to the fancy boy on the floor. "It drops like a trapdoor."

He looked back at me through eyes that seemed to pulse every time his heart beat. Both his hands were on the floor, palms down, his body rising and falling with his labored breathing. Under a trim moustache his chin fell away a little, quivering like the rest of him. A hairline that had once swept across his forehead now lay like low tide on the back of his head, graying a little, but not much. There was a scar on one lip and his nose had been twisted out of shape not too long ago, but when you looked hard you could still see through the wear of the years.

He was just what I expected. "Hello, Mallory," I said, "or should I say, Nelson?"

I could hardly hear his voice. "W . . . who are you?"

"Don't play games, sucker. My name is Mike Hammer. You ought to know me. I bumped one of your boys and made a mess of the other awhile back. You should see him now. I caught up with him again. Get up."

"What . . . are you going . . . to do?" I looked down at the .45. The safety was off and it was the nastiest-looking weapon in existence at that moment. I pointed it at his belly.

"Maybe I'll shoot you. There." I indicated his navel with the muzzle.

"If it's money you want, I can give it to you, Hammer. Please, get the rod off me."

Mallory was the tough guy. He edged away from me, holding his hands out in a futile attempt to stop a bullet if it should come. He stopped backing when he hit the edge of the desk. "I don't want any of your dough, Mallory," I said, "I want you." I let him look into the barrel again. "I want to hear something you have to say."

"I . . ."

"Where's Miss Grange . . . or should I say Rita Cambell?"

He drew his breath in a great swallow and before I could move swung around, grabbed the pen set from the desk and sent the solid onyx base crashing into my face.

Fingers clawed at my throat and we hit the floor with a tangle of arms and legs. I brought my knee up and missed, then swung with the gun. It landed on the side of his neck and gave me a chance to clear my head. I saw where the next punch was going. I brought it up from the floor and smacked him as hard as I could in the mouth. My knuckles pushed back his lips and his front teeth popped like hollow things under the blow.

The bastard spit them right in my face.

He was trying to reach my eyes. I tossed the rod to one side and laughed long and loud. Only for that one moment did he possess any strength at all, just that once when he was raging mad. I got hold of both his arms and pinned them down, then threw him sideways to the floor. His feet kicked out and kicked again until I got behind him. With his back on the floor I straddled his chest and sat on his stomach, both his hands flat against his sides, held there by my legs. He couldn't yell without choking on his own blood and he knew it, but he kept trying to spit at me nevertheless.

With my open palm I cracked him across the cheek. Right, left, right, left. His head went sideways with each slap, but my other hand always straightened it up again. I hit him until the palms of my hands were sore and his cheek split in a dozen places from my ring. At first he flopped and moaned for me to stop, then fought bitterly to get away from the blows that were tearing his face to shreds. When he was almost out, I quit.

"Where's Grange, Mallory?"

"The shed." He tried to plead with me not to hit him, but I cracked him one anyway.

"Where's the Cook girl?"

No answer. I reached for my rod and cradled it in my hand.

"Look at me, Mallory."

His eyes opened halfway. "My hand hurts. Answer me or I use this on you. Maybe you won't live through it. Where's the Cook girl?"

"Nobody else. Grange . . . is the . . . only one."

"You're lying, Mallory."

"No . . . just Grange."

I couldn't doubt but what he was telling the truth. After what I gave him he was ready to spill his guts. But that still didn't account for Cook. "Okay, who does have her then?"

Blood bubbled out of his mouth from his split gums. "Don't know her."

"She was Grange's alibi, Mallory. She was with the Cook dame the night York was butchered. She would have given Grange an out."

His eyes came open all the way. "She's a bitch," he mouthed. "She doesn't deserve an alibi. They kidnapped my kid, that's what they did!"

"And you kidnapped him back . . . fourteen years later."

"He was mine, wasn't he? He didn't belong to York."

I gave it to him slowly. "You didn't really want him, did you? You didn't give a damn about the kid. All you wanted was to get even with York. Wasn't that it?"

Mallory turned his head to one side. "Answer me, damn you!"

"Yes."

"Who killed York?"

I waited for his answer. I had to be sure I was right. This was one time I had to be sure.

"It . . . it wasn't me."

I raised the gun and laid the barrel against his forehead. Mallory was staring into the mouth of hell. "Lie to me, Mallory," I said, "and I'll shoot you in the belly, then shoot you again a little higher. Not where you'll die quick, but where you'll wish you did. Say it was you and you die fast . . . like you don't deserve. Say it wasn't you and I may believe you and I may not . . . only don't lie to me because I know who killed York."

Once more his eyes met mine, showing pain and terror. "It . . . wasn't me. No, it wasn't me. You've got to believe that." I let the gun stay where it was, right against his forehead. "I didn't even know he was dead. It was Grange I wanted."

Even with his shattered mouth the words were coming freely as he begged for his life. "I got the news clipping in the mail. The one about the trouble in the hospital. There was no signature, but the letter said that Grange was Rita Cambell and she was a big shot now and if I kidnapped the kid, instead of ransom I could get positive information from York that his kid was my son. I wouldn't have snatched him if it wasn't so easy. The letter said the watchman on the gate would be drugged and the door to the house open on a certain night. All I had to do to get the kid was go in after him. I was still pretty mad at York and the letter made it worse. I wanted Myra Grange more than the old man, that's why when those crazy lugs I sent after the kid lost him I made a try for her. I followed her from her house to another place then waited for her to come out before I grabbed her. She was in there when York was killed and I was waiting outside. Honest, I didn't kill him. She didn't know who I was until I told her. Ever since that time when York stole my kid I used the name Nelson. She started to fight with me in the car and hit me over the head with the heel of her shoes. While I was still dizzy she beat it and got in her car and scrammed. I chased her and forced her off the road by the river and she went in. I thought she was dead. . . ."

The footsteps coming up the stairs stopped him. I whipped around and sent a shot crashing through the door. Somebody swore and yelled for reinforcements. I prodded Mallory with the tip of the rod. "The window and be quick."

He didn't need any urging. The gun in his back was good incentive. That damn warning trip. Either it went off someplace else or the boys on the doors got suspicious. Egghead was starting to groan on the floor. "Get the window up."

Mallory opened the catch and pushed. Outside the steel railings of the fire escape were waiting. I thanked the good fathers who passed the law making them compulsory for all three-story buildings. We went out together, then down the metal stairs without trying to conceal our steps. If I had a cowbell around my neck I couldn't have made more noise. Mallory kept spitting blood over the side, trying to keep his eyes on me and the steps at the same time. Above us heavy bodies were ramming the door. The lock splintered and someone tripped over the mug on the floor, but before they could get to the window we were on the ground.

"The boathouse. Shake it, Mallory, they won't care who they hit," I said.

Mallory was panting heavily, but he knew there was wisdom in my words. A shot snapped out that was drowned in a sudden blast from the orchestra, but I saw the gravel kick up almost at my feet. We skirted the edge of cars and out in between the fenders, then picked an opening and went through it to the boathouse. The back of it was padlocked.

"Open it."

"I . . . I don't have the key."

"That's a quick way to get yourself killed," I reminded him.

He fumbled for a key in his pocket, brought it out and inserted it in the padlock. His hands were shaking so hard that he couldn't get it off the hasp. I shoved him away and ripped it loose myself. The door slid sideways, and I thumbed him in, closing the door behind us. With the gun in the small of his back I flicked a match with my fingernail.

Grange and Cook were lying side by side in a pile of dirt at the far end of the boathouse. Both were tied up like Thanksgiving turkeys with a wad of cloth clamped between their jaws. They were out cold. Mallory's mouth dropped to his chin and he pointed a trembling finger at Cook. "She's here!"

"What the hell did you expect?"

His face grew livid until blood flowed afresh from his mouth. Mallory might have said something in anger if the match had not scorched my finger. I dropped it and cursed. He pulled away from the gun at the same time and ran for it. I took four steps toward the door, my arms outstretched to grab him, but he wasn't there. At the other end of the room one of the girls started to moan through her gag. A knob turned and for a second I saw stars in the sky at the side of the wall. My first shot got him in the leg and he fell to the floor screaming. In the half-light of the match I hadn't seen that side door, but he knew it was there. I ran over and yanked him back by the foot, mad enough to send a bullet into his gut.

I never had the chance. There was a blast of gunfire and my rod was torn from my grasp. The beam of a spotlight hit me in the eyes as Dilwick's voice said, "Freeze, Hammer. You make one move and I'll shoot hell out of you."

The light moved over to the side, never leaving me. Dilwick snapped on the overhead; one dim bulb that barely threw enough light to reach both ends. He was standing there beside the switch with as foul a look as I ever hope to see on a human face and murder in his hands. He was going to kill me.

It might have ended then if Mallory hadn't said, "You lousy rat. You stinking, lousy rat. You're the one who's been bleeding me. You son of a bitch."

Dilwick grinned at me, showing his teeth. "He's a wise guy, Hammer. Listen to him bawl."

I didn't say a word.

Dilwick went over and got my gun from the floor, using his handkerchief on the butt, never taking his eyes from either of us. He looked at me, then Mallory, and before either of us could move sent a shot smashing into Mallory's chest from my .45. The guy folded over in a quarter-roll and was still. Dilwick tossed the still-smoking gun down the room. "It was nice while it lasted," he said, "but now it will be even better."

I waited.

"The boss had a swell racket here. A perfect racket. He paid us off well, but I'm going to take over now. The hell with being a cop. It'll make a pretty story, don't you think? I come in here and see you shoot him, then shoot you. Uh-huh, a very pretty story and nobody will blame me. You'll be wrapped up cold for a double murder, first that copper and now him."

"Sure," I said, "but what are you going to do about Grange and her pal?"

Dilwick showed his teeth again. "She's wanted for York's murder, isn't she? Wouldn't it be sweet if they were found dead in a love tryst? The papers would love that. Boy, what a front-page story if *you* don't crowd them off. Grange and her sweetie doing the double Dutch in the drink instead of her cooking for the York kill. That would put a decent end to this mess. I got damn sick and tired of trying to cover up for the boss anyway, and you got in my hair, Hammer."

"Did I?"

"Don't get smart. If I had any sense I would have taken care of you myself instead of letting that dumb bunny of a detective bollix up things when you were tailing me on that back road."

"You wouldn't have done any better either," I spat out.

"No? But I will now." He raised the gun and took deliberate aim at my head.

While he wasted time thumbing back the hammer I tugged the snub-nosed .38 from my waistband that I had taken from the punk with the wrecked face and triggered one into his stomach. His face froze for an instant, the gun sagged, then with all the hatred of his madness he stumbled forward a step, raising his gun to fire.

The .38 roared again. A little blue spot appeared over the bridge of his nose and he went flat on his face.

Mine wasn't the only gun to speak. Outside there was a continual roar of bullets; screams from the house and commands being shouted into the dark. A car must have tried to pull away and smashed into another. More shots and the tinkling of broken glass. A man's voice screamed in agony. A tommy went off in short bursts blasting everything in its path. Through the door held open by Mallory's body the brilliant white light of a spotlight turned the night to day and pairs of feet were circling the boathouse.

I shouted, "Price, it's me, Mike. I'm in here!"

A light shot in the door as hands slid the other opening back. A state trooper with a riot gun pointed at me slid in and I dropped the .38. Price came in behind him. "Damn, you still alive?"

"I look it, don't I?" Laughing almost drunkenly I slapped him on the shoulder. "Am I glad to see you! You sure took long enough to get here." Price's foot stretched out and pushed the body on the floor.

"That's . . ."

"Dilwick," I finished. "The other one over there is Mallory."

"I thought you were going to keep me informed on how things stood," he said.

"It happened too fast. Besides, I couldn't be popping in places where I could be recognized."

"Well, I hope your story's good, Mike. It had better be. We're holding people out there with enough influence to swing a state legislature, and if the reason is a phony or even smells like one, you and I are both going to be on the carpet. You for murder."

"Nuts, what was all the shooting about outside?"

"I got your message such as it was and came up here with three cars of troopers. When we got on the grounds a whole squad of mugs with guns in their hands came ripping around the house. They let go at us before we could get out of the cars and there was hell to pay. The boys came up expecting action and they got it."

"Those mugs, chum, were after me. I guess they figured I'd try to make a break for it and circled the house. Dilwick was the only one who knew where we'd be. Hell, he should have. I was after Grange and the Cook girl and he had them in here."

"Now you tell me. Go on and finish it."

I brought him up to date in a hurry. "Dilwick's been running cover for Mallory. When you dig up the books on this joint you're going to see a lot of fancy figures. But our boy Dilwick got ideas. He wanted the place for himself. He shot Mallory with my gun and was going to shoot me, only I got him with the rod I took off the boy whose car I flipped over. Yeah, Dilwick was a good thinker all right. When Grange didn't show up he did what I did and floated down the river himself and found how the eddies took him to the shore. At that time both he and Mallory were figuring on cutting themselves a nice slice of cash from the York estate. Grange was the only one who knew there was evidence that Ruston wasn't York's son and they were going to squeeze it out of her or turn her over to the police for the murder of York."

Price looked at the body again, then offered me a cigarette. "So Grange really did bump her boss. I'll be a so-and-so."

I lit the butt slowly, then blew the smoke through my nostrils. "Grange didn't bump anybody."

The sergeant's face wrinkled. He stared at me queerly.

"This is the aftermath, Price," I reflected. "It's what happens when you light the fuse."

"What the hell are you talking about?"

I didn't hear him. I was thinking about a kidnapping. I was thinking about a scientist with a cleaver in his skull and the chase on for his assistant. I was thinking about Junior Ghent rifling York's office and coming up with some dirty pictures, and then getting beat up. I was thinking about a shot nicking Roxy and a night with Alice Nichols that might have been fun if it hadn't been planned so my clothes could be searched and my skull cracked afterward. I was thinking about a secret cache in the fireplace, a column in the paper, a cop trying to kill me and some words Mallory told me. I was thinking how all this might have been foreseen by the killer when the killer planned the first kill. I was thinking of the face of the killer.

It was a mess. I had said that a hundred times now, but what a beautiful mess it was. There had never been a mess as nasty as this. Nope, not a dull moment. Every detail seemed to overlap and prod something bigger to happen until you were almost ready to give up, and the original murder was obscured by the craziest details imaginable. Rah, rah, sis boom bah, with a fanfare of trumpets as the police come in and throw bullets all over the place. Was it supposed to end like this? I knew one thing. I was supposed to have died someplace along the line. The killer must be fuming now because I was very much alive. What makes people think they can get away with murder? Some plan it simple, some elaborately extreme, but this killer let things take care of themselves and they wound up better than anyone could have hoped for.

"Don't keep secrets, Mike, who did it?"

I threw the butt down, stamped on it. "I'll tell you tomorrow, Price."

"You'll tell me now, Mike."

"Don't fight me, kid. I appreciate all that you did for me, but

I don't throw anyone to the dogs until I'm sure."

"You've killed enough people to be sure. Who was it?"

"It still goes. I have to check one little detail."

"What?"

"Something that makes a noise like a cough."

Price thought I was crazy. "You tell me now or I'll hold you until you do. I can't stick my neck out any further. I'll have hot breaths blowing on my back too, and they'll be a lot hotter if I can't explain this mix-up!"

I was tired. I felt like curling up there with Dilwick and going to sleep. "Don't squeeze, Price. I'll tell you tomorrow. When you take this little package home . . ." I swept my hand around the room, ". . . you'll get a commendation." Over in the corner a trooper was taking the bonds from the girls. Grange was moaning again. "You can get her side of the story anyway, and that will take care of your superiors until you hear from me."

The sergeant waited a long moment then shrugged his shoulders. "You win. I've waited this long . . . I guess tomorrow will be all right. Let's get out of here."

We carried Grange out together with the other trooper lugging the Cook girl over his shoulder. Myra Grange's pupils were big black circles, dilated to the utmost. She was hopped up to the ears. We got them into one of the police cars then stood around until the casino gang was manacled to each other and the clientele weeded out. I grinned when I spotted a half-dozen Sidon cops in the group. They had stopped bellowing long ago, and from the worried looks being passed around it was going to be a race to see who could talk the loudest and the fastest. There would be a new police force in Sidon this time next week. The public might be simple enough to let themselves be bullied around and their government rot out from underneath them, but it would only go so far. An indignant public is like a mad bull. It wouldn't stop until every tainted employee on the payroll was in a cell. Maybe they'd even give me a medal. Yeah, maybe.

I was sick of watching. I called Price over and told him I was going back. His face changed, but he said nothing. There was a lot he wanted to say, but he could tell how it was with me. Price nodded and let me climb into my car. I backed it up and turned around in the drive. Tomorrow would be a busy day. I'd have to prepare my statements on the whole affair to hand over to a grand jury, then get set to prove it. You don't simply kill people and walk away from it. Hell, no. Righteous kill or not the law had to be satisfied.

Yes, tomorrow would be a busy day. Tonight would be even busier. I had to see a killer about a murder.

chapter twelve ▆▆▆▆▆▆▆▆▆▆

IT WAS TEN after eleven when I reached the York estate. Henry came out of his gatehouse, saw me and gaped as though he were looking at a ghost. "Good heavens, Mr. Hammer. The police are searching all over for you! You . . . you killed a man."

"So I did," I said sarcastically. "Open the gates."

"No . . . I can't let you come in here. There'll be trouble."

"There will if you don't open the gates." His face seemed to sag and his whole body assumed an air of defeat. Disgust was written in the set of his mouth, disgust at having to look at a man who shot a fellowman. I drove through and stopped.

"Henry, come here."

The gatekeeper shuffled over reluctantly. "Yes, sir?"

"I'm not wanted any longer, Henry. The police have settled the matter up to a certain point."

"You mean you didn't . . ."

"No, I mean I shot him, but it was justified. I've been cleared, understand?"

He smiled a little, not quite understanding, but he breathed a sigh of relief. At least he knew he wasn't harboring a fugitive in me. I pulled up the driveway to the house, easing around the turns until the beams of my brights spotlighted the house. Inside I saw Harvey coming to the door. Instead of parking in front of the place I rolled around to the side and nosed into the open door of the garage. A big six-car affair, but now there were only two cars in it, counting mine. A long time ago someone started using it for a storeroom and now one end was cluttered with the junk accumulated over the years. Two boys' bicycles were hanging from a suspension gadget set in the ceiling and underneath them a newer model with a small one-cylinder engine built into the frame. Hanging from a hook screwed into an upright were roller skates and ice skates, but neither pair had been used much. Quite a childhood Ruston had.

I shut the door of the garage and looked up. The rain had started. The tears of the gods. Of laughter or sorrow? Maybe the joke was on me, after all.

Harvey was his usual, impeccable, unmoving self as he took my hat and ushered me into the living room. He made no mention of the affair whatsoever, nor did his face reveal any curiosity. Even before he announced me, Roxy was on her way down the stairs with Ruston holding her arm. Billy Parks came out of the foyer grinning broadly, his hand outstretched. "Mike! You sure got your nerve. By gosh, you're supposed to be Public Enemy Number One!"

"Mike!"

"Hello, Lancelot. Hello, Roxy. Let me give you a hand."

"Oh, I'm no cripple," she laughed. "The stairs get me a little, but I can get around all right."

"What happened, Mike?" Ruston smiled. "The policemen all left this evening after they got a phone call and we haven't seen them since. Golly, I was afraid you'd been shot or something. We thought they caught you."

"Well, they came close, kid, but they never even scratched me. It's all finished. I'm in the clear and I'm about ready to go home."

Billy Parks stopped short in the act of lighting a cigarette. His hands began to tremble slightly and he had trouble finding the tip of the butt.

Ruston said, "You mean the police don't want you any longer, Mike?" I shook my head. He gave a little cry of gladness and ran to me, throwing his arms about me in a tight squeeze. "Gee, Mike, I'm so happy."

I patted his arm and smiled crookedly. "Yep, I'm almost an honest man again."

"Mike . . ."

Roxy's voice was the hoarse sound of a rasp on wood. She was clutching the front of her negligee with one hand, trying to push a streamer of hair from her eyes with the other. A little muscle twitched in her cheek. "Who . . . did it, Mike?"

Billy was waiting, Roxy was waiting. I heard Harvey pause outside the door. Ruston looked from them to me, puzzled. The air in the room was charged, alive. "You'll hear about it tomorrow," I said.

Billy Parks dropped his cigarette.

"Why not now?" Roxy gasped.

I took a cigarette from my pocket and stuffed it between my lips. Billy fumbled for his on the floor and held the lit tip to mine. I dragged the smoke in deeply. Roxy was beginning to go white, biting on her lip. "You'd better go to your room, Roxy. You don't look too good."

"Yes . . . yes. I had better. Excuse me. I really don't feel too well. The stairs . . ." She let it go unfinished. While Ruston helped her up I stood there in silence with Billy. The kid came down again in a minute.

"Do you think she'll be all right, Mike?"

"I think so."

Billy crushed his cig out in an ashtray. "I'm going to bed, Mike. This day has been tough enough."

I nodded. "You going to bed, too, Ruston?"

"What's the matter with everybody, Mike?"

"Nervous, I guess."

"Yes, that's it, I suppose." His face brightened. "Let me play for them. I haven't played since . . . that night. But I want to play, Mike. Will it be all right?"

"Sure, go ahead."

He grinned and ran out of the room. I heard him arrange the seat, then lift the lid of the piano, and the next moment the heavy melody of a classical piece filled the house. I sat down and listened. It was gay one moment, serious the next. He ran up and down the keys in a fantasy of expression. Good music to think by. I chain-lit another cigarette, wondering how the music was affecting the murderer. Did it give him a creepy feeling? Was every note part of his funeral theme? Three cigarettes gone in thought and still I waited. The music had changed now, it was lilting, rolling in song. I put the butt out and stood up. It was time to see the killer.

I put my hand on the knob and turned, stepped in the room and locked the door behind me. The killer was smiling at me, a smile that had no meaning I could fathom. It was a smile of neither defeat nor despair, but nearer to triumph. It was no way for a murderer to smile. The bells in my head were rising in a crescendo with the music.

I said to the murderer, "You can stop playing now, Ruston."

The music didn't halt. It rose in spirit and volume while Ruston York created a symphony from the keyboard, a challenging overture to death, keeping time with my feet as I walked to a chair and sat down. Only when I pulled the .45 from its holster did the music begin to diminish. My eyes never left his face. It died out in a crashing maze of minor chords that resounded from the walls with increased intensity.

"So you found me out, Mr. Hammer."

"Yes."

"I rather expected it these last few days." He crossed his legs with complete nonchalance and barely a glance at the gun in my hand. I felt my temper being drawn to the brink of unreason, my lips tightening.

"You're a killer, little buddy," I said. "You're a blood-crazy, insane little bastard. It's so damn inconceivable that I can hardly believe it myself, but it's so. You had it well planned, chum. Oh, but you would, you're a genius. I forgot. That's what everyone forgot. You're only fourteen but you can sit in with scientists and presidents and never miss a trick."

"Thank you."

"You have a hair-trigger mind, Ruston. You can conceive and coordinate and anticipate beyond all realm of imagination. All the while I was batting my brains out trying to run down a killer you must have held your sides laughing. You knew pretty well what killing York would expose . . . a series of crimes and petty personalities scrambled together to make the dirtiest omelet ever cooked. But *you'd* never cook for it. Oh, no . . . not you. If . . . if you were found out the worst that could happen would be that you'd face a juvenile court. That's what you thought, didn't you? Like hell.

"Yes, you're only a child, but you have a man's mind. That's why I'm talking to you like I would to a man. That's why I can kill you like I would a man."

He sat there unmoving. If he knew fear he showed it only in the tiny blue vein that throbbed in his forehead. The smile still played around his mouth. "Being a genius, I guess you thought I was stupid," I continued. With every word my heart beat harder and faster until I was filled with hate. "It was getting so that I thought I was stupid myself. Why wouldn't I? Every time I turned around something would happen that was so screwy that it didn't have any place in the plot, yet in a way it was directly related. Junior Ghent and Alice. The Graham boys. Each trying to chop off a slice of cash for themselves. Each one concerned with his own little individual problem and completely unknowing of the rest. It was a beautiful setup for you.

"But please don't think I was stupid, Ruston. The only true stupidity I showed was in calling you Lancelot. If I ever meet the good knight somewhere I'll beg him to forgive me. But I wasn't so stupid otherwise, Ruston. I found out that Grange had something on York . . . and that something was the fact that she was the only one who knew that he was a kidnapper in a sense. York . . . an aging scientist who wanted an heir badly so he could pass on his learning to his son . . . but his son died. So what did he do? He took a kid who had been born of a criminal father and would have been reared in the gutter, and turned him into a genius. But after a while the genius began to think and hate. Why? Hell, only you know that.

"But somewhere you got hold of the details concerning your birth. You knew that York had only a few years to live and you knew, too, that Grange had threatened to expose the entire affair if he didn't leave his money to her. Your father (should I call him that?) was a thinker too. He worked out a proposition with Alice to have an affair with his lesbian assistant and hold that over her head as a club, and it worked, except that Junior Ghent learned of the affair when his sister told him that York had proposed the same deal to her, too, and Junior wanted to hold that over Grange's head, and Alice's, too, so that he could come in for part of the property split. Man, what a scramble it was after that. Everybody thought I had the dope when it was lying beside the wall out there. Yeah, the wall. Remember the shot you took at Roxy? You were in your room. You tossed that lariat that was beside your bed around the awning hook outside her window, swung down and shot at her through the glass. She had the light on and couldn't see out, but she was a perfect target. You missed at that range only because you were swinging. That really threw me off the track. Nice act you put on when I brought the doctor in. You had him fooled too. I didn't get that until a little while ago.

"Now I know. You, as an intelligent, emotional man were in love. What a howl. In love with your nurse." His face darkened. The vein began to throb harder than ever and his hands clenched into a tight knot. "You shot at her because you saw me and Roxy in a clinch and were jealous. Brother, how happy you must have been when the cops were on my back with orders to shoot to kill. I thought you were simply surprised to see me when I climbed in the window that time. Your face went white, remember? For one second there you thought I came back to get you. That was it, wasn't it?"

His head nodded faintly, but still he said nothing. "Then you saw your chance of bringing the cops charging up by knocking over the lamp. Brilliant mind again. You knew the bulb breaking would sound like a shot. Too bad I got away, wasn't it?

"If I wasn't something of a scientist myself I never would have guessed it. Let me tell you how confounded smart I am. Your time doesn't matter much anyway. I caught up with one of your playmates that snatched you. I beat the living hell out of him and would have done worse to make him talk and he knew it. I'm a scientist at that kind of stuff. He would have talked his head off, only he didn't have anything to say. You know what I asked him? I asked him who Mallory was and he didn't know any Mallory. Good reason too, because ever since you were yanked out of his hands, your father went by the name of Nelson.

"No, he didn't know any Mallory, yet you came home after the kidnapping and said . . . you . . . *heard . . . the . . . name . . . Mallory . . .* mentioned. When I finally got it I knew who the killer was. Then I began to figure how you worked it. Someplace in the house, and I'll find it later, you have the information and Grange's proof that you were Mallory's son. Was it a check that York gave Myra Grange? Somehow you located Mallory and sent him the clipping out of the back issue in the library and the details on how to kidnap you. That was why the clipping was gone. You set yourself up to be snatched hoping that the shock would kill York. It damn near did. You did it well, too, even to the point of switching Henry's aspirins to sleeping tablets. You set yourself up knowing you could outthink the ordinary mortals on the boat and get away. You came mighty close to failing, pal. I wish you had.

"But when that didn't do it you resorted to murder . . . and what a murder. No sweeter deal could have been cooked up by anyone. You knew that when York heard Mallory's name brought into it he'd think Grange had spilled the works and go hunting up his little pet. You thought correctly. York went out there with a gun, but I doubt if he intended to use it. The rod was supposed to be a bluff. Billy heard York leave, and he heard me leave, but how did you reach the apartment? Let me tell you. Out in the garage there's a motorbike. Properly rigged they can do sixty or seventy any day. The noise like a cough that Billy heard was you, Ruston. The sound of the motorbike, low and throaty. I noticed it had a muffler on it. Yeah, York had a gun, and you had to take along a weapon too. A meat cleaver. When I dreamed up all this I wondered why nobody spotted you going or coming, but it wouldn't be too hard to take to the back roads.

"Ruston, you were born under an evil, lucky star. Everything that happened after you surprised York in that room and split his skull worked in your favor. Hell seemed to break loose with everybody trying to cut in on York's dough. Even Dilwick. A crooked copper working for Mallory. Your real father needed that protection and Dilwick fitted right in. Dilwick must have guessed at part of the truth without ever really catching on, and he played it to keep Mallory clear and in a good spot to call for a rake-off, but he got too eager. Dilwick's dead and the rest of his lousy outfit are where they're supposed to be, cooling their heels in a cell.

"But where are you? You . . . the killer. You're sitting here listening to me spiel off everything you already know about and you're not a bit worried. Why should you be? Three or four years in an institution for the criminally insane . . . then prove yourself normal and go back into the world to kill again. You have ethics like Grange. There was a woman who probably loved her profession. She loved it so much she saw a chance to further her career by aiding York, then using it as a club to gain scientific recognition for herself.

"But you . . . hell." I spit the word out. "You banked on getting away scot-free first, then as a second-best choice facing a court. Maybe you'd even get a suspended sentence. Sure, why not? Any psychiatrist would see how that could happen. Under the pressure of your studies your mind snapped. Boy, have you got a brain! No chair, not for you. Maybe a couple of years yanked from your life-span, but what did it matter? You were twenty years ahead of yourself anyway. That was it, wasn't it? Ha!

"Not so, little man. The game just doesn't go that way. I hate to go ex post facto on you, but simply because you're nicely covered by the law doesn't mean you'll stay that way. I'm making up a new one right now. Know what it is?"

He still smiled, no change of expression. It was almost as if he were watching one of his experiments in the rabbit cage.

"Okay," I said, "I'll tell you. All little geniuses . . . or is it genii? . . . who kill and try to get away with it get it in the neck anyway."

Very deliberately I let him see me flick the safety catch on the .45. His eyes were little dark pools that seemed to swim in his head.

I was wondering if I were going to like this.

I never killed a little genius before.

For the first time, Ruston spoke. "About an hour ago I anticipated this," he smiled. I tightened involuntarily. I didn't know why, but I almost knew beforehand what he'd say.

"When I threw my arms around you inside there feigning happiness over your miraculous reappearance, I removed the clip from your gun. It's a wonder you didn't notice the difference in weight."

Did you ever feel like screaming?

My hand was shaking with rage. I felt the hollow space where the clip fitted and swore. I was so damn safety conscious I didn't jack a shell into the chamber earlier either.

And Ruston reached behind the music rack on the piano and came out with the .32.

He smiled again. He knew damn well what I was thinking. Without any trouble I could make the next corpse. He fondled the gun, clicking the hammer back. "Don't move too quickly, Mike. No, I'm not going to shoot you, not just yet. You see, my little knowledge of sleight of hand was quite useful . . . as handy as to know how to open locks. The Normanic sciences weren't all I studied. Anything that presented a problem afforded me the pleasure of solving it in my spare time.

"Move your chair a little this way so I can see you to the best advantage. Ah . . . yes. Compliments are in order, I believe. You were very right and very clever in your deductions. Frankly, I didn't imagine anyone would be able to wade through the tangle that the murder preceded. I thought I did quite well, but I see I failed, up to a certain point. Look at it from my point of view before you invite any impetuous ideas. If you turned me over to the police and proved your case, I would, as you say, stand before a juvenile court. Never would I admit my actual adulthood to them, and I would be sent away for a few years, or perhaps not at all. You see, there's a side to my story too, one you don't know about.

"Or, Mike, and this is an important 'or' . . . I may kill you and claim self-defense. You came in here and in a state of extreme nervous tension hit me. I picked up a gun that dropped out of your pocket . . ." he held up the .32, ". . . and shot you. Simple? Who would disbelieve it, especially with your temperament . . . and my tender years. So sit still and I don't think I'll shoot you for a little while, at least. Before I do anything, I want to correct some erroneous impressions you seem to have.

"I am not a 'few' years ahead of my time . . . the difference is more like thirty. Even that is an understatement. Can you realize what that means? Me. Fourteen years old. Yet I have lived over fifty years! God, what a miserable existence. You saw my little, er, schoolhouse, but what conclusion did you draw? Fool that you were, you saw nothing. You saw no electrical or mechanical contrivances that had been developed by one of the greatest scientific minds of the century. No, you merely saw objects, never realizing what they were for." He paused, grinning with abject hatred. "Have you ever seen them force-feed ducks to enlarge their livers to make better sausages? Picture that happening to a mind. Imagine having the learning processes accelerated through pain. Torture can make the mind do anything when properly presented.

"Oh, I wasn't supposed to actually feel any of all that. It was supposed to happen while I was unconscious, with only the subconscious mind reacting to the incredible pressures being put upon it to grasp and retain the fantastic array of details poured into it like feed being forced through a funnel down a duck's gullet into its belly whether it wants it or not.

"Ah, but who is to say what happens to the mind when such a development takes place? What may happen to the intricate mechanism of the human mind under such stimulation? What new reactions will it develop . . . what new outlets will it seek to repel the monster that is invading it?

"That is how I became what I am . . . but what I learned! I went even farther than was expected of me . . . much farther than the simple sciences and mathematics *he* wanted me to absorb. I even delved into criminology, Mr. Hammer, going over thousands of case histories of past crimes, and when this little . . . circumstance . . . came to my attention, I knew what I had to do . . . then figured out how I could do it.

"I researched, studied and very unobtrusively collected my data, putting myself not *ahead* of you in the commission and solution of criminal actions, but on an approximate level. With your mind highly tuned to absorb, analyze and reconstruct criminal ways, your close association with the police and past experience, you have been able to run a parallel course with me and arrive at the destination at the same time."

He gave me a wry grin. "Or should I say a little behind me?" With his head he indicated the gun in his hand, ". . . seeing that at present I hold the most advantageous position."

I started to rise, but his gun came up. "Remain seated, please. I only said I didn't *think* I would shoot you. Hear me out."

I sat down again.

"Yes, Mr. Hammer, if I had but given it a few days more study your case would have been a hopeless one. Yet you did find me out with all my elaborate precautions, but I still have a marvelous chance to retain my life and liberty. Don't you think?"

I nodded. He certainly would.

"But what good would it do me? Answer me that? What good would it do me? Would I ever have the girl I love . . . or would she have me? She would vomit at the thought. Me, a boy with an adult mind, but still a boy's body. What woman would have me? As the years passed my body would become mature, but the power of my mind would have increased ten-fold. Then I would be an old man within the physical shell of a boy. And what of society? You know what society would do . . . it would treat me as a freak. Perhaps I could get a position as a lightning calculator in a circus. That's what that man did to me! That's what he did with his machines and brilliant thoughts. He crumpled my life into a little ball and threw it in the jaws of science. How I hated him. How I wish I could have made him suffer the way he made me suffer!

"To be twisted on the rack is trivial compared to the way one can be tortured through the mind. Has your brain ever been on fire? Have you ever had your skull probed with bolts of electrical energy while strapped to a chair? Of course not! You can remain smug and commonplace in your normal life and track down criminals and murderers. Your one fear is that of dying. Mine was of not dying soon enough!

"You can't understand how much the human body can suffer punishment. It's like a giant machine that can feed itself and heal its own wounds, but the mind is even greater. That simple piece of sickly gray matter that twists itself into gentle shapes under a thin layer of bone and looks so disarming lying in a bottle of formaldehyde is a colossus beyond conception. It thinks pain! Imagine it . . . it thinks pain and the body screams with the torture of it, yet there is nothing you can call physical in the process. It can conceive of things beyond normal imagination if it is stirred to do so. That is what mine did. Things were forced into it. Learning, he called it, but it might as well have been squeezed into my brain with a compressor, for it felt that way. I knew pain that was not known by any martyr . . . it was a pain that will probably never be known again.

"Your expression changes, Mr. Hammer. I see you believe what I say. You should . . . it is true. You may believe it, but you will never understand it. Right now I can see you change your mind. You condone my actions. I condone them. But would a jury if they knew? Would a judge . . . or the public? No, they couldn't visualize what I have undergone."

Something was happening to Ruston York even as he was speaking. The little-boy look was gone from his face, replaced by some strange metamorphosis that gave him the facial demeanor I had seen during the wild mouthings of dictators. Every muscle was tense, veins and tendons danced under the delicate texture of his skin and his eyes shone with the inward fury that was gnawing at his heart.

He paused momentarily, staring at me, yet somehow I knew he wasn't really seeing me at all. "You were right, Mr. Hammer," he said, a new, distant note in his voice now. "I *was* in love with my nurse. Or better . . . I am in love with . . . Miss Malcom. From the moment she arrived here I have been in love with her."

The hard, tight expression seemed to diminish at the thought and a smile tugged faintly at the corners of his mouth. "Yes, Mr. Hammer, love. Not the love a child would give a woman, but a man's love. The kind of love you can give a woman . . . or any other normal man."

Suddenly the half-smile vanished and the vacant look came back again. "That's what that man did to me. He made an error in his calculations, or never expected his experiment to reach such a conclusion, but that man did more than make me a mental giant. He not only increased my intellectual capacity to the point of genius . . . but in the process he developed my emotional status until I was no longer a boy.

"I am a man, Mr. Hammer. In every respect except this outer shell, and my chronological age, I am a man. And I am a man in love, trapped inside the body of a child. Can you imagine it? Can you think of me presenting my love to a woman like Roxy Malcom? Oh, she might understand, but never could she return that love. All I would get would be pity. Think of that . . . pity. That's what that bastard did to me!"

He was spitting the words out now, his face back in the contours of frustration and hatred, his eyes blankly looking at me, yet through me. It had to be like this, I thought, when he was on the brink of the deep end. It was the only chance I had. Slowly, I tucked my feet under me, the movement subtle so as not to distract him. I'd probably take a slug or two, but I'd lived through them before and if I managed it right I might be able to get my hands on his gun before he could squeeze off a fatal one. It was the only chance I had. My fingers were tight on the arms of the chair, the muscles in my shoulders bunched to throw myself forward . . . and all the time my guts were churning because I knew what I could expect before I could get all the way across that room to where he was sitting.

"I have to live in a world of my own, Mr. Hammer. No other

world would accept me. As great a thing, a twisted thing that I am, I have no world to live in."

The blankness suddenly left his eyes. He was seeing me now, seeing what I was doing and knowing what I was thinking. His thumb pulled back the hammer on the .32 to make it that much easier to trigger off. Behind the now almost colorless pupils of his eyes some crazy thought was etching itself into his mind.

Ruston York looked at me, suddenly with his boy-face again. He even smiled a tired little smile and the gun moved in his hand. "Yes," he repeated, "as great as I am, I am useless."

Even while he had talked, he had done something he had never done before. He exposed himself to himself and for the first time saw the futility that was Ruston York. Once again he smiled, the gun still on me.

There was no time left at all. It had to be now, *now!* Only a second, perhaps, to do it in.

He saw me and smiled, knowing I was going to do it. "Sir Lancelot," he said wistfully.

Then, before I could even get out of the chair, Ruston York turned the gun around in his hand, jammed the muzzle of it into his mouth and pulled the trigger.

The Body Lovers

THIS IS FOR BOB SHIFFER
WHO WAITED A LONG TIME

chapter one ▬▬▬▬▬▬▬▬▬▬▬▬▬

I HEARD THE screams through the thin mist of night and kicked the car to a stop at the curb. It wasn't that screams were new to the city, but they were out of place in this part of New York that was being gutted to make room for a new skyline. There was nothing but almost totally disemboweled buildings and piles of rubble for three blocks, every scrap of value long since carted away and only the junk wanted by nobody left remaining.

And there was a quality to the screams that was out of place too. There was total hysteria that only complete terror can induce and it was made by a child.

I grabbed the flashlight from the glove compartment and climbed out, picked a path through the mounds of refuse and ran into the shadows, getting closer to frenzied shrieks, not knowing what to expect. Anything could have happened there. A kid playing in those decayed and ruptured ruins could be trapped without having to do more than nudge a board or jar an already weakened wall. Aside from the occasional street lamps, there wasn't a light for blocks, and even the traffic detoured the section that handled the heavy equipment of the demolition crews.

But there wasn't any accident. He was just sitting there, a kid about eight in baggy jeans and a sweater, holding two hands clawlike against his face while his body wracked with his screaming. I reached him, shook him to get his attention, but it didn't do any good. I had seen the signs before. The kid was hysterical and in a state of shock, his entire body rigid with fear, his eyes like two great white marbles rolling in his head.

Then I saw what he was screaming about.

They had dropped the body behind a pile of cement blocks from a partly shattered wall, pulling a broken section of sheetrock over it to hide it from casual view. But there's nothing casual about a little kid who liked to play in junk and found himself stumbling over the mutilated body of what had been a redheaded woman. At one time she would have been beautiful, but death had erased all that.

I bundled the kid in my arms and got him back to the car. Along the way the breath had run out of him and the screaming became muffled in long, hard sobs. His hands clutched my arms like small talons and very slowly the knowledge that he was safe came into his eyes.

There was no use trying to question him. At this stage he was too likely to be incoherent. I started the car, made a U-turn and headed back toward the small trailer the construction company used for a watchman's shack.

From outside I could hear a radio playing and I shoved the door open. A stocky, balding guy was bending over a coffeepot on the portable stove and turned around startled. "Hey . . ."

"You got a phone here?"

"Listen, mister . . ."

"Can it, buddy." I flipped my wallet out so he could see my New York State P.I. license and when he did he got a quick look at the .45 automatic in the shoulder sling. "You got trouble here. Where's the phone?"

He put the pot down shakily and pointed to a box built against the wall. "What's the beef? Look, if there's trouble . . ."

I waved him down and dialed Pat's office number downtown. When the desk sergeant answered I said, "This is Mike Hammer. Captain Chambers there?"

"Just a second, please."

Pat came on with, "Homicide, Captain Chambers."

"Mike, pal. I'm on the Leighton Construction site in the watchman's shack. You'd better get a crew and the M.E. down here in a hurry."

Almost seriously, Pat said, "Okay, who'd you kill now?"

"Quit being a comedian. There's a body all right. And get an ambulance here. I have a sick kid on my hands."

"Okay, you stay put. I'll get this put on the air and be there myself. Don't touch anything. Just let it be."

"Forget it. You tell the guys in the squad cars to look for my light. Somebody might still be there . . . and there may have been more than one kid involved. I'll leave this one with the watchman. Maybe a doctor can get something out of him."

I hung up, went outside and brought the kid in and put him down on the cot the watchman used. The guy wanted to know what it was all about, but I cut him off, covered the kid up and told him to stay there until the police arrived. He didn't like it, but there wasn't anything else he could do. Then I got back in the car, drove up the road to where I had found the kid, parked up on the remains of the sidewalk so my headlights could probe the darkness of the buildings and hopped out.

Rather than silhouette myself against their glare, I skirted the beams, picking my way with the flash, the .45 in my hand on full cock. It was doubtful that anybody would stay around a body he had disposed of, but I didn't want to take the chance.

When I reached the sheetrock I stood still and listened. Across town the thin wail of sirens reached me, coming closer each second. But from the interior of the buildings there was nothing. Even a rat crossing the loose litter in there would have made a sound, but the silence had an eerie, dead essence to it.

I pointed the flash down and looked at the body beneath the hunk of sheetrock. She had been in her late twenties, but now time had ended for her. She lay there on her back, naked except for the remnants of a brilliant green negligee that was still belted around her waist. Her breasts were poised in some weird, rigid defiance, her long tapered legs coiled serpentine-like in the throes of death.

She hadn't died easily. The stark horror etched into the tight lines of her face showed that. Half-opened eyes had looked into some nameless terror before sight left them and her mouth was still frozen in a silent scream of pain.

I didn't have to move the body to know how it had happened. The snake-tail red welts that curled up around her rib cage and overlapped all the way down her thighs showed that. Dried clots of blood mottled the nylon of her negligee, stiffening it to boardlike hardness, some of it making the edges of her long hair like an old paintbrush. Tendrils of her life streaked her calves and the back of her neck, but the entire naked front of her was oddly untouched.

Somebody had strung her up and whipped her to death.

The flat of my hand touched the cold flesh of her stomach.

Whoever it was had had plenty of time to get away. She had been there a good twenty-four hours.

Behind me the sirens screamed to a stop and the bright fingers of their spotlights swung in arcs, focused on me and held there. A voice yelled for me to stand still and a half-dozen shadowed figures began clambering over the rubble in my direction.

Pat was the second one to reach me and he told the uniformed cop holding his service .38 on me to put it away. Then I stepped back and watched the mopup operation go into action.

The Medical Examiner had come and gone, the morgue attendants had carted the body away to the autopsy room, the reporters and photogs had left the area strewn with burned-out flash bulbs that winked like dead eyes in the floodlights the search team had set up and the kid had been taken to the hospital. Pat finished his instructions and nodded for me to follow him back to the car.

Not too far away was an all-night diner and we picked out an empty booth in the back corner and ordered coffee. Then Pat said, "Okay, Mike, let's have it."

"I gave it to you."

"Friend, I don't like that coincidence angle. I've found you on top of kills before."

I shrugged and took a sip of the coffee. "I'm not protecting a client, kid. Since noon I was out checking an accident report for Krauss-Tillman on the new Capeheart Building. That's five blocks north of the spot where I found the kid."

"I know where it is."

"So check on me."

"Hell, if I didn't know better, I would. Just don't make this any of your business."

"Why should I?"

"Because you have a big nose. That's what you told me at dinner last night. I'll be damn glad when you marry Velda and she nails your shoes down."

"Thanks a bunch," I grinned at him.

He nodded, picked up his coffee and tasted it, not answering.

Pat and I had been friends too long. I could read him too well. He could say as much without saying a word as he could in a conversation. The years since we first met had hardly left a trace on him; he still resembled a trim business executive more than he did a cop . . . until you got to his eyes. Then you saw that strange quality that was a part of all professional cops, that of having seen trouble and violence so long, fought it step for step, that their expression was like seeing instant history, past, present and future.

I said, "What's on your mind, Pat?"

And he knew me too. I was the same as he was. Our fields were different, but allied nevertheless. We had been together on too many different occasions and we had stood over too many dead bodies together for him not to get my implication.

"It was that thing she wore," he told me.

"Oh?"

"Remember that blonde we fished out of the river last month . . . a schoolteacher from Nebraska?"

"Vaguely. It was in the papers. What about her?"

"She wore a gimmicky robe just like that one, only it was black."

I waited and he looked at me across the coffeecups. "It's on the books tentatively as a suicide, but our current M.E. has a strange hobby, the study of chemically induced death. He thinks she was poisoned."

"He thinks? Didn't he perform an autopsy?"

"Certainly, but she had been in the water a week and there was no positive trace of what he thought could have caused it."

"Then what shook him?"

"A peculiarity in the gum structure common to death from that cause. He couldn't pin it down because of time submerged in water polluted from a chemical treatment unit that was located nearby. He wanted to do some exhaustive tests, but the possibility was so remote and the evidence so inconclusive that we had to release the body to the girl's parents, who later had it cremated."

"Something else is bugging you," I reminded him.

He had another pull at the coffee and set the cup down. "If the M.E. was right, there's another factor involved. The poison he suggested was a slow-acting one that brought death about very gradually and very painfully. It is used by certain savage tribes in South America as a punishment to those members who have committed what they consider to be a serious offense against their taboos."

"Torture?"

"Exactly." He hesitated a second, then added, "I got a funny feeling about this. I don't like your being involved."

"Come on, Pat, where the hell would I come in? I dumped it in your lap and that's as far as I go."

"Good. Keep it like that. You know how the papers handle

anything you're involved in. It's a field day for them. You always did make good copy."

"You worrying about the new administration?"

"Brother!" Pat exploded. "The way our hands are tied between politics and the sudden leniency of the courts it's like trying to walk through a mine field without a detector."

I threw a buck down on the table and reached for my hat. "Don't worry about me," I said. "Let me know how it turns out."

Pat nodded and said, "Sure." But there wasn't any conviction in his voice at all.

The morning was colored a New York gray, damp with river fog that held in suspension the powdered grime and acid grit the city seemed to exhale with its breathing process. It came from deep inside as its belly rumbled with early life, and from the open wounds on its surface where antlike people rebuilt its surface. Everyone seemed oblivious to the noise, never distinguishing between the pain sounds and the pleasure sounds. They simply followed a pattern, their own feet wearing ruts that grew deeper and deeper until there was no way they could get out of the trap they had laid for themselves. Sometimes I wondered just who was the master and who was the parasite. From the window of the office I looked down and all I could see was a sleeping animal covered with ticks he could ignore until one bit too deep, then he would awaken to scratch.

Behind me the door opened and the faint, tingling scent of Black Satin idled past on the draft from the hall. I turned around and said, "Hi, kitten."

Velda gave me that intimate wink that meant nothing had changed and dropped the mail on the desk. She was always a surprise to me. My big girl. My big, beautiful, luscious doll. Crazy titian hair that rolled in a pageboy and styles be damned. Clothes couldn't hide her because she was too much woman, wide shouldered and breasted firm and high, hollow and muscular in the stomach and flanked with beautiful dancer's legs that seemed to move to unheard music. She was deadly, too. The tailored suit she wore under the coat hid a hammerless Browning and her wallet had a ticket from the same agency that issued mine.

Pretty, I thought, and I was such a damn slob. We never should have let it go this long. I had tasted her before, felt that wild mouth on my own and fallen into the deep brown of her eyes.

Crazy world, but she was ready to play the game out as long as I had to.

"See the papers?" she asked me.

"Not yet."

"You did real well. I can't leave you alone for a minute, can I?"

I picked up the tabloid and shook it out. I was there, all right. Page one. The department had held back the details, but it was a big spread anyway. The inside story gave the account of what had happened in general, me hearing the kid and finding the body, but no mention was made of the way the girl had died. Most of the yarn concerned the kid who had been playing on the site and accidentally came across the corpse when he lifted the sheetrock.

As yet no identification had been made of the woman and no witnesses to the disposal of her body had been located, but my accidentally stumbling on the scene was played up and some of my history rehashed for the public benefit. The writer must have been somebody I bucked once, because the intimation was that it involved me personally. Coincidence was something not acceptable to him. At least, not with my background.

I tossed the paper down and pulled a chair up with my foot. "Here we go again."

Velda shrugged off her coat and hung it up. I recited the incident all over again and let her digest it. When I finished she said, "Maybe it'll be good for business."

"Nuts."

"Then stop worrying about it."

"I'm not."

She turned and smiled, the even white edges of her teeth showing beneath that full, rich mouth. "No?"

"Come on, sugar."

"Get it out of your system. At least call Pat and find out what it's about."

"Dames," I said, and picked up the phone.

His hello was cool and he didn't repeat my name, so I knew he had company in the office. He said, "Just a minute," and I heard him get up, walk to the filing cabinet and slide a drawer open.

"What is it, Mike?"

"Just my curiosity. You get anything on that kill?"

"No I.D. yet. We're still checking the prints."

"Any dental work?"

"Hell, she didn't even have a filling in her mouth. She looked like a showgirl type so she might have a police registration someplace. You talk to any reporters yet?"

"I've been ducking them. They'll probably dig me out here, but there's nothing I can tell them you don't know. What's the matter, you don't sound happy."

"Mitch Temple from *The News* spotted the similarity in those flimsy robes that were on the bodies. He got lucky in checking out the labels and beat us to the punch. They were purchased in different spots—those shops that specialize in erotic clothes for dames. No tieup, but enough to hang a story on."

"So what can he say?"

"Enough to stir up some of these sex-happy nuts we have running loose around here. You know what happens when that kind of stuff hits the papers."

"Anything I can do?"

"Yeah . . . if you know Mitch well enough, tell him to lay off."

I grinned into the phone. "Well now, this can be a fun afternoon."

Pat grunted and said, "I suggested you *speak* to him, buddy."

"Sure, buddy. The point is loud and clear. When do you want my official statement?"

"Right now if you can get the lead out."

When I hung up I gave Velda the rundown and reached for my hat. She gave me that funny quizzical look and said, "Mike . . ."

"Yeah?"

"Did Pat notice the color relationship of those negligees?"

"Like what?"

"Black on a blonde and green on a redhead."

"He didn't mention it."

"They aren't exactly conservative. They're show-off things to stimulate the male."

"Pat thinks the last one was a showgirl."

"The other was a schoolteacher though."

"You're thinking funny thoughts, girl," I said.

"Maybe you ought to think about it too," she told me.

chapter two ▰▰▰▰▰▰▰▰▰▰▰

MY RECEPTION AT headquarters wasn't exactly cordial. I gave a detailed statement to a police stenographer in Pat's office, but when he got done with the routine interrogation the new assistant D.A. took it from there, trying to sweat out some angle that connected me to the case. Luckily, Pat deliberately checked out my movements and corroborated them ahead of time, getting both of us off the hook, but not without getting the eager-beaver assistant D.A. red in the face. He gave up in disgust and stamped out of the office after telling me to stay in town.

"He must have read that in a book somewhere," I told Pat.

"Don't mind him. The front office gets spooked when sensational cases hit the papers in an election year."

"Don't kid with me, Pat. It smells like they're setting you up to be the patsy if something goes sour."

"You know how they're shaking up the department. Too many of the good ones already retired out in disgust."

"Don't let those political slobs ride you."

"I'm a paid employee, buddy."

I grinned at him. "Well, I'm not, and I got a big mouth. Outside a dozen reporters are waiting for me to show and I can do a little sounding off when I get rubbed wrong."

"Knock it off."

"Hell, no trouble."

"Forget it. You get to see Mitch Temple?"

"Not yet."

"Do that much and you'll do me a favor. That's all I ask. The rest we can handle just fine right here."

"I told you before I'm not in this."

"Tell it to the boys waiting outside." He got up and waved to the door. "Let's go. Your public awaits."

Pat sweated out the interview with me, watched me stand for pictures and nodded with approval when I parried the questions. For a change I didn't have to dodge and they knew it was because my story was a straight one. A couple wanted my opinion on the kill, but I shrugged it off. So far it was only Mitch Temple who had tried to tie in the earlier murder with the redhead, so there wasn't anything from that direction. If there was a tieup, Pat would find it. Right now it was only guesswork.

When they finished with me we went down to the coffee urn and drew a couple of cups. "You did pretty well back there."

"Nothing to tell them."

"Thanks for not guessing. Maybe I have something to tell you."

"Maybe I'd just as soon not know."

"Yeah," Pat said sourly. "So far there's no definite connection with those negligees. If the first one was a suicide, it's common enough. More than half who do the dutch act go out naked or partially dressed, though damned if I know why."

"You said *if*, Pat."

"Our little M.E. friend pursued his hobby further than I thought. Before they carted the corpse off he took tissue samples for further study. He won't commit himself positively, but he seems satisfied that his diagnosis was correct. As far as he's concerned, that first dame was poisoned, slowly and painfully."

"What can you do about it?"

"Nothing. There's no body to exhume and no way of proving those tissue samples came from the original corpse. Given a few more days and there won't be any trace of the chemical that was administered. It's deteriorated."

"And the other one?"

"A whip that left pretty definite imprints on the flesh. They match specialty items shipped from Australia for a few circus and stage acts."

"Trace the buyers?"

Pat nodded. "The regulars buy them in dozen lots. Straight people. The trouble is, the import house plants them around in all sorts of places . . . even to advertising them in those fetish magazines. We checked their orders and they've sold hundreds by mail alone. It would be damn near impossible to trace one back."

"That leaves her prints."

"And her pictures. The photo lab did a pretty good job of reconstructing her as she must have looked." He held out a four-by-five glossy and I scanned it closely. "Faces like that get remembered," he told me. "She was quite a beauty."

"Can I keep this?"

"Be my guest. It'll be in the paper anyway."

"Good deal. I'll call you after I see Temple."

"Think it'll do any good?"

I let out a short laugh. "I know a few things he wouldn't want to get around."

At twelve-thirty I met Mitch Temple at the Blue Ribbon Restaurant on Forty-fourth Street. He had been an old-line reporter who finally made it with a syndicated column and success seemed to have made him more cynical than ever.

I didn't have to tell him what I was there for. He had laced the facts together as soon as I had called him, and when we had a drink and put our order in he said, "How come you're the errand boy, Mike?"

"Because I might be able to squeeze harder."

He gave me a lopsided grin. "Don't hound me about that party on the yacht. You've used that twice already."

"Then how about the story you never wrote about Lucy Delacort? That house she ran . . ."

"How did you know about that?"

"I got friends in strange places," I told him. "Old Lucy really went for you, didn't she? In fact . . ."

"Okay, enough, enough. What do you want?"

"Pat says to lay off the negligee angle in those two deaths."

His face became strangely alert. "I was right," he said softly, "wasn't I?"

"Got me, Mitch. Pat doesn't want to stir in a sex angle, that's all. It gives the wrong people ideas. Give him a few days to work it out and you can do what you please. Can do?"

"That louses up a lot of legwork. I busted my tail tracking down those labels."

"How much did you get?"

Mitch shrugged. "The probable sales outlets. The clerks couldn't give me anything definite because they were hot items. You know, out-of-towners getting something sexy for the wife back home, servicemen making points with a broad, buying exotic goodies in the big city . . . dames trying to stir a little life into the old man with a little nylon lust."

"That's all?"

"I couldn't get a description to save my tail. Except for a couple of limp characters who took sizes they could wear themselves. Apparently they were regular customers. I could run them down all right, but I don't think it would do any good. Maybe you have an idea."

"Fresh out," I said. "Velda mentioned the color combinations, green with the redhead and black with the blonde if it means anything."

"Hell, they were the fastest selling numbers. They didn't even have a pink or a white in stock. Nobody's modest these days." Mitch leaned back in his chair. "Maybe you'd better tell Pat I'm still working on it."

"So's he."

"I'm surprised nobody else made the connection. It isn't a big one, but it's a connection."

"Probably because that schoolteacher was a suicide."

"Now I'm beginning to wonder about that too," Mitch growled.

"So's Pat, but he's seen other suicides go out in their scanties. Seems to be a common practice."

"Yeah, I know. She could have had a coat on before she hit the river. Nobody would have noticed her then. If she dropped it any one of that crowd along the docks would have picked it up and hocked it for a drink without thinking about it."

"What'll I tell Pat?"

"I'll play along for a week. Meanwhile, I'll still try to get an angle on those gowns." He looked across his glass at me. "Now what about you, Mike? You've always made interesting copy. Where do you stand?"

"Out of it. I'm a working stiff."

"You're not even curious?"

"Sure," I grinned, "but I'll read about it in *The News*."

After lunch I walked to Broadway with Mitch, turned north and headed back to the office. The morning damp had turned into a drizzle that slicked the streets and turned the sidewalks into a booby trap of umbrella ribs. The papers on the newsstands were still carrying front-page stories of the death of the redhead and the afternoon edition of one had a nice picture of me alongside the body shot of the corpse and one of the kid. I bought three different papers, stuffed them in my raincoat pocket and turned in at the Hackard Building.

Velda had left a note saying she was going to do some shopping and would be back later. Meanwhile, I was to call the Krauss-Tillman office. I dialed Walt Hanley at K-T, got his instructions on another job, hung up and added a postscript to Velda's note saying that I'd be out of the city for a few days and to cancel our supper date.

She was going to be sore about that last part. It was her birthday. But I was lucky. I had forgotten to buy her a present anyway.

The few days were a week long and I stopped by the office at a quarter to five. Velda sat there typing and didn't even look up until she had finished the page. "Happy birthday," I said.

"Thanks," she said sarcastically.

I grinned and tossed down the package I had picked up ten minutes ago. Then she couldn't hold the mad any longer and ripped the paper off it. The pearls glinted a milky white in the light and she let out a little squeal of pleasure. All she could say was, "They real?"

"They'd better be."

"Come here, you."

I leaned over and sipped at the rich softness of her mouth and felt that same surge of warmth that came over me whenever she did those woman-things to me.

I pushed her away and took a deep breath. "Better quit while you're ahead."

"But I thought you were winning."

"You were drowning me, kitten."

"Just wait till later."

"Stop talking like that, will you?" I said. "I've been stuck in the bushes a week until I'm ready to pop."

"So I'll pop you."

I rumpled her hair and perched on the edge of the desk. She had my mail stacked up in three piles, circulars, business and personal, and I riffled through them. "Anything important?"

"Haven't you been reading the papers?"

"Kid, where I've been there wasn't anything but hills and rocks and trees."

"They identified the redhead that was killed."

"Who was she?"

"Maxine Delaney. She was a stripper on the West Coast for a while, was picked up twice in a suspected call-girl operation, but released for lack of evidence or complaints by parties involved. She was last heard of in Chicago where she was registered with a model agency and did a few nudies for a photographer there."

"I meet the nicest people, don't I? Any mail?"

"Nothing special. You got a package there from a pen pal, though."

In the personal pile was a flat, six-inch square package with a box number address and a postmark from that famous city on the Hudson that harbors New York's more notorious ex-citizens. I tore it open and took the lid off the box inside.

A stenciled letter informed me that the enclosed was made by a prison inmate and any voluntary contribution I cared to make would go in the recreational fund. The enclosed was a neat black handmade leather wallet and tooled on the front in an elaborate scroll was MICHAEL HAMMER, INSURANCE ADJUSTER. And it was such a nice piece of work too.

I tossed it in front of Velda. "How about that?"

"Your reputation has gone to the dogs." She looked up, read the letter and added, "They have a complaint department?"

"Send five bucks. Maybe it's deductible." I dropped the wallet in my pocket and slid off the desk. "Let's have some supper."

"Okay, insurance adjuster."

We were going out the door when the phone rang. I wanted to let it ring, but Velda was too much a secretary for that. She answered it and handed it to me. "It's Pat."

"Hi, buddy," I said.

I couldn't quite pin down his tone of voice. "Mike . . . when did you see Mitch Temple last?"

"A week ago. Why?"

"Not since?"

"Nope."

"He give you a hard time or anything?"

"Hell no," I told him. "I gave you all the poop on that deal."

"Then tell me this . . . you got a straight alibi for, say . . . twenty-four hours ago?"

"Buddy, I can have my time and places verified by three witnesses for the past seven days to this minute. Now what gives?"

"Somebody bumped Temple in his own apartment, one knife thrust through the aorta, and he died all over his fancy oriental rug."

"Who found him?"

"A girl friend who had a key to his apartment. She managed to call us before she went to pieces. Get up here. I want to talk to you."

I hung up and looked at Velda, knowing my face was pulled tight. "Trouble?" she asked me.

"Yeah. Somebody killed Mitch Temple."

She knew what I was thinking. "He was poking around on that girl's murder, wasn't he?"

I nodded.

"Then what does Pat want with you?"

"Probably every detail of our last conversation. Come on, let's go."

Mitch Temple had an apartment in a new building on the east side, a lavish place occupied by the wealthy or famous, and the uniformed doorman wasn't used to seeing squad cars and police officers parked outside the ornate doorway.

The cop on duty recognized me, passed me through and we took the elevator up to the sixth floor. Two apartments opened off the small lobby, one apparently belonging to an absent tenant, the other wide open, the cops inside busy with routine work.

Pat waved us in and we skirted the stain on the floor near the door and followed him across the room to where the body lay. The lab team wound up their work and stood to one side talking baseball. I said, "Mind?"

"Go ahead," Pat told me.

I knelt by the body and took a look at it. Mitch Temple lay sprawled on his side in a pool of blood, sightless eyes glazed with death. One hand was still stretched out, clawing at his suitcoat he had jerked off the chair back, his fingers clutching the white linen handkerchief he always wore in his breast pocket. I stood up and looked at the trail of blood from the door to the hole in his chest. It was a good twenty feet long.

"What do you make of it, Pat?"

"Looks like he opened the door to answer the bell, took a direct stab from an eight-inch knife blade and staggered back. Whoever killed him just closed the door and left."

"A wound like that usually drops a man."

"Most of the time."

"What was he after in his coat?"

"Something to stop the flow of blood is my guess. Nothing seems to have been touched. I'm surprised he lived long enough to get that far. So was the Medical Examiner. He fell twice getting to his coat and crawled the last few feet."

"Nobody comes into these apartments without being announced downstairs first," I reminded him.

Pat gave me a disgusted look. "Come on, we haven't pinpointed the time of death yet, but a pro could manage it at the right time. These places are far from foolproof. We're checking out the tenants and anybody else who was here, but I'm not laying any bets we'll come up with something. The type who live here don't want to be involved in any way. They don't even know their next-door neighbors."

"That's New York," I said.

"Now how about you." It was a statement, not a question.

I looked at him and shook my head. "Count me out. I haven't had contact with him since I saw him last. I told you what he said . . . he'd lay off his story for a week, but meanwhile he'd keep on working that negligee angle. Think he found something? He had a lot of sources."

Pat shrugged. "Neither his paper nor his secretary had any record of his movements. She said he was gone a lot, but he turned out his column regularly. We're backtracking the items he reported in case it ties in with one of them."

"How about that series he did on the Mafia last month?"

"They're too smart to buck the press. It wouldn't stop anything and throw too much light on them. They want anonymity, not publicity. This is something else."

"Those damn negligees?"

"It's a possible. I hoped you'd come up with something."

I reached in my pocket for my cigarettes and got the wallet instead. "Hell, I'm only an insurance adjuster," I grinned. "It says so right here." I tossed the wallet to Velda. "Here, you can have it." She caught it, and like all women, dropped it in her pocketbook. "Sorry, Pat. I can't give you a damn thing. That is, unless the police department wants to employ me."

"Yeah," he grunted. "I can picture that. Well, you might as well get out of here before the press arrives. They'll blow this one sky high as it is and I don't want them getting cute followup angles involving you."

"Count me out, old buddy."

"If you hear of anything, let me know."

"Sure will."

"There's a side entrance. Take that out."

We started for the door and I turned around as I reached it. "Mind letting me know how things shape up?"

Pat's mouth twitched into a smile. "Okay, nosy."

Supper was a steak in Velda's apartment, a homey little arrangement she set up deliberately, a perfect man trap if there was one. She wore a quilted housecoat of deep blue, belted loosely enough so that when she walked each step exposed a satin length of calf and thigh, provocatively out of reach as she passed by. Sitting opposite me, the lapels stretched over the deep swell of her breasts, and with the gentlest motion of her shoulders, fell apart so I could be taunted by her loveliness.

I finally pushed the plate away, the steak finished, but untasted. She poured the coffee, grinned and said, "See what you're missing?"

"You're a nut." I fished my cigarettes out and stuck one in my mouth. "Light me, will you?"

Velda reached for her pocketbook, dumped some of the stuff out until she found matches and lit my butt. When she was putting the things back she paused with the wallet in her hand and said, "Why would an inmate send you that?"

"You saw the letter. It's part of their rehabilitation program."

"No, I don't mean that. If they're sent to well-known people, certainly they wouldn't mistake their occupation. Especially not yours. It's too bad there's no name of the maker."

"Let's see that." I took the wallet and flipped it open. It was of standard design with card pockets, an identification window and a section for bills. I felt in all the compartments, but nothing was there. "Empty," I told her. "Besides, these things would be checked to make sure nobody was sending messages outside. It could be a cute gimmick."

"Maybe it has a secret compartment," she laughed.

But I didn't laugh. I stared at the wallet a long moment, then felt around the folded edges until I found it, a cleverly contrived secret pocket that cursory examination would never uncover.

That's where the note was.

It was written in pencil, printed in tiny caps on toilet paper. I read it twice to make sure of what I had, digesting every word. *Dear Mike, Heard about that redhead on the radio. My sister knew her and the Poston dame. Didn't think much about it when the Poston kid died, but this one bothers me. I ain't heard from Greta in four months. You find her and make her write and I'll pay you when I get out.* It was signed, *Harry Service.*

Velda took the note from my fingers and read it over, frowning. "Poston," she said softly. "Helen Poston. That was the school-teacher who committed suicide."

"That's the one."

"But this Harry Service . . . wasn't he the one . . . ?"

"Yeah, I got him sent up."

"Why would he write to you?"

"Maybe he doesn't hold a grudge. Besides, he's not the type to confide in cops. He wouldn't give them the sweat off his butt."

"What're you going to do about it, Mike?"

"Damn it," I said, "what can I do?"

"Let Pat have it."

"Great. Then word gets around I'm a first-class fink. Harry went to all that trouble to get this to me. The insurance adjuster bit was supposed to tip me and I'm thick-skulled about it."

Velda handed the slip back to me. "You don't owe this Service any favors."

"Not in the ordinary sense. Even though I nailed him in that robbery and he tried to kill me, he still figures I'm square enough to deal with." I glanced at the note again. "It's a crazy request."

"What you're thinking is even crazier."

"A wild kind of a client."

She gave a little shrug of resignation. "Pat doesn't want you playing with this thing. You're only asking for trouble."

"Hell, all I'm doing is locating a missing person."

"You're rationalizing," she said. "But go ahead, you'll do it anyway. Only don't start tonight, okay?"

"Okay."

"Okay then," she repeated with an impish grin and came into my arms. On the way she tugged at the belt and I felt wild little fingers crawl up my spine.

chapter three

THE FILE ON Harry Service listed his sister Greta as next-of-kin. He had taken a seven-to-fifteen-year fall on that armed robbery rap a year and a half ago and at that time her address was listed as being in Greenwich Village. I never remembered her being at the trial, but when I went through the back issues of the paper there was one photo of the back of a woman in a dark coat squeezing Harry's arm after he was sentenced.

It was a little after two when Hy Gardner got to his office. He waved me into a chair and sat down behind his typewriter. "What's on your mind, Mike?"

"The Service trial."

"You did him a favor slamming him in the cooler. That way he won't make the chair. You're not trying to spring him now, are you?"

"Not me."

"Then what's the problem?"

"When he was sentenced there was a dame there to see him off. It may have been his sister. Your paper had a picture of her back, but that's all. If you know any of the photogs who covered the thing, maybe one of them might have clipped a shot of her face."

"Something doing?"

"She might be a witness in something else, but I want to be sure."

"I can check," he said. "Hang on."

Twenty minutes later a clerk came up from the morgue with

two four-by-five glossies that showed her face. One was a partial profile, the other a front view. The last one was the best. The coat hinted at the fullness of her body and the wide brim of her hat didn't conceal a face that devoid of makeup was pretty, but with it could have been beautiful. They hadn't printed the picture because Harry Service's face was turned away, but the notation on the back of the photo named her as *Greta Service, sister.* Three others were identified as Harry's lawyer, the D.A. and the owner of the store he was trying to rob.

"Can I have this, Hy?"

"Be my guest," he said without looking up from his notes. "When you going to tell me about it?"

"It's just a little thing. Might be nothing at all."

"Don't con me, kiddo. I've seen you with that look before."

"Maybe I better not play poker."

"Not with me. Or Pat."

I got up and stuck on my hat. "So you want to come along?"

"Not me. I'm cleaning up here and heading for Miami. I know when to cut out. Write me about it when it's over."

"Sure thing," I said. "Thanks."

The Greenwich Village number was a weatherbeaten brownstone that was part of the old scene, a three-story structure that could have been anything once, but had been converted into studio apartments for the artists and writers set. Inside the small foyer I ran my fingertip along the names under the mailboxes, but there was no Greta Service listed. It wasn't surprising. In view of the publicity given her brother, she could have changed her name.

Now it was all legwork and luck. I pushed the first bell button and shoved the door open when the latch began to click. A guy in a pair of paint-stained slacks stuck a tousled head out the door and said, "Yeah?"

"I'm looking for a Greta Service."

He gave me a twisted grin and shook his head. "Now friend, that sure ain't me. I'm the only straight man in this pad. This is a dame you're talking about, ain't it?"

"That's what I was told. She lived here a year and a half ago."

"Before my time, feller. I've only been here six weeks."

"How about one of the other tenants?"

The guy scratched his head and frowned. "Tell you what . . . as far as I know that kookie bunch on the next floor moved in about four months ago. Student type, if you know the kind. Long hair, tight pants and loose, and I mean like loose, man . . . morals. Me, mine are lax, but not loose. They're real screamers up there.

Odd jobs and checks from home to keep them away from home. If I was their old man . . ."

"Who else is there?"

He let out a short laugh. "You might try Cleo on the top floor. That is, if she's available for speaking to. She ain't always. They tell me she's been around a while."

"Cleo who?"

"It's *whom*, ain't it?" he said. "Anyway, who cares? I don't think I ever heard any other name."

"Thanks, I'll give it a try."

When he had ducked back behind the door I picked my way up the stairs to the second-floor landing and stood there a few seconds. Inside the apartment a couple was arguing the merits of some obscure musician while another was singing an accompaniment to a scratchy record player. It was only ten A.M., but none of them sounded sober. I took the guy's advice and followed the stairs up to the next floor.

I knocked twice before I heard the languid tap of heels come toward the door. It opened, not the usual few inches restricted by a guard chain women seem to affect, but fully and with a single sweeping motion designed to stun the visitor. It was great theatrical staging.

She stood there, hands against the door jambs, the light from the French windows behind her filtering through the silken kimono, silhouetting the matronly curves under it. Poodle-cut hair framed a face that had an odd, intense beauty that seemed to leap out of dark eyes that were so inquisitive they appeared to reach out and feel you, then decide whether you were good enough to eat or not.

For a second the advantage was hers and all I could do was grin a little bit and say, "Cleo?"

"That's me, stranger." Then the eyes felt me a little more and she added, "You look familiar."

"Mike Hammer."

"Ah, yes." She let a little laugh tinkle from her throat. "The man on the front page." Then she let her hands drop, held one out and took my arm. "Come in. Don't just stand there."

This time I let my own eyes do the feeling. They ran up and down the length of her asking questions of their own.

Cleo laughed again, knowing what I meant. "Don't mind my costuming. I'm doing a self-portrait," she said. "It does kind of rock you at first though, doesn't it?"

"Pretty interesting," I agreed.

She gave a disgusted toss of her head. "Men like you have lived too long. Nothing's new. I could slaughter you." She grinned again and ran her fingers through her hair. "But you should see what it does to the other kind."

"I don't know the other kind."

"Naturally."

She led me inside and slid up on a wooden bar stool in front of an easel while I looked around the room. Unlike most of the village pads, it was a completely professional setup. The windows and skylight were modern and cleverly arranged for maximum efficiency, wall shelves stocked with every necessity, and on the far end, equipment for engraving and etching stretched from one side to the other.

Every wall was covered with framed pictures, some original art, others black and white or full color glossy reproductions. Every one bore the simple signature, *Cleo.*

"Like them?"

I nodded. "Commercial."

"Hell yes," she told me. "The loot is great and I don't go the beatnik route. I don't expect you to recognize them . . . you don't look the type to read women's fashion magazines, but I happen to be one of the best in the field."

I walked over to the easel and stood beside her. The picture she was painting would never make any family magazine. The face and body were hers, all right, but the subject matter was something else. Even unfinished you knew what she was portraying. She was a seductress for hire, promising any man anything he could possibly want, not because money was the object, but because she desired it that way herself. It was a total desire to please and be pleased, but whoever succumbed to the lure was going to be completely devoured with the excesses she could provide to satisfy her own pleasures.

"How about that," I said.

"You got the message?"

"I got the message," I repeated. "Still life."

"Drop dead," she smiled.

"It isn't commercial."

"No? You'd be surprised what some people would buy. But you're right, it isn't commercial . . . or rather, not for sale. I indulge myself in the hobby between assignments. Now, you didn't come up here to talk art."

I walked over and eased myself down into a straight-backed chair. "You ever know Greta Service?"

There was no hesitation. "Sure. She lived downstairs for a while."

"Know her well?"

She shrugged and said, "As well as you ever get to know anybody around here. Except for the old-timers, most are transients or out-of-towners who think the Village is the Left Bank of New York."

"What was she?"

"An out-of-towner. I forget where she came from, but she was doing some modeling work and moved into the Village because it seemed the thing to do and the rent comparatively cheap."

Casually, I asked, "What are you doing here?"

"Me," Cleo smiled, "I like it. I guess I read too many stories about the place years ago too. Right now I'm one of the old-timers which means you've been here over ten years. Only thing is, I'm different."

"Oh?"

"I make money. I can support my habit of fine foods and a big bar bill. Around here I'm an oddball because of it. The others dig my hobby but sneer at my crass commercial works, yet they still take the free drinks and stuff their pockets as well as their stomachs whenever I toss a neighborhood soirée up here." She glanced at me seriously. "What's with this Greta Service?"

"A friend wants to locate her. Got any ideas?"

Cleo thought a moment, then shook her head. "You know about her brother?"

I nodded.

"Not long after that she moved out. As far as I know, she never said a word about where she was going. Her mail piled up in the box downstairs, so apparently she never left a forwarding address."

"How about her friends?"

"Greta wasn't exactly the friendly type. She was . . . well, remote. I saw her with a few men, but it wasn't like . . . well, whether she cared they were there or not. I did get an impression however. Unless they were wealthy, she wasn't interested."

"Gold digger?"

"What an archaic term," Cleo told me. "No, not quite that. She just was determined to get money. Several times she said she had enough of scraping by. It was there to be had if you looked hard enough." Cleo slid off the stool and stretched elegantly, the sheer silk of the kimono pulling taut across the skin beneath it. "She was a determined kid," she said. "She'll make it somehow."

"But how?"

"Women have ways if they want something badly enough. There are always hidden talents."

"Yeah, sure," I said.

"Cynic."

"Anybody around here who might know where she'd be?"

She gave me a thoughtful look and said, "Possibly. I'd have to ask around some."

"I'd appreciate it."

Cleo grinned at me. "How much?"

"What're you asking?"

"Maybe you'd like to pose for me."

"Hell, I'm not the still-life type," I said.

"That's what I mean," she said impishly.

I got up with a laugh. "I'm going to squeal to your boss."

"Oh, you'd like her."

"Dames," I said. I walked to the door and turned around. Cleo still had the window at her back and the shadow effect of her body was a tantalizing thing. "I'll check back later," I told her.

"You'd better," she said.

The R. J. Marion Realty Company on Broadway owned the Village building Greta Service had occupied. The receptionist introduced me to a short, balding man named Richard Hardy who handled the downtown rentals and after he waved me to a chair and I explained what I wanted he nodded and said, "Greta Service, yes, I remember her, but I'm afraid I can't help you at all."

"No forwarding address?"

"Nothing at all. We held her mail here for a month before returning it to the senders, hoping she might notify us, but there was no word whatsoever. Incidentally, this isn't exactly uncommon. Some of the tenants down there are, well, peculiar. They come and go and sometimes don't want anyone to know where they've been."

"Any of that mail here now?"

"No . . . but it wouldn't help anyway. It was mostly bills from some of the better stores, a few from model agencies and a lot of circulars. Her rent and utilities were paid up, so we didn't think much of it."

I thanked the guy, left him to a desk full of paperwork and went down to the street. New York still had her gray hat on and the air had a chilly smell to it. I edged to the curb side and followed the crowd up to my corner and headed toward the office.

Velda was on the phone when I walked in. She finished talking and hung up. "How'd you make out?"

I gave her what information I had and picked up a couple of folders from her desk. "What's this?"

"Background on Helen Poston and Maxine Delaney. I thought you'd want it. They're mostly newspaper clips, but they cover as much as the police have. I reached some people in the Poston girl's home town who knew her . . . the school superintendent, the principal, two teachers and the man who sold her a used car. She had a good reputation as far as her work was concerned, but I got the impression that teaching wasn't her main ambition in life."

I glanced up from the folder and stared at her. "Like how?"

"Nothing definite . . . it was an impression. The car salesman was the one who put his finger on it. You know the type . . . a real swinger ready to sound off about anybody. He was the one who said he'd like to see her in a bikini. She bought the car to make a trip and seemed pretty excited about getting away from the home town and all he could think of was a small-town teacher in a big city having a ball away from the prying eyes of the school board. I said I was doing a feature story on her and he made sure I spelled his name right."

"And Maxine Delaney?"

"I called Vernie in L.A. and he checked with the arresting officer who picked her up. His opinion was that she was one of the lost tribe who inhabit the movie colony with stars in their eyes until disillusionment sets in, then she didn't give a damn any more. Bob Sabre reached the Chicago outfit she posed for and said they didn't bother with her because she didn't project. Nice face and body, but she lacked that intangible something. She still thought she was a star and played it that way."

"Two of a kind," I said.

"There's a similarity." She pinched her lower lip between her teeth a moment, then said, "Mike . . ."

"What?"

"I can see the green on the redhead, but that black didn't fit the blonde Poston girl. She wasn't the type."

"They change when they hit the big town, kid."

"Everybody said she was extremely conservative."

"That was at home. There weren't any eyes watching her here."

"Could there be a connection?"

"If there is, it'll come out. Right now I want you to check all the charge accounts at the better stores and see what you can get on Greta Service. She might have left a forwarding address with their billing departments. I can't see a dame giving up charge accounts or lousing up her credit if it can be avoided."

Velda grinned up at me. "You going to leave a forwarding address?"

"Yeah," I said, "yours. I'll call in later."

"Thanks a lot."

"Only because I love you, baby."

"Oh boy," she said quietly and reached for the phone.

Donald Harney had an office on the ninth floor of the Stenheim Building, sharing space with three other lawyers who hadn't made the high-income cases yet. The legal library was all secondhand and it was plain that any attempt at putting up a front was a lost cause a long time ago. The community receptionist told me to go right on in and I pushed through the door to his private cubicle.

Harney didn't stand on ceremony in his own back yard. He sat there in his shirtsleeves with a pencil over his ear editing a brief, shoved his hair out of his eyes and got up for a handshake. Our last meeting at Harry Service's trial had been short, on the witness stand, and then only for a few perfunctory questions regarding his arrest. It had been a plea of guilty and his concern was getting Harry off with as light a sentence as possible.

When he sat back relaxed he said, "What brings you here, Mike? My client bust out?"

"Harry isn't the type," I told him. "He'd rather sweat out a parole. Look . . . I'd like some facts about him."

"It's still privileged information."

"I know, but it concerns the welfare of your client . . . and mine." I grinned at him. "Funny as it sounds, Harry asked me to do him a favor." I held out the note he had sent and let Harney read it over, then tucked it back in my wallet.

"How'd he get that to you?"

"Guys in stir can think up a lot of ways. Know anything about his sister?"

Harney squinted and swung in his chair. "Harry's case was assigned to me by the court. He didn't have any funds to provide for a defense. The trial lasted three days only because the prosecution was trying to tie Harry into a few other unsolved robberies. The last day his sister appeared out of nowhere, damn well upset, too. Apparently they had been pretty close in their earlier days, then split up after their parents died and hadn't kept in touch."

"It was too late to do anything then."

Harney shrugged and nodded. "She seemed to blame herself . . . a sort of maternal instinct coming out. When they were kids he was quite a hero to her. Later he helped her out financially when she was off working."

"What did she do?"

"She never said. Anyway, the day Harry was sentenced she told him she was going to make sure they never had to worry again, that she'd get things ready for his release . . . you know, the usual emotional outburst."

"Was it?"

Harney gave me a puzzled look. "Well, she seemed serious enough, but I've been through those situations before. It sounds good at the time, but how the hell can a dame alone do all that?"

"There are ways."

"Which brings us up to why you're here."

"Yeah. She's missing and Harry's worried. Tell me, have you seen him in prison?"

"Twice. I went up there on other business and took the time to say hello."

"He mention anything?" I asked him.

"Only that things were fine, his sister came to see him often and he was working toward a parole. You can't always tell, but he seemed convinced that crime was more trouble than it was worth. In fact, he even asked about you. Once he called you a 'nice bastard' because you could have killed him and didn't."

I stuck a butt in my mouth and lit it. "There's an odd factor here, you know?"

"The way Harry Service contacted you?"

"He could have gone through you."

Harney let out a grunt and shook his head. "You know those guys, Mike. I represent the law. Face it, in your own peculiar way, you don't. With your reputation you're closer to being one of their own kind. I can see his point. Now, what can I do to help out?"

"Get a line on Greta Service and buzz me." I grinned a little and added, "I'll split the fee when Harry gets out."

For a few seconds Harney studied my face. "You got more going than Harry Service, haven't you?"

"I don't know. There's a possibility. At least we can wrap up this bit for Old Harry."

"You don't owe him anything."

"He asked me for a favor."

A small twitch of humor touched the corner of his mouth. "You tough guys are all alike."

"Will do?" I asked.
"Will do," he said.

Greenwich Village is a state of mind. Like Hollywood. There really isn't such a place left any more. It exists in the memories of the old ones and in the misconceptions of the new ones. It's on the map and in the vocabulary, but the thing that made Hollywood and the Village has long since gone and thousands prowl the area where they once were, looking for the reality but finding only the shadow.

A few landmarks are still around; the streets do their jig steps and the oddball characters wrapping up their life on canvas or in unpublished manuscripts are attractions for the tourists. But the city is too big and too fast-growing to contain a sore throat and coughed-up phlegm. The world of commerce has moved in, split it with the beatniks who clutched for a final handhold, and tolerates it because New York still needs a state of mind to retain its image while the computers finally take over.

For those who lived there, night, like Gaul, was divided into three parts. The realists occupied it early, the spectators came to browse during the second shift, then the others waited for the all-clear to sound and came out of the dream world to indulge their own fantasies.

I sat in a smoke-shrouded bar nursing a highball, watching the third stage drift in. Since midnight I had been buying the bartender a drink every third round and the last hour he had been getting friendly enough to pour me a legitimate jolt and spend time down at my end growling about the type of trade he had to put up with. After a couple paid for beer in nickels and pennies he came back, mopped down in front of me, moving my bills out of the way and said, "What are you doing here? You're from uptown, ain't you?"

"Way uptown."

"This place gives me the creeps," he said. "I shoulda stayed with the Department of Sanitation. My old lady didn't like being married to a garbage man. Now look. I serve garbage to garbage. Damn, what a life."

"It's tough all over."

"You looking for action?"

"That I can get uptown."

His eyes ran over my face. "I seen you before. You with the Vice Squad?"

"Hell no."

"Too bad. You'd have a ball in this place only you'd never have jail room." He stopped and squinted at me. "Where did I see you?"

I flipped one of my cards out of my coat pocket and held it out.

"Ain't that something," he said. "I knew I seen you someplace. What's with this joint?"

"The end of the road, looks like. I've been trying to run down Greta Service all night."

"So why didn't you ask?"

"You know her?"

The guy hunched his shoulders and spread his hands out. "She used to come by here some. Lived a few blocks over, I think. She in a jam?"

"Not that I know of. Her brother wants to locate her."

"The one who got pinched? Hey . . . you were on that job, weren't you?"

"I nailed him. Now he wants me to find her."

"Boy, she ain't been around a while. She moved outa her pad down here, but came back sometimes for hellos. Went native once."

"What?"

"You know, hanging on the arm of some gook with a funny hat. He wasn't no American. The guy had bucks and shelled it out, but when she started mixing it with some of her old friends he made her cut out."

"Recognize him?"

The guy picked up the bar rag and mopped at nothing in particular. "Hell, who knows from who around here? They all look alike. Most of that type are down at the Flagstaff anyway. I don't pay no attention to nobody nohow. Stay out of trouble like that."

"Ever see her with anybody else?"

"Couple of times she was with the dykes what come in, only in this joint that ain't unusual. She'd sit with some of the local kids for a few drinks sometimes. Can't say I ever seen her with anyone special except that gook." He picked up my glass, built me a fresh drink on the house and set it down in front of me. He let me taste it, nodded approvingly, and said, "Come to think of it, I stopped by Lew Michi's place after I closed up here and she was with some good-looking dame and one of those foreigners then too. This one didn't wear a gook hat, but he was real native."

"How's that?"

He made another gesture with his hands and said, "You know, dark like, maybe one of those Hindoos or something. They was having a pretty good time, laughing and talking. That was some broad she was with, a real doll. Plenty expensive, too. Some of them tourists come down here dressed like a party at the Ritz."

"Remember when that was?"

The bartender frowned, reached back in thought and told me, "Long time ago. I don't remember seeing her after that at all. Guess she moved out."

I finished the drink and slid a couple of singles across the bar to him. "Not much I can do here then. Thanks for the talk."

"No trouble. Come back any time. Some nights this place gets real jumpy."

I grinned at him. "I bet."

Outside, the night people were rendezvousing on the corners, ready to swing into the usual routine. Headquarters was a bar or a restaurant where they could sip coffee or a beer and talk interminably about nothing anyone else could understand.

A couple of squad cars cruised by slowly, the cops scanning faces, checking each place for trouble before going on. Nobody paid any attention to them at all. I reached Seventh Avenue, turned right and walked south a block toward a cab stand ready to call it a night.

Then I saw Cleo sitting at the end of the bar on the corner and pushed in through the door and sat down beside her.

"Hello, big man," she said without looking up from her paper.

"Got eyes in the back of your head?"

"Nope. Just good peripheral vision." Then she folded the paper with a throaty chuckle and flipped it aside. "You're still haunting our house."

"It's not like the old days, Cleo."

"Things change. Find out anything about Greta?"

"Not much. She didn't leave much to start from." I waved the bartender over and told him to bring me a Four Roses and ginger ale. "You ever know who she worked for?"

Cleo gave me a small negative shake of her head. "She was registered with most of the agencies. I know she got jobs here and there . . . at least enough to support herself. Most of them were with the garment industry, modeling for the trades. You really have to hustle to make a buck in that business. I sent her up to see Dulcie once. . . ."

"Who?" I interrupted.

"Dulcie McInnes, my boss. Super fashion editor of the Proctor

Group. Money, society, international prominence among the fashion set who buy three-thousand-dollar gowns. Greta got her interview, but it ended there. Her appearance was earthy rather than ethereal and the Proctor girls have to be gaunt, long-necked and flat-chested. Greta photographed like a pin-up doll."

"Tell me something," I said. "How much do these kids make?"

"If you're one of the top twenty you can climb into the fifty-thousand-a-year bracket. Otherwise you stay in the crowd, squeeze out a hundred or two a week for the few years nature lets your face stay unwrinkled and hope for a break or somebody who wants to marry you."

"How about you, kid?"

Cleo gave me another of those deep chuckles and said, "I made my own breaks and when it comes to men, well, after two sour early marriages, I'll take them when I want them."

"You'll fall."

"It'll take a guy like you to do it." She reached over and pinched the back of my hand. "I'm the aggressive type, watch out."

I tasted the drink and put it down. "Think Greta could have lit out with some guy?"

She made a wry face and shook her head. "Greta had more on her mind than men, I told you. She was the money type and had enough to attract it." She paused and picked up her drink. "How far are you going to go to locate her?"

"Beats me, kid. She had a pretty big head start."

"Look, there's one thing about the city . . . pretty soon you bump into someone you know. Maybe some of the gang around here might have seen her. If it means that much to you we can tour a few of the places she played in."

"I've had enough gin mills for one night."

Cleo finished her drink and slid off the stool with a rustle of nylon, a funny little smile playing around her mouth. "Uh-uh, big man. Little Greta had peculiar tastes. The oddball intellectuals were more to her liking."

"Lead on," I said.

If there was a host, nobody pointed him out. Introductions were a casual affair of no last names and preoccupied acceptance. The smell of weed mixed in the tobacco smoke that hung in the air like a gray smog and a few were already flying away into a dream world on something stronger.

Cleo and I drifted around the fringes a few minutes before she leaned over and whispered, "The weekly gathering of the clan, big man. Greta made the meetings pretty often. Some of them would have known her. Go ahead and cruise. Maybe you'll come up with something. Give me a nod when you've had enough."

Most of the two dozen crammed into the apartment sprawled on the floor listening to the pair strumming guitars on the window seat. A cropped-haired girl in tight jeans sang a bitter song against the world with her eyes squeezed tight, her hands clenched in balled fists of protest.

I gave up after the second time around and joined the two guys at the makeshift bar back in the kitchen and made myself a decent drink for a change. An empty fishbowl beside the bottles was partly filled with assorted change and few lone singles, waiting for contributions to help pay the freight. I dug out a five, dropped it in and the guy with the beard grinned and said, "Well, well, a banker in our midst." He lifted his glass in a toast. "We salute thee. That denomination doesn't appear very often around here."

I winked at him and tried the highball. "Nice party," I said.

"Hell, it stinks. It was better when we had that horsy belly dancer up for laughs." He tugged at his beard and grimaced. "You dig this gravy?"

"Nope."

"You didn't look like the type."

"I can give you the first ten lines of 'Gunga Din,' " I said.

He let out a short laugh and took a long pull from his beer bottle. "I must be getting old. Guys like you are easier to read. Me, I'm scratching thirty-four and still going to college, only now the freshman cap doesn't fit too well and I'm beginning to think that maybe my old man was right after all. I should have gone into the business with him. When you get that attitude, the kick is gone." He paused reflectively. "Maybe I'll start off with a shave."

"Try a haircut too."

"The freshman cap wouldn't fit," he laughed. "How'd you make it here?"

"Cleo brought me."

"Ah, yes. The lady of the loins. Some great stories are told about that one, but methinks it's all talk. Not a Simon around who wouldn't want to sample her pies. You tried it for size yet?"

"Nope."

"Ha. That's a different answer. Anyone else would have happily lied about it. Intend to?"

"I haven't thought about it."

"Brother rat, with an attitude like that, you can't miss. Cleo just can't stand indifference. How'd you ever meet her?"

"Looking for Greta Service. She lived in the same building."

The guy gave me a surprised glance. "Greta? Good grief. She's long gone." His eyes ran up and down me. "She give you the brush too?"

"Never even met her."

"That's good. Guys flipped for that one and she wouldn't go the route. A few hearts are still bleeding around here. Sol saw her once uptown but she shook him loose in a hurry. Didn't want anything to do with her old buddies."

"Who's he?"

He indicated a lanky kid in a red plaid shirt curled up against the wall, chin propped in his hands while he contemplated the trio whanging out the folk songs. "Wait a minute, I'll go get him."

Sol Renner turned out to be a sometimes-writer of ads and captions for the women's trades and had met Greta Service through a mutual account. My story was that I had a message from a friend who had a job lined up for her, but Sol grimaced and told me to forget it.

"She didn't need a job when I saw her last. She was coming out of a fancy restaurant with some joe, all decked out in furs and diamonds and all I got was a quick 'hello, glad to see you' and out. I asked her if she heard about Helen Poston, but she just gave me a funny look and nodded, then got into a cab."

"Helen Poston?"

"Yeah. Crazy kook drowned herself. She and Greta did a couple of jobs for Signoret Fashions where I worked and kind of hit it off like dames do. Guess they were friendlier than I thought. So I boo-booed. She sure picked herself a beauty, though."

"Who?"

"Greta," he said. "The duck she was with was a Charlie Chan type, short, dark and dumpy with b.b. eyes and a mustache. He hustled her in the cab in a hell of a hurry."

"Got any idea where I could find her?"

He grinned and said, "Try New York."

"Great."

"Maybe some of the others might know?"

"Ixnay. I'm the only one around here who saw her. The kid's found her mark. My guess is she doesn't want to be disturbed. Anyway, she's not with the working masses any more, that's for sure."

The singers got started on a new theme about war and I finished my drink. Cleo was cornered in the alcove by two straggly-haired kids sucking on beer bottles, trying their damndest to make man talk. I eased them apart; smiling so as not to hurt their feelings and took Cleo's arm.

"Time to go, sugar."

One of the kids grabbed my hand and said, "Hey!" indignantly, so I wrapped my fingers around his forearm and squeezed a little bit. "Yes?"

My smile showed all the teeth and he read me right. "Nothing," he said, so I let him go. Cleo forced back a laugh and hooked her arm under mine and we headed for the door.

"Big man," she said. "Big, big man. Come home for coffee. I have something to show you."

I kicked the door shut and she flowed into my arms, her mouth a wild little volcano trying to pull me into its core. Deliberately, she took my hand, pressed it against the warmth of her belly, then forced it up to cup her breast. Beneath my fingers she hardened, her body twitching spasmodically, pressing against me in a plain language of desire.

Very gently I pushed her away and held her hands in mine. Her eyes were full of soft fire, lovely and wise, her lips moist and trembling. She looked at me for a long second, then said, "No coffee?"

"Rain check?"

She smiled ruefully and touched my face with her fingertips. "How can you do this to me, big man?"

"It isn't easy."

"The next time I'll make it real hard for you."

"Shut up," I grinned.

chapter four ■■■■■■■■■■■■■■■■■■■■■■■■■■

I CAME IN out of the rain, threw my coat over the back of the desk chair and picked up the coffee Velda had waiting for me. She let me finish half of it before she came over and laid a two-page report down in front of me. "Rough night?"

Women. I didn't bother playing her game. "Not bad. I got a line on Greta Service."

"So did I."

"Brief me," I said.

"She had six hundred dollars in charges she had been paying off monthly. She cleaned them all up at once with cash payments, didn't draw on any more purchases and never left a forwarding address. One woman in the credit department knew her from when she was a saleswoman and waited on her. From what she hinted at, Greta Service was wearing finer clothes than the store supplied. Where were *you* last night?"

"Working." I synopsized the details of last night for her, emphasizing the relationship Greta Service had had with Helen Poston. Velda made a few notes on a scratch pad, her face serious. "Want me to follow it up?"

"Yeah, ask around her neighborhood. They'd remember a suicide, all right. Lay on a few bucks if you have to grease anybody. As far as they're concerned, you're a reporter doing a follow-up yarn. Just be careful."

"Like you?" She gave me a poke with her elbow.

I looked up at her and a teasing smile was playing with the corner of her mouth. "Okay, I won't bug you," she said. "Only you could have put on a clean shirt without lipstick on the collar."

"I'm a show off," I said.

"That you are, chum. Sometimes I could kill you." She refilled my cracked cup from the quart container and asked, "What do you think?"

"A pattern's showing. Greta came up with money from some area. It looks more like she found a sponsor than a job."

"That's what the credit manager suggested. Did you check the m.p.'s with Pat?"

"No good. Who'd report her missing? Harry came directly to me. From now on it's legwork around probable places she might spend time in."

"Would they recognize her from that photo Hy gave you? It isn't very good."

"No, but I know where I can get a better one," I told her.

Velda picked up her coffee and sat on the arm of the chair beside me. "And I'll do the work while you carouse . . . is that it?"

"That's what I got you for, baby," I said cheerfully.

"You're asking for it," she growled back. "All this for a con."

"It goes further than that. Has Pat called?"

"No, but Hy has. He washed out the Miami trip for a few days to do a couple of features on Mitch Temple. You'd better buzz him."

"Okay." I finished the coffee and reached for my coat. "I'll check in this afternoon."

"Mike . . ."

"What, kitten?"

"It's those negligees. . . ."

"Don't worry, I didn't forget. Mitch Temple wasn't killed for nothing. Pat'll run that lead right into the ground. When he has something I'll know about it."

The Proctor Group was located in the top half of a new forty-story building it had just built on Sixth Avenue, a glass and concrete monument to commercialism with the sterile atmosphere of a hospital.

Dulcie McInnes was listed on the lobby directory as Executive Fashion Editor with offices on the top floor. I got in the elevator along with a half dozen women who eyed me speculatively and seemed to pass knowing little glances between them when I pushed the top button.

It was a woman's world, all right. The decor was subtle pastels, the windows draped with feminine elegance and footsteps were muted by the thick pale green carpeting. Expensive oil paintings decorated the walls of the reception room, but something seemed to be missing.

The two harried little men I saw scuttled around like mice in a house full of cats, forcing badgered smiles at the dominant females who wore their hats like crowns, performing their insignificant tasks meticulously, gratefully acknowledging the curt nods of their overlords with abundant thank you's. What was missing were the whips on the wall. The damn place was a harem and they were the eunuchs. One looked at me as if I were a peddler who came to the front door of the mansion, was about to ask me my business when he caught the reproving eye of the receptionist and drifted off without a word.

She was a gray woman with the hard eyes and stern mouth of the dean of a girls' school. Her expression was one of immediate rejection and no compromise. She was the guardian dog at the portals of the castle, not there to greet, but to discourage any entry. Her suit had an almost military cut to it and her voice held a tone of total hostility.

"May I help you?"

Help? She was wanting to know what the hell I was doing there in the first place.

"I'd like to see Dulcie McInnes," I said.

"Do you have an appointment?"

"Nope."

"Then I'm afraid it's impossible." The dismissal was as fast as that. To make it more pointed, she went back to sorting her mail.

Only she had the wrong mouse this time. I walked to the side of the desk, leaned over and whispered in her ear. Her eyes went wide open almost to the point of bursting, her face a dead white, then a slow flush began at her neck and suffused her cheeks and the stammer that came out of her mouth had a little squeak to it.

"Now," I said.

Her head bobbed and she tried to wet her lips with a tongue just as dry. She pushed back from the desk, got up and edged around me nervously and stepped inside the door marked *Private* beside her. In ten seconds she was back, holding the door open timorously to let me in, then closed it quickly with a short gasp of horror, when I grinned at her.

The woman on the couch wasn't what I expected at all. She had a mature beauty only middle age can bring when nature cooperates with fashion demands and scientific treatment. A touch of gray added a silvery quality to hair that fell in soft waves around a face that held a gentle tan. Her mouth was full and rich, curved in a welcoming smile. She put the layout sheets on the coffee table and stood up, sensing my immediate approval of the way the black sheath dress encompassed the swell of her breasts and dipped into the hollow and flare of her hips.

But it was her eyes that got you. They were a bright, unnatural emerald green full of laughter.

"Miss McInnes?"

Her teeth sparkled white under her smile and she held her hand out. "Whatever did you say to Miss Tabor? She was absolutely terrified."

"Maybe I'd better not repeat it."

"She never even got your name."

Her hand was firm and warm in mine, enthusiastic for the few moments she held it. "Mike Hammer," I said. "I'm a private investigator."

"Now that's a novelty up here," she laughed. "No wonder Miss Tabor was so upset. Haven't I read about you?"

"Probably."

She walked back to the couch and sat down, held out a box of cigarettes to me when I took the chair opposite her and lit us both with an ornate gold lighter.

"You've got me curious about your visit. Who's being investigated?"

I blew out a cloud of smoke and took the photograph from my pocket. "Nothing spectacular. I'm trying to find this woman. Greta Service . . . she's a model."

Dulcie McInnes took the photograph from my hand and studied it a minute. "Should I know her?"

"Probably not. She applied here for photographic work one time at Cleo's suggestion and . . ."

"Cleo?" Her head tilted with a gesture of interest. "She's one of our finest contributors."

"Think you may have some test pictures of her?"

"Undoubtedly. Just a moment." She picked up the phone, pressed a button on the base and said, "Marsha? See if we have any photos of Greta Service in our personnel files. No, she's a model. Bring them up, please."

When she hung up she asked, "Did she work for us?"

"Opinion is that Greta was, well . . . a little too stacked for high fashion jobs."

"Luckily for us we're only concerned with the woman's opinion. You men . . . all you want is pin-ups."

I looked at her and felt my mouth twist into a smile.

She threw back her head and laughed, her eyes sparkling in the light. "No, I'm not the high fashion type either, thank goodness. I'd hate to have to starve myself into a size six."

"I don't think that would help much either. When you're endowed, you're endowed. Don't knock it."

"Words like that rarely pass through these portals." Her eyes were filled with a mocking challenge. "I assume you're an expert on these matters."

"I haven't heard any complaints."

Before she could answer there was a knock on the door and a tall, slim girl walked in with a folder, handed it to her boss and threw a nervous little glance toward me before she left. "You made quite an impression outside," Dulcie McInnes said and handed me the folder after examining it.

Inside was a typed résumé listing Greta Service's statistics and qualifications. Her address was the one in the Village. Several news clippings from the garment industry's trade papers showed her in various costumes with her face partially obscured by either a coat collar or wide-brimmed hat, and there were four composite photos with the Proctor Group stamp on the back.

Greta Service was all that was said about her. No dress could do justice to a body that was so obviously made for a bikini. There was no way of erasing the odd, sensual appeal of her face so beautifully framed by long jet black hair, and no matter how she posed, you got the impression she would rather be naked than in a dress of any price.

"You see it too?" she asked me.

"Lovely."

"I didn't mean that. She just isn't a Proctor Girl. It's one of the hazards of the business."

I picked the best of the lot and held it up. "Can I have this?"

"Certainly, if it will help. We keep the negatives on file downstairs. Occasionally we do have requests from certain manufacturers for this type, but not often."

I rolled it up and slipped it in my pocket. "Think anybody here might know anything about her?"

"I doubt it," she said. "Her application date was quite a few months ago and they interview girls daily down there. Women are such a common commodity in this business you can't tell one from the other after a while. I remember getting Cleo's note about this girl, but I passed it on to personnel to handle. She wasn't the first Cleo submitted and we have used several others she suggested. Top-notch free-lancers like Cleo aren't easy to find and they usually make a good choice. In this case, I imagine Cleo was doing a little wishful thinking. The Service girl would do better with one of the men's magazines."

"What's the going rate with them?"

She shrugged, thought a moment and said, "Only a fraction of ours. Once a Proctor Girl, the sky's the limit. Quite a few have wound up in Hollywood."

I got up and pulled my coat on. "That's it then. Thanks for your time, Miss McInnes."

"Glad you came." Her emerald eyes seemed to dance with my own. "It's made for an enjoyable morning." A tiny furrow creased her forehead. "Would you mind letting me know if you find her?"

"Sure."

"It's ridiculous, I know, but I get a maternal feeling about these girls. It isn't a bit easy for them at all."

She held out her hand and I wrapped my own around it. I squeezed too hard, but she didn't wince and her own grip was firm and pleasing. "You'll hear from me," I said.

"Don't forget."

The receptionist made a frightened, crablike move to get out of the way when I stepped through the door, her face flushing again when I looked at her. Then she sniffed with indignation and faked ignoring me. She was the only one. The other few in the room looked at me with open curiosity, their eyes full of speculation.

I pushed the down button and waited, listening to the rush of air in the elevator well behind the door. The noise stopped and the doors parted sullenly. A swarthy man clutching a black attaché case stepped out, his sleepy eyes sweeping over me carelessly before he headed toward the reception desk. I got in and pressed the lobby button, picked up several employees and a few who were obviously models on the way down and reached the street smelling of assorted imported perfumes.

Sixth Avenue had lost its identity over the last ten years. It was an empire now.

The lunch crowd had left the Blue Ribbon Restaurant when I met Hy Gardner and we had the corner table in the bar to ourselves. I sat with my back to the wall while Hy dug out a sheaf of notes and laid them on the table while he fished for words. He looked like a guy who couldn't scratch his itch and finally he said, "What the hell are you into now, Mike?"

"Ease off, buddy," I told him. "Clue me in first."

"Okay." He sat back and shoved his glasses up on his forehead. "You're on top of the Delaney kill, you had a contact with Mitch Temple before he was knocked off, then you were there with Pat at the apartment after Mitch was bumped and we couldn't even get in."

"Wait a minute . . ."

"Quit dicing. One of the guys saw you take the side exit out. But you wanted something on Greta Service and if you think I don't think this is all part of one of your packages, you're crazy."

"Hy . . ."

"Look," he interrupted, "my Miami trip is loused up, one of our own guys got killed and you're playing footsies with me. Since when?"

"Can you cool it if I spell it out?"

"What am I, a kid? Man, after all we've been through . . ."

"All right, I'm not even sure there's a connection." I took five minutes and laid out the details for him while he jotted them down on the back of one of his papers. When I got done I said, "Make anything of it?"

"According to Harry Service his sister knew both the Poston and the Delaney girl. Your report verified the Poston tie-in, anyway.

In their business it wouldn't be unusual—they probably have plenty of mutual friends. Dozens of them line up for one job and they're always meeting at the agencies. So far as you know, Greta Service is around someplace and the only one worried is her brother, and that's because he heard about the two deaths and the fact that his sister knew both of them."

"Greta disappeared," I said.

"Not disappeared," Hy stated. "Her immediate whereabouts are unknown. You think that's something new in this town? Hell, let a broad in that racket hook a guy who'll keep her in minks and she'll drop the old gang in a second. Since when do I tell you that?"

"You're not, friend. I got the same picture. It's just that I got a funny feeling about it."

"Oh boy," Hy said. "Oh, boy. I don't even like you when you get that look. You'll screw the works up for sure."

"Maybe. What's the news on Temple?"

Hy pulled his glasses down on the end of his nose and peered at me over them. "You don't hit one of us that easily. It gets everybody edgy and we have too many inside sources we can work. In our own way we're like cops. News is where the trouble is and we're right there. Right now everybody is in the field on this assignment and little things are drifting in the cops never even heard about."

"Like what?"

"Mitch was around too long not to keep a daily record. Bobby Dale dug it up in his personal effects in the office. The only thing hot he had going was the Poston and Delaney tie-in. He left a page full of speculation about that, including Pat Chambers' request through you to lay off running it."

"Don't blame Pat for that."

"I'm not. But it didn't stop Mitch from pushing the angle. He hit every damn store he could find who sold negligees like the ones those kids wore and spent over three hundred bucks making purchases in various ones. The boxes started arriving at the office the day he was killed."

"What came of it?"

"He found something that killed him, that's what. The day he was knifed he was all excited about something and spent a full hour in the morgue file going through stock photographs. He didn't pull any or there would have been a record of it and the attendant there didn't notice what section he was working in so we can't point it up from there."

"Any record of that?"

"It either happened too fast or he was too excited to put it down."

"That doesn't fit him at all."

"I know. Dale said he kept a private reference on him at all times."

"Nothing like that was found on the body."

"That doesn't mean it wasn't there. The position he died in was reaching for his coat. All he grabbed was that handkerchief, but he could have been trying to protect those papers. Whoever killed him simply lifted the stuff."

"But they couldn't be sure he didn't make a duplicate copy," I reminded him.

"It was a chance they took and it paid off. Right now everybody's backtracking Mitch's movements and something will show sooner or later. One thing we just found out was that Mitch made four calls to Norman Harrison, the political columnist on his paper. Norm wasn't home and his answering service took the message to call back. Mitch died before he could reach him. Ordinarily, Mitch and Norm rarely saw each other, so the request was kind of odd."

I went to say something, but Hy held up his hand. "Wait, that isn't all. The day he was poking around in the morgue file Mitch sent a note by messenger to a man named Ronald Miller. He's an engineer for Pericon Chemicals in their foreign division. We contacted him in Cairo and he said Mitch wanted to see him on an important matter, but he was leaving for Egypt that day and couldn't make it. He didn't have any idea of what Mitch wanted, either. Their relationship was normal . . . they had served in the army together, got together occasionally and Mitch reviewed a couple of books this Miller wrote on his experiences in the Far East."

"It makes sense?"

"I pulled the books from the library and went through them. One was an adventure novel and the other a technical travelogue. Neither sold very well. There wasn't a single thing in either one that fits this case."

"How long ago did he write them?"

"About ten years back."

"Nothing new since then?"

"No. Why?"

"Maybe he was intending to write another one."

"So what?"

"He could be an authority on something by now," I said.

"What's on your mind?"

"I don't know yet. How much of this has Pat got?"

"Everything. We're cooperating right down the line."

I grinned at him. "Late enough to get a head start, but cooperating."

"We're in business too," Hy agreed. "We still know the law on withholding evidence."

"And you decide what's evidence?"

For the first time Hy let a smile break through. "You ought to know, Mike. Now, where do you go from here?"

"Looking for Greta Service."

"Still on that kick."

"It's the only one I got."

"Suppose it leads to Mitch?"

"He was my friend too, Hy."

"Yeah. Maybe you're right. It's better if we cover all the angles. There's no reason for anybody else to take it from that end except you. I hope you come up with something."

I took the photo of Greta Service from my pocket and held it out to Hy. "Your bunch can help out. How about running off a batch of these and passing them around. Somebody might spot her around Manhattan. And get the original back to my office. I'd like an excuse to see that McInnes doll again when I hand it back."

Hy nodded and grinned. "Not that it'll do you any good, kid. She's class and you don't fit in that kind of company. You'd have to wear a monkey suit and there wouldn't be any place to hide that damn gun you carry."

Pat met me in his office, his hair mussed and shadows under his eyes, looking like he had been up all night. He said, "Sit down," answered the phone twice, then leaned back in his chair and wiped the back of his hand across his face. "Sometimes I wonder if it's worth it."

"Who's on your back now?"

"You must be kidding. I told you this was an election year. Everybody's passing the buck this time. That Temple kill really stirred the fudge."

"Got anything on it yet?"

He shook his head slowly. "Nothing but boxes of women's nightgowns. We hit all the stores they were bought at and most of the salesgirls remembered selling them, but that's about all.

Mitch told the girls he was trying to match one a friend bought for his wife and looked for a description of anyone who bought either black or green, but both colors were so popular the girls couldn't come up with anything concrete."

"Why did he bother buying them then?"

"Got me. Probably just to make it look good. Come here, take a look."

The office next to Pat's was empty, but the desk and chair were piled high with empty boxes and a table along the wall was covered with a mound of filmy garments. I went over and separated them, looking at the labels. None were expensive, but the designs were clearly erotic and not intended for the average housewife. Half the pile were black numbers, the rest all shades of red, green and blue with two canary yellow styles.

"Find out which one he bought last?"

"No. Four of the sales slips were dated the same day he died and all were bought in the morning, but nobody could pinpoint the time. Each one of those stores sold a bunch of these things to men and women the same day. We have a team out trying to nail something down, but all we get is a big, fat zero. Why the hell do these things have to be so complicated?"

"Wish I could help."

"Don't do me any favors," Pat said. "I'm still getting nudged by the brains upstairs about how you happened to be the one to find the Delaney girl."

"What's new on her?"

"One thing for sure . . . neither she nor the Poston girl were identified as buyers of those gowns. We got a make on the Delaney kid by way of left field. About a month ago Vice raided a pornographic photography ring selling sixteen-millimeter stag reels and she was one of the featured players. One of our guys recognized her. The ones who sold the stuff couldn't put a finger on the ones who filmed it, but there was a scene with a window in the background that spotted certain buildings and we were able to locate the hotel they made it in. Right now we have a partial description of the ones who occupied the place and have the hotel covered in case they show again."

"Fat chance. That bunch shift around."

"It's the only chance we have. Dames who make money that way don't pay social security and rarely use their own names. We still got the body on ice. She has one distant relative in Oregon who wants nothing to do with the situation, so there we stand."

"And the Poston woman?"

"You know that angle."

"Don't tell me you aren't digging into probable sources of the poison that might have killed her."

Pat relaxed and grinned at me. "You think too much, Mike," he said. "Sure, we're on it, the Washington agencies have been notified, but the possibilities of getting a lead are so remote I'm not hoping we'll get the answer that way. The M.E. got off some letters to friends in the profession who share the same hobby. He thinks they might be able to supply the answers if anybody has imported that particular drug."

"This deal has some peculiar sexual connotations," I said.

"Most of them have."

"But not like this."

"So far nobody knows they're tied in yet. We're not even sure ourselves. Luckily, the papers are cooperating."

"What happens if they break it first?"

"All hell breaks loose. Think you can use a partner?"

"Any time," I laughed.

"Which brings us to why you came up here in the first place."

I said, "Remember Harry Service?"

Pat nodded.

"He wants me to find his sister. She hasn't contacted him in a long time."

"*You?* He wants *you* to do this?"

"Come on, Pat, he isn't the kind to go to the cops."

"How'd he reach you?"

"Supposing I forget you asked that question."

Pat gave me a disgusted look and said, "Okay, okay. What do you want from me?"

"A letter from the brass getting me in to see Harry. Somebody in the front office has got to be the friendly type."

"Not as far as you're concerned."

"I can push it if I have to."

"I know you can. Just don't. Let me see what I can do." He gave me a quizzical glance and stuck his hands deep into his pockets. "One thing, old buddy. And tell me true. Harry contacted *you,* right?"

"If you don't believe it I can show you how."

"Never mind."

"Why?" I asked him.

"Because if you initiated the contact I'd say it was tying into my immediate business."

My laugh didn't sound too convincing, but Pat bought it. "You know me," I said.

"That's what I'm afraid of."

The attendant at the morgue file of the paper was a crackly little old guy who used to be one of the best rewrite men on the staff until the demands of age caught up with him. Now he was content to spend his time among the artifacts of journalism, complaining about the new generation and how easy they had it.

I said, "Hi, Biff," and he squinted my way, fished for his glasses and got them on his nose.

"Mike Hammer, I'll be damned." He held out a gnarled hand and I took it. "Nice of you to visit an old man," he said with a smile. "I sure used up a lot of adjectives on you in the old days."

"Some of them weren't very nice."

"Company policy," he laughed. "You always made a great bad guy. But how the hell did you always come out clean?"

"That's my policy," I said.

He came around the counter lighting the stub of a chewed cigar. "You got it made, Mike. Now, what can I do for you?"

"Mitch Temple was in the other day. . . ."

He coughed in the cigar smoke and regarded me with amazement. "You're in this?"

"Sideways. Can you keep it quiet?"

"Sure. I'm not on a beat."

I gave him a quick picture of my meeting with Mitch Temple and the possibility that his death might be involved in something I was working on. Biff knew I wasn't putting it all on the line, but it was to be expected and he didn't mind. Let him alone and he'd put some of the pieces together himself.

Biff said, "All I can do is tell you what I told the others. Mitch came down and spent a while here going through the files. I was busy at the desk and didn't pay any attention to him. He didn't ask for anything and didn't check anything out."

"His column doesn't often carry photographs."

"That's right. When it did they were usually new ones supplied by some press agent. Then they were filed away down here."

"What section was he working in?"

"Hell, Mike, I can't see beyond that first tier. He was out of sight all the time. All the rest asked me that same question. I could hear him banging drawers, but that was all."

"Anybody else come in while he was here?"

Biff thought a moment, then said, "I know where he wasn't.

All the show-biz and Broadway files are on the left there. He was back in the general news section, but they're cross-indexed alphabetically, by occupation and a few other headings. Hell, Mike, Al Casey who does the feature crime yarns even dusted around for Mitch's prints on the cabinets and didn't come up with anything. I don't know where he was poking around."

I didn't pay any attention to the other old guy in the coveralls who was pushing a broom around the floor until he said, "I sure know where he was."

Both of us turned around slowly and looked at him. He never stopped his sweeping. My voice came out in a hoarse whisper. "Where?"

"The P-T section. He left all the damn butts squashed out on the floor and I had to scrape 'em up."

"Why didn't you say something?" Biff said.

"Nobody asked me," he growled.

I said, "Show me," and Biff led me back around the floor-to-ceiling rows of files until we came to the section between P and T.

Then all we did was stand there. There were forty separate drawers in the section, each a good four feet deep and crammed with folders. Biff said, "You know how many items are in this place?" I shook my head. "Figure at least a hundred to the drawer and each folder with at least ten photographs. You got a lot of looking to do, friend. Maybe you can suggest something."

"How do you get to the top drawers?"

"There's a stepladder down the end."

I waved for Biff to follow me and found the old guy emptying his sweepings into a trash can. "Did Mitch Temple have that ladder out when he was here?"

"Yep." He spit into the can, slid the top on and walked away.

"I know," Biff muttered, "nobody asked him. Now what?"

"Half of those files are eliminated. If Al Casey has the time he might try working over the other half."

"If I know him, he'll make the time," Biff said.

"Just do me a favor, keep me out of it," I told him.

Biff's face twisted into a puzzled expression. "You mean I'm supposed to have had the idea?"

"You've had them before, haven't you?"

"That was before."

"Well, you got one again."

I grabbed a cruising cab on Forty-second Street and had him take me back to the Hackard Building. The working crowd had cleared out an hour ago and the city was going through its momentary lull while the night closed in around it. I took the elevator up to the eighth floor and walked down the corridor to my office, my heels echoing hollowly in the empty space.

My keys were in my hand, but I didn't put them in the lock. Tacked to the frame was a white sheet of paper that covered one of the panes of frosted glass with the simple typewritten note, *Back Later,* across it.

I slid the .45 out of the sling, thumbed the safety off and the hammer back and moved so my shadow wouldn't fall across the door. I had had other notes stuck on my door, but this one had been written on my own brand of bonded paper in the brown typing we always used and had to come from inside the room. Only it was something neither Velda nor I would have done.

I reached over and pulled the paper away. There was a fist-sized hole in the pane right by the lock that a glass cutter had made and the note was tacked over it so nobody would notice it and possibly report it downstairs.

They didn't even bother to lock up after they had left. The knob turned under my hand and I shoved the door open. I reached in, flicked the light on, then walked inside and kicked the door shut with my foot.

Somebody had been very neat about it. Thorough, but neat. The place had been given a professional shakedown from one end to the other and not one thing had been missed. The desk drawers and cabinets had been emptied, but their contents were in inverted piles, systematically scrutinized and left lying there. Nobody ripped up seat cushions any more, but each one had been turned over and inspected for signs of fresh stitching and all the furniture had been pulled out to see if anything had been concealed behind it.

Now it was getting interesting. Somewhere out there in the maw of the city somebody was concerned about my participation in something. I sat down in my chair, swung around and looked out at the lights that outlined New York.

The possibilities were limited. To somebody, the fact that I was the one to find the Delaney girl could have seemed like more than a coincidence. With her background, she could have been involved in something heavy enough to warrant investigation from private sources and I was on her tail.

Or was it Greta Service? The prison grapevine could have passed along Harry's concern about his sister's absence and his contact with me and if Greta had been wrapped up with the wrong people, they wouldn't want me poking around.

Then there was Mitch Temple. A guy like that could always pop an exposé that was worth a kill if it could be kept quiet.

Somebody wanted to know how much I knew. Somebody didn't know I knew about the thread that tied all three of those people together.

I picked up the phone and dialed Velda's apartment. After four rings her service answered and when I identified myself, said she hadn't called in since that afternoon. I left a message for her to contact me at the usual places and hung up.

There was no sense dusting the place down for prints; a pro would have worn gloves anyway. Nothing was missing as far as I could see and the data Velda had compiled for me would be in the safe at Lakland's—a precaution we always took.

I used a piece of cardboard and covered the hole in the glass from the inside, then snapped the lock, walked out and closed the door.

Silence has a funny sound. You hear it in the jungles when everything is too still and you know there's somebody in the trees with a gun ready to pick you off. You hear it in a crowded room when everybody turns off the conversation when you walk in the door and you know the hostile element is ready and waiting.

I could hear it in the corridor and before the parrots could scream with indignation of sudden movement and the monkeys jump with alarm at shattering blasts, I hit the floor and rolled, the .45 in my hand spitting back at the half-opened door behind me where the guy in the black suit was trying to bring me into the sights of his automatic and getting nowhere because his bullets were tearing aimlessly into the tile and ricocheting off the walls while mine had already punched three holes into his chest.

chapter five ■■■■■■■■■■■■■■■■

HE LAY FACE down in the half-opened doorway, death so new that it hadn't erased the look of surprise on his face. I nudged the door open, flipped the light switch with the tip of my finger and looked around the room. There was nothing fancy about the Hackard Building or the offices it rented. This one was a minimum setup with a wooden desk, a pair of chairs and a coat rack. A layer of dust was spread evenly over everything, the window was grimy and the floor scuffed and splintered from the countless pieces of equipment that had been moved in and out.

The guy had drawn up a chair close to the door to be able to listen to any activity in the hall outside. Chances were that he had shaken my place down, found nothing and waited for me. If the door had opened from the other side he would have had a clear shot at my back before I could have done anything about it and Pat would have had me in his statistical columns instead of his address book.

I went through his pockets, found sixty-two bucks and some change, a pair of rubber gloves you could buy anywhere and two fairly stiff plastic strips that I slipped into my own pocket. None of his clothes were new. His suit had come from a large chain and looked about a year old, matching everything else. Unless the police had a record on the guy, or could come up with something out of the lab, getting a make on him wasn't going to be easy. He looked to be in his late forties, on the thin side and about five ten or so. His dark hair had receded, but there was no gray showing, so my guess at his age could have been off. I studied his face again, taking in the sharp features and the odd skin coloration. There was a death pallor there but it couldn't obliterate some of the characteristics common to some Europeans or Latin Americans.

One thing was sure, it wasn't a plain contract kill. Those guys specialize in one field and don't bother with any shakedown job to boot. Either there were two involved or this one was on assignment to find out what I knew or make sure I didn't find out any more.

But what the hell had I found out?

I stepped over the body and went back into the corridor. The elevator was still where it had left me and nobody had come to investigate the shots. It wasn't strange. The old building was solidly built and could muffle noise almost completely.

There was still a way to play it. I'd be asking for trouble, but it would keep me from doing too much explaining and it was simple enough to look right. Three of the offices down the hall from mine were occupied by small businesses that could conceivably keep something of value on the premises. In the door of each one, I knocked a hole in the glass panes, reached in and opened the lock, hoping none of them had alarms wired to them. Every room got the same treatment, a little disturbance that would indicate a search and the rubber gloves in the guy's pocket would explain the lack of prints. In the last place there was a gold wrist watch lying on top of a desk and I took it out and dropped it in the dead man's pocket for a clincher.

Then I went back to my own office and called Pat.

By nine-thirty they had bought my story. The guy at the newsstand downstairs had remembered the guy coming in after everybody had left and as he was closing up. Two of the men who rented the other offices said they did a cash business, but never left money in the office overnight, but for someone who didn't know it, they were probably targets for a robbery. The watch in the corpse's pocket made the deal firm. My version was that I had seen the broken windows, checked my own office and started out to see if anyone was still around when he tried to nail me. The manager admitted that a lot of the empty offices were unlocked, so the probability was that the guy had heard the elevator coming up, slipped into one to hide, and when he started out to make a getaway, saw me, panicked and started shooting.

I knew better. He had come prepared to handle a lock with those plastic strips. My door wouldn't give in to that technique so he had broken the window, but they made it easy for him to wait me out in a convenient empty office.

Pat drove me downtown and took my statement there. Before I finished, one of the detectives came in and told him there was no make on the guy yet, but that the gun was a .38 Colt Cobra licensed to a jeweler that had been stolen in a robbery two months before. The lab hadn't come up with any laundry marks on the guy's clothes and the only lead they had was that he had been wearing shoes made and sold in Spain but they were probably as old as his clothes. His prints had been wired to Washington and pictures were telephotoed to Interpol in case he was a foreign national.

Pat took my statement, read it through once and tossed it on his desk. "I almost believe it," he said. "Damn it, I almost believe it."

"You're a spooky slob," I grunted.

"I'm supposed to be, buddy. Right now I'm spooked more than ever. First the Delaney thing, now this."

"At least this one's cut and dry."

"Is it?" he asked softly.

"Nobody's looking for your scalp."

He interlocked his fingers and smiled at me, his eyes cold. "Are they looking for *yours*, Mike?"

I smiled back at him. "They'll have a hard time getting it."

"Don't con me."

"You have statements from five witnesses besides me that put a common robbery motive behind this, a stolen gun, gloves, a paraffin test that shows he shot at me, the position of the corpse proving concealment, so what more do you want?"

"I could tell you another way things *might* have been arranged," Pat said. "The only reason I'm not hammering at it is because the manager's statement is the only one that sticks with me . . . the fact he admitted that occasionally some empty offices are left unlocked. There was one other open one on your floor, but the rest were locked."

"Okay, I was lucky. I was there with a gun. Anybody else would have been written off and you'd have an unsolved one on your hands."

"We're not done with this one yet, you know."

"I hope not. I'd like to know who he was myself."

"You'll find out. Think it might tie into something you're on?"

I got up and stretched, then slapped on my hat. "The only thing I'm on is trying to locate Greta Service."

"Maybe I can help you on that." He reached in his desk drawer, took out an envelope and handed it to me. "Authorization to see old Harry. Your conversation will be recorded. Tomorrow you'll probably hear from the D.A. on your court appearance. Don't stay away too long."

"Thanks, chum."

"No trouble. You interest me. I always wonder how far you'll get before you wind up with your ass in a sling."

On some people prison life had a therapeutic effect. Harry Service was one of them. He had slimmed down and his face had lost the hostility it had worn at the trial and he was genuinely glad to see me. There was a momentary surprise, but he knew all the tricks and expected that I did too and anything taken down on tape for analysis later wasn't going to add up any hard points for him.

I said, "See your sister lately?"

"Nope. She sure knows how to worry a guy."

"She's big enough to take care of herself."

"That I wouldn't mind. What bugs me is she wants to take

care of me too. I tried to tell her I'd make out. . . . After this stretch I'm going legit, believe me."

"Well," I said, "I wish I could tell you something, but I couldn't locate her. She moved from her last place. One of her friends saw her uptown once, but that was the end of it. I wouldn't sweat it if I were you."

"You ain't me though, Mike. She's all I got for family."

"Maybe you know some of her friends."

He looked at me meaningfully. "Not any more."

"Yeah," I said. "Tell me . . . what was she like when she visited you last?"

Harry squirmed in his seat and frowned. "Well, she was . . . well, different."

"How?"

"I don't know how to say it. She wouldn't tell me nothing. She said pretty soon everything was going to be all right because she was going to get a lot of dough. I didn't think about it much because that's what she said right along. This time, though, she wouldn't say how. Like it was a big secret. The part I don't like is that her face was the way she looked as a kid when she done something she shouldn't of."

"Did she mention any of her former . . . friends?" I asked him.

"That was before the last time," Harry said. "Something was cooking and she didn't say, but I caught on that they all might have part of the action. Funny thing, Greta wasn't one what makes friends fast. The ones she usually took to were kind of oddballs, sort of misplaced types."

"Mixed up?" I suggested.

Harry shook his head. "No, not that. Kind of don't-give-a-damn people. I think that was why she stayed in the Village."

"You're not much help," I said.

"I know," Harry nodded. "Only thing I could put my finger on was when she was here last she opened her pocketbook and I saw a letter in there that was postmarked . . ." He paused, and wrote with his forefinger on the countertop, *Bradbury*. "I remembered it because I almost pulled a job there once," he said. "Then, when I mentioned it to her she snapped the pocketbook shut and said it wasn't nothing at all and I knew damn well she was lying."

"You mean out on the Island?"

"That's the place." He ran his tongue over his lips and added as an afterthought, "Something else . . . that letter was light green, kind of. It was long, like a business would use."

I looked at my watch. The time was almost up. "Okay, kid, I'll see what I can do."

"You'll try real hard, okay, Mike?"

"The best I can."

Harry stood up and looked at me anxiously. "And Mike . . . I ain't got no hard feelings about being in here. It's my own fault. I'm just glad I didn't shoot you."

"You're luckier than most, Harry," I told him, but he hadn't heard about last night and didn't get the meaning at all.

On the way back to the city I picked up a newspaper at a gas stop and flipped through the pages. All the local news was obscured by the latest trouble spot in the world and the statements from the U.N. idiots who fostered the whole mess and were trying to explain their way out of it. Right now they were trying to make the United States the goat again and we were falling for it. I spit out the window in disgust and read the small blurb that detailed the shooting in the Hackard Building. Space was so limited that they didn't bother going into my background again except to mention that I was the one who had discovered the Delaney girl's body. The story simply stated that I had interrupted a burglar and killed him when he tried to shoot his way past me. So far the dead man had not been identified.

Velda and Hy Gardner were having coffee in the office when I got there. They sat on opposite sides of the room making small talk, deliberately avoiding the big thing that was on their minds. The place seemed charged with some unseen force that oozed from both of them.

Hy took the cigar out of his mouth and said, "Well, you did it again."

I tossed my hat on the rack. "Now what?"

Something like a look of relief passed over Velda's face. "You could have let me know where you were."

"What's everybody worried about me for?"

"Mike . . ." Hy drained his cup and put it on the desk. "Pat's sitting on this latest bit of yours. You think we don't know it? It was a good story, friend, but we all know better."

Velda said, "The D.A. called. You have a court appearance this Monday. He's after your license."

"So what else is new?"

She grinned and poured me a cup of coffee. "Ask Hy."

I looked over at him. "Got something?"

"Something you started. Old Biff down at the morgue got Al Casey back and they pulled about thirty folders Mitch handled when he was poking around in the morgue. They catalogued the photos Mitch handled and it's the damndest conglomeration you ever saw, from polo players to politicians. Right now he thinks you know more than you're telling and they want you to see what Mitch was looking for."

"Biff said he didn't check anything out."

"Hell, Mike, he could have stuck it in his pocket if he had wanted to."

"What for? If he was looking for an I.D. on somebody he would have gotten it right there."

Hy scrutinized my face closely. "Do you know what it was?"

"No," I said simply.

"Then why did somebody try to kill you?"

"I don't know that, either."

For a few seconds Hy was silent, then he nodded and stuck the cigar back in his mouth and stood up. "All right, I'll go for it." He pulled a manila envelope out of his pocket and flipped it on the desk. "The copies of Greta Service's photos you asked for. I passed the rest out. The gang will keep their eyes open."

"Thanks, Hy."

He picked up his coat, headed toward the door and stopped beside me. "Just tell me one thing off the record to satisfy my curiosity. That guy you shot . . . it didn't happen like you told it, did it?"

I grinned at him and shook my head. "No."

"Damn," he said and walked out.

Velda locked the door behind him and went back to her desk. "It's pretty deep, isn't it?"

"We're on something. It's not tangible, but it's got somebody worried all to hell." I briefed her on my conversation with Harry Service and the details of the gunfight in the corridor, watching her face furrow with concern.

"I asked around the neighbors where Helen Poston lived. A few of them were able to describe a friend of hers that tallied with Greta. One old biddy turned out to be a people-watcher who drew a lot of her own conclusions, but the main thing she brought out was that Helen Poston was neither happy nor doing too well until after she met Greta. From then on she started turning up in new clothes and staying away from the house on weekends. Greta had a car the woman couldn't identify and on Friday nights they'd leave, Helen with a suitcase, and get back sometime Monday. One night she didn't come back at all and that's when she was found dead."

"That's the first I heard about a car," I said.

"Rented, probably. A kid described it as a black compact with no trim, so we can assume it was an agency vehicle. You want me to check with the garages that handle them?"

"Yeah . . . and get the mileage records. Did Greta—or whoever it was—show up after the Poston kid died?"

"Apparently not. There was a police investigation and her parents picked up her clothes. Three days later her room was rented to somebody else."

"Anybody else asking around there?"

"Not as far as I could find out. I played it cool enough so nobody would identify me again in case you're worried."

"I'm worried," I told her. "From now on we'll stay away from the office. You take a room at the Carter-Layland Hotel and get me one adjoining. . . ."

"Oh boy," she grinned.

I faked a swing at her and she faked ducking. I looked at my watch. It was three-thirty. "Let's cut," I said.

Pat had identified the guy who tried to kill me. We sat at one end of the bar in the Blue Ribbon having a sandwich and beer before the supper crowd came in and he let me scan the report that had gotten to his office an hour before.

Interpol, through their Paris office, had picked his prints and mug shots out of their files and transferred them to New York immediately. His name had been Orslo Bucher, accredited with Algerian citizenship, an army deserter and minor criminal with three convictions. He had escaped from a prison camp three years ago and been unheard from since. The report said there was no present evidence of him having applied for a passport from any country they serviced.

"Illegal entry," I suggested.

"We get a few hundred every year. There are probably thousands in the country we don't know about. A lot of the traffic comes up through Mexico and the Gulf coastline."

"Why here, Pat?"

He said, "The Washington Bureau thinks it's because they want political sanctuary. They have enemies in other countries. Because of their criminal records they can't come in legally."

"And this one?"

Pat shrugged and took a bite of his sandwich. "Who knows? We traced him to a room in the Bronx he had occupied for a year and a half. He did odd jobs, seemed to have enough money to keep him going, though nothing fancy, and didn't cultivate any friends except for a couple of jokers at the neighborhood bar. He serviced a whore every two weeks or so without any unnecessary conversation. The only thing she remembered was that the last time around he made her change a fifty instead of giving it to her in the assorted bills he usually did."

"New money?", I asked him.

He got the point. "If he had any more, we didn't find it. I'd figure that if you were the target for a contract kill it would go higher than what he was showing and the gun hand would have had a little more class. That's why I'm still letting your story stand, old buddy."

I grinned at him and hoisted the beer. "He was an army type and that pistol he carried wasn't a zip gun."

"Hell, I figured that, but who isn't ex-military any more? And with his background you could expect him to tote a little hardware. It isn't that hard to come by." He paused and put down his sandwich. "Incidentally, we found some burglar tools and some goodies lifted in a previous robbery in his room."

I kept my face straight and nodded. Pat was really scrambling it now. He was throwing the possibility that the guy really had tried to knock off my office for something of monetary value instead of having either Velda or me as a primary target and all I did was add to the picture by phonying the other break-ins.

"And now the case is closed," I said.

Pat washed his last bite down and shoved the glass back. His eyes went over my face and the lines that played with the corners of his mouth weren't a smile. "Is it?" he asked me.

When a few seconds went by, I said, "Don't nudge me, Pat."

"Last night we exhumed a body. It was that of a young girl supposedly killed in a car crash about four months ago. She was burned beyond recognition, but we got a make from a routine inquiry on her dental work a month later. The lab reports said she was loaded to the gills, and that quite literally. Anybody with the alcohol content she had shouldn't have been able to drive at all. However, making exceptions for certain tolerances people show, we had to assume that's what caused it. She was known as a heavy drinker and a wild kid who could really hold the stuff. She was last seen alive in a slop chute in the Village and said she was going on a party somewhere without saying anything more. The ones she was with were well alibied and told us it was nothing new. She took off in her car and what happened wasn't totally unexpected."

"Then what's your angle, Pat?"

"A more detailed autopsy showed injuries not normally sustained in a car crash, even one of that magnitude. Even the heat couldn't account for certain aspects of her condition."

"You're not saying much, kiddo."

"Ever hear of the rack?"

"Come off it, Pat!"

"Nasty thought," he said, "but look at this." He held out a photo and let me look at it. It was a reduced studio picture of a lovely, well-built girl in her middle twenties, swathed in a sheer, Grecian-style dress, posed languidly against an artificial column, a seductive expression in her dark eyes and the trace of a smile creasing her mouth.

"What about her?"

"Registered with the police department as a night-club entertainer. Good appearance, but a lousy voice so she didn't make out. Her agent couldn't sell her except as a hostess in a few joints and said she picked up money from the johns in the places she worked and seemed to do all right. Orphaned at sixteen with a crippled brother in Des Moines who drew a full World War Two disability pension and ran a moderately prosperous market on the side. He sent the money to bury her."

He gave me another long, steady look. "Tie in the others and what do you have?"

"Somebody loves nice bodies," I said.

"There's one other thing."

"So?"

"This one knew Greta Service," Pat said. "They both worked for the same two outfits in the garment district at the same time, modeling identical lines. Phil Silvester photographed them together for their brochure."

"Got a pick-up out on her?"

"In five states." He paused and glanced at me out of the corners of his eyes. "We covered some of your ground but didn't get too much cooperation. How did you make out?"

"No better."

"Harry Service wouldn't talk, either."

"Put him in jail," I said.

"Quit trying to be funny, Mike. He mentioned a letter to you without giving the postmark. The tape was clear at that point."

"He didn't say," I told him.

"Withholding evidence isn't a pretty matter, chum."

"Evidence of what? All I have is privileged information. I'm working for Harry, remember?"

"Balls." Pat's face grew tight. "I'm not going to play you down, Mike. Right now I want an opinion. Do you think there's any tie-in between these women?"

I waved to Ed to bring me another beer and finished half of it before I answered him. "Look, Pat . . . we have three kids in allied professions. It's possible they all knew each other. It's a damn tight business so it's likely they ran into each other. Let's assume they did. Two are dead and one is missing."

"You forgot the fourth one."

"For the moment that's pure speculation. Check your statistics and you'll see how many die every hour."

"Think maybe Greta Service is dead?"

"No. A friend of hers saw her alive and not too far from here not long ago."

"Mike, they were show kids, no family ties and not in the big time. Any of them would hustle for a buck."

"And you and I know plenty like that. You're angling for the Jack-the-Ripper bit, aren't you?"

"It's possible. There's a curious part to it. None of those girls were sexually molested prior to their deaths."

"If it's one man he's got a damn good operation going. Just tell me this . . . and it's your thought . . . why go so far out for a remote poison to knock off the Poston girl? How would he have access to the stuff if it's that scarce? It doesn't fit the pattern."

"But there's a pattern," Pat insisted.

"Sure, if you look at it like that."

Pat swung around and looked straight at me. "Which brings us straight back to you, friend."

"Now you're sweating me."

"Nope. That'll come later, old pal. Right now I'm just wondering about one thing. That business with Orslo Bucher. Did it happen the way you said it did?"

"Funny, Hy asked me the same thing."

"What did you tell him?"

"Does Macy's tell Gimbel's?"

Pat threw his half of the lunch money on the bar top. "Don't get too deep, Mike. You don't go solo in this world very long. We've played a lot of games together. Let's not quit here. I know how you think, so I'm going along with you for now, but remember that upstairs, people are after your neck. If you fall, I can too, so stay loose."

"I'm so loose I jingle."

"Just one more time. For me. And off the record. The bit with Bucher . . . *did it happen* like that?"

I shook my head. "Nope."

"You know what you are, don't you?"

"I've been told often enough," I said.

Orslo Bucher's neighborhood wasn't new to me. It lay in the fringe area adjoining a slum section that was marked for urban renewal when they could figure out where to put the people that were already there. You could feel the depression that hung over the buildings like an emotional smog, see it in the gray wash that dangled from the clotheslines between the buildings and in the restless hostility of the inhabitants. It was a place that existed on the gratuity of the city's Welfare Department, but the bars were filled and the curbs lined with an assortment of misused cars.

Two years ago we had mopped up a bunch who had peddled home-made booze that had killed off fifteen people at a party, and there would still be some around who liked the feel of the cash I had laid out to get a line on the slobs. The police would get a few reluctant facts, a squeeze on their informers might get them a little more, but when they saw the long green and knew I wasn't submitting official reports they'd lay it out for me.

Max Hughes was the night bartender at the Seville, a grungy corner slop chute. He had just come on the shift when I walked in, mopped the bar top down with a dirty rag and gave me the barest glance of recognition. Without being asked, he slid a beer in front of me and changed the twenty I put down.

"Orslo Bucher," I said. I tapped the ten-spot on the counter and watched it disappear under his fingers.

He leaned forward, propping his elbows on the mahogany. "You the one who bumped him?"

I nodded.

"Thought it was you. Hell, he was asking for it."

"Why?"

"Petty crap. He was always pulling something."

"Alone?"

"Strictly," Max said. "Nobody much wanted him around anyway. Kind of a mean one. I tossed him out a couple of times when he was loaded and he looked like he wanted to kill me."

"He make any trouble around here?"

"No . . . but I'd lay odds he was the one pulled that armed stickup on Arnie's liquor store last month. I felt that iron he carried when I heaved him out."

"Who'd know about him, Max?"

"Like I said . . . nobody. He was either in his pad, one of the joints or gone. Nobody cared." Max squinted and rubbed his chin. "Funny thing though, once I seen him getting into a big new car over on Lenox Avenue. He got in the back and the car had a chauffeur. I didn't see who he was with, except the guy wore a homburg and seemed to know him. It wasn't the kind of company Bucher usually kept."

"Sure it was him?"

"Positive." He frowned again and tapped the back of my hand with his finger. "Come to think of it, old Greenie said he seen the same thing once. I didn't believe him because Greenie's bombed out on booze and can't think straight. He kept telling me it was a dipple car, whatever the hell that is, but he's always got a screwy name for everything."

"Suppose I talk to Greenie."

Max grunted and said, "You'll have to go six feet down to do it. He got clipped by a truck two months ago and died in Bellevue."

I was getting nowhere in a hurry. When Max couldn't supply any answers there weren't any to be had. I said, "What about that whore Bucher used?"

"Rosie? Man, that one's on the last time around. She'll bang for a beer or a buck and lucky to get either. The only ones she gets is the bums the other hustlers won't touch. Lucy Digs and Dolly gave Bucher the brush when he tried to warm their pads, that's why he wound up with Rosie, and when them two turn anything down, it got to be pretty sad. Nope, old Bucher wasn't too popular around here. He ain't going to be missed none at all. Not none. If it wasn't for the cops nosing around nobody would have given him a thought."

"Okay, kid, if that's the best you can do."

"Sorry, Mike. That's the way it is. Suppose something turns up?"

I took out a card and wrote the name of the hotel on it. "Call me here if you think it's important." He looked up at me with shrewd eyes. "I'll mail you a check," I said.

Hy was just getting ready to leave his office when I reached him. He had been trying to get me for the past hour and was about to give up. Too many people were around for him to talk, so he told me to meet him at Teddy's place as fast as I could. I walked up a block, grabbed a cab and gave him the address of the restaurant in the lower end of Manhattan.

He was waiting for me in a private section and he wasn't alone.

He pointed to a seat and indicated the tall lanky guy next to him. "You know Al Casey?"

"I've seen you around." I held out my hand and he took it. "Biff told me about you going over the morgue files. Come up with anything?"

"That's what we wanted to talk to you about," Hy said. "Sit down."

I pulled out a chair and he nodded to Al. "Fill him in."

Al eased back in his chair and had a sip of his coffee. "First, we think we found Mitch Temple's last contact. He was in a woman's clothing shop on Broadway asking about those damn negligees and finally bought one. He had given his name and the office address to the salesgirl and laid down twenty bucks for a twelve-dollar item. The girl left to ring up the sale and when she came back he was gone. Now on Broadway, people don't just leave tips like that, so the girl remembered the incident after a little bit of persuasion. She hadn't mentioned it before because she didn't want the manager to know she had taken any cash on the side. The second thing she remembered was that while she was writing up the sales slip, Mitch kept looking at another customer down further in the store who was poking around a clothes rack and was preoccupied enough so that she had to ask him twice about the address before he gave it to her. She never saw either one again."

"What did Mitch buy?"

"A black nylon shortie outfit. Real sexy, she said. What we figure is, he recognized the other guy and followed him out. The date on the sales slip tallies with the day he first started to go through the morgue files."

"Anybody else recognize the other one?"

"No. There was one new girl who might have waited on him, but apparently he didn't buy anything. If it was the one she *thought* she remembered, it was just a man who asked if that were all the colors they had in stock. She said that was it and he left. What was peculiar about it . . . there was a complete color assortment of new stock that had just been put out that morning."

I looked at the two of them and felt my mind fingering out the bits and pieces until there was only one little piece left.

"Complete except for one," I said.

Al Casey shook his head. "Every color. I even checked their stock records."

"Not white," I told him.

Both of them looked at each other and a frown began to form

between Al's eyes. "That's right," he said. "There wasn't any white. But how would you know?"

"Mitch Temple told me. That's why he was reaching for that white handkerchief in his pocket. Not for anything else he had."

Hy shoved his glasses up on his forehead and stared at me hard. "I don't get it, Mike."

"Velda spotted it first," I told him. "Green for redheads, black for blondes. What color dame would look best in white?"

After a moment Hy said, "A brunette or black-haired doll."

"Like Greta Service," I added.

chapter six ∎∎∎∎∎∎∎∎∎∎∎∎∎∎∎∎∎∎∎

THERE WAS A pattern coming out now. All it took was for that first piece to fall in place. Pat might have put his finger on it after all. Police records were spotted with psycho types who would go to any extremes to satisfy their own strange desires. They could be as devious as a snake and harder to track down. They could weave their own schemes into such fantastically intricate designs that there seemed to be no beginning nor end of the confusion. It wasn't so much a pattern as a suggestion of one, but it was there.

I said, "How much of this has Pat got?"

"His own squad made the same rounds. If they got different answers that's their tough luck."

"How long do you expect to sit on it?"

"Until we get one step further," Al told me. "Norm Harrison got back from Washington today where he was covering the latest Senate subcommittee investigations. He was going to go through all his papers to see if Mitch dropped a note to him after he couldn't reach him by phone. There was a mail chute in Mitch's apartment house, so it's a possibility."

Hy lit his cigar and blew the match out through a cloud of smoke. "I'm going to see him tonight. He's covering a political bash one of the U.N. members is giving for a newly admitted country. One of those splinter groups from Africa we're supporting. You want to go along?"

"Why me?"

"Because you're in this as deep as we are and damn well know it. We're not passing up any chance of missing an angle on Mitch's death even if we have to play along with you."

"Thanks, pal," I grinned. I looked at Al Casey. "And you?"

"Back to those files. I think I know the system Mitch used in going through them. It wasn't alphabetical. If I can find the last folder he hit we'll narrow it down pretty well. Even if something's missing, we can check it against the negative files."

I pushed back from the table and got up. "Okay, buddy, I'm with you."

The town house of Gerald Ute was a newly restored three-story building just off Fifth Avenue opposite Central Park. My own knowledge of Ute came from sketchy newspaper accounts and on the way over Hy briefed me on his background. He owned several flourishing corporations that had expanded into the multimillion-dollar class since 1950, but he himself hadn't erupted onto the social scene until his wife decided Chicago was too restrictive for their new position and coerced him into a move to New York. She lasted a year before she made him a widower, but Ute had gotten to enjoy the high life of society circles he could afford and he widened his activities so that he was everything from patron of obscure arts to unofficial host to visiting dignitaries.

Apparently Ute was smart enough to stay out of the political jungle, though on several occasions his influence was used to mollify ruffled feathers among the U.N. members he cultivated. His activities didn't seem to interfere with his businesses, which were still climbing on the big board in the Stock Exchange, and at sixty-two, he was pretty well out of the scandal class.

The muted sounds of a string quartet floated through the rooms against the background of quiet murmuring. A butler took our hats and behind him the guests were gathering in small groups, waiters circulating with trays of champagne glasses. There was little formality. Most of the men were in business suits, a few in black ties, while the women fed their vanities in Paris originals winking with diamonds.

Gerald Ute knew the value of good public relations. I saw Richie Salisbury who usually covered the Washington beat, Paul Gregory whose "Political Observations" were featured in a national magazine and Jean Singleton who usually handled the foreign news coverage. Ute was talking to Norman Harrison when we walked in, stopped long enough to come over and say hello to Hy and be introduced to me.

For all of his years, he was still ruggedly handsome, though starting to bulge out at the middle. He had the sharp eyes of the shrewd speculator that could laugh at locker-room jokes or cut ice if they had to. When they focused on mine they were reading me like a computer being programmed and he said, "Mr. Hammer. Yes, you've made some headlines recently."

"Accidentally," I said.

"But good for business." He dropped my hand and smiled.

"Sometimes."

"It's too bad I can't write half the things I know about him," Hy put in.

"Why don't you?"

Hy let out a laugh. "Because Mike might decide to write a biography and I'd be in it. How's the party going?"

"Fine, fine. It's just a welcoming thing for Naku Em Abor and his party . . . getting him acquainted with the city and all that. People will be drifting in and out all evening. Suppose I introduce you around."

Hy waved him off. "Don't bother. I know everybody anyway. If I don't, I will."

"And you, Mr. Hammer?"

Before I could answer Hy said, "Don't worry about him, Gerald. You never know who this guy is buddies with."

"Then let me introduce you to our hostess for the evening." He walked between us to the nearest couple, a woman in a black strapless gown that flowed over her body like a silvery fluid who was talking to a small oriental in a tuxedo. He said, "My dear . . . if you have a moment . . ."

She turned around, her hair still glinting like a halo, eyes twinkling and touched so that they seemed to turn up at the corners, and when they looked at me, widened with pleasure and Dulcie McInnes said, "Why, Mike, how nice to see you here!"

Hy nudged Gerald Ute with his elbow and whispered, "See what I mean?"

Our host laughed, presented James Lusong, talked for a few moments, then the three of them went back to the others, leaving me with Dulcie and a glass of champagne.

"From fashion editor to hostess," I said.

"Our advertisers appreciate the association." She took my arm and steered me through the crowd, nodding to friends and occasionally introducing me. I saw Hy to one side speaking quietly to Norm Harrison, but couldn't overhear what they were saying. "It adds class to our publications," Dulcie told me.

"It won't if you're seen with me," I said.

"Ah, but you add excitement. Society girl on safari with white hunter."

"That doesn't make for healthy relationships."

Her fingers squeezed my arm and she grinned up at me. "No, but interesting ones. After you left the office there were all sorts of speculation going on. I rather thought our employees read only the more gentle periodicals, then I find they like sensationalism too. You seem to have supplied it for them. A few discreet questions and I learned a lot about you."

"I'm surprised you'll still speak to me, Miss McInnes."

"You know women better than that," she said. "And the name is Dulcie. Now . . . satisfy my curiosity. . . . Since you weren't on the guest list, how did you make it here?"

"Power of the press. Friend Hy Gardner was invited and dragged me along. Not that I'm much on these bashes, but we have an appointment later."

"Any friend of the press is a friend of Gerald's. I'm glad you made it. Anyone here you'd like to meet?"

In four different spots around the room, men were clustered in a tight circle, laughing occasionally, talking with that odd intensity they developed when the nucleus of the circle was a pretty woman. "Maybe the Proctor Girls," I suggested.

Dulcie poked me with her finger. "Uh-uh. They're just eyewash. Besides, they're too young for you."

"How about them?" I indicated the men around the girls. Not one of them would ever see fifty again.

She looked at them and laughed lightly. "Funny, isn't it? When the Assembly is in session they're at each other's throats or thinking up some scheme to transform the world. Now here they are simpering at twenty-year-olds like schoolboys. There's nothing like a pretty face to keep peace and quiet at a party."

"You ought to try it at the U.N. Maybe that's what they need."

"Oh, I've given it a thought. Gerald didn't exactly favor the idea the first time, but the Proctor Girls were such an asset he insists we invite them. Actually, it was his wife's idea originally."

"How did you get involved with being his hostess?"

"I'm a social climber, or haven't you heard?"

"Rumors," I admitted. "I'm not a member of the set myself."

"Fact is, I was born to this sort of thing. My family was Midwestern blue book and all that, I attended the right schools and made the proper friends, so that all of this comes naturally. I rather enjoy it." She sipped her champagne thoughtfully and said, "Every one of those Proctor Girls you see are from important families. One is engaged to a junior congressman, one to the son of a wealthy industrialist and the other two are being signed by a Hollywood studio."

"Lucky."

"No . . . they work for it. The qualifications for a Proctor Girl are quite rigorous. If they weren't, we couldn't afford to have them here." She put her empty glass on the tray of a passing waiter and took another. "By the way . . . have you found the girl you were looking for?"

"Not yet. It's a big city and it's easy to get buried in it. I'm giving it a little more time."

"Did the photographs help at all?"

I shrugged and shook my head. "Nobody's seen her. But you don't forget a face like that."

Dulcie turned and cocked her head, her eyes thoughtful. "You know, I'm wondering. . . ."

"What?"

"Teddy Gates . . . the one who photographed the girl you wanted. He has contracts independent of ours and sometimes uses models we turn down. It could be possible he kept a listing on her. He's done it before."

I could feel my neck muscles tighten with the thought of the possibility. "How can I reach him?"

"You won't have to. He keeps an office in our building and I have the keys." She looked at her watch and said, "It's eight now. We'll be breaking up here about midnight. Are you intending to stay?"

"No."

"Then suppose you meet me in the lobby of my building . . . say at twelve-thirty. We'll take a look."

"You don't mind?"

"Uh-uh. I like white hunters. Now let me go play hostess. Have fun."

I watched her walk away, appreciating the patrician stride that was so full of purpose, yet so totally feminine. Other eyes caught her as she passed, and watched regretfully when she was out of sight.

Norm Harrison hadn't found any communication from Mitch Temple. He had gone through his files and his notes without seeing even an interoffice memo. The kid who did his desk work said he remembered Mitch trying to contact him, but his conversation was hurried and the main point was for Norm to call him back when he came in. The kid didn't remember anything else.

We were all together in the library trying to figure out Mitch's reason for the call, but Norm couldn't put his finger on it and all he could speculate on was the one time they had been together at a party was when Mitch queried him about the political repercussions of his series on the Mafia. Since then Norm had been assigned to cover the general political situations in the U.N. and the forthcoming elections in the States, neither of which touched Mitch's area of operation.

One of the maids came in, told Hy he was wanted on the phone and we waited while he took the call. When he came back he had a look of excitement on his face, waited until we were alone and said, "Al Casey located the cabbie he thinks picked up Mitch. He had him follow another cab and passenger to a store on Twenty-first Street. They waited outside for about fifteen minutes, then this man came out with a package under his arm, walked to the end of the block and got into a private car he apparently had called for. They tailed him out to the Belt Parkway, but the other car was going like hell and when the cabbie tried to keep it in sight, he got stopped by a police cruiser and picked up a ticket. Mitch had the guy drive him back uptown and got out near his apartment."

"He was sure it was Mitch?"

"The cabbie identified his photo. What made him remember was that Mitch tipped him enough to pay for the ticket."

"But no I.D. on the other car?" I asked.

"They never got close enough. It was getting dark, traffic was heavy and he said it was either a dark blue or black sedan. He didn't remember the make."

"How about the store?"

"None of the clerks were specific about the customers, but one did sell a white negligee that day. Al checked the sales slips. It was a cash purchase with no name or address."

I looked at Hy thoughtfully. Something was bugging me and I couldn't reach out and touch it. I said, "Pat better have this now."

"He's already got it," Hy said. "But what good's it going to do if we don't know who the hell we're looking for?"

"Mitch recognized him."

"And Mitch knew a hell of a lot of people."

"But why him?" I insisted. "What would make one guy stand out of a crowd buying sexy clothes for his doll?"

Norman said quietly, "Maybe he's done it before . . . been messed up in this sort of thing."

"We can find out," Hy told us. "Pat will be checking the M.O.'s and we can give him a hand. Want to come, Mike?"

"No, you go ahead. I'm going to try a different direction. I'll call you later."

Hy had that puzzled look back on his face again. "Look, Mike . . ."

"It's only an idea," I interrupted him. "We have to play this from all sides."

Gerald Ute seemed sorry to see us go, but wasn't insistent on our staying. We said good-by to a few of the others and Dulcie McInnes came over to walk us to the door. I told her something had come up I wanted to check on, but would see her at the Proctor Building as we planned.

Outside, Hy had flagged a cab, dropped me off opposite the News Building without asking any questions and went downtown. There was a small bar close by that the newspaper fraternity kept filled between shifts. Tim Riley was on his usual stool with his usual martini in his usual endless discussion of the New York Mets with the bartender. He was an old sports reporter assigned to the rewrite desk now, but he couldn't get baseball out of his system.

He gave me a big grin when I sat down next to him, but I didn't let him get started on the Mets. I said, "Favor time, Tim."

"Mike, I haven't got a ticket left. I . . ."

"Not that. It's about Mitch Temple."

He put his glass down, his face serious. "Anything. Just ask."

"Did he save carbons of his columns?"

Tim grimaced with his mouth and nodded. "Sure, they all do in case they need a reference later."

"I want to see them."

"You can go through back issues and . . ."

"That'll take too long. I'd sooner see his carbons."

He finished his drink with one swallow, pushed a bill across the bar and got off the stool. "Come on," he said.

Mitch Temple's cubicle of an office had the stale smell of disuse. An old raincoat still dangled from the hook behind the door and the ashtray was filled with snubbed butts. Somebody had gone through his drawers and left his papers stacked on his desk. Two three-drawer filing cabinets stood side by side, a couple of the drawers only partially closed, but since they only contained his original typewritten carbons stapled to their printed counterparts, there had been no thorough examination. Each folder contained his turnout for the month and they were dated back to two years ago. Some of the folders had cards clipped to their fronts cross-indexing Broadway items, rumors turning into fact, things of interest concerning personalities to be elaborated on later. I snagged the swivel chair with my toe, pulled it up in front of the files and sat down.

"Something I can help you with?" Tim asked me.

"I don't know what I'm looking for myself."

"Well, take your time. Nobody's going to bother you in here. And Mike . . . if you find anything, you yell, hear?"

"Don't worry, Tim. And thanks."

Mitch Temple had been more than an ordinary Broadway gossip columnist. Here and there little gems appeared that I remembered turning into cold, hard news stories later on. He had roved from one end of town to the other, Broadway his theme, but branching off into sidelines that turned him into a part-time crusader when he got hold of something. His series on the Mafia caused a full investigation of their activities with several convictions. Twice he got on politics and made a few faces red around town.

Dulcie McInnes and Gerald Ute appeared here and there when they either hosted a party or were guests at one. Some of Dulcie's escorts at society soireés were international figures in politics or finance. She was top-echelon jet set, traveling all over the world for the Proctor Group. Although Mitch reported her as being at different affairs of state and involved with pleasantries accorded the United Nations delegates, she didn't seem to show any political persuasion or be attached to anyone in particular.

Gerald Ute came in for a little closer coverage. He was always financing some far-out project or sounding off on things from scouting to the foreign problems. Twice, there was a romantic link to some prominent matron, but nothing came of it. In one column Mitch hinted that he had used his influence with the delegate of the deposed dictator of a South African nation to nail a fat mineral-rights contract for one of his companies, but in today's business arrangements, that's par for the course.

There were other names I recognized and others I didn't. For three consecutive weeks Mitch hammered at the hypocrisy of the United Nations regarding their commitments, naming Belar Ris, who had come out of obscurity after World War Two with a fortune behind him and had led an uprising that turned his country's colony into an independent nation that elected him their U.N. delegate. He was trying to force an acceptance of the part-

Arabian complex headed by Naku Em Abor. Well, Mitch lost that one, I thought. The country was in and old Naku was being feted at Gerald Ute's party right now. Mitch tried a lot, but he didn't win them all. Despite his personal investigation and reporting of facts, two labor unions kept top hoods in office, an outlaw strike damn near destroyed the city and a leading politician was re-elected even though he had a close affiliation with the Communist Party.

I had another ten minutes before I had to leave, so I took out the last of the folders in the drawer. They made interesting reading, but weren't at all informative. Belar Ris's name came up again, once when he got flattened by some playboy in a gin mill and once when the Italian government accused him of being associated with a group marketing black-market medicines for huge profits. There were a few other hot squibs about show-business personalities and some minor jabs at the present administration that weren't unusual.

About a third of Mitch's columns had been covered, and as far as I was concerned, it had been a waste of time. It had taken more than what he had written to cause him to be killed. Anybody with any common sense wouldn't want to tackle the entire newspaper staff and the police. And right there was the rub again. Supposing it wasn't someone with common sense . . . just a plain psychopath?

At twelve-twenty-five I was in the lobby of the Proctor Group Building getting a nervous look from a night watchman. Five minutes later Dulcie came in with a wave to both of us and he looked relieved to see her. Someplace she had changed to a skirt and sweater with a short coat thrown over her shoulders and she looked like a teen-ager out on a late date.

"Been here long?"

"Five minutes. Good party?"

"A social success. You left early or you would have met the great heads of great nations."

I said one word under my breath and she suppressed a giggle, her eyes laughing at me.

She had the key to a private elevator that whisked us up to the tenth floor, the area reserved for the photographers. She found the switch, threw the lights on and led me down the corridor past the vast film-developing and processing laboratory, the stages where the models were posed against exotic backdrops, down to the offices where we found the one labeled *Theodore Gates*.

"Here we are." She pushed the door open and stepped inside,

turned the button on the desk lamp and walked to the cabinets along the wall. "Service, wasn't it?"

I nodded. "Greta Service."

She slid the drawer out, thumbed through a few envelopes and drew out one with Greta's name typed across the top. Inside were duplicate photos of the ones in the master file and a résumé of Greta's experience. The address was the one in Greenwich Village.

"No good," I said. "We'll need a later address."

She stuffed the folder back and shut the drawer. "Wait a minute." There was a rotary card file on Gates' desk and she flipped it around, stopped and said, "Could this be it?"

I looked at it. The notation listed her name, the Village number with a line drawn through it and another at the Sandelor Hotel, a fourth-rate fleabag on Eighth Avenue. A series of symbols at the bottom of the card may have been significant to Gates but didn't mean anything to me. In the bottom corner was another name, *Howell*.

"Well?"

"It's the only lead I got. I'm going to follow it up."

"Perhaps you could call first and . . ."

"No . . . I don't want to spook her off." I laid my hand over hers. "Thanks, kitten. I appreciate this."

There was a sad little expression in her eyes. "Would it be too much to ask . . . well, you *do* have me curious . . . can I go with you?"

I took her arm. "Sure, why not?"

We got out of the cab at the Sandelor Hotel and went into the lobby. It was a place for transients and permanent guests too impoverished or old to go any further. A musty smell of stale smoke and hidden decay hung in the air where it had been gathering for decades. The carpet was threadbare in front of the sagging cracked leather chairs, and in line to the desk and staircase. Drooping potted palms were spotted in the corners, two in front of the elevator that had an OUT OF ORDER sign on it.

The desk clerk was another relic, half asleep in a chair, three empty beer bottles beside him. I walked up and said, "You have a Greta Service here?"

He looked at me through half-opened eyes and shook his head. "Nobody by that name."

"You sure?"

"I said so, didn't I?"

Then I remembered the name on the bottom of the card and said, "How about Howell?"

He turned partly around, glanced at a chart pinned to the wall and nodded. "Second floor, two-oh-nine." He reached for the phone.

"Forget it," I told him.

For just a second he started to get irritated, then he took one hell of a good look at me, seemed to shrink back a little, made a motion with his shoulders and settled back into the chair. I took Dulcie's arm and steered her toward the stairs.

I knocked on the door twice before I heard a muffled sound from inside. When I knocked again a sleepy voice said, "All right, all right, don't knock the door down." I heard a chair being kicked, a soft curse, then a stripe of light showed under the door. The chain slid back, the lock clicked and the door swung open.

I said, "Hello, Greta."

It was her. It wasn't the Greta Service of the photographs, but it was her. Some of the beauty had eroded from her face, showing in the texture of her skin and the momentary void of her eyes. Her jet black hair was tangled and fell around her shoulders while she clutched the front of a cheap bathrobe together to keep it closed.

I pushed her inside, took Dulcie with me and closed the door. Greta had gone pretty far down the line. The room was bare as the law allowed. One closet showed only a few clothes and an empty gin bottle lay on the nightstand beside the bed with a broken glass on the floor.

She looked from me to Dulcie, then back to me again. "What do you want?"

"You, Greta," I said.

"What for? What the hell do you mean by . . .?" She stopped, took a longer look at me, then added, "Don't I know you?"

"Mike Hammer."

Then she knew me. "You bastard," she hissed.

"Ease off, kid. Don't blame your brother's fall on me. He was the one who wanted me to find you."

Greta took a step back, faltering a little. "Okay, you found me. Now get out of here." For some reason she avoided looking at my eyes.

"What's with this bit?" I asked her.

Her head came up hesitantly, her lips tight. "Leave me alone."

"Harry wants to see you."

She spun around, staring dully into the dirty glass of the window. "Like this?"

"I don't think he cares."

"Tell him for me that I'll see him when I'm ready."

"What happened, Greta?"

We exchanged glances in the reflection of the glass. "I didn't make it, that's all. I had big ideas and they didn't work out."

"So what do I tell Harry?"

"I'm working," she said. "I make a buck here and there. My time will come." There was a funny catch in her throat. When I didn't answer she spun around, her hands going to her hips. The robe came open as she stood there glaring at me and under the nightgown her body was outlined in lush perfection. "Just tell him to stay off my back until I'm ready, you hear me? And quit following me around. I'll do what I want to do my own way and I don't need any interference. He didn't do so good his way either, did he? All right, at least I'm on the outside doing what I can. Now lay off me and get out of here!"

"Greta . . . want to talk about Helen Poston?"

There was no physical reaction at all. "She's dead. She killed herself."

"Why?"

"How would I know? She'd been brooding over some man. If she was stupid enough to kill herself over one she deserved it."

"Maybe she didn't kill herself," I said.

A small shudder crossed her shoulders and her hands were clenched into fists. "When you're dead you're dead. What difference does it make any more?"

"Not to her. It could to somebody else. Feel like talking about it?"

She turned angrily and walked to the closet, tore the clothes from the hangers and threw them into a suitcase on the floor. "Damn it," she muttered, "I'll go someplace where nobody can find me." She looked back over her shoulder, eyes blazing. "Go on, get out of here!"

Dulcie said, "Can't we do something?"

"No use. This is what I came for. Come on, let's go."

On the street there were a pair of cabs parked off the corner. I put Dulcie in the first, told her to wait a second, then walked back to the other cab. I wrapped a five-spot around my card and handed it to the driver. He took it cautiously, his eyes wary. I said, "There may be a woman coming out of that hotel in a few minutes. If she takes a cab, you pick her up. Let me know where she goes and I'll make it worth your while."

He held the card under the dash light and when he looked up

there was a big grin on his face. "Sure, Mike," he said. "Hot damn."

Dulcie McInnes lived in a condominium apartment that rose alongside the park with quiet splendor that only the very wealthy could afford. I knew some of the names of others who owned their premises there and I was surprised Dulcie could afford it. She saw the question in my face and said, "Don't be surprised, Mike. The Board of Directors of Proctor insisted on it. Something to do with image-making, and since they own the building, I am happy to comply with their wishes."

"Nice. I should have a job like that."

"At least you can share my luxury after taking me to that . . . that place tonight."

"It's pretty late."

"And it's coffee time . . . or are you a little old-fashioned?"

I let out a little laugh and followed her into the elevator. The air whooshed in the tunnel we were being sucked up in, the quiet sound of unseen machinery humming in some distant place. Little voices, I thought. They were saying something, but were too far away to be heard. It wasn't like the old days any more. I could think faster then. The little things didn't get by me. Like tonight at the Sandelor Hotel. Everything was fine. I could tell Harry that. I did what he wanted me to do. Greta was on her uppers, but well enough and I couldn't blame her for not wanting Harry to see her. She could have known the dead girls, but that wouldn't be unusual at all. Greta was alive. She wanted it the way it was. Then what was so damn peculiar?

I hadn't realized the elevator had stopped and I was staring past Dulcie, who stood in a small foyer, past the arch into a magnificent living room whose windows looked like living pictures of New York with its myriad of winking lights.

"Remember me?" she smiled. "We're here." She reached her hand out, took mine and led me inside. "Drink or coffee?"

"Coffee," I said. "You sure your friends won't object to me being here?"

"Friends?"

"Some of the company you travel in ranks pretty high."

Dulcie giggled again, a disturbing quality that made her seem schoolgirlish. "Some are just rank. Now sit down while I put the coffee on." She disappeared into the recesses of the house, but I could hear her making domestic sounds, unconsciously whistling snatches of a new show tune. I turned the record player on, slipped a few Wagnerian selections on the spindle and turned the volume down so the challenging themes were reduced to mere suggestions of their intent.

She came back with the coffee and set it on the marble-topped table in front of the sofa and sat down beside me. "You're awfully pensive. Do I affect you that way?"

I took the coffee from her and studied her face. Even this close, maturity had only softened her beauty to classic form. Her breasts swelled beneath the sweater, melted into hips poised in an arrogant twist, with her legs crossed, one in gentle motion. "Not you," I grinned.

"Thinking about Greta Service, weren't you?"

"A little."

She stirred her coffee and tasted it. "Weren't you satisfied?"

"Not really. I wish I knew why."

Dulcie put her cup down and leaned back thoughtfully. "I know. Unfortunately, I've seen it happen before. Some of these girls never realize what a tough world this is. There are thousands of beautiful faces and gorgeous bodies. They aspire for greatness and when it doesn't happen to them they can't understand it. The road downhill is steeper than the one going up."

"It's not that. She's been kicked around before. I thought she was a more determined type."

"Frustration can be a pretty terrible thing," she said. "What can you do?"

"Nothing, I guess. I'll just lay it out the way it is. Her brother will have to be satisfied with it."

"And you'll never have another reason for disrupting my routine again," Dulcie smiled impishly.

"Maybe I'll think of one."

The light glinted from her eyes when she stared at me, the pupils dark little pools under long, curling lashes. Her tongue stole out, moistened her lips and very softly, very directly, she said, "Think of one now," then reached up and turned off the light above us.

She was a gentle, lovely flower that budded slowly, then erupted into a wild blossom of incredible delight. Her hands were tight on my wrists, directing their motion, controlling pressures to her own satisfaction, then, knowing I understood, began a searching of their own. Her mouth was a delectable pillow of warmth that moaned with pleasure when I kissed her, her entire body a writhing masterpiece of sensuality.

When the gray light of the false dawn touched the city outside, I left and took a cab to the Carter-Layland Hotel. I got the key to my room, went in quietly and kicked off my shoes. The door to the adjoining bedroom was closed, so I lay down on the bed and stared at the ceiling, my hands under my head.

All I could think of . . . was it over or just beginning?

chapter seven ▬▬▬▬▬▬▬▬▬▬▬

I NEVER REMEMBERED having fallen asleep. I awoke with the fading light of day suffusing the room and the mice feet of rain on the window beside the bed. My watch said ten minutes to four and I swore under my breath for letting time get away from me.

When I rolled out of the sack a note fell off my chest. *Blue Ribbon at six, stinker,* it read and was signed with Velda's elaborate V. A quick shower straightened me out, I shaved the stubble off my face and pawed through the suitcase of clothes she had brought for me and got dressed. Automatically, I checked the action on the .45, slipped it into the holster and pulled my coat on.

Last night had been a rough one. I grinned, reached for the phone and dialed Dulcie's office number. The one who answered was Miss Tabor, the old maid I had ruffled so badly the first time around. When I asked for Dulcie she said Miss McInnes had left for Washington on the ten o'clock plane and would be out of town for several days. She asked who was calling and when I told her I could hear her quick gasp and she stammered that she would tell Miss McInnes that I had called.

I hung up the phone and started to get up when it rang. I picked it up again and said, "Yes?"

"This Mike Hammer?"

"You got him."

"Ray Tucker, Mike. I'm the cab driver you told to follow that girl last night."

I had damn near forgotten about that. "Sure, Ray. Where'd she go?"

"Well, it's hard to say. She came out and flagged me down and I took her to that five-story public parking lot on Eighth and Forty-sixth. She hopped out and went inside. The gate was closed on one side so I cruised around the other and waited a few minutes, then a car came out I think was her. I was going to follow her a ways, but a passenger boarded me and I was laying back too far to really tail her. She drove down to Seventh, then turned right again on the block where there's a southbound entrance to the West Side Highway. That's the best I could do."

"Get the make of the car?"

"A light blue Chevy sedan. A new one. Couldn't spot the plates," he said. Then suddenly he added, "Oh, yeah, there was a dent in the right rear fender. Just a little one."

"Okay, Ray, thanks. Let me know where to reach you and I'll send you a check."

"Forget it, Mike. Them things are kind of fun." He hung up and I put the phone back.

There it was again. Something that didn't belong there. You don't own a new car while you're bedding down in the squalid quarters of the Sandelor Hotel. But Ray Tucker wasn't sure, either, and if the driver in the car wasn't Greta Service, she could have used the parking lot as a cute gimmick to check on anyone following her. I knew the place, and while one side was open to traffic, the gate on the other merely admitted a person and not a car. If she thought I might have been on her tail it would have been a perfect spot to dump me.

I grabbed my hat and raincoat, went downstairs, checked for messages, then went out and waited five minutes before a cab pulled over for me. I gave him the address of the Sandelor Hotel and sat back. I don't usually get mistaken for a tourist, but the cabbie took a chance on it. He caught my eyes in the rear-view mirror and said, "If anybody steered you to the broads in that place, buddy, drop it."

"No good?" I asked absently.

"Crap. You'd do better with a pick-up from one of the joints. That's real gook stuff there."

The tautness started across my mouth. "Oh?"

"Sure, foreign seamen, weirdie boys, all that. Maybe half a dozen broads work outa that place and I wouldn't pay five cents to throw a rock at it."

"I'm not after a dame. There may be a friend of mine there."

He shook his head sympathetically. "Tough," he muttered. "That's a real bughouse."

There was a new man on the desk this time, a tall sallow-faced guy in a worn blue serge suit with rodent eyes that seemed to take everything in at once without moving at all. When I passed the desk he said, "Say . . ." in a whispery voice and I turned, walked back again and stood there for a good ten seconds without taking my eyes off him.

He tried to bluster it out, but it was the kind of situation he didn't like. "Can I . . . help you?"

"Yeah. You can stay right there and keep your mouth shut. Is that plain enough?"

Those narrow little eyes half shut and the rodent look turned snakelike. He passed it off with a shrug and went back to his bookkeeping. I went up the stairs and down the corridor to the room I had been in last night.

This time the light was already on, and inside a man's hoarse voice was spitting obscenities at a girl. She came back at him with some vile language, then there was the fleshy sound of a hand cracking across a jaw and I shoved the door open.

She sprawled on the floor against the wall, momentarily stunned, one hand pressed against her cheek, a dirty blonde life had prematurely aged. The guy was a big one, heavy under the sport coat and slacks, his face showing the signs of a losing ring career. His nose was flattened and twisted, one ear lumpy and a scar dragged down one corner of his mouth.

He looked at me with a sneer and said, "You got the wrong room, buster."

"I got the right one."

Surprise turned the sneer into a half-smile of anticipation. "Out, out. Like maybe you don't know any better?"

I just stood there. He let two seconds go by, then dropped into a familiar crouch and came at me. He started to feint with his left to cross one over to my jaw, only I never let him get that far. I put a straight jab in his mouth that jarred him back, then hooked him in the gut and again under the chin before he realized what had happened. His legs went rubbery and he went into a sagging dance of defeat. I made sure of it with another right that almost snapped his head off and he crashed against the lone dresser and knocked the lamp off it.

The girl was looking up at me with outright fear, wide awake now. "What . . . did you do . . . that for?"

"Be happy, kid. He belted you, didn't he?"

She started to struggle to her feet. I yanked her up, led her to the bed and let her sit down. "We . . . hell, he's my . . . we work together." Anger flooded her face and she spoke through clenched teeth. "You damn fool, now he'll beat the hell out of me. You crazy or something? What did you make trouble for? Why don't you go . . . .?"

I held out my wallet so she could see the glint of metal inside. Like I figured, she wasn't the kind who wanted to question a badge so far as even take a good look at it. Tiny white lines etched the corners of her mouth and she threw a nervous glance at the guy on the floor. "Let's start with names," I said.

There wasn't any anger in her voice any more. "Listen, mister . . ."

"Names, kid. Who are you?"

She looked down at her feet, her fingers twisting at the bed-clothes. "Virginia Howell."

"Where's Greta Service?"

I saw her frown, then she looked up at me. "I don't know any Greta Service."

Too many times I had put up with lying broads and I could tell when they were spinning one off. *This one wasn't. Now it was all back to where it started again.*

"Let's start with last night, Virginia. Where were you?"

"I was . . . out on a trick." She dropped her eyes again.

"Go on."

"It . . . was a hotel on Forty-ninth. Some john from out of town, I guess. Probably from one of the ships. He . . . he wasn't nothing, but he gave me a hundred bucks and I spent the night with him."

"Where'd you pick him up?"

"I didn't." She pointed to the guy on the floor. "He arranged the date like most of the time. He don't like me doing my own business." A touch of irony came into her voice. "I suppose I got to split with you too. Well, get it off him. He got it all now. Never even let me keep my percentage because I gave him some lip."

"You let anybody use your room?"

"Who the hell wants to use this dump?"

"I didn't ask that."

"No," she said.

I stepped over the guy on the floor. He was breathing heavily through his nose and a trickle of blood was dribbling down his chin. I opened the door of the closet. The same rack of clothes and suitcase was there that I had seen last night.

Virginia said, "You'd better blow, mister. He hates cops."

"Who is he, kid?"

"Lorenzo Jones. He used to fight."

"He's not doing so good right now."

"Just the same, he's mean. Don't think he won't look for you."

I bent over and plucked Lorenzo Jones' wallet from his pocket. He had five hundred and thirty bucks in it, a driver's license issued to himself giving the hotel as his permanent address and two tickets to the fight at the Garden next week. "Where's his room?"

Virginia made a disgusted grimace. "Who knows? He's got six girls in his string. Whoever's empty that night is where he stays. He won't pay for anything. He says he lives here. That's a lot of bull. He used to before he took on the other girls."

"Let's get back to last night again."

She sighed, squeezed her eyes shut and named the hotel, the room and the man as simply "Bud." He was middle-aged, dark, had a trace of an accent and a scar on his chin. Lorenzo Jones had met her at their usual place at eleven o'clock, told her where to go and she went. The whole arrangement had been customary as far as she was concerned except that Jones had bragged about how he had taken the sucker for a bundle. Remorsefully, she added, "You know something, mister? Two years ago I was getting two hundred bucks a night every time."

"These streets go two ways, kid. You don't have to stay around."

"Cut it out. Where the hell is there to go?"

I threw Lorenzo's wallet on the bed and reached down to jerk him to his feet. The voice from the doorway said, "Just hold it like that."

A pair of them stood there, one blocking the doorway with his body, the other slapping a billy against his palm suggestively. They were gutter punks trained in countless street brawls and the kind of predators who were turning the city into a shambles. They were in their late twenties, dangerous as hell because they liked what they were doing and were completely equipped for it.

The first one sensed what I was going to do and moved like a cat. Before I could get the .45 in my hand he was on me, swung the billy in a flat arc and I got my arm up just in time to deflect it. The thing caught me high on the shoulder and my whole arm went numb. He started a backhand swing when I chopped a short one up between his legs. He let out a breathless yell, but I hadn't caught him squarely enough and he was back again, cursing through his teeth. The other one came in from the door, launched a roundhouse right into my ribs, knocking me back against the bed and sending Virginia to the floor. He saved my neck because he knocked me out of the way of the billy, but I didn't have time to think about it.

Maybe they thought I was going to use my hands. They should

have known I had been through the mill too. I braced myself, kicked out and smashed the second guy's face to a pulp with my heels, rolled, got to my feet, stepped into the clear and let the one with the billy make another try for me. He came in grinning, tried to fake me out and brought his arm around. I went under it, caught his forearm, threw him into a lock and went against the elbow joint with such leverage that the bone splintered under my fingers and the guy jerked like a crazy puppet with the agonizing pain that tore through his body. For one second his mouth opened to scream, then he went limp in a faint and I let him drop to the floor. The other one was on his hands and knees, trying to get up. I kicked him in the face again and he flopped back like a big rag doll.

Virginia Howell was crouched in the corner, hands pressed to her mouth, eyes great staring orbs of fear. There wouldn't be any use trying to talk to her now. I picked up my hat and looked around.

Lorenzo Jones was gone.

I went downstairs and when the desk clerk saw me coming, he turned pale. He didn't move when I grabbed his shirt front, didn't make a sound when I backhanded him across the mouth three times. He was caught short and was paying for it, hoping the others would be as easy on him. While he watched, I picked up the phone, called Pat and told him what happened. Everything was turning screwy and we'd want a pickup on Greta Service no matter what the excuse would be, and one on Lorenzo Jones, which would be easy to make stick. He told me to stand by to give the details to the squad car that was on the way, but I didn't have any intention of doing that at all. Those boys knew how to get what they wanted and the ones upstairs would still be here when they arrived.

In fifteen minutes I was supposed to meet Velda. She was going to have to wait. I went back into the rain, walked two blocks north along the curb, trying to spot an empty cab, finally flagged one down and had him take me to the Proctor Building.

The attendant in the lobby had just come on duty and told me the staff had already left for the day, but he was the same one who had been there last night and remembered me being with Dulcie. I told him she had asked me to get something from Theodore Gates' office, that it was damn important and some-body's head would roll if her wishes weren't complied with. He was so eager to please that he called his assistant in to watch the lobby and took me upstairs himself.

When we reached Gates' office I went directly to his rotary card file and spun it around to the G's. What I wanted was those symbols he had inscribed there and to get them translated. I thought I had missed her name and tried again, then a third time to be sure.

Greta Service's card was missing.

The attendant was watching me closely. "Find what you needed, sir?"

I didn't answer him. Instead, I asked, "Who's the receptionist on this floor?"

He thought a moment, then: "A Miss Wald, I believe."

"I want her home phone."

"There's probably a directory in the desk there." He went to the top drawer, pulled out a slide and ran his finger down it. "Here you are." He read the number off to me. I picked up the phone and dialed it. After four rings a young voice answered and I said, "Miss Wald, I'm calling for Theodore Gates. Was he in the office today?"

"Why, yes, he was. He came in about ten, but canceled his appointments and left."

"Know where I can reach him?"

"Did you try his home?"

"Not yet."

"Then I don't know where he could be. You'll have to wait until tomorrow."

I told her thanks and hung up. I found his home number, dialed it, let it ring a dozen times before I was sure there was nobody there, then hung up and jotted down his address.

"Will that be all, sir?"

"Yeah," I said. "For now."

Gates had a combination studio apartment in a renovated brownstone in the Fifties. Two other photographers occupied the building and apparently the one on the bottom floor was working because the lights were on and the foyer door open. I went inside, up the stairs to the second floor and pushed the buzzer to Gates' apartment.

Nobody answered.

I tried six picks on the lock before getting one that worked, stepped inside and felt for the light, the .45 tight in my fist. I flipped it on, moved sideways and covered the room. The place was a maze of equipment, smelling of hypo and water-colored backdrops, but it was empty. I tried each of the rooms to make

THE BODY LOVERS 561

sure. Theodore Gates wasn't there. Two closets were still full of
his clothes, his dresser drawers well filled and orderly, but there
was no telling whether or not he had taken anything with him.

In the studio itself was a desk cluttered with photographic supply
catalogues and opened mail, another of those rotary files centered
on it. I thumbed through this one too, but there was no Greta
Service in it either. Along one side was a row of metal filing
cabinets and I pulled out the one under "S." A folder of proofs
on Greta Service was there, all right, duplicates of the ones in the
Proctor Building. I was about to shut the drawer when I noticed
that the contents had been alphabetically arranged from the P's
to the T's. Out of curiosity I thumbed the first few back.

Then I saw the name *Helen Poston.*

Only four proofs were in the folder, but they were enough.
Teddy Gates had posed her so that every inch of her lush form
was visible through the sheer Grecian gown, the same one Greta
had modeled in. She wasn't a Proctor Girl, but neither was Greta.
It was too bad. They made the Proctor Girls look pretty sickly.
I put the proofs back and tried the "D" file and came up with
three on Maxine Delaney. The redhead wore a sarong, but the
effect was the same. All woman, but no Proctor Girl. There was
too much breast and thigh, too much inborn seductiveness rather
than the lean emaciated look the fashion magazines demanded.

I closed the drawers and checked the rotary file again. Neither
Helen Poston nor Maxine Delaney had an index card there. That
I could expect. They were both dead. Taking their photos out of
the files would come with a general cleanup. But Greta Service's
had been there and wasn't any longer.

Any prints I might have left, I wiped off, then went downstairs,
back to Broadway where I picked up a cab and headed for the
Blue Ribbon.

Velda had almost given me up and was on her last cup of
coffee. Angie was trying to keep her company at a table in the
back, but they had run out of conversation just as I arrived. She
had sparks in her eyes and if there had been something to throw
I would have caught it, but she took one look at my face where
the guys at the Sandelor had worked me over and the anger
subsided into an expression of concern and she grabbed for my
hand.

Angie brought me coffee and a sandwich and while I finished
it I gave her the details. The little fine points I would liked to
have elaborated on wouldn't come out. They were still ideas that
wouldn't congeal into a solid and until they did they just lay there

dormant, oozing through my mind, waiting to be recognized.

Velda had had a phone pickup service put on the office line and the only ones who had called were Hy and Pat. Pat had two possibles on persons who had been convicted on sex charges, later paroled and were presumed to be in the area. Both were parole violators and an intensive search was on for both. The men who jumped me were in custody, accusing the desk clerk of having hired them to lay me out. I was supposed to go in and press charges. There was a tracer out for Lorenzo Jones, but a guy like that could disappear anywhere in New York. Virginia Howell came up with the names and addresses of his other women, but he wasn't at any of those places.

Hy wanted to see me as soon as possible. Al Casey had come up with something he wanted corroborated and I was to meet him at ten at his office.

When Velda had given me the information she said, "What does it look like?"

"It smells. When it gets this damn complicated there's something else going on."

"I found the car Greta Service used. It was a rental job and she had it out twice. Both times it was registered to her and the mileage figures were nearly identical. The first time it was 118 miles, the second, 122." She reached in her pocketbook and brought out a map of the New York, Jersey and Long Island area.

"Figuring it as a round trip each way," she said, "I laid out a general sixty-mile radius from the city. Here it is." She shoved the map to me and sketched the circled area with her forefinger.

"That's a hell of a lot of square miles," I told her.

"We're only interested in the perimeter."

"If she went directly to her target, yeah."

"We'll have to assume some things. Anyway, she had Helen Poston with her and women don't usually get too devious when they're driving."

I traced the line of her circle, picking out the cities the line touched. Peculiarly, there weren't many that it intersected at all. According to the diagram, the extent of Greta's trip would have led her to some pretty remote spots.

There was one that it did come close to, though. It was on Long Island and the name was *Bradbury*. I took out my pen and drew a circle around the town. "We'll start here."

She looked across the table at me and nodded. "The origin of that letter Greta had."

"When Harry mentioned it she cut him off. It may mean something."

"I know the section, Mike. When I was a kid it was a very exclusive place for the wealthy. It's come down a lot since the general population move to the suburbs, but there are still a lot of big people out that way."

"Who would Greta know there?" I asked her.

"A beautiful woman might know anybody. At least it's a lead. Supposing I check into a hotel out that way and see what I can do. I'll call you when I'm located."

"You watch it. You're a beautiful doll too."

"It's about time you noticed." She gave me a big grin. "And when I think of those lovely adjoining rooms going to waste . . ."

"I'm hurting too, kitten."

She looked at her left hand and the ring I had given her. "I can come closer to getting married than any girl in the world. Why did I have to pick you?"

"Because we're made for each other," I told her. "Now get moving."

I could tell when Pat was burning. He stared at me with those cold eyes of his as if I were a suspect and let me go through my story for the third time around before he said, "Just tell me why you didn't hold Greta Service."

"For what reason?"

"You could have called me."

"Sure, and if there was something backing up this mess and she's involved she would have clammed right up."

"That doesn't cut it with me, Mike."

"No? I'd like to see what a lawyer would do to you if you tried it. I played it my way and that's the way it is. Any word on Lorenzo Jones or Gates yet?"

"Not a damn thing. Jones is holed up somewhere and the best we got on Gates was a statement from the elevator operator in the Proctor Building that he left sometime after ten. He carried no luggage and seemed to be in a hurry. The cleaning woman who took care of his place said everything was still there as far as she knew, but she had the idea he kept a woman somewhere and a change of clothes at her apartment. We're still looking. Incidentally, the other desk clerk at the Sandelor Hotel handed us a blank. He knew the Howell dame but couldn't identify Greta. He's generally half in the bag and can't see too well anyway. We leaned on him a little but couldn't cut it at all."

"And Dulcie McInnes?"

"She was on live TV from Washington this afternoon M.C.-ing a fashion show for some big women's organization. She's a house guest of a woman who's the wife of one of our biggest lobbyists and couldn't give us a lead to Gates at all. She suggested that he might have gone off on an independent assignment. Our men didn't think so because the equipment he would have carried is still at his studio."

I leaned back in the chair with my hands folded behind my head. "Not much is being said in the papers about Mitch Temple."

"Which is the way we wanted it and they're cooperating."

On the wall the clock ticked the seconds away. Pat finally said, "The M.E. had replies to his queries about the poison that was used on the Poston girl. It wasn't as exclusive as he thought it was. There are certain other derivatives from similar sources that have been used by the Orientals for centuries. It went out of fashion when the royalty class was deposed by the rabble, but available. Interpol reported its use several times during some big family vendettas in Turkey."

"I'm missing your point," I said.

Pat picked up a pencil and doodled on a pad on the desk. "There isn't any. I'm just throwing it up for grabs."

"Sorry, buddy."

"We hit a dead end on the whip that killed the Delaney kid."

"You still have one more to go. Find out who owns a rack."

Pat shot me an annoyed glance. "Mike . . . this could be an individual. A nut. He preys on one type. He uses gimmicks." He threw the pencil down and slapped the desk with an open hand. "Damn it, I haven't got the feeling that it is and neither do you."

I didn't say anything.

"Damn it, Mike . . ."

"Something's wrong. Too many things miss being on the line by a fraction. There are people involved who have no right being there at all. Kills like this generally touch only certain persons . . . they don't get spread out all over the map like this one." I stopped and let the chair ease forward. "No, I don't think it's an individual. It's too well coordinated. If it were an individual somebody would have seen something. If those kills were related there was nothing spontaneous about them."

"Get to it, Mike."

"Theodore Gates could be the key. He knew three of them. Photos of them were in his files. I saw Greta's name in his personal index and the next time it wasn't there at all. He had the time to destroy it. Greta could have called him after I left there to tell him I had located her. A little thought would put his finger on what happened. He took the card out and disappeared."

"Why?"

"And therein lies the rub," I quoted. "Why? Unless he and Greta had something going for them. Somebody obviously paid off Lorenzo Jones to use Virginia Howell's room that night. I'll take her word for it she didn't know what the scoop was."

"We'll get him."

"Sure, but what good will it do? He's a pimp, a punchy pimp. If there's a hot one here nobody's going to invite him in on the deal. That type is too likely to blow it to pieces. No, he was used somehow. I can see how a guy like Gates might have had contact with Jones. Gates had outside assignments that could have led to Jones or he just could have been one of the guy's clients. When you get a file on Gates that stuff will come out. We just can't wait around, that's all."

Pat got up and stalked to the window, snapping his fingers with impatience. "Mitch Temple puts it all in the same package," he said. "He spotted the same similarity and followed it up. He recognized somebody and died for it." He turned around and squinted at me. "Then there was that guy who tried for you. Nothing came of that either. We're dealing with a cast of nobodies."

"But they're there."

"Sure. And we're here. Three punks are in the can on an assault and battery charge. Great record. You know what the papers will be doing to this office if there's no action before long?"

I nodded. "Every reporter in the city is working overtime."

"The difference is, friend, that they don't have to be the goats."

"Pat," I said quietly.

"Yeah?"

"What's out at Bradbury?"

"Now what hole in your head did that come out of?"

"It came up along the line," I said.

Pat's smile was a tight thing that barely crinkled his mouth. There was no humor in it at all. Before he could push it I added, "Harry Service mentioned Greta having a letter from there once. He didn't see it."

Some of the frost left his face. "When was this?"

"Her last visit."

Pat went over it in his mind a moment and told me, "It's a resort area along the coast and a residential area for the wealthy further in. I haven't been there for five years."

"Nothing else?"

"You pushing an angle?" he demanded.

"Curious, that's all."

"She could have been there. The place is public beaches, a yacht harbor and motel area now. Some of the Fire Island crowd took it over and ran it down. It's getting a reputation of being an artists-and-models colony. The old permanent residents complained, but it didn't help any. I guess they thought it would ruin their image, especially after a couple of the embassies bought into the area there."

"What embassies?"

"Oh, the French have a place there . . . so do one of the Russian satellite countries. I think one of the Middle East outfits moved out there a couple of years ago too."

I laughed with surprise. "And I thought if it didn't happen in the city here you wouldn't know about it."

"The reason I know is because some of our best officers retired from the force to take up security jobs there at twice the pay."

"Not at the embassies?"

"No, they have their own security. The town has a jazz festival every year that brings in a mob of town wreckers. The public finally anted up for a bigger force before somebody caused an international incident. It's gotten worse every year. It's too damn bad Gerald Ute wouldn't be philanthropic in other fields."

"Ute?"

"Yeah, the one you met the other night."

"He's got a place out there?"

"Not him. He simply financed the jazz festivals. He turned his place into a communal recreation center for the bigwigs of the U.N. The city runs it, but on a pretty restricted basis. It was a grand gesture and got him a lot of publicity, but it got a white elephant off his hands too . . . along with a fat tax deduction."

He sat down, swinging idly in his chair, watching my face. "Velda's out there," I said.

"So are a hundred agents from Washington to make sure nothing happens to the housecats from the U.N. These days nobody wants to take a chance of having some politico scratched. Hell, the way diplomatic immunity goes these days we can't even give out parking tickets."

I didn't want Pat to see my face. He didn't know it, but he had just been the catalyst that jelled one of those thoughts that had been so damn elusive.

When I got up I tossed a note on Pat's desk. "Can you see

Harry gets this? It's a report that his sister is alive."

"Okay. You going to press charges against those three we're holding?"

"Right now."

"You're going to have a lot to talk about when you're in court on that kill."

chapter eight ▬▬▬▬▬▬▬▬▬

FOUR OF THEM were in the office when I got there. Al Casey and Hy were at the desk and two old-timers from the morgue file, passing them from one to another, identifying the subjects and making terse comments on their background.

I threw my coat and hat on a chair, took one of the containers of coffee from the sack and looked over Hy's shoulder. "What have you got?"

Hy nudged Al. "Tell him about it."

He fanned out a dozen pictures in front of him. "Mitch Temple pulled out a lot of folders, but his prints were only on the edges, from where he thumbed through them. However, on the photos in two of the folders his prints were all over them, so he had taken a lot of time going through them."

"These?"

"Yeah. Sixty-eight of them in the 'General Political' classification. We have everything from the mayor's speech to a union parley. We tried the cross indexes and can't see what ties in. Everybody in the foreground of the shots is identified and so far we have over three hundred names with repeats on about half, all of whom are fairly prominent citizens."

"How many did the paper use?"

"About a third. They're stamped on the back with the dates."

"There's a common denominator there though, isn't there?"

Hy nodded. "Sure. We nailed that right away. All were taken in New York within the last year. Try to make something out of that."

I picked some of the photos from the pile on the end and scanned through them. Some I remembered having seen in the paper, others were parts of the general coverage given the occasions by one or more photographers. There were faces I knew, some I had just heard about and too many that were totally unknown.

Every so often somebody would spot a possible connection and it would be checked out with another index, but every time they'd draw a blank. There didn't seem to be any possibility of a connection between their activities and Mitch Temple's death. Nevertheless, the pictures made repeated rounds among all of us.

I grinned when I saw Dulcie McInnes at a charity function and another of her at a ball in a Park Avenue hotel dancing with an elderly foreign ambassador in a medal-decorated sash. Then I stopped looking at faces and concentrated on the names typed and pasted to the back of the sheets.

The only one whose name had come up before was Belar Ris. He was greeting a diplomatic representative from one of the iron curtain countries who was getting off an airplane and Belar Ris had the funny expression of a man who didn't particularly care about being photographed. He seemed to be tall and blocky, suggestive of physical power even tailor-made clothes couldn't conceal. His face didn't show any trace of national origin except that he was swarthy and his eyes had a shrewd cast to them. His out-stretched arm was bared to the cuff of his coat, his wrist and forearm thick. Belar Ris was a short-sleeved-shirt man, the kind who wanted no obstacles in the way of a power move.

Al saw me concentrating on the photo and asked, "Got something?"

I tossed the picture down. "Mitch had some column items on this one."

He looked at it carefully. "Who didn't? Belar Ris. He's a U.N. representative. There's another picture of him in tonight's paper raising hell at an Assembly meeting."

"Anything special on him?"

"No, but he's publicity-shy. There are a dozen like him at the U.N. now . . . the grabbers. He'll play both ends against the middle to keep things going back home. Anything to protect his interests. It's too bad the idiots appoint people like that to represent them."

"They have to." Al separated some of the shots in front of him and picked one out. "Here's another of Ris. It was right after that Middle East blow-up. The guy he's talking to was ousted the next week and killed in a coup."

One other person was in the picture, but the lighting didn't make his features too distinguishable. "Who's this?"

Al took the picture from me, scanned it and shook his head. "Beats me. Probably in the background. He's not mentioned on the back."

"He looks familiar," I said.

"Could be. That's right outside the U.N. complex and he could be part of a diplomatic corps. It doesn't look like he's standing with Ris."

He was right. The guy wasn't with Ris or the other one, but it didn't look as if he were going anywhere either. He seemed to be in an attitude of waiting, but even then, with a stop-action shot, you couldn't tell. There was something vaguely familiar about him, a face you see once and couldn't forget because of the circumstances. I ran it through my mind quickly, trying to focus on possible areas of contact, but couldn't make a connection and put the picture back on the pile.

I spent another twenty minutes with them, then got up and wandered down the corridor to the morgue where old Biff was reading his paper. He waved and I said, "Mind if I take a look in your files?"

"Be my guest."

I went down the rows until I came to the "R's" and pulled out the drawer. There was a file on Belar Ris, with three indistinct photos that hadn't been used. There was the shadow of his hat, a hand apparently carelessly held in front of his face and a blur of motion that didn't quite make him recognizable. The ones he was with were identified, but I didn't make any of them. All of them seemed to have some prominence, to judge by their clothes, the attaché cases they carried or the general background. I closed the files and walked back to the desk.

Hy was standing there looking at me.

"Okay, Mike," he said, "you pulled something out."

"Belar Ris," I told him. "There's nothing in the files."

"Why him?"

"Nothing special. He was the only one I recognized that Mitch wrote about."

"Can it, Mike. There *is* something special. What?"

"The guy doesn't seem to like having his picture taken."

"A lot of them are that way."

"Attached to a diplomatic staff? They're all publicity hounds."

"What do you know about Ris, Mike?"

"Only what Mitch wrote."

"Maybe I can tell you a little more. He's got a hush-hush background. Black-market activities, arms dealing, tricky business dealings, but I know a lot of others on top of the political situation that were just as bad. Right now he's being treated mighty carefully because guys like that can sway the balance of power in the U.N. Now look . . . there's something else about Ris, so don't you tell me . . ."

"There isn't anything, buddy. I was swinging wild."

Biff shoved the paper across the desk before Hy could answer me and said, "This the one you're talking about?"

It was Belar Ris on the front page, all right. He was talking to two of our people and a French representative during a break in the session and his face was hard and one finger pointed aggressively at our man who looked pretty damn disgusted. The caption said it was a continuation of the argument over having admitted the government represented by Naku Em Abor, who had just proposed some resolution inimical to the western powers.

Hy said, "Does that look like a guy who doesn't want his picture taken?"

I had to admit that it didn't.

Biff grinned and said, "Don't fool yourself, Hy. Charlie Forbes took that shot and he doesn't work with a Graflex. Ten to one it was a gimmick camera hidden under his shirt."

I tapped Hy on the shoulder. "See what I mean?"

He handed the paper back. "Okay, Mike. I'll buy a little piece of it. We'll poke around. Now how about the rest of it?"

"The boys on the police beat have big ears."

"When it concerns you, yeah."

I gave him the story on finding Greta Service without mentioning all the details, simply that Dulcie McInnes had suggested checking Teddy Gates' files and I had come up with another address. He knew he wasn't getting the whole picture, but figured I was protecting a client's interest and since the job was done as far as Harry was concerned, it ended there.

When I left the building it was pretty late, but for what I wanted to do, the night was just starting.

The stable of girls Lorenzo Jones ran was a tired string operating out of run-down hotels and shoddy apartments. They all had minor arrest records, and after each one, simply changed the locality of their activities, picked up a new name and went back into the business. Like most of the girls who were on the tail end of the prostitution racket, they had no choice. Jones ran things with an iron fist and they didn't dispute his decisions. The operation was pretty well confined to the section catering to the waterfront trade, the quickies and drunks who patronized the dives where he made the contacts for his broads.

None of the first three I found had seen him and they seemed to be wandering around in a vacuum, not knowing whether to hit the streets or wait for Jones to arrange their appointments. Two of them had turned repeat tricks for old customers out of habit and one had solicited a couple of customers on her own because she was broke.

For some reason they were anxious to see Jones show up again, probably because on their own they'd get sluffed off if they tried to hustle, while Jones got the money in advance and the customer took what he was offered whether he liked it or not.

Talking wasn't part of their makeup. They had taken too many lumps from Jones and their customers over the years and there was no way to lean on them.

But the fourth one wasn't like that. Her name was Roberta Slade and she was the last one Jones had added to his firm. I found her in a place they called Billy's Cave sipping a martini and studying herself in the mirror over the back bar.

When I sat down her eyes caught mine in the glass and she said with a voice the gin had thickened just a little bit, "Move to the rear of the bus, mister."

She turned insolently and I could see that one time she had been a pretty girl. The makeup was heavy, her eyes tired, but there was still some sparkle in her hair and a little bit of determination in the set of her mouth. "Do I know you?"

I waved for a beer and pushed some money across the bar. "Nope."

"Well, I'm taking the day off." She turned back and twirled the glass in her hand.

"Good for you," I said.

I finished half the beer and put the glass down. "Shove off," she said softly.

I took twenty bucks out and laid it down between us. "Will that buy some conversation?"

A little grin split her lips and she glanced at me, her eyebrows raised. "You don't look like one of those nuts, mister. I've given a hundred different versions of my life history embellished with lurid details to guys who get their kicks that way and I can spot them a city block away."

"I'm not paying for that kind of talk."

Quickening interest showed in her face. "You a cop? Damn, you look like one, but any more you can't tell what a cop looks like. The vice squad runs college boys who look like babies; dames you take for schoolteachers turn out to be policewomen. It's rough."

"I'm a private cop, if you want to know."

"Oh boy," she laughed. "Big deal. Whose poor husband is going to get handed divorce papers for grabbing some outside stuff?" She laughed again and shook her head. "I don't know names, I'm lousy at remembering faces and all your twenty bucks could buy you would be a lot of crap, so beat it."

"I want Lorenzo Jones."

The glass stopped twirling in her fingers. She studied it a moment, drained it and set it on the bar. "Why?" she asked without looking at me.

"I want to give him a friendly punch in the mouth."

"Somebody already did."

"Yeah, I know." I laid my hand palm down on the bar so she could see the cuts across my knuckles. "I want to do it again," I said.

Very slowly, her face turned so she was smiling up at me and her eyes had the look of a puppy that had found a friend and was trying his best not to run away. "So I have a champion."

"Not quite."

"But you laid him out, didn't you? Word gets around fast. You were the one who raised all that hell in Virginia's room, weren't you?"

"I was on a job."

Her grin turned into a chuckle and she motioned with a finger for the bartender to fill her glass again. "I wish I could have seen it. That dirty bastard took me apart enough times. He hated my guts, you know that? And do you know why?"

"No."

"I used to work a hatcheck concession in a joint he hung out in. I wasn't like this then. He tried his best to make me and I brushed him off. He was a pig. You know how he gets his kicks? He . . . well, hell, that's another story."

Her drink came and I paid for it. For a few seconds she stirred the olive around with the toothpick absently, then tasted it, her eyes on herself in the back bar mirror. "I almost had it made. I was doing some high-class hustling, then I got a guy who liked me. Nice rich kid. Good education." She made a sour grimace and said, "Then Jones queered the deal. He got some pictures of me on a date and showed them to the kid. That was the end of that. I went to pieces, but he picked them up fast. He had me worked over a couple of times, picked up by the cops so I had a record, then he moved in and took over when I didn't have any place to go." Roberta took a long pull of the martini and added sadly, "I guess this is what I was cut out for anyway."

"Where's Jones now?"

"I hope the bastard's dead."

"He isn't."

She ran the fingers of one hand through her hair, then lightly down the side of her cheek. "The cops are looking for him too."

"I know."

"Why?"

"There are a couple of dead girls he might know something about."

"Not Lorenzo Jones. They can't make any money for him dead. He'd keep them alive."

I said, "He's just a lead. I want him, Roberta."

"What will you do to him if you find him?"

"Probably kick the crap out of him."

"Promise?"

I grinned at her. She wasn't kidding at all. "Promise," I said.

"Can I watch?"

"My pleasure."

She picked the drink up, looked at it a moment, then put it down unfinished. The twenty was still there, but she didn't touch it. "My treat," she told me.

The rain had slicked the pavement and was coming down in a fine drizzle, throwing a misty halo around the street lights. I wanted to call a cab, but Roberta said no and we walked two blocks without talking. Finally I said, "Where to?"

"My place." She didn't look at me.

"Lorenzo there?"

"No, but I am." She didn't say anything after that, crossing the avenues in silence, then down another two blocks until we came to the doorway between a pair of stores and she took my arm and nodded. "Here."

She put a key in the lock and pushed the door open, stepped in and let me follow her. I went up the stairs behind her, waited at the first landing while she opened up again and switched the light on. I had been in a lot of cribs before and they were usually dingy affairs, but she had taken a lot of trouble with this one. It was a three-room apartment, clean, furnished simply, but in good taste.

Roberta saw me take it in with a single sweep of my eyes and caught my initial reaction. "My early upbringing." She walked to the closet, reached deep into the shelf and came out with a cheap pad stuffed with papers and held together with a rubber band. She handed it to me and said, "He dropped it one night. It's a tally sheet on us, but you'll find receipts in there from a few places. We knew he had a place he stayed when he wasn't in with one of us, but nobody knew where. That is, until I found this one night. You'll find him there, but let me go find me first."

I looked at her, wondering what the hell she was talking about, and when she left, sat down and opened the pad. The kids had made plenty for Lorenzo Jones, all right, but I wasn't interested in his take. What I saw were paid bills from three different small hotels, each covering a period for about three months, and the last was dated only a month ago and if the pattern fit, he'd be there now. Only he wasn't listed as Lorenzo Jones. His name on the bill head was an imaginative J. Lorenzo, room 614 of the Midway Hotel.

Roberta Slade came back then. She wasn't the same one who had left and I saw what she meant about finding herself. She smelled of the shower and some subtle perfume; the makeup was gone and the outfit she wore was almost sedate. She pulled on a maroon raincoat, stuffed her hair under a silly little hat and smiled gently. "There are times," she said, "when I hate myself and want to go back to what I think I could have been."

"I like you better this way."

She knew I meant it. There was an ironic tone in her voice. "It isn't very profitable."

"You could give it a try, kid."

"That depends on you. And Lorenzo Jones. He's got a long memory."

"Maybe we can shorten it up a little."

The Midway Hotel rented rooms by the hour or the day, and if you paid in advance no luggage was required. The going rate for accommodations was steeper than the place deserved because the management got its cut for providing its service of keeping its mouth shut and overlooking the preponderance of Smiths in the register.

I signed in as Mr. and Mrs. Thompson from Toledo, Ohio, passed the money over and took the key marked 410. The clerk didn't even bother to look at my signature or thank me for letting him keep the change of my bill.

There was no bellhop, but this place had an early-model self-service elevator that took us to the fourth floor where we got out.

We walked to the room and when I opened the door she gave me an odd look, a wry little smile, shrugged and walked in.

I grinned at her, but there wasn't any humor there. "No tricks, kid. I can't go busting in his door up there and he damn well won't open it for me."

"Nothing would surprise me any more. I'm sorry."

I went to the window, forced it up and looked out at the back of the building. Like most, it had an iron fire escape with landings that covered the windows of several rooms at each floor. I shucked my raincoat and threw it to Roberta. "Give me fifteen minutes to get up there, then come pay a visit."

"You won't start without me, will you?"

"No . . . I'll wait."

Outside, thunder rumbled across the sky and for a second there was a dull glow over the city. I stepped out to the iron slats and closed the window behind me. The rain waited for that second and came at me like a basket of spitting cats, daring me to go any further.

I swung my legs over the railing and got my feet set, hanging on to the metal bar behind me. The rain pelted my face and I couldn't be sure of the distance to the other fire escape frame. Then the sky lit up with that dull gray incandescence and I could see it, and while the image was still there, jumped, my fingers clawing for the iron rail.

My hands made it, but my feet slipped, smashing me into the uprights. I hung on, pulled myself up until I found a toehold, then climbed over and stood there to get my breath and see if anybody had heard the racket. There wasn't any need to worry; the rain kept the windows closed and the thunder drowned out any noise I thought I made. Two flights up where room 614 was, the window was outlined in yellow behind the drawn shade.

I took the .45 out of the sling, cocked it and started up the stairs.

The window was open about four inches from the bottom with the shade pulled below the level of the sill. Inside a radio was playing some tinny music and the smell of cigar smoke seeped out the opening. There was a cough, the creak of bedsprings and somebody twisted the dial of the radio savagely until another station was on. I tried the window. The damn thing was stuck fast.

Behind my back the wind came at me, driving the rain through my clothes, making the shade flop against the sill. I edged to one side, reached out with my fingers, got the shade, pulled it down on the roller and let it go. The thing snapped up under the tension of the spring and flapped wildly around its axis and the guy on the bed jumped up with a curse, startled, a snub-nosed gun in his hand. He took a look at the shade, let out another curse, stuck the gun in his waistband and came to the window, reaching up to pull down the blind.

And saw me standing there with the .45 aimed at his middle through the glass.

"Open it," I said.

For a moment I thought he was going to try it, but the odds were just too big and he knew it. His face was a pasty white, his hands shook going to the window, and when he forced it up he stood there with the sweat running down his forehead into a crease in his flattened nose and he couldn't get a sound out of his throat.

I stepped inside, yanked the gun out of his pants and smashed him across the jaw with it. His head snapped back and he stumbled against the bed just as a knock came on the door. I walked over, opened it and let Roberta in. She gave me a hurt look and said, "You promised."

"It was just a teaser, kid," I told her. "The main course comes up later."

Lorenzo Jones got his voice back. "Mister . . . look, I didn't do nothing. . . . I . . ."

"Shut up." I locked the door behind me, went over and pulled down the window, closed the shade and, very deliberately, turned the volume of the radio up.

Lorenzo Jones got the message loud and clear. His eyes in their heavy pads of flesh grew a little wild. They didn't want to look at mine. They tried to appeal to Roberta, then he saw who she was. "Look mister . . . if she paid you to do this, I'll pay you more. That bitch . . ."

"She didn't pay me, Lorenzo."

"Then why . . .?"

"Shut up and listen to me, Lorenzo. Listen real good because I'm only going to say it once. I'm going to ask you questions and if you don't answer them right you're going to catch a slug someplace." I motioned to Roberta. "Get me a pillow."

She pulled one from the bed and tossed it to me. I wrapped it around the rod in my fist and walked over to Jones. He tried to swallow and couldn't. I said, "Who paid you to use Virgina Howell's room?"

"The . . . the girl. She . . ."

"Not the girl."

His nod was desperate. "It was, I'm telling you. She gimme the dough. . ." I leveled the .45 at his kneecap. "Cripes, don't shoot me, will ya! I'm telling ya, the girl gimme the money. Ali said she'd pay me. . . . It wasn't the first time. He wanted a room somewhere for himself or his friends, I'd clear Virginia out and let 'im use it. Always whoever used the room would pay me. He . . ."

"Roberta?" I asked.

"He's pulled that plenty of times, usually with Virginia. A lot of those bums don't want to sign a register. A couple of times he stuck somebody up there who was hot."

I looked back to Jones again. "How long was Greta supposed to stay there, Lorenzo?"

His shrug was more like a big shudder. "I . . . dunno. Ali never told me. She got out on her own, then that stupid Virginia came back when I told her to stay away until I saw her. That's why I smacked her. She was givin' me a hard time. She didn't like nobody using her place. That other one messed up her clothes, threw them in a suitcase, knocked them down. . . ."

"That other one was putting on an act for me, Lorenzo. She wanted me to think she lived there." I stopped a second, watched him and said, "Was she there before?"

"How do I know? I don't ask Ali no questions. Maybe she was. I ain't gonna complain when . . ."

I cut him off. "Who's Ali?"

"Hell, that's all I know. Just Ali. He's a guy."

"You're getting close to hopping, Jones." I grinned at him and my mouth was a tight line across my teeth. I could feel my fingers starting to squeeze the gun.

Lorenzo Jones knew it too. His breath sucked in so hard he almost choked and he tried to double up in a ball. "Who's Ali?" I repeated.

His tongue ran over dry lips. "He's . . . on a ship. Some kind . . . of a steward."

"More."

"He brings things in. You know, he . . ."

"What does he smuggle, Jones?"

He couldn't keep his hands still and the sweat was dripping off his nose. "I . . . I think it's H. He don't tell me. His customers are . . . special. He ain't . . . in the rackets. He does it special."

"That puts him in the money class," I said.

Lorenzo jerked his head in a nod.

"How would he contact a slob like you?"

"I . . . got him some broads one time. He like to . . . well, he wasn't right. He did some crazy things to 'em, but he paid good."

"What things?"

Lorenzo Jones was almost babbling, but he said, "Cigarettes. He burned 'em, things like that. He'd . . . bite them. Once he . . ."

Roberta came up and stood beside me, looking at Jones with loathing. "I knew two of those kids. They never talked about it, but I saw the scars. One wound up in the mental ward at Bellevue and the other stepped in front of a subway train when she was dead drunk."

"Describe them, Jones."

His mind didn't want to work. He couldn't keep his eyes off the pillow that covered the gun in my hand. I grinned again and it was too much for him. His mouth began to contort into words. "He . . . he's kind of not too big like. He talks funny. I tried to get something on him so I could maybe score with him but he's careful. I seen him in the Village sometimes. Him and a silly hat. He goes with them oddballs down there for kicks. Look, I don't know him. He's just some gook."

I got that feeling again, a surging of little streams running together to churn into a more powerful feeder that would eventually build to a raging torrent. How many people had called other people a gook? It was old army slang for any native help, the baggy-pants bunch that toted your barracks bags and did your washing. The kind who'd beg with one hand and kill with the other, to whom petty theft was a pastime, robbery a way of life and to be caught was kismet and your head on a pole outside the city.

"Okay, Lorenzo, now one more for the big go and don't muff it. You said you tried to get something so you could score on him. That means you tailed him. You know he comes off a ship." I paused, then said, "Which ship?" and held the gun on his gut.

He didn't hesitate at all. "The *Pinella*."

I nodded. "Why you holing up, Lorenzo?"

No words came out. His eyes seemed sunk in the back of his head.

I said, "Maybe you did find out something. Maybe you found out this man would kill you the first time you ever messed anything on him."

Jones got his voice back at last. "Okay, so I seen those broads. I know guys like him. He even told me. He . . ." His voice lost itself in the fear that was so alive it drenched him with sweat.

"Now, Roberta?" I asked.

"Now," she said.

I took my time with him and any little sounds he was able to make were drowned in the noise of the radio. He came apart in small splashes of blood and livid bruises he was going to wear a long, long time. I talked to him quietly while I did it and before his eyes were closed all the way I made him look at Roberta and see what he had done to her and when he couldn't see any more, made him remember what he had done to the others. I made sure he knew that this could only be the start of things for him because a lot of people were going to know who he was and what he did and wherever he went somebody else would be waiting for him and Lorenzo Jones knew I wasn't lying, not even a little bit.

When it was over I took his wallet, emptied out the three grand it held and handed it to Roberta. She could split it up with the others and they could get the hell away from the mess they were in if they had the guts to. At least I knew she would.

I stuck the snub-nose gun in my pocket, put the .45 back and went downstairs with Roberta. I tossed the room key on the desk and the clerk put it back on the hook without looking at me. The rain had settled into a steady downpour and I called a cab and put her in it.

She looked out the window, took my hand and said, "Thanks."

I winked at her.

"I don't even know your name," she said.

"It doesn't matter."

"No, it really doesn't, does it? But I won't forget you, big feller."

chapter nine ▮▮▮▮▮▮▮▮▮▮▮▮▮▮▮▮▮▮▮▮

IT WASN'T TOO difficult to get a rundown on the *Pinella*. She was a freighter under Panamanian registry that accommodated ten passengers in addition to cargo. She had been in port eleven days taking on a load of industrial machinery destined for Lisbon and would be here another five days before sailing. The crew was of mixed foreign extraction under a Spanish captain and at the moment, most of them were ashore.

But it was almost impossible to get anything on the steward. His name was Ali Duval. He attended the passengers, generally engineers who traveled with the equipment, the crew and kept to himself on the ship. In port he left at the first possible moment and didn't return until just before sailing time. Both the Treasury men and the customs officials gave the ship and crew a clean bill of health. No contraband had ever been found on board, none of the crew had ever been apprehended trying to take anything illicit ashore and no complaint had ever been lodged against the vessel or its personnel.

During the lunch hour I circulated among some of the dock workers trying to pick up any information, but no one had anything to offer. A check through a friend of mine got me the story that the *Pinella* was owned by several corporations, but it would take months to unravel the front organizations and the real owners who buried themselves in a maze of paperwork to beat taxes.

I grabbed a bite to eat in a little restaurant, watching the dark creep up on the waterfront. The rain had stopped earlier, but it still was up there, threatening. The night lights came on along the wharves making the ships in their berths seem unreal and whoever walked between the lights and the hulls would throw a monstrous shadow along the steel sides momentarily, then dissolve into the dark further on.

I was going to grab a cab and head back uptown when I saw the night watchman come on duty across the street and decided to make another stab at it. In five minutes I found out he was a retired cop from the New York force who had been at this job ten years and glad to have somebody to talk to. The nights were long and lonely and conversation was the only thing left he had to enjoy.

And he knew Ali Duval. At least he knew who he was. On the ship he wore a uniform, but when he hit the beach he was wearing expensive clothes, which was pretty fancy for a low-paid steward, but he accounted for it by saying how guys like that saved their money and blew it in one big bust the minute they hit the shore. He used to wonder what it was he carried in the paper bag when he left the ship, then on two different occasions he had seen him drive up in a new black limousine wearing "one of them native hats like the Shriners wear."

I said, "A fez?"

"Yeah, that's it. With a tassel. He got out of the car, put it in the bag and went on board with his suitcase. Some of these foreigners are nuts."

"Who was in the car?"

"Got me. They were friends though. They sat and talked a few minutes, before he got out. I couldn't see the car. Sure was a dandy. Probably was a relative. Plenty of these guys got people over here, only usually they ain't so well off."

"Ever been on the ship?"

"Few times," he said. "The chow's pretty good."

"They get any visitors up there?"

"Not when I'm on. Hell, who wants to see a freighter? This one's better'n most, but she's still a freighter."

"Listen," I said, "how can I recognize this Duval?"

"Well, if he ain't got his hat on, you might say he's medium, kinda foreign-looking and has an accent. If you can read faces, I'd say this one could get mean if he wanted to, or maybe that's just the way some foreigners look. It's just that he's got . . . well, there's something."

"I know what you mean. Got any idea how I can find him?"

"Not a one. Couple of times the mate tried to dig him up, but that bird didn't show. He goes someplace and gets himself lost. Dames, probably. All them sailors think of is dames. The last time the mate chewed him out and wanted to know where the hell he was and Duval just looked at him like he wasn't even there and went up on deck. Guess he figures his shore time's his own. I know he don't go with none of the others. That bunch hardly ever gets more than six blocks away from here anyway. They're back and forth for their clothes, picking up money they left stashed away so they wouldn't get rolled for the whole wad the first night out and picking up chow on board when they go broke. This Duval, he just leaves and comes back as sharp as when he left. Sharper even. He's always got new clothes on."

I spent five more minutes with the old guy before I left but there wasn't any more he had to offer, so I thanked him and crossed the street to a bar and went in the back to a pay phone. I finally reached Pat at his apartment, told him I was coming up and to put the coffee on.

We sat there at the kitchen table of his bachelor digs and he listened while I gave him the bit at the Midway Hotel and the follow-up at the *Pinella*. When I got done he glared at me across the table and tossed his spoon halfway across the room in disgust. "Damn, when are you going to learn, Mike?"

"Jones wouldn't have told you any more."

"You know we have ways to handle guys like that."

"Balls. Those girls wouldn't file a complaint anyway."

"They don't have to. You think we couldn't get a witness to go against him?"

"So some judge would throw thirty days at him and let him go back into the business? Come on, Pat, you're smarter than that. He won't be operating in this town any more."

"Neither will you if the D.A. hears about it."

"Who's to tell?" I grinned. "Anyway, how about checking with Interpol to see if they have anything on Ali Duval."

"And then what?"

I finished my coffee and slid my chair back from the table. "Let's put the pieces together, Pat. You have three dead women who might have had some mutual relationship. I had one live one who's tied into the picture. We have a guy named Theodore Gates who knew at least three of them. I go looking for Greta Service and the lead took me to the Proctor Group. Dulcie said I caused a lot of talk up there. . . . It was right after the big spread they had on me in the papers, so supposing this Gates gets the word?"

Pat nodded agreement and rubbed his eyes.

"Okay," I said, "so he remembered the file he had on Greta listing her with the Howell dame. Who knows what kind of photography he was doing? Half the pornography made is done in those joints. He got up to his office but the damage had already been done. He lifted the card out of the rotary file too late. Greta didn't want to be found, Gates didn't want her found, and when I did, Greta cut out. She could have contacted Gates and he took off when he saw things coming apart."

"I can punch holes in that," Pat said.

"But at least it's a place to start. And it gets us back to Mitch Temple. He was interested in the Delaney and Poston deaths too. He recognized somebody and followed him, somebody who was buying a white negligee."

Pat held up his hand. "That hasn't been proven."

"Screw the proof. Let's guess a little and see what we have. Now two things could have happened. Either the person Mitch saw and followed recognized him and backtracked Mitch to his apartment, or Mitch pulled a stupid trick. We know he tried to call Norm Harrison and missed him. We know he poked around in the morgue looking for a photo to confirm his suspicions. Supposing he decided to make a direct inquiry to the one he was after to bring him out into the open?"

"That's pretty damn dumb."

"Not if he thought the guy was too big to try the direct approach.

He underestimated the opposition, but it could have paid off. Don't forget, he was waiting to see Norm Harrison. He could have expected it to be him at the door that night."

"And what have you got so far, Mike?"

"Everything's related so far. From the girls, to Mitch, to Greta, to Gates, to Jones, to Ali Duval. It's stretching it pretty thin, but one thing holds it together . . . the thing that started the whole ball rolling . . . those negligees. If that one factor was removed, if those girls had been dressed differently, we never would have been where we are. That is, until Harry Service got into the act."

"Mike," Pat said seriously, "do you realize that we haven't anything tangible to go on? Take the guy you so nicely knocked off. . . ."

"And you get the other part of the picture," I said. "He had a contact with somebody in a big car. A chauffeur-driven one. Ali has a contact with someone in a big limousine. Now there's one thing that's been running throughout this business since I first got on it. I keep hearing the word gook kicked around. They told me that in the Village about Greta Service being seen with one. Jones calls Ali a gook. They called Orslo Bucher a gook. We have a foreign ship in port, Ali spotted by Jones as working some kind of racket and if it weren't for a couple of plain old American girls involved I'd say we had some kind of international intrigue going."

"You're going," Pat said. "You're not happy until you make a mess of everything."

"Yeah, then explain your interest in the way those girls died, old buddy. You were pretty sure you had something, or are you still on the sex-fiend kick?"

"It seems a little more logical than the web you're trying to weave."

"Does it?"

Pat grimaced and filled the cups again. "Let me tell you something else, Mike. This afternoon we get another possible. You remember the Corning case about three years ago?"

"No."

"Well, it was kept pretty quiet. He committed six sex murders, all mutilations and pretty messy. He was caught and sent to a state institution for the criminally insane. After two and a half years of being a vegetable, he suddenly regained his senses and escaped. They got him in an abandoned house, but rather than surrender he burned the place down around himself. That's what they thought. There wasn't much of the corpse left to get a positive identification. This afternoon we get a call from someone who knew him well who said he saw Corning right here in the city. Now . . . if you want to know if I'm on a sex-fiend kick, maybe I am."

"You'll still keep Gates on the wanted sheet, though?"

"We can do that."

"What about the poison angle on the Poston kid?"

"The M.E. is making that his project. He's tracing sources. If something shows we'll follow that line too. Just so you can't say we're not covering every route I'll see what Interpol has on Ali Duval and have them pick up anybody in a fez who isn't a Shriner."

"What're you so nervous about, kid?" I grinned.

Pat gave me a pointed stare and said, "If you had those papers breathing down your neck the way I've had you would know why."

"You do it when a cop gets killed," I reminded him.

"That's different."

"Not for those guys. Besides, nothing's been printed yet."

"Only because they haven't turned up something either, but it's coming. If something doesn't break damn soon they'll cut loose at the department, then the action starts." He put his cup down on the table and tilted back in his chair. "Incidentally, your buddies with the papers put a squeeze on the D.A. All you'll be required to give in court is a reasonable explanation."

"Nice of them."

"Maybe they're just saving you to be a goat too in case it all falls apart."

"One goat's enough. I'll let it be you."

"Great. Thanks."

I grinned at him, slapped my hat on and said good night. He had enough troubles for one day.

When I got back to the hotel there were four messages in my box to call Velda at a number in Bradbury. I got up to the room, shucked my coat and had the operator put me through. The place was a motel outside of the town and her room didn't answer, so I said I'd call back and hung up. I waited an hour and tried again. She still didn't answer so I lay back on the bed and snapped the light off.

At two-thirty she called me back, jarring me out of a sleep.

"Mike?"

"Here, kid. Go ahead."

"Look, I don't know whether this means anything or not, but

this morning I made a contact in the bus station."

"Who was it?"

"Just a girl. She was in the ladies' room crying and I tried to find out what was wrong. When she finally got past the tears and started talking, she said she was stranded in town and had no way back to New York."

"Hell, that's a sucker story, honey. How many times . . .?"

"Will you listen!" I lay back on the bed and told her to go ahead. She was always picking up wet birds in the street anyway. "I took her outside and bought her some coffee and let her spill it. She was brought out here last night by some man she met in a bar downtown when she was a little high. He said he was going to take her to a real party that would make New York look like a playground. On the drive out he said he worked at one of the embassy retreats and knew how they could look in on the whole show.

"Driving out she started to sober up and her new friend didn't look so good to her any more. His talk scared her to death. Twice he stopped the car and tried to make a play for her, but both times other cars coming made him drive on. She fought him off, but couldn't get away. He kept telling her his boss really knew how to make a woman come around. All you had to do was hurt them enough and there wasn't anything they wouldn't do, anything at all. By this time she was nearly hysterical. He got to Bradbury, stopped for gas, but didn't have money to pay the attendant so he left his watch for security and said he'd pick it up tonight. That was as much as she heard. While he wasn't watching she got out of the car and ran for it, but she left her purse in the car and had no way to get it back."

"Didn't she ever hear of the Travelers Aid Society?" I said.

"Quit being funny," Velda told me. Her voice had an angry bite to it. "Anyway, I gave her fifteen dollars so she could get cleaned up—she spent the night sleeping in the bushes—and she was to meet me at the bus station later and point out the man when he came to reclaim his watch."

I nodded in the dark and said, "So you waited and waited and the little doll never showed up."

"No, she didn't."

"Kiss your fifteen bucks off, kitten."

"But I found the gas station she had mentioned. The guy had already reclaimed his watch. The attendant didn't know him, but verified the fact that he stopped there occasionally and apparently did work for one of the embassies because he used one of their cars on occasions."

Velda could have stumbled over something. I said, "What are the schedules out of there?"

"Three buses and two trains daily. I checked both places, but nobody answering her description bought a ticket. There was very little outbound traffic and she would have been spotted."

"Maybe she walked out a ways and flagged a bus down."

"I asked about that. They don't stop except for their regular stations."

"She could thumb," I suggested.

"Doubtful. There's an enforced law about that around here. Besides, after that one experience I don't think she'd want to lay herself open to another. My guess is that's she's still here in town. I'm going to canvass the resort area motels where they have off-season rentals and see if she checked into one of them. She was still shaken up and might not have wanted to travel in that condition. She had enough money for both her room and her fare besides."

"You get her name?"

"Certainly. Julie Pelham. I called the phone at her address and her landlady said she hadn't come in yet. She gave me a description that fit this girl but didn't seem too concerned about what had happened."

"Okay, check it out. Maybe you'll get your money back yet."

"One more thing, Mike," she said. "I asked around the local stores about the activities around the embassies. One of them has started laying in the usual supplies they get when a party's in the making. They spread it around trying to cover it up, but the signs are there."

"Which one?"

"I don't know yet. It isn't easy to get near those places. Besides their own security there are a lot of men in unmarked cars riding double around the area."

"They're our people."

"Yes, I know. They don't seem to like their jobs. What can you do with a crowd having diplomatic immunity?"

"Not much," I said, "so you forget that part and see if you can run down the girl. I'll check back with you tomorrow, so leave word for me. If you can't get to me, reach Pat or Hy."

"Suppose . . ."

"Don't suppose anything. Just do as I tell you to."

"Or what?"

I laughed into the phone. "I'll punch you right in the mouth with my lips."

"Hit me, man," she said and hung up.

I picked up the morning paper at the desk and flipped through the pages. There was a short piece inside about the police researching Mitch Temple's files to see if he had uncovered anything that might have led to his death and a short recap of his murder. Another mentioned that Maxine Delaney's death was still unsolved, but the police were expecting a break momentarily. Nothing was said about Corning being at large, so Pat was probably keeping it squashed until it could be confirmed or the man apprehended. Most likely he had all available manpower out trying to track the guy down, but didn't release the information to the press to avert any panic. Most of the news was still political, split between the current foreign crisis and the last minute moves at the U.N. before the Assembly paused for a recess.

Hy's column mentioned that Dulcie McInnes had returned to town after a successful invasion of Washington and was resuming her position as unofficial hostess of New York's society set.

I tossed the paper down and called Hy's office. His secretary said he wasn't expected in for an hour, so I tried Al Casey, told him I wanted to see him and he said to come on up.

Al was curious about why I wanted to know the details of Gerald Ute's grand gesture of giving up his property in the Bradbury area to the various legations for recreational use, but didn't try to quiz me on it. He took me to the section smelling of old newsprint where they kept their clippings, found Ute's file and dragged it out.

Besides the news reports of the transaction, several of the columnists had discussed it, both pro and con, but nothing unfavorable went against Ute. The transfer did give him a tax break, but he was wealthy enough so that it didn't matter one way or another. Publicity wise, it gave him good coverage. His philanthropies covered a lot of angles and this was just another. There didn't appear to be any direction to his giveaway program, except that most of the causes seemed to be good ones and the grants justified.

The town of Bradbury wasn't pleased entirely—their local paper resented the intrusion of iron curtain members in their midst, but since other friendly members were represented in the grant, it could have been an all round show of good will.

I said, "Al, you been up to Bradbury?"

"When Ute opened the places I was. After that most of the places closed their gates. You know how these foreigners are. They don't want anybody prying around. As far as I know, everything's peaceful up there except when they bring in that jazz festival, but that's over on the beach section anyway."

"No rumors?"

He squinted at me, trying to fathom my meaning. "What are you getting at?"

"I don't know."

"Then there're no rumors. If there were any, we'd sure know about it. The locals up there will pick up any kind of gossip."

"Al," I said, "this Belar Ris . . . he's with the legation that uses one of those places up there, isn't he?"

"You know, Mike, that's the second time you brought that guy into it. Why?"

"Mitch took off on him in his column."

"I know. The guy's a modern day pirate, but so what? He's not the only one. That's the way they operate over there. The money boys run things so they can make more money. Mitch rapped him and others like him in his column, but that had been going on for a year. If Ris was going to move in on Mitch he'd buy the paper and fire him. Frankly, I don't think Ris gave a damn. He's still got diplomatic immunity."

Why was it that every time I heard those words something crawled up my back?

Al fingered through the file and pulled out an aerial photo of Gerald Ute's former estate. "Here's what interests you so much. Ten years ago he bought the old Davis-Clendenning property. It takes in about a thousand acres. What those fieldstone monstrosities represented to those two old men, I don't know, but they built a half dozen mansions around, rarely used them, then they were sold after they died. Ute picked it up, did some minor developing, couldn't find a use or a buyer for it and rather than let taxes chew him up, gave the place away. Over here is another section he donated to be used for civic affairs. That's where the jazz bash is held. He got a few others to chip in to build the amphitheater and practically finances the rest of the venture alone."

I wasn't interested in the jazz site. I said, "Which legation building is Ris associated with?"

Al scowled, looked at the photo and tapped the one in the northeast corner. "This one, I think. Hell, I don't remember." His eyes caught mine. "You got a lead on something?"

"An idea maybe," I said.

"Something we can help with?"

"Not yet."

"If it's got to do with Mitch, I'd like it now."

"You'll know about it if it does."

I left Al sitting there puzzled, then went downstairs and found a pay phone, dropped in a dime and dialed the Proctor Group number and asked for Dulcie. Miss Tabor let out another one of those horrified gasps, but put me through.

Dulcie McInnes came on with a pleasant laugh and said, "Mike, how nice. I was hoping you'd call."

"Me?"

"Yes, you. For some reason you seem to bring a little excitement into an otherwise staid life." Then she turned serious a moment with, "Mike . . . the girl we saw . . ."

"I notified her brother. That was all I could do. He wanted to be sure she was safe, that's all."

"Well, it sure caused a flurry around here. Do you know the police have been here inquiring about Teddy Gates?"

"What about him?"

"I don't know. Nobody knows where he is. He isn't at home and he hasn't shown up at work. I wish you'd tell me what's going on."

"He may be caught in the middle of a big one," I said. "If he's found he'll supply a lot of answers."

For a second she didn't say anything, but I could hear her steady breathing. "Mike . . . can this hurt the Proctor Group? You know, will there be any publicity?"

"I don't see how. If he was engaged in something outside the office it shouldn't touch you."

"Please, Mike. Be sure. If they find out . . . well, even though I helped you . . . the Board certainly won't like it. I can't afford to be involved in anything sensational and neither can the magazine."

"We can keep a lid on it. Look . . . can I see you again?"

"I'd love to, Mike. When?"

"As soon as possible. I want you to exert a little of your influence for me."

"Oh?"

"I want to meet Belar Ris."

Her laughter was a clear tinkle. "Social climber," she told me. "I should think you could do better. Now there are several young ladies of respectable and wealthy parents who . . ."

"I'm not kidding, Dulcie. Can it be arranged?"

She caught the imperativeness in my voice and got serious again. "Do you have a black tie?"

"I'll get one."

"Tonight there's a reception at the Flamingo Room for one of the delegations. Mr. Ris will be there. I'm invited and I'll be happy to have you escort me. Suppose you meet me at seven-thirty in the lobby. Now, can you tell me why?"

"Later."

"Mike . . ."

"What?"

"If you hear anything about Teddy Gates . . ."

"Don't worry, he'll turn up. I'll make sure we keep a lid on it."

"Thank you, Mike."

"See you tonight."

When I hung up I waited a few seconds, then tried the number in Bradbury that Velda had given me. There was no answer in her room and no messages for me either.

I tried Pat and got him in. He told me he had to go uptown and to meet him at the Blue Ribbon in an hour.

New York was still under its blanket of gray. There was a damp, clammy chill in the air and the streets were devoid of their usual crowds. I had forty-five minutes to waste, so I headed west, taking it easy, and got to the Blue Ribbon in time to have coffee with George before Pat got there. He came in exactly on schedule, tossed his hat on the rack and pulled out a chair opposite me. He looked tired, tiny lines pulling at the corner of his eyes and mouth.

He waited until his own coffee came before he said, "The Corning deal washed out."

"What happened?"

"We picked up the guy in the neighborhood he was spotted in. It was one of those damn look-alike situations and I couldn't blame the guy who fingered him. He was pretty indignant, but played the good citizen bit and even let us print him for a positive I.D. The guy was clean . . . service record in Washington, executive job in Wall Street for fifteen years. A real bust."

"Scratch one sex fiend."

"There's something else." Pat reached into his pocket and pulled out two folded white sheets and handed them to me. There was a peculiar look in his eyes and he edged forward in his chair. "Our M.E. ferreted this out. Remember me telling you about chemical substitutes that induce the same symptoms he found in the Poston girl?"

I nodded.

"There's the formula. The stuff isn't even produced in this country at all. It's made in limited quantities by a French firm and distributed to selected outlets that use the stuff for chemical analysis tests in locating certain rare elements in earth samples. One of those buyers is Pericon Chemicals."

I looked up from the report and felt my eyes start to narrow. "Ronald Miller, Mitch Temple's friend. He's with them."

"Yeah, his army buddy, the book writer."

"We got hold of him this morning," Pat told me. "He confirmed the use of this product . . . called it C-130 . . . and even knew of its side effects. In fact, its properties are clearly stated on the containers. Before they handled it properly, the stuff killed a lot of people by being induced through skin abrasions. It's been manufactured since 1949 and a record is kept of its sales and use.

"Now here comes the kicker. A year ago part of an order going to Pericon Chemicals was stolen in shipment. None of it has ever been recovered, although the manufacturers conducted an exhaustive search and even issued notices as to its deadly effects. A check with the company showed that two previous inquiries had been made to them requesting a sale of the product, but were turned down because they only sell to specific companies for specific purposes. Both inquiries were by phone. And now here it is—that C-130 was being shipped on board the *Pinella* on a trip from Marseilles to Tangiers."

"Ali Duval," I hissed.

"He was a steward on the ship then too."

"There's a weak point there, Pat."

"I know," he said. "Mitch Temple didn't know for sure how the Poston girl might have died. He had no reason to check with Miller on that angle."

"He wanted something, *that's* for sure," I said.

Pat nodded. "Pericon Chemicals got involved in some litigation over the theft and we're going into that for what it's worth. There's got to be some connection."

"How expensive is that stuff?"

"It sells for twelve hundred dollars an ounce."

"That's more than H."

"And a half liter is missing."

I let out a low whistle. "That's a lot of loot. Somebody was still taking a chance on handling it."

"The package wouldn't be very large. It could be moved around. Hell, the stuff is even soluble in water and can be impregnated into clothes and recovered later the same way."

"No sign of Ali Duval?"

"Nothing yet. He was of French Arabian parentage and we're covering all the places he might go to find his own kind. Photos of Duval are being circulated and if he's around, we'll find him."

"And charge him with what?"

"We'll break him down."

"I didn't ask that."

"That's the other hole in the picture. I'd rather not think about it right now. If he's wrapped up in anything, maybe another country will want to pick him up. The inquiry to Interpol is out now and I'm waiting for an answer." Pat paused and finished his coffee. He put the cup down carefully, his eyes watching my face. "Have you got anything more to add?"

"Not yet."

He would have known if I were lying. He nodded and said, "I'm going to check a couple of belly dance places tonight. Native music . . . the real stuff they say. Want to tag along?"

"Not tonight. I got a date."

"Better than a belly dancer?"

I looked at him with a slow grin. "Much."

Pat felt in his pocket, extracted a two-by-two photo and tossed it on the table. "Here's a passport telephoto of your boy Duval. You might want to know what he looks like."

I said thanks and Pat walked off. I looked at the picture, studying the ineptitude of some photographer. The telephoto process and subsequent reproduction had modified the features, taking out the sharpness of the original photo, but Duval was still distinguishable. He was a tanned face with nothing spectacular about him until you saw the eyes and the innate savagery that lay behind them.

chapter ten ■■■■■■■■■

THE CURB IN front of the hotel on Park Avenue was lined with limousines. Photographers roamed the sidewalks, picking their way through the curious, trying for a spot to snap the greats of the international set for their society pages.

Most of the cars were chauffeur-driven, and pulled away after discharging their passengers, but another group bearing DPL plates parked wherever they wanted to, insolently occupying the space in the no-parking zones. Two mounted cops on horseback disgustedly ignored them and concentrated on keeping traffic moving the best they could.

I got out of my cab and went into the lobby past one of the photographers who looked at me uncertainly a second before he spotted someone he was sure of. I stood in line, checked my hat and coat, then drifted off looking for Dulcie. From any side except the front, most of the males were indistinguishable in their identical tuxedos, but the women stood out in the plumage and I wondered what the hell ever happened to the order of things. In nature, the males wore the gaudy colors and the females were the drab ones.

You could tell the pecking order of this barnyard by the preferential treatment accorded the greater luminaries. They were fawned upon, deferred to and waited on incessantly, always surrounded by their retinue. The babble of sound was punctuated by foreign tongues and the shrill laughter of the women, stuffy animals who strutted for the benefit of anyone who would look.

This is society, I thought. Brother.

Some of them had already formed their little coalitions and were drifting toward the elevators, deep in conversation, the women trailing behind them, their attitudes artificial, their posturing inane. There were some who had the earmarks of complacency and I figured them for either the genuine articles, born to build and control empires, or those who just didn't give a damn.

A couple of times I caught sight of myself in one of the mirrors and I looked uncomfortably out of place. Twice, men I cased as security personnel went by and we nodded imperceptibly. I was being taken for one of their own and their eyes didn't miss the way the jacket was tailored to conceal a gun or the mark of the professional any more than my own did.

At seven-thirty Dulcie arrived with several others, made her rounds of formal cheek-kissing and handshaking, but all the while searched the faces around her for me. I waved, let her get done with it all, check her wrap, then walked over trying not to grin like an idiotic schoolkid.

Dulcie wasn't the peacock type at all. Her gown was a black sheath that fitted as though there was nothing beneath it at all. Her hair was up in a mass of soft waves with lights bouncing off the silver accents like an electrical display. There was a diamond necklace at her throat and a thin diamond bracelet watch on her wrist.

But she was the most striking thing there.

I said, "Hello, beautiful."

Her fingers grabbed my hand and she tilted her head back and laughed softly. "That's not a proper society salutation, big man."

"It was the only thing I could think of."

"You did fine," she said and squeezed my fingers. "I like." She ran her eyes up and down me and said with approval, "You make quite a figure in that tux."

"Only for you, baby. I'm not a clothes horse."

"That's what I thought. I was afraid you might not come."

"Wouldn't miss it for the world. I could use exposure to some of the nicer things in life."

Dulcie threw me a tilted glance. "Don't expect too much. Some of these people come from strange corners of the world. It's still rough out there." She hooked her arm under mine. "Shall we go up to the Flamingo Room?"

"That's what we came for," I said. We started in the direction of the elevators, mingling with the others. While we waited I asked her, "Any thing new on Gates?"

"No. One of the other boys took over his appointments. He's left quite a gap in things. Mike . . . what do you think happened to him?"

"If I knew I'd be making him spill his guts out. He's got himself in some kind of bind and is riding it out."

"I went to the trouble of calling the agencies who give him assignments. He isn't out on any of theirs. What he had to do was either for us or for himself in his own studio. One of his friends had a key to his apartment and inventoried his equipment. He didn't take anything with him at all."

"He won't get far."

Dulcie shook her head, her face thoughtful. "I don't know. Matt Prince who does our developing and Teddy were pretty close. He said Teddy kept a lot of money in his office desk. It isn't there now."

"How much?"

"Over a thousand dollars. He was always buying new cameras or lenses. Matt said Teddy never worried about leaving it around. He had plenty of money anyway."

"He could go a long way on a grand."

The elevator came before she could answer me and we stepped back in the car. Going up Dulcie introduced me to a few of the others there who looked at me strangely, not sure who I could be, but certain I must have some importance since I was with her.

The Flamingo Room was a burst of color and noise when we walked into it, a montage of patterns made up of people in motion, under the flags of all the nations that dangled from the ceiling, waving in idle motion under the pressure of some unseen breeze. An orchestra was at the rear, varying its selections to suit every national taste, and tables were arranged around the sides piled with delicacies from countless countries. Champagne corks popped constantly and the clink of hundreds of glasses punctuated the hum of voices.

"What ever happened to the poverty program?" I asked her.

She poked me and said, "Hush!" with a stifled laugh.

Dulcie had an incredible memory for names, even the tongue twisters. She mingled easily, the right words always ready, her capacity for pleasing others absolutely incredible. More than one man looked at me enviously for being her escort, trying to catalogue me in their minds.

When I had to I could play the game too. It didn't come as easily and began to wear thin after the first hour. I hadn't come to hobnob and Dulcie sensed my irritation and suggested a cocktail at the bar.

We had just started toward it when Dulcie said casually, "There's Belar Ris," and swerved toward one corner of the room where three men were grouped, talking.

One dog can always tell another dog. They can see them, smell them, or hear them, but they never mistake them for anything but another dog. They can be of any size, shape or color, but a dog is a dog to a dog.

Belar Ris stood with his back angled to the wall. To an indifferent observer he was simply in idle conversation, but it wasn't like that at all. This was an instinctive gesture of survival, being in constant readiness for an attack. His head didn't turn and his eyes didn't seem to move, but I knew he saw us. I could feel the hackles on the back of my neck stiffening and knew he felt the same way.

Dog was meeting dog. Nobody knew it but the dogs and they weren't telling.

He was bigger than I thought. The suggestion of power I had seen in his photographs was for real. When he moved it was with the ponderous grace of some jungle animal, dangerously deceptive, because he could move a lot faster if he had to.

When we were ten feet away he pretended to see us for the first time and a wave of charm washed the cautious expression from his face and he stepped out to greet Dulcie with outstretched hand.

But it wasn't her he was seeing. It was me he was watching. I was one of his own kind. I couldn't be faked out and wasn't leashed by the proprieties of society. I could lash out and kill as fast as he could and of all the people in the room, I was the potential threat. I knew what he felt because I felt the same way myself.

He had the skin coloration of one of the Mediterranean groups. His eyes were almost black under thick, black brows that swept to a V over a hawklike nose that could have had an Arabian origin. Pomaded hair fitted like a skullcap and his teeth were a brilliant white in the slash of his smile.

Dulcie said, "Mr. Ris, how nice to see you. May I present Mr. Hammer?"

For the first time he looked directly at me and held out his hand. His forearm that protruded from his jacket sleeve showed no cuff and I knew I had been right. Even under a tux he wore a short-sleeved shirt.

"Delighted, Mr. Hammer." His voice was accented and deep, but devoid of any of the pleasure his smile feigned.

"Good to see you, Mr. Ris." The handshake was brief and hard.

"And are you a member of our great United Nations group? I don't remember having seen you. . . ."

I wasn't going to play games with him. "Hell, no," I said. "I'm a private cop."

For a split second there was a change in his eyes, a silent surprise because I couldn't be bothered acting a part. For Dulcie's sake he played it with an even bigger smile and said, "I certainly approve. Anyone as charming as Miss McInnes certainly needs a protector. But here, my dear, as if there was any danger . . ." He let his sentence drift and glanced at me questioningly.

"Half these people here are fighting one another a few thousand miles away," I said.

Belar Ris wouldn't drop his smile. "Ah, yes, but here we are making peace. Is that not so?"

"That'll be the day," I said. I knew what my face looked like. I wore my own kind of grin that happened automatically when an enemy was in front of me and felt my eyes in a half squint and a funny relaxed feeling across my chest.

"You are not one of those who have confidence in the United Nations then, Mr. Hammer. That is too bad. It is such a monument to . . . to . . ." He paused, searching for words. "The integrity of the world."

I said, "Bullshit."

"Mike!" Dulcie's face had turned pink and she nudged me with her elbow. "What a terrible thing to say."

"Ask the boys who were in Korea or Viet Nam or Stanleyville. Ask . . ."

Belar Ris threw his head back and let out a deep chuckle. "That is perfectly all right, Mr. Hammer. You see, it is people like you who must be convinced, then you will be the most firm advocates of the united world. It will take much discussion, many arguments and positive persuasions before things are resolved." He held out his hand to me again. "Good evening, Mr. Hammer." His fingers tightened deliberately and I threw everything I had into the grip. I could do it that way too. He felt me buck him, then let my hand go. "It is a good thing to have the opinion of . . . the man on the street," he said. He nodded to Dulcie, gave her a small bow that was typically European. "Miss McInnes."

He walked away, his blocky figure the picture of confidence. Dulcie watched him a moment, then turned to me. "Is that what you came for? If I thought it was to get in a political argument . . . You embarrassed him!"

"Did I?"

Then she let the laugh go, trying to stifle it with a hand. "It was funny. Even when you said that awful word."

"So wash my mouth out with soap."

"Really, Mike. Now can you tell me why you wanted to meet him?"

"You wouldn't understand, kid."

"Are you . . . satisfied?"

I took her arm and steered her toward the bar. "Perfectly," I said. "Someplace in the pattern there's a place for him."

"You're talking in riddles. Let's have our drink and you can take me home. I have a big weekend with a new issue of the magazine in front of me and can't afford any late nights until it's put to bed."

"That's too bad," I said.

Her fingers tightened on my arm. "I know." She rubbed her head against my shoulder. "There will be other times."

I left Dulcie outside her apartment and told the cab driver to take me back to my hotel. Upstairs, I got out of my tux, mixed myself a drink and slouched in a chair with my feet on the window sill, looking out at the night.

Sometime not too long ago a point had been reached and a bridge crossed. It was too dark to see the outlines of it, but I could feel it and knew it was there. Too long that little thing had been gnawing at the corners of my mind and I tried to sift it out, going over the puzzle piece by piece. One word, one event, could change the entire course of the whole thing. Out there on the streets Pat and his men and the staff of the paper were scouring the city for that one thing too. Somebody had to find it. I finished my drink, made another and was halfway through it when my phone rang. It was my answering service for the office number with the message that I had several calls from the same number and the party gently insisted that they were urgent.

I dialed the number, heard it ring, then Cleo's voice said, "Mike Hammer?"

"Hello, Cleo."

"You never came back."

"I would have."

"You'd better come now," she said.

"Why?"

"Because I know something you'd like to know." There was a lilt to her voice as if she had been belting a few drinks.

"Can't you tell me now?"

"Nope. I'm going to tell you when you get here." She laughed gently and put the phone back. I said something under my breath and redialed her number. It rang a dozen times but she wouldn't answer it. I cradled the receiver, then got up and climbed into my clothes. It was eleven-thirty and one hell of a time to be starting out again.

There are times when something happens to Greenwich Village. It gives a spasmodic heave as if trying for a rebirth and during its convulsions the people who dwell in her come out to watch the spectacle. It's hard to tell whether it's the inanimate old section or the people themselves, but you know that something is happening. Windows that never show light suddenly brighten; figures who have merely been shadows in doorways take life and move. There is an influx from neighboring parts, people being disgorged from taxicabs to be swallowed up again in the maw of the bistros whose mouths are open wide to receive them.

The peculiar ones with the high falsettos, skin-tight pants and jackets tossed over shoulders capelike display themselves for public viewing, pleased that they are the center of attraction, each one trying for the center of the spotlight. Their counterparts, sensing new prey available, ready themselves, then stalk toward their favorite hunting grounds, masculine in their movements, realizing that sooner or later someone will respond to the bait being cast out, then the slow, teasing struggle would begin, and they, being the more wise, would make the capture.

A sureness seemed to be the dominant attitude. Everybody seemed so sure of themselves for that one single night. The heavy damp that should have been oppressive worked in reverse, a challenge to stay outside and dare the elements, a reason to go indoors to expend the excessive energy that was suddenly there.

I got out of the cab on Seventh Avenue and walked through the crowds, watching them pulsate across the streets at the change of the lights, feeling the static charge of their presence. I wasn't part of them at all and it was as though I were invisible. They had direction of purpose, to be part of the pleasure of the rebirth. I had direction of course only and picked my way to the house where Greta Service had lived and pushed Cleo's bell.

The buzzer clicked on the lock and I went inside, let the door shut behind me and went up the stairs to the top floor and stood there in the dark. I didn't knock. She knew I was there. I waited a minute, then her door opened silently, flooding the landing with a soft rose glow from the lights behind her and she was wearing one of those things you could see through again.

"Hello, Mike."

I walked inside, let her take my hat and coat from me and picked up the drink she had waiting on top of the table. Her project had been finished and her work area was rearranged, her tools and equipment placed to become part of the decorative concept of the room. Through the skylight and the full French windows I could see the outline of New York above the opaque surfaces of buildings around her.

"Pensive tonight, aren't you?" She went over and pulled a cord, then another, closing out the view through the windows. It was like pulling the covers over your head in bed.

"Sorry," I said.

"No need to be. You'll loosen up. Even if I make you."

"It's one of those nights," I told her.

"I know. You felt it too, didn't you?"

I nodded.

She walked past me, the sheer nylon of the full-length housecoat crackling, the static making it cling to her body like another skin. She switched the record player on and let Tchaikovsky's *Pathétique* seep into the room. She turned, swirling the ice in the glass in her hand as the subtle tones began their journey into life. "Fitting music, isn't it?"

I looked at her and tasted my drink. She had built it just right.

"They don't know it out there," she said. "They take time out of their expressionless little existences trying to find something vital here and leave things as they found them. They really go away empty."

"What did you have to tell me, Cleo?"

She smiled, crossed one arm under her breasts, balanced the other on it and sipped her drink. "But you aren't one of them."

"Cleo . . ."

She paid no attention to me. She walked up, took the drink I didn't know I had finished from my hand very slowly and went and made me another. "Do you remember what I told you when you were here?"

"No."

"I said I wanted to paint you."

"Look . . ."

"Specially now." Her eyes viewed me with an odd interest. She turned her head from side to side, moved to study me in a different light, then said, "Yes, something has happened to you since the last time. It's better now. Like it should be. There isn't any softness at all left."

I put the drink down and she shook her head very gently. "It's something you want to know, Mike, but you'll have to do what I want you to do first."

I said, "I found Greta."

"Good," she said, and smiled again. "It's more than that now though, isn't it?"

"Come on, Cleo. What have you got on your mind?"

She walked up to me, turned her back and took my hands, wrapping them around her waist. Her hair brushed my face and it smelled faintly of a floral scent. "I work for the Proctor Group too, or have you forgotten? I knew when you went up to see Dulcie McInnes. You should never have said what you did to her Miss Tabor. That old harridan can't stand dominant males."

"I was there," I admitted.

She turned in my arms, her body a warm thing against mine. "And I was jealous." She smiled, let her arms crawl up my sides, her hands going to my face, then lacing them behind my head. "I saw you first," she grinned. "Am I teasing well enough?"

"I'm hurting. Don't lean on me too hard."

"There was some strange speculation about Teddy Gates. Now he's missing after you paid another visit up there. People are talking, yet nobody really knows anything at all."

"Except you."

"Except me," she repeated. "You found Greta Service, but it couldn't have ended because you're here now to find out something else."

I ran my fingers down the small of her back and felt her body arch under them. "What's your price, Cleo?"

"You," she said. "I'm going to paint you first. I want you permanently inscribed so I can look at you and touch you and talk to you whenever I want and know you'll never fade away." She raised herself on her toes and her mouth touched mine lightly. Then she let herself down and pushed away from me, her eyes sad little imps dancing in far off places.

"I'm a funny woman, Mike. I'm young-old. I've seen too much and done too much in too short a time. What I really want I can never have, but I have sense enough to realize it, so I take what I can get when I can get it, or is that too complicated?"

"I understand."

"This is Cleo's last stand here." She swept her arm around to take in the room. "It's very little, but it's a sanctuary of a sort. From here I can see the other part of the world and nobody can touch me. I can stay here forever and ever with all the good parts of me right where I want them, never changing, never turning their backs. Do I sound too philosophical?"

"You can do better."

The imps in her eyes danced again. "But I don't want to. I'm alive here, Mike. Now I'm going to make you part of that life. I won't sell you. I won't give you away. I'm going to keep you. You're going to be mine like nobody else ever had you."

"Cleo . . ."

"Or what you want to know won't be yours."

I put the drink down. "Your show, kid. Do I loosen my tie?"
"You take off your clothes, Mike."

She painted me that night. It wasn't what I had expected. The
background was a jungle green with little bright blobs of orange
that seemed to explode outward from the canvas, distorting the
sensation of seeing a flat surface. There was a man in the picture
and it was me, but not so much the physical representation as
the mental one. It was the id rather than the ego, the twilight
person you were only when you had to be. She had seen things
and caught them, registering them for all time as we know it and
when I saw myself as she did it was the same as looking at the
face of an enemy. The short hairs on the back of my neck raised
in sudden anger at the confrontation and I knew what Belar Ris
had seen just as I had seen him. My .45 was there too, exact in
detail almost to seeming three-dimensional, but it was away from
my hands as if I didn't need it.
    During the hours she had discarded the sheer nylon, working
unfettered, concentrating solely on the portrait. I could study her
abstractly, enjoying the loveliness of her body, then in the stillness
my mind had drifted to other things and Cleo was only a warm
outline of motion, of long smooth sweeps of pink, blossoming
mounds that were half hidden behind the easel, then quickly there
again. I had time to think in an unreal world where thinking was
all there was to do. The extended strands of the web began to
join together with the cross sections of odd conjecture, and little
by little, piece by piece, the thing that was possible became
probable.
    She let me have that one brief look, then turned the canvas to
face the wall.
    "You're mine now," she said. Her finger touched a switch and
the lights faded gradually into nothingness and the two of us were
there alone, people again, barely visible, whitish silhouettes against
the velvet of night.
    Behind the curtains a false dawn marked the beginning of a
new day. The spasm outside was over and whether the Village
was in the agony of rebirth or the throes of death, I would never
know. We had bought the hours at a price. We had spent excesses
we had accumulated during that time, and for a little while there
was that crazy release that was a climax and an anticlimax that
left no time for work or thought any more.
    I looked at the day crawling through the skylight. She had pulled
back the blinds so that the glass was a huge square of wet gray

overhead, wiggling with wormy raindrops that raced to the bottom to form a pool before dripping off the edge of the sill.

I rolled off the couch and reached for my clothes. I could smell the aroma of coffee as I got dressed and called for her twice without getting an answer. I dressed quickly, found an electric percolator bubbling in the kitchen, poured myself a cup hurriedly and swallowed it down.

Then I saw her note.

It was written in charcoal on a sketching pad, just a few lines, but it said enough.

> Mike Darling . . . the man Sol Renner saw Greta with has his picture in the paper beneath. Thank you for everything, it was lovely. You'll never leave me now.
> Good-by,
> Cleo.

I yanked the paper out from under the pad. It was the same copy Biff had shoved under my nose the other night. The man in the picture was Belar Ris.

The web was pulling tighter, but I still couldn't see the spider. I put my hat on and went back through the studio. The easel was still in place, but the picture was gone. The place still smelled of her perfume and the nylon thing was lying across the back of the chair. *Pathétique* was still playing, the record never having been rejected.

She had chosen a good piece. Symphony No. 6 in B minor, Opus 74. Tchaikovsky should have stuck around to write another. This one would be even better.

chapter eleven

I STOPPED BY the hotel, showered and changed into fresh clothes. No calls had come in and when I phoned Velda's number there was no answer and no messages. I left word for her to call me as soon as she arrived and dialed Pat. The desk sergeant told me he had left an hour ago and hadn't reported in yet, but had asked if I had tried to contact him. I thanked him and hung up softly though I felt like slamming the receiver back on the cradle.

I called Hy's office and that didn't answer.

Dulcie's phone didn't answer either, then I remembered it was Saturday. Modern technology had given us two days of rest. I got so damn disgusted I went downstairs to the lobby and picked up a copy of the paper and flipped through it without really seeing anything until I came to the center fold.

Somebody had snapped a shot of Belar Ris, Dulcie and me talking, but my back was to the camera and all you could see was Dulcie and Belar Ris and it looked for all the world as if we were enjoying ourselves.

I threw the paper on a chair and was about to go out when the desk clerk stopped me. I wasn't signed in under my right name, but he knew the room I was in and pointed to a row of phones against the wall. I picked it up and said, "Yeah?"

"Mike?"

"Speaking."

"Pat. What's got hold of you?"

"Listen . . ."

"You listen. Meet me at the Blue Ribbon about six-thirty. Have you called Hy?"

"He wasn't in. Why?"

"Because they found Gates," he said. "Some tramp tripped over the body under a culvert that goes over the Belt Parkway. Gates shoved a .22 pistol in his mouth and pulled the trigger, or at least that's the way it looked. He's been dead since the day he left according to the M.E.'s estimate on the spot."

"Where does Hy fit in?"

"Tell him to squash the story until we can move on it."

"The last time I tried that Mitch got killed."

"Mike . . ."

"Okay. I'll leave word. Just one thing . . . did he have any money on him?"

"Damn right, almost nine hundred bucks in cash."

"He didn't get very far," I said.

"What?"

"Nothing. I'll see you at six-thirty."

Now Gates, I thought. That opens the web again, but just a little bit. The spider was still inside.

Pat was late. I sweated him out for an hour, playing with the coffee George had sent up to the table. Outside, the rain blasted down with the furious derision nature can have for humans, laughing at the futile attempts people put up to avoid her.

Pat finally came in whipping the rain from his hat, one of the young lawyers from the District Attorney's staff behind him. He introduced him quickly as Ed Walker and they sat down opposite me. Walker was looking at me as if I were a specimen in a zoo and I felt like slamming him one.

Pat said, "Reach Hy?"

"I told you I'd leave word. It was the best we can do."

"Good enough."

"Why?"

"The county police accepted Gates' death as suicide. We're not sure. How'd you tap the money angle?"

I told him what Dulcie had mentioned to me.

"That might figure in."

"Pat," I said, "don't get lost in this. A guy with a grand in his pocket doesn't knock himself off without a big run first."

"That's what I mean," he told me. "Any coroner's jury would direct a verdict of suicide the way it was set up. He used his own gun, even the cartridges and the clip had his fingerprints on it and there was a possible motive behind his own death."

I pushed my coffee away and flipped a butt between my lips. "Get to it."

"Tell him, Ed."

Walker opened his briefcase, took out several sheets of paper and referred to them. He looked at Pat, then me, shrugged once and laid them flat on the table. "You guys have the screwiest deal I ever saw."

"He's been in this from the beginning."

"But I haven't. Damn, my curiosity is worse than a cat's and someday it's going to get me the same thing."

Pat said annoyed, "Come on, Ed."

Walker nodded and adjusted his notes. "I pushed a few people overseas and got the details of the litigation the Pericon Chemical Company hit the steamship line with concerning the theft of that C-130. During the hassle the Pericon people uncovered the true owners of the shipping line. The majority control belonged to Belar Ris."

I said, "Oh?" and wondered why it came out so casually.

Pat's eyes were all over me, picking me apart. "That isn't the end of it. I have the report from Interpol. Ali Duval has been associated with Belar Ris since the late forties. He started off as an Algerian terrorist fighting the French, was picked up by Ris somewhere along the line and used by him as an enforcer in several of his enterprises. Duval is suspected of having committed nine different murders and an assault on a political personage from Aden. We might be able to get him held on the last charge. Once they get him in their hands they'll make him talk. It's a lousy way of doing things, but a threat to turn him over to them might work wonders."

"You're sure you can nail him then?"

"He'll leave on the *Pinella.*"

"Where is he now?"

"Nobody seems to know," Pat said.

"And Ris?"

"He's had a tap on his phone for the last twelve hours. We know where he is." Pat gave me a laconic grin and said, "He called your erstwhile friend Dulcie McInnes at three-fifteen this afternoon and confirmed his appointment to pick her up for some affair they're having out at the estate in Bradbury this evening. We're going to cover that place like the lid on a pan tonight and if Duval shows we'll nail him."

"What about Ris?"

"Those damn dipples can get away with murder and we can't do a thing about it."

"Those what?"

"Dipples," Pat repeated. "DPL plates. Diplomatic immunity. He'll get away clear until he's declared *persona non grata* and tries to re-enter the country."

And there it was. The guy Mitch Temple chased who could get away with speeding on the Belt Parkway while he got stopped in the cab. The guy who made the contact with Orslo Bucher. The guy in the black official limousine who dropped Ali Duval off. Damn, it was there all the time. The *dipple* car. *Old Greenie had even called it that!*

I got up without saying anything and went to the wall phone and dropped in a dime. I gave the operator Velda's number. The manager of the motel said she hadn't returned to her room, but if I was to call to tell me that the answer was in Bradbury and she was going inside to get her fifteen dollars back. She'd be at G-14. The guy sounded puzzled.

The phone almost fell from my fingers. I wanted to yell, "No, don't try it alone"—but nobody would have heard me.

I didn't bother to pick up my coat. George didn't question me, but just gave me the keys to his car when I asked for them and I went out the front way leaving Pat and Walker still sitting there waiting for me, got the car out of the garage and headed out of the city.

Saturday was just another night in Bradbury. Two hours from New York put it another world away in another dimension. I stopped at a gas station on the edge of town, filled the tank and had the attendant point out the direction of the former Gerald Ute estate. In twenty minutes I reached the edge of the area he described to me, a rise in the road that gave a panoramic view of the landscape below.

Here and there in the distance lights winked between the trees, and when I had them located, drove past them. Every so often another car would pass going in the opposite direction, and once one drew abreast of me while the occupant scrutinized my face, then sped ahead and cut off at a side road.

Our people, I was thinking. The whole place was under constant surveillance. They'd keep up a running conversation on their car radios to keep me spotted until they were sure I had left their section. George's car didn't have DPL plates. There would be other security if I could get inside their compounds that would be even tighter. How did Velda think she could make it?

I circled the whole region until I came back to the outskirts of the city. There wasn't one way of telling just where the hell she was! Those buildings were scattered in haphazard fashion behind their towering walls and if I tried them one at a time I could be too late.

But what was it the guy had said on the phone? Velda would be at G-14. She'd expect me to know what that was. She had more sense than to try and hit a target like that by herself. The message wouldn't be too cryptic. It would be something I should recognize.

It was. It took me long enough to get it. I found a service station that I generally used, went in and got one of their standard road maps of the local area and looked at the grid markings on the side. The point where the vertical G and horizontal 14 intersected was two miles from my present position. I thanked the guy, got behind the wheel and turned around.

There were no lights showing in the building at all, but there was the barest reflection from the chrome trim of the cars that were parked in front of it to tell me it was far from deserted. I had run George's car into the brush beside the wall, nosing it in far enough so as to be practically invisible from the side road I had turned onto. From the roof I was able to reach the top of the wall and pull myself up. I flattened out, getting my eyes adjusted to the darkness, then swung over and dropped to the ground. Now I was thankful for the rain we had had. The bush I hit crumpled wetly, rather than crackling under the impact. I stood there fighting the urge to run, the .45 in my hand, the hammer back.

It was almost too quiet and that eerie stillness saved my neck. I heard the whispering thud of feet, the breath and the guttural snarl the same second I ducked to one side and felt something brush my arm and heard the wicked snap of teeth closing on air. The dog's leap took him into the same bush I had landed on, but to him it was more of an obstacle. I could see him then, clawing to break loose from the entangling branches, a sleek muscular killer, attack-trained to kill silently and quickly in the dark.

I whipped the .45 down across his head, saw him sag, recover, then go down again the second time when the muzzle of the gun smashed his skull. There would be more than one dog on the premises. They'd be like sentinels making their rounds. The others hadn't gotten the smell of me yet, and when they did, would come in almost silently and unseen like the other one.

I stayed close to the tree line, ran across the open lawn to the parking area and lost myself in the dozen or so cars parked beside the house for a few minutes, trying to figure a way in. As near as I was I could see the vague outlines of the windows and the lights that filtered past drawn curtains.

The main entrance was to my left, but I didn't want to hit the doors. Those would be well guarded. The larger windows that opened on the main rooms wouldn't be any good either. I didn't know what I was going into and had to feel my way there.

I could see the place now. It was built in a Victorian style of native brick and looked like a great stone fortress. But all fortresses had chinks and this one was in its style of architecture. The gingerbread ornaments that littered its face made perfect handholds. I shoved the .45 back in the sling, edged to the side of the building and began climbing.

Twenty feet up I had almost reached the second level. Down below I heard a snarl of impatience, then a door opened and a shaft of light illuminated the front of the building. Another dog, a huge Doberman, padded by, stood in the light a moment sniffing the air, then a voice said, "What is it?"

Another one answered with, "Nothing. They are always like that."

The door closed and the night took back its own. The dog snarled again, but from another point this time.

I didn't take any chances with the windows. The odds were that they had alarms rigged to them. I kept climbing until I felt the cornice of the roof under my hands and wiggled myself over the top. I lay there and looked at the ground a long way below, and when I was satisfied no one had seen me, picked my way to the cupola that sat like a silly little hat right in the middle of the building.

They hadn't bothered to wire these windows. I leaned my elbow against one until it gave, shattered gently and fell inside with a noisy tinkle, then picked out the larger pieces, opened the catch and swung it in on its rusted hinges.

No practical purpose was served by the cupola. It was dirty and empty, just the remnant of an era long past. I found the stairwell leading down, cupped a lit match in my hand and went down to the door. It had a large, old-fashioned latch that moved easily when I lifted it, and when I pushed against the door it swung out without a sound.

I was on the third level of the building in a corridor dimly lit from the light that rose from an open staircase at the far end. A series of rooms led off the hall, four on each side. I tried a couple of the doors, smelled the mustiness and dust that oozed out of the rooms and knew they weren't used. At one time they were probably designed for servants' quarters and had been vacant a long time.

From below I could hear the sound of voices and I followed the hall to the staircase and looked around it. There was a landing below, a ninety degree bend in the stairs and nothing was visible. I started down the first step, saw the small movement of a shadow on the wall beneath me and drew my foot back. They had that area covered by a guard.

Several times when I was a kid I had been in old houses like these and I remembered that they generally had a service exit to the other floors for the servants. I went back down the hall, around the bend and found what I was looking for. The steps were old and dry and creaked under my feet, so I stayed as close to the wall as I could get. I made it to the second level and pushed the door open.

This time I almost wasn't lucky at all. The man sitting there with his chair tilted back against the wall tried to come to his feet and reach for the gun in his belt at the same time. The movement was too sudden and the chair slid out from under him.

Even then he almost had time. He rolled, pulled the gun and was bringing it up when my toe caught him under the chin and almost took his head off. His jaw was tilted at a wild angle, his bottom teeth cutting into his cheek. His eyes were wide open, but he wasn't seeing anything. I took the gun from his hand, spun the cylinder to make sure it was loaded, then dragged him back into the shadows under the stairs and put the chair back where he had it. If anyone came checking on him they might think he only left his post for a minute and wouldn't be too worried.

Once past the guard I was able to get a better impression of the layout of the house. It rambled in all directions, doors opening into well-stocked pantries, linen closets and storage rooms. I had spotted two more men at critical points, but there was no way to move in on them without being seen. One gunshot would bring others running and I couldn't afford that.

Somewhere inside the house there was a burst of sound, voices laughing, muffled by the thickness of the walls. I stood in the niche of a doorway watching the man at the end of the corridor, saw him stretch, bored, then turn and walk in my direction. He got fifteen feet away, stopped, seemed to sense something, then shrugged and turned his back and returned to his original position.

Behind me the door I was leaning against opened with the faintest squeak. The guard stopped again, looked back over his shoulder, then decided to investigate and walked back. I had no choice except to step back through the door and close it, hoping he wouldn't notice the movement. His feet passed, then came by again as he satisfied himself that there was nobody there.

Now he'd be alert. I swore at myself for not jumping him when I could have, but it was too late now. I lit my last match, found myself in a kitchen cluttered with dirty dishes piled high on the sink, and an ancient gas range littered with used pots. Four rolling serving trays were lined against the wall next to a corridor that led somewhere into the bowels of the house.

The match flickered and went out, but I had my direction fixed and followed it in my mind.

And I found what I came for. Or at least some of it.

The two great sliding doors that opened onto the room were shut, but age had shrunk them so that a quarter-inch crack showed in their vertical alignment. I pressed my eye to the aperture to get a wider angle of vision and saw them, a small crowd, some in chairs, some standing smoking, enjoying the spectacle on the stage in the middle of the room.

A cage had been erected there about eight feet square, finger-thick bars covered with a thin wire mesh. She stood in the middle, absolutely motionless, uncomfortably poised on a small block of wood, her ink-black hair a startling contrast against the white negligee that had parted down the front and was thrown back over her shoulders. A false smile of frozen horror looked like it had been painted on her face, a look of total disbelief, yet somehow tinged with grim determination. Not a muscle in her body moved, and in the weird blue light that enveloped her I could see a reflection in her eyes as they followed the insidious motion of the two diamondback rattlesnakes that writhed restlessly just inches from her legs, their tongues nervous little feelers sensing danger in this strange atmosphere, their tails buzzing with anger.

I had found Greta Service again.

How long she had been there I couldn't tell, but the terrible agony of the position she was forced to hold was evident in the muscular tension of her legs. Any movement, no matter how slight, would bring those snakes striking to an attack.

A figure moved from behind a chair and I saw Belar Ris. For a second the light caught him and I could see his smile of enjoyment. He sat on the arm of the chair and draped his hand across the shoulder of the one sitting there.

From one side a voice said, "How long has it been, Belar?"

He looked at his watch. "Forty minutes."

Then the one in the chair said, "You're going to lose your bet, Belar. She's going to win your fifty thousand dollars."

My skin crawled all over because the answer was all right there in that room. *The voice was Dulcie McInnes'.*

And Belar Ris said, "No, I won't lose. You'll have your pleasure."

How long had you been doing it, Dulcie . . . finding the kind of woman who would submit to this kind of pleasure-seeking? You were in the right position for it. How many more were dead that we didn't know about? And how many ever did win the bet that they could outlast a distorted thirst for pleasure? And what was your gain, Dulcie . . . a greater social acceptance because of your associations? Who else did you entice into this tight circle who could be blackjacked politically because he had become a blood brother to depravity?

It must have shaken her when I came into the picture because until then it all would have been so carefully planned and executed. They had the money and the means to operate with and always the knowledge that the shield of diplomatic immunity was there for them.

What was your shield, Dulcie? Or was money and power sat-isfaction enough?

I could see more of the faces now. They were the faces of those from countries of sudden wealth and emergence into power, but who still reveled in the savageries of the near-primitive. But not all. Several I had seen at the Flamingo Room the other night enjoying their respectability.

Dulcie's choice of subjects had been excellent. They were women alone with no one to care about them. They would do anything for a chance at a small fortune.

The exception had been Greta who did have somebody who cared about her. She was willing to take the big gamble because she cared about somebody too. Harry Service might not have been worth it, but he was all she had and she was going to keep her promise to him.

Her face was tighter now than before, fighting the unbearable strain of her position and the proximity of the snakes.

Too bad Mitch Temple couldn't see what he had stumbled upon. He started chasing down a murderer because a single thread seemed to tie in the deaths of two girls, two inexpensive, sexy nylon negligees. He did the legwork in countless shops and was lucky enough to spot Belar Ris buying another one. Even when he published Belar Ris's activities in his column, he might not have made any personal contact with the man, so he verified his identification by going through the morgue files until he located Ris's picture.

Even his call to Norm Harrison fitted in. You couldn't openly accuse a man in his position unless you had positive proof. But Norm had been out of town. Mitch did have another source of information going for him. Ronald Miller probably had told him about his company's litigation with Belar Ris in the theft of the C-130. That fitted in too. Ali Duval could have seen the shipment, recognized its potential to Ris and gotten it ashore.

Mitch's trouble was, Ronald Miller had left too and Mitch had no place to go to except the source itself. It would be like him to call Ris, ostensibly to arrange for an interview on some matter or other, then try to draw him out. But Ris had something going for him too. Mitch's picture was at the top of his column. Ris could have recognized Mitch and seen through the whole skein and stopped it right there with a single knife thrust through Mitch's heart.

Yet it *didn't* stop there. I was looking for Greta and Greta could have led me to them if I pushed hard enough. She had already been recruited and was ready for them regardless of what happened to the other girls who went ahead of her. She had probably been held right here for this very night and she was doing it of her own volition.

They didn't know what I had though. The papers had made a big thing of my reputation and they couldn't take a chance. Orslo Bucher was one of their own nationals and could be called upon for the small jobs. He searched my place, then tried for me and died doing it. That threw it back at them again.

I still kept looking for Greta.

So they let Greta come to me.

Ali Duval arranged to use Virginia Howell's room through Lorenzo Jones, a far-out contact that could have no possible connection with anyone. It was a simple thing for Dulcie to drop a card into Teddy Gates' rotary file and lead me to it, and just as simple to remove it again and send Gates off on an appointment that would lead to his death. The red herrings and the wild geese were all over the place to foul up the trail.

The thing they didn't plan for was Lorenzo Jones' curiosity about Ali. Jones could smell a buck and would chase it, but he could smell trouble too and was scared to death of it. They didn't plan on me pushing it any further after I had seen Greta. She was there because she wanted to be there. She had to be there if she wanted the chance at the big stakes she coveted so desperately.

Dulcie, you damn fool. It couldn't last. You couldn't keep it covered forever.

There was a hum of voices, then a cold hush. I looked through the crack again. Greta had tottered on the block and both the snakes were poised, tongues flicking to find the source of movement, their buttons a steady, sharp buzz in the quiet.

It had to be now.

I jammed the two guns in my belt, felt for the handles that were indented into the frames of the doors and got my feet braced. I was ready to tear them apart when I heard the shouting and saw a tall guy run in from an alcove and point behind him.

"The dog. It has been killed. Someone is inside."

The one in front of the door was too intent on what the other had said and didn't hear me until I was almost through the opening. He whirled, struck out at me and caught the side of the .45 across his face and went down with a scream.

Confusion was immediate. They tried to run and had no place to go. There were more of them than I expected, but they had no way of knowing how many were coming behind me and their first thought was to get out. They were there for pleasure and stayed for panic and when the guy at the door blasted two quick shots in my direction it added to the turmoil. The crowd parted in front of me, faces and bodies just a blur in the dim light.

Not Greta though. She never moved. She couldn't.

I let go two quick blasts through the cage and took the heads off the snakes just as she let herself go and crumpled up on top of their thrashing bodies.

They came in fast from all sides, gun muzzles winking death, the roar lost in the screams and hoarse shouts of the ones trying to get away. I caught one in the chest and shot the leg out from under another, but they weren't the ones I wanted.

Belar Ris was my target and he was someplace in the dark.

I almost had it made. I took down one who blocked the exit and I almost made the door. I could have brought those agents patrolling the area swarming onto the place with a couple of fast gunshots into the night and they could have taken over and finished the job.

That *almost* was the big one. My luck ran out. I felt the searing finger crease my skull and I went down on my face, hoping the blackness would come before the pain.

The lolling motion of my head woke me up. Dizzy waves of pain swept over me and my stomach heaved in the spasms of nausea. I felt twisted out of shape and tried to pull myself together but couldn't move. My feet were tied and my hands bound together behind my back. I forced my eyes open, saw the two who carried me, and beside the ones who held me under the arms, Dulcie and Belar Ris.

Dog met dog again. He saw me looking at him and said, "You are a fool."

But I didn't answer him. I looked at the other dog and said to Dulcie, "Hello, bitch."

She didn't answer me. The one carrying my feet stopped and said, "In here, Belar?"

"Yes, with the others, Ali."

He let my feet go and turned, taking a set of keys from his pocket. This time I got a good look at his face. I had seen it twice before. Once in a news photo standing near Belar Ris. But the first time was when I was leaving Dulcie's office and he stepped out of the elevator.

The picture was complete. Only no one was going to see it. Like the one Cleo painted of me, I thought. That was all that was left. My eyes closed and I felt my head fall again, but I could still hear them.

Dulcie said, "You think it's safe?"

Belar's voice was a deep rumble. "The windows are barred and the door is triple locked. They'll keep until we can dispose of them."

"But . . ."

He cut her short. "You get upstairs and quiet the others. Someone could have heard the shooting. If there's an inquiry we can arrange to have the guards say there was a prowler on the grounds. If not, we'll simply sit down, let everyone return to normal and discuss how we can get rid of the bodies this one provided us with."

I heard the door swing open, then I was tossed inside and the door closed with a metallic clang behind me and the bolts shot home. I lay there waiting, retching at the pain that was like a hot iron against my head, the cold concrete of the floor grinding against my face.

Then there was the rasp of a match and a light blossomed in the corner of the room and a familiar voice said, "Mike?"

Surprise shook me back to normal. I saw her face in the light, grimy with dirt, but smiling. "Hi, Velda." You'd think we were meeting for lunch.

She laughed, reached up and pulled a cord. A single bulb suspended from the ceiling came on, the light barely reaching the corners of the room. She came over, untied my hands and feet, watched while I rubbed the circulation back into them and looked at the cut on my scalp. It was superficial, but painful. At least I wouldn't die from it.

When I could stand up she pointed behind me. Greta Service was lying there, hands and feet tied, a large, blue bruise on her forehead. "They brought her here first," Velda said. "Are there any others?"

"No."

She bent down and untied Greta, then massaged her into gradual consciousness. I let her get done, made sure Greta was all right, then pulled Velda up to me. "Let's have it, kitten. How the hell did you get here?"

"Julie Pelham. That man found her. He must have been looking for her and forced her into the car, then didn't know what to do with her. I saw them go by, grabbed the plate number and had it checked out. It was registered to one of the ones in the legation that occupies this building. I tried to come in through a back way, got cornered by one of those dogs and a guard grabbed me. They were having a conference on what to do with me when some of the others began arriving, so they tied me up and dumped me in here. It took me about an hour to break loose, but at least I wasn't shut up in the dark."

"What happened to the girl?"

Velda pointed toward the far corner with her thumb. "Look."

Two bodies were curled together in a heap. "They both made mistakes," I said. "He couldn't explain the girl, but she explained him." I glanced around me peering into the shadows. "Have you checked this place out?"

"It's part of an old laundry. Those are washtubs down there and there's an old gas stove that leaks. That one window leads out to the ground level. I think we're in the back of the house somewhere, but I'm not sure. The window bars go right into the cement."

She tried to sound matter-of-fact about it, but I could feel the rising fear in her inflection. "Take it easy, kid. Let me look around."

There was no chance of going through the door. It was too heavy and too securely bolted. The only other way out was the window. The glass was on the other side of the bars, coated with black paint. I felt the bars themselves, inch-thick pieces of metal with only a surface coating of rust. At a first glance they seemed to be an impregnable barrier, but the iron had feet of clay.

The old cement they were imbedded in had been eroded by dampness and leakage and I could scratch a groove in it with my fingernail. I went over to the old stove, pulled off one of the grates and began chipping away. It powdered at first, then the cracks appeared and I pulled it loose by chunks. In ten minutes I had the bars wrenched out of place. I didn't have a gun any more, but those bars would make a good weapon if we needed one.

Greta moaned and sat up, one hand going to her head. She was still only half conscious and unaware of what was going on. I got my arms around her to pull her to her feet when I heard a short muffled buzz and held up my hand for Velda to be quiet. After a few seconds it came again, then once more and was cut off in the middle. I let Greta go and went over to the cabinet beside the stove. I pulled the door open.

Inside on the shelf was an old phone buried under a heap of moldy towels. I picked the receiver up gently, but whoever was on the other end was just hanging up. I held the hook down, let it go and listened but there was no dial tone.

The expectant look on Velda's face disappeared when I shook my head. "It rings on an incoming call, but you can't call out. It's an old model they forgot to disengage when they installed the new ones. It only works because there's a crossed wire somewhere."

"But if someone calls in . . . we could tell them . . ." She stopped, realizing the improbability of it.

Yet . . . *something* could be done with that phone. We might not make it out of the grounds, but we could leave our fist behind us. I pulled it out as far as I could, pried the guts out of it so that only the ringing mechanism was left. I unscrewed the bells and tied a nail to the clapper with a shoelace for greater leverage. Then I fastened the crazy rig to the light bulb so that when the phone rang that bulb was going to be smashed to bits.

Velda watched me, but I didn't take the time to explain it to her. When I was through I went to the window, swung it outward on its hinges and helped Velda climb through. She and I both managed to get Greta out and when they were ready I went back, pulled the burners off the stove so the gas would come through at full pressure and climbed out the window. When I pushed it back in place I picked up the iron bars, handed one to Velda and said, "Let's go."

And the lady with the luck smiled on us. This time she was giving us a free roll of the dice. The night was our friend and the shadows our love. The guards were still there, but their anxiety made them too alert and they exposed themselves so we were able to skirt around their positions. The cool wind was at our backs so no scent reached the dogs and we made the wall and found a way over it.

The car wasn't too far away, still concealed where I had hidden it and we got in and I started up and pulled out on the dirt road. A quarter mile down other cars paraded in their vigil, protecting those behind the walls from those outside.

It was the wrong way around, I thought.

We passed through Bradbury, found an open gas station and went in and cleaned up. I looked at the clock. In a little while the sun would be coming up.

I used one of George's credit cards he kept in the glove compartment to wangle some cash out of the station attendant. He figured us for Saturday-night drunks and had that happen to him before and the tip was worth his handing me the change.

I made one call to Hy from the pay station outside and told him to get me the number of the phone in the building Belar Ris' group occupied. Hy called back in five minutes, but I wouldn't give him any information. I said I'd tell him later and I would. It was a shame he'd never be able to print it.

Velda and Greta Service came out and got in the car. I was dropping a dime in the slot when a city patrol car drove up and a uniformed cop got out, fishing in his pocket for some change. He saw me in the booth and stood outside waiting patiently while I dialed.

By now that single room would be gas-packed, a monstrous potential of destruction waiting to be triggered into instant hell.

In my ear I heard the stutter of the ringing phone.

Six miles away a brilliant glow of orange blossomed like a night flower into the sky, lasted seconds at its apex and died with the speed of its blooming. There were more seconds of night-quiet, then the thunderous roar came in with its wave of shock that rattled the windows in the buildings behind us.

The cop's mouth dropped open, his face still taut with surprise. "What the hell was that!"

"Wrong number," I said and walked to the car.

Survival...Zero!

TO JACK AND PEGGY McKENNA
WITH THANKS FOR THE MANY HAPPY RETURNS

chapter one ▰▰▰▰▰▰▰▰▰▰▰▰▰▰

THEY HAD LEFT him for dead in the middle of a pool of blood in his own bedroom, his belly slit open like gaping barn doors, the hilt of the knife wedged against his sternum. But the only trouble was that he had stayed alive somehow, his life pumping out, managing to knock the telephone off the little table and dial me. Now he was looking up at me with seconds left and all he could do was force out the words, "Mike . . . there wasn't no reason."

I didn't try to fake him out. He knew what was happening. I said, "Who, Lippy?"

His lips fought to frame the sentence. "Nobody I . . . not the kind. . . . No reason, Mike. No reason."

And then Lippy Sullivan died painfully but quickly.

I went out in the hallway of the shabby brownstone rooming house and walked up to the front apartment that had SUPER scrawled across the top panels in faded white paint and gave it a rap with the toe of my shoe. Inside, somebody swore hoarsely and a chair scraped across bare wood. Two locks and a bolt rasped in their sockets and the door cracked open on a safety chain.

The fat-faced guy with the beery breath squinted up at me in the light from behind him, then his eyes narrowed, not liking what he saw. "Yeah?"

"You got a phone, buddy?"

"What if I do?"

"You can let me use it."

"Drop dead." He started to close the door, but I already had my foot in the crack.

I said, "Open up."

For a second his jowls seemed to sag, then he got his beer courage back up again. "You a cop? Let's see your badge."

"I'll show you more than a badge in a minute."

This time he didn't try smart-mouthing me. I let him close the door, slide the chain off, then pushed in past him. The room was a homegrown garbage collection, but I found the phone behind a pile of empty six-pack cartons, dialed my number and a solid Brooklyn voice said, "Homicide South, Sergeant Woods."

"Captain Chambers in? This is Mike Hammer."

Behind me a beer can popped open and the fat guy slid onto a chair.

When the phone was picked up I said, "Hi, Pat. I got a stiff for you."

Softly, Pat muttered, "Damn, Mike . . ."

"Hell," I told him, "I didn't do it."

"Okay, give me the details."

I gave him the address on West Forty-sixth, Lippy's full name and told him the rest could wait. I didn't want the guy behind me getting an earful and Pat got the message. He told me a squad car was on the way and he'd be right behind it. I hung up and lit a butt.

It was an election year and all the new brooms were waiting to sweep clean. The old ones were looking to sweep cleaner. It was another murder now, a nice, messy, newspaper-type murder and both sides would love to make me a target. I'd been in everybody's hair just too damn long, I guess.

When I turned around the fat guy was sweating. The empty beer can had joined the others on the table beside him.

"Who's . . . the stiff?"

"A tenant named Lippy Sullivan."

"Who'd want to kill him?"

I shoved my hat back and walked over to where he was sitting and let him look at the funny grin I knew I was wearing. "He have anybody in with him tonight?"

"Listen, Mister . . ."

"Just answer me."

"I didn't hear nothin'."

"How long you been here?" I said.

"All night. I been sitting here all night and I didn't hear nothin'"

I let the grin go a little bigger and the grin wasn't pretty at all. "You better be right," I told him. "Now sit here some more and think about things and maybe something might come back to you."

He gave me a jerky nod, reached for another beer and watched me leave. I went back to Lippy's room, nudged the door open and stepped inside again. Somebody was going to give me hell for not calling an ambulance, but I had seen too many dead men to be bothered taking a call away from somebody who might really need it.

Death was having a peculiar effect on the body. In just a few minutes it had released the premature aging and all the worry had relaxed from his face. I said softly, "Adios, Lippy," then took a good look at the room. Not that there was much to see. There were hundreds more just like it in the neighborhood, cheap one-room fleabags with a bed, some assorted pieces of furniture and a two-burner gas range on top of a secondhand dresser in one corner. The only thing that looked new was an inexpensive daybed against the far wall and from the way the mattress sagged on the brass four-poster I could see why he'd needed it.

I used a handkerchief, pulled out the dresser drawers, and fingered through the odds and ends that made up Lippy's wardrobe. Nothing was neat or orderly, but that was Lippy, all right. Just another guy alone who didn't give a damn about having ironed socks and shorts. The closet held a single wrinkled suit, some work clothes carelessly tossed onto hooks, two pairs of worn shoes and an old Army raincoat. I patted the pockets down. One pair of pants held three singles and a lunch ticket. There was nothing else.

Outside I heard the whine of a siren coming closer, then cut out when the squad car reached the building. I went over and elbowed the door open. Two uniformed cops came in properly geared for action. I said, "Over here." Another car pulled up and I heard a door slam. Pat hadn't wasted any time.

The lab technicians had dusted, photographed and taken the body away. All that was left of Lippy was a chalked outline on the floor beside the sticky damp sawdust that had soaked up his blood. I walked over and sat on the couch and waited until Pat slumped wearily into a chair that looked as tired as he was.

Finally Pat said, "You ready now, Mike?"

I nodded.

"Want me to take notes?" Pat asked.

"You'll get the report in the morning. Let's make it real official."

"We'd better. I know people who'd like to burn your ass for anything at all. They might even make it on this one. So let's hear the story. Once more, from the top."

"Lippy . . . Lipton Sullivan," I said. "We went to school together. He dropped out at the ninth grade and we met up again in the Army for a while. No record I know of. Just a hard-luck character who couldn't make it in this world. Two years ago I got him a job checking out groceries in a wholesale warehouse."

"See him often?"

"Only once since then. We had a couple of drinks together. He insisted on buying. Nice guy, but a born loser."

Pat rubbed his hand across his eyes before looking up. "Heavy drinker?"

"Nope. He rarely touched the stuff."

"Broads?"

"I told you he was a loser. Besides, he never was a big one for women. They seemed to be mutually unattractive to one another."

This time Pat waited a long time before he spoke. "I don't like it, Mike."

"I can't blame you."

"No . . . I don't mean that."

"So?"

"You're involved, old buddy. I know what happens when you get involved. Right now you sit there and play it cool, but you know you're damn well involved . . ."

"Nuts," I said. "He was a guy I knew, that's all."

"He didn't call the cops, Mike. He called you. When was the last time he did that?"

"When I got him that job. He thanked me."

"That was two years ago, you said. You changed your number since then."

I grinned at him and reached for a cigarette. "You're still pretty sharp, kid," I told him. "No phone directory here, no memos in the papers on him so he must have memorized my new number."

"Something like that."

"Maybe he wanted to thank me again."

"Can it."

"So I'm his only famous friend." I fired up the butt and blew a stream of gray smoke toward the ceiling.

"Let's take the other reason why I don't like it."

"Go ahead."

"For a nothing guy like him it's too nasty a kill. Now suppose we see how smart you still are, friend."

I glanced over at the discolored sawdust and felt my mouth turn sour. "One of three things. A psycho kill, a revenge kill or a torture kill. He could have stayed alive a long time with his belly slit open before somebody pounded the knife into his chest."

"Which one, Mike?" Pat's voice had a curious edge to it.

My own voice sounded strange. "I don't know yet."

"*Yet?*"

"Why don't you handle it your own way?" I said.

"I'd love to, but I got that funny feeling again, Mike. Sometimes I can smell the way you think."

"Not this time."

"Okay, I'll buy it for now. See you in the morning?"

"Roger, kiddo."

The Blue Ribbon Restaurant on West Forty-fourth had closed an hour ago, but George and his wife were keeping Velda company in a corner booth over endless pots of coffee, and when I came in she gave me one of those "You did it again" looks and propped her chin on her hands, patiently waiting for an explanation. I sat down next to her, brushed my lips across that beautiful auburn pageboy roll of hair that curled around her shoulders and patted her thigh gently. "Sorry, honey," I said.

George shook his head in mock wonder and poured my coffee. "How you can stand up somebody like your girl here gets me, Mike. Now you take a Greek like me . . ."

His wife threw the hooks right into him. "To see *my* husband, I have to work the cash register. He loves this place more than he does me."

"Business is business," I reminded her.

Velda let her hand fall on top of mine and the warmth of her skin was like a gentle massage. "What happened, Mike?"

"Lippy Sullivan got himself sliced to death."

"*Lippy?*"

"Don't ask me why. That cat never did anything to get himself a smack in the eye. Somebody just got to him and took him apart. It could have been for any reason. Hell, in that neighborhood, you can get knocked off for a dime. Look at that wino last week . . . murder for a half bottle of muscatel. Two days before and a block away some old dame gets mugged and killed for a three-dollar take. Great. Fun City at its best. If the pollution doesn't get you, the traffic will. If you live through those two you're fair game for the street hunters. So stay under the lights, kids, and carry a roll of quarters in your fist. The damn liberals haven't outlawed money as a deadly weapon yet."

Velda's fingers squeezed around mine. "Did they find anything?"

"What the hell would Lippy have? A few bucks in his pocket, an almost punched-out lunch ticket, and some old clothes. But the lab'll come up with something. Any nut who killed like that wouldn't be careful about keeping it clean. It's just a stupid murder that happened to a nice guy."

"Nobody heard anything?" Velda asked me.

"The way he got sliced he wasn't about to yell or anything else. Anybody could have walked in there, knocked on his door, got in and laid a blade on him. The front door was open, the super had his TV going and a belly full of beer and if anybody on the block saw anything they haven't said so this far."

"Mike . . . you said he had a few dollars . . ."

"Stuffed into his watch pocket," I interrupted. "They don't even make pants with them any more."

"There has to be a reason for murder, Mike."

"Not always," I told her. "Not any more. It's getting to be a way of life."

We finished our coffee, said so long to George and his wife and grabbed a cab on the corner of Sixth Avenue. It was a corner I couldn't remember any longer. All the old places were gone and architectural hangovers towered into the night air, the windows like dimly lit dead eyes watching the city gasping harder for breath every day.

New York was going to hell with itself. A monumental tombstone to commercialism.

When we reached Velda's apartment she looked at me expectantly. "Nightcap?"

"Can I pass this time?"

"You're rough on a woman's ego. I had something special to show you.".

"I'd be lacking appreciation tonight, kitten."

Her gentle smile told me all I needed to know. She had been around me too long not to recognize the signs. "You have to do it, Mike."

"Just to make sure. The damn thing bugs me."

"I understand. I'll see you at the office tomorrow." She leaned over, tasted my mouth with hers and brushed her fingers down

my cheek. I said good night, watched her go into the building
and told the driver to take me home.

The killing of Lippy Sullivan was only a one-column squib in
the morning papers, the body being reported as having been
discovered by a friend. Political news, a suspected gangland rubout
of a prominent hood and the latest antics of a jet set divorce trial
made Lippy the nonentity in death that he was in life.

My official statement had been taken down by a bored steno,
signed, and Pat and I sat back to enjoy the cardboard-container
tasting coffee. Ever since I had come in he had been giving me
a funny, wary-eyed look and I was waiting for him to spit out
what was on his mind. He took his own sweet time about it,
swinging around in his swivel chair and making small talk.

Finally Pat said, "We were lucky on this one, buddy."

"How?"

"Your name didn't bring the grand explosion I thought it would."

I shrugged and took a sip of the coffee. It was bitter. "Maybe
the old days are gone."

"Not with this bunch in office. When Schneider got knocked
off last night it gave them something bigger to play with."

I put the empty container on his desk and sat back. "Quit
playing games, Pat," I said.

He stopped swinging in the chair and gave me another of those
looks again. "I got the lab report. A practically untraceable knife,
no prints on the weapon at all . . . nothing. The only prints on
the doorknob were yours, so the killer apparently used gloves. Six
other sets of prints were picked up in the room . . . Lippy's, the
super's, two guys from the furniture store on Eighth Avenue who
moved in a couch for him and two unidentified. The super had
the idea that Lippy was friendly with a guy upstairs who used to
have a beer with him now and then. He moved out a week ago.
No forwarding address."

"And the other set?"

"We're running them through R and I now. If we don't have
anything, Washington may come up with a lead."

"You're sure going to a lot of trouble," I said.

"Murders are murders. We're not concerned with a pedigree."

"This is old Mike you're jazzing now, friend. You're making
like it was a prime project."

Pat waited a minute, his face tight, then: "You holding back,
Mike?"

"For Pete's sake, what the hell kind of a deal is this? So I knew the guy. We weren't roommates. You get a lousy kill in your lap and right away you got me slanted for working an angle. Come off it."

"Okay, relax. But don't say I haven't got just cause, kid. Knowing a guy's enough to get you kicking around and that's just what I don't want."

"Balls."

"All right," he told me, "we checked Lippy out . . . his employers gave him a clean bill. He worked hard at a low-paying job, never any absenteeism, he was a friendly, well-liked guy . . . no previous history of trouble, didn't drink, gamble, and he paid his bills. He got himself killed, but he had memorized your number beforehand."

Pat stopped for a second and I said, "Go on."

"The lab came up with something else. There were traces of tape adhesive around his mouth. Nobody heard him yell because he didn't. Your friend Lippy was gagged, tortured and finally stabbed to death. The way we reconstructed it was that the killer simply walked in off the street, knocked on the door, was admitted, knocked Lippy out, searched the place and when he didn't find what he was after, took him apart with a knife."

I looked at Pat curiously and said, "Nice, real nice. Why don't you fill in the holes? I was there too."

Pat nodded and sat back again, still watching me. "There was a contusion behind Lippy's ear that apparently came from a padded billy. Certain articles were out of position indicating a search of the premises. Or did you poke around?"

"A little," I admitted. "I didn't disturb anything."

"This was a search. Expert, but noticeable."

"For what?"

"That's what I'd like to know." I got another one of those long searching looks again. "He was your friend, Mike. What aren't you telling me?"

"Man, you're a hard one to convince."

"Let the details filter upstairs to one of those new bright boys in the D.A.'s office and they'll be even harder to convince. Right now there's not much noise because Lippy wasn't much of a guy, but somebody's going to read these reports, and somebody's going to start making waves. And, friend, they'll break right over your head."

"Once more around the track, Pat," I said. "You know everything I know. Just hope those prints show something. If I can think of anything you'll get it fast and in triplicate. Who's assigned to the case?"

"Jenkins and Wiley. They've been drawing all blanks too. Nobody saw or heard anything. Wiley's been using an informer we have on the block and the guy says the talk is square. The oddballs are coming and going in that neighborhood all the time and nobody pays any attention to them. They might come up with a lead, but the longer it takes the slimmer the chances are."

"Sorry about that."

Pat grunted and gave me a relieved grin. "Okay, pal. I don't like to lay it on either. I guess there can be one kill in the city that doesn't have to have you involved in it."

I stood up and put on my hat. "Hell," I said, "I'm too old for that crap any more anyway."

He gave me another of those unintelligible grunts and nodded thoughtfully. "Yeah, *sure* you are," he said.

The cabbie wanted to edge out of the heavy traffic so he cut over to Eighth Avenue going north and stayed in the fire lane, making the lights at a leisurely pace. I cranked the window down and let the thick air of the city slap at the side of my face, heavy with smells from the sidewalk markets, laced with the acrid tang of exhaust fumes that belched out of laboring trucks and buses. The voice of the city kept up its incessant growl, like a dog who didn't know whom to pick on and settled on everybody in general. *Most people out there never even heard the voice, I thought. Even the smells were the natural condition of things. Someday I was going to get the hell out of here. I was glad I had nothing to do about Lippy. So he was a guy I knew. I knew lots of guys. Some were alive. Some were dead.*

Then we were almost at Forty-sixth Street and I wondered who the hell I thought I was fooling and told the driver to pull over and let me out. I handed him a couple of singles, slammed the door, watched him pull away and crossed the street over to where Lippy Sullivan had died such a messy death. All I could say to myself was, *"Damn!"*

chapter two ■■■■■■■■■■

THE FAT LITTLE super who smelled of sweat and beer didn't give me any lip this time. It wasn't because of the first time or because he had seen me there in the midst of the homicide squad with a gold shield cop my buddy. It was because I was the same kind of New York he was, only from a direction he was afraid of. There was nothing he could put his finger on; a squawk wouldn't bother me and could hurt him, and if he didn't play it nice and easy he could play it hard and get himself squeezed.

So he played it right and whined how he had told everything he knew which wasn't anything at all and let me into Lippy's room with his passkey, idly complaining about how he had to clean up the mess that had been left around before the flies got into it and the stink got worse than it was. Nobody paid him extra and the damn nosy cops wouldn't let him rent the room out until the investigation was over and he was losing a commission.

I shoved him out of the room, slammed the door in his face and flipped the overhead light on with my elbow. The stain was still there on the floor, but the sawdust was gone and so was the chalked outline of Lippy's body. And so was Lippy's new couch. I had seen it in the super's apartment when he had opened the door for me.

There wasn't anything special to look for. The cops had done all that. What I wanted was to know Lippy just a little bit better. I could remember a skinny little kid with a banana stalk in a street fight, swinging it out against the Peterstown bunch, then the soda bottle collection to pay for the six stitches the doctor over Delaney's Drugstore had to put in his eyebrow. Some stupid sergeant gave him a B.A.R. to tote during the war and he hauled it all over Europe until he finally got a medal for using it in the right place at the right time. Then he just went back to being Lippy Sullivan again with nobody except the Internal Revenue Service and me ever knowing his real first name, and now he was dead.

So long, Lippy. Wish I had known you better. Maybe I will.

I had been in too many pads like this not to pick up the little signs. It wasn't what *was* there. It was what *wasn't*. There was that little Spartan touch that flipped you right back into an Army barracks where what you had you kept in your pocket. Lippy had been here almost two years and he hadn't collected anything at all. The shade on the lamp had been patched and painted to match the fabric, the old chair in the corner had been repaired where it was possible and the cracks in the plastered walls had been grouted to keep the roaches contained and the drafts out.

The one cupboard held an assortment of chili, hash, a half-dozen eggs, some canned vegetables, two boxes of salt and an oversized can of pepper. Lippy didn't exactly live high off the hog. But then again, he didn't ask for much, either. He sure didn't ask to get killed.

I took my time and went through his stuff piece by piece and wound up wondering what he had that made him valuable enough to die like he did. There wasn't one damn place he could have hidden anything and not the slightest sign that he even tried.

Yet somebody had sliced him up to make him talk.

Without thinking I sat on the edge of his bed, then stretched out and folded my hands behind my head and looked at the ceiling. It was a lousy bed but a lot better than what we had in the Army sometimes. Come on, Lippy, what was it? Did you have something? Did you *see* something? Why remember my phone number?

I let a curse slip across my lips because Lippy himself had given me the answer. What was it? Yeah . . . *"No reason, Mike . . . no reason."* And at a time like that a guy just doesn't lie.

But he had called for me and without having to say it, told me not to let him go out like that, a nothing nobody with a first name the world would never remember, but with that single phone call he had begged me not to let him be just another statistic in the massive book of records the great city keeps for its unrecognizables.

All right, Lippy. You are a somebody. Get off my back, will you? Maybe you didn't think there was a reason, but somebody else sure as hell had a good one for killing you.

I slid off the bed and picked my hat off the floor, then got to my feet and walked to the door. To the empty room I said, "Mike, you're getting old. The edge is off. You're missing something. It's right here and you're missing it."

The super popped the door open before I even knocked. I walked in past him to the couch against the wall, pulled the cushions off and unzipped the covers. Inside was a foam rubber pad and nothing else. I turned it over and felt around the burlap and canvas bottom, but there was nothing there either. I knew the cops had gone through the same routine so I wasn't really expecting to find anything anyway. When I finished I left it like it was and looked at the slob with the half-empty beer can who was hating me with his eyes. "Put it back where you got it," I said.

"Look, I had to clean . . ."

"I'll clean *you,* buddy. I'll turn you inside out and let the whole neighborhood watch while I'm doing it."

"Nobody even paid me . . ."

"You want it now?" I asked him.

The beer can fell out of his hand and he belched. Another second and he was going to get sick.

"Put it back," I told him again.

Jenkins and Wiley were ten minutes away from being off duty, having coffee in Raul Toulé's basement hideaway. I pulled a chair out with my foot, waved for Raul to bring me a beer and sat down. Jenkins curled his beefy face up into a grin and said, "Ain't it great being a private investigator? He don't have to drink coffee. He gets a beer. Just like that. How's it going, Mike?"

"So-so. I just came out of Lippy's place."

Wiley nodded and took a sip of coffee. "Yeah, we got the word. Mumpy Henley spotted you getting out of the cab. Ever since you busted him on that assault rap he'd like to peg you. Doing anything illegal, Mike?"

"Certainly."

"That's good. Just do it to the right people."

"I try." I took my beer from Raul and downed half of it. "You guys get anything?"

Jenkins ran his hand through his mop of hair and shook his head. "Dead end. You know what we got in an eight-block area this past month? Four kills, eight rapes, fourteen burglaries and nine muggings. That's just what was reported."

"Should keep you guys pretty busy."

"Natch. We solved six murders, none of the rapes wanted to prosecute, two burglars were apprehended, one by an old woman with a shotgun and another by Sid Cohen's kid . . . and those two bragged about a hundred something they pulled around here. Only that crazy Swede policewoman nailed a mugger. She broke his arm. Nice place to live, but don't try to visit."

I said, "What about Lippy?"

Wiley fingered some potato chips out of the bowl in front of him and stuffed them in his mouth. "Not a damn thing. His employers vouch for him, the few neighborhood places he did business with give him an okay, nobody can figure out any reason why he should have been knocked off like that, so what's to say? Most everybody around here thinks it was some nut. It wouldn't have been the first time."

"How long you figure on staying on it?" I asked them.

"Not much left to do unless we get a break," Jenkins said. "Now we wait. If it was a psycho he'll probably hit again. Trouble is with that kind, you never know what they're going to do."

"It wasn't any psycho," I told him quietly.

They both looked at me, waiting.

"Just something I feel," I added. "You saw the lab reports. The place was searched."

"For what?" Wiley finished his coffee and pushed his cup away. "Your friend didn't have anything worth looking for."

"Somebody thought he did."

"Well, if they make anything out of those two sets of prints, we may get lucky. Look, I'm going to call in. Who's buying?"

I grinned at him and picked up the tab. Wiley fished a dime out of his pocket and went to the phone booth while I paid the bill. When he came back he had an amused frown on his face. "You could have been right, Mike."

"Oh?"

"Lippy did have something worth looking for only it wasn't in his room. Captain Chambers took a flyer and checked the local banks. Lippy had over twenty-seven hundred bucks in the Commerce National. Odd deposits every so often. No specific amounts."

"Nobody found a bankbook on him," I said.

"It was in his locker where he worked. He had it stuck under a batch of order forms. So now we have a motive."

"Murder for that kind of money?" I asked him.

"Hell, around here you could buy a dozen kills for that."

Siderman's Wholesale Groceries was a busy little place filled with the tangy odors of a farmhouse pantry with all the activity of an anthill. Young Joe Siderman led me back to his office, tossed me an apple and told me to sit down.

"Tough about Lippy," he said. "He was a good guy. They know who did it yet?"

I shook my head. "The police think somebody knew about that twenty-seven hundred he had saved up and maybe had it in his room."

"Crazy world, ain't it?"

"You see that bankbook of his?"

"Sure, I found it in his stuff. Nobody woulda known about it for months maybe if that Captain Chambers didn't get me poking around for it."

"Remember any of the deposits?"

"You know me, Mike. I'm a nosy bastard, so sure, I took a look. Like mostly from ten to fifty bucks each time. No special dates of deposits though. Sometimes twice a week, sometimes once."

"Lippy make that much here?"

Joe shined his apple on his sleeve and took a bite of it. "So we pay minimum wages for his job. It wasn't exactly skilled help. Lippy took home maybe sixty bucks a week. He never made no complaints about it. I don't know how he coulda saved that much these days. He didn't handle no cash here so he wasn't hitting the till. Maybe he played the horses."

"Nobody's that lucky, Joe."

"He got it from somewhere."

"Think maybe one of the others he worked with would know?"

"Doubt it. He got along good with everybody, but he never really buddied up to nobody special."

"Screwy," I said. "Why would he keep a bankbook stashed here?"

"That ain't unusual," Joe told me. "Half these guys what live in furnished rooms ain't got no families and think the job's their home. A coupla guys keep everything in their lockers here. Hell, Lippy even had his Army discharge and his rent receipts in that box. You want me to ask around a little? Maybe somebody knew him better than I thought."

"I'd appreciate it," I said. I tossed one of my business cards on his desk. "You can reach me here if anything turns up."

"Sure. Want another apple? They're pretty good. Come from upstate."

"Next time. Thanks for the talk."

I got up and started for the door when Joe stopped me. "Hey, one thing, Mike."

"What's that?"

"Was Lippy livin' with a broad?"

"Not that I know of. He never played around. Why?"

"Just something funny I thought of. We sell the help groceries at wholesale, you know? So always they buy just so much on payday. A few weeks back that Lippy doubled his order three weeks running then cut back down again."

"He ever do that before?"

"Nope, but I'll tell you something. It didn't surprise me none.

You know what I think? He was always a soft touch and he was feeding somebody who was harder up than he was. Like I said, he was a nice guy."

"Yeah. So nice that somebody killed him."

"Times are tough all over."

The haze over the city had solidified into lumpy gray masses and you could smell the rain up there. I picked up the afternoon paper at a newsstand on Broadway and went into the Automat for coffee. Upstairs at an empty table I went through both sections of the edition without finding anything on Lippy at all. Tom-Tom Schneider was getting a heavy play, but he was a big hood in the policy racket, handling all the uptown collections. Be honest, I thought, be forgotten. Convicted criminals who bought two .38 slugs in the brain for crossing the wrong man get the big splash. At least they go out with everybody knowing their names. Even then, old Tom-Tom was being crowded a little by the political news, the latest Met scores and a mystery death in the Times Square subway station.

Somebody behind me said, "Hello, Mike, doing your homework?"

I looked over my shoulder and grinned. Eddie Dandy from WOBY-TV was standing there with a tray of milk and two kinds of pie, looking more like a saloon swamper than a video news reporter.

"You got my favorite table," he said.

I pushed a chair out for him. "Be my guest. I thought you guys ate free in all the best places in town."

"You get tired of gourmet foods, kid. I go for a little home cooking now and then. Besides, this place is closest to the job."

"Someday you're going to shave and wear an unwrinkled suit in the daytime and nobody's going to know you," I told him. "A dandy you are by name only."

Eddie put his pie and milk down, set the tray on the empty table beside us and picked up his fork. "That's what the wife keeps telling me. We people in show business like to change characters."

"Yeah, sure."

Between bites he said, "Petie Canero saw you down at headquarters. That Sullivan thing, wasn't it?"

I nodded and took another pull at my coffee. "It's still cold."

"You got to be a big man to get any action nowadays. Like

Schneider. They'll spend a bundle going after his killers and wind up with nothing anyway."

"Maybe not."

"Oh hell, it was a contract kill. Somebody hired an out-of-town hit man and that was it for Tom-Tom. He's been stepping on too many toes trying to get on top. Everybody saw it coming. For one thing, he steps outside without his two musclemen beside him and it's bingo time. The cops ask questions but who's going to talk?"

"Somebody always does."

"When it's too late to move in. Right now I wish somebody would say something about that body in the subway. I never saw such a damn cover-up in my life. We all got the boot at the hospital . . . nice and polite, but the big boot just the same. What gets me is . . . ah, hell."

I frowned and looked across the table at him. "Well . . . what about it?"

"Nothing. Just that coincidences make me feel funny."

"Afraid I'll scoop you on your own program?"

Eddie finished his first piece of pie, washed it down with half a glass of milk and reached for the other. "Sure, man," he grinned. "No, it's just funny, is all. Remember when I did the news for the Washington, D.C., station? Well, I got to know a lot of the local citizenry. So when I went down to the hospital I spotted a couple of familiar faces. One was Crane from the State Department. He said one of his staff was in with an appendectomy and he was visiting. Then I saw Matt Hollings."

"Who's Hollings?"

"Remember that stink about the train loaded with containers of nerve gas out West . . . the stuff they were going to dump in the ocean only they wouldn't let it travel across the country?"

"Yeah."

"Hollings was in charge of the project originally," Eddie said. "So when I saw Hollings and Crane talking I checked on Crane's friend. She was there with an appendectomy, all right, but she was a young girl in the steno pool who had only been with State six weeks. Seems funny they could have gotten that close in such a short time."

"She could have been a relative."

"Unlikely. The girl was a native Puerto Rican."

"Guys and gals are a strange combination," I said.

"Not with a wife like Crane's. Anyway, it was a coincidence and I don't like coincidences. They get admittance, we get the boot. All because some bum twitches to death on a subway platform. If they got a make on him it wouldn't have been so bad, but there was no identification at all."

"It's a shame you guys work so hard for a story," I laughed.

Eddie finished his pie and milk, belched gently and got up. "Back to the grind, buddy. I got to get my garbage ready for tonight."

I looked at him, nodded silently and watched him leave. Eddie Dandy had just told what I had forgotten. Damn, I thought.

Outside it had started to rain.

The kid perched on the steps of the brownstone lifted the cardboard box off his head and peered up at me. The super, he said, went down to the deli for his evening six-pack of beer. From there he'd go to Welch's Bar, have a few for starters, tell some lies and make a pass at Welch's barmaid before he came home. That wouldn't be for another hour yet. Smart, these kids. Twelve going on thirty. I tossed him a quarter and he put the box back on his head so he could listen to the rain hammer on it and ignored me.

I didn't bother to wait for the super. I went to the back of the hallway, found the stairs to the basement and snapped my penlight on. I had to pick my way around the clutter of junk to the bottom, then climb over trash that had been accumulating for years before I came to the current collection. Four banged up, rusted cans, each half filled with garbage, were nested beside the crumbling stairwell that led to the backyard and the areaway to the street. Tomorrow was collection day.

Garbage. The residue of a man. Sometimes it could tell you more than what he saved.

I turned the cans over and kicked the contents around on the floor, separating the litter with my foot. A rat ran out over my toe and scurried away into the darkness. Empty cans, crumpled boxes and newspaper made up most of the contents, the decayed food smell half obscured by the fumes from some old paint-soaked rags at the bottom of one can. A fire inspector would flip over that. There was a pile of sticky sawdust in a stained shopping bag that was all that was left of Lippy. It almost made me gag. Farther down was some broken glass, two opened envelopes and a partially crushed shoebox. The envelopes were addressed to Lipton Sullivan. One was a notice from the local political organization encouraging him to vote for their candidate in the next election. The other

was a mimeographed form letter from a furniture store listing
their latest sale items.

I tossed them back and picked up the box, ripping the folded-
in top back with my fingers.

Then I was pretty sure I knew where all of Lippy's bank deposit
money had been coming from. The box was loaded with men's
wallets and some goodies that obviously came from a woman's
purse. There was no money anywhere.

My old friend Lippy had been a damn pickpocket.

Velda was already at my apartment when I got there, curled
up like a sleek cat at the end of the sofa, all lovely long legs that
the miniskirt couldn't begin to hide and a neckline it didn't try
to. Those gorgeous breasts were still high and bouncy, flaring out
in a wild challenge, her stomach flat until it took that delicious
swell outward into her thighs and always that silky pageboy of
auburn hair framing a face that was much too pretty for anybody's
good.

"You look obscene," I said.

"It's a very studied pose," she reminded me. "It's supposed to
have an effect on you."

"And it does, kitten. You know me." I tossed the box on the
coffee table.

"Why don't you get out of those wet clothes and then we'll
talk."

"Don't mind the garbage smell," I said. "It's a dirty business.
Make me a drink and take a look at that stuff. Don't touch
anything. I'm going to take a hot shower. This racket is beginning
to get to me."

The impish grin she had greeted me with was lost in the look
of concern and she nodded. I walked into the bedroom, peeled
off my coat, yanked the .45 from the shoulder rig, tossed it on
the dresser and got rid of the rest of my clothes. I spent fifteen
minutes under a stinging needle spray, got out, wrapped a towel
around my middle and walked back into the living room trailing
wet footsteps.

Velda handed me my drink, the ice clinking in the glass. "Now
you look obscene. Why don't you ever dry yourself off?"

"That's what I got you for," I said.

"Not me. I'd only make you wetter."

"Someday I'm going to marry you and legalize all this nonsense."

"You know how long I've been hearing that?"

I tasted the drink. She'd hit the blend right on the button. "At least you're engaged," I said.

"The longest one on record." I grinned at her and she smiled back. "That's okay, Mike. I'm patient." Her eyes drifted toward the box on the table. She had dumped out the contents and sorted things out with the end of a ball-point pen. "Sorry about Lippy, Mike. Pretty disappointing. I always had him figured for a right guy."

"He gave that impression," I said. "What do you make of it?"

"Plain enough. Somebody knew what he did in his spare time and tried to heist his take. He wouldn't tell where he hid it because it wouldn't have done any good since it was in the bank. So he was killed. Getting rid of the stuff is part of the pattern. They take the money and dump the rest. He probably could have tried using some of the credit cards in those wallets, but that doesn't fit a pickpocket's usual routine."

"Sure looks that way."

"You go through any of that yet, Mike?"

"I didn't have time. Why?"

"Because Lippy didn't hit just anybody. That's the money crowd you see there. Wait until you check it out. If Lippy was a working dip he wouldn't be allowed inside their circles. He even got to a woman."

"I saw that compact."

"Gold with real diamonds. Expensive, but not pawnable."

"Why not?"

"Look at the hallmark and the inscription. It's a Tiffany piece given to Heidi Anders."

"The actress?"

"The same. The donor signed himself Bunny, so we'll assume it's Bunny Henderson with whom she's been seen these last few months. Playboy, jet setter, ne'er do well, but carries a load of power in his back pocket."

"What's it worth?" I asked her.

"My guess about five thousand. But that would be nothing to her. She's loaded with gems. To her that compact was more utilitarian than ornamental. I'm surprised a pickpocket specializing in wallets would tap a woman's handbag."

"Women aren't generally wallet carriers, kitten. He could have gotten a handful of money and that at the same time."

"Your buddy got plenty." She nodded toward the table. "Check it."

I walked over and took a look at some of the wallets she had spread open. All of them were expensive leather items, the plastic windows filled with top-rated credit cards. I picked up a pen and turned a few of them over, then stopped and tapped the inside of the large pigskin job. The top half of two pink pieces of cardboard were sticking up out of the slot. "There's your answer, kid. Theater tickets. He was working the new Broadway openings. Those ducats are being scalped at fifty bucks a pair which is a little more than the ordinary workingman can afford."

"Mike . . . those bank deposits. They weren't all that big."

"Because the people he was hitting didn't work with cash. They're all on the credit card system. But at least he knew he was always sure of something."

"You missed something, Mike."

"Where?"

Velda pointed to the worn black morocco case at the end. "He didn't have any credit cards, but there's a driver's license, some club memberships and a very interesting name on all of them."

I finished half my drink, put my glass down and studied the wallet. Ballinger. Woodring Ballinger. Woody Ballinger to his friends and the cops alike. Big-time spender, old-time hood who ran a tight operation nobody could get inside of.

"Great," I said.

"He could have run Lippy down and put some heat on him."

"Not Woody. He wouldn't take the chance. Not any more. He'd lose his dough and let it go at that."

"So it had to be someone who knew what Lippy was doing."

"Pat still has two sets of prints he's checking on."

"What will you do with this stuff?"

"Take it down to Pat tomorrow and let them process it. The suckers will be glad to get their credit cards back."

"Mike . . ."

"What?"

"You could have brought this right to Pat, you know."

"Yeah, I know. And they could have gone to the trouble of poking around in Lippy's garbage too."

"That puts you right in the middle. You're going to stick your neck out again."

"Something's too off balance for me. If Lippy were big enough they'd be giving this a rush job like they are with Tom-Tom Schneider. Everything gets priority when you're a big name. So now Lippy goes down in the books as a pickpocket knocked off for his loot. Maybe one day they'll get his killer on another charge. End of story."

"But not for you."

"Not for me."

Velda shook her head and gave a mock sigh. "All right, I took down the names and addresses of everybody heisted. The list is over there." She pointed to a half-used steno pad on the TV set.

"You always try to outthink me, don't you?"

"Generally," she said. A smile started in the corner of her eyes. "Know what I'm thinking right now?"

With a quick motion of her hand she reached out and flipped the towel from around my waist and let it fall to the floor. Those beautiful full lips parted in the rest of the smile and she said, "Yes, I know what you're thinking."

chapter three

PAT MADE A bit production out of the glare he was giving me, but the edge was all mine because his group should have found the stuff in the first place, not me. It's great to be public-spirited, but not when you're soaking wet, stinking from cellar garbage and alone with a beautiful broad.

He finally said, "Okay, Mike, you're off the hook, but you can still get a stinger up your tail if the D.A.'s office decides to probe."

"So cover for me," I told him. "Now, any of that stuff reported missing?"

Pat flipped through the report sheets on his desk and nodded. "Practically all of it. The credit cards have been canceled, two license renewals have been applied for and you'll be three hundred dollars richer. Reward money."

"Forget it. That way the D.A.'ll really nail it down. How about that compact?"

"Miss Heidi Anders thought she had mislaid it. She never reported it as missing or possibly stolen. Incidentally, it was well insured."

"Great to be rich. Did any of them know where the stuff was lifted?"

"Not specifically, but they all felt it was on the street somewhere. Three of them were positive it was in the theater area, William

Dorn pinpointed his on Broadway outside of Radio City Music Hall. He had used his wallet money to pay off a cabbie and remembered being jostled in the crowd outside the theater. A block later he felt for the wallet and it was gone."

"How did Ballinger take it?"

Pat shrugged and put the reports back in the folder. "Surly as usual. He said he had a couple hundred bucks in his wallet that we could forget about. Getting his driver's license back is good enough. We can mail it to him."

"Nice guys are hard to find."

"Yeah," Pat said sourly. "Look, about those rewards. My advice is to take them before they insist and put through an inquiry that might attract attention." He tore a sheet off his memo pad and passed it to me. "Irving Grove, William Dorn, Reginald Thomas and Heidi Anders. There are the addresses. You don't exactly have to lie, but you don't *have* to mention you're not with the department."

"Hell, cops don't collect rewards."

"People are funny. They like to do favors too."

"I'll donate it to the Police Athletic League."

"Go ahead."

"What about Lippy, Pat?"

"Hard to figure people out, isn't it? You think you know them, then something like this happens. It isn't the first time. It won't be the last. Someday we'll nail the guy who did it. The file isn't closed on him. Meanwhile, just leave it alone. Don't bug yourself with it."

"Sure." I got up and tossed my raincoat over my shoulder. "Incidentally, any news on Tom-Tom Schneider?"

"He thumped his last thump. A contract kill. One of the slugs matched another used in a Philly job last month."

"Those boys usually dump their pieces after a hit."

"Maybe he was fond of it. It was nine millimeter Luger ammo. Those pieces are getting hard to come by."

"How'd you do with that body in the subway?" I asked him.

Pat's face stiffened and he stopped swinging in his chair. His eyes went cold and narrow and his voice had a bite to it. "What are you getting at, Mike?"

I stuck a cigarette in my mouth and held a match to it. "Just curious. You know how I pick up bits and pieces of information. New York isn't all that tight."

He didn't move, but I saw his knuckles whiten around the arms of his chair. "Buddy, how you get around is unbelievable. Why the curiosity?"

I took a guess and said, "Because you have every available man checking the guy out. Even some Feds have moved in, but when it comes to Lippy it's a one-day deal."

For a moment it looked like Pat was going to explode, then he looked at me, his mind trying to penetrate through mine to see if I was guessing or not. It was my mention of the Feds that put the frown back on his face again and he said, "Damn," very softly and let go the arms of the chair. "What do you know, Mike?"

"Want an educated opinion?"

"Never mind. It's better that you knew so you wouldn't be guessing in front of the wrong people."

I took a pull on the butt and blew a shaft of smoke in his direction. "So?"

"A sharp medic in the hospital didn't like the symptoms. They autopsied him immediately and confirmed their suspicions. He was infected by one of the newer and deadlier bacteria strains."

"Unusual?"

"This was. The culture was developed in government laboratories for C.G. Warfare only. They're not sure of the contagion factor and don't want to start a panic."

"Maybe he was a worker there."

"We're checking that out now. Anyway, just keep it to yourself. If this thing gets around we'll know the source it came from."

"You shouldn't be so trusting then."

"Oh, hell, get out of here, Mike."

I snubbed out the butt in his ashtray, grinned and went through the door. Eddie Dandy would give his left whoosis for this scoop, but I wasn't in the market for left whoosises.

I managed to reach Velda just before she went out to lunch and told her I wouldn't be in the rest of the day. She had already cleaned up most of the paperwork and before she could start in rearranging the furniture I said, "Look, honey, one thing you can do. Go to Lippy's bank and find the clerk he deposited that money with."

"Pat has a record of that."

"Yeah, of the amounts. What I want to know is if he remembered what denominations of bills were deposited."

"Important?"

"Who can tell? I'm just not satisfied with the answers, that's all. I'll check back with you later."

I hung up and went back into the afternoon rain. A couple were getting out of a cab on the corner and I grabbed it before anyone else could and told the driver where to go.

Woodring Ballinger had a showpiece office on the twenty-first floor of a Fifth Avenue building but he never worked there. His operating space was the large table in the northeast corner of Finero's Steak House just off Broadway, a two-minute walk to Times Square. There were three black phones and a white one in front of him and the two guys he was with were in their early thirties with the total businessman look. Only they both had police records dating back to their teens. That businessman look was one that Ballinger never could hope to buy. He tried hard enough, with three-hundred-buck suits and eighty-dollar shoes, but he still looked like he just came off a dock after pushing a dolly of steel around. Scar tissue laced his eyebrows and knuckles, he always needed a shave and seemed to have a perpetual sneer plastered on his mouth.

I said, "Hello, Woody."

He only half looked at me. "What the hell do you want?"

"Tell your boys to blow."

Both of them looked up at me a little amused. When I reached for my deck of cigarettes they saw the .45 in the holster and stopped being amused. Woody Ballinger said, "Go wait in the bar."

Obediently, they got up, went past me without another glance and pulled up stools at the bar with their backs to us. I sat down opposite Woody and waved the waiter over to bring me a beer.

"You lost, Hammer?"

"Not in this town. I live here. Or have you forgotten?" I gave him a dirty grin and when he scowled I knew he remembered, all right.

"Cut the crap. What d'you want?"

"You had your wallet lifted not long ago."

His fingers stopped toying with his glass. The waiter came, set the beer down and I sipped the head off it. "What's new about that? The cops found it."

"*I* found it," I said. "Yours wasn't the only one in the pile."

"So okay. I get my license back. There wasn't no money in it. The bum who lifted it grabbed that. Two hundred and twelve bucks. Where'd you find it?"

"Doesn't matter. The guy's dead who was holding it. Somebody carved him apart for nothing. The money was all in the bank."

"Hell, I'd sure like to get my hands on the bastard. Hittin' me, the dirty punk. Maybe he's better off." Woody stopped then, his eyes screwing half shut. "Why tell me about it anyway?"

"Because maybe you might know what dips are working the area. If you don't know, maybe you can find out."

"What for? If the guy's dead he . . ."

"Because I don't like to think it was the guy who was killed. So poke around. You know who to ask."

"Go ask them yourself, buster."

"No, you do it, Woody. I haven't got time." I finished my beer, threw a buck on the table and got up. When I went by the bar I tapped one of the business types on the shoulder and said, "You can go back now."

They just looked at me, picked up their drinks and went back to their boss without a word. Ballinger chose his people carefully.

It wasn't too long ago that the East Side past Lexington had been just one long slum section with a beautiful vitality all its own you couldn't duplicate anywhere in the world. Then they had torn down the elevated and let the light in and it was just too much for the brilliant speculators to miss.

Oh, the slums were still there, isolated pockets nestling shoulder to shoulder with the sterile facades of the expensive high rise apartments, tiny neighborhoods waiting for the slam of the iron ball to send them into an oblivion of plaster dust and crumpled bricks. If an inanimate thing could die, the city was dying of cancerous modernism. One civilization crawling over another. Then there would be ruins laid on top of ruins. I could smell the artificially cooled air seeping from the huge glassed doorways around the uniformed doormen and thought, hell, I liked it better the other way.

Miss Heidi Anders occupied 24C, a corner patio apartment on the good side of the building where the sun came in all day and you weren't forced to see how others lived just a ninety-degree turn away from you. The doorman announced me, saying it was in connection with the compact she had lost and I heard her resonant voice come right out of the wall phone and say, "Oh, yes, the policeman. Please send him up."

The doorman would have liked to mix a little small talk with me but the elevator was empty and I stepped inside, pushed number twenty-four and took the ride upstairs.

I had only seen production photos of Heidi Anders, commercial pictures in the flowing gowns she generally wore in the Broadway musicals. For some reason I had always thought of her as the big robust type who could belt a song halfway across the city without a mike. I wasn't quite ready for the pert little thing in the white hip-hugger slacks and red bandanna top that left her all naked in between. The slacks were cut so low there was barely enough hip left to hug them up. And if the knot on the bandanna top slipped even a fraction of an inch it was going to burst right off her. What got me, though, were the eyelashes she had painted around her navel. The damn thing seemed to be inspecting me.

All I could say was, "Miss Anders?"

She gave me a nervous little smile and opened the door all the way. "Yes . . . but please, call me Heidi. Everybody does. Come in, come in." Her tongue made a quick pass across her lips and her smile seemed a little forced. No wonder cops were lonely. Even if they thought you were one they got the jumps.

"Hammer. Mike Hammer."

She took my coat and hat, slipped them on a rack, then led me into the spacious living area of the apartment. She didn't walk. She had a gait all her own, a swaying, rolling, dancing motion that put all her muscles into play. Unconsciously, she flipped the lovely tousle of ash-blonde hair over her head, spun around with her arms spread in a grand theatrical gesture and said, "Home!"

It might have been home to her, but it looked like some crazy love nest to me. It was all pillows, soft couches and wild pictures, but it sure looked interesting. "Nice," I said.

She took a half jump into one of the overstuffed chairs and sank down into it. "Sit, Mr. Hammer. May I make you a drink? But then, policemen never drink on duty, do they?"

"Sometimes." I didn't trust the couch. I pulled an ottoman up and perched on the edge of it.

"Well, they never do on TV. Now, are you the one who found my compact?"

"Yes, Ma'am." I hoped it was the proper TV intonation.

Once again she gave me that nervous little smile. "You know, I never even realized I had lost it. I'm so glad it has been recovered. You're getting a reward, you know."

"I'd appreciate it if you'd just make a donation to the P.A.L."

"The Police Athletic League? Oh, I did a benefit for them one time. Certainly, if that's the way you want it. Do you have it with you?"

"No, you can pick it up from the property clerk after you've identified it. It's a Tiffany piece so they'll have a record of it and your insurance policy will have it described. No trouble getting it back."

Her shoulders gave an aggravated twitch, then she ran her fingers through her beautifully unruly hair and smiled again. "I don't know what I'm impatient about. I've been without it all this time, another day won't matter. I guess it's just the excitement. I've never really been involved with the police except to get my club permit and that was years ago. They don't even do that any more now, do they?"

"No more. Look, maybe I will have that drink. Show me where the goodies are."

"Right behind you." She pointed. "I'll have a small Scotch on the rocks."

I got up, made the drinks, and when I got back she had changed from the chair to the couch looking like she was half hoping she was going to get raped. I hated to disappoint her, but I handed her the Scotch and took the ottoman again to try my tall rye and ginger. She toasted me silently, tasted her drink and nodded approvingly, then: "You know . . . since you didn't bring my compact, and you won't accept any reward, was there something you wanted to talk to me about?"

"Not many of us get a chance to see a luscious actress in the flesh. So to speak," I added. Her navel was still looking at me.

"You're sweet, but you're lying," she smiled. She tasted her drink again, leaned forward and put it on the floor between her feet. The halter top strained uncertainly, but held.

I said, "I was hoping you might remember when and where you lost that thing."

"Oh, but I do. I didn't think about it at first, but when I put my mind to it I remember quite well."

I took another pull at my drink and waited, trying to keep my eyes off her belly.

"I went to the theater to catch Roz Murray in the opening of her new show. During the intermission I went to the powder room and found it gone. I never suspected that it had been stolen, but I'm always misplacing things anyway, and I supposed I had left it at home. I was sure of it when I found that two fifty dollar bills and some singles were gone too. I thought I had scooped some out of my drawer before I left, but I was in such a damn rush to meet Josie to make curtain time I could have pulled a boo-boo."

"How did you get to the theater?"

"Josie picked me up downstairs in a cab and paid the bill."

"And you never bothered checking for it later?"

"Oh, I kind of looked around. I always keep a few hundred

dollars loose in the drawer and the rest was still there and I didn't bother to count it. I figured the compact was simply tucked away someplace else."

I rattled the ice around in the glass and tried the drink again. "One more thing. At any time that evening do you remember being crowded?"

"Crowded?"

"Hemmed in with people where somebody could make a pass at your handbag."

She looked thoughtful a moment, then reached down for her drink again. It was a very unsettling move. Over the glass her eyes touched mine and her tongue made that nervous gesture again, passing quickly over her lips. "No . . . not really . . . but, yes, while we were going in there was this one man . . . well, he sort of cut across in front of us and had to excuse himself. He acted like he knew somebody on the other side of us."

"Can you describe him?"

She squinched her eyes and mouth shut tight for a good five seconds, then let her face relax. Her eyes opened and she nodded. "He was about average height . . . smaller than you. In his late forties. Not well dressed or anything . . . and he had funny hair."

"What kind of funny?"

"Well, he should have been gray but he wasn't and it grew back in deep V's on either side."

I knew it showed on my face. The drink turned sour in my mouth and that strange sensation seemed to crawl up my back. She had just described Lippy Sullivan.

"Is . . . something wrong?"

I faked a new expression and shook my head. "No, everything is working out just right." I put the glass down and stood up. "Thanks for the drink."

Heidi Anders held out her hand and let me pull her up from the depths of the cushions. "I appreciate your coming like this. I only wish . . ."

"What?"

"You could have brought the compact. Police stations scare me."

"Get me your insurance policy, a note authorizing me to pick it up for you, and you'll have it tomorrow."

For the first time a real smile beamed across her face. "Will you?" She didn't wait for an answer. She broke into that wild gait, disappeared into another room and was back in three minutes with both the things I asked for.

She walked me to the door and held my coat while I slipped

into it. When I turned around her face was tilted up toward mine, her mouth alive and moist. "Since you wouldn't take the reward, let me give you one you *can* keep."

Very gently, she raised herself on her toes, her hands slipping behind my head. Those lips were all fire and mobility, her tongue a thing that quested provocatively. I could feel the hunger start and didn't want it to get loose, so just as gently I pushed her away, letting my hands slide down the satin nudity of her back until my fingertips rested on the top of those crazy hip huggers and my thumbs encircled her almost to those exotic areas where there is no turning back. I heard her breath catch in her throat and felt the muscles tauten, her skin go damp under my palms, then I let her go.

"That was mean," she said.

"So is painting that eye around your belly button."

The throaty laugh bubbled up again and she let her hands ease down from my neck and across my chest. Then the laugh stopped as she felt the .45 under my coat, and that nervous little glint was back in her eyes.

"Tomorrow," I said.

"Tomorrow, Mike." But she said it like she really didn't mean it at all.

The afternoon papers were still splashing the death of Tom-Tom Schneider all over their pages. The D.A.'s office was running a full-scale investigation into all his affairs and connections, the State Committee on Organized Crime had just been called into executive session for another joust at the underworld and anybody with a political ax to grind was making his points with the reporters. Everybody seemed agreed that it was a contract kill and two columnists mentioned names of known enemies and were predicting another gangland war.

Someplace there would be another meeting and the word would go out to put a big cool on activities until the heat had died down and someplace else a contract was being paid off and spent.

Lippy Sullivan had been forgotten. Maybe it was just as well. The guy who died on the subway station wasn't mentioned at all either. When I finished with the paper I tossed it in the litter basket and went into the cigar store on the corner and called Velda.

When she came on I asked her how she made out at the bank and she said, "The teller remembered Lippy all right, Mike. Seemed like they always had a little something to talk about."

"He remember the deposits?"

"Uh-huh. Tens, twenties and singles. Nothing any bigger. From what was said he gathered that Lippy was in some small business enterprise by himself that paid off in a minor fashion."

"Nothing bigger than a twenty?"

"That's what he told me. Oh, and he always had it folded with a rubber band around it as if he were keeping it separate from other bills. Make anything out of it?"

"Yeah. He was smart enough to cash in the big ones before depositing them so nothing would look funny." I told her briefly about Heidi Anders identifying Lippy in the crowd.

All she said was a sorrowful, "Oh, Mike."

"Tough."

"Why don't you leave it alone?"

"I don't like things only half checked out, kid. I'll push it a little bit further, then dump it. I wish to hell he hadn't even called me."

"Maybe you won't have to go any further."

"Now what?"

"Pat called about twenty minutes ago. He had pictures of Lippy circulating around the theater areas all day. Eight people recalled having seen him in the area repeatedly."

"Hell, he lived not too far from there."

"Since when was Lippy a stage fan? He never even went to the neighborhood movie house. You know what his habits were."

"Okay, okay. Were they reliable witnesses?"

"Pat says they were positive ID's. Someplace Lippy learned a new trade and found a good place to work it."

"Nuts."

"So make Pat sore at you. He's hoping this new bit will keep you out of their routine work. Now, is there any reason why you still have to go after it?"

"Damn right. Only because Lippy said there wasn't any reason to begin with."

"Then what else can I do?"

"Go ask questions around Lippy's place. Do your whore act. Maybe somebody'll open up to you who won't speak to me or the cops."

"In that neighborhood?"

"Just keep your price up and you won't have any trouble."

She swore at me and I grinned and hung up.

I was only three blocks away from Irving Grove's Men's Shop on Broadway and there was still time to make it before the office buildings started disgorging their daily meals of humans, so I ducked back into the drizzle and walked to the corner. A little thunder rumbled overhead, but there were a few breaks in the smog layers and it didn't look like the rain was going to last much longer. In a way, it was too bad. The city was always a little quieter, a little less crowded and a lot more friendly when it was wet.

Irving Grove was typical of the Broadway longtimers. Short, stocky, harried, but smiling and happy to be of service. He turned the two customers over to his clerks and ushered me into his cubicle of an office to one side of his stockroom, cleared a couple of chairs of boxes and invoices and drew two coffees from the battered urn on the desk.

"You know, Mr. Hammer, it is a big surprise to know my wallet was found. Twice before this has happened, but never do I get them back. It wasn't the money. Three hundred dollars I can afford, but all those papers. Such trouble."

"I know the feeling."

"And you are sure there will be no reward?"

"The P.A.L., remember?"

He gave me a shrewd smile and a typical gesture of his head. "But you are not with the police force, of course. It would be nothing if . . ."

"You don't know me, Mr. Grove."

"Perhaps not personally, but I read. I know of the things you have done. Many times. In a way I am jealous. I work hard, I make a good living, but never any excitement. Not even a holdup. So I read about your . . ."

"Did you ever stop to think that there are times I envy you?"

"Impossible." He stopped, the coffee halfway to his mouth. "Really?"

"Sometimes."

"Then maybe I don't feel so bad after all. It is better to just read, eh?"

"Much better," I said. "Tell me, are you a theatergoer?"

"No, only when my wife drags me there. Maybe once a year if I can't get out of it. Why?"

"Whoever lifted your wallet was working the theater crowds."

Irving Grove nodded sagely. "Ah, yes. That is possible. I see what you mean." He put his cup down and picked a half-smoked cigar from an ashtray and lit it. "See, Mr. Hammer, I live on the West Side. For years yet, always the same place. I close here and on nice nights I walk home. Maybe a twenty-minute walk. Sometimes I go down one street, sometimes another, just to see the people, the excitement. You understand?"

I nodded.

"So pretty often I go past the theaters just when they're going in. I watch what they're wearing. It helps for my trade, you know. It was one of those nights when my wallet was stolen. I didn't even realize it until the next morning, and I couldn't be sure until I came back to the store to make sure I hadn't dropped it here somewhere. Right away I reported it and canceled all my credit cards."

"What denomination bills did you have with you?"

"Two one hundred dollar bills, a fifty and one five. That I remember. I always remember the money."

"Where did you carry it?"

"Inside my coat pocket."

I said, "Maybe you can remember anybody that pushed or shoved you that night. Anybody who was close to you in the crowd who could have lifted it?"

Grove smiled sadly and shook his head. "I'm afraid I'm not a very suspicious person, Mr. Hammer. I never look at faces, only clothes. No, I wouldn't remember that."

I crushed my paper cup, tossed it in the wastebasket and thanked him for his time. He was just another blank in a long series of blanks and all it was doing was making Lippy look worse than ever. Velda was right. I should have just left it all alone.

So I got out of there, walked over to Forty-fourth and The Blue Ribbon, pulled out the chair behind my usual table and had the waiter bring me a knockwurst and beer. Jim waved hello from behind the bar and switched on the TV so I could watch the six o'clock news.

Eddie Dandy came on after the weather, freshly shaven, his usual checkered sportscoat almost eyestraining to watch whenever he moved, his voice making every piece of dull information sound like a world-shattering event. George came over and sat down with his ever-present coffee cup in his hand and started in on his favorite subject of food. He had just asked me about a new specialty he was thinking of putting on the menu when I stopped him short with a wave of my hand.

Eddie Dandy had changed the tone of his voice. He wasn't reading from his notes, he was looking directly into the camera in deadly seriousness and said, ". . . and once again the public is being kept in the dark about a matter of grave importance. The unidentified body found in the Times Square station of the subway has been secretly autopsied with the findings kept locked in government files. No information has been given either the police or the press and the doctors who performed the autopsy are being confined in strict quarantine at this moment. It is this reporter's opinion that this man died of a virulent disease developed by this government's chemical-germ warfare research, one that could possibly lead to severe epidemic proportions, but rather than inform the public and institute an immediate remedial program, they chose to avoid panic and possible political repercussions by keeping this matter completely in the dark. Therefore, I suggest . . ."

I said, "Oh, shit!" Then threw a bill on the table and dashed to the phone booth in the next room. I threw a dime in the slot, dialed Pat's number and waited for him to come on the phone.

I said, "Mike here, Pat."

He was silent a second, then through his breathing he told me, "Get your ass down here like now, buddy. Like right this damn minute."

chapter four ▃▃▃▃▃▃▃▃▃▃▃▃▃▃▃▃

PAT WOULDN'T TALK to me. He didn't even want to look at me and for the first time since we had been friends I felt like telling him to go to hell. I didn't. I just sat there beside him in the patrol car and watched the streets roll by on the way to the office building on Madison Avenue where the watchdogs had their cute little front they thought nobody knew about. And this time even Pat was surprised when I got out first, went inside to the elevator and punched the 4 button without being told. There was a NO SMOKING sign in the elevator so I took out my deck, shook a cigarette loose and struck a wooden kitchen match across the NO. Then he knew how I felt too. He started to say something, only I got there first.

"You should have asked me," I said.

The others were all waiting, quiet and deadly, their faces full of venom, tinged with total dislike and anticipating selective revenge. *Screw them too,* I thought.

There weren't any introductions. The big guy with the bulging middle and the florid face simply pointed to a chair and after I looked at it long enough and decided on my own to sit down, I sat, then spun my butt into the middle of their big, beautiful mahogany company table and grinned when another one glared at me a second before picking it up and dropping it in a huge ceramic ashtray.

Everyone sat down with such deliberate motion you'd think we were about to go into a discussion of a successful bond issue. But it wasn't like that and I wasn't about to let them open the meeting. I waited until the last chair had scraped into position and said, "If you clowns think you're about to steamroller me, you'd just better start thinking straight. Nobody asked me here, nobody advised me of my rights, and right now I'd just as soon kick any or all of you on your damn tails . . . including my erstwhile buddy here . . . and all you need to start the action is one little push."

"You're not under arrest, Hammer," the fat one said.

"Believe it, buddy, that I'm not. But I'm sure interested in getting that way."

When they looked at each other wondering what kind of a cat they had caught in their trap I knew I had the bull on them and I wasn't about to let go. For the first time I looked directly at Pat. "I saw Eddie Dandy's show tonight myself. You've already been informed by Captain Chambers here that I was a recipient of confidential information. It was given me in way of explanation so I wouldn't do any loose talking, so I assume everyone here figures I picked up a few fast bucks by passing that information on. Okay, right now, hear this just once. It was Eddie Dandy who suggested the idea and I just made a few discreet inquiries that shook up my good pal Pat to the point where he had to fill me in on the rest." I tapped out another butt and lit it. Somebody shoved the ashtray my way. "Pat, I said nothing, you got that?"

He was still the cop. His expression didn't change an iota. "Sorry, Mike."

"Okay, forget it."

"It can't be forgotten," the fat guy said. "Do you know who we are?"

"Who the hell are you trying to kid?" I asked him. "You're all D.C. characters playing political football with something you can't handle. Now you got Eddie Dandy on your backs and can't get him off."

One of the others snapped a pencil in two and stared at me,

his face tight with rage. "He'll be here to explain his part in this."

"There *isn't* any part, you nut. All you can do now is offer excuses or start lying. Which is it? Or do you discredit Eddie? Tell me, is it true?"

Everybody wanted to talk at once, but the fat guy at the end silenced them with one word. Then he looked down the table at me and folded his hands with all the innocence of a bear trap. "Tell me, Mr. Hammer, why are you so militant?"

"Because I don't dig you goons. You're all bureaucratic-nonsense, tax happy, self-centered socialistic slobs who think the public's a game you can run for your own benefit. One day you'll realize that it's the individual who pulls the strings, not committees."

"And you're that individual?"

"I can pull more than strings, friend, that's why you got me here. Right now I'm all for going out and really sounding off about what I know. How about that?" I sat back and listened to the quiet.

Pat broke the eerie stillness. "Don't push him, Mr. Crane. The whole thing shook me for a minute, but I'd rather have him on our side."

"Protecting yourself, Captain?"

"Another remark like that and you'll be protecting yourself, Mr. Crane. I'll rap you right in the mouth."

The big man from the State Department took one look at Pat's face and the knuckles of his interlocking fingers whitened. "Captain . . ."

"You'll be better off just telling him, Mr. Crane. He isn't kidding."

They could talk with their eyes, this bunch. They could just look at each other and have a conversation, hash the problem out and come to a decision. When it was made, Crane gave an almost imperceptible nod and stared at me again, his eyes cold. "Very well. I don't approve, but considering how far out on a limb we are, we'll give you the story."

"Why?" I asked.

"Simply because we can't afford to have anyone prying into this affair. After Eddie Dandy's report we'll have everyone in the news media asking questions. They don't like negative answers. They'll go directly to Dandy and we're hoping you can influence him to state that he was wrong in his premises."

"Brother!" I snubbed my butt out and sat back in my chair. "You don't know reporters very well, do you? Where is Eddie now?"

"Being briefed on the incident. He'll be here shortly."

"You better have something good to tell him. Or me."

Crane nodded. "I think we have."

"I'm listening."

"Of course you realize the confidential nature of this matter?"

"I did before," I said.

Mr. Crane managed a little of his State Department pomp and leaned back, mentally choosing his words. When he was satisfied, he said, "In 1946 a Soviet agent was planted in this country by the regime then in power with specific instructions that at a certain time, when the economic and political factors were right, to totally sabotage certain key cities through the use of biological or chemical means. His orders were irrevocable. He was given the properties to accomplish his mission, and the persons he could contact who would relay the schedule of destruction. This was a top secret project that could in no way be canceled out. This agent had one contact who, like him, was only to relay the information of when it would take place, then set in motion the machinery that would take over after the destruction finished our present system of government."

"And that guy is dead," I said.

"Very dead. Now we know the system he used. It was bacteriological. He's set everything in motion. It's a time delay affair. Unfortunately, he somehow got exposed himself and died."

I looked over at Pat. "You said it came out of our labs."

Crane didn't let him answer. "All research seems to come to the same conclusions. The strain of bacteria was similar, but not identical."

"You got troubles, Mr. Crane, haven't you? We have ICBM's, Polaris, all the new goodies stored up in silos around the country that can reach anywhere around the world, and now that you know what's on our necks we can get in there for a first strike, only you're not striking. Why?"

That caught them a little off base. Maybe they thought I couldn't figure it out. Crane gave me a perceptive brush of his eyes and said, "Because the Soviets are caught on their own horns. They don't want it either. They want it stopped right now and they're cooperating. There's a new regime in power and their entire political system has been changed in view of the Chinese situation. They can't afford to be hit from both sides. Only one of their personnel was able to hint at this development, but that was enough to get leads, process them and get the story. Do you see now why we can't afford a panic?"

"So you're buying time."

"Exactly."

Before he could answer another of the gray flannel boys came in, walked up and spoke to him. Crane nodded and said, "Bring him in."

Eddie Dandy looked like he had been wrung out in an old Maytag. Sweat had plastered his hair to his forehead, his sports jacket was rumpled and he couldn't keep his hands still at all. But his face still bore that hard stamp of the veteran newscaster with the "show me or else" look. Apparently they hadn't mentioned me to him at all and his eyes registered momentary surprise when he saw me sitting there. I waved nonchalantly and winked and I knew damn well things were beginning to add up to him.

They gave him the same rundown they gave me, but he had saved up his little shocker for them. When Crane insisted just a little too hard on Eddie divulging his source of information, he simply said, "Why it was you and Mr. Hollings who tipped me off." I applauded with a laugh nobody appreciated. Pat gave me a tap with his foot.

"Please don't think everybody is stupid," Eddie told them. "I have to research news items and the death of that guy in the subway had certain earmarks that were familiar to me. Or did you forget the death of all those sheep out west when that nerve gas went in the wrong direction? Or the two lab workers whose families raised such hell about the cover-up when they kicked off? Seeing you two in the hospital was all it took to pin the probability down . . . that and a few inquiries made to knowledgeable scientists who don't approve of the more sophisticated methods of modern warfare."

Somehow they all seemed to stop communicating then. Their exchanges of looks didn't bring any responses. Red-faced, Crane mustered all his eloquence and put the proposition right on the line. Eddie could be the turning point of panic. Until the location of the destruct cannisters could be determined and destroyed, Eddie was to retract his broadcast and maintain that position.

He looked at me and I shrugged. I said, "There's a possibility a mass search for the stuff might help."

"You'll get mass exodus from the cities and panic, Mr. Hammer," Crane told me. "No, we have competent people experienced in these matters and with help from the Soviets I'm confident it can be accomplished."

"Sure, you trust the Soviets and you know what you'll get. You get screwed every time and you slobs are all afraid of screwing back. What happens if you *don't* find the stuff?"

"We're not even considering that possibility," he shot back. "No . . ."

But Eddie cut him off right there. "You're forgetting something. Now my neck is out with the network and the audience. I'll be coming off looking like a bumbling amateur. I'll be lucky if I can hang on to my job. So we make a deal."

"Yes?"

"No other reporter, broadcaster or what-have-you gets any part of this story if you pull it off. All I need is a hint that this has been leaked and I'll blow the whole thing all over your faces. *If* you manage to lock this thing up, I get first crack at releasing it along with verbal progress reports in the meantime. You haven't got much choice, so you can take it or leave it."

"We'll take it, Mr. Dandy," Crane said. This time the communication was complete. Everybody else agreed too.

Pat took Eddie Dandy and me to a late supper at Dewey Wong's wild restaurant on East Fifty-eighth Street as a way of apology. I gave him a little private hell, but it didn't take long to get back on our old footing. He was red-faced about it, but too much cop to let it bother him. What really had him going was the maximum effort order that was out in the department, recalling all officers from vacation, assigning extra working hours, canceling days off and hoping to keep the reason for the project secret long enough to get the job done. With the same thing going on all over the country, it wasn't going to be easy. Until it was finished, every other investigation was going to be at a standstill. When we finished, Eddie took off to start working on his end and I rode back downtown with Pat. In the car I said, "Velda told me about Lippy working the theater areas."

"I hope it satisfies you."

"Ahh . . ."

"Come on, Mike, stay loose. It's pretty damn obvious, isn't it?"

"There's still a killer around."

"More than one, buddy, and we're not concentrating any on your old pal. From now on we'll be going after the biggest and the best for one reason only . . . to give the papers all the hot news they can handle so maybe they'll skip over this latest incident. We're in trouble, Mike."

"Never changes. There's always trouble."

"And I don't need any with you."

I handed him the insurance papers and note Heidi had given

me. He glanced at them and handed them back, his face masked with total astonishment. "By damn, you land right in the middle of the biggest mess we've ever had and all you want is a passkey to some broad's tail. Man, you never change! You damn horny . . ."

"Lay off, Pat. I could have had that for free yesterday."

"Then why . . ."

"It'll keep you off my back if for no other reason."

"For that I'll do anything. Look, take every one of those wallets and give them back personally. It won't be hard to arrange at all. Then go get drunk or shack up for a week or get lost in the mountains . . . just anything at all!"

"My pleasure," I said.

He slammed his hand down on his knee with a disgusted gesture and shut up again. But he meant what he said. He packaged the whole lot for me, had me sign for each item and let me leave so he could handle all the traffic that was beginning to jam the room.

Outside, I set my watch with the clock in a jeweler's window. It was a quarter to eleven. The night was clear and an offshore breeze had blown the smog inland. You could see some of the stars that were able to shine through the reflected glow of the city lights. Traffic was thin downtown, but up farther, New York would be coming to life. Or death, whichever way you looked at it. For me, I couldn't care less because it had always been that way anyway. At least the little episode with all the forces of national and international governments had bought me the same thing it had bought them . . . time. Everybody would be too busy to be clawing at my back now. I grinned silently and flagged down a cruising cab.

Finero's Steak House was jammed with the after-theater crowd, a noisy bunch three deep around the bar and a couple dozen others waiting patiently in the lobby for a table. I waved the maître d' over, told him all I wanted was to see Ballinger and he let the velvet rope down so I could go in.

He was like something out of a late-late movie, sitting there flanked by two full-blown blondes in dresses cut so low they seemed more like stage costumes than evening wear. His tux was the latest style, but on him it was all eyewash because he was still the dock-type hood and no tailor was ever going to change him. One of the blondes kept feeling his five o'clock shadow and murmuring about his virility. The other was doing something else and Ballinger was enjoying the mutual attention. The others respectfully ignored the play, paying due attention to their own dates. The original pair were there, but a new one had been added, a punk named Larry Beers who had been a *pistolero* with the Gomez Swan mob when he was nineteen and graduated into the upper echelon brackets when he had beaten a rap for gunning down two of the Benson Hill bunch. I didn't know Ballinger had him on his side until now. Old Woodring was paying high for his services, whatever they were, that was for sure.

This time Woody put on an act for everybody's benefit. I got a big smile, an introduction to the girls whose names all sounded alike, the pair named Carl and Sammy, but when he came to Larry Beers I said, "We've met." His handshake was very wary. "Been a long time, Larry.

"Let's make it longer the next time."

"Why not?"

Ballinger gave me a big smile that was all snake with the fangs out, his heavy-lidded eyes asking for trouble. "Join us, Hammer?"

"Not tonight, Woody. I got better things to do."

"Ah, come on, I'll get you a broad and . . ."

"I'm a leg man, myself," I said.

The blonde on his left stuck her tongue out at me. "I have those too, you know."

"I hope so. It's just that I enjoy a certain style and design."

She laughed and put both her hands on the table. Woody seemed annoyed at the sudden attention I was getting and let his smile fade. "You want something?"

I reached in my pocket, took out his wallet and tossed it on the table. "Just saving some embarrassment by having you go down and get it. Seems funny, an old pro like you letting a dip grab his poke. You do what I asked you?"

He was too happy to know I was leaving not to answer me. He stuck the wallet back in his pocket without looking at it and said, "Not yet, but soon."

"Real soon, okay?"

I looked at them all briefly, remembering their faces, nodded and went back to the street. I could feel Woody Ballinger's eyes boring into my back all the way.

On the way to the East Side I stopped in a gin mill on Sixth Avenue and put in a call to Velda at her apartment. I let the phone ring a dozen times, but there was no answer. I tried the office too in case she decided to work late. Same thing. The answering service for my apartment number told me there had been no calls for me at all. I wasn't about to worry about her. She had a P.I. ticket and a nasty little .32 hammerless automatic

SURVIVAL . . . ZERO!   663

to go with it and when the chips were down she could take care of herself. Right now she probably was following orders, purse swinging with the come-on look in Lippy's neighborhood, seeing how the other half lived.

Near-midnight callers on actress tenants mustn't have seemed unusual to the doorman. He was the same one who had admitted me earlier and when I asked him if he ever slept he chuckled and said, "Changed shifts with Barney. He's courting and the night work was ruining his love life. You want to see Miss Anders, go right up. She got in a little while ago and for her it's like the middle of the afternoon." He gave me a knowing look and added, "You want I should call her?"

"Give her a buzz. Hammer's the name."

"Yes, sir." He plugged in the jack, flipped the toggle twice and waited. Then: "Miss Anders, I have a Mr. Hammer . . ."

Her voice, ringing with that odd quality that could carry right through a phone, came right over his, but this time with a hurried urgency that seemed to have a catch in it. "Yes, please, send him right up."

The doorman hung up and made a wry face at me. "Funny broad, that."

"How come?"

"Any guy she can get, but always picks the wrong ones who give her a hard time. Like tonight she comes home, eyes all red, sniffling and jumpy. You'd think she'd blow this coop and start over somewheres."

"The mortality rate is pretty high in show business. Those dames can attract some oddballs."

"Yeah, but no reason to. They're just people same as anybody else. They got a face and a body and you'd think they'd make out okay, but this one is always miserable. It's a wonder she'll even speak to a guy any more. A big star, plenty of money and always down in the dumps. Me, I'm plain glad to be what I am."

"I know the feeling," I said.

This time I didn't have to touch the bell. The door was cracked and she was waiting for me, a pert thing with crazy ash-blonde hair, belted into a sheer black housecoat that clung so magically to all the curves and hollows that it seemed like she didn't have anything on at all.

But she wasn't quite as pretty as the last time. Her eyes were too red and feverish looking. The nervousness was more acute and the smile she gave me was strained to its limit. She swallowed with a tiny, jerky motion of her head and reached for my sleeve.

"Come in, Mike. Please come in. I guess you must think I'm awfully strange to be having guests so late, but it's really nothing for me. Nothing at all." She tried a laugh on as she shut the door and took my hat. It had a hollow, flat sound. "You'll have to excuse me if I'm not at my best. It's just that . . . well, I imagine everyone has personal problems and . . ."

"Don't let it bother you, honey."

Heidi Anders' fingers squeezed hard on my arm and she nibbled gently on her lower lip. Something like a shudder ran through her, then she tugged and let me feel the warmth of her body beside me as she took me into that nutty love nest of hers. Maybe it was the maid's day off, but the place wasn't like it had been. Too many things were out of place; cushions strewn around, a lamp on the floor, ashtrays filled with lipstick-smeared butts. They weren't party signs or trouble signs . . . just diffident neglect as if nobody gave a damn about the place.

She pushed me onto the couch, forcing gaiety into her tone. "Can I make you a drink, Mike?"

"A short one maybe. I can only stay a minute."

"Oh?" I couldn't tell whether it was fright or disappointment in her expression.

"I only came to bring your compact back." I reached in my pocket, took out the diamond-studded case and her insurance papers and laid them on the coffee table.

For all she seemed to care it could have been a piece of junk. She turned quickly, called back, "Thank you. It was very kind," over her shoulder, and went to the small mahogany bar in the corner and made me a drink. She came back and handed it to me. The ice in the glass clinked against the sides and she put it down quickly so I wouldn't notice her hand tremble.

I said, "None for you?"

"No . . . not now." She pulled a tissue from one slash pocket and touched her nose and eyes with it, the corners of her mouth crinkling in a smile. "I guess I shouldn't be so sentimental over small things," she said. "You'll have to excuse me." She reached for the compact and the insurance policy. "Maybe I'd better put these where they won't get lost again. Be right back."

I nodded and tasted my drink. She had made it too strong, but it was still good. She disappeared into her bedroom and closed the door behind her. I took another sip of my drink and got up and walked around the room, studying the decorations. There were framed photos of Heidi in her lavish stage costumes, others deliberately posed, provocative bikini scenes taken against white sand and palm tree backgrounds. Some were ornaments that could have been taken for the ruins of Pompeii. The oil paintings were original and unique, all with a carefully guarded sexual motif. The pieces that were obviously foreign were rare and expensive, half of them reflecting the phallic theme, but the other half a little out of place since they were the result of good and expensive taste. Too bad there weren't more of them. I finished my drink and put the glass back on the bar.

I started back to the couch when Heidi said, "Sorry I took so long. I had to freshen up."

When I turned around I felt my mouth go dry and the muscles tightened across my shoulders. It was Heidi, all right, but the curtain had gone up and it was another Heidi altogether. The fever in her eyes had turned into a deep sultry azure. The smile was real, tantalizing, and when she walked toward me the sway was there, the slow, female gesticulations with the hips and thighs that could make them all so damn sure of themselves because they knew what it could do to a man. She had rearranged the housecoat so that the lapels were thrown open to the shoulders, the translucent fabric passing over breasts only half covered, to the belt at her waist. Her eyes held mine, letting me take her all in, then she stopped in a deliberate pose and the rest of the housecoat parted so that I could see all of her at once. Luscious, firm, silken, with the lightest of tans that offset hair that was tousled and ash-blonde, *and not tousled and not ash-blonde*.

The tableau was only momentary before she came to me and took my hand. This time hers wasn't shaking at all. I turned her around, put my fingers under the chin and tilted her head up to me. Very slowly, her tongue licked her lips, making them glisten softly, her eyes intense and sleepy looking. But I didn't kiss her. I let my fingertips run under her sleeves, caressing her skin gently, then I led her to the couch and eased her down. She quivered gently and smiled, squirming into the soft cushions, her eyes still sleepy and hungry.

"I'll be right back," I said and she nodded dreamily.

I went into the bedroom and it only took me two minutes to find the compact and another one to locate the catch that let the back of it drop open. It was made to hold another type of powdered cosmetic, and what was there was a powder, all right, but it wasn't cosmetic. The syringe was in a velvet case in her large jewel box. I took them both back to the living room and walked to the couch.

Heidi was lying there waiting. She had opened the belt and

thrown the housecoat wide open. One hand half cupped a breast and her thighs were parted in invitation. Her eyes were closed but the one in the center of her belly was watching me avidly.

I said, "Heidi," her eyes came open and she smiled. "You're a junkie."

Then her eyes went wide and the smile stopped.

"No wonder you needed that compact so badly, kid. Who cut off your supply?"

No vibrancy in her voice now at all. Nothing but sheer childish fear, weak and hesitant. "Mike . . ."

"You're a great actress, kid. You faked it nicely, but then, you didn't have much of a choice. A real loud beef about the loss might have brought in a smart insurance investigator who would have found your stash, or a trip to the police lost-and-found meant taking a chance talking to a wised-up cop who spotted your symptoms and got the picture right away."

"Please, Mike . . ."

"You're lucky, doll." I tossed the compact down on the table. "It's your problem, not mine, and I'm not making it mine. I could dump this stuff but you'd only find another supplier. I could turn you in but some sweet judge would only turn you out again, especially if it were your first rap. The resulting publicity could kill you altogether or could make you bigger than ever. That's happened too. All I want to tell you is that you're a jerk. The complete clown. A raggedy-ass damn fool idiot and right now you're able to know what I'm talking about. You're probably not on too bad, but you're hooked and you're scared to bust it. All you can do is go downhill and lose everything you ever worked for and pretty soon you'll be working even harder peddling your behind ten times a day for enough to buy a jolt. You look great lying there right now and if you were for real I'd join the fun and games and come away with a great memory, but you're not for real any more and I wouldn't waste my time at it. So give it a big thought, baby, if you're capable of it. Think about it every day and do what you please. You can come back to the land of the living or start getting all your papers and photos in order so that when they find your lovely little corpse in the river or on the floor with a deliberate overdose because it all got too much for you, the newshounds will be able to give you a nice, lurid send-off in the obit columns."

She had never stopped watching me. Those azure eyes were wide open, unconsciously wet. One hand pulled the front of the housecoat across the slow heave of her stomach and her breasts moved with a quick intake of breath.

I got my hat from the table beside the door and got the hell out of there. I walked eight blocks toward my apartment before I bothered to flag down a cab. When I got home I showered, had another drink and flopped down on the bed, looking at nothing on the ceiling.

Stupid, idiotic broad. But I was just as sore at myself. Something about the whole deal should have told me something and I was too aggravated to put it in its right place.

chapter five

BY NOONTIME I had reduced Lippy's haul to two undelivered wallets. The owner of the rather shabby job lived and worked in Queens and made an appointment to meet me at my office on Saturday to pick it up. The other belonged to William Dorn who was about to donate to the P.A.L. like the others. A maid gave me his office number and when I called him he was appreciative and invited me to lunch at The Chimes, a sedate and expensive restaurant on East Fifty-seventh Street. My taste didn't run to exotic French cuisine, but the change could be different and I made a one o'clock date to see him there. I tried another call to the office and Velda's apartment but she was at neither place so I rang Eddie Dandy and he was glad to take a beer break with me for a half hour.

I had to laugh when I saw him. It wasn't the hell he had caught from the network for making waves or the embarrassment of sweating out the snide remarks from the rest of the staff. It was the agony of having to sit on a story he knew was hot and not being able to release it.

He downed a tall schooner of lager without stopping, belched once and called for another. "Only one thing got me, buddy. Suppose somebody else pieces it together the same way I did."

"Quit worrying. By now they have it all nicely organized with everybody briefed properly and they'll be able to con the best cynic into taking their word for it. Right now it's a dead issue."

"Not to a couple of guys I know. They couldn't picture me doing an about-face like that. You catch my retraction?"

"Missed it."

"That's the trouble with color TV. They could see the egg all over my face in bright yellow against screaming red. It wasn't easy, pal. I hope when I make the next announcement I'm not a pasty white. If they don't get that stuff this whole country could be wiped out. You know anything about the germ warfare developments?"

"Just what I read in the papers."

"Well, it isn't pretty and you're not going to be reading much about it at all. That stuff is as top secret as it can get. Right now they're flooding us with news stories from every direction you can think of just to keep the public's mind off my big squeal. It may work and it may not. We've had the switchboard lit up like a star burst since I broke it and have operators working overtime with nice pat explanations. They're even sending form letters out to those who want them. It's rough, boy, rough. What are you up to?"

"Some simple legwork on a simple matter," I said.

"You still on that Sullivan deal?"

I nodded.

"A lost cause, Mike. They pull the cops in to track down Schneider's killers, they schedule a special political parade to cover the vacation wipe-out, the Crime Commission is laying it on heavy and you couldn't bust a cop loose for special detail work for anything. Nope, you won't get any leg up from the cops until this is over."

"I'm not asking for any."

"Okay, you know the story. You're making a federal case out of a simple murder and robbery. Why?"

"Beats me," I told him. "Maybe because I believed something nobody else believed."

"Hell, people will believe anything. Look what happened with me."

"So waste time. So feel lousy. What's left to do?"

"I told him about the wallets and my date with Dorn. I didn't mention Heidi Anders at all.

"William Dorn?" he asked.

"Know him?"

"Park Avenue offices?"

"That's the one."

"Sure, he's chairman of the board of Anco Electronics, his

March Chemical Company engineered that new oil refining process the industry has turned to and now he's gone heavy in mining. You're traveling in fancy company, kiddo. I never thought I'd see the day. Ole Mike Hammer, denizen of the side streets, partying with café society. Better not let it get to be a habit."

I looked at my watch. "Well, if it does, it starts now." I finished my beer, flipped Eddie for the drinks, won the toss and told him so long. At one o'clock on the nose I walked into The Chimes, got a disapproving stare from the maître d' until I asked for Mr. Dorn's table, then his professional subservient attitude returned with a fawning nod and he bowed me to a table in a hand-carved, oak-paneled booth on the dais-like section of the main room that was obviously reserved for only the most select clientele.

Most actors would like to age into a man like William Dorn. A few have, but only a few. He was tall and lean with a tanned, rugged face and intelligent eyes under a thick shock of wavy hair streaked with gray. When I took his hand he had a strong, sure grip and I knew he wasn't as lean as he looked. Suddenly I felt like a slob. He was one of those guys who could look good in anything and I knew why the amused woman, with the hair so raven black it was darker than the shadows she sat in, could be so much at ease with him.

"Mr. Hammer," he said in a pleasantly deep voice, "William Dorn, and may I present Miss Renée Talmage."

She had held out her hand and I took it gently. "A pleasure," I said.

"Very nice to see you, Mr. Hammer." Her smile broke around a set of even gleaming white teeth and she added, "Please sit down."

"Miss Talmage is head of accounting at Anco. Have you heard of us?"

"Just this afternoon."

"Don't let it bother you, Mr. Hammer. Our business is not one that goes in heavily for publicity and promotion. Care for a drink before lunch?"

"Rye and ginger'll do," I said.

The waiter hovering behind me took the order and disappeared. I pulled Dorn's wallet from my pocket and handed it to him. He took it, flipped it open and scanned his credit cards and held it up to show Renée Talmage. "Now that is efficient police work. Imagine."

"Strictly accidental, Mr. Dorn." I pushed a receipt and my pen across to him. "Mind signing for it?"

"Not at all." He scrawled a signature in the proper place and I folded the receipt back into my pocket.

He said, "In a way, it's a shame to put you to all the trouble. I've already canceled the credit cards, but my driver's license and club cards are really the valuable items."

"Sorry you didn't get your money back too. It rarely happens, though, so feel lucky you even got anything."

"Yes, I do. Very. There's a matter of a reward that I mentioned."

"A check to the Police Athletic League will do nicely, Mr. Dorn."

For the first time Renée Talmage leaned out of the shadows. She was even lovelier than I had taken her to be. I figured her age in the early thirties when a woman was at her best, but it was almost impossible to pin it down accurately. "Mr. Hammer . . . your name is very familiar."

I had to give her a silly grin. "Yeah, I know."

"Are you . . ."

I didn't let her go any further. "Yeah, I'm the one," I said.

Dorn let out a little laugh and gave us both a quizzical look. "Now what is this all about? Trust Renée here to come up with something odd about even the most complete stranger."

"What she means, Mr. Dorn, is that I'm not with the police department at all. I'm a licensed private investigator who gets into enough trouble to make enough headlines to be recognized on occasions, which, funny enough, is good for business but hell on the hide occasionally. It was a guy I once knew who had your wallet among others. I located them and I'm paying my last respects by getting them back where they came from."

Dorn recognized the seriousness in my voice and nodded. "I understand. Quite long ago . . . I had to do something similar. And this person you knew?"

"Dead now."

The drinks came then and we raised our glasses to each other, two Manhattans against a highball, tasted them and nodded our satisfaction and put them down. Renée Talmage was still looking at me and Dorn gave me another chuckle. "I'm afraid you're in for it now. My bloodthirsty co-worker here is an avid follower of mysteries in literature and films. She'll press you for every detail if you let her." He reached over and laid his hand on her arm. "Please, dear. The man was a friend of Mr. Hammer."

"It doesn't matter," I said. "I have more than one friend with an illegal pastime. Too bad it caught up with him. So far it's tabbed as murder that came out of an attempted robbery."

"Attempted?" Renée Talmage leaned forward, the interest plain on her face.

"They never got what they went after. The money was all banked, squirreled away in a neighborhood account."

"But the wallets . . ."

"Discarded," I told her. "With a guy like him it would be too chancy to risk using credit cards. He just wasn't the type to own one."

"And that's your story," Dorn said to her. "I think we can talk about more pleasant things while we eat."

"Spoilsport," she grimaced. "At last I have a chance to talk to a real private cop and you ruin it." She looked at me, eyes twinkling. "Look out, Mr. Hammer, I may deliberately cultivate you, regardless."

"Then start by calling me Mike. This Mr. Hammer routine gives me the squirms."

Her laugh was rich and warm. "I was hoping you'd ask. So then, I am Renée, but this is William."

Dorn looked at me sheepishly. "Unfortunately, I never acquired a nickname. Oh, I tried, but I guess I'm just the William type. Odd, don't you think?"

"I don't know. Look at the trouble our last Vice President had. He had to settle for initials. At least you look like the *mister* belongs there."

We ordered then, something in French that turned out to be better than I expected, and between courses Dorn drifted into his business. He had started out during the war years assembling radar components under military contract, developed a few patentable ideas and went on from there. He admitted freely that World War II, Korea and the Vietnam thing made him wealthy, but didn't hesitate to state that the civilian applications of his products were of far more benefit than could be accrued by the military. Hell, I didn't disagree with him. You make it whenever and however you can. Separate ethics from business and you get a big fat nothing.

Apparently Renée Talmage had been with him for ten years or so and was a pretty valuable asset to his business. Several times she came up with items of interest that belonged more in a man's world than a woman's. Dorn saw my look of surprise and said, "Don't mind the brainy one, Mike. She does that to me sometimes . . . the big answers from those pretty lips. I pay her handsomely for her insight and she hasn't been wrong yet. My only concern is that she might leave me and go in business for herself. That would be the end of my enterprises."

"I can imagine. I got one like that myself," I said.

At two thirty I told them I had to split, waited while Dorn signed the tab and walked to the street with them. Someplace the sun had disappeared into the haze and a bank of heavy, low clouds was beginning to roll in again. I offered to drop them off, but Dorn said they were going to walk back and gave me another firm handshake.

When Renée held out her fingers to me her eyes had that sparkle in them again and she said, "I really *am* going to cultivate you, Mike. I'm going to get you alone for lunch and make you tell me everything about yourself."

"That won't be hard," I said.

Dorn had turned away to say hello to a foursome that followed us out and never heard her soft, impish answer. "It will be, Mike."

I got back to the office and picked up the mail that had been shoved through the slot in the door and tossed it on Velda's desk. For five minutes I prowled around, wondering why the hell she didn't call, then went back to the mail again. There were bills, four checks, a couple of circulars and something I damned near missed, a yellow envelope from the messenger service we sometimes used. I ripped it open and dumped out the folded sheet inside.

The handwriting was hers, all right. All it said was *"Call Sammy Brent about theater tickets. Will call office tonight."* The envelope was dated one fifteen, delivered from the Forty-fifth Street messenger service office. Whatever she was getting at was beyond me. Sammy Brent ran a tiny ticket office dealing mainly in off-Broadway productions and dinner theaters in the New York-New Jersey-Connecticut area.

The Yellow Pages listed his agency and I dialed the number, getting a heavy, Lower East Side accent in an impatient hello twice. I said, "Sammy?"

"Sure, who else? You think I can afford help here?"

"Mike Hammer, buddy."

"Hey, Mike, whattaya know?"

"Velda said I should call you about theater tickets. What the hell's going on?"

"Yeah, yeah. That crazy broad of yours shows up here like some Times Square floozie on the loose and I didn't even know her. Man, what legs! She's got her dress up to . . . good thing the old lady wasn't around. Man, she's got a top and bottom you can't . . ."

"What's with the tickets?"

"Oh." His voice suddenly went quiet. "Well, she was asking about Lippy Sullivan. Real sorry about that, Mike."

"I know."

"Good guy, him. You know, he was hustlin' for me."

"What?"

"He picked up extra change scalping tickets. Not for the big shows, but like the regular ones I handle. Conventions come in, those guys got a broad and no place to go, he'd meet them in bars and hotels and hustle tickets."

"What!"

"He was a good guy, Mike."

"Look, how'd you pay him?"

"Cash. He'd get a percent of the price over the going rate. Like maybe a buck or two. It was a good deal. We was both satisfied. You know, he was a good talker. He could make friends real easy. That's why he did pretty good at it. No fortune, but he picked up walking-around money." When I didn't answer him he said, "It was okay, wasn't it, Mike? Like I ain't the only one who . . ."

"It was okay, Sammy. Thanks."

And it was starting to spell out a brand-new story.

I searched my memory for the return address that had been on the envelope in Lippy's garbage, finally remembered it as being simply NEW USED FURNITURE on Eighth Avenue and dug the number out of the directory.

Yes, the clerk remembered Lippy buying a couch. It wasn't often they sold a new one in that neighborhood. He had picked it out on a Saturday afternoon just a couple of weeks before he died and paid for it in cash with small bills. No, he didn't say why he wanted it. But permanent roomers in the area often changed furniture. The landlords wouldn't and what transients usually rented with their meager earnings were hardly worth using. I thanked the clerk and hung up.

When I looked down the .45 was in my hand, the butt a familiar thing against my palm. It was black and oily with walnut grips, an old friend who had been down the road with me a long time.

I slid it back in the holster and walked to the window so I could look out at the big city of fun. The clouds were rolling around the edges, melting into each other, bringing a premature darkness down around the towering columns of brick and steel. It's a big place, New York. Millions of people who run down holes in the ground like moles, or climb up the sides of cliffs to their own little caves. Most were just people. Just plain people.

And then there were the others, the killers. There was one out there now and that one belonged all to me.

Okay, Lippy, the pattern's showing its weave now. Sammy nailed it down without knowing it. You worked your tail off for an honest buck but you were just too damn friendly. Who did you meet, Lippy? What dip hustling the theater district did you pick up to move in with you? Sure, I could understand it. Dames were out of your line. It was strictly friends and how many did you have? You were glad to have somebody get close to you, to yak with and drink with. You found a friend, Lippy, until you found out he wasn't honest like you were. You latched onto a lousy cheap crook. What happened, pal? Maybe you located his cache and stuck it where he couldn't get to it, then dumped those wallets in the garbage. So he came back and tried to take it from you. No, Lippy, there wasn't any reason at all for it, was there? You would have shared your pad, your income, your beer . . . anything to keep him straight and your friend that you could believe in and trust. No reason for him to kill you at all. Only I have a reason, friend, and my reason is bigger than the one you didn't have.

All I had to do was find the right pickpocket.

So I sat there and ran it over in my mind until I could see it happen. It shouldn't be too much of a job now I knew in which direction to take off. There was only that little nagging thought that something was out of focus. Something I should see clearly. It wasn't that complicated at all.

Outside, the darkness had sucked the daylight out of the city and I sat there watching it fight back with bravely lit windows in empty offices and the weaving beams of headlights from the street traffic. In a little while the flow would start from the restaurants to the theaters and it would be the working hour for the one I wanted. If he was there.

Meyer Solomon was a bailbondsman who owed me a favor and he was glad to pay it back. I asked him to find out if anybody had been booked on a pickpocket charge within the last two days and he told me he'd check it out right away. So I stayed by the phone for another forty minutes until it finally jangled and I picked it up.

"Mike? Meyer here."

"Let's have it."

"Got six of 'em. Four were bums working the subway on sleepers and the other two are pros. You looking to hire one of 'em?"

"Not quite. Who are the pros?"

"Remember Coo-Coo Weist?"

"Damn, Meyer, he must be eighty years old."

"Still working, though. Made a mistake when he tried it on an off-duty detective."

"Who else?"

"A kid named Johnny Baines. A Philly punk who came here about three years ago. Good nimble fingers on that guy. The last time he was busted he was carrying over ten grand. This time he only had a couple hundred on him but it wasn't his fault."

"Why not?"

Meyer let out a sour laugh. "Because he was only three hours out of the clink where he spent ninety days on a D and D rap. He never really had a chance to get operating right. You going bail for somebody, Mike?"

"Not this time, Meyer. Thanks."

"Anytime, Mike."

I hung up and went back to the window again.

He was still out there somewhere.

I called downstairs, had a sandwich, coffee and the evening papers sent up. The hunt was getting heavier for Schneider's killers and the reporters were hitting every detail with relish. Another time it would have been funny, because contract killers who blasted one of their own kind seldom got that kind of attention. Right now they'd be running scared, not only from the cops, but from the guy who gave them the job. Their business days were over. Two National Guard units were being called out on a security maneuver, detailed upstate. The same thing was happening in five other states. In view of the tense international situation the military deemed it smart policy to stay prepared. It made for lots of space, dozens of pictures and if somebody was lucky they might come up with something. Somehow I didn't feel very excited about sitting on the edge of annihilation.

At twelve fifteen the phone went off beside my ear and I rolled off the old leather couch and grabbed it. My voice still sounded husky from being asleep and I said, "Yeah?"

"Mike?" Her voice sounded guarded.

"Where the hell have you been, Velda?"

"Shut up and listen. I rented one of those fleabag apartments across the street from Lippy's rooming house, downstairs in the front. If you called Sammy Brent then you have it spotted . . . the tickets and all?"

"Loud and clear. Lippy had somebody staying with him."

"That's what it looks like, but he was never seen going in or out and nobody seems to know a thing about it. Apparently he

was a pretty cagy character to get away with that, but I know
how he did it. In this neighborhood at the right hours he wouldn't
be noticed at all."

"All right kid, get with it."

"Somebody's in Lippy's old room right now. I spotted the beam
of a pencil flash under the window shade."

"Damn!"

"I can move in . . ."

"You stay put, you hear? I'll be there in ten minutes."

"That can be too late."

"Let it. Just watch for me. I'll get off at the corner and walk
on up. Cover the outside and keep your ass down."

I grabbed an extra clip for the .45 out of the desk drawer,
slammed the door shut behind me and used the stairs instead of
waiting for the elevator. A cab was ahead of me, waiting for a
red light at the corner and I reached it as the signals changed and
told him where to go. When the driver saw the five I threw on
the seat beside him he made it across town and south to the
corner I wanted in exactly six minutes and didn't bother to stick
around to see what it was all about.

It was an old block, a hangover from a century of an orgy of
progress, a four-storied chasm with feeble yellow eyes to show that
there still was a pulse beat somewhere behind the crumbling
brownstone facades. Halfway down the street a handful of kids
were playing craps under an overhead light and on the other side
a pair of drifters were shuffling toward Ninth. It wasn't the kind
of street you bothered to sit around and watch at night. It was
one you wanted to get away from.

I flashed a quick look at the rooftops and the areaways under
the stoops when I reached Lippy's old place, found nothing and
spotted Velda in the doorway across the street. I gave her the
"wait and see" signal, then took the sandstone steps two at a
time, the .45 in my hand.

A 25-watt bulb hung from a dropcord in the ceiling of the
vestibule and I reached up and unscrewed it, making sure I had
my distance and direction to the right door clear in my mind.
The darkness would have been complete except for the pale glow
that seeped out from under the super's door, but it was enough.
His TV was on loud enough to cover any sound my feet might
make and I went past his apartment to Lippy's and tried the
knob.

The door was locked.

I took one step back, planted myself and thumbed the hammer

back on the rod. Then I took a running hop, smashed the door open with my foot and went rolling inside taking furniture with me that was briefly outlined in the white blast of a gunshot that sent a slug ripping into the floor beside my head.

My hand tightened on the butt of the .45 and blew the darkness apart while I was skittering in a different direction, the wild thunder of the shot echoing around the room. Glass crashed from the far end and a chair went over, then running legs hit me when I was halfway up, fell and I had my hands on his neck, wrenched him back and banged two fast rights into his ear and heard him let out a choked yell. Whoever he was, he was big and strong and wrenched out of my hands, his arms flailing. I swung with the gun, felt the sight rip into flesh and skull bone. It was almost enough and I would have had him the next time around, but the beam of a pencil flash hit me in the face and there was a dull, clicking sound against the top of my head and all the strength went out of me in one full gush.

A faraway voice said almost indistinctly, "Get up so I can kill him!" But then there were two popping sounds, a muffled curse, and I lay there in the dreary state of semiconsciousness knowing something was happening without knowing or caring what until a hazy dawn of artificial light made everything finally come into misty focus that solidified into specific little objects I could recognize.

Velda said, "You stupid jerk."

"Don't be redundant," I told her. "Where are they?"

"Out. Gone. The back window was open for a secondary exit and they used it. If I hadn't fired coming into the building you would have been dead by now."

The yelling and screaming of the fun watchers on the street were coming closer and a siren was whining to a stop in front of the house. I pushed myself to a sitting position, saw the .45 on the floor and reached for it. I thumbed out the clip, ejected the live slug in the breech, caught it and slid it back into the clip, then reloaded the piece and stuck it back in the holster. "You see them?" I asked.

"No."

I took a quick look around the room before they all came in. The place was a shambles. Even the paper had been torn off the walls. "Somebody else figured it out too," I said.

"What were they after, Mike?"

"Something pretty easily hidden," I told her.

chapter six

PAT CAME IN while they were taking my statement, listened impassively as I detailed the events at Lippy's place and when I signed the sheets, walked over and threw a leg over the edge of the desk. "You can't keep your nose clean, can you?"

"You ought to be happy about extra diversions from what I hear," I said.

"Not your kind." Pat glanced sidewise at Velda. "Why didn't you call for a squad car?"

Velda threw him an amused smile. "I wanted to be subtle about it. Besides, I wouldn't want to get fired."

I said, "Why the beef, Pat? We interrupted a simple break-in and attempted robbery."

"Like hell you did."

"Nothing illegal about it. Any citizen could pull it off."

"You managed to goof," he reminded me. "They got away."

"They didn't get what they were after."

"What *were* they after, Mike?"

I gave a meaningless shrug.

Pat picked up a pencil and twirled it in his fingers. Let's have it, Mike," he said softly.

"Lippy was right, Pat. He got killed for no reason at all. He was a hardworking slob who made friends with some dip working the area and took him into the rooming house with him. That's the one they were after."

Pat's eyes half closed, watching me closely. "Something was in one of those wallets . . ."

"Maybe not," I said. "Apparently the guy was with Lippy a few weeks before Lippy got onto him and booted him out. That bunch of wallets was probably just his last day's take. You know who they all belonged to."

"And one guy was Woody Ballinger."

"Yeah, I know."

"Keep talking," Pat said.

"How many good pickpockets do you know who never took a fall?"

"They all do sooner or later."

"None of the prints you picked up from the apartment got any action, did they?"

Pat's lips twisted in a grin. "You're guessing, but you're right.

678

The set we sent to Washington turned out negative. No record of them anywhere, not even military."

"That gives us one lead then," I said. "Most people stay within their own age groups, so he was a 4-F in his late forties."

"Great," Pat said.

"And without a record, maybe he wasn't a regular practicing dip at all. Somebody could have been after him for what he did before he took up the profession."

"That still leaves us with nothing."

"Oh, we have something, all right," I said.

"Like what?" Pat asked me.

"Like what they didn't get yet. They'll keep looking."

The other two cops and the steno collected their papers, nodded to Pat and left the three of us alone in the room. Pat swung off the desk in that lazy way he had and stared out the window. Finally he said, "We haven't got time to throw any manpower into this right now." There was something tight in his voice. I felt Velda's eyes on me, but didn't react.

"I know."

"You be damn careful, Mike. My neck's out now too."

"No sweat." I lit a cigarette and tossed the match in the wastebasket. "Any progress yet?"

He didn't look at me. "No."

"The lid on pretty tight?"

"Nothing will ever be tighter." He took a deep breath and turned around. In the backlight from the window his face looked drawn. "If you turn up anything, keep in touch. We still have a primary job to do."

"Sure, Pat."

I picked up my hat and reached for Velda's arm. I knew the question was on her lips, but she said nothing except for a so long to Pat. When we got down on the street to hunt up a cab she asked evenly, "What was that all about?"

It was a nice night for New York. The wind had cleaned the smog out of the skies and you could see the stars. Kids walked by holding hands, traffic was idling along and behind the lighted windows families would be watching the late news. Only nobody was telling them that the biggest news of all they wouldn't want to hear. They were all living in wonderful ignorance, not knowing that they might be living their last night. For one second I wished I was in the same boat as they were.

I took Velda's hand and started across the street to intercept a cab going north. "Just some departmental business," I said. "Nothing important."

But she knew I was lying. There was a sadness in the small smile she gave me and her hand was flaccid in mine. Keeping details from Velda wasn't something I was used to doing. Not too long ago she had taken a pair of killers off my back without a second's hesitation. Now she was thinking that I couldn't trust her.

I said, "Later, kitten. Believe me, I have a damn good reason."

Her hand snuggled back into mine again and I knew it was all right. "What do you want me to do now?" Velda asked.

"Back on the trail. I want that dip. He could still be in the area."

"Even if he knew somebody was out to kill him?"

"There's no better place to hide than right here in the city. If he's any kind of a pro he's been working. If he's moved in on somebody else's turf they'll be the first to dump him. So make your contacts and buy what you have to. Just lay off any hard action. I'll take care of that end."

"How do we clear any messages?"

"Let's use the office. I'll keep the tape recorder on and we can bleep in any cross information." Both of us carried electronic units that could activate the tape in either direction so it wasn't necessary to have someone in the office all the time.

"Where are you going to be, Mike?"

"Seeing what an old enemy is up to."

"Woody Ballinger?"

"Uh-huh."

"He can't afford to lose any more," Velda said.

"Neither can I, sugar," I said.

"What brings you back to him again?"

All I could think of was Heidi Anders' compact. What she had in it put her life on the line. I said, "Somebody's not after money. Woody used to keep all his business in his head. Maybe he put some of it in his wallet this time. A smart dip could have spotted it and tried a little blackmail."

But first I had to be sure.

They wouldn't talk to the cops. To a uniform or a badge they were deaf, dumb and blind, but I wasn't department material and they could read it in my face. I was one of them, living on the perimeter of normalcy and the ax I was grinding was a personal one because Lippy had been my friend and they had tried to knock me off too.

The redheaded whore called Skippy who had her crib across the back court from Lippy had seen them come out the window, two guys in dark suits she could tell didn't come from the neighborhood. They had jumped the fence and gone through the alley between her place and the dry cleaner's. No, she didn't see their faces, but the light hit one and she knew he was partially bald, but not too old because he could run too fast. She took the twenty I gave her since the excitement scared off the john she had in the pad and it was too late to turn another trick.

Old lady Gostovitch had seen them go right past her when she was coming in from her nightly bash at the gin mill, but her eyes were bad and she was too bagged to make their faces. All she could tell me was that they were in dark suits, climbed into a car and drove away. When she crunched the bill I handed her in her fist she added one more thing.

Between wheezes she said, "One wore them heel things."

"What heel things?"

"Clickers."

"Clickers?"

"Clickers. Like kids got, y'know?"

"No, I don't."

"Sheee-it, boy. They drag 'em over the floor and scratch everything up. Like dancers got on their shoes, y'know?"

"Metal taps?"

"So I call 'em clickers. Only on his heels. Maybe I don't see so good no more, but I hear. Boy, I hear everything. I even hear the cat pissin'. Thanks for the scratch." She looked down at the bill in her hand. "How much is it?"

"Ten bucks."

"Maybe I'll buy glasses." She looked up and gave me a gummy smile.

I said, "How many?"

"Enough to get slopped. Makes me feel young again, y'know?" She spit on the sidewalk and hunched her shabby coat around her shoulders, her eyes peering at me. "Sure, *you* know. Boy like you knows too damn much."

When she had shuffled off I started toward the corner, then stopped midblock to watch a convoy of Army trucks rumble by, escorted by a pair of prowl cars with their flashers on, each giving a low growl of their sirens at the intersections as they went through the red lights. There were four jeeps and thirty-eight trucks, each filled with suddenly activated and annoyed-looking National Guardsmen. It hadn't been since the summer encampments that the city had seen one of these processions. I was wondering what excuse they were going to give the public if the public bothered to ask.

Overhead a cool northeast wind suddenly whistled through the TV antennaes on the rooftops and swirled down into the street, picking up dust and papers along the curbs and skittering them along the sidewalks. *Hell,* I thought, *it's going to rain again. Maybe it's better that way. People don't like to come out in the rain and if they don't they can't ask questions.*

Someplace Velda was roaming around the area doing the same thing I was doing only from a different direction and she could do it just as fast. And right now time was our enemy.

I shoved the bar door open and inched past the uglies with their serapes, the virgin-hair muttonchops and shoulder-length curls. They were the boys. The girls weren't any better. They smelled better, except the smell was artificial and I wondered if it were to enhance the little they had or cover up what they lacked. One idiot almost started to lip me until I squeezed his arm a little bit, then he whited out and let me go by with a sick grin his old man should have seen if he had chopped him in the mouth ten years ago when there was still hope for him.

Velda had called to say she had canvassed the neighborhood with no results so she was going back into the barnacle she had rented and keep a watch on Lippy's old apartment.

The other call was from Renée Talmage. "Mr. Tape Recorder," she said, "please tell Mr. Hammer that I am going to be waiting ever so impatiently for him in Dewey Wong's restaurant on Fifty-eighth Street, snuggled against the wall close to the window where all those lovely men will know I'm waiting for someone and perhaps not try to pick me up. And Mr. Tape Recorder, tell him that Dewey says he will stay open very late just to make sure Mr. Hammer gets here."

I hung up and looked at my watch. It was one twenty-five. Outside the phone booth the uglies were making time with the idiots. In New York, the uglies are the long-haired idiot guys. The idiots are the short-haired ugly girls. It isn't easy to tell one from the other. One ugly didn't realize it, but he was kissing another ugly. In a way he was lucky. The idiot he was with was even uglier.

So I said the hell with it and grabbed a cab up to Dewey Wong's and got around the corner of the bar, sat down next to her and told beautiful Janie who was filling in for her old man behind the bar to bring me a rye and ginger.

"Pretty isn't she?" Renée asked.

"A mouth waiting to be kissed," I said.

"Dewey seems pretty capable."

"Ever since he's been colonialized," I told her.

"Colonialize me," Renée said. A little half laugh played around her mouth and her eyes were full of sparkles.

"Now?"

She lifted her glass in a challenge, the big black pupils inside all those gold flecks watching me closely. Carelessly, she said, "Why not?"

I let my hand run up the bare leg that was crossed over the other one until my fingers had the top of her bikini pants under their tips and said, "Ready?"

Her glass went back to the bar top very slowly, every movement deliberate and slow to make sure nobody was watching. Even the smile was unsure of itself. "You're crazy, Mike."

"I could have told you that."

"Take your hand out of my pants."

"I'm not done yet," I said. I took a drink of my highball. Janie grinned and turned away to serve another customer. At least she knew what was happening.

Almost pathetically, Renée said, "Please?"

"You wanted to be colonialized," I told her.

"But not in front of all these people."

"Tough," I said. She felt my fingers curling around that silly little hem they build into bikini pants. I wondered what color they were.

"I know a better place to find out," Renée told me.

I'm an old soldier. I grew up watching Georgia Sothern, Gypsy Rose Lee, Ann Corio and the rest on the stage of the old Apollo and Eltinge theaters and got my lessons in basic female anatomy from the best of them. There's never been a shape or size I couldn't slam into one category or another no matter what part I was looking at and get clinical about it at the same time. Women are women. The female counterpart. They're supposed to be something special, intelligent, loving, pneumatic, sexy as hell, incredibly beautiful, with that little thing they're instinctively supposed to do that can make a man turn inside out. Hardly any fit the pattern. Oh, I knew some.

Now I knew another.

She just stood there in the middle of the room and let the

funny little smile do the teasing while she unzipped slowly and let the dress fall in a heap around her feet.

"Better?" Renée asked.

I nodded. But casually, because she still hadn't caught up to Georgia Sothern. That one could *really* take off her clothes. She used to do it to "Hold that Tiger," but that music would sound silly these days. "You're doing fine," I told her.

"Can I have a drink?"

I tasted my own highball and loosened my tie. "If that's what you need to uninhibit yourself, baby, the bar's right behind you."

She lifted herself on tiptoe, nothing on but a flesh-colored bra and bikini pants with other colors dominating the sheer mesh, and grinned at me like she was running all the plays. "Like?"

"I like," I said.

She hooked her thumb in the top of those bikini pants and pulled them down a bare inch. A little tumble of dark hair spilled out over the top. "Like?" Her voice was provocatively inquisitive.

"I like," I said again.

She took off her bra. She spilled out there too, full and high, heavy breasted with round, square-tipped, demanding nipples emerging from their even darker cores.

"Still like?" she asked. I watched her eyes drift down me, all stretched out on my own damn couch. For a second she was puzzled.

I said, "I'm a leg man, kid."

Then she grinned again and took off those flesh-colored bikini pants.

Naked women are pretty. Damn, but they're pretty. Any size, any shape you look, and when they're built like all those pinups we used to have on the inside of locker doors and the kind they plaster up in garages to keep your mind off the repair bills, they can con you into anything.

And Renée knew what I was thinking. "For real?" she asked.

"You must be one hell of a business asset," I said.

"William never saw me like this."

"Why not?"

She twirled around, picked the drinks off the bar and handed me another one. "He never put his hands inside my pants," she said.

"Stop being vulgar," I told her.

"Ho . . . yeah. Keep talking, fingers."

"I barely touched you."

"Except in the right spot," Renée said.

"Sorry about that."

"Yes, you are. Little scarred feathers extending from your wrist, delicate, woman-killing tentacles that touch and excite. Look at me, totally bare and throwing it at you, and you lying there with a drink in your hand and all you have off is your top collar button because your tie is too tight."

"Like?" I said.

"Like, you dumbhead," Renée smiled. "I often wondered what I could do to a nasty slob like you." She took a big sip of her drink, put it back on the bar and walked toward me, the fingers of her hand spread out over the delicious swell of those sleek, wide hips.

"I think you're impotent," she said.

The laugh stayed behind my lips. I put my drink down and looked at her, big and naked and lovely, all nice high titties and a dark curly snatch, her smile almost a sneer, and I said very softly, *"Oh, brother."*

"What?"

"In the Army we said you were ready to be rued, screwed, blued and tattooed."

"You're not doing anything."

"I'm wondering why I should."

"Perhaps you can't."

As carefully as I could I slid off the couch and shrugged my coat off. I picked the .45 out of the shoulder holster and laid the leather on the floor. Then I picked off my tie, unbuttoned my shirt and flicked the belt out of its restraints. My pants were only a hindrance. I let them go around my feet and kicked them aside.

"So you're not impotent," she said after a long, hungry glance.

I sat down on the couch again and picked up my drink. All I had was ice left. "I could have told you that."

"Talking isn't proving."

"Sugar," I told her, "you're forgetting something. There's nothing I have to prove. I get what I want whenever I want it. I can name the time, place and position. Twenty years ago I would have hosed a snake if somebody held it down for me, but now I'm selective. It's still a man's world, baby, but you have to be a man to live in it. Then again, I'm still curious."

Her forehead wrinkled inquisitively. "Curious? About what? There's nothing more to show you unless I turn inside out."

"Don't do that. I just had the rug cleaned." I grinned at her.

Then she laughed, picked up her drink and sat down in my Naugahyde recliner like she was at a presidential reception. "Curious," she said again. Her eyes went up and down me twice, her smile getting broader. "We make a great couple. Naked six feet apart. What can be more curious than that?"

I got up, mixed another drink and went back to the couch again. "Why you came on so strong. This is our second time out, kid. Two hellos and you're ready to go fifteen rounds in the hay. You're class, big business and big money with enough style to snag any guy you want . . ." I held up my hand to cut off her interruption ". . . and suddenly you get the hots for a lousy beat-up old soldier in the shadow police business."

Renée's teeth glistened in her smile and she raised her glass in a mock toast to me. "Crude, but very astute, Mike. But I told you I was going to cultivate you, didn't I?"

I nodded.

"And I told you it would be hard, didn't I?"

I grinned back and adjusted my position. There were times when a guy could be quite uncomfortable.

"So the answer should be obvious," she said. "I enjoy my position, I enjoy my wealth, I take pleasure from my social obligations, but oh, they're so *damned* dull." She nodded toward the window. "There aren't any challenges left out there. I operate on a man's level, but they won't let me get in there and swing. Everybody's so hellishly condescending and polite, patting my head because I did my homework and came up with the right answers. Then when nobody's looking they try to pat my fanny and always seem to miss. Sometimes I wish one of them would get me alone in the stockroom or something."

"Attagirl, tiger," I said.

"Stop laughing. It's serious."

"Why don't you marry William?"

"Because he's already married."

"Oh?"

"To corporate structure," she said. "Commerce is his wife, children and mistress. Women are nothing unless they are an adjunct to the business. We are nurtured, tolerated and exploited according to our abilities to perform."

"Come on, honey, you like the guy."

"He's the biggest challenge of all, but the only game you play without any possible chance of winning."

"That sure pigeonholes me, doesn't it?" I asked her.

Renée tried her drink again, then swirled the ice around in the glass, making it clink musically. "Who can win with you, Mike?"

"Nobody, unless I let them," I said.

"Are you going to let me?"

"No."

"You dirty dog. Why not?"

"Right now you're having too much fun sitting here talking about it. The experience is new and exciting. It's like kicks, doll. It's even better than having a guy roped to stakes in the ground and standing over him with a whip. The only thing that bugs you is that I laid down the ground rules."

"What a bastard you are."

"How come everybody says that to me?"

"Because you are. I can even tell what you're thinking."

I looked at her and waited.

She said, "You're getting kicks out of it, too, sitting there naked and horny, watching me suffer, knowing damn well there's going to be a next time and when that happens it's going to be something incredible."

"You called me, remember?"

"And I'll call you again." She let her teeth show in another brilliant smile. "I don't care if you *are* a bastard. I wish you didn't know so much about women, though. Tell me one thing, Mike . . ."

"What?"

"You could have stopped it all by having a casual drink with me and turning the conversation into more normal avenues. Why didn't you?"

I finished my drink, studied the empty glass a moment then put it on the floor. "It's been a rough few days, sugar. I lost a friend, got shot at, clobbered, interrogated by . . . oh hell. You were a welcome relief, a lift to the old ego. You have to get up to bat before you know if you can hit or not."

"Now you're going to make me get dressed and send me home," Renée said.

I felt a laugh rumble out of my chest. "Roger, doll. So hate me. You'll always wonder what it would have been like."

Her glass went down to the floor too and her laugh had a throaty tinkle to it. "I'll find out. Cultivating you may take longer than I thought. You may turn out to be the biggest challenge of all."

"Not tonight."

"I know. But since you've been such a bastard, will you do something for me?"

"Maybe."

She pushed herself out of the chair slowly, all naked, smooth skin radiating warmth and desire, little pulse beats throbbing erotically in the lush valleys. She reached out, took my hand and encouraged me to my feet until flesh met flesh, insinuating themselves together in a way that only flesh can.

"Kiss me," Renée said. After the briefest pause. *"Hard."*

I climbed out of bed and stood in front of the window watching the thin patter of rain dribble down the dust-caked glass. The morning crowds were at their desks inside their offices and the shoppers hadn't started out yet. Two blocks away a fire siren howled and a hook and ladder flashed through the intersection, an emergency truck right behind it. *Damn games,* I thought. *I lost a night; I started out for Woody Ballinger and almost wound up doing bedroom gymnastics.* I wiped my face with my hand, feeling the stubble of a beard under my fingers, then grinned at my reflection in the window pane. Hell, I needed the break. Even near-sex could be good therapy. "Buddy," I said out loud, "maybe you still got it, maybe you haven't, but either way they think you have and want some of it."

Okay, so a guy needs an ego boost occasionally.

I switched on the television, dialed in to a news station and went to the bathroom to shave and clean up. I was putting a new blade in the razor when I heard the announcer talk about a shooting during an attempted robbery on West Forty-sixth Street, one that was broken up by a civic-minded passerby.

Thanks, Pat, I said mentally.

While I shaved there was news about the troop movements going into critical areas of the state, sections where power stations and reservoirs were located, their training missions all highly secretive. Results of the operations would be analyzed and announced within two weeks.

Two weeks. That's how much time they knew they had. Success meant announcement. Failure meant destruction. There would be no need for an announcement then. Somehow I still couldn't get excited about it. I wondered what the city would look like if the project failed. New York without smog because the factories and incinerators had no one to operate them. No noise except the wind and the rain until trees grew back through the pavement, then there would be leaves to rustle. Abandoned vehicles would rot and blow away as dust, finally blending with the soil again. Even bones would eventually decompose until the remnants of the race were gone completely, their grave markers concrete and steel tombstones hundreds of feet high, the caretakers of the cemetery only the microscopic organisms that wiped them out. Hell, it didn't sound so bad at all if you could manage to stick around somehow and enjoy it.

A commercial interrupted the broadcast, then the announcer came back with news of a sudden major-power meeting of the United Nations. A possible summit meeting at the White House was hinted at. The dove factions were screaming because our unexpected military maneuvers might trigger the same thing in hostile quarters. The hawks were applauding our gestures at preparedness. Everything was going just right. Eddie Dandy's bomb was demolished in the light of the blinding publicity that seared the unsuspecting eyes of the public.

And all I wanted to do was find me a pickpocket. Plus a couple of guys who had tried to knock me off.

I finished my shower, got dressed, made a phone call, then went down to the cabstand on the corner. Eddie Dandy met me for coffee in a basement counter joint on Fifty-third, glad to get away from the usual haunts where he was bugged about his supposed TV goof. He was sitting there staring at himself in the polished stainless steel side of the bread box, his face drawn, hair mussed, in a suit that looked like it had been slept in. Somehow, he seemed older and thinner and when I sat down he just nodded and waved to the counterman for another coffee.

"You look like hell," I said.

"So should you." His eyes made a ferret-like movement at mine, then went back to staring again.

I spilled some milk and sugar into my coffee and stirred it. "I got other things to think about."

"You're not married and got kids, that's why," he said.

"That bad?"

"Worse. Nothing's turned up. You know how they're faking it?" He didn't let me answer. "They've planted decoy containers in all shapes and sizes that are supposed to be explosive charges. Everybody's out on a search, Army, Navy, C.D. units, even the Scouts. They're hoping somebody will turn up something that isn't a decoy and they'll have a starting place. Or a stopping place."

I grabbed a doughnut and broke it in two, dunking the big end in my coffee. "That bad?"

"Oh, cool, Mike, cool. How the hell do you do it?"

"I don't. I just don't worry about it. They got thousands of people doing the legwork on that one. Me, I have my own problems."

"Like getting shot at in Lippy's apartment."

"You get around, friend."

"There was a news leak out of Kansas City and Pat had me in again. I heard him talking about it to the guy with the squeaky voice from the D.A.'s office. All I did was put two and two together. What happened?"

"Nothing." I gave him the details of the episode and watched him shrug it off. Nothing was as big as what he was sitting on right then.

"Maybe you got the right attitude after all," Eddie finally said. He sipped his coffee and turned around. I knew his curiosity would get the better of him. "When you going to ask me something you don't know?"

I stuffed the rest of the doughnut in my mouth, wiped the jelly off my fingers and grinned at him. "Woody Ballinger," I said.

"Come on, Mike." His voice sounded disgusted with me.

"Two months ago you did that crime special on TV," I reminded him. "Part of the exposé touched his operation."

"So what? I made him a typical example of hoods the law doesn't seem to tap out, always with enough loot to hire good lawyers to find the loopholes. He hides everything behind legitimate businesses and goes on bilking the public. You saw the show."

"I'm interested in what you didn't say, friend. You researched the subject. You got some pretty weird contacts too. You were fighting a time element in the presentation and the network didn't want to fight any libel suits, even from Woody."

"Mike . . . what's to know? He's in the rackets. The cops know damn well he's number two in the policy racket uptown but can't prove it. It used to be bootlegging and whores, then narcotics until he rubbed Lou Chello wrong and the mob gave him that one-ended split. He has what he has and can keep it as long as his nose stays clean with the lasagne lads. They'll protect their own, but only so far."

"A year ago there was a rumble about buddy Woody innovating a new policy wrinkle in the Wall Street crowd. Instead of nickels and dimes it was a grand and up. Winning numbers came from random selections on the big board. There was a possibility of it being manipulated."

"Balls. Those guys wouldn't fall for it," Eddie reminded me.

"They're speculators, kid," I said. "Legit gamblers. Why not?"

Eddie waited while the counterman poured him another coffee and left to serve somebody else. "I checked that out too. Nobody knew anything. I got lots of laughs, that's all."

"Wilbur Craft supposedly made a million out of one payoff," I said.

"Nobody saw it if he did. Or maybe he paid it to his lawyers to get him off that stock fraud hook. I spoke to him up in Sing Sing and he said it was all talk."

"Maybe he didn't want to get hit with an income tax rap on top of everything else. He only drew three years on the fraud rap."

"Keep trying, Mike."

"Craft still has his estate in Westchester."

"Sure, and the place in Florida and the summer place in Hawaii. It was all free and clear before they rapped him."

"Upkeep, pal. It takes a lot of dough," I said.

"I know. I got a five-room apartment on the East Side."

"Suppose Woody did run a big operation independently?"

"Then he'd be sticking his neck way out there just asking it to get chopped off. The dons would have their pizza punks out there with their shooters in his ears for even trying it. No dice, Mike."

"Guys get big," I said. "They don't want somebody else's hand in their affairs. They think they're big enough to stand them off. They have their own shooters ready to protect the territory."

"Unknown powers can do it. Not slobs who like to parade it in public."

"Egos like to be recognized," I said.

"That's how they get dead."

"Just suppose," I asked him.

Eddie blew on his coffee and tasted it. He had forgotten the sugar, made a face and stirred some in. "He'd have to do it in his head. No books, no evidence. All cash, personal contacts, and hard money payoffs."

"Woody's a thinker, but no damn computer."

"Then a minimum of notations, easy to hide, simple to destroy."

"But it could be done?"

"Certainly, but . . ." Eddie put his cup down and turned around to look at me, his eyes squinted half shut. "Either you're trying to make me feel good by getting my mind off things or you got something. Which?"

"You'll never feel good, kid. I was just confirming something I thought of."

"Damn, you're a bastard," Eddie said with a quick grin.

"*Why* does everybody call me that?" I asked.

chapter seven ▪▪▪▪▪▪▪▪▪▪▪

VELDA HAD LEFT a recorded message at ten fifteen stating that she had located Little Joe, the no-legged beggar who pushed himself along on a skate-wheeled platform. Little Joe had seen Lippy and a tall, skinny guy together on several occasions. They were obviously friends, but Little Joe didn't buy the other guy at all. He figured him for a hustler, but didn't ask any questions. His own business was enough for him. He could probably recognize the guy again if he saw him, but the skimpy description was the best Little Joe could do. Velda had left him my numbers to call if he saw him again and if it turned up right Little Joe earned himself a quick hundred. Meanwhile, Velda was going to stay in the area and see what else she could pick up.

Tall and skinny. Probably a million guys like that in the city, but at least it was a start. Eliminate the squares, look for a hustler in a ten-block area during a critical time period when the theater crowds were going in and out and you could narrow it down to a handful. The trouble was, that handful would be the cagy ones. They wouldn't be that easy to spot. They had their moves plotted and a charted course of action if somebody made them. They could disappear into a hundred holes and nobody was going to smell them out for you. I put the phone back, turned my raincoat collar up and went outside and waited for a cab.

Pat's office wasn't the madhouse I thought it would be. All officers available for duty were out in the field and only a lone bored-looking reporter was on a telephone turning in a routine report. A dozen empty cardboard coffee cups stuffed with drowned cigarette butts littered the desk, holding down sheafs of paper.

I said, "Hi, buddy," and he turned around, his face seamed with fatigue lines, his eyes red-veined from lack of sleep. "You look beat."

"Yeah."

I pulled a chair up, sat down and stretched my legs. "Since when does an operation this size involve homicide?"

"Ever since that guy died in the subway."

"Anything new?"

"Not a damn thing."

"Then why don't you try sleeping in a bed for a change?"

"We're not all private citizens," Pat growled.

"How's the general reaction so far?"

"We're managing."

"Somebody's going to wonder about the Russia
a summit meeting and the bit going on in the U.N.

"There's enough tension in the world to make it l
You have four shooting fracases going on right now
those involved have nuclear capabilities if they decide t
There's reason enough for international concern. Wash
handle it if certain parties who know just a little too da
can keep quiet."

"Don't look at me, buddy. It's your problem."

Pat gave me a lopsided grin. "Oh no. Some of it's yours
you're immune to certain deadly diseases."

"They isolate it yet?"

"No."

"Locate the agents that were planted here?"

"No."

"You talk too much," I said.

Pat leaned back and rubbed his eyes. "There's nothing to
about. For the first time the Reds are as bugged about it as
are. They know we have a retaliation policy and damn well kno
its potential. Nobody can afford to risk a C.B. war. They haven
been able to run down a single piece of written evidence on this
business at all. If there ever was any, it's been deliberately destroyed
by that previous regime. That bunch tried to keep a dead hand
in office and they did a pretty good job. We have to work on
rumor and speculation."

"Did the technicians at Fort Detrick come up with anything?"

His eyes gave me an unrelenting stare.

"Come on, Pat. There's nothing really new about our chemical-
biological warfare program being centered there."

"What could they come up with?" he asked me softly.

"Like nuclear physics, problems and solutions seem to be arrived
at simultaneously. When that agent was planted here that bacteriological program would have been developed to a certain point.
Now it's twenty-some years later, so they should be able to guess
at what he had as a destructive force."

"Nice," Pat said. "You're thinking. They can make a few educated guesses, all right, but even back then, what was available
was incredibly destructive. Luckily, they worked on antibiotics,
vaccines and the like at the same time so they could probably
avoid total contamination with a crash immunization program."

I looked at him and grinned. "Except that there isn't enough
time to go into mass production of the stuff."

Pat didn't answer me.

t means only a preselected group would be given immu-
n and who will that group consist of . . . the technicians
ave it at hand, a power squad who can take it away from
or selection by the democratic method of polls and votes?"
ou know what it means," Pat said.
ure. Instant panic, revolution, everything gets smashed in the
cess and nobody gets a thing."
"What would you do, Mike?"
I grinned at him again. "Oh, round up a few hundred assorted
yles of females, a couple of obstetricians, a few male friends to
hare the pleasure and to split the drinks, squirt up with antibiotics
and move to a nice warm island someplace and start the world
going again."

"I never should have asked," Pat said with a tired laugh. "At
least now I'll be able to get some sleep knowing the problem has
been solved." He yawned elaborately, then stifled it. "Unless you
got another one."

"Just one. Did ballistics get anything on those shots in Lippy's
apartment?"

Pat moved a coffee cup aside and tugged out a stained typewritten
sheet of paper. "They dug a .38 slug out of the floor. The ejected
cartridge was a few feet away. The ring bands on the lead were
well defined so it was either a new piece or an old gun with a
fresh barrel. My guess would be a Colt automatic."

"You check the sales from local outlets?"

"Peterson did. Everything turned up clean since the new law
in the state went into effect, but prior to that there were thousands
of sales made outside the state that would be almost impossible
to run down. Anybody intending to use a gun illegally is going
to be pretty cagy about it, especially buying one through a legitimate source. I wouldn't pin any hopes on tracking that job down
unless you locate the gun itself. Or have you?"

"Not yet."

"I wish I had the time or inclination to nail your pants to a
chair," Pat said. "Right now I couldn't care less. Incidentally," he
added, "I might as well give you a little fatherly advice. Although
several people in rather high places who seem to know you pretty
well have vouched for your so-called integrity, the skeptics from
the bureaus in D.C. decided a little surveillance wouldn't hurt.
They didn't like the contact between you and Eddie Dandy this
morning."

"I didn't have any tail on me."

"Eddie did. He works in a more sensitive area than you do. It wouldn't surprise me a bit if he went into custody until this thing was over."

"They wouldn't be that stupid."

"Like hell they wouldn't. He tell you about that business in Kansas City?"

"He mentioned it."

"Plain luck we stopped it this time."

"It'll get a lot stickier if anybody *really* wants to get inquisitive," I said. "How about some lunch?"

"Thanks, but I'm too bushed. I'm grabbing some sleep. Tonight I got a detail covering the reception at that new delegation building they just opened. The Soviets and their satellite buddies are throwing a bash and everybody's got visions of fire bombs and bullets dancing through their heads."

"Crazy," I said. "Can I use your phone?"

"Go ahead."

I dialed my office number, waited for the automatic signal, held the tone gimmick up to the mouthpiece and triggered it. Four faint musical bleeps came out, there was a pause and a voice with a laugh hidden in it said, "Please, Mr. Tape Recorder, inform your master that his cultivator is available for an afternoon drink. He has the office phone number."

I felt myself grinning and hung up.

"Has to be a broad," Pat said. "It has to."

"It was," I told him.

"Just how many broads you figure you collect any given month, pal?"

"Let's put it this way," I said. "I throw away more than most guys get to see."

Pat wrinkled his face and waved for me to get the hell away from him. Some perennial bachelors are different from others.

The bar at Finero's Steak House was packed three deep with a noisy crowd fighting the martini-Manhattan war, the combatants armed with stemmed glasses and resonant junior-executive voices. A scattering of women held down the barstools, deliberately spaced out to give the stags room to operate, knowing they were the objects of attention and the possible prizes. The one on the end was nearly obscured by the cluster of trim young men jockeying for position, but for some reason the back of her head and the way her hair tumbled around her shoulders was strangely familiar to me. She swung around to say something and laugh at the one behind her who was holding out a lighter to fire up her cigarette when her eyes reached out between the covey of shoulders and touched mine.

And Heidi Anders smiled and I smiled back.

The two young men turned and they didn't smile because they were Woody Ballinger's two boys, Carl and Sammy, and for one brief instant there was something in their faces that didn't belong in that atmosphere of joviality and the little move they instinctively made that shielded them behind the others in back of them was involuntary enough to stretch a tight-lipped grin across my face that told them I could know.

Could.

From away back out of the years I got that feeling across my shoulders and up my spine that said things were starting to smell right and if you kept pushing the walls would go down and you could charge in and take them all apart until there was nothing left but the dirt they were made of.

So I made a little wave with my forefinger and Heidi Anders said something to her entourage, put her glass down on the bar and came to me through the path they opened for her and when she reached me said, "Thank you, Mike."

"For what?"

"Yelling at me. I looked in the mirror. It's worse than the camera. It tells you the truth without benefit of soft lighting, makeup men and development techniques."

"Sugar," I asked her, "when did you last pop one?"

"You were there."

"And it was cold turkey all the way? Kid, you sure don't look like you're in withdrawal."

A flash of annoyance tugged at her eyes and that beautiful mouth tightened slightly. "I had help, big man. I went for it right after you left. Dr. Vance Allen. You've heard of him?"

I nodded and studied her. Vance Allen wasn't new to me. He was a longtimer in the field of narcotic rehabilitation. Some of his measures were extreme and some not yet accepted into general practice, but his results had been extremely significant.

"Hurt any?"

"At first. You're looking at an experiment with a new medication. In a way I'm lucky. I wasn't hooked as badly as you thought."

"Who put you on it?"

"That's one of those things I'd rather not talk about. In time it will be taken care of. Meanwhile, I'm working at being un-hooked."

I shook my head and looked past her. "Not yet. Right now you're nibbling at another line."

Heidi tilted her face and squinted at me, not understanding.

"That pair you're with are a couple of hoods."

"Oh . . . don't be silly." She gave me a disgusted grimace. "They work for Mr. Ballinger and Mr. Ballinger . . ."

". . . is a legitimate businessman," I finished for her. "One day try old issues of the newspapers . . . about July, four years ago, or check into your nearest friendly precinct station. The desk sergeant will fill you in on his background."

"I don't believe . . ."

"You got any reason *not* to believe me?"

"No." But her voice was hesitant.

"Somebody tried to kill me last night." I looked past her to the bar again and she almost turned to follow my gaze.

"But . . ."

"When you go back there," I said, "tell your friends that I'll be looking them up. Right after I see their boss. We have a little business to discuss too."

Some of the color drained out of her face and she gave an annoyed toss of her head, her lower lip pinched between her teeth. "Damn! You men . . ."

"Just tell them, Heidi."

"I don't know why . . ."

"Tell them. And have the message passed on to Larry Beers too."

I winked at her and left her standing there a moment watching me before she walked back, that wild hip-swaying walk reflecting her annoyance. Carl and Sammy weren't going to be too happy with the news. They'd been too used to doing the chasing and calling the shots when and where they wanted them.

The maître d' and headwaiter had seen Woody Ballinger earlier, but he had left about an hour ago. His office secretary had called a little while back looking for him, so he wouldn't be there. I just told them that they could tell Woody Mike Hammer was looking for him on a "business matter" and if he didn't find me I'd find him. Let Woody sweat a little too.

Between three and four in the afternoon the New York cabbies change shifts. It's bad enough on a nice day trying to fight the women shoppers and the early commuters for one, but in the rain, forget it. You could stand in the street and get splashed by their wheels or try walking, but either way you'd get soaked. For once the weatherman had been right and they were predicting three more days of the same. Intermittent heavy rain, occasional clearing, windy and cool. It was a hell of a time to be on the streets.

A girl walked by the store entranceway I was nestled in, head lowered into the slanted rain, her plastic coat plastered to her body, outlining her scissoring thighs as she doggedly made her way to the corner to make a green light. At least she reminded me of something. I went inside the store, bought a pack of cigarettes, walked back to the phone booth, put a dime in the slot and dialed a number.

The secretary told me to hold, checked me out, then put Renée Talmage on the line. She chuckled once and said, "Hello, teaser."

"But fun, kid."

"Too frustrating, but yes . . . fun. At least different. Where are you?"

"A couple blocks away and soaking wet."

"There's a nice little bar downstairs in the building where you can dry out while we have a drink."

"Fine," I told her. "Five minutes."

It was closer to fifteen and she was part of the way through a cocktail, totally engrossed with the bartender in a discussion about the latest slump in the stock market, when I got there. I tossed my soggy trench coat and hat on the back of a chair and climbed on the barstool next to her. "Must be great to be intelligent. Bring me a beer," I told the bartender.

She stopped in the middle of Dow-Jones averages and tilted her head at me. "And I thought you had class. A beer. How plebian."

"So I'm a slob." I took the top off the beer and put the glass down with a satisfied burp. "Good stuff, that. You have to raise your hand to get out of class?"

"Recess time." She laughed and sipped her cocktail. "Actually, the day is done. William is socializing with the wheels of the world and I'm left to my own devices for the time being."

"You got nice devices, kid," I said. The dress she had on wasn't exactly office apparel. The vee-neckline plunged down beside the naked swell of her breasts to disappear behind a four-inch-wide leather belt. "Don't you have anything on under that?" I asked her.

"We women are exercising our newfound freedom. Haven't you heard about the brassiere-burning demonstrations?"

"Yeah. I heard. Only I didn't figure on being this close to the ashes. It's distracting."

"Well?"

"Don't guys find it hard to keep their eyes off you?"

Renée looked at me with an amused smile, her mouth formed into a tiny bow. "Very hard."

"Cut it out."

Her smile got deeper. "Me? You're the one making all the dirty remarks."

I almost spilled my beer before I managed to get it down.

"Now what have *you* been doing to get so wet . . . tailing a suspect?"

"Not quite. There are better ways of nailing them. I've been walking and remembering a dead friend who shouldn't have died and thinking out why he died until things begin to make a little sense. One day, one second, it's all going to be nice and clear right in front of me and all those targets will be ready to be knocked off."

The funny little smile on her face warped into a worried frown and some deep concern showed in her eyes. "Is it . . . that personal, Mike?"

"All the way."

"But you're serious . . . about killing."

"So was somebody else," I told her.

Renée looked into her glass, started to raise it, then put it down and looked at me again. "Strange."

"What is?"

"My impressions. I read about people in your line of work, I see the interpretations on TV and in movies . . . it's rather hard to believe there really *are* people like that. But with you it's different. The police . . ."

"Cops are dedicated professionals, honey. They're in a tough, rough, underpaid racket with their lives on the line every minute of the day. They get slammed by the public, sappy court decisions and crusading politicians, but somehow they get the job done."

"Mike . . . I thought I knew people. I'm personally responsible for the actions and decisions of several thousands and answerable only to William Dorn. I can't afford to make mistakes in selecting them for sensitive positions, but I would have made a mistake with you."

"Why?"

"Because . . . well, there are different sides of you that nobody can truly see."

"You've just lost touch with the lower class, kid. You work on too high a level. Get out there on the street where the buying public is and you'll see a lot of other faces too. Some of them probably work for you too. Not everybody is in an executive position. Macy's and Sears Roebuck still do a whopping big business by catering to their tastes."

"Take me with you, Mike," she said.

"What?"

"You could be right. I'd like to see these people."

"Renée, you'd get your clothes dirty, your nails broken, and your ass patted. It's different."

"I'll survive it."

She was so serious I had to laugh at her. I finished the fresh beer the bartender set in front of me and thought, what the hell, a change of pace could be good for her. It was one of those evenings where nobody was going anyplace anyway, so why not? We could cruise through the entrails of the city and maybe pick up pieces here and there that were lying around loose.

Down at the end the bartender had switched on the TV to a news station and the announcer finished with the weather and turned the program over to the team who handled the major events. Somebody in Congress was raising a stink about the expenses involved in calling up National Guard and Army Reserve units for a practice maneuver that apparently had no meaning. Film clips taken by some enterprising photographer who had slipped past the security barrier showed uniformed figures slogging through mud and water, flashlights probing the darkness. Another shot had a group locating and dismantling some apparatus of destruction around a power station. He even included the information that they were deliberately planted decoys with a minimum explosive capacity to sharpen the soldiers' abilities. It seemed that most of the activity was centered around the watershed areas in key areas across the nation with chemical analysis teams right in the thick of things. The commentator even speculated briefly on sophisticated chemical-biological warfare techniques and this exercise was possibly for training in detection and neutralizing an enemy's attack from that direction.

He never knew how nearly right he was.

Tom-Tom Schneider's killers had escaped a trap laid by the Detroit police. Somebody had passed the word where they could be found and there was a shoot-out in the Dutchess Hotel. Two cops were wounded, a porter killed, and it was believed that one of the suspects was shot during the exchange. An hour later a known police informer was found murdered with three .38's in his chest along a highway leading from the city. It was going to make a good pictorial spread in tomorrow's papers.

The mayor was screaming for more crime control and was setting up a panel to study the situation. Good luck, mayor.

"Great world out there," I said.

"I'd still like to see it with you."

"Okay. Finish your drink."

I hoped I wouldn't run into Velda. Women don't exactly appreciate other women's plunging necklines.

Caesar Mario Tulley was a professional panhandler who bused over from Patterson, New Jersey, every day, picked up a hundred bucks in nickels and dimes from the tourist suckers, then went back to his flashy suite in a midtown hotel. He had pageboy hair, a faceful of stringy whiskers and a motley outfit of clothes held together with beads and chains that no decent hippie would be caught high in. But it was his gimmick. That and the lost look in the young-old face and tired eyes. The women felt sorry for him and the men flipped their quarters in his hand to pay for the snide remarks that went with the coin. Hell, he probably was making out better than any of them.

He saw me and Renée squeezed together under her umbrella, half stepped out of the shoe store doorway, then recognized me and those deliberately tired eyes pepped right up. A loose-lip grin split the whiskers and he said, "Oh, hi, Mike. Almost put the bite on you."

"Fat chance," I told him. "How you doing, Caesar?"

"Lousy tonight. Tried working Radio City and got rousted by the fuzz. Then some drunk belts me in the chops figuring I was his own kid and tried to drag me back to Des Moines, Iowa. I was halfway to the Forty-second Street subway before I shook him loose. What kind of kooks they got around here these days?"

"Look in the mirror, kid."

"Man, I'm straight! A working stiff! You think I'd go this route if it didn't pay off! Twice a week I take acting classes and already I got a future lined up. You see me on TV the other night?"

"Great show." Last Tuesday they did a special on the hippies in town and managed to round up a few of the real pros like Caesar. Twenty-seven runaway kids in Greenwich Village were recognized and picked up by their parents, four narcotics pushers were spotted by sharp-eyed detectives and hauled in on possession charges, and the public had a good idea of what the city was coming to.

"Pig's ass it was a good show," Caesar said sullenly. "Practically everybody spots me. I even got a call from the Internal Revenue Service. Making it ain't so easy now."

"So act."

"What do ya think I'm doing? It ain't Shakespeare, but it sure takes talent."

"And nerve." Renée smiled.

"Lady, come on. It's all part of the game." He rattled his beads and stepped back into his doorway shelter again. "What you doing out, Mike?"

"Trying to find somebody. Tall, skinny, in his forties and boosting wallets in the theater district. Got anything?"

He cocked his head and peered at me, eyes squinting. "Hey, some hustler was asking the same thing. Big chick, long dark hair, real knockout. Don't know why she was hustling, but I tried to make out and she brushed me off. Me! How about that? I wanted to give her a twenty . . ."

"You would have had your head handed to you," I said, grinning again. Caesar boy had run into Velda.

"Fuzz?" he asked, incredulously.

I nodded, not explaining all of it.

"Man, they sure make them real these days. She coulda busted me for panhandling. Awful pretty for fuzz though, even under that face crap."

"The guy I mentioned, Caesar?"

"Hell, I don't butt in to somebody else's . . ."

"You buck the theater crowds, Caesar. He would have been in the same area."

He shrugged, giving a small negative shake to his long hair, but his eyes didn't want to look at me. I stepped out from under the umbrella and got up close to him. "Compared to withholding information, panhandling is a chintzy rap."

"Mike . . . you ain't the fuzz. You . . ."

"My license makes me responsible to turn certain facts over to them, buddy."

"Hey, I thought we was pals."

"After office hours."

Caesar Tulley made a resigned gesture and ran his fingers through his hair. "There was some talk. Wooster Sal saw this guy hit a couple of jobs and tried to cut himself a chunk. He got a busted lip for it."

"You see him?"

"I saw him pop Wooster Sal. Like a sneak punch. Wooster shoulda kept to his own racket."

"Anything special about him . . . facial characteristics . . . you know?"

Another shrug. "Just a guy. I didn't get a real good look. Anyway, I didn't want one. I'm opposed to violence."

"What about this Wooster Sal?"

"Hell, after that he dug out for the West Coast. Gone like two weeks now."

"Keep looking, okay? I'm in the phone book."

I flipped him a wave and started to walk away when he called me back. "Hey, Mike, there was one thing."

I turned and waited.

"He wore a red vest. Pretty dumb in his business."

One more little piece to add to the pile. In time it would mount up to a face and a body. One red vest, and it probably wasn't dumb. It was a good luck charm, vanity or any other of a dozen reasons a petty crook could consider imperative.

I hooked my arm through Renée's and pushed the edge of her umbrella out of my face. "You have odd friends, Mike. Those newsstand dealers, the pair at the hamburger stand . . . who else do you know?"

"You'd be surprised," I said. "Still feel like prowling?"

Renée glanced at her watch and tightened her hold on my arm. "It's almost ten, my big friend. I told you I had to meet William at that reception in a half hour."

It was the same one Pat had mentioned to me, the opening of the new Soviet delegation buildings. "Since when are you people messed up in politics?"

"Since Teddy Finlay from the State Department invited us. One of the new delegates was a foreign supplier for our Anco Electronics before we bought him out. Finlay thought it would be beneficial to have a less formal introduction to him."

"And where do you come in?"

"I pick up William's memos he made at the meeting today, give him his tickets for his Chicago trip tomorrow, murmur a few pleasantries and leave. Impulsively, she added, "Why don't you come along?"

"We aren't exactly in evening clothes, baby."

"But we won't be going to the reception proper. I'm to meet him in office A-3 in the west annex, not where the crowd will be. Please, Mike?" She nudged me expectantly, her leg touching mine in a long-legged stride. The wind gusted and blew the rain under the umbrella into my face. Hell, it would be good to get out of it for a few minutes.

"Why not?" I said.

The two uniformed cops covering the annex entrance scanned. Renée's admittance card and checked our ID's. The older one, sweating under his rubber raincoat said, "Hold a second," then walked across the street to a squad car, talked through the window and stepped back when the door opened. I let out a grunt of amusement when Pat got out, hunched against the rain, his hands in his pockets.

When he saw me his face finally registered something besides tired boredom. "Now what are *you* doing here?" he asked me.

"Personal invitation, old buddy."

"His name isn't on the card," the cop told him. "What do you think, Captain? The dame's okay."

Pat flipped the rain from the brim of his hat and stepped away, nodding for me to follow him. He swung around, his voice a low growl. "This stinks. No matter what you tell me, it plain stinks. What are you building?"

"Not a thing, Pat. Miss Talmage has a business appointment with her employer there and invited me along. Can anything be simpler?"

"With you, nothing's simple," Pat said. "Look, if you pull anything . . ."

"Unwind, will you buddy? Can't I talk to you any more?"

For a long few seconds he studied my face, then let a smile crack the corners of his mouth. "Sorry, Mike. I guess I got too much bugging me. There's more than one meeting going on in there."

"So the Soviets really are cooperating on that C.B. deal?"

"You called it. And they're scared stiff. All the top brass from Fort Detrick arrived at seven with a limousine of Russkies straight off a chartered nonstop plane from Moscow right behind them."

"Military types?"

"Hardly. Some were too old for that."

"Specialists in chemical-biological warfare," I suggested.

"Could be."

"Any newspapers covering it?"

"Only the social end. They missed the first batch. That's why you spook me. Nothing better interrupt that meeting."

"Quit worrying about me. Anything turn up yet?"

"One lonely probability. A couple on a honeymoon camping

trip spotted a guy wandering around the Ashokan watershed area. He seemed to be sick . . . kind of stumbling, fell a couple of times. They were going to go over to him but he wandered up to the road and must have thumbed a ride. The rough description they gave was similar to the guy we found in the subway."

"The Guard in the area?"

"Like a blanket. Boats, divers, foot by foot search. They cut off the water flow from that district and that they *can't* keep a secret, so they'd better come up with some imaginative excuse before morning."

"Oh, they will," I said casually.

Pat jammed his hands back into his pockets and grimaced in my direction. "They better do better than that. Right now you can realize what it's like to be in death row with no reprieve in sight."

"Yeah, great," I said. "By the way, you ever get tipped to a pickpocket who works in a red vest?"

"Go screw your pickpocket in a red vest," Pat said sourly. He waved an okay sign to the two cops and headed back toward his car.

The ramrod-stiff butler with the bristly gray hair scrutinized the admission card, verified Renée with an inaudible phone call and apparently described me after giving my name. The reply was favorable, because he took our wet clothes, hung them in a closet in the small foyer and led us to the office door in the rear. Unlike my coat, his hadn't been tailored to conceal a heavy gun and it bulged over his left hip. For him, butlering was a secondary sideline. He had been plucked right off an army parade ground.

William Dorn introduced me to the five of them as a friend of his, his eyes twinkling with amusement. They all gave me a solemn handshake, the one-jerk European variety with accented "How-do-you-do's" except Teddy Finlay. He waited until Dorn and Renée were exchanging papers and the others talking animatedly over drinks, then pulled me aside to the wall bar and poured a couple of highballs.

He handed me one, let me taste it, then: "How long have you been a 'friend' of William, Mike?" He laid it heavy on "friend" so I'd know he made me.

"Not long," I said.

"Isn't being here an imposition?"

"Why should it bother you? The State Department doesn't work on my level."

"Mr. Robert Crane is my superior. It seems that you were trying to work on his. Nobody is pleased having you know what we do."

"Tough titty, feller. Crane didn't like it because I wouldn't take his crap. I won't take yours either, so knock it off."

"You still didn't answer my question." There was a hard edge in his voice.

"I have a contract to bump the Russian Ambassador. That sound like reason enough?"

"One phone call and you can be where Eddie Dandy is, Mr. Hammer."

I took another pull of my drink, not letting him see how tight my fingers were around the glass. "Oh? Where's that?"

"On vacation . . . in protective custody. He was getting a little unruly too."

When I finished the drink I put the glass back on the bar and turned around to face him, the words coming quietly from between my teeth. "Try it, stupid. I'll blast a couple of .45's into the ceiling and bring every damn cop and reporter around in this joint. Then just for fun I'll run off nice and fat at the mouth and really start that panic you're working your ass off to avoid. That loud and clear?"

Finlay didn't answer me. He just stood there with white lines showing around his mouth and his forehead curled in an angry frown. Two of the Czech representatives had been looking curiously in our direction, but when I turned, faking a smile, they stopped watching and went back to their conversation. Dorn and Renée had finished their business and were laughing at some remark Josef Kudak had made and waved me over to join them. Kudak was the new member of the Soviet satellite team, but it was evident that the three of them were old friends despite political differences.

"Good joke?" I asked.

William Dorn chuckled and held a match to a long, thin cigar. "My friend Josef thinks I'm a filthy rich, decadent capitalist and wants to know how he can get that way too."

"Tell him?"

"Certainly not. I bought him out for three million dollars and I'd wager he hasn't spent a penny of it yet."

"You don't know my wife *or* our tax structure, friend William," the Czech said. He was a small, pudgy man with a wide Slavic face and bright blue eyes. "Between them they have reduced me to poverty."

"There are no poor politicians," I put in.

Renée looked startled, but Dorn laughed again and Kudak's face widened in a broad smile. "Ah," he said, "at last a candid man. You are right, Mr. Hammer. It is all a very profitable business, no? Should it be otherwise? Money belongs to those who can get it."

"Or take it," I said.

"Certainly, otherwise it would rot. The peasants put their gold into little jars and bury it. They die of old age without revealing where they have hidden it, so afraid are they of having it stolen. With it they buy nothing, do nothing. It is for the businessmen, the politicians to see that money is kept circulating."

It was hard to tell if he was joking or serious, so I just grinned back and lit up a smoke. "I wish some of it would circulate my way."

Kudak's eyebrows went up a little in surprise. "You are not a politician?"

"Nor a good businessman," I added.

"But you must have a profitable specialty . . ." He looked from me to Dorn and back again.

"Sometimes I kill people," I said.

Dorn let out a long laugh at the expression on Kudak's face and the way Renée grabbed me to make a hurried exit after a quick handshake with everybody I'd met. When she got me outside in the rain she popped her umbrella open with typical feminine pique and said, "Men. They're all crazy!" She stretched her arm up so I could get in beside her. "What a thing to say to a man in high office. Doesn't anything ever embarrass you?"

"Wait till he finds out it's true," I said.

"I'll never take you with me again."

"Never?"

"Well, at least not where there's people. Now, where are we off to?"

I looked at my watch. It was twenty after eleven and raining. Inside the main building the reception was going full force and the sound of a string quartet was almost drowned out by the steady hum of voices. On the street at least fifty uniformed cops stood uncomfortably in assigned positions waiting for their shift to end. Pat's car was gone, but the pair of harness bulls still stood at the fenced entrance. It was the kind of night when New York slept for a change. At least those who knew nothing of the man in the subway.

And maybe the guy in the red vest.

I turned my coat collar up and threw my cigarette into a puddle where it fizzled out. "Suppose I check my office, then we go out for supper."

"No more prowling?"

"I've had enough for one day."

I signed us in at the night desk and steered Renée to the open elevator on the end of the bank, got in and pushed the button for my floor. She had that impish grin back, remembering the look the night man had given us downstairs, and said, "The direct approach is very fascinating, Mike. Do you have a couch and champagne all ready?"

"No champagne. Might be a six-pack of Pabst beer in the cooler though." .

"How about a bathroom? I have to piddle."

"And so ends a romantic conversation," I said as the door slid open noiselessly.

"Well, I really have to," she insisted.

"So go," I told her.

She was taking little mincing steps walking down the corridor to my office, and to make sure nothing would stay between her and the john, I got ahead, stuck my key in the lock and pushed the door open.

Not really pushed. It was jerked open with me leaning on the knob and I tumbled inside knowing that the world would be coming down on my head if all the reflexes hadn't been triggered in time. But there are some things you never seem to lose. They drilled them into you in the training camps, and made you use them on the firing line and what they didn't teach you, you learned the hard way all at once or you never lived to know about anything at all. I was in a half roll, tucking my head down, one hand cushioning my fall and the other automatically scrabbling for the .45 when heavy metal whipped down the back of my head into my shoulders with a sickening smash. Then you know there's still time because the pain is hot and wet without deadening numbness and the secondary impulses take over immediately and whip you away from the force of the second strike.

I was on my back, the flat of my hand braced for leverage, bringing my foot up and around into flesh and pelvic bone in a high, arching kick that gouged testicles from their baggy sockets with a yell choked off as it was sucked down a throat in wild, fiery agony. I could see the shadowy figure, still poised for another smash at my head, the bulk of a gun in his hand, then it jerked toward me convulsively and the flat of my .45 automatic met frontal bone with all the power I could put behind it. Time was measured in tenths of a second that seemed to take minutes, but

it was enough to buy me time. Two blasts of flame went off in my face, pounding into the back of the one on top of me and something tore along the skin of my side, then Renée was screaming in the doorway until another shot rocketed off and cut it off abruptly. I saw the other one run, saw her fall, but couldn't get out from under the tangle of limp arms and legs that smothered my movements in time. Crazy words spilled from my mouth, then I got the body off me, pushed to my feet with the .45 still cocked and staggered into the corridor.

Down the hall the blinking lights of the elevator showed it was almost halfway to the ground floor. None of the others were operating and I could never beat it down the stairway. I shoved the gun back in the speed rig under my coat and knelt down beside Renée. She was unconscious, her eyes half open, a heavy red welt along her temple, oozing blood where the bullet had torn away hair and skin. She was lucky. In her fright she had raised her hands and the heavy ornamental knob of the umbrella handle had deflected the slug aimed for her face and turned sudden death into a minor superficial scratch. I let her lie there for a minute, went back into my office and switched on the light.

The body on the floor was still leaking blood that soaked into the carpet and all I could think of was that the next time I'd get a rug to match the stains and save cleaning costs. I put my toe under the ribs and turned it over. The two exit wounds had punched gaping holes in the chest and the slash from my rod had nearly destroyed his face, but there was enough left to recognize.

Larry Beers wouldn't be renting his gun out to the highest bidders any more. One slug that had gone right through him and grazed me was still imbedded in the carpet, a misshapen oval of metal standing on edge. There were no alarms, no sirens, no voices; the office building was deserted and we were too high up for gunshot sounds to reach the street.

I stood up and looked around at the absolute destruction of all my new furniture, the mess of cotton batting from torn cushions, papers from the emptied files and remnants of furniture that had been systematically destroyed. But they had started to work from one side to the other and stopped three quarters of the way across. I knew what had happened. They had located the automatic taping system built into the wall behind the street map of New York City. Somebody had played it. Then somebody had destroyed it. The ashes were still warm in the metal wastebasket in the corner of the room.

Like a sucker punch in the belly the picture was clear. There

was a call on that tape, probably from Velda. It meant something damn important, enough to kill for. Now one was dead, but the other was still loose and if Velda had identified herself they'd know who to look for and probably where. If she had gotten hold of something she'd want to meet me and would have set a time and a place.

Larry Beers, Ballinger's boy. Out of curiosity I looked at the bottom of his shoes, saw the half-moon-shaped pieces of metal imbedded in the heels that old lady Gostovitch had called clickers and felt good because one was down who deserved it, and the one paying the price would be the guy who ran off and the one who was paying for the hit. It was Woody I had to find before he found Velda. There was one little edge I still had, though. They couldn't be sure I wasn't dead, and if I wasn't I'd be looking for Woody too, and he had to reach me fast because he knew he'd be on my kill list just as sure as hell.

Behind me a small, frightened voice said, "Mike . . ."

Renée was standing in the doorway, hands against the frame, her face white and drawn. She saw the body on the floor but was still too dazed to realize what had happened. She tried a painful smile and lifted her eyes. "I . . . don't think I like your friends," she said.

chapter eight ▰▰▰▰▰▰▰▰▰▰▰▰

THERE WAS NO way of determining the actual cause of the wound, so the doctor accepted her explanation without question. The tip of an umbrella whipped in a sudden cross-directional gust had caught her, we said. He applied an antibiotic, a small compress she hid behind her hair and had me take her home. She still had a headache, so she took the sedative the doctor had given her, a little wistful at me having to leave, but knowing how urgent it was that I must. She had been caught up in something she had never experienced and couldn't understand, but realized that it wasn't time to ask questions. I told her I'd call tomorrow and went back into the rain again. My shirt was still sticking to my side with dried blood, stinging, but not painful. That could wait.

The doctor never saw that one because he would have known it for what it was and a report would go in.

Back in the office a body still sprawled on the floor in its own mess, a note to Velda on its chest to check into the hotel we used when necessary and hold until I contacted her. The door was locked, the "OUT" sign in place, now Woody Ballinger could sweat out what had happened.

The night clerk in the office building had heard the elevator come down, but was at the coffee machine when the occupant left the lobby and all he saw was the back of a man going out the door. Four others had signed the night book going in earlier and he had assumed he was one of those. When I checked the book myself the four were still there on the second floor, an accountancy firm whose work went on at all hours. Woody's boys had it easy. A master key for the door, time to go through my place and time to phone in whatever information they found on the tape. Then they just waited. They couldn't take the chance of me getting that message and knew that if I did I'd want to erase it on the chance that Woody would make a grab for me after I made it plain enough to his boys that I was ready to tap him out.

Okay, Woody, you bought yourself a farm. Six feet down, six long and three wide. The crop would be grass. You'd be the fertilizer.

I stood under the marquee of the Rialto East on Broadway, watching the after-midnight people cruising the Times Square area. The rain had discouraged all but a few stragglers, driving them home or into the all-night eating places. A pair of hippies in shawls and bare feet waded through the sidewalk puddles and into the little river that flowed along the curb, oblivious to the downpour. One lone hooker carrying a sodden hatbox almost started to give me her sales pitch, then obviously thought better of it and veered away. She didn't have to go far. A pair of loud, heavyset conventioneer types had her under their arms less than a half block away. What they needed around here was the old World War II G.I. pro stations. Nowadays the streetwalkers carried more clap than a thundercloud. Syph was always a possibility and galloping dandruff a certainty.

Earlier, a dozen phone calls to the right people had gotten me the same piece of information. Woody Ballinger had been missing from the scene ever since this morning. Carl, Sammy and Larry Beers were gone too. I had lucked into snagging the apartment Carl and Sammy shared, but the doorman told me they had left in the morning and hadn't returned. He let me confirm it myself by rapping on their door.

And now I was worried. Nobody had seen Velda since four hours ago. Her apartment phone didn't answer and the place she had taken opposite Lippy's old place was empty. The small bag she had taken with a few extra clothes was in the closet, two sweaters on hangers and a few cosmetics on the ancient dresser beside the bed.

When she worked in the field, Velda was a loner. Except for a few personal contacts, she didn't use informants and stayed clear of places she would be recognized. But Woody knew her and if she were spotted it wouldn't be too hard to grab her if they went at it right.

I knew what she was wearing from what was left over in her luggage and had passed the word around. Denny Hill was pretty sure he had seen her grabbing a coffee and a hot dog in Nedick's, but that had been around seven o'clock. I found Tim Slatterly just closing his newsstand and he said, sure he had seen her early in the evening. She was all excited about something and he had made change for her so she could use the phone in the drugstore on the corner.

"Thought she was a hooker." Tim laughed. "You shoulda seen the getup she had on." He pulled off his cap, whipped the rain off it and slapped it back on again. Then he looked at me seriously. "She ain't really . . ."

"No. She was on a job for me."

He let the smile fade. "Trouble?"

"I don't know. You see which direction she came from?"

Tim nodded toward the opposite side of Seventh Avenue going north. "Over there. I watched her cross the street." He paused a second, rubbing his face, then thumbed his hand over his shoulder. "Ya know, this probably was the closest place to call from. Two blocks up is another drugstore and one block down is an outside booth. If this one was closest she probably came from that block right there."

So she was in a hurry. She wanted to make a phone call. *That could have been the one to me recorded on the tape that was destroyed.* And what she found could have come from that direction.

"You see her come out, Tim?"

"Yeah," he nodded. "She had a piece of paper in her hand. At first she started to flag down a cab, then gave it up and headed back over the West Side again. Look, Mike, if you want I'll call over to Reno's and the guys can . . ."

"It'll be okay, buddy. Thanks."

"Oh . . . and Mike, she ever find that guy? The one with the fancy vest? She asked me about that too."

"When?"

"That was, lemme see . . . right after I came on this morning. Like I told her, I see them things sometimes. One guy been coming here eight years always wears one. He owns a restaurant downtown. Rich guy. There's another one, but he kind of drifts by once in a while at night. I figured him for a pimp."

I edged back under the protection of the overhang, the rain draping a curtain around us. "Tall and skinny, about forty-some?"

Tim bobbed his head quickly. "Yeah, that's him."

"When did you see him last?"

"Hell, about suppertime. He was still drifting along when everybody else was hustling to get outa the wet. I remember because the bum picked a paper outa the trash can somebody tossed away instead of buying one. A wet paper yet." Tim stopped, watching me intently, then added, "So he started to cross the street heading west too. I wasn't really watching."

"Good enough, Tim," I said.

And now the reins were pulling in a little tighter. The possibilities were beginning to show themselves. It was me who had put Woody onto it in the beginning. He had his own sources of information and it wouldn't have taken him long to spot the association between Lippy and me and dig around the same way I did. If I had found anything Lippy's former friend had lifted from Woody, the police would have had it by now and he'd be squatting on an iron bunk in the city jail.

But no charges had been leveled, so whatever he was after was still up for grabs. I let the rain whip at my face and grinned pointlessly. So he double-checked Lippy's pad with his boys and they damned near knocked me off. They had taken off fast, not knowing how long I had stayed around, and maybe if I looked hard enough I could have uncovered the item. It wouldn't be big. Large enough for a wallet and easy enough to hide.

It made sense then. They had to take me out to be sure. They ransacked my office first, then waited for me. They had to. After my bit earlier about "doing business" with Woody, he could have assumed I had the stuff and was ready to sell it to him. That would be "business" in his language. Or Velda could have come up with it and phoned in the information on the tape recorder and they couldn't take a chance of me getting it. They'd try to tap me out first, then Velda.

Damn it all to hell, why didn't she stay in the office where she belonged?

From a quarter mile down the avenue came a whine of sirens and tiny red dots winked in the night. I waited and watched another convoy of Army trucks rumble by, escorted by two prowl cars clearing the way. All of them were way above the speed limit. The last four were ambulance vehicles and a jeep. When they passed by I crossed to the other side of Seventh Avenue and started working my way west across town.

At four A.M. I checked out a single lead and came up with a guy in a red vest, a stew bum conked out on wine, sleeping in a doorway on Eighth Avenue. I said something under my breath and walked down to the bar on the corner that was just about to close up for the night. I tried Velda's apartment first, but there was no answer. I tried the hotel I wanted her to use, but nobody using our cover names had checked in. My office phone rang twice before it went to the recorder with the fresh spool I had inserted. There were no messages. By now Larry Beers' corpse would be cold and stiff, his blood jellied on the floor. Pat was going to give me hell.

He did that, all right, standing there over the body and chewing me out royally, his eyes as tired and bloodshot as my own. Outside the windows the sky had turned to a slate gray, the rain had stopped, but poised and waiting until it could be at its most miserable best when it let loose again.

The body of Larry Beers had been carted off in a rubber bag, the room photographed, the basics taken care of, now two detectives were standing outside the door getting a muffled earful as Pat lit into me.

All I could say was, "Listen, I told you I had a witness."

"Fine. It better be a good one."

"It is."

"You better have a damn good excuse for the time lapse in reporting this mess too."

"Once more for the record, Pat, my witness got hurt in the shuffle. I took her to a doctor who will verify it."

"He had a phone."

"So I was in a state of shock."

"Balls. You know the kind of lawyer Ballinger has to protect his men? You think that other guy's going to admit laying for you? Like hell . . . they'll say you set a trap and touched it off yourself deliberately in front of a witness. Nice, eh? You were even supposed to get the other one, but he got away. So maybe your bullets aren't in him. The other guy was firing in self-defense."

"Look at the office."

"You could have done that yourself. You told me you didn't see them in the act of wrecking it. Your witness couldn't help there, either."

"Well, you know better."

"Sure, *I* do, only I'm just a cop. I can investigate and arrest. I don't handle the prosecution. Your ass is in deep trouble this time. Don't think the D.A.'s office is going to buy your story on sight. What you *think* happened won't cut any grass with that bunch. Even the shooting at Lippy's won't help any. That could have been staged too. You try using the witness you got there and all you'll get is a cold laugh and a kiss-off. Even your own lawyer wouldn't touch them."

"Okay, what do you want from me?" I asked him.

"Who's your witness, damn it!"

I grinned and shrugged my shoulders. "You know, you forgot to advise me of my rights, Captain. Under that Supreme Court decision, this case could be kicked right off the docket as of now."

Pat let those red eyes bore into me for ten seconds, his teeth clamped tight. Then suddenly the taut muscles in his jaw loosened, he grinned back and shook his head in amazement.

"I don't know why I'm bothering with you, Mike. I'm acting like this is the first homicide I ever stumbled over. After all the nitheaded times you and I . . . oh, shit." He swabbed at his eyes with his hands and took a deep breath. "The whole damn country's in line for extermination and I'm letting you bug me." He dropped his hands, his face serious. "Anyway, by tomorrow you wouldn't even make the back page."

I didn't say anything. His face had a peculiar, blank look.

Finally, Pat dropped his voice and said, "They found a canister at the bottom of the Ashokan Reservoir. It was a bacteriological device timed to open six days from now."

I couldn't figure it. I said, "Then why the sweat if you got it nailed down?"

Pat brushed some torn remnants off the arm of the chair and lowered himself down to it. "The guy found dead in the subway was the same one those honeymooners spotted, all right. They searched the area where they saw him and came up with the canister." His eyes left the window and wandered over to mine. "It must have been the last one he planted. It was marked #20—

ASHOKAN. Someplace scattered around are nineteen others like it, all due to release in six days."

"And the papers got this?"

"One of the reservists in the group that handled the stuff was a reporter fresh out of journalism school. He figured he had a scoop and phoned it in. He didn't know about the other nineteen they didn't find."

"There's still time to squelch the story."

"Oh, they're on that, don't worry. Everybody connected with that guy's paper is in protective custody, but they're screaming like hell and they're not going to be held long. There's a chance they might have spouted off to their friends or relatives, and if they did, it's panic time. People aren't going to hold in a secret like that."

"Who's handling it . . . locals?"

"Washington. That's how big it is." Pat reached for his hat and stood up. "So whatever you do doesn't really matter, Mike. You're only an interesting diversion that keeps me from thinking about other things. Six days from now we can all pick out a nice place to sit and watch each other kick off."

"Brother, are you full of piss and vinegar tonight."

"I wish you'd worry a little. It would make me feel better."

"Crap," I said sullenly. There was no mistaking Pat's attitude. He was deadly serious. I had never seen him like that before. Maybe it was better to be like the rest of the world, not knowing about things. But what would they be like when they found out?

"Six days. When it happens you can bet there's going to be some kind of retaliation, or expecting it, the other side fires first. A nuclear holocaust could destroy this country and possibly the bacteria too. If I were on the other side I'd consider the same thing." Pat let a laugh grunt through his teeth. "Now even the Soviet bunch is thinking along those lines. I heard they all tried to get out of the country when we found the thing, but the Feds put the squeeze on them. In a way they're hostages for six days and they'd better run down a lead before then or they've had it too."

"Sounds crazy," I said.

"Doesn't it?" Pat waved me to the door. "So let's have a coffee like it all never happened and then we'll check into the ballistics report on those slugs that tore up your buddy Beers."

I lay stretched out on the bed, not quite awakened from the druglike sleep I had been in. The window was a patch of damp gray letting the steamy smells of the city drift into the room through the open half. The clock said ten after two, and I pulled the phone down beside me and dialed the office number. Nothing. Velda's apartment didn't answer either.

Where the hell was she? Until now Velda had always called in at regular intervals, or if necessity warranted it, longer ones, but she always called. Now there were only two answers left. Either she was on a prolonged stakeout or Woody Ballinger had found her. I tried another half-dozen calls to key people I had contacted, but none of them had seen Woody or any of his boys. All his office would say was he had left town, but Chipper Hodges had gone into his apartment through a window on a fire escape and said his bags were in a closet and nothing seemed to be missing.

Pat had slept in his office all night and his voice was still a hoarse growl with no expression in it at all. "Sorry, Mike," he said, "still negative. Nobody's seen Ballinger around at all."

"Damn it, Pat . . ."

"We'd *like* to see him, though. Ballistics came up with another item besides those slugs in Beers coming from that same gun that shot at you in Lippy's apartment. That same gun was used to kill the cop who stepped into the cross fire when he was raiding that policy place uptown. Supposedly one of Woody's places."

"And now you got men on it."

"Uh-huh. As many as we can spare. Don't worry, we'll find Ballinger."

"He might have Velda. There isn't much time."

"I know," he told me softly, "not for any of us," then hung up.

Back to *that* again, I thought. Six days . . . no, five days left. In a way there was almost a comic angle to the situation. The ones who didn't know what was impending couldn't care, and those who knew about it didn't. A real wild world, this. Trouble was coming in from so many sources that another one, no matter how big, was no more than an itch to be scratched. Maybe the world wouldn't give a damn either if it did know. Nobody seems to think that big. *Sufficient unto the day are the evils thereof.* How long since Hiroshima and Nagasaki? You sit on a time bomb so long you get to ignore it. The object of destruction gets to be a familiar thing and one more wouldn't matter anyway. Defusing the problem was somebody else's job and somehow in some way it would be taken care of. That's what we have a government for, isn't it? So why worry, have another beer and watch the ball game. The Mets are ahead.

I picked up a paper at the stand on the corner and riffled through the pages. The *News* had a two-column spread on page four about how the special Army teams in their exercise maneuvers upstate had located a possible contamination source in the Ashokan Reservoir, and although the water supply to New York City and adjacent areas had been temporarily curtailed, there was no actual shortage and the Army experts were expected to clear the matter up shortly.

Further on was another little squib about a certain Long Island newspaper suspending operations temporarily due to a breakdown in their presses. Washington was putting the squeeze on, but good. I wondered how Eddie Dandy was making out, wherever he was. By now he must have a mad on as big as his head. Somebody was going to catch hell when they released him, that was for sure.

Little Joe was working his trade on Broadway, pushing himself along on a homemade skateboard. For a beggar he was ahead in his field, peddling cheap ball-point pens instead of pencils, gabbing with all the familiar figures who kept him in business with the daily nickels and dimes.

I drew his attention by fluttering a buck down over his shoulder into his box and he spun around with a surprised grin when he saw me. "Hey, Mike. Thought I just got me a big spender. You want a pen?"

"Might as well get something for my dollar."

He held up his box. "Take your pick."

I pulled out two black ones and dropped them in my pocket. "Velda told me she saw you," I said.

"Yeah," Joe said, craning his neck up to look at me. "She was looking for that dip I saw with old Lippy."

A curious tingle ran across my shoulders. "She didn't say what he was. You didn't know, either."

"That was *then*. Me, I ain't got much to do except look, and besides, you two always did get me curious. So I look and ask a few people and pretty soon I get a few answers. Since Lindy's closed I moved my beat up here a couple of blocks and you'd be surprised how much can go on just a pair of traffic lights away. Like another world."

"Don't yak so much, Joe."

"Mike . . . when do I get the chance to? Like you're a captive audience." Then he saw the impatience in my face and nodded. "He came in from Miami about two months ago where he was working Hialeah. That was his thing, working the tracks where the cash money was and the crowds and the excitement. Only the security boys made him and he got the boot."

"Who fed you that?"

"Banjie Peters. He hustled tout sheets. He even knew the guy from a few other tracks that kicked him out. So the only place he don't get the boot is Aqueduct and he comes up here for the season. He works it one day and blammo . . . security spots him and gives him the heave. He was lucky because he didn't even have time to make his first touch. They find him with anything on him and it's curtains out there."

"They have a name for him?"

"Sure, a dozen, and no two alike." He gave me a funny little grin and fished around in his legless lap for something. "I kind of figured you'd be around so I had Banjie con his buddies in security outa a picture they had. They mugged him at Santa Anita and sent copies around."

He held out a two-by-two black and white photo of a lean, sallow-looking face with a mouth that was too small and eyes that seemed to sneer at the world. His hair had receded on the sides and acne scars marred the jawline. The picture cut him off at chest level, but under his coat he had on an off-shade vest with metal buttons that could have been red. His description on the back put him at age forty-six, five feet eleven tall and one hundred fifty-two pounds. Eight aliases were given, no two remotely alike, and no permanent address.

Now I knew what he looked like.

Little Joe said, "He couldn't score at the track, that's why he started hustling around here. You remember Poxie?" While I nodded Joe went on. "When he ain't pimping he keeps his hand in working other people's pockets. This boy sees him working Shubert Alley and beats the crap outa him. Like he laid out a claim and was protecting it. Over there's where he and Lippy used to meet up. You know, Mike, I don't think Lippy knew what the guy was doing."

"He didn't," I said.

"Maybe he found out, huh? Then this guy bumped him."

"Not quite like that, pal. You know where he is now?"

"Nope, but I seen him last night. He come outa one of them Greek language movies on Eighth Avenue and hopped a cab going uptown. I woulda taken the cab number so you could check out his trip sheet, only I was on the wrong side of the street."

"Good try, kid."

"If you want, I'll try harder."

I looked at him, wondering what he meant.

Little Joe grinned again and said, "I saw Velda too. She was right behind him and grabbed the cab after his."

The knot in my stomach held fast, not knowing whether to twist tighter or loosen. "What time, Joe?"

"Last show was coming out. Just a little after two thirty."

And the knot loosened. She was still on her own then and Ballinger hadn't caught up with her. She had located our pickpocket and was running him down.

Little Joe was still looking at me. "I saved the best until last, Mike," he said. "The name he really goes by is Beaver. Like a nickname. He was in Len Parrott's saloon when Len heard two guys ask about him. This guy drops his drink fast and gets out. They were asking about a red vest too and the guy had one on." A frown drew his eyebrows together. "They was Woody Ballinger's boys, Mike."

I said, "Damn" softly.

"The bartender didn't tell them nothing, though."

I let a five-spot fall into Little Joe's box. "I appreciate it, buddy. You get anything else, call Pat Chambers. Remember him?"

"Captain Pat? Sure, how could I ever forget him? He shot the guy who blew my legs off with that shotgun fifteen years ago."

If you can't find them, then let them find you. The word was out now in all the right places. It would travel fast and far and someplace a decision would have to be made. I was on a hunt for Sammy and Carl to throw a bullet through their guts and do the explaining afterward. They'd start to sweat because there was plenty of precedent to go by. I had put too many punks they knew under a gun for them to think I wouldn't do it and the only way to stop it would be to get me first. They were the new cool breed, smart, polished and deadly, so full of confidence that they had a tendency to forget that there were others who could play the game even better. Who was it that said, *"Don't mess around with the old pros"*?

I finished straightening up the wreckage in the office, pulled a beer out of the cooler and sat down to enjoy it. From the street I could hear the taxis hooting and thought about Velda. She was a pro too and it would take a pretty sharp article to top her. She knew the streets and she knew the people. She wasn't about to expose herself and blow the whole job no matter how far into it she had gotten. If the chips went down, she'd have that little rod in her hand, make herself a lousy target and take somebody down too. At least in New York you heard about shootings.

I switched on the transistor radio she had given me and dialed the news station. For ten minutes there was a political analysis of the new attitude the Russians had taken, seemingly agreeable to acting in harmony with U.S. policy along certain peace efforts, then the announcer got into sports. Halfway through there was a special bulletin rapped out in staccato voice telling the world that the hired killers of Tom-Tom Schneider had been located in a cheap hotel in Buffalo, New York, and police officers and F.B.I. troops had surrounded the building and were engaged in a gunfight, but refraining from a capture attempt because the pair had taken two maids as hostages.

Okay, Pat, there's your news blast for tomorrow. Plenty of pictures and plenty of stories. It would cover all news media in every edition and the little find at the Ashokan Reservoir would stay a one-column squib that nobody would notice and you had one more day without a panic.

There was a four-car wreck on the West Side Highway. A mental patient leaped from the roof of an East Side hospital, landed on a filled laundry cart and was unhurt. No other shootings, though, and the regular musical program resumed.

All I could do was wait awhile.

At six thirty in the morning I woke up when my feet fell off the desk. Daylight had crept into the office, lighting the eerie stillness of a building not yet awake. There was a distant whine of the elevator, probably the servicemen coming in, a sound you never heard at any other hour. I stood up, stretched to get the stiffness out of my shoulders and cursed when a little knife of pain shot across my side where the slug had scorched me. Two blocks away a nice guy I knew who used to be a doctor before they lifted his license for practicing abortions would take care of that for me. Maybe a tailor could fix my jacket. Right now the spare I kept in the office would do me.

At eight fifteen I picked up the duplicate photo cards Gabin's Film Service had made up for me, mug shots of the guy they called Beaver with his résumé printed on the back. A half hour later I was having coffee with Pat and gave him all but three of them.

He called me two dirty names and stuck them in his pocket. "And you said you wanted nothing to do with it," he reminded me.

"Sorry about that," I said.

"Yeah. Professional curiosity?"

"Personal interest."

"You're still out of line. Regulations state you're supposed to represent a client." He dunked a doughnut in his coffee and took a bite of half of it.

"Be happy, friend. I'm giving you no trouble, I'm paying for the snack and staying out of your way. You should be glad citizens take an active interest in affairs like this. Besides, you haven't got the time."

"So why the photos?"

"You still have routine jobs going. Pass them along to the plainclothes boys. Maybe you got bigger things on your mind, but this is still an open murder."

"For you it's not open."

"I'm just throwing back the foul balls."

"Mike," he said, "you're full of shit. Sometimes I wish I had never known you."

"You worry too much, friend."

"Maybe you should. The days are going by fast."

I took a close look at his face. The lines were deeper now, his eyes a lined red, and when he spoke it was almost without moving his lips. Somehow he couldn't focus on me, seeming to look past me when he spoke. "Our Soviet friends have come up with another piece of information. When we wouldn't let them out of the country they really began digging. That strain of bacteria the former regime packaged and sent here was more virulent than even they suspected. If it's loose there's no hope of containing it, none at all. The lads at Fort Detrick confirmed it and if we don't get a break pretty damn quick it's all over, Mike, all over."

"That doesn't sound like police information."

"Crane broke down when he got the news. I was there when he went hysterical and blew it."

"How many others know this?" I asked him.

"You're the eleventh." He finished the doughnut and sipped at his coffee. "Kind of funny. We sit here like nothing's happening at all. We want a pickpocket in a red vest, I watch the teletype to see how they're doing in Buffalo with those contract hoods, everybody else is plugging through the daily grind and in a few days we'll all be part of the air pollution until nature figures a way out of it in a couple million years."

"Man, you're a happy guy today."

Pat put the cup down and finally got his eyes fixed on mine. "Mike," he said, "I'm beginning to figure you out."

"Oh?"

"Yeah. You're crazy. Something's missing in your head. Right now I could lay odds that all you're thinking about is a dame."

"You'd lose," I said. I picked up the tab and stood up. "I'm thinking about two of them."

Pat shook his head disgustedly again. "Naked?"

"Naturally," I said.

chapter nine ▬▬▬▬▬▬▬▬▬▬▬▬▬▬▬▬▬▬▬

SOMETHING HAD HAPPENED to the Broadway grapevine. Nobody had seen Velda and although a half-dozen of the regular crowd were able to spot the red-vested Beaver by his photograph, nobody had seen him either. Woody Ballinger, Carl and Sammy were in the nothing pocket too and I was beginning to get those funny little looks like it was *"Watch out, Mike, you're tangling with the trouble crowd now"* time. Not that it was a new experience, but they were beginning to watch and wait, hoping to be there when the action started.

Some people liked car races. You could see the big kill happen there too. Others took it where they could find it, and now they were beginning to get a blood smell and watched the field leaders to see who was going to crowd who in the turn and wind up in pieces along the walls of Manhattan. By noon the sunny day had turned overcast again, the smog reaching down with choking little fingers, and I had reached Lexington Avenue where I had another cup of coffee in a side-street deli just to get out of it.

The counterman used to work for Woody and he couldn't give me a lead at all. It was nearly my last straw until I remembered how close I was to that crazy pad in the new building just a few blocks away, and finished the coffee and picked up a pack of butts at the cashier's desk while I paid my bill. There was somebody else who knew the people I was looking for.

The doorman flipped a fingertip to his cap and said, "Afternoon, sir."

"Your partner still courting?"

"He'll never learn. Last night he got engaged. I do double shifts and don't get any sleep, but I'm sure making the bucks. Just wait until he starts buying furniture."

"Miss Anders in?"

"Sure. Different girl, that. Something happened to her. Real bright-eyed now. I think maybe she dumped that clown she was going with. Playboy, no good at all. Too much money. Last night she got in at ten, and alone. You want me to call up, officer?"

I grinned at him, wishing Pat could have been here. He would have turned inside out. To Pat I was always the other side of the fence, with my face always the prime type to get picked up in a general dragnet.

"Don't bother," I said. I returned his casual wave and walked to the elevator.

Heidi Anders saw me through the peephole and snapped off the double locks on the door. It opened a scant three inches on the chain and that pert face with the tousled ash-blonde hair and full-lipped mouth was peering at me with a disguised smile and I said, "Trick or treat?"

The door closed and I heard the chain come off. When it opened again her head was tilted in a funny smile, the upslanted eyes laughing at me. "Trick," she said. Then added. "But if you come in, it'll be a treat."

"I'll come in."

She let the door open all the way and I walked inside. I was treated. Heidi Anders was standing there bare-ass naked, prettier than any centerfold picture in a girlie magazine and no matter how lovely those uniquely rounded breasts were, or how all that ash-blonde hair contrasted, all I could see was that crazy navel with the eyelashes painted around it like an oversexed Cyclops.

"I just got up," she said.

"Don't you ever take your makeup off?"

"It's part of my personality," she told me. "Most men have an immediate reaction." She closed and locked the door behind me. "I wish you had."

"I want to wink at it."

"At least that's different." She smiled and walked down the hall, not bothering to take my hat this time. That wild gait was still there, but naked it had a totally new sway. I let her get all the way into the living room before I moved. Then I went in slowly, watching all the corners just to be sure, glad to have been in enough games not to get wiped out at the first charge of the opposition.

She didn't know it, but my hand was hooked over my belt, the palm comfortable against the butt of the .45. Too many times naked women and death walked side by side.

Heidi had thrown back the draperies and stood there in the cold gray light that brought out the tan marks on the flesh, then turned around slowly to face me. "Do I look different, Mike?"

The navel still watched me. Crazy eye. Blind, but crazy and watching. The lashes were extra long.

"Different," I said.

"You did it. You yelled at me. Mike . . . you were pretty rough."

"A broad like you shouldn't get hooked on H. There's too much going for you." I picked a cigarette out of my deck and lit it up. "Sorry about yelling at you."

"It wasn't that." She picked up something filmy from the chair and drew it through her hands. "I saw your face when I turned you off. I was lying there all ready and waiting and I turned you off. That never happened to me before. I wanted to get laid and I was right there waiting for you and I turned you off. You yelled. I felt like . . . you know what I felt like?"

I nodded. "No retractions, kid."

"Good. We did well, the doctor and I."

"How about Woody Ballinger's goons?"

For a second I thought I had played it wrong, then she kinked her lips in a tiny smile and her eyes lit up again. "I asked around," she said. "You were right, you know."

I reached up and slipped my hat off casually, and held it in front of me. "Will you get dressed?"

I got that grin again. "I asked around about more than Woody Ballinger." Once more I got that provocative, tilt-headed glance. "I didn't think you were so sensitive." Then she sway-walked over to me and held out her hand. "Can I take your hat?"

"Don't be smart-ass," I said. "Just make me a drink."

"They were right." She stepped back and looked at me with feigned wide-eyed amazement. "They were really right."

But she made the drinks, a long cooler for me and a short one for herself, and sat down opposite me in all that colorful nudity and crossed her legs like she was at a tea party in a Pucci dress and let me have the full impact of that little eye in her navel that never blinked and just looked at me with an unrelenting stare.

"Uncomfortable?" she asked flippantly.

But age has its benefits and experience its knowledge. I tossed my hat on the couch and grinned at her. "Nope."

Her smile turned into a mock frown. "Damn, I hate you older

men. You have too much control. How do you do it?"

"Science, kitten."

"Impossible."

"See for yourself."

"I do but I don't believe it. How can I turn you on again?"

"By quitting the damn hippie talk and answering some questions."

Heidi raised her glass and tasted it, her eyes on mine. "One favor deserves another."

"Where's Carl and Sammy? And Woody?"

Her glass stopped just short of her mouth. "What?"

"You heard me."

"But . . ."

"I told you to pass the word along."

"Mike . . . I told them what you said."

"No reaction? No nothing? You aren't the type of broad they pick up at a bar and not one they leave alone. Those damn slobs can buy tail or crook a finger and it'll come running out of their stables for them. You're a class broad and for you they'll give an excuse. They were both on the make the other night and the way they were pushing they wouldn't just bust out of a date. Where are they, Heidi?"

Her fingers were stiff around the glass and she had tucked her lower lip between her teeth, looking at me intently. "Mike . . .

"Sammy . . . he . . . well, he wanted to see me again and we, well, we sort of made a date, but he called and said it would have to wait."

"Why, honey? Girls don't let a guy off the hook that easily."

"Woody wanted him to . . . do something. He couldn't cancel it."

"Has he called again?"

She nodded, glanced at her drink, then put it down. "Today. An hour ago, I guess."

"Where was he?"

"He didn't say. All he told me was that he'd see me tonight. His job would be done then."

"Where'd he call from?"

"I don't know."

"Damn it, think!"

"Mike . . ."

"Look," I told her. "Remember back. Was he alone? Quiet?"

"No," she said abruptly. "It was noisy, wherever he was. I could hear the tooting."

"Tooting?"

"Well, it was like two toots, then while we were talking, three toots."

"What the hell is a *toot?*" I asked her.

"A toot! You never heard a toot? A horn toot. No, it was a whistle toot. Oh, balls, I don't know what was tooting. It just tooted. Two, then three."

"Heidi . . ."

"I'm not drunk and I'm not high, damn it, Mike . . ."

"Sorry." I let a little grin seep out. How the hell can you get sore at a naked dame four feet away who was so excited she even forgot and uncrossed her legs like she had a dress on. "He say when he was going to see you?"

"Just tonight." She saw the look on my face and frowned too. "If it helps . . . he said he'd call me today sometime to let me know when."

"There are a lot of hours in the day, kid."

"Well, I got mad and said I'd be gone all afternoon and if he wanted to call me it had better be before noon."

I looked at my watch. Noon was an hour away. And in an hour anything could happen. "Let's wait," I said.

Heidi grinned and picked up her drink again. The eye in her navel seemed to half close in its own kind of smile and never stopped watching me. She got up with studied ease, little muscles rippling down her thighs, her breasts taut and pointed and came across the few feet that separated us. Very gently she sat down on my lap.

"Hurt?"

"No," I said.

"Ummmm." Heidi finished the drink and tossed the empty glass on the sofa, then turned around, her hand behind my neck. "I really don't want to see Sammy anyway, Mike."

"Do it for me."

"I owe you more than that."

She squirmed and the glass almost fell out of my hand. She was all sleek and sweet smells and the heat from her body emanated in all directions like some wild magnetic force. Her hand found mine and pressed it against her stomach and all the concerted thought I had had for what was happening outside started to drift away like smoke in an updraft and her mouth kept coming closer and closer, the lips rich and red and wet.

But the phone rang, that damn, screaming, monstrous necessity with the insistent voice that demanded to be answered.

I had to push her to her feet, put her hand on the receiver and wait another second until the shock of the change registered sadly in her eyes.

"Get it," I said.

She picked up the phone, my ear close to hers at the receiver. "Hello?"

The voice was partly hoarse, a muffled voice trying to be heard over some background noise. "Heidi?" Something rumbled and I heard three short faraway sounds and knew it was what she had called *toots*.

"Hello . . . Sammy?" she asked.

Then there was another voice that said, "You crazy!" and the connection was chopped off abruptly.

Heidi let the phone drop back into its cradle, her face puzzled. "It was him."

"Somebody didn't want him making a call," I said.

"I heard those toots again."

"I know. They're blasting warnings around construction sites. Three of them was the all-clear signal."

"Mike . . ."

I reached for my hat, feeling the skin tight around my jaws. "He won't be calling back, Heidi. Not right now."

Someplace things were coming to a head and here I was fiddling around with a naked doll, letting her wipe things right out of my mind. I picked up the phone, dialed my office number and triggered my recording gimmick. One call was from a West Coast agency wanting me to handle some Eastern details for them, the other was from a local lawyer who needed a deposition from me, and the third was from William Dorn who wanted me to call him as soon as possible. I let the tape roll, but there was nothing from Velda or anybody else. I broke the connection, waited a second, then dialed Dorn's office. His secretary told me that he had been trying to reach me, but had gone to a meeting in his apartment thirty minutes ago and I should try him there. She gave me the number and his address and hung up. When I dialed his place the phone was busy, so I gave it another minute and tried again. It was still busy. I said to hell with it, hung up and slapped my hat on.

Heidi had made herself another drink, but none for me. She knew it was over now. I said, "Tough, kitten. It might have been fun."

She took my hand and walked the length of the corridor, then turned and stood on her toes, all naked and beautiful, and reached for my mouth with hers. I let my hands play over her gently, my fingers aching with remorse because there wasn't time to do all the things I wanted to do with her.

Gently she took her mouth away and smiled. "Another day, Mike?"

"Another day, Heidi. You're worth it now."

"I think it will be something special then."

My fingers squeezed her shoulder easily. "Dump those bums of Woody's."

"For you, Mike, anything." She stepped back two paces, an impish grin teasing her mouth, and did something with her stomach muscles.

That nutty eye that was her navel actually winked at me.

The doorman in the towering building on Park Avenue was an old pro heavyweight decked out in a blue uniform trimmed with gold braid that was too tight across his shoulders and his face was enough to scare off anybody who thought they could cross those sacred portals without going through the elaborate screening process that was part of the high rent program.

He half-stepped to intercept me when I came through the glass doors and I said, "Hi, Spud. Do I say hello or salute?"

Spud Henry squinted at me once, then stepped back with a grin that made his face uglier but friendlier and held out a massive paw to grip mine in a crushing handshake. "Mike, you old S.O.B.! How the hell are you?"

"Back to normal when you let go my hand." I laughed at him. "What're you doing here? I thought you had saved your money."

"Hell, man, I sure did, but try retiring around that old lady of mine. She drives me bats. All the time wants me to do somethin' that don't need doin'. *Take the garbage out.* What garbage out? *Who cares, take it out. Paint the bathroom.* I just painted the bathroom. *The color stinks. Get those kids outa the backyard.* Whatta ya mean, get 'em out, they're our kids. Man, don't never get married. It was easier fightin' in the ring."

"How many kids you got, Spud?"

"Twelve."

"How old's the youngest?"

"Two months. Why?"

"Some fighting you do."

Spud gave me a sheepish grin and shrugged. "Well hell, Mike, ya gotta take a rest between rounds, don't ya?" He paused and cocked his head. "What you doin' up this way? I thought you was a side-street type."

"I have to see William Dorn. He in?"

"Sure. Got here a little while ago. He got a crowd up there. Some kind of party?"

"Beats me. What's his apartment?"

"Twenty-two, the east terrace. Real fancy place. Since when you goin' with the swells?"

"Come on, Spud, I got a little class."

"That's *big* class up there, Mikey boy. Man, what loot, but nice people. Big tippers, always polite, even to me. Just nice people. When the last kid was born he gimme a hundred bucks. One bill with a fat one-zero-zero on it and it was like the days back in the Garden when they used to pay off in brand-new century notes. You want me to announce you?"

"Never mind. He called me. I didn't call him."

"Take that back elevator. It's express. Good to see you, Mike."

"Same here. Tell the missus hello."

I got off at the twenty-second floor into an elaborate gold-scrolled and marble-ornamented vestibule that reeked of wealth only a few ever got to know, turned east to a pair of massive mahogany doors inlaid with intricate carvings and set off with thick polished brass fixtures. I located the tiny bell button set into the frame, pushed it and waited. No sound penetrated through the doors or walls, nothing came up from the street and I didn't hear anything ring. I was about to touch it again when bolts clicked and the door opened and William Dorn stood there, a drink in one hand and a sheaf of papers in the other.

His surprise was brief, then he pulled the door open and said, "Mike . . . good to see you. Come in. I didn't know you were on the way up."

I didn't want to get Spud in a jam so I said, "I slipped by the doorman while he was busy. Sneaky habit I can't get out of."

Dorn laughed and closed the door. From the other room a subdued murmur of voices blended into a monotonous hum. I could see the backs and shoulders of a dozen men in quiet conversation and when one looked around I spotted Teddy Finlay with Josef Kudak beside him and a few feet away the six-foot-six beanpole from the Ukraine who made all those anti-U.S. speeches in the United Nations last month. This time they all seemed to be pounding at one nail with no disagreement for a change.

"Didn't mean to break in on your party," I said.

"Business meeting," Dorn told me. "Glad you could come. Let's go into the library where we can talk. Care for a drink?"

"No thanks."

He folded the papers in his hand and stuffed them in his pocket. "This way."

The library was another example of class and money. It was there in rare first editions and original oils, genuine Sheraton furniture giving obeisance to a great Louis XIV desk at one end of the room that nestled there like a throne.

"You ever read all those books?" I asked Dorn.

"Most of them." He waved me to a chair. Before I got comfortable he asked, "What happened to Renée?"

"She got creased by a bullet."

Dorn nearly dropped his drink. His mouth pulled tight and I saw his shoulders stiffen. "She didn't tell me . . ."

"Don't worry, she's okay."

"What happened?"

"Nothing I'm going to talk about right now. Why?"

"She . . . well, she's important to me, damn it. Right now we have a big expansion move on and . . ." He looked at me, shook his head and glanced down at his hands that were clasped together too tightly. Finally he looked up. "It might be better if you said what you were thinking, Mike. I'm a callous person so wrapped up in business and finance that nothing else matters. Nothing is expected to interfere with those vital affairs."

"Don't sweat it, William. She'll be okay."

"Is she . . ."

"Just a crease. She was real lucky. I'm surprised she didn't tell you about it."

"Renée can keep a confidence, even from me. I knew she was with you, but it was unlike her to . . ."

"It was justified. Hell, doesn't she ever get sick?"

"Never."

"A dame got to get her period once in a while. That's usually a good excuse."

"Not with Renée. She treats . . . commerce, let's say, almost as I do. You're the first one she ever took an active interest in."

"You don't know what you're missing," I said.

For a second a flash of annoyance creased his eyes, then disappeared into a wry smile. "You may be right. I've heard that before." He picked up a pencil and tapped it against the polished wood of the desk. "Mike . . . do me a favor."

I nodded.

"Check on her. She won't answer the phone and I'd rather not bother her after what you just told me."

"Be glad to."

"And Mike . . ."

"If it can be avoided, don't expose her to . . . well, anything more in your line. I'd appreciate that."

"I didn't expose anybody. It just happened. She wanted to see how we lived on the other side of the tracks. I could have told her it could be just as rough where she came from too because I've been on the other side of the bridge myself. Nobody ever seems to learn anything, do they?"

The seconds ticked by while he looked at me, finally nodding agreement. "And you, Mike. Do you ever learn?"

"Always something new," I said. I got up and took a last look at all the money that surrounded me. "I'll check in on Renée for you. She'll be fine, so quit worrying."

Dorn held out his hand and I took it. "Sorry you couldn't get me at the office. I didn't mean for you to go out of your way. I guess it really wasn't that important after all."

"No trouble," I said.

He walked me to the door and behind me the hum of voices had grown louder. One was edgy and hoarse, but I recognized it as Crane's from the State Department. The one he was talking to said, "Nyet, nyet!" then subsided while Crane finished talking. I said, "So long" to Dorn at the door, took the elevator back down again and looked for Spud. He was gone, and a tall kid with a sad face had replaced him. He had his hair tucked under the back of his visored cap and didn't look happy about it. They probably even made him shave off his beard. He couldn't have run off a Bowery panhandler.

Rain. Someday they'd cover New York like the Astrodome and you wouldn't have to worry about it. The computers had predicted partly cloudy and had sat back in their oiled compartments with all the whirring and clacking, giving off with mechanical laughter at the idiots who had believed their programming. The smart one knew the city. Never predict New York. Never try to outthink it. The damn octopus could even control the weather and when it wanted everybody to be miserable, everybody was miserable.

I looked up at the tops of the buildings and watched the gray blanket of wet sifting down to slick the streets and fog the windows, wondering why the hell I didn't get out like Hy Gardner did. A cab pulled up and disgorged a fat little man who threw a bill at the driver and trotted across the sidewalk to the protection of the building entrance and before the elderly couple frantically waving at the cabbie from the corner could make the run, I hopped in and closed the door. The driver saw my face in the rearview mirror and didn't try for the Sweetest Cabbie of the Year award. I gave him Renée's address and sat back while he pulled out into the traffic and U-turned at the corner to head north.

The ends. Why the hell don't they meet? It wasn't all that complicated, just a simple rundown of a lousy pickpocket who lost his haul to an honest guy who tried to keep him straight and killed to get it back. A lousy pickpocket who had hit the wrong pockets and now there were others looking for him too, but why? What did Woody Ballinger have to lose? Heidi Anders had a compact with her life wrapped up in white powder in a false bottom. She would have done anything for a single pop of the junk and damn near did until I creamed her out. Now it was Woody trying to beat me to Beaver.

The driver's radio blared out another of those special bulletins the networks loved to issue. In Buffalo, New York the police had shot and killed Tom-Tom Schneider's killers. The hostages were unharmed. Tomorrow the papers and TV would carry the full account and Pat Chambers could count on another day free of panic. But where the hell was Velda? Where was that lousy dip Beaver in the red vest and where were Woody Ballinger and his boys? The rain splattered against the windows and the radio went back to Dow-Jones averages and the cab pulled into the curb. I peeled off a five from my roll and handed it through the window to the driver.

The little patch on her head around the shaved area of her scalp was nearly unnoticeable, her hair covering it with the usual feminine vanity. I grinned at her, lying there under the covers and she smiled back, her eyes twinkling. "I know," she said, "under the covers, the nightgown . . . I'm stark naked."

"Lovely," I said.

"X-ray eyes?"

"Absolutely. I walk down Fifth Avenue and all those broads in their fancy clothes think they're hiding something? Hell, I look right through them and all I see is skin and hair and toenails that need cutting. Everybody's naked, sugar."

"Am I naked?"

"My X-ray eyes are out of order."

Renée looked at me and smiled, then pushed the covers down

to her midriff, then all the way to her feet with a quick flip of her hand. Without taking her eyes off mine, she tugged at the nightgown, then slipped it over her head and tossed it to the floor.

"*Now* you're naked," I said.

"You don't sound excited."

"I'm an old dog, kid. I had this happen before lunch." I lit up a butt and took a deep drag, then let the smoke blow across the bed.

"I could kill you."

"You are."

"How can you resist me?"

"It isn't easy. Luckily, you're a sick woman."

"Horse manure," Renée said. "Tell me how pretty I am."

I looked at her lying there. "You look like a perfect biological specimen. Everything's in the right place, the titties are pointing in the right direction, but a little saggy because you're flat out like that. The snatch is cute, very decorous, but for a connoisseur like me, maybe a little bushy. A touch with a pair of scissors might sharpen up the angles and trim it down to size. . . ."

"Oh, you dirty . . ."

"Ah-ah . . . you're a sick woman, remember?" I help up my hand to stop her. "But you look kissable and parts of you are wet and inviting and if I didn't have all the moral turpitude I was born with, do you know what I'd do?"

"I wish you'd just screw me and shut up."

"You got no class, Renée."

"You got no dick, Mike Hammer."

"Want references?" I asked her. "How's the head?"

She touched her scalp with her fingertips and winced. "Sore, but not that sore. I've been deliberately taking advantage of my . . . condition, and staying bedridden."

"I know. And your boss is up in the air over your disappearance. It seems that he can't get along without you. I'm here on a rescue mission to get you back to work."

Her mouth formed a fake pout. "I thought you just wanted to see me."

"Right now I'm seeing all of you there is to see."

"You've missed the other side."

"Leave something to the imagination, will you? Besides, suppose that maid of yours walks in here?"

"Oh, she'll understand."

I shook my head and laughed. Dames. "Get up and get dressed. If you hustle I'll have a coffee with you while I use your phone."

Renée grimaced and tossed a pillow at me. "Your casual treatment is making me feel married, you big slob. How can you resist me like this?"

"It isn't easy at all, sugar. If I had the time I'd tear you apart."

"Nothing but promises."

I threw the pillow back at her and went back to the living room. The chubby little maid with the odd accent had her coat on and asked me to tell Miss Talmage she was leaving for the afternoon, but would be back around five to prepare supper. If she was needed, she could be reached at her sister's. Miss Talmage had the number.

When she left I picked up the phone and called Henaghan at the New York City Department of Public Works. His second secretary found him and put him through.

"Hey, Mike," he yelled. "What's new?"

"Need some information, Henny."

"Well, this is a public department."

"See if you can check and find out what construction units have been issued permits for blasting inside the city limits. Can do?"

There was a small silence and Henaghan said, "Aw, Mike, have you taken a look around lately? This town is like a beehive. They're putting up stuff all over the place."

"Yeah, but they only blast during the ground operation. It shouldn't be all that difficult."

"Look, I'll give you a number . . ."

"No dice. I'll get handed from file clerks to petty officials who'll want explanations and authorizations and still come up with year-old information. I could do better touring the city in a taxi taking notes and I haven't got that much time. You do it for me."

"Mike . . . " Henny sounded harried.

"Or do you forget me having to run up to Albany to get you out of the can last summer? Or that time in Miami when . . ."

"Okay, okay. Don't remind me. The memories are too painful. Where are you?"

I gave him the phone number.

"Stay there. It may take a little while, but I'll expedite things."

From the bedroom I heard the shower cut off and clothes hangers rattling in a closet. I stared absently at the rain slashing against the window and picked up the phone again, dialed my office number and activated the tape recorder.

And Velda had finally called in. Her voice was crisp and hurried, no words wasted at all. She said, "Suspect located at Anton Virelli's area and running fast. Ballinger's right behind him with his men but haven't pinpointed his location. If you haven't hit it yet, suspect goes by name of Beaver and knows he's being tracked. He's been working his way uptown and has something on his mind, probably a safe place to hide out. He should be making a move soon if he sticks to his timetable. My guess is he'll come out of the west end of the block so I'm going to take a chance and cover the Broadway side. I'll call back as soon as he shows."

That was the end of the message and I was about to hang up when another click signaled a further message and a voice said, "Uh, Mike? Like this is you or a machine. Mike?" There was a pause, then, "So you're automated. Everything's gone automated." I felt like telling that silly Caesar Mario Tulley to hurry up and get with it, but you don't rush the new generation. "You know how you was asking about that guy in the red vest? So I split a joint with an old friend and we get to talking and I asked and sure enough, he knows a guy who knows him. I'm going to see him later, so if you get down this way I'll be working around the Winter Garden. Maybe I'll have something for you. Uh . . . how the hell do you say so long to a machine anyway?" He mumbled something else and the connection was ended.

Damn, it was closing in fast. The ends were beginning to meet, but they were all tied up inside a tape recorder and I had to wait for the spool to roll. But Velda had narrowed it down somewhat. Anton Virelli was a bookie who operated from a storefront on Ninety-second Street just off Broadway. At least now I knew what area to concentrate on. I called Pat and rousted him out of bed at home. He hadn't had much sleep, but he softened the growl in his voice and listened when I gave him the information. He thought he could tap a couple of plainclothesmen to probe the area for Beaver and he could get a warrant out for Woody and his boys that might slow them down long enough for us to reach our man first. I thanked him and hung up.

A lovely voice behind me said, "Beaver. What an odd name. The people you know."

I turned around and Renée was standing there, fresh from the shower, her hair piled on top of her head, wrapped in a heavy white terry-cloth robe belted tightly enough to make her a living hourglass. She smelled of summery fragrances and bath oils and she pirouetted gracefully so I could see all of her, then wrinkled her nose at me, brought in a tray with a coffee pot and two cups and sat down.

"Great," she said. "Naked, I get no reaction. Completely covered in an old robe you simper like a kid. What's with you men?"

I took the coffee she handed me. "We like the mystery better."

"Liar. Business is more important to you. What have you been so busy about and who is Beaver? Another one of your friends who shoot at people?"

"I never met the guy."

She gave me a hurt look. "All right, you don't have to tell me anything. But don't blame me for being curious, please. After all, I did get shot and it was a new experience, one that I wouldn't like to repeat, and I thought some kind of explanation might be in order."

Wind from the river rattled the window and the rain tried to claw its way in. I looked at her and grinned. Hell, she was entitled. I fished in my pocket and took out the three photos of Beaver, handing her one. I let her look at it while I started from the beginning and brought her up to date. But it was really me I was talking to, trying to jell the details in my mind, picking out the strange little flaws and attempting to force in things that didn't belong or should have.

She handed the picture back and I stuck it in my pocket.

The phone still sat there, impassive and unconcerned with it all.

The muscles were tight across my back and my hands were knotted into balls of rage.

"Mike . . ." she came over to me and unbuttoned my jacket, then slipped it off, her hands kneading the back of my neck. I closed my eyes and felt the tension begin to melt under the gentle pressure of her fingers. She tugged the shoulder harness off then and let the .45 drop to the floor, then it was my tie and my shirt, her hands working their way across my chest and arms. Her palms pushed me back on the couch and her fingers worked at my belt and I just let her go ahead until she was done. I felt her stand up, heard the soft whisper of cloth and let my eyes slit open a bare fraction and watched her standing there warmly nude and smiling. "Don't move," she said.

I closed my eyes again, wiping out all thought for the minute she was gone, then heard her come in and opened them again. She threw a pillow on the floor beside the couch, knelt down with her arms outstretched and the vibrator she had attached to her hand started to pulsate crazily as she started at my neck and began a slow, deliberate journey into other areas.

Time went by in slow, lazy circles, then the erotic tingling of the vibrator stopped and a more intense sensation replaced it until time erupted into an explosive spiral that diminished out of sight and left me gasping for breath.

On the table the phone had come to life.

I opened my eyes and Renée said, "Good?"

"Beautiful."

I reached over and picked up the receiver.

Henaghan told me I probably could have done better with the taxi ride, but came up with five places conducting blasting operations at the moment. I wrote them all down, thanked him and hung up, looking at the list in my hand.

Only one place was above Fifty-second Street, an area off Columbus Avenue at One Hundred-tenth Street. And that wasn't anywhere near Anton Virelli's territory at all. If Velda was holding down a stakeout around Ninety-second and Broadway, she was doing it alone. Somehow Beaver had cut loose earlier and with more manpower to cover the exits, Woody and his boys had caught his move and had him cornered in another location.

In a way it was a relief to me. She was out of the action now and I wanted to keep it that way. If Velda didn't tumble to the fact that Beaver was gone I could move in alone without sweating about her catching a slug. I looked at the paper again and swore softly. An area, that's all it was. A big flat area with hundreds of holes to crawl into. Those blasting signals were clear, but distant, tonal enough to penetrate phone booth walls or old apartments. There wasn't any chance of tracking down every telephone in the neighborhood at all. What I needed was an address. Beaver was heading for one definite spot, that was sure. One place where he figured he'd be safe. He was enough of an old hand to stay out of the hands of other pros so far and he'd be playing it smart and cagy.

Caesar Mario Tulley was going to get me that address.

Renée had slipped back into her robe and was sitting on the end of the couch, watching me with a small, wistful smile. "I hate telephones," she said.

"Things are beginning to move."

"I know. You came, now you have to go."

"Your turn the next time," I said.

"It's all right, Mike. Some things are more important than others." She saw me frowning, not knowing how to answer her, and nodded. "Really, I understand," she added.

"Beaver's someplace around Columbus and a Hundred-tenth Street, Woody's boys have him hemmed in. He's probably pinned down temporarily, but not located yet. I want first crack at that bastard."

"You know where he is?"

"No, but somebody else might have the answer."

"Mike . . ." Renée's face went soft and worried. "Please be careful. I would like to see you again."

"You will."

"This wild business of yours . . . well, I guess I've been in a pretty distant world." She licked her lips and shook her head in disbelief. "Dead people . . . I've been shot . . ." her eyes met mine then, " . . . and you, Mike."

"Things aren't all that bad," I said.

She tried to smile, but it was forced. I suddenly felt pretty silly standing there without any clothes on. She knew what I was feeling, faked a grin, then stood up and frowned. Her hand shot out to the table to support herself.

"You all right?" I asked her.

She touched the side of her head, blinked, then nodded, taking a deep breath. "Just my head. I still can't move too quickly. I get dizzy when I do." Her smile came back, this time with natural ease. "Why don't you go inside and get dressed? I'm going to call my maid back. There are times when I just don't like to be left alone."

I picked up my clothes, somehow feeling guilty, and went into the bedroom. I showered quickly, climbed into my clothes, snugged the .45 down in its sling and went back into the living room.

For a minute I thought she wasn't there, then I saw a small upturned palm sticking out from behind the chair and half ran to where she was lying. Her eyes were partially slitted open and a trickle of blood was oozing down from under the pad on her scalp.

I got my hands under her arms and lifted her to the couch, stretching her out with a pillow under her feet. A couple of ice-cold wet towels finally brought a flicker to her eyes and she moaned softly. "What the hell happened, kid?"

She let her eyelids close, then open. "I was . . . calling Maria . . . and I fainted." I looked at the compress on her head. One end had come loose from where it had evidently hit something. She winced and pushed my hand away.

"You want me to get a doctor?"

"No . . . I'll be all right. Please . . . don't leave until Maria gets here."

"Sure, kid. How do you feel?"

"Awful . . . headache."

Luckily, Maria's sister only worked three blocks away and she was there in ten minutes. She helped me get Renée into bed, but kept looking at me suspiciously as though she didn't believe what really had happened. She made me leave while she got a nightgown on her, then came bustling back into the living room, frowning. Just in time I kicked the vibrator under the couch before she saw it. "You stay. I'm going to the drugstore for something to make her sleep."

I got that guilty feeling again and just nodded.

From the bedroom I heard Renée call my name and I walked in and took her hand. There was a fresh bandage in place and the blood had been wiped from her hair. "Mike . . . I'm sorry.

"Forget it."

"Go do what you have to do," she said softly.

I looked at my watch. It was still early. Caesar liked to work the later crowds; he looked a little more pitiful under the night lights. "I got time," I told her.

It was thirty minutes before Maria got back with a plastic bottle of capsules, and another thirty before the drowsiness came over Renée's eyes. Just before they closed, she said, "It *was* nice, wasn't it, Mike?"

"Crazy, but beautiful," I answered.

Maria gave me another of those stern looks and nodded toward the door. "Now you go."

And I went.

I called William Dorn's apartment from the first open bar I came to. A maid answered and said Mr. Dorn was in a business conference and couldn't be disturbed at the moment.

"Give him a message for me, please."

"Certainly, sir."

"Tell him Miss Talmage suffered a slight relapse and has been given a sedative, but there's nothing to worry about."

"Oh . . . then she won't be at the meeting this evening?"

"I'm afraid not."

"Yes, thank you, Doctor. Is there anything Mr. Dorn can do?"

"Nothing at all."

"Very well, Doctor, and thank you again."

I hung up and grunted. I didn't think I sounded like a doctor at all.

The rain was coming down harder and I turned up my collar against it. Somewhere Beaver was hiding and Woody and his boys were waiting.

It was going to be a trouble night.

chapter ten

THEY COULD ONLY hold the story back just so long. When more than one person knows, there is no secret. The final edition of the evening paper carried the opener that was the crack in the whole faulty scheme of security. An unmentioned source had leaked the information that the dead guy in the subway station had died of a highly contagious disease and upon further investigation nothing could be learned from officialdom about the matter. There were vigorous denials, but no one offered other explanation. The Newark paper went a little further, an editorial demanding an answer over a body-shot of the corpse.

So far nobody had put the obvious pieces in place . . . the sudden show of harmony between the U.S. and the U.S.S.R., the burst of activity from the armed forces reservists and the presence of the Fort Detrick C.B. warfare teams. But it was coming. No amount of security was going to stop people with imagination from thinking along certain lines, then proving out their theories. Tomorrow a few more questions would be asked, then when no answers were forthcoming the dam would burst and every end of the news media would be jamming down the throat of bureaucracy. Tom-Tom Schneider was dead, his killers were dead. What other pieces of sensationalism could they dig up to bury the biggest news story of them all?

I walked up Broadway past the offices of WOBY-TV and wondered how Eddie Dandy was doing. On impulse, I turned in out of the wet, found the receptionist just going out for a coffee break and asked her.

Eddie Dandy had just come in an hour ago. He was in his office and wasn't to be disturbed. I thanked her, let her go for her coffee and took the elevator upstairs. I spotted the two guys by his door before they saw me, turned right instead of toward his office, rounded the corridor until I found an empty desk and picked up the phone and dialed Eddie's number.

His hello was tired and curt and I said, "Mike Hammer, Ed. How goes it?"

"Stinking, kid. Where are you?"

"Right down the hall. Can you break away from the watchdogs long enough to go to the john?"

"Yeah, sure, but look, buddy . . . I'm strictly off limits. Anybody caught talking to me gets the same solitary confinement treatment."

"Balls."

"Man, they did it to me."

"I'm not you. Give me five minutes, then cut out."

The men's room was across the corridor, out of sight from the pair, and I went in without being seen. Nobody else was there, so I stepped into the end booth and closed the door. Five minutes later I heard the outside door hiss shut and walked out of the cubicle.

Eddie looked tired, but his eyes were bright and his mouth tight with constrained rage. "You look terrible," I said.

His eyes went toward the door. "Quiet. They're standing outside."

"How'd you shake loose? I thought they had you under wraps."

"A few nosy buddies of mine started poking around when I didn't show. The big wheels figured I'd be better off where I could be seen and answer monitored phone calls that could be chopped off fast if I started to squawk. Brother, when this is over asses are going to burn, and I mean burn."

"It isn't over yet," I reminded him.

His face turned gray and he seemed ten years older. "I was in on some high level discussion, Mike. You really know how bad it is?"

"Maybe I'm better off not knowing."

Eddie didn't even hear me. "There's no place to hide. Everybody would be running for cover, but *there's no place to hide!* They've isolated that damned disease and it's the worst thing they ever came up against. Once it gets started there's no stopping it, no vaccines, no natural barriers . . . nothing. The damn stuff is so self-perpetuating it can even feed on itself after it's done feeding on everything else. Maybe a few guys will escape it for a while. The men in the Antarctic on Operation Deepfreeze will miss it because intense cold is the only thing that can stop it, but where will they be when the supply planes stop coming in?"

"Eddie . . ."

"Hell, for years they talked about the atom bomb, the big boom that could wipe out the world. They should have talked about something else. At least that would have been quick. This makes nuclear fission look like a toy."

"There's still a chance."

"Not much, friend. Only one guy knew where those containers were planted and now he's dead."

I shrugged and looked at him. "So what's left to do?"

He finally broke a grin loose and waved his arms in mock disgust at me. "I wish I could think like you, Mike. No kidding, I really do. I'd go out, find a few broads and start banging away until it was all over. Me, I'm just going to sit and sweat and swear and worry until my time comes to check out, then maybe I'll cry a little, get drunk as hell and not have to fight a hangover.

"Pessimists are a pain in the butt," I said.

"You're absolutely nuts, Mike. How can you stand there and . . ."

"I have my own business to take care of."

Eddie let out a grunt of disbelief. "Still Lippy Sullivan? Just like things weren't . . ."

"It keeps me busy," I interrupted. I brought him up to date and by the time I was done he had almost forgotten about what was happening outside.

"Woody Ballinger's a rough boy to snag in a trap, Mike. He's been around. If that dip lifted something from his wallet and tried to shake him down for it, he was plain asking to be killed. You ought to let Woody do you a favor and knock him off."

"Not this guy. As long as we still have murder one punishment, I want him to go through the whole damn torturous process."

"So what can I do?"

I looked at my watch again. Time was going by fast. Outside, darkness had blacked out a wet city and the rain was still scratching against the windows. "Do me a favor," I said. "Get a call through to Pat Chambers for me and tell him to drop the area around Ninety-second and get his men over to Columbus and One Hundred-tenth. If they spot Velda, don't tip her to the move. Can you do that?"

"Sure. Those kind of calls I can make, so long as I stay off the Big Subject."

"They letting you broadcast?"

"Nothing live. I have to tape it first. They thought of everything." I looked around the room and grinned. "Except this."

"Yeah. Who makes appointments in men's rooms except sexual deviates?"

"Don't let it get around. That might make more news."

Suddenly his eyes clouded. "Wait until tomorrow. They really got a beaut cooked up. The public will flip, Wall Street stocks will tumble and the news outlets will eat it up. There won't be room enough in any paper or broadcast for anything else."

"Oh? Why?"

"The President is scheduled to have a serious heart attack," he said.

Caesar Mario Tulley hadn't shown up and nobody had seen him around since earlier in the day. Little Joe had taken up his usual rainy night station in the back booth of Aspen's Snack Bar, peering out the window, sipping one coffee after another.

He shrugged when I asked him and said, "Don't worry about him, Mike. He'll show. A night like this, the kid makes out, all wet and sorry-looking. Wish I could make half of his take. The suckers feel worse over a long-haired kid in dirty clothes panhandling nickels than a guy like me with no legs."

"Quit complaining," I said. "You got it made."

Little Joe laughed and took another sip of his coffee. "If I didn't I wouldn't be inside. Man, I had my times out there on nights like this. It was good hustling, but hell on the health. You look for him over at Leo's?"

"They didn't see him."

"How about Tessie . . . you know, Theresa Miller, that cute little whore from the Village. She never stops. If there's a live one on the street she'll tap him."

"She saw him this afternoon, not since," I said. "Look, he told me he was going to see a friend. You know who he hangs out with?"

"Come on, Mike. Them hippies all look alike to me. Sure, I seen him with a few creeps before, but nobody I could finger. Hell, I don't even want to get close to 'em. He works his side of the street, I work mine. Look, why don't you try Austin Towers? Tall, lanky guy with a scraggly goatee. Always hangs out by the paper kiosk the next block down. He sells them kids pot and if anybody would know, he would."

I told Little Joe thanks and flipped him a five-spot.

He grabbed it and grinned. "I never refuse money," he said.

Austin Towers didn't want to talk, but he thought it was a bust and didn't have time to dump the two paper bags he had in his raincoat pocket and gave me a resigned look and followed me into the semilit entrance of the closed shoe store.

"I want to talk to a lawyer," he said.

All I did was look at him.

For a second he stared back, then dropped his eyes nervously and a tic pulled at the corner of his mouth.

I still didn't say anything.

"Listen, Mister . . ."

I let him see the .45 under my coat and his eyes widened and he tried to swallow the lump in his throat. His voice was a hoarse whisper when he said, "Man, look, look . . . I'm just pushing grass. I ain't crowding nobody. I don't hold no hard stuff, not me. Man, it's all grass and who puts heat on grass? You guys want me out, I go pick another spot and . . ."

"Where can I find Caesar?"

The relief that flooded his face swept over him like a wave. "Oh, man, he ain't nothin', that guy. He just . . ."

"You see him today?"

"Sure, about four. He bought some stuff so he and a friend . . ."

He was talking fast and furiously, happy to know it wasn't him I was leaning on. I cut him short. "Where is he?"

"His pal got a pad on Forty-ninth. First floor over the grocery in the front."

"Show me."

"Mister . . ."

I didn't want him making any phone calls that would scare off my birds. "Show me," I said again.

And he showed me. A stinking, miserable two-room flop that reeked of garbage and marijuana smoke where Caesar Mario Tulley and a scruffy-looking jerk in shoulder-length hair were wrapped in Mexican serapes, stretched out on the floor completely out of their skulls from the pot party.

I said, "Damn!" and the word seemed to drop in the room like soft thunder.

Austin Towers started edging toward the door. "Like I showed you, man, so now I gotta cut, y'know?"

"Get back here, freak."

"Man . . ."

"Killing you would be a public service." My voice had such an edge to it that he scurried back like a scared rat, his head bobbing, eager to do anything that would keep him alive. "How long are they going to be out of it?"

"How would I know, man?"

I snapped my head around and stared at him, watching his breath catch in his chest. "You sold him the stuff. You know how much they had. Now check them to see what's left and make a guess and make a good one or I'll snap your damn arms in half."

He didn't argue about it. One look at my face and he knew I wasn't kidding. He bent over the pair, patted them down expertly, finding the remnants of the joints they had gone through, then stood up. "Used it all. Man, they tied one on, them two. Maybe three-four hours you might reach 'em if you're lucky."

This time I grinned, my lips pulled tight across my teeth. "Maybe if *you're* lucky it'll be one hour. One. You're in the business, boy, so you'd better know all the tricks. You start working on them and don't stop until they're awake. Don't bother trying to run out. You couldn't run fast or far enough that I couldn't nail you, so play it sweet and cool and you might get out of this in one piece. One hour, kid. Get them back and I don't give a damn how you do it."

"Man, you don't know this stuff!" His voice was nearly hysterical.

"No, but you do," I told him.

Velda had called in again. She was still on the stakeout but getting edgy because there had been no tip-off to Beaver's whereabouts. She was going to give it one more hour and then try another possible lead. That left me forty-six minutes to work ahead of her.

The taxi dropped me at the corner of Columbus Avenue and a Hundred-tenth Street and when I looked around the memories of the old days from when I was a kid came rushing back like an incoming tide. There were changes, but some things never change at all. The uneven rooftops still were castle battlements, each street a gateway in the great wall. The shufflers still shuffled, oblivious to the weather, urchin noises and cooking smells mingling in this vast stomach of a neighborhood. Plate glass windows protected with steel grilling, others unconcernedly dark and empty. The perennial tavern yellow-lit behind streaked glazing, the drugstore still sporting the huge red and purple urns, the insignia of its trade. On a good night the young bloods would be gathered on the corners, swapping lies and insults, protecting their turf. The hookers would cruise for their johns and the pushers would be clearing the path to an early grave for the users.

They didn't know me here, but they knew I wasn't an outsider. I was born part of the scene and still looked it and they didn't mind me asking things and didn't mind answering. I showed the photo of Beaver to the bartender in Steve's Bar and Grill. He didn't know the guy, but took it to the back room and showed it to somebody else. One guy thought he looked familiar, but that was all.

In the candy store, the old man shook his head and told me the man in the picture looked like somebody good to stay away from and tried to talk about the old days until I thanked him and went back outside.

A gypsy cab driver having coffee and a doughnut in his car scanned the photo and said he was pretty sure he had seen the guy around, but didn't know where or when. It was the eyes, he said. He always looked at people's eyes, and he remembered seeing him. He told me to look for Jackie, the redheaded whore who swore she was a prostitute because she wanted money to go to college. Jackie knew everybody.

Jackie knew Beaver, all right. He had bought her pitch about two weeks ago, gone to her apartment and parted with ten bucks for sexual services rendered, leaving her with a few welts and bruises. She had seen him once after that, getting into a taxi down the block. She knew he didn't live in the area, but assumed he dropped up to see a friend who did. No, she couldn't even guess at who it was. The neighborhood was full of itinerants and strange faces. She took my ten bucks and thought I was a nut for not getting the whole go for the money.

Now, at least, I was in the area.

There were three construction sites within two blocks. One was a partial demolition job and the other two were leveled. The last one had wiped out a row of three brownstones all the way to the corner and the cut went deep into the solid rock that was the bed of the city. The hole was spotted with small ponds of rainwater and a yellow backhoe tractor stood lonely and dead-looking in the middle of the gorge, its toothed claw ready to pounce into the granite, but dead, like a suddenly frozen prehistoric beast.

Silent air compressors and equipment shacks lined one side of the street, abutted on either end by battered dump trucks. A square patch of dim light outlined the window of the watchman's stubby trailer and from behind the locked door I could hear Spanish music working toward a finale of marimbas and bongo drums before the announcer came on to introduce the next number.

I knocked on the door and it opened to a toothy grin and a stale beer smell and the young-old guy standing there said, "Come in, come in. Don't stand in the rain."

"Thanks." I stepped inside while he turned down the radio.

"Not much of a place," he said, "but I like it."

"Why not?"

"Sure, why not? It's a living. I got my own house and nobody to bitch at me. Pretty damn noisy in the daytime, then I got so I could sleep through anything. Maybe that's why they keep me on. Me, I can stay awake all night and sleep daytimes like they want. Don't get much company, though. Now, what can I do for you?"

I showed him the picture of Beaver and let him study it. "Ever see that man?"

He looked at it intently, then handed it back. "Can't say.

Daytimes I sleep, y'know. After a while them damn compressors get to be like music and they put me right to sleep. Know something? I got so's I can't sleep without 'em going."

"You're sure?" I asked.

He nodded. "Don't remember him. We've been here a month already and I don't remember him. Know most everybody else, though. Especially the kids. The ones who like to climb all over things."

I was about to leave when I turned around and looked at him. "The crew work in the rain?"

"Hell no! They finished up right after it started and shut everything down. Them boys got the life, they have. Busted up my sleep real awful. When the compressors went off, I woke up. Shit, feller, I haven't been able to get back to sleep since. Everything's just too damn quiet. Look, you want a beer?"

"No thanks."

"You a cop? Maybe for the company?"

"Private investigator."

"Oh, about that stuff the kids took last week. Hell, we got it all back before they could hock it."

"You been cooped up here all day?"

Naw, I walked around some. Didn't leave the block, though. Just bought some grub and beer, walked around to stretch out. Never leave the place alone long, and never at night. That's why they keep me on."

I pulled up a folding chair with my toe and hooked my leg over it. "See any strange faces around at all?"

"Ah, you got bums comin' through all the time. They go from . . ."

"Not bums. These wouldn't be bums."

"Who'd come down this way if they wasn't bums? Maybe some kids from . . . hey . . . yeah, wait a minute. When I went for the beer . . . before it got dark."

"So?"

"I see this car go by twice. New job with two guys in the front seat. It stopped halfway up on the other side and one got out. Then the car went up further and parked. I really didn't pay no attention to it on accounta it was raining so hard. When I came back the car was gone."

"A late-model, black, four-door job?"

"Yeah, how'd you know?"

"It's parked up on Columbus outside the drugstore," I said. "You got a phone here?"

"Under the blankets on the cot there. I like to keep it muffled. Can't stand them damn bell noises."

Pat wasn't in, but I got hold of Sergeant Corbett and told him to get a message through and gave him my location. He told me Pat had assigned an unmarked cruiser to the area earlier, but they were being pulled out in another thirty minutes. Too much was happening to restrict even one car team in a quiet zone on a quiet night and I was lucky to get the cooperation I did.

I said, "It may not be so damn quiet in a little while, buddy."

"Well, it won't be like the U.N. or the embassy joints. Everybody's in emergency sessions. You'll still be lucky if you get thirty minutes."

I hung up and tossed the covers back over the phone. The watchman was bent over the radio again with a beer in his hand, reading a comic book lying open on the floor.

My watch said Velda had left her post fifteen minutes ago. Somehow, someway, she'd find a thread, then a string, then a rope that would draw her right to this block.

I went out, closed the door and looked up the street, then started to walk slowly. On half the four-floor tenements were white square cardboard signs lettered in black notifying the world that the building was unfit for tenancy or scheduled for demolition. The windows were broken and dark, the fronts grime-caked and eroded. One building was occupied despite the sign, either by squatters with kerosene lamps or some undaunted tenant fighting City Hall. In the middle of the block was one brownstone, the basement renovated years ago into a decrepit tailor shop no wider than a big closet. A tilted sign on the door said a forlorn OPEN, and I would have passed it up entirely if I hadn't seen the dot of light through the crack in the drawn blind.

Sigmund Katz looked like a little gnome perched on his stool, methodically handstitching a child's coat, glasses on the end of his nose, bald head shiny under the single low-watt bulb. His eyes through the thick glasses were blue and watery, his smile weak, but friendly. An old-world accent was thick in his voice when he spoke. "No, this man in the picture I did not see," he told me.

"And you know everyone?"

"I have been here sixty-one years, young man." He paused and looked up from his needlework. "This is the only one you are looking for?" There was an expression of patient waiting on his face.

"There could be others."

"I see. And these are . . . not nice people?"

"Very bad people, Mr. Katz."

"They did not look so bad," he said.

"Who?"

"They were young and well dressed, but it is not in the appearance that makes a person good or bad, true?"

I didn't want to push him. "True," I said.

"One used the phone twice. The second time the other one stopped him before he could talk. I may not see too well, but my hearing is most good. There were violent words spoken."

I described Carl and Sammy and he nodded.

"Yes," he said, "those are the two young men."

"When they left here . . . did you see where they went?"

The old man smiled, shook his head gently and continued sewing. "No, I'm afraid I didn't. Long ago I learned never to interfere."

I unclenched the knots my fingers were balled into and took a deep breath. *Time, damn it, it was running out!*

Before I could leave he added, "However, there was Mrs. Luden for whom I am making this coat for her grandson. She thought they were salesmen, but who would try to sell in this poor neighborhood? Not well dressed young men who arrive in a shiny new car. They knock on doors and are very polite."

I watched him, waiting, trying to stay relaxed.

"Perhaps they did find a customer. Not so long ago they went into Mrs. Stone's building across the street where the steps are broken and haven't come out."

The tension leaked out of my muscles like rain from my hair and I grinned humorously at Mr. Katz.

His eyes peered at me over his glasses. "Tell me, young man, you look like one thing, but you may be another. By one's appearance, you cannot tell. Are you a nice man?"

"I'm not one of *them*."

"Ah, but are you a nice man?"

"Maybe to some people," I said.

"That is good enough. Then I tell you something else. In Mrs. Stone's building . . . there are not just two men. Three went up the first time, then a few minutes ago, another two. Be careful, young man. It is not good."

And now things were beginning to shape up!

I ran back into the rain and the night, cut across the street and found the building with the broken steps, took them two at a time on the side that still held and unsheathed the .45 and thumbed the hammer back. The front door was partially ajar and I slammed it open with the flat of my hand and tried to see into the inkwell of the vestibule. It took seconds for my eyes to adjust, then I spotted the staircase and started toward it.

And time ran out.

From a couple of floors up was a crash of splintering wood, a hoarse yell and the dull blast of heavy caliber guns in rapid fire, punctuated by the flatter pops of lighter ones. Somebody screamed in wild agony and a single curse ripped through the musty air. I didn't bother trying to be quiet. I took the steps two at a time and almost made the top when I saw the melee at the top lit momentarily in the burst of gunfire, then one figure burst through the others and came smashing down on top of me in a welter of arms and legs, gurgling wetly with those strange final sounds of death, and we both went backward down the staircase into an old cast iron radiator with sharp edges that bit into my skull in a blinding welter of pain and light.

chapter eleven ▬▬▬▬▬▬▬▬▬▬

VELDA WAS CRYING through some distant rage. I heard her say, "Damn it, Mike, you're all right! You're all right! Mike . . . answer me!"

My head felt like it was split wide open and I felt myself gag and almost threw up. The light from Velda's flash whipped into my eyes, beating at my brain like a club for a second until I pushed it away.

"Mike . . .?"

"I'm not shot," I said flatly.

"Damn you, why didn't you wait? Why didn't you call . . ."

"Ease off." I pushed to my knees and took the flash from her and turned it on the body. There was a bloody froth around the mouth and the eyes were glassy and staring. Sammy had bought his farm too.

Across the street people were shouting and a siren had started to whine. I let Velda help me up, then groped my way up the stairs to the top. The pictures would take care of all the gory news the public was interested in. Carl was sprawled out face down on the kitchen floor of the apartment with half his head blown away, a skinny little guy in a plaid sports coat and dirty jeans was tied to a chair with a hole in his chest big enough to throw a cat through, his toupee flopping over one ear. Like the little whore had told me, one was partially bald. Woody Ballinger was in a curiously lifelike position of being asleep with his head on an overturned garbage sack, one hand over his heart like a patriotic citizen watching the flag go by. Only his hand covered a gaping wound that was all bright red and runny.

That was all.

Beaver wasn't there.

I walked over and looked at the broken chair beside the table with the ropes in loose coils around the remnants. Somebody else had been tied up too. Behind the chair was a broken window leading to the rear fire escape and on one of the shards of glass was a neat little triangle of red wool. The kind they make vests out of.

The flash picked out an unbroken bulb and I snapped it on. In the dull light it looked even messier and Velda made heaving noises in her throat.

I looked at the table top and knew why Woody wanted Beaver so badly. His policy code sequence identifying the workings of his organization was laid out there on a single sheet of typewritten paper that had been folded so that it would fit a pocket wallet.

And that was why Woody wanted Beaver. But who had wanted Woody?"

My head felt like it wanted to burst. In a minute the place would be crawling with cops. And outside, there still was Beaver, and *I wanted him.*

I shoved the unfired .45 back in the sling and turned to Velda. "You stay here and handle it, kitten. Give them as much as you know, but give me running time."

"Mike . . ."

"This was only one stop on Beaver's route. He's heading someplace else." I went over to the window and put one leg through. "How did you know about this place?"

"One of Anton Virelli's runners saw Woody's car here. He reported in."

"You see anybody leave the building?"

"I'm . . . not sure. I was looking for you."

"Okay, sugar. Stall 'em. They're coming up."

* * *

Austin Towers had had more than the hour he expected and he hadn't wasted any of it. Caesar and his friend were sitting up, shivering under cold wet sheets, trying to keep their feet off the sodden rug on the floor. The dull luster was still in their eyes, but they were awake enough to mumble complaints at Towers who threatened them with another bucket of ice water if they tried to get up.

When he heard me come in he almost dropped the pail and stood stiff in his tracks, waiting to see if I approved or not. Caesar let his head sag toward me and managed a sick grin. "Hi, Mike. Get . . . get this bastard . . . outa here."

"Shut up, punk." I took the pail from Towers and sat it on the floor. "How good are they?"

"Man, I tried. Honest . . . "

"Can they think coherently?"

"Yeah, I'd say so. It ain't exactly like a booze hangover. They . . . "

"Okay then, cut out." He started to move around me and I grabbed his arm. Very slowly I brought the .45 up where he could see it. His face went pasty white and his knees started to sag. "This is the kind of trouble that stuff brings. You're not invulnerable . . . and kid, you're sure expendable as hell. Start thinking twice before you peddle that crap again."

His head bobbed in a nod and new life came back into his legs. "Man," he said, "I'm thinking! I'm thinking right now."

I let him go. "Scram."

He didn't wait for me to repeat the invitation. He even left his coat on the back of the chair. Caesar chuckled and tried to unwrap himself from the sheet. "Thanks, old pal Mike. That guy . . . he sure was bugging us. Gimme a hand. I'm freezing to death."

"In a minute." I glanced at the other guy, slack-lipped and bony, like a sparrow under the wet cloth. "This the guy you were going to meet about Beaver?"

"Sure, Mike." He let out a belch and moaned, his teeth chattering. "So we meet like I said."

"You were going to meet me too, Caesar."

His face tried to scowl. "Look, if you're going to be like that . . . " He saw me pick up the pail. "Okay, okay. I'm sorry. It ain't the end of the world."

I almost felt like telling him right then.

"Hey, Mister." The other one looked like he was coming apart at the seams. "I did like Caesar asked. My friend, he told me where this guy . . . the one in the red vest, where he flops."

"Where?"

He gulped and tried to look straight at me. "Take . . . this sheet off, huh?"

I hated to waste the time, but I couldn't afford to put up with a stubborn idiot. I undid the knots Tower had twisted the ends into and yanked the wet cloth away and he stumbled out of his chair and reached for the coat Towers had left and pulled it tightly around him, still shivering.

"Where?" I repeated.

"Carmine said he seen him at the Stanton Hotel. They're on the same floor."

"He describe him?"

"Tall. Skinny. Like kind of a mean character. He ain't there all the time, but he hangs onto his pad."

"What else?"

"Always the red vest. Never took it off. Like it was lucky or something." I started to leave, then: "Mister . . ."

"Yeah?"

"You got a quarter? I'm flat."

I tossed five bucks on the chair. "Unwrap the idiot there and you can both blow your minds. Someday take a look in a mirror and see what's happening to you."

I picked up a cruising cab on Eighth Avenue and gave him the address of the Stanton. Before the turn of the century it had been an exclusive, well-appointed establishment catering to the wealthy idler who wanted privacy for his extramarital affairs, but time and changes in neighborhood patterns had turned it into a way station for transients and a semipermanent pad for those living on the fringes of society.

A fifteen-truck Army convoy was blocking traffic, white-helmeted M.P.'s diverting cars west, and the driver cut left, swearing at all the nonsense. "Like the damn war, y'know? You'd think we was being invaded. The way traffic is already they could hold them damn maneuvers someplace else."

"Maybe they hate the mayor," I said.

He growled in answer, swerved violently around a timid woman driver who was taking up a lane and a half and yanked the cab through a slot and made a right on Tenth Avenue. I looked at my watch. Five after ten. An hour and a half since the slaughter uptown. Enough time for Beaver to collect his gear and make another run.

I didn't wait for change. I threw a bill on the seat beside the driver and got out without bothering to close the door. Fingers of rain clawed at my face, wind-whipping the drenching spray around my legs. Inside the lobby of the Stanton clusters of men trying to look busy were staying away from the night. A uniformed patrolman, a walkie-talkie slung over his shoulder, finished checking the groups and pushed through the doors, looked up at the sky in disgust, then lowered his head against the wind and turned west.

I went in, cut across the lobby to the desk where a bored clerk with a cigarette drooping from the corner of his mouth was doing a crossword puzzle on the counter.

He didn't bother looking up. "No rooms," he said.

I flipped the puzzle to the floor and knocked the cigarette from his mouth with a backhanded swipe and his head snapped up with a mean snarl and he had his hand all cocked to swing when he saw my face and faded. "You got bad manners, friend."

"If you're looking for trouble . . ."

"I *am* trouble, kiddo." I let him look at me for another few seconds, then he dropped his eyes and wiped his mouth, not liking what he saw. I reached in my pocket for the photos of Beaver. There were two left. Someplace I had left one, but it didn't matter now.

The clerk had seen cards like those before, but cops carried them, and I got the eyes again because he had figured me first for one thing, now he was trying to make me for another and it didn't jell. I put the card on the counter facing him. "Recognize him?"

He didn't want to talk, but he didn't want to know what would happen if he didn't either. Finally he nodded. "Room 417."

"There now?"

"Came in earlier. His face was swollen and he was all bloodied up. What'd he do?"

"Nothing that would interest you."

"Listen, Mac . . . we're trying to stay clean. This guy never gave us no fuss so why are you guys . . . "

I grabbed his arm. "What *guys?*"

"There was another one before. Another cop. He wanted him too."

"Cop?"

"Sure. He had one of these mug cards."

Pat might have made it. One of his squad just might have gotten a lead and run it down. Enough of them had copies of the photos and one way or another Beaver could be nailed.

"You see them come out?" I asked him.

"Naw. I don't watch them bums. You think I ain't got nothin' better to do?"

"Yeah, I don't think you have. Just one more thing . . . stay off that phone."

A swamper in filthy coveralls was oiling down the wooden steps, so I pushed the button beside the elevators instead of walking up. The ancient machinery creaked and whined, finally groaning to a halt. The door slid open and two drunks were arguing over a bottle until one behind them pushed through with a muttered curse, almost knocking them down. He looked familiar, but I had seen too many lineups with these characters playing lead roles, so any of them could be familiar. The other two guys that pushed their way through were Vance Solito and Jimmy Healey, a pair of the Marbletop bunch who ran floating crap games on the side. I shoved the two drunks out to do their arguing and punched the button for the fourth floor.

Outside 417 I stopped and put my ear to the door. No sound at all. I slid the .45 out, thumbed the hammer back and rapped hard, twice. Nobody answered and I did it again with the same result. Then I tried the knob. The door was locked, but with the kind of lock it only took a minute to open. When I had the latch released I stepped aside and shoved it open and stared into the darkness that was intermittently lit by the reflected glow from a blinking light on the street below.

I waited, listening, then stepped around the door opening inside, flipped the light switch on and hit the floor. Nothing happened. I stood up, put the .45 back and closed the door. Nothing was going to happen.

Beaver was lying spread-eagled on the floor wallowing in his own blood, as dead as he ever was going to be, his stomach slit open and a vicious hole in his chest where a knife thrust had laid open muscle and bone before it carved into his heart. There were other carefully planned cuts and slices too, but Beaver had never made a sound through the tape that covered his mouth. His face was lumpy, bruised from earlier blows, with nasty charred and blistered hollows pockmarking his neck from deliberate cigarette burns.

But this was different. Woody had taken care of the first assault, but he hadn't gotten around to killing him and when the break came Beaver had dumped himself out of his chair, broken loose and gone through the window while all the action was going on. But this was different.

No, this was the same. It had happened before to Lippy Sullivan.
I took my time and read all the signs. It finally made sense
when I thought it out. Beaver's break wasn't as clean as he had
figured. He had been tailed to his safe place, hurting bad and
terrified as hell. And when the killer finally reached him he couldn't
run again. He was supposed to talk. He was tied up, his mouth
taped while the killer told him what he wanted and what he was
going to do to him if he didn't talk and just to prove his point
the killer made his initial slashes that would insure his talking.

*Except Beaver didn't talk. He fainted. There were more of those
nicely placed slices, delivered purposely so the pain would bring
him out of the faint. But Beaver didn't come out of it . . . there
had been too much before it and he lay there mute and unconscious
until the killer couldn't wait any more and made sure he'd never
talk to anybody else either. And when he was done killing he had
torn the room apart, piece by piece, bit by bit.*

I followed the search pattern looking for anything that might
have been missed, fingering through the torn bedding, reaching
into places somebody already had reached into, feeling outside
around the window ledges, going through the contents of the single
dresser whose drawers were stacked, empty, along one wall.

Beaver wasn't a fashion plate. He only had two suits and two
sport jackets. The pockets were turned inside out and the coat
linings ripped off. On the floor of the closet was a bloodstained
shirt and a crumpled red vest with more blood, stiff and dried,
staining the fabric.

I took another twenty minutes to make sure there was nothing
I had missed and finally sat down on the edge of the bed, lit up
a cigarette and looked at the mutilated body of Beaver on the
floor.

I said, "You weren't lucky this time, chum. That red vest didn't
bring you any luck at all, did it?"

Then I started to grin slowly and got up and went back to the
closet where the red vest lay in a crushed lump. It wasn't much.
It was old and worn and it must have been expensive at one time
because it still held its color. Beaver had thrown it there when he
took off his bloodied clothes, hurting and not caring about his
lucky charm. It was too carelessly tossed off and not much for
the killer to search because it didn't have pockets.

*But it had been Beaver's lucky charm once and a place to hide
all his luck, something that was always with him and safe.*

I found where the hand stitching was around the lower left
hand edge, picked at the thread and pulled it out of the fabric.

The sheet of onionskin paper folded there slid out and I opened it, scanned it slowly, then went to the phone and gave the desk clerk Eddie Dandy's number.

He said he knew how he could give his watchdogs the slip, but if he did that was the end of him in broadcasting, in life, in anything. He had been given the word strongly and with no punches pulled. He wanted to know if it was worth it.

I told him it was.

chapter twelve ▬▬▬▬▬▬▬▬▬▬▬▬

I LET HIM vomit his supper out in the toilet bowl and waited until he had mopped his face with cold water and dried off. He came back in the bedroom, trying to avoid the mess on the floor, but his eyes kept drifting back to the corpse until he was white again. He finally upended one of the drawers and sat on it, his hands shaking.

"Relax," I said.

"Damn it, Mike, did you have to get my ass in a sling just to show me this?"

I took a drag on my cigarette and nodded. "That's right."

Very slowly his face came out of his hands, his eyes drifting up to mine, fear cutting little crinkles into the folds of skin at their edges. "You . . . did you . . ."

"No, I didn't kill him."

Bewilderment replaced the fear and he said nervously, "Who did?"

"I don't know."

"Shit."

I went and got him a glass of water, waited while he finished it, looking out the window at the glassy-wet tops of the buildings across the street. Down below a police cruiser went by slowly and turned north at the corner. "Quiet out," I said.

Behind me, Eddie said softly, "It'll be a lot quieter soon. Just a few more days. I don't know why I was worrying about coming here at all. What difference can it make?"

"It hasn't happened yet."

"No chance, Mike. No chance at all. Everybody knows it. I wasted all that time worrying and sweating when I could have been like you, calm as hell and not giving a damn about anything. Maybe I'm fortunate at that. In a few days when the lid comes off and the whole world knows that it's only a little while before it dies, everybody else will go berserk and I'll be able to watch them and have an easy drink to kiss things goodbye." He let out a little laugh. "I only wish I could have been able to tell the whole story. They talk openly now. It doesn't seem to matter any more. You didn't know the Soviets ran down more of the story, did you?"

I shook my head and watched the rain come down, only half hearing what he said.

"That other regime . . . they never thought the strain of bacteria was so virulent. It would be contained pretty much in this hemisphere and die out after a certain length of time. They made tests on involuntary subjects and decided that one out of ten would be immune, and the vaccine they had developed would protect those they wanted protected. It wasn't just two agents who were planted in this country. There were twenty-two of them, and each was supplied with enough vaccine to immunize a hundred more, all key people in major commercial and political positions who would be ready to run the country after the plague was done wiping out the populace. Oh, they could sit back and not give a damn, but there was one thing they never got to know. The vaccine was no damn good. It was only temporary. They'll last a month or two longer after the others have died, but they'll die harder because it is going to take longer. Only they're not going to know this because everyone involved in the project is dead and there's nobody to tell them. They were going to know when it happened, because the single unknown, the key man who was going to plant the stuff around the country, was the only one who knew who the others were and he was going to notify them so they could set all their grand plans into motion."

"Nice," I said.

"So he planted the stuff . . . all those containers. My guess is he lucked out because of the vaccine he was injected with. There was a possibility it could do that. Funny, isn't it?"

"Why?"

"Because they have that organization all set up. They're ready to move in and set up another semislave state. The elite few get it all and the rest get the garbage. Not bad if you're one of the elite few and have the only guns around to back you up. It doesn't even make any difference if those agents were given the date or not. Either way they think they'll be ready to grab it all. It might screw up their timing, but that's about all. They move in, think they have it made, then all of a sudden it hits them too."

"It won't happen."

Eddie Dandy laughed again, a flat, sour laugh that ended in a sob. "Mike, you're mad."

I turned around and looked at him perched on the edge of the drawer, muscles tightened with near hysteria bunching in his jaw. I grinned at him, then picked up the phone. It was five minutes before they located Pat Chambers and I let him take me apart in sections before I said, "You should have gone with me, friend. It wouldn't have taken all this time."

"What are you talking about?"

"You can buy next year's calendar, Pat. You'll be able to use it."

For ten seconds there was a long silence on the other end of the line. He knew what I was talking about, and his voice came back with a tone of such absolute consternation that I barely heard him say, "Mike . . ."

"It was all wrapped up in Lippy Sullivan," I told him. "Handle this gently, Pat. And Pat . . . you'd better pass the word that the President doesn't have to have a heart attack tomorrow. There'll be plenty of news for everybody to chew on . . . and when you're passing the word, pass it high up where it counts and none of those eager lads with all that political ambition will be able to get their teeth in my ass for what's going to happen. Tell the thinkers to get a good story ready, because there's going to be the damndest cover-up happening tomorrow you ever saw in your life, and while it's happening I'm going to be walking around with a big grin, spitting in their eyes."

Before he could answer I told him where I was and hung up. Eddie Dandy was watching me like I had gone out of my mind. I handed him the sheet of onionskin paper.

"What's this?"

"The exact location of every one of those containers. You have the manpower already alerted and placed, the experts from Fort Detrick on hand to decontaminate them and the biggest scoop of your whole career. Too bad you'll never really be able to tell about it." I looked at him and felt my face pull into a nasty grin, "Or the rest of it."

I tried one more call, but my party wasn't at home, which confirmed what I already knew. I took the two last photos of

Beaver out of my pocket, looked at them and threw them down beside the body. He didn't look like that any more.

Spud Henry didn't know how to say it, the white lies not quite fitting his mouth. Finally he said, "Oh, hell, Mikey boy, it's just that I got orders. He gimme special orders on the house phone. Nobody goes up. It's an important business meeting."

"How many are up there?"

"Maybe six."

"When'd the last one come in?"

"Oh, an hour ago. It was then I got the call. Nobody else."

"Look, Spud . . ."

"Mike, it won't make no difference. They got the elevator locked up on that floor and there ain't no other way. All the elevators stop the next floor down. There's a fire door, but it only opens from the inside and you can't even walk up. Come on, Mike, forget it."

"Sorry, Spud."

"Buddy, it's my job you got in your hands."

"Not if you didn't see me."

"There's no way in that I can't see you! Look, four of them TV's cover the other exits and I got this one. How the hell can I explain?"

"You won't have to."

"Oh boy, will I catch hell. No more tips for old Spud. It's gonna be real dry around here for a while. Maybe that longhaired relief kid will get my job."

"Don't worry," I said.

"So go ahead. Not even a monkey can get there anyway."

The elevator stopped at the top, the doors sliding open noise-lessly. It was a bright blue foyer, decorated with modern sculpture and wildly colorful oil paintings in gold frames. The single door at the end was surrealistically decorated with a big eye painted around the peephole and I wondered how long ago it was that I was watched by another painted eye.

I touched the bell and waited. I touched it again, holding it in for a full minute, then let go and waited some more. I wasn't about to try to batter down three inches of oak, so I took out the .45 and blew each of the three locks out of their sockets. The noise of the shots was deafening in that confined space, but the door swung inward limply. I wasn't worried about the sound. It wasn't going to reach anyplace else. The tenants here were paying for absolute privacy that included soundproofing. Tomorrow the shattered door would even be an asset when the explanations started.

I walked through the rooms to the back of the building and into the bedroom that faced the fire escape, covered the catch with my sleeve, twisted it open, then raised the window the same way. All around me New York was staring, watching me with curious yellow eyes in the darker faces of the other buildings, seeing just one more thing to store away in memories that could never be tapped.

Gusts of wind whipped around the corner, driving the rain in angular sheets. I grinned again and started up the perforated steel steps to that other window and leaned against it with my shoulder, putting pressure to it gradually until the small pane cracked almost noiselessly. The pieces came out easily and I got my hand through the opening, undid the lock and shoved the window up. A swipe at the catch wiped out any prints and I was inside.

When I eased the door open I heard the subdued murmur of voices, the words indistinguishable. I was in a small office of some type, functional and modern, the kind a dedicated businessman whose work never stopped would have.

Maybe there would be things in there, I thought, *but let somebody else find it.*

I leaned on the ornate handle of the latch and tugged the door open.

The maid heard me, but never had time to see me. I laid a fast chop across her jaw as she turned around and she went down without a sound. I pulled her into the little office and closed the door on her. And I was in a dining area with the voices a little louder now because they were right behind the one more door I had to go through.

One of the voices smashed a hand on a table hard and in choked-up anger said, "How many times do I have to tell you? There was nothing! I looked everywhere!"

"It *had* to be there!" I *recognized that voice.*

"Don't tell me my job! It was *not* in the room. It was like all the other places. Maybe he did not have it at all. To him, what would it mean? Nothing, that's what. A single piece of paper with names of places written down. Why would he have kept that?"

Then there was another voice I recognized too, a cold, calm voice that could be jocular and friendly at other times. "He didn't have to know what it meant. It was something that came from the wallet of an important person who would keep only important things on that person. It would have a certain value. Why else would he have made those calls?" The voice paused a moment, then added. "You know, it would have been easier to have paid his price."

The other one said, "A blackmailer could have photostated it. If it were valuable to me, it would have been equally as valuable to someone else."

"To whom would he sell?" the cold voice asked.

"Who knows how a mind like his would work? Perhaps a newspaperman, or by now he might have even suspected just what he did hold. You realize what it would be worth then, the price he could demand for it? That's all it would take to smash everything we have built. We couldn't take the chance."

"I'm afraid the chance has already been taken," the flat voice stated. "Now there is no time for any alternative. We simply have to wait. At this point there is little possibility that we will fail. If the document is hidden or destroyed, it will stay hidden or destroyed. There is not enough time left for anyone to pursue the matter further. I suggest you ring for that maid again and inquire about our drinks so we can conclude this affair."

From another room I heard the annoyed sound of a buzzer. It rang again, then a voice I knew so well said, "Stanley, go see what's keeping her."

I stepped away from the door and crowded behind the angle of an ornate china closet. The door opened and clicked shut on its own closing device and I saw the face of the man who had come in, a still angry face at having been chewed out for bungling the job. It wasn't a new face. I had seen it twice before this night, once in a burst of gunfire at the top of the stairs and again coming out of an elevator in the hotel where Beaver had been sliced to death like Lippy Sullivan.

Like Lippy Sullivan.

The man called Stanley crossed the room and pushed open the swinging door that led into the kitchen calling loudly for somebody named Louise. He never heard me follow him in, but when he didn't find Louise he spun around and I let him see me, one big surprised look, and he knew who I was and why I was there and before he could get the knife out of his belt with an incredibly fast snatch and thrust, I leaned aside and threw a fist into his face that sent his features into a crazy caricature of a human and left teeth imbedded in my knuckles and a sudden spurt of blood spraying both of us.

I should have shot him and had it over with, but I didn't want it to happen that fast. I was a pig and wanted him all for myself and slowly and almost made a mistake. He was a pro and strong. He was hurt and death could be the next step and he was moving and thinking even before he hit the floor. He didn't waste breath yelling. What strength he had left kept the knife in his hand, his feet scrabbling for survival.

The blade flashed around when I jumped him, the gun forgotten now. All I wanted was to use my hands. I got my fingers in his hair and yanked his head around, pounding my fist against his ear. I saw the knife come up and blocked it with my knee, the razor edge slicing into my skin, then I let go of his hair and grabbed his wrist.

He was strong, but I had gotten to him first and he wasn't that strong any more. He was flat out under me and I was bringing his own knife up under his throat and this time he knew it couldn't be stopped and he tried to let out the yell he had held in. Then my knee caught him square in the balls with such impact he almost died then, eyes bugging out of his head in sheer agony.

He still fought, and he was still able to see what was happening when his own hand drove the knife completely through his neck until it was imbedded in the floor behind.

I picked up my rod and eased the hammer back.

Okay, Lippy, it was almost paid for.

You shouldn't stop and think back. I should have known that. All the years in the business and I forgot a little thing that could kill you. It wasn't instinct that turned me in in time. It was an accident. I should have known they'd send another one out to see what had happened and he was standing there behind me with a gun coming out of his pocket, a flat, ugly thing with a deadly snout ready to spit.

But you don't beat a guy to the draw who already has a gun in his fist, and I triggered the .45 into a roaring blast that caught him just off center from his nose and threw the entire back of his skull against the door. I was over him before he had crumpled to the tiles and met the other one coming in and this time I was ready. He only saw me as the slug was tearing his chest apart, dropped the Luger and stood there in momentary surprise, then fell in a lifeless heap, blocking the doorway.

Chairs crashed backward outside and there was a shrill scream cutting through the curses. I kicked the corpse out of the way, yanked the door open in time to see that smiling, pleasant Mr. Kudak who was so political, who had come from one regime into another without anybody ever knowing about it, picking himself up off the floor. He didn't have a gun, but he had a mind that was even more dangerous so I blew it right out of its braincase without the slightest compunction and ran across the room, jumping the knocked-over furniture, and reached the door just as it was locked in my face.

They shouldn't have bothered. One shot took the lock away and I kicked the door open and stood there with the .45 aimed at William Dorn who was pulling a snub-nosed revolver from the desk drawer, then swung the .45 to cover Renée Talmage who was standing there beside him. They never saw me thumb the empty .45 back into the loaded position.

"Don't bother, William," I said. "Toss it in the middle of the floor."

For a second I thought he'd try for me anyway and I got that strange feeling up across my shoulders. *I knew what would happen if he did.* But there are those who can plan violence and those who could execute it. He wasn't one of those who could pull the trigger.

Right now he was thinking and I knew that too. I could take them in, say what I had to say, and while the police held them the big death would be released and all he had to do was wait long enough and everybody would be gone except them and they could walk out easily enough.

I grinned and said, "It couldn't happen that way, William."

They looked at each other. Finally he straightened and tried to regain his composure. "What?"

"You could be in a cell. So everybody's dead. You'd still be in a cell and you'd starve to death anyway."

Renée spoke for the first time. "Mike . . ."

"Shut up, Renée. For a whole lifetime I'm going to have to look back and remember that I liked you once. It's going to be a damn nasty memory as it is, so for now, just shut up."

Now there was something about the way they looked at each other. And I was enjoying myself. It was going to be fun bringing them in like this. They'd hate me so hard after it they would never be able to live with themselves.

"You never should have killed the wrong man, William," I said. "Just think, if your bright boys had really been on the ball when they went after that pickpocket and found where he was living, you would have won the whole ball game. But no, they put the knife to the wrong boy, and the right one hit the road. He was a sharp article too and when he knew what was chasing him he pulled out all the stops. Right then he knew what he had was important and started playing his own game."

"See here . . ."

"Knock it off. It's over, William. The trouble with Beaver was, he didn't know who really was out to kill him. The only stuff worth while was what he had from you and Woody Ballinger. He tried to tap you both and almost got tapped out by Woody first. Old Woody has manpower too.

"I guess you thought I was a real clown getting into the act, stumbling all over trying to square things with a nobody who had gotten himself knocked off. Brother, you should have done your homework better. I work on the dark side of the fence myself."

Renée was watching me, her hands clasping and unclasping, something desperate in her eyes. "You're a cutie, honey," I told her. "The act in your apartment was neat, real neat. You saw those pictures I had of Beaver and slipped one out of my pocket when I was lying there all nice and naked and getting beautifully vibrated. You slipped it to your maid to deliver to William here when she was supposed to go to the drugstore. It doesn't take a half hour to go to a drugstore a block away. Then all the manpower went into high gear again. I went and laid out the story for you in detail that made things nice and easy. You got bullet-creased by an enemy I was on to so I thought you were square with me . . . not the real enemy after all. I'm getting old, chums. I'm just not thinking hard enough, I guess. In my own way I have a little luck here and there, and people make mistakes. Like William's maid mentioning the meeting here tonight and you not being sharp enough to have your maid tell me you were sleeping in case I called.

"Maybe all the excitement was too much for you. Things were coming to a head and you were ready to be king and queen. Now I'm going to tell you something. You never would have made it. That vaccine doesn't make you immune."

This time their eyes met, held a second, and the fear was there all the way.

I said, "We know the story, at least most of it. Now there will be time to dig the rest of it out. Nobody will ever know about it though and that's the way it should be. Maybe now some of this crappy rivalry between countries will slow down and there will be some sensible cooperation. I doubt it, but it may happen for a while and even that's better than nothing. I found your little sheet of onionskin, William, all nicely detailing where those canisters were planted and right now every one of them is being located and deactivated. If you don't believe me I'll name a few."

I gave him four and he knew for certain then.

"By tomorrow there will be some other things added. It won't take the pros long to get all the names of your people and the net will tighten quickly and tightly and all your beautiful hopes will go up in smoke."

Something about them had changed. It had started when they looked at each other. It had grown fast, and now they looked at each other again, a resigned look that had a peculiar meaning to it and William Dorn said, "We go nowhere, Mr. Hammer."

"You're going with me," I told him. "Consider yourself lucky. At least here you get due process of law. Your own people would kill you the slowest way they know how."

"They would manage somehow anyway, I'm afraid."

"That's your tough luck," I said.

"No, long ago we prepared for such an eventuality. The preparation was drastic and simply an eventuality, but the time has come and now there can be no other way. We both have been fitted with cyanide capsules, Mr. Hammer. I'm sorry to spoil your fun."

Once more, they looked at each other, both nodding almost imperceptibly, and there was a minute movement of the lines of their jaws.

I could see the death coming on, but they sure as hell weren't going to spoil my fun.

"Too bad," I said. "You still had another way out." I looked at the stubby revolver that was lying on the floor near their feet and very slowly I raised the .45 to my own temple. I pulled the trigger and there was only that flat, metallic click of the hammer snapping shut on nothing.

They both tried to scream a protest at the world and lunged for the gun on the floor at the same time. They could take me with them . . . the final pleasure would be theirs after all.

Renée had the gun in her fingers and William Dorn was trying to tear it from her when the cyanide hit them with one final spasm.

And I was laughing in a very quiet room.